CW01261035

blackwell

the complete series

Blackwell: The Complete Series
Amanda Richardson
Copyright 2024 Amanda Richardson
www.authoramandarichardson.com

Cover Design: Emily Wittig

This is a work of fiction. Names, characters, businesses, places, events and incidents are either the products of the author's imagination or used in a fictitious manner. Any resemblance to actual persons, living or dead, or actual events is purely coincidental.

All rights reserved. This book or any portion thereof may not be reproduced or used in any manner whatsoever without the express written permission of the author except for the use of brief quotations in a book review.

CONTENTS

LORDS OF DARKNESS	1
Book One	
LADY OF DARKNESS	185
Book Two	
PRINCES OF SIN	367
Book Three	

LORDS OF DARKNESS
BOOK ONE

AUTHOR'S NOTE

This is book one in a dark reverse harem romance series. Please note that this book is **dark**. Let me say that again, as I know some of you have been with me since I started writing romance: ***this book is dark.*** Darker than anything I've ever written. You will love the heroes, and then you will hate them before you love them again. If you're looking for villains who eventually turn good, that doesn't happen in this book. They are the antithesis of a romantic hero in every way. Proceed with caution.

For a list of triggers, please visit my website:
www.authoramandarichardson.com/triggers

For everyone who always wanted to hate f*ck the villain

Hell is empty and all the devils are here.

William Shakespeare

CHAPTER 1

ALARIC

Cracking my neck and popping my knuckles, I look down at the bound and gagged man kneeling before me. He's screaming behind the duct tape, his icy-blue eyes wide and bloodshot. Well, one of them. The other one is swollen shut, thanks to Gideon's forceful punches.

I'm surprised at the lack of remorse on my part for what I'm about to do. Then again, it's not every day that our order is betrayed by one of our own. We're all closer than brothers. We may not share blood, but we share a bond that's over a thousand years old—and we have rules that have existed since the Middle Ages. Our quintet is something sacred, something to *revere*.

And yet, he threw it all away. He threw us to the wolves, and for that, he will be shown zero mercy.

The proverbial knife he stuck in my back will be the same knife I kill him with.

"We all swore an oath. Five families. Five Lords. And tonight, you betrayed us," I say in a deceivingly calm voice, looking down at Charles. "Do you have any last words for us?"

Gideon steps forward and unties his hands before ripping the tape from his mouth. I'm eager to hear his bullshit excuse. I'm sure he's been thinking of what to tell us for *years*.

Fool.

Arrogant, stupid fool.

"Alaric," he gasps. "You're making a terrible mistake. Please, let me explain—"

Reaching down, I yank him up by his shirt collar so that he's inches from my face. He's a large man—ten years our senior, though he can outrun us and lift heavier in the gym. Still, his physical health won't help him now. He knows we've found him out.

And he's going to pay fiercely.

"A *mistake*? You should be ashamed of the brand you wear on your skin," I spit, baring my teeth. "We live by our oaths, and we die by them, too. You have given your life to the Lords, and yet you have squandered it." I throw him back down onto the concrete. "Do it," I tell Gideon. I'm too angry, too *hurt*, to deal with Charles. It feels so much heavier than our usual kills. The weight of the energy in the air right now is nearly suffocating me.

Turning away, I walk back to where Sterling and Theo are bending over a laptop. I know Theo is downloading the entire drive so we can access it later if needed—and I'm sure, given Charles's betrayal, that it's ripe with information.

"The conversations go back years," Theo says, his face lit up from the light of the screen. He glances up at me, a look of unguarded fury on his face. It doesn't surprise me that he's angry. We're all angry. We never thought we'd be here. After all, Charles taught us everything we know. He was our guardian angel, our mentor.

But the winged angel has fallen, and the punishment for that is death.

"He's been giving them information since before we joined," he adds.

"Of course he has," I say, turning my gaze back to Charles.

He sold us out to our enemies. Someone looking in might wonder why we're surprised. We are the Lords of Darkness, after all. It's not like we abide by any rules, and most people would consider us the goddamn grim reapers. But I am surprised. We all are. Our order is not like the others—that's why we've survived so long. Closer than brothers. A hive mind. If one limb of our quintet is missing, we all flounder.

Charles screams. Gideon pins him down with a knee on his neck to keep him from moving. Naked from the waist up, Charles screams again as Gideon's butterfly knife pierces the flesh on his bicep. In a slow, precise movement, he begins the process of carving the scarred brand from Charles's flesh.

"No, please!" Charles begs, his dark blue eyes finding mine.

For a second, I falter. Those eyes have been my guide for so long. But then I remember what he did—and how he so thoroughly betrayed us. The fury returns, and I grit my jaw.

"We're well within reason to eliminate you, Charles." I glance at Gideon, who is nearly done removing a large portion of his flesh. "Don't be gentle. Our forefathers would want it to hurt."

"Let me explain," Charles sobs, sounding pathetic. Blood streaks down his arm as Gideon continues his carving without pause.

I click my tongue. "I thought you'd have more of a backbone," I muse, walking closer. "But you're a weakling. A rotting limb. We're simply choosing to amputate the rot."

Gideon throws a bloody piece of tissue onto the floor before me. I want to walk over and step on it to prove a point—grind it into the stone—but that would mean mucking up my shoes. Charles looks up at me with tear-stained cheeks.

Kneeling before him, I grab his chin and force him to look into my eyes. "You are hereby removed as a Lord of Darkness, Charles Blackwell. Your son will become your replacement when he comes of age."

"No," he garbles. "Not Archie."

I chuckle, grabbing the knife from my back pocket. Charles's eyes widen when he sees it. An iron blade, and a handle carved from bone. Over a thousand years old. Passed from Lord to Lord since our order was formed in 1066 A.D. It's symbolic. We were all initiated with this blade—made some of our first kills with this blade—and now, a member would be eliminated with it. Unfortunately, he wouldn't be the first.

"I'm afraid you don't get a say anymore," I hiss, pressing the sharpened tip into his neck. "You fucked everything up." Pushing through the rubbery resistance of his skin, I slowly begin to slit his throat, making sure to angle my hand away from the spurting blood so I don't get my hands dirty.

He makes a choking noise. I fucking love the sounds that come from a man as I'm slitting his throat. Juicy, watery, a garbled last plea to let them live, as if it'll save them.

Too bad he's irredeemable.

In thirty seconds, he'll bleed out all over the floor, and his heart will stop pumping. His organs will fail, and he'll go into a coma.

Good fucking *riddance.*

29... 28... 27...

"Harlow," he sputters.

I narrow my eyes, pulling my hand away. "Who the fuck is Harlow?"

He makes a gurgling sound, his hand going up to the wound. The blood dribbles out in timed surges with each beat of his weakening heartbeat.

"My daughter."

I lower my head. Now he's just playing games, and I *really* don't appreciate it when people fuck around.

"You don't have a daughter, you lying bastard."

His eyelids begin to drop, and his skin goes white as the blood runs down his chest, forming a puddle on the ground beneath him.

10... 9... 8...

"Harlow Windsor."

I grit my teeth, but before I can ask him who the fuck he's talking about, the light leaves his eyes, and he slumps over.

3... 2... 1...

His body falls onto the ground with a sickening thud.

I've killed enough men to know how long exsanguination takes. Forty percent of your blood drains quicker than you'd think.

Especially when you nick the carotid artery.

I turn and look at the guys, unease coiling in my core. "Who the fuck is Harlow Windsor?"

"He's lying," Sterling answers, pushing off from the wall. He's been watching everything unfold, quiet and menacing as always. He doesn't know when to lighten up, though I know he blows off steam being a goddamn sexual deviant.

Looking at Theo, his brows furrow. "Do you think he was lying?"

"I don't know," Theo says simply. "But I can find out for sure."

I'm sure as fuck he can. Theodore Wolf can sniff anything and everything out. He's a goddamn computer genius. Getting on his bad side sends shivers down my spine. He can hack anything, control any heavy machinery—including cars, planes, cargo ships... the power he has is terrifying. He could send the world into complete darkness if he wanted to.

We all look between each other, dumbfounded as I rub my mouth. "I didn't hear a thing," I say quickly, looking back at Charles's body. "I'm not about to hunt down some long-lost daughter when we have a perfectly acceptable heir two miles away."

"Archie is two," Theo muses, and I glare at him.

"Do you have a better idea?"

"Our fathers must've known, right?" Sterling asks, his expression serious. "If he had another child?"

Gideon snorts, flicking his bloody knife open and closed. "It's not information that was ever passed on to me," he replies, smirking. "If they knew, they withheld it on purpose."

"Okay, then. I'm putting my foot down. We forget Charles ever mentioned it. The order dictates it can be any blood relative. We use Archie when he comes of age."

"In sixteen years," Gideon says, his jaw feathering. He looks at all of us. "That's a long ass time to wait. Being down a man puts us at risk." Looking right at me, he crosses his arms, the knife still clutched in his bloodied hand. "I vote we find his daughter."

"Me too," Sterling says. "Sixteen years is too long. We'll be middle-aged by then."

"Me three," Theo interjects. "*If* she exists. And if she doesn't, we have a backup."

I grind my teeth together. "You were all perfectly willing to wait for Archie before we fucking killed a fellow Lord," I grind out, running a hand through my hair. This was not a part of the plan. And if there's one thing I hate more than playing games, it's being unprepared. *Fuck.* "How do we know he wasn't lying?" I ask, looking at them.

Gideon shrugs as he kicks at Charles, rolling him over onto his back. "I guess there's only one way to find out." Unlike me, Gideon doesn't mind getting dirty. His blue button-up shirt is stained with blood. "Fucker's bleeding a lot," he adds, looking down at Charles.

"He was taking blood thinners," I tell him, straightening my suit and stepping around the growing puddle of crimson. I turn my attention to Sterling. "Come on, let's get this over with."

Sterling drags Charles to the pile of wood in the middle of the barn. I grab a cigarette from my suit pocket, flicking the solid gold lighter and inhaling as the end begins to burn. The nicotine buzz hits my brain instantly.

Blowing out a puff of smoke, my eyes scan the barn as Sterling checks

Charles's pockets, removing his wallet, phone, and keys. He hands Theo the phone—and I know Theo will extract every morsel of information he can get.

I check my watch as I wait for them to finish with the lighter fluid. We've got to get the timing just right—dark enough to hide the smoke, but not too late to arouse suspicion. It's eight-thirty, which is ideal, so I guess we're doing this now.

I take one last drag, the sweet taste of tobacco snaking down my throat. Walking up to Charles, I flick the lit cigarette onto his body, and everything ignites instantly. We all take a few steps back and watch. The smell of burnt pork roast permeates the air.

In an hour, all the flesh will be gone.

So, we wait. Watching in silence. Saying our goodbyes to our fellow Lord.

He doesn't deserve our respect, but we give it to him anyway.

I check my phone, but there are no notifications.

Because we're all here.

The four—now three—people I communicate with the most. There's something depressing about that—about four men walking in, and only three walking out.

Once the flames die down, the guys use a shovel to sever the skull from the spine. There's a cracking sound, and a second later, I hear them roll it over to where I'm standing. I pull on my thick gloves. Looking down at the smoking skull, I cock my head, reaching down and picking it up. I stare into the eye sockets, a small frown tugging on my lips. *Why'd you have to betray us, Charles?* The flesh has been burned off entirely, the planes of the thick bone smooth, and a creamy white color.

A lot of people think bones turn black when they're burned, but that's not entirely true. At a high degree of heat, bones do turn black—but as it gets hotter, they burn white.

We leave the rest of the bones to denature, only ashes remaining as we depart.

I walk over to the back room, placing the skull next to Charles's father's skull. Removing my gloves, I take a step back, admiring the shelf carved into the wall hundreds of years ago.

A place to house every single Lord of Darkness before us.

One day, we'd be here, too—our children or nephews or cousins setting our skulls to rest here for eternity.

To be forgotten, hidden, amongst other monsters.

Because that's what we are. *Monsters.* Death incarnate, but with royal blood.

We are going to need our quintet. We can't function properly without it, and waiting sixteen years would mean we'll be without a vital branch of our order for that long. Gideon is right. It will leave us vulnerable. And I am not going to let this fucking empire fall on my watch. Not after a thousand years. We'd worked too hard, for too long, to give up now.

I turn to face the others, my hands in my trouser pockets. They're watching me expectantly, and I realize with a jolt that Charles's death makes me the next leader.

First in, first up.

I give myself a few seconds to let that all sink in. Pinching the bridge of my nose and closing my eyes, I think of what our ancestors would've done. The answer is obvious.

"Find her."

Their monstrous, wicked grins are their only responses.

CHAPTER 2

Harlow

I stand in front of Blackwell House and look up at the gothic stone manor. I haven't been here since I was a kid, but it hasn't changed at all. My eyes sweep over the round lines of the mansard roofing, the dormer windows, and the newly planted rose bushes along the perimeter. I shift my weight from one foot to the other uncomfortably, shielding my eyes as I take it all in. The heat is oppressive. I'd forgotten about that. I'm used to New York heat—the stifling, damp, unmoving air. The kind that keeps me up at night, tossing and turning on my flat sheet. But this? This is an entirely different beast. This is an *older*, more menacing heat—one that comes for you when you least expect it, nestling into the crevices of your skin folds and dripping down your back with the slightest movement.

The driver grabs my two large suitcases and leads us toward the grand entrance. I can see the rose garden out back, with every perfectly trimmed bush clumped together by color. The brass fences and plaques gleam against the bright sun. Wrinkling my nose against the cloying smell, I follow the driver inside. The wind picks up, making my blouse flutter. I nearly groan at the relief, at the small repreive of cool air.

Once inside the house, I look around. The furniture and art are the same as I remember—stuffy and old-fashioned. I never felt at home here, not even as a teen. Everything was for looking, not touching. The art was for gazing upon, and the furniture was not for sitting. I learned that the hard way once when I was seven.

The driver greets the housekeeper. I don't know either of them. The ones that were here when I was a child are long gone by now.

"Miss Windsor," the housekeeper says, her hair pulled back into a tight bun. She's wearing the same uniform all the help wears—a grey smock dress and white apron. "Welcome back to Blackwell House." I'd forgotten how this part of the world was still stuck in the Downton Abbey era. "Let me show you to your room." I nod without answering, waving goodbye to the driver. Grabbing my bags, she clicks her tongue. "Don't worry about those. I will have them sent up."

"I don't mind—"

She reaches out for my hand gently, cupping it in hers. "That's what we're here for." Dropping my hand, she gestures for me to follow her upstairs.

I know she's just trying to put me at ease, but I don't like the way she says that. Though, who am I to question the status quo? I came here with one purpose, and one purpose only—to help Cecelia with the funeral, and then to get the fuck out of here. I can't afford to get attached, and I certainly have no right to change the way things are done. My father was set in his ways. It's not like my being here was going to suddenly change an entire class system overnight.

We walk up the stairs, my hand grazing the polished walnut wood. The soft padding of the runner feels nice on the soles of my feet. I'd made the mistake of wearing a pair of new boots, and the bottoms of my heels ache from the day of travel to get here from New York. I'm excited to sit down and decompress—maybe revel in the fact that I flew internationally all by myself.

I wasn't sure I'd be able to do it.

"Here you are," the housekeeper says, throwing a door open.

I look around at the dark room. It hasn't changed since the last time I was here. From the looks of it, no one has been inside since then, either. It's clean, but the smell of musty carpet permeates the air.

"I'm Rose, by the way," she says warmly.

"Thank you, Rose. It's nice to meet you."

"Cecelia and Archie should be home shortly. She was disappointed that she couldn't receive you herself."

"It's fine."

She shuffles a bit, her face pinching into a look of pity. I know exactly what she's going to say before she says it.

"I was so sorry to hear about your mother. And now..." Her voice breaks, and she swallows down a sob. "Your father was a good man. You've experienced so much loss in such a short amount of time. If there's anything I can do to make the transition more comfortable, please do let me know..." she trails off, her green eyes wide and watery.

"Thank you, Rose," I respond as I set my purse down on my bed.

She nods once before leaving, and I'm left staring at the room I once used to love. The bed is the main attraction—something that made me feel so special as a young child. It was massive for a little girl, and I felt like a princess every time I stayed here. The billowing, white voile fabric is pulled tight to each bedpost, and the dark, wooden poster frame was luxurious for me, having come from a small bed in New York.

I take in the rest of the bedroom—the bold floral wallpaper, the antique walnut dressing table and matching stool, the dark green, velvet chaise lounge next to the window... it's all the same, except it feels smaller, somehow. Less grand. I suppose that's what happens when you grow up. My eyes flick to the bathroom. The brass fixtures must've been recently polished, as they're gleaming and shiny. I turn back to the window and take a seat on the chaise lounge.

As much as I hate the idea of being back here, the village of Blackwell is very quaint. From my vantage point on the third story, I can see the stone cottages that line the outskirts of town. The Blackwell Minster sits to the left of the Blackwell market square. My gaze traces the road to the left—the one that veers up a winding hillside. Though it's an affluent place, it still holds a sense of community and old-fashioned whimsicalness. The rolling hills behind town are dotted with white sheep, and the cars that drive along the two-lane road are black and gleaming—again, because people here have money.

Blackwell is nestled between Oxford and London, a tiny, hidden place where the gross median income is ten times that of an average town in England. Dukes, Lords, Counts, Viscounts... all titles that have since mostly disappeared in the modern age.

Except for here.

And then there's me. *Not* a Lady—despite my father being a Duke. But since my parents never married, I'm just a bastard child. The charity case. I was fine with that. I'd never felt a connection to this part of my life, and I'd stopped visiting after everything happened. Flying, being in a different country, being stuck in this old house... they were triggers for me.

Most things were triggers for me now.

So, being back here so soon was not supposed to be in the cards. Then again, no one expected my father to have a stroke at forty-two, but here we are.

At least I had a place at NYU Tisch School of the Arts this fall. I wouldn't be staying here for long. Just a week, maybe two. And I'm only here as a favor to Cecelia, a woman I'd never met, and her two-year-old son, Archie.

My half-brother.

Sighing, I play with my dark curls, twisting my hair around one of my fingers nervously as dark clouds begin to roll in, overtaking the bright blue sky. Well, *that's* a metaphor if I've ever seen one. I grind my jaw as the sky unleashes, sending rain pouring down in thick droplets. It cascades along the side of the window in thick rivulets, and I watch it, mesmerized.

I get up and walk to my purse, popping one of my anti-anxiety pills under my tongue.

This place gives me the creeps. As a child, the two weeks I spent here every summer always felt endless and dire. My father was a busy man, always locked in his office or away on business. Cecelia wasn't around back then, so I spent most of my time wandering the halls and countless rooms of the manor. And now? He's gone, and I have to pick out funeral flowers and a casket, as if I knew him. Which isn't true at all. We were never close.

And I guess now we'd never get the chance.

I take a quick shower and freshen up, changing into black leggings and a loose, dark grey Nirvana sweatshirt. The sun is fading below the horizon, so I flick on one of the lamps in my bedroom. I look at myself in the full-length mirror, adjusting the hem of my sweatshirt. My dark, curly hair is pulled up haphazardly, and my face looks ashen and exhausted. I inherited my father's golden complexion, but right now, it's jetlagged and weary, with bags shadowing my eyes. I pinch the bridge of my nose and close my eyes, inhaling deeply as I feel the familiar tendrils of anxiety beginning to skitter across my skin.

Hopefully, my medication works soon, but still...

I take another deep breath.

You are safe here.

He can't find you in England.

You are safe here.

When I'm done with my mantras, I shoot a quick text to Gemma—my best friend in New York—so that she knows I've arrived safely.

I'm just setting my phone down when there's a loud rapping on my door. I walk over and throw it open, and before me stands a woman who I can only assume is Cecelia Crawford-Blackwell—all five-foot-one of her, wearing a light green summer dress and white sandals.

"Hi, Harlow," she says, her voice breathy as she rushes forward, pulling me into a hug. "I'm so sorry about what happened, and that we're meeting under these circumstances."

My hug is limp compared to hers. I'm not a big hugger—but apparently, she is.

"How are you doing?" I ask, pulling away.

Stupid question. Her fucking husband just died.

I don't know Cecelia well at all. My father married her a few years ago, and my mom and I knew about the engagement, wedding, and subsequent birth of Archie. He'd been born a few months before my mother... well... before she died. We've spoken more on the phone in the last week than we ever have, but so far, she seems friendly.

"I'm okay," she answers. Her voice is soft, her accent neutral and light. She looks up at me, her brow slightly furrowed. "I mean, as okay as one can be in this shitty situation. Fortunately, Archie is too young to really understand what's happening."

"Well, I am here to help you," I tell her, and I mean it sincerely.

I'd gotten news about my father's death last week, two days before graduating from high school. I'd planned on spending the summer working, earning money for my first year at NYU. But all of that would have to wait a couple of weeks, as I'd flown here as quickly as I could. I knew Cecelia was going to need help planning, and since she offered to fly me out, so I couldn't really say no. I feel a sense of obligation to help her, and I want to get to know my half-brother. Death has a strange way of making you cling to any semblance of comfort, and my mother's death eighteen months ago meant my father, and his family here, were all I had left.

"Thank you," she hiccups, her eyes welling up with tears. "I don't even know where to start. This house is so big, and Charles didn't keep very good records of things. I tried sorting through his office, but I don't understand any of it—" she cuts off with a sob, covering her mouth. Taking a deep breath, she composes herself and stands up taller. "I'm trying to say that I'm very grateful for the help. I suppose we're family now, right?"

I give her a grim smile. "Yeah. In a weird, fucked up way."

She barks a laugh. She's pretty—and young. She can't be older than thirty. Short dark hair. Large green eyes. Red lips. I wonder if we'd be friends under different circumstances.

Her eyes land on mine, and she gives me a wan smile. "We can deal with everything after a proper meal. Nothing makes sense when you're faint with hunger. Come on, let's go. You can finally meet Archie, too. He's hunkered down in front of the iPad."

Heading down the stairs, I wish I could tell my mom about all of this. I wish I had someone other than Gemma to confide in. She got the brunt of it after my mom died. Her family took me in, letting me stay with them as I finished my junior and senior year at Berkeley Carroll School. It's a good thing Gemma and I are self-sufficient as fuck, though, because her parents were almost never around.

Cecelia is right. We are sort of a family now.

The only family I have left.

Arriving in the dining room, I see Archie seated at the table, a plate of cut up pizza before him as he watches something on the iPad.

"Archie," Cecelia says, walking over to the toddler. My experience with little kids is limited. In fact, they sort of scare me. His dark curls hang in front of his face, and his cheeks still have that baby roundness to them. "Want to meet your sister, Harlow?"

Archie turns and looks up at me. Giving me a lopsided grin, he waves briefly before flicking his eyes back to the screen.

Cecelia sighs. "I feel like a horrible mother, sticking him in front of the screen like this," she says, watching him.

I reach a hand out, rubbing her arm. "Hey. You're doing the best you can do, okay?"

She nods once and then takes a seat at the table. I notice the head of the table—where my father used to sit—has a place set for him, too.

"It feels weird not to include him," she says, as if reading my mind.

I smile at her, staring down at the soup before me. Placing a napkin on my lap, I take a sip.

"Before he..." She pauses, squeezing her eyes shut before opening them and continuing. "Charles told me you got into NYU," she says, daintily using her spoon to sip her soup.

"Yes. I'm very excited."

"I'm sure you'll be busy, but just know that you're welcome to visit us in England any time."

I swallow thickly as I rub my chest with my free hand. "Thanks," I say quickly, quelling the emotion building up inside of me.

Because my father and I were never close, I clung tight to my mom. They got pregnant with me when they were very young. Mom was twenty, and he was twenty-four. She was in love with him, and he loved her, too, but his family and his title kept them apart. They agreed that I would spend two weeks at Blackwell House every summer, so that's exactly what I did from the time I was old enough to fly without a chaperone. Usually that age is twelve, but my father, being who he is, hired a private jet. I've been flying to England alone since I was five, spending most of my summer vacations in a large, stuffy manor until I turned sixteen.

Until my life changed.

I admired my father's wealth, but it never really felt like something I could relate to. He never felt accessible, or like a true father. Sure, I was beholden to him, because he covered my tuition at Berkeley Carroll, and I knew he paid child support to my mother. And after her death, money miraculously showed up in my bank account. But the older I got, the more I saw through the façade. The more I realized how much of a jerk he was for abandoning my mother when she was pregnant with me. She would've married him, too, but apparently, she wasn't good enough.

So when I found out he died, I was sad, but I also felt a sense of relief. Like the burden of trying to better our relationship was over.

The chef takes our soup dishes, and a minute later, plates with steak, potatoes, and a green salad appear.

I've never been good at small talk, so I cut my steak and pop a piece into my mouth just as Cecelia begins filling the silence.

"They wouldn't let me see his body, you know," she says hesitantly.

I go still. "Really? But you said he collapsed at a work dinner."

She nods. "He did. But there was a mix-up at the morgue, and he was sent to be cremated. That's what he wanted, so I guess it's for the best." She pushes her food around. "I have this dream sometimes that he's not dead. That there was just some kind of misunderstanding, and he's actually alive."

I swallow thickly. "I can tell you loved him a lot."

"I did. I do," she corrects. "I'm not sure where all that love is supposed to go." The corners of her eyes drag down, the sadness clear in her expression. Looking at Archie, I follow her gaze. "In a way, I'm glad this happened when Archie was so young. But on the other hand, it makes me sad that he won't remember his own father."

My chest aches as I look at my half-brother. He's bouncing around in his seat, chewing pizza, completely oblivious.

"I can take him to the park or something while I'm here," I offer. "Give you some alone time?"

She smiles grimly, exhaustion written all over her face. "Thank you, Harlow." She stands up, and I see that she's barely touched her food. "I apologize, but I'm suddenly so tired. Would it be alright with you if we push the funeral planning until tomorrow?"

I didn't know much about death and wills, but even in his young age, my father at least had the foresight to draft a living trust. Cecelia and I would handle the stuff on the surface—booking a place for the service, flower arrangements, and the guest list. His attorney and personal secretaries would handle everything else.

Thank God.

I nod. "Of course not. I'll see you in the morning," I say warmly, watching as she collects Archie.

"Thank you. If you need anything, I'm sure Rose would be happy to assist you."

Just then, Rose comes in from the kitchen and collects Archie from Cecelia. "Come on, lad. Let's take a proper bath and get ready for bed."

"Thank you, Rose," Cecelia says, giving Archie a kiss and walking away.

Rose clucks her tongue after she's gone. "Poor thing. She hasn't been herself since the duke passed away. She's barely eating. I know it's the grief, but she needs to keep strong for the babe," she adds, rocking Archie on her hip. He giggles and places his palm on her cheek.

"Rosie," he gurgles. Looking over at me, he grins. "Sissy."

My throat constricts. He's too cute for his own good.

"Maybe I can talk to Cecelia tomorrow."

Rose nods. "I hope you can get through to her. Lord knows we've tried and failed," she says with a sad but hopeful smile, bouncing Archie some more.

I smile back as the chef sets down some sticky toffee pudding. Mouth watering, I dig in. "I know a lot about grief, and it can be fickle," I tell her softly, taking a small bite.

Rose's expression softens. "Of course you do, love."

She walks upstairs with Archie, and I'm left looking around the room. It's so large, I feel swallowed up being here.

I can't imagine how Cecelia feels.

After I finish my dessert, I spend the better part of my evening digging around this old, creepy house.

I spent a lot of my summers as a kid exploring Blackwell House, always feeling like I was in a movie, or had discovered a spooky, haunted mansion. It looked nothing like anything in New York—crumbling stone, rich tapestries, gilded furniture. I couldn't wrap my mind around this amount of wealth. And since my father and Cecelia were married, she will automatically inherit all of this if she wants it. I'm not sure what happens if she doesn't. I don't envy her—the heavy burden of being a Duchess in a house like this? No, thank you. I was lucky to be able to walk away from it all.

I walk up to my room a couple of hours later and open the curtains, glancing out. The rain is pouring down now, thunder echoing against the stone. A lightning strike flashes in the distance, illuminating the driveway and front gate. I blink rapidly. It looks like four hooded figures are standing under the gate, but by the time I rub my eyes and look again, the illusion is gone.

I'm seeing things.

With goosebumps covering my skin from head to toe, I snap the curtains closed and head to the bathroom. Drawing a bath, I sit on the edge as the tub fills.

I just need to get some sleep, and then tomorrow, I can handle everything that needs to be done.

CHAPTER 3

G‍ideon

"On your knees," I growl, grabbing a fistful of Olivia's hair and pushing her head down.

She huffs in protest, but then she grabs my hips and unzips my trousers with her teeth. *Good little slut.* I hiss as she frees my cock, grabbing onto one of the iron sconces in the dark corner of the hallway for leverage as I thrust between her thick, pert lips.

"Lord St. Claire—" She makes a choking sound when I shove myself deeper, and her long nails dig into my ass in protest. I keep going, looking down as her eyes water. When her face starts to turn purple, I pull out as she gasps for air.

I can see the fear in her eyes.

Is it too much to ask for someone who won't back down from a challenge? Someone who won't *"Yes, Lord"* every goddamn minute? I need a fighter. A brat. Someone who likes to be punished.

A minute later, I come all over Olivia's tits.

Even though she acts like she enjoys being sprayed with my come, there's still something missing. Some link or connection that I keep hunting for. The problem is that these girls are too easy.

I'm a hunter in search of his prey.

I yearn for the chase—to hunt someone down and watch as I try to snuff the life out of them. To get them a breath away from the precipice of death before pulling back.

It's always been my thing—life, death, what happens after. That's why I'm so fascinated with weapons—with the idea of a small sliver of metal being able to take down someone like Charles Blackwell.

I like death so much that I have to touch it, *feel* the steel of my favorite blade constantly.

I think we're all naturally morbid as fuck. You have to be with our jobs.

I fuck to feel, to give my life more purpose than being a killing machine.

But right now, Olivia is looking at me like I just gave her the world.

I wish she'd have some respect.

"Go," I command, and she scurries away, fixing her apron.

To be honest, I can't even remember when we started fucking around, or why. Boredom, maybe? She was constantly eyeing me at the coffee shop, and one day I asked her out to lunch, only to drag her into the old hallway of our office and fuck her senseless against the stone wall. The ground level wasn't really used by us, and since we owned the building, it made sense to bring her here.

I won't be seeing her again, though.

She's not quite my type.

A few minutes later, I'm sitting alone at my desk on the second story, flicking my knife open and closed, when Theo walks in carrying a sheet of paper. He has a dour expression on his face. I know he and the guys were at Wolf Manor earlier, Theo's main place of residence. He has his whole setup there—monitors and flashing machines, capable of almost anything. Working in an office is relatively new for us. But we couldn't pass up the opportunity to diversify our investments when this place came onto the market.

A medieval prison tower? Hell, yes.

"Who died?" I ask sarcastically, cocking my head.

Theo slaps down a sheet of paper, and I go still. It's a picture. "What am I looking at?"

"Harlow Windsor. Eighteen. Graduated from Berkeley Carroll School in New York City last week. Charles had been making tuition deposits for years."

"Hmm," I say, my eyes grazing over the image. Dark, thick curls hang down her narrow shoulders. She has the same navy-blue eyes as Charles. Sharp cheekbones, a smattering of light freckles and full lips have me captivated. But it's her sun-kissed complexion that has my eyes wandering down to where her shirt dips, revealing a sizable cleavage. She's not the type of woman I normally gravitate toward, but Harlow Windsor is stunning in a natural kind of way.

I can't help but want to taste her—to lick that golden skin and devour her whole.

"Are we sure she's his daughter?"

Theo gives me an incredulous look. Sometimes I forget I'm dealing with the biggest computer nerd in the world.

"Positive. She did one of those ancestry tests a couple of years ago. And there's the fact that she's here now, in Charles's house."

I stiffen. "She's here? Why? Were they close?"

He shrugs. "No idea."

I look down at the second paper he set down. Excellent grades. An acceptance letter to NYU Tisch School of the Arts. Chosen major: Art. I flick through the portfolio examples Theo printed out, not really caring about them. I mean, she's good, but art isn't really my thing. There's an Instagram account with a few thousand followers. *Impressive.* From the looks of it, her area of interest is street art, and she goes by the pseudonym MONSTER for that. Getting to the last page, my eyes scan the text. It's a newspaper clipping from eighteen months ago, detailing a murder in an apartment building.

"Her mother," Theo supplies, and I look up at him.

"And we just fucking killed her father," I grit out.

"She's an orphan now. Makes it easier to pluck her right out of New York to join the Lords."

"Technically, she'd be a Lady," I say, glancing down at the papers again.

"Haven't had one of those in a while," he replies. I hand the papers back to him—all of them except the picture of Harlow. That's for me to keep. "What if she says no?"

I huff a laugh, leaning back in my chair. "She won't."

"She might," he argues, glaring down at me. "And by telling her about our order, we're exposing ourselves."

I smirk. "Then let's make sure she doesn't say no."

The Lords of Darkness are the oldest order in the world—the Illuminati meets Al Capone. We rule the underground of Britain, and our web of power extends out in five directions. Hence the five families. Formed by five companions of William the Conqueror, the same five families had been doing this job since the eleventh century.

It's not glamorous, and it involves a lot more blood and gore than Alaric likes, but we have no choice. As actual Lords, our blood is considered elite—*royal*. We are a branch of English nobility with the most important job in the world, and when someone is born into one of the families, they have no choice but to become a Lord of Darkness.

We don't see it as a burden.

We see it as an honor.

"So, what's the plan, then?" Theo asks.

"We find her, and we make her a Lady."

Harlow Windsor was about to regret the day she met us.

CHAPTER 4

Harlow

I wake up just as the sun is rising the next morning, feeling groggy and unsure of where I am. Sitting up, I groan as I remember I'm in Blackwell. Throwing the covers off, I decide to make the best out of a shitty situation and go for a walk to reacquaint myself with the village. Maybe I'll even do some art if I can find a discreet place. Slipping into leggings and a baggy red sweatshirt, I throw my thick hair up and slide a headband on before stepping into my sneakers. Grabbing my backpack, which has limited supplies thanks to customs, I head downstairs and tuck my phone into the side pocket.

I'm not hungry, so I just pluck a takeaway cold brew from the fridge and walk out the front door. I go slower under the gate, trying not to overthink the shoe outlines in the mud. *The four figures...* It's just a coincidence that there are eight footprints. Right? Who in their right mind would be standing out here ominously in the rain, watching me?

No one.

It's just my anxiety talking.

You are safe here.

He can't find me here.

You are safe here.

Which reminds me...

Reaching into my backpack, I grab my travel bottle of meds and pop one under my tongue since I forgot when I woke up.

I continue to meander down the road leading to the center of town. Every block or so, I survey the surfaces available to me. The farther I go down the hill into town, the foggier it gets. I can feel the cool air sticking to my lungs, but instead of wanting to cough, it's refreshing.

The view opens before me when I get into town. The village is quaint and idyllic—completely different from my life in Brooklyn. Stone houses, a large ruin behind the large minster, and timber-framed shops line the main cobblestone road. No one is out and about now, so it feels like the entire village is mine. I walk slowly through the market square, and a bell chimes quickly to signal half-past six. I turn right on one of the side streets. It's winding and picturesque, and I hate that I love it so much.

Loving it will just make it that much harder to leave, and I need to leave because this place reminds me of my life before everything changed—of when things were easier, simpler. This place also reminds me of my mom, and everything she would never have.

I end up on the other side of the town, and I take the main road that leads to Blackwell Park, and beyond it, Drago Lake.

All of Blackwell sits in a shallow valley, while the houses of the elite sit up on the hills surrounding the village. I'm panting as I walk up the hill toward Blackwell Forest, my heart hammering in my chest when I make it to the top.

I stop and catch my breath as I look around.

I don't know much about my father's personal life other than what's on paper, but being here reminds me of a story he once told me as a child. It was about five princes who lived in a small English village. Each house represented a different part of England. It was their job to protect their country. There was the house to the northwest, that represented the Northwestern part of the country. The house to the northeast, that represented the east part of the country. The house to the southwest, that represented the southwestern part of the country. The house to the southeast, that represented the southeastern part of the country. And there was one house in the middle—protecting the village, and London, the capitol. All the houses were on a hill, overlooking the village. Overlooking the country.

So now, naturally, any time I see a house on a hill, I think of that story.

I turn around, starting my trek back to Blackwell village. I know the morning will only get busier as the tourists come into the village on the train, so if I'm going to do this, it needs to be now. Finding a space of wall on the underpass of a bridge, I drop my backpack and look around. The coast is clear, but just to be safe, I decide to move quickly. I pull the lettered stencils out of my backpack, quickly unscrewing the cap of the kid's paint that I brought with me. Spray paint wouldn't have made it past security, obviously, so I had to make do. I'll need to replenish my supplies as soon as possible.

I pull my logo stencil out—**MONSTER**. That's the name I use, mostly because I couldn't think of anything else.

Standing back, I admire my work.

We're all trapped in the Underworld.

I added a yellow crown over the 'O' in underworld, using excess paint so that it drips down a bit, making the whole thing look a bit messy.

Art is subjective, of course, but my art means something to me, and that's all that really matters. It reflects my current emotions, thoughts, feelings... and right now, I feel trapped in a place that's pretty on the outside, with secrets lurking just beneath the surface.

I take a picture and post it to my Instagram account, leaving a minute later.

I can't deny that half the reason I love street art so much is because it puts *me* in power. It gives me some semblance of control. No one back home knows about it. Not even Gemma. After I lost my mom, and then everything else happened, I had to pull myself up by my bootstraps once I recovered. I was truly alone, and that caused me to grow up quickly. I got on medication for the anxiety issues, and then I put my head down, determined to get into NYU. I needed the art. It gave me a reason to keep going, to keep pushing past the grief of losing my mom and my entire life as I knew it.

I was in charge of my destiny, and every time I create something, it grounds me.

I had worked my ass off at Berkeley Carroll, and I had gotten myself into NYU with a full scholarship, majoring in art.

No one could take that away from me.

After it all happened, my father offered several times to come out and help me, but at the time, I didn't really want to see him. A part of me regrets that, because now he's gone and I'm essentially an orphan. That feeling hangs heavy over me, and I'm sure it will for a long time.

When I pass through the village this time, it's much livelier. The baker's door is open, and several people are out with coffees walking their dogs. I get back to the house and head into the kitchen, grabbing a pastry before making my way upstairs. If Cecelia and Archie are awake, they're in some other part of the house, so I make a vow to find them after I shower—which I gladly do a minute later.

Changing into a loose, dark green dress, I pull my hair up into a messy bun. I didn't wash it, because washing this mop of fur entails an hour of drying, and I can't be bothered today. Glancing down at my phone on the bed, I see that I have a message from someone on Instagram. I don't have a ton of followers, but the ones I do are loyal as fuck. Clicking over, my stomach drops when I read the message.

Pretty dress.

Swallowing, I go to their profile, but it's blank. *User.1954012876*.

Before I exit, three dots appear, indicating that they're writing something else. It appears, then disappears. I bite my lower lip, my thumb hovering over the keyboard.

Monster: Who are you?
User.1954012876: A new fan.
Uneasiness slithers through me.
Monster: From NY?
User.1954012876: No.
It's not him.
It's not him.
It's not him.

Monster: Why the comment on my dress?
User.1954012876: That green really brings out the golden hue of your skin. I want to lick that skin from head to toe.

Holy shit. My palms sweat as I respond.

Monster: Leave me alone.
User.1954012876: I wish I could.
Monster: Who are you?
User.1954012876: You'll find out soon enough.

Dropping my phone, I frantically look around. Unease slithers through my bones. My hands are shaking when I pick my phone back up, seeing I have another message.

User.1954012876: Stop looking around. You won't find me.

I instantly block the number and delete the messages.

Sitting on the bed, I lean back and take a few calming breaths. Their statement was generic and meant to creep me out. I've worn this dress before, so chances are, someone from high school saw me in it at some point and they're just pranking me.

It's nothing.
It's not him.

Turning my phone on silent, I shake myself off and head downstairs to find Cecelia and Archie.

They're both in the rose garden, and I walk up to where Cecelia is sitting, her phone in her hand. Archie is running around in circles, chasing the pigeons.

"Hey," I say, glancing around suspiciously. The hairs on the back of my neck stand on end, and it feels like someone's watching me. But when I scan the garden, it's just the three of us.

Cecelia sits up straighter. "How was your night? Did you sleep okay?" She's more casual today—skinny jeans, sneakers, and a loose t-shirt. When I take in her face, I notice the bags under her eyes.

"I did, thank you. What about you?" I pry.

She gives me a grim smile. "I had them bring Archie's cot into my bedroom after Charles..." she trails off. "I couldn't take being alone, or the thought of Archie being in another room. But he still wakes up every few hours, so it feels a bit counterproductive. Now I'm sad *and* exhausted."

A pang of sympathy washes through me. Here I am, wallowing in the fact that my father and I would never be close, and Cecelia is so afraid to be alone after his death that she's bunking with her toddler. I mean, I don't blame her. But it hits me then that she's lost her life partner. Her future just went from something tangible to... being a single mom.

Which is daunting as fuck.

"Do you want me to watch him while you take a nap?"

I don't know why I offer. I've never spent alone time with a child before, but he *is* my half-brother.

She shakes her head. "That's okay. I can handle it. But thank you." Standing up, she brushes herself off, even though the iron bench we were sitting on was nowhere near dirty. "Shall we go inside and begin? I was thinking we could finalize a date, time, and venue for the funeral so that we can start letting people know. I anticipate that a lot of people will want to attend, considering his status."

I look over at Archie.

"I can have Rose watch him," she says, walking over and picking him up. He leans down and kisses her on the forehead, and for the first time since I met her, she looks happy as she kisses the tip of his nose.

"Sure," I say, swinging my arms awkwardly.

A few minutes later, once Archie is settled with Rose, we begin sorting through my father's will. He was organized enough to recommend the Blackwell Minster for the wake, as well as the mortuary and crypt he'd like to be placed into. Apparently, there's a Blackwell mausoleum. *That's not creepy as fuck or anything.* Cecelia and I decide the best date and time is tomorrow at noon, and once we finalize the announcement and the venues, she goes upstairs for a nap.

I casually begin to go through the rest of my father's office, making piles of my own. Most of it is meaningless drivel—bills, receipts, contracts. I scan whatever seems important into Cecelia's laptop. We still haven't found his computer, but I'm sure it'll turn up soon.

Like all the other Dukes of England, my father didn't have a *job*, per se, but he owned this land. His title meant he was often away doing who knows what, being important and mysterious. He did die at a business dinner, though the specifics weren't given.

My eyes land on a small sculpture on the right side of his desk. A skull wearing a crown. As my finger grazes the gold crown, a shiver works down my spine. The sculpture doesn't go with his old man aesthetic at all, but something about it feels familiar. Something catches in my mind, and I vaguely recall a memory of him. I was young, maybe seven or eight, and he'd spilled coffee on his shirt during breakfast. He's taken his shirt off at the table before going up to his room to change, and...

The scar on his bicep. *A skull with a crown.*

I'd completely forgotten about that.

When I asked him about it, he just smiled and told me it was something he did when he was young and stupid.

Shaking my head, I forward the drafted funeral announcement to Cecelia's private secretary. He will send everything out and coordinate RSVPs. I suppose nobility has its perks. Once I'm sure we're all set for tomorrow—and after googling how to prepare for a funeral, just in case we missed anything—I log off and lean back in my father's chair.

The hairs on the back of my neck begin to prickle, and I glance out into the black, endless night outside my father's office window.

My stomach drops, but no one is out there.

Or at least, no one I can see.

CHAPTER 5

Harlow

Of course it's pouring as Cecelia and I arrive at Blackwell Minster the next day. The large, stone edifice is normally a light grey, but today, the rain makes it look dark and foreboding. Rose must have Archie because I haven't seen him all morning. Cecelia and I greet the guests at the door, and I'm surprised at how everything came together so easily. The wake passes quickly. The priest's eulogy is bracketed with dramatic organ music every few minutes. Cecelia remains stoic, and I look down at my black boots too often. All in all, though, it's a pleasant wake.

Everyone starts the quarter mile walk to the cemetery for the committal. It's raining, but the people in attendance have prepared and brought umbrellas. Cecelia carries Archie under her massive umbrella, her expression serious and forlorn. She looks so elegant, though, in a form-fitting black dress, black stilettos, and an elegant, black fascinator.

On the complete opposite end of the spectrum is me, wearing a long, black, flowy dress with wide sleeves, complete with lace-up boots. I didn't do anything to my hair, as per usual, so my curls fall down my back in a messy heap. I look and feel like a medieval witch, and the setting only exacerbates that feeling. Rainy days in England remind me of the old, gothic romance novels I used to love as a teenager.

Once we get to the cemetery, the mood shifts, and I get that same sensation of someone watching me. There are over a hundred people in attendance. Maybe more. Cecelia decided not to open the funeral to the public, as is sometimes done with funerals for nobility. Instead, we kept the guest list short and concise, not wanting a huge ordeal. Which is why, as I look around, I'm surprised to see four large men standing near the back of the crowd.

They *definitely* weren't at the wake.

I would've remembered them, as we watched every single person file in carrying an official invitation per the instructions. But these guys are young. Good-looking. I would've remembered them because they would've stood out in a sea of middle-aged bodies.

Their murderous expressions highlight their chiseled, clenched jaws, like they're angry for some reason. Their whole demeanor is gloomy and foreboding. They're standing at the back, watching over everything, like the four horsemen of death.

Who are they? And why are they here?

Swallowing roughly, I study their appearances, my eyes raking over the suits that must've been tailored to their individual forms. There's no way a man could look that good in a suit off the rack. They're clean-shaven except for one of them. Probably English nobility if their shiny watches and polished shoes are any indication. The man farthest to the left has black curly hair that's longer on top. His eyes are dark, yet his skin is pale. He looks the most put together, like a GQ model. *Billionaire Daddy.* The second guy has wavy dark blonde hair that's pulled into a messy bun, with piercing blue eyes. *Trouble.* He's also the only one with scruff, and the only one not wearing a watch. Plus, instead of the leather dress shoes the others are wearing, he has on black, leather converse. *Hmm.*

The third guy has short, dark hair and green eyes. His skin has a more golden, bronzed hue, and he's scowling into the crowd like he has something up his ass. His cheekbones look sharp to the touch, and though he appears as put together as the first guy, he has thick rings on each finger, like he's out getting in bar fights. *Mr. Grumpy.* The fourth guy looks like a goddamn golden retriever next to the rest of them. White-blonde hair that's longer on top and slicked back. His light blue eyes sparkle mirthfully, and I instantly want to touch his hands—the biggest hands I've ever seen. His expression turns serious, and I get goosebumps. Okay, maybe he's not like a golden retriever. *Murder Puppy.*

Despite my observations and funny nicknames, though, something about them scares me. They give off a menacing vibe, like they're about to kidnap someone or collect on a debt. They're dressed nicely, sure, but something about them feels off. Not to mention, they're all tall with large, muscular frames. If I had to guess, they're probably all at least a foot taller than me.

Guy number one—*Billionaire Daddy*—locks eyes with me, and my blood runs cold at the contact. He adjusts his suit, his eyes boring into mine with the kind of intensity that makes my whole body feel like it's vibrating.

"Who are they?" I ask Cecelia, nudging my chin in their direction.

Cecelia glances back to the four men. "Oh, they're the other Blackwell elites. They were friends with your father." She steps a little closer. "The man on the left is Lord Alaric Cross. Next to him is Lord Gideon St. Claire. Then Lord Sterling Beauchamp. And all the way to the right is Lord Theodore Wolf. I've met them a few times."

I raise my eyebrows. "All of them are Lords? Like my dad?"

She nods. "They're nice, but they sort of keep to themselves. They all have houses in Blackwell."

For some reason, I'm reminded of the story my father told me about the five princes. I keep my eyes forward, but that same feeling of someone watching me continues through the rest of the committal. I don't dare look back until it's over, and when I do, the four Lords are gone.

After the funeral, I hang out with Archie for a bit while Cecelia takes a nap. The two of them are headed to her parents' house in the Cotswolds tomorrow morning, and my flight back to New York is later this week. As Archie shows me his endless supply of magnetic blocks, mumbling words that are only somewhat coherent, I try to muster some grief for my father, but I can't dredge up anything. I feel sorry for Cecelia and Archie, but we weren't close enough for me to feel genuinely sad. People were crying today, asking how Cecelia and I were, but how could I tell them that I didn't feel a thing?

Maybe I really am a monster.

We all eat a quick dinner, and I can tell Cecelia is eager to go to bed. I know being around her family for the next couple of weeks will help her massively, and the house will be just fine without her, thanks to Rose and the rest of the household staff. And once she feels better, she'll come back and take up residence as the Duchess of Blackwell. She doesn't seem interested in that position, but I don't push the subject. Whatever she decides to do, when Archie comes of age, he will become Lord Blackwell. My involvement in this little nest of nobility is fluid. I can pop in and out of their lives, focusing on my art in New York. In a way, I'm grateful that my parents never married and left me without a title.

As I get ready for bed, I think of my mother, and how much she would've liked Cecelia and Archie. How she would've loved seeing the resemblance between him and me. I miss her so much, and my eyes prick with tears as I think about the hole in my chest that's been there since that fateful night. I wish I could tell her about everything, ask her about this village, and what she saw in my father.

Wiping my cheeks, I look at myself in the mirror. I can't ask her. I can't change the past and bring her back. But I *will* always have this tiny pocket of family here, and that has to count for something. I didn't exactly want to come back here, but I'm glad I did. Cecelia was right. They are my family now, and even though it took my father's death to get to know them, I will be grateful we all came together.

I slide my bare legs between the thick duvet and the bottom sheet, reveling in the comfort. Being here for a couple more days will be nice. I can get to know Rose, I can discover more about who my father was, and I can connect with my ancestors. I can't remember what year my father said the Blackwell family settled here, but I know it was a *long* time ago. In the 1200s, I believe. As much as I fight against it, I share his blood, which means this house and this village are connected to me in a strange way. I might as well get to know the area a bit better.

I grab my kindle and switch off the room light, sighing contentedly. I thought this whole trip would trigger another episode for me, but it hasn't so far. I'm pleasantly surprised about how well I'm handling everything. I fall asleep quickly, my eyes growing heavy. Just as I feel the tug of sleep pulling me under, that same prickling sensation of being watched slams into me, and my eyes snap open.

Three figures are standing in the darkness at the edge of my bed.

I open my mouth to scream, but a warm hand comes to my mouth, and a second later, I feel the distinct, sharp tip of a knife against my windpipe.

CHAPTER 6

※

Sterling

"Don't move, or I'll slit your pretty little throat," I growl.

Harlow doesn't whimper or cry like I expect her to. Instead, she just glares right up at me, her face full of fury. Though, she does flinch away from me slightly, and that reaction has me all sorts of confused about where my allegiance lies.

Average height, curvy in the right places, with dark, curly hair and uptilted blue eyes. I can't take my attention off her as her chest rises and falls more quickly. She flicks her eyes to Alaric, Gideon, and Theo at the end of the bed, and then her nostrils flare delicately as she turns her blue-eyed gaze back to me. Her breath is warm against my hand.

"I will not hesitate to kill you if you scream," I add, removing my hand from her mouth. When I do, she flinches again, and I nearly break my teeth from clenching my jaw so hard. Someone hurt her once, and that thought alone makes me feel downright fucking *murderous*.

She scowls. "Who the hell are you, and how did you get into my bedroom?"

"I know the security password."

Her brows furrow slightly, and I can see the wheels spinning in her mind. My eyes take in her heart-shaped face and full lips. It's too dark to see them, but I know—from studying the picture Theo sent around—that there are light, delicate freckles lining the bridge of her nose. *God, she'd look incredible on her knees.* So many women have that artificial feel, like they've sprayed, plucked, and plastered on anything beautiful about them. But not Harlow. She's perfect in every way. Though if she tries anything, I won't hesitate to kill her.

"Come on, let's get this over with," Alaric muses, moving to the other side of the bed.

"Let him do his thing," Theo adds, sounding amused.

"You didn't answer my question," she grits out, narrowing her eyes at me before turning them to the others. "Who. Are. You," she bites out.

I pull the knife away from her skin as her eyes scan each of us thoroughly. She knows she's outnumbered, and hopefully, she's not stupid enough to try anything. I hold the knife at my side just in case, though I can tell she's scared and trying to hide it. Her eyes flick between us again, assessing us. *Studying* us. Maybe she knows who we are, and that fact alone keeps her from screaming for help. Around here, we're respected. *Worshipped.* And most people never see beyond the aristocratic veil we've hung up. Most people never see the monsters hiding in plain sight.

"I'm Lord Sterling Beauchamp," I say.

"I know who you are," she bites back. "I saw you all earlier at my father's funeral."

"Observant little monster," Gideon mutters.

She snaps her gaze to his face. "*You* were the one messaging me on Instagram," she accuses.

He grins. "Good girl."

Jesus Christ, she's gorgeous. And the way she's acting like she doesn't give a fuck about anything is hot as hell. My cock hardens when I think about pinning her against this bed, about *dominating* her.

Muffling her screams.

Watching her eyes widen with fear.

And then watching them roll into the back of her head as I make her little cunt pulse around my leaking cock.

"What Sterling is trying and failing to tell you is that you are one of us now," Gideon says from the end of the bed. He's toying with his goddamn knife again.

"One of you? Like hell I am," she retorts. Her voice shakes slightly.

"Do you want the short version or the long version?"

Harlow sits up on her knees, and the covers fall away from her body. She's not wearing pants, and her thin camisole means that we can see her peaked nipples, and the red panties grazing her voluptuous ass. *God, what I'd do to push her down on the bed right now, swipe those panties to the side, and make her ass shake as I drive into her.* Licking her lips, she crosses her arms. "I don't want any version. I want you out of my room," she says defiantly.

I rub my mouth. "Unfortunately, that's not an option."

"Your father was a Lord of Darkness," Alaric says, standing across from me, obviously tired of playing cat and mouse. "Five families. Five bloodlines. We have ruled the underbelly of England for a thousand years. Your father's death means the next heir is... you."

"Well, technically, it's you *and* Archie," Theo interjects, shrugging.

"Archie?" Harlow looks at me. "He's a baby."

I tilt my head and crawl onto the bed, scooting closer on the mattress so that my body is an inch away from hers. She visibly shrinks away from me.

"We were prepared to wait sixteen years. But then we found out about you," I add, running a finger down the side of her face before she smacks my hand away.

I ignore the rumbling of anger inside of me at her defiance. It makes me want to punish her, makes me want to give her nightmares about what I'd do to her.

"Well, neither of us are joining your stupid cult."

"Jesus fuck," Gideon murmurs. Flicking his blade out, he walks over to Harlow and slams her down by her neck so that she's face down. This close to her, I can hover over her face as Gideon does his thing. My fists curl at my sides.

"Hey! Stop, let me go!" she screams, her panicked voice muffled from being shoved into the duvet.

Gideon's hand holds her neck, and he places a knife at the back of her knee. "The popliteal artery runs close to the joint capsule of the knee," he snarls, poking the tip of the knife against her flesh. "One more bratty comment, and I'll slice it. You'll bleed out in ninety seconds."

Harlow takes a shuddering breath. Twisting her face to the side, she looks at me with daggers in her eyes.

"Fine. Give me the short version."

I stand up, frowning. "For a thousand years, people in our five families have kept secrets. We've assassinated public figures. We've worked both with the crown and against it. We swear allegiance only to ourselves."

She rolls her eyes. The *fucking* audacity. "Can you explain in plain English, please?"

Alaric coughs and looks away as I grind my teeth together. "We are considered the oldest and most powerful organized crime group in the world."

"Yeah, got that part," she huffs.

Baring my teeth, I reach over and grab a fistful of her hair, yanking her neck backward. "I dare you to keep talking back," I seethe.

Something akin to a whimper escapes her throat, so I grip harder, enjoying the way I seem to be inflicting pain, yet hating myself for being the one to cause her hands to tremble. "Over the last thousand years, we have maintained our ancient rites, passing them down orally, member to member, and through secret codes. Our order is based exclusively on blood ties, like I said earlier."

I wait for her to speak back, but she just breathes heavily as she glares up at me. I release my hold on her hair.

"We deal with drug trafficking, mainly, competing only with the Sicilian mafia in that regard. There's also arms trafficking, money laundering, extortion—and there's a *lot* of extortion—and loan sharking. We do not kill women and we do not deal with prostitution. A large part of our order is hunting down the bad guys and killing them slowly."

"Like Robinhood," Theo chimes from the end of the bed.

"*No*, nothing like Robinhood."

Theo frowns. "Hey, fuck you, man. Robinhood was totally based on the order."

Jesus. Theo and Gideon are always fucking around. It's like they don't take this seriously at all, even though I know they'd take a bullet for me in a heartbeat.

I always seem to be the only one taking my job seriously.

"Anyway," I continue, ignoring Theo. "We have a relationship with just about every cartel member, mafia organization, and oligarchy in the world."

Harlow raises her hand. She *fucking* raises her hand.

The sass, I swear to God.

"I have a question."

"Go ahead," I grit out.

"You're saying my father did all of this?"

"He *taught* us all of this."

She narrows her eyes, but this time, it's out of curiosity. "Okay. Keep talking."

I pace back and forth in front of the bed, some of my annoyance dissipating with each breath. "We are capable of heavily influencing local and national politics. We infiltrate every single sector of this country. Our activities make up a large portion of England's GDP. We don't have official employees. We run the show ourselves, utilizing our relationship with other organizations. Sometimes they betray us. Sometimes we betray them, though that's rare. There is murder, and there is danger lurking around every corner. But we also have access to every secret, every historical artifact that has gone into hiding. Have you heard of the Illuminati?"

She grunts. "Yes, I have read a Dan Brown novel before."

"Give us more sass, I dare you," Gideon growls, gripping her knee tighter.

Harlow quiets after that, albeit reluctantly.

"There was no Illuminati. Not really. It was us. The secrets people think are lost, the documents and evidence that no one can find? We hid it. We house more secrets than anyone else in the world."

Gideon removes his knife from the back of her knee, and she crawls away from both of us. Pulling her knees into her chest, she glares right at me as she says, "Prove it."

Fuck, she's feisty.

I begin to unbutton my shirt. Her eyes watch my fingers for a second, catching on my muscled core before they come back up to my eyes. I don't miss the way her mouth drops open and snaps closed. In fact, her perusal of my body *almost* makes me want to smile.

And I never smile.

Pulling off my shirt, I show off the scar on my right bicep.

"Look familiar?" I ask.

Her lips part as she sits up quickly. "My dad—he has that same skull and crown on his desk."

"I got that for him for his fortieth," Gideon muses.

She looks at Gideon, her brow furrowed. "So you were all close?"

I nod. "Closer than brothers." I look between the guys, and we silently convey what we're *not* going to tell her: namely, that we are responsible for her father's death.

That's a story for another day.

Harlow swallows, blinking rapidly. "So... what? Am I just supposed to drop my entire life to hunt down bad guys?" Her throat bobs as Theo lets out a low laugh.

I glare at her. "Let's rephrase that. You *will* drop everything. Or, if you choose to go back to New York, we will recruit Archie when he's old enough."

I know I've hit a nerve when her eyes widen. "And it has to be one of us?"

I nod. "The title of Lord—or Lady—of Darkness is passed down by blood only."

"So, Archie will have to do this if I say no?"

I can see the argument she's having with herself. If she walks away, she's condemning Archie to this life as Charles's only other heir.

Her face falls as she takes everything in. Sitting back down on the bed, her posture is hunched, and she rubs her face with her hands.

"We'll give you the night to think about it," I tell her.

Gideon walks over and places a finger underneath her chin. "Don't be scared, little monster. You've just inherited a whole goddamn family. Your blood runs black, just like ours. Welcome to the Lords of Darkness, Lady Blackwell."

CHAPTER 7

Harlow

Fuck. This.

After they leave rather abruptly, I give myself a few minutes to quell my nerves before I climb out of bed and begin to pack my bag. I don't know what else to do. I've managed to keep my anxiety at bay, but when I think of what they said... what they did as they touched me...

Just like he touched me.

I close my eyes and shake the thoughts away. It won't do me any good to blindly panic. As long as I can think straight, I will find a way out of this predicament. As I begin to toss clothes into a bag, I have this heavy, tugging feeling that I should wait until the morning. That way, I can say a proper goodbye to Cecelia and Archie.

On the other hand, maybe it'll be easier if I just slip back to New York early. I'm sure Cecelia will understand, and I'm sure as hell not waiting around to see what else the *Lords of Darkness* have in store for me. There's no fucking way I'm joining their order, or whatever the fuck they called it. If I warn Cecelia about them, maybe she can go into hiding with Archie–

My phone chimes from my bedside table, and I glance over at the lit screen. Walking over, my eyes scan the text as shivers skitter down my spine.

I wouldn't go anywhere if I were you. You can't outrun us, little monster.

I let out a groan of frustration, slamming my phone face down and flopping myself onto the bed.

What the fuck.

What the fuck.

I knew my dad was someone of importance. But I had no idea it was something like this. How come he never said anything? Then again, he never said much of anything. But if I was going to take over for him one day, surely, he would have warned me?

Maybe he didn't get a chance.

It suddenly occurs to me that maybe he didn't have a stroke, that if being a Lord of Darkness is as dangerous as the guys made it out to be, maybe he died *on the job.*

Grabbing my phone, I begin typing a response furiously.

Me: Did my father really die of a stroke? Or did he die on the job?
Alaric: Does it matter?
Theo: It was a stroke, Harlow.
Sterling: Stop asking questions.

I stare at my phone in surprise. They all come in succinct order. Why are their names programmed into my phone? When I open the group chat, it seems they've all been added to my phone as contacts. Alaric, Gideon, Sterling, Theo. Underneath the company for each of their names is the skull emoji. *Very funny.*

Me: Did you hack into my phone?!
Theo: We hacked into everything.
Theo: We can see your pictures, your texts, your browser history, your kindle library...

My cheeks burn.

Me: WTF.
Gideon: You have quite the taste for sex books, don't you?

I hate them. I really, truly, genuinely *hate* them. The fact that they're attractive and beguiling in some weird, fucked up way means *nothing.* It's the accent. British men always appear hotter because of the accent. That's all it is.

Me: They're romance books, and they're amazing.
Me: Why am I even defending myself? I'm not ashamed.
Sterling: Let's get back on topic now, shall we?
Theo: I want to hear more about the sex books.

I growl with frustration and slam my phone down. They can't just waltz into my life like this and take over. An hour ago, I had no idea who they were, and now I'm just supposed to drop everything and join their stupid order? Because my father died? Absolutely not.

But if I don't... Archie would have to.

Fuck.

Reality comes crashing back into me. I need to *think.* Focus. If this is true, and if I run away, Archie will be slated to take over in sixteen years. Sweet, chubby-cheeked Archie. My brother.

Admitting that out loud, that he's my brother, my family...

Swallowing through the lump in my throat, I rub my neck. What kind of person would I be if I went back to New York and let Archie take my place? What if something happened to him? I could never forgive myself.

Or...

Maybe there's a way to keep us both safe.

There's no way either of us are going to join the Lords of Darkness.

I'll find a way out for Archie, Cecelia, and me. I'll figure out a way to keep us all safe. But until then, I need to let them think I was considering it, or I would be risking all our lives.

Me: I have one condition.

Sterling: There are no conditions.

Me: If you want me to join the stupid Lords of Darkness cult, there most definitely are conditions.

Sterling: You seem to think you're running the show, but that couldn't be further from the truth.

Me: Well, you're kind of relying on me to say yes, right? If I say no, you can't stop me. And I assume you'll be one man short for sixteen years. You need me. Admit it.

I smirk. *Ha.* Gotcha.

They think they could just walk into my life and irrevocably alter the course of my future? Hell to the no. I'm in charge of myself now.

I didn't come this far just to give it all up. I didn't overcome what I did just to succumb to four men who say I have no choice.

I would take my fate back into my own hands.

Alaric: What is your condition?

Me: I will join your order. In four years. After I'm done with art school.

This would give Archie and Cecelia time to make a run for it. And it would give me time to figure a way out of this. I stare at my phone, waiting for a response. My heart is racing, and my stomach flutters nervously. It's a fair compromise on paper, but I have no idea if they're the compromising type. If they are, great. If not... I am fucked. But at least I can say that I tried.

Gideon: Do you really think we'd allow you to leave?

Sterling: We don't accept that condition.

Fuck. I need to get Archie and Cecelia the fuck out of England, then.

Alaric: Do you realize how dangerous it is for you to be out in the open right now? We've made ourselves a great number of enemies over the years. Soon, they will find out about you—and that's if they don't already know, considering you were at the funeral. Do you want to know what they'd do to you if they found you?

I roll my teeth over my bottom lip, my thumb hovering over the screen. *Fuck.*

Theo: That's not even considering that Archie would be in danger, too. You will both be hunted until one of you joins the order. After you join us—because you basically have no choice—they'd have to get through us first, little monster. And that's sure as fuck never going to happen once you're officially ours.

My breathing hitches, and my stomach swoops low. I'm not sure why. These guys are my enemies, whether they want to believe it or not. It doesn't matter how many proclamations they make like this. At the end of the day, they are bad guys. And they want to drag me down to hell with them.

I *will* find a way out of this. I have to.

Me: I need more time to think about it.
Sterling: You can have until tomorrow.
Rolling my eyes, I respond.
Me: SO generous of you. Thank you, sir.
Sterling: Don't call me sir unless you're ready to get on your knees for me.
Again, my breath stutters.
Alaric: There's a formal dinner tomorrow night in London. You will be there.
Me: Fuck that.
Sterling: You will be there, or we will have no choice but to assume you've declined our invitation. And that you've accepted the risk to both you and Archie.
Fuck.
Me.
Okay, I need to figure out my plan of escape soon, then.
Theo: A car will pick you up. Be ready at 17:00.
Me: Fuck you.
Sterling: Goodnight, Harlow.

Groaning, I roll over and put my arm over my face. How the hell did I get myself into this position? Screw my dad for never telling me about this, for never preparing me. Though, what if these guys are lying? I pick my phone back up and do a Google search. Of course, nothing comes up about the Lords of Darkness, and I go back eighteen pages. How have they never been mentioned anywhere over the last thousand years? What if they *are* lying?

But *why* would they be lying?

I think of my father's office. Of the skull and crown, which seemed to be made of solid gold. Of the scar on his bicep. I didn't say anything to them about that memory of my father with the burn identical to Sterling's. I didn't want to admit that their story made sense. Not in front of them, at least.

They exude power. The way they watched me during the funeral. The way they were able to circumvent the security system at Blackwell House...

Somehow, I know in my gut that they're not lying.

I sigh heavily, feeling a headache start to come on. The pounding begins behind my eyes, and I curl up in my duvet, shoving all thoughts of the Lords of Darkness out of my mind. It takes me a few minutes, but finally, the lull of sleep pulls me under.

CHAPTER 8

Theo

I grab the to-go coffees, making my way back down the narrow street to the old tower in the city that encompasses our office. It's not exactly an office, per se—we don't do any actual work there. But for tax purposes, we bought Crowne Tower to do business for our "consulting" firm. It's the place we can get out of our respective houses and talk or coordinate our next target. Plus, the building is cool as fuck. A medieval tower with dark beams, stone walls, and an ancient prison cell in the basement—which has come in handy numerous times.

Using my keycard, I grant myself access to the office, taking the narrow, stone steps up two flights of stairs. When I push the modern door open, our loft-style workspace comes into view. Alaric is at his desk, scowling at his computer. Gideon is on the couch, one leg over his knee, scrolling on his phone. And Sterling is at the window, looking out onto the street with his hands in his pockets.

"Got coffee for you fuckers," I mutter. "Maybe it'll perk you all up."

Gideon pockets his phone and looks at me. "I still think we should've taken her back here last night."

Handing him his black coffee, I shake my head. "No. We need to lull her into a false sense of security. Once she's branded, she's not going anywhere. But if we come on too strong, I get the feeling she'll spook."

"How do we know she hasn't already?" Sterling asks, twisting around.

I hand him his cappuccino. "Because I have surveillance cameras in the house. She hasn't left." Reaching into my pocket, I show him my phone. It's been playing a constant loop of the front door of Blackwell House, Harlow's bedroom, and the rose garden—just in case she tries to escape through the back door. "See?" The footage cuts to Harlow's room, and she's still asleep in her bed.

Sterling takes my phone and narrows his eyes. "Good. Keep an eye on her." Handing it back, he takes a sip of his coffee.

"How does she work into our plan for tonight?" Alaric asks, glancing up from his screen. "This is an important job, so if—"

"I know it's an important job," I say casually, walking his macchiato over to him and setting it down. "I'm keen to see how she performs under pressure."

His brows knit together. "What the fuck are you insinuating?"

I cock my head and sip my triple espresso. "We all have our strengths and weaknesses. If she's going to be a part of our order, we need to figure out what hers are."

Gideon snorts. "Or we could just ask her."

I give him a coy smile. "We could. Or we could have fun with it."

"You're going to exploit her, aren't you?" Alaric asks, giving me an amused look. "Work your magic and shit?"

I sit down at my desk, moving my mouse to power up my computer. "I have one true gift," I joke, logging in with my thirty-digit password. If anyone can dig up any dirt on her, it's me. If anyone can break a person by knowing their deepest, darkest secrets, it's me. I'll find out what makes her scream with terror—what gives her nightmares.

And I'll use it against her.

"You're sick," Alaric adds.

"We were all tested," I argue. "By her father, I might add." I grimace when I think of the shit we had to do, fresh off our eighteenth birthdays. Back then, Charles worked alone. Our fathers had been killed a week prior. *Betrayed* is more like it. He was desperate to restore the order back to the five branches quickly, so he rode us hard.

Our little monster wouldn't be exempt from that same rigorous preparation.

"So, what? We're going to ask her to complete the job tonight?"

I shrug. "I'm not sure. I haven't thought that far in advance."

"It's too risky," Sterling says seriously. "If she fails, if our target gets away..." he trails off, scowling at each of us. "We can't risk it."

"Fine. Then we make her watch," I reply.

Gideon snorts. "*That's* going to be entertaining. Let her watch as we slaughter another man."

Alaric tilts his head, plucking a piece of visible lint off of his pristine suit jacket. "It's not the worst idea. There are ways to keep her quiet in case she puts up a fight."

"You realize that would make her a witness?" Sterling interjects. "How the hell do we know she won't narc?"

I smirk. "Because the first thing we're going to do is make her ours. *Officially.*"

They all look at me with questioning eyes. Gideon speaks first.

"Fuck. I forget how fucking crazy you are under that golden boy persona."

I give him an evil grin. "She won't be able to run to the cops after. Because she'll bear the mark of the Lords of Darkness."

CHAPTER 9

Harlow

I hardly ever sleep in, so when I wake up at half-past nine, I climb out of bed and rub my eyes, disoriented. I think I hear Archie chortling about something downstairs, and that reminds me that they're leaving soon. Throwing on some sweatpants and a sweatshirt, I pull my hair into a low bun before walking down the stairs, ignoring the sinking feeling when I remember what happened last night.

Yeah, I'm going to need to take care of that soon.

Cecelia is trying to wrangle two massive suitcases while Archie points at the door, yelling, "Go! Go! Archie go!" and then cackling like a little psycho.

Smiling, I saunter up to them.

"Oh, good," Cecelia breathes, looking visibly relieved. "I didn't want to wake you, but I was hoping we'd get to say goodbye."

Before I can respond, she pulls me into a tight hug.

"You guys are leaving right now?" I ask, and I realize suddenly that I don't want them to go. I don't want to be here all alone.

Cecelia pulls away. "Yep. Car's waiting outside." She gives me a warm smile. "I've really enjoyed getting to know you, Harlow. You remind me of Charles, and that brings me comfort," she says, her voice wrought with emotion. "I hope you know you're welcome back any time."

Looking down at Archie, he grins up at me with perfect little chicklet teeth.

"Sissy," he says, running up to my leg and wrapping himself around it. "I lub sissy."

Well, shit.

I swallow the emotion clawing up my throat and look back up at Cecelia.

"I've actually been thinking of staying for a little longer," I tell her slowly. "Get to know Archie when you guys get back. Maybe learn a bit more about my heritage and ancestry."

Figure out a way to make sure we're all safe somewhere on the other side of the world...

Cecelia's face brightens. "Oh, that would be wonderful! I'm not sure how long we'll be gone..." She trails off as her expression turns sad again. "But it would be so nice for Rose to have you around."

I smile. "Why not."

Bending down so that I'm crouching, I hold my arms out. "Have a nice trip, Archie," I tell him gently. He runs into my arms and gives me a tight hug. I close my eyes, inhaling his baby scent.

There's no fucking way those sickos are ever going to touch him. I'll make damn sure of that.

Saying goodbye, I wave from the front door, with Rose at my side as they drive away in a black SUV.

"I think it'll be good for her," Rose mutters. "She needs to be with family right now."

I nod. "I agree."

"I honestly wonder if she'll ever come back," Rose adds. "Your father was the only thing tying her here."

I don't know what to say to that.

"Oh, I almost forgot. You've had a package delivered this morning," she says brightly, walking back into the house.

Closing the door, I follow her to the dining room, where a large grey box is sitting. A crisp white ribbon is wrapped around it with a perfect bow on top.

"Vivienne Westwood," Rose mutters, clucking her tongue. "Very posh." She walks away, leaving me with the gift.

I already know who it's from.

It's surprisingly light as I carry it up the stairs. After setting it on the bed, I close my door and walk over to it, untying the ribbon. When I lift the top of the box off, I gasp at the gold dress folded neatly inside. The material is a mix of gold silk and small, shining gold beads, and it falls through my fingers just like liquid metal would. Holding it up, I look at myself in the mirror. I've never been a big gold person. But this? It brightens my eyes, and brings out the golden hue of my skin. I pull my lower lip between my teeth, contemplating.

If I try the dress on, they win.

If I ignore the dress, they still win.

Might as well look pretty while I lose.

Taking my clothes off, I step into it. There's no zipper since the material is stretchy. I step over to the mirror and stare at myself with wide eyes.

Holy shit. I look... *good?* I've never worn a dress this nice. The neckline drapes low, but not too low, and the material hugs my curves like cling wrap. I turn around and admire my backside. Somehow... *somehow...* they'd managed to find the perfect dress for me. The back is open, held together by two thin straps. It flows from my hips all the way to the floor, and the material barely grazes the

Persian rug, not a millimeter too long or too short. It's like they had a cardboard cutout of my body and tailored this dress around me. *How?*

My phone chimes from my bed, and I walk over, reading the text.

Gideon: Send us a picture.

How the hell did they know I was wearing the dress?

I look around warily. Is there a hidden camera in here, or are they just being creepy?

Me: Screw you.

Sterling: Remember to be ready at 17:00.

Me: I don't have shoes. I can't go.

Sterling: On it.

I scowl at my phone and turn it off, laying down in my dress and grabbing my kindle. Once I power it up, I notice my book selections have broadened, and my library is filled with books I've never read.

War and Peace.

Ulysses.

Catch-22.

Gawking at my screen, I find at least fifty new books in my library—all classic literature.

The *nerve*.

Deleting them all one by one, I click into my newest rom com about a woman who discovers she's the long-lost heir to a country in Europe. Swallowing, I click out of it. *Too close to home right now.* I find one of my favorite smutty books about a priest, settling down into the duvet—still in my dress, mind you. I assume they'll want this back after, so I might as well wear the shit out of it.

An hour later, Rose knocks on my door with another box.

"Another deliver—" She gasps. "Is that the dress?" she asks, setting the small box down on my dresser.

I sit up. *Dammit.* What do I tell her? I open my mouth to make up an excuse when she narrows her eyes and gives me a coy smile.

"Are you seeing someone?"

I snap my mouth shut before opening it again. "Yes. It's very new, and he's taking me to London tonight."

She grins and does a little shimmy. "My, my. You sure do work fast!"

I shrug. "It's nothing serious. We met online."

"Well, please be safe. I've heard horror stories about online dating." She wrings her hands nervously. And I'm not sure why I open my stupid mouth. Maybe it's because I don't want her to worry, and knowing that I'm with my father's peers might set her at ease.

"It's Alaric Cross," I tell her quickly. "That's who I'm going to see tonight."

Her face brightens. "Oh, Lord Cross! How lovely. He's such a handsome young man."

I can't even fight her on that one. The man looks like he should be on a runway somewhere.

"Yep. Anyway, he's sending a car for me at five."

Rose does that same shimmy again, and her whole body shakes with excitement. "Oh, shall I send for hair and makeup?"

I almost say no—*almost*. But when else will I have this kind of opportunity? I'm not going to slither my way out of this deal today. It's going to take a few days—maybe even a few weeks—to get all my ducks in a row. I have to pretend I'm going along with it in the meantime.

"That would be great, thank you."

"How exciting! Your father was very fond of Lord Cross."

So you were all close?

Closer than brothers.

I give her a tight smile. "I'm sure he was."

"I'll have everyone arrive at half-past one?" She looks at my mess of hair, still pulled into a messy low bun. "Or maybe one on the dot, so you have time to get your hair washed?"

"Sounds great. Thank you, Rose."

She skips—literally *skips*—to the door. "I'll bring some food up for you, Miss Windsor."

Nodding, I wave as she walks away, and then I flop myself back onto my bed.

What the hell did I just agree to?

Remembering the box she brought up, I walk over to it, opening the lid to find four-inch black stilettos.

Nope.

Closing it back up, I toss the box to the back of my walk-in closet, and then I go back to reading about confessional blow jobs.

⁂

Five hours later, I can't believe the transformation. The two hairdressers in my room flit around, packing their things up. The makeup artist is watching me closely, trying to decide what else she can pluck or blot, I'm sure. I've never been a high-maintenance girl. I usually wear minimal makeup, and my hair is too crazy to tame, so I gave up years ago, other than my yearly haircut. But right now? I hardly recognize myself.

The hairdressers had some contraption for the bath so that they could wash my hair without getting me wet. Fancy shampoo and conditioner meant my hair was easy to brush through. After a quick trim, they blew it dry and straightened it. I never wear it straight, and because of that, I didn't realize how long it was. It falls nearly to the top of my butt. And my makeup? It's insane what a little contour can do. Add in smokey eyes, nude lipstick, and false lashes... and I look better than I've ever looked. I'd taken a quick shower before everyone arrived, pulling on my only thong so that my panty line didn't show through the dress.

Not my underwear of choice—but it's all for *the* dress. I don't even need a bra since the dress holds my ladies up nicely.

Rose walks in and gasps again, holding her hand to her mouth. "You look stunning!"

Smiling, I sit down on the bed and begin to pull my Doc Martens on.

"Oh, my..." she whispers, staring at me. "Are those the shoes you're wearing?"

I snort. She's bouncing from foot to foot, trying to be mindful and kind. "Unless you want me to break my ankle, then yes."

"I'm sure Cecelia has something. What size are you—"

"It's fine," I interrupt. "You can hardly see my shoes when I stand up."

To prove a point, I stand as the dress cascades down to the floor, covering my footwear of choice.

"What about a jacket? Cecelia has a nice fur shrug—"

"I have one," I say, grabbing the only jacket I thought to bring. A genuine leather moto jacket. Pulling it on, it makes me look like a total baddie. I hold my hands out and pop a hip. "See?"

Rose, to her credit, just beams at me as the hair and makeup people depart.

"Very lovely. Shall I wait up for you tonight? Or..." she trails off, winking.

I groan. "I am not sleeping with him if that's what you mean. But he's been very mysterious about what we're doing, so I'm not sure when I'll be home. There's no need to wait up."

I see the wry smile begin to form, so I hold my hand out. "I want to reiterate *again* that no sex will be had," I tell her.

She smirks as she walks out, and I sit on my bed, waiting for 17:00.

I check my phone—it's 16:46. I pop my anti-anxiety pills into my purse and head downstairs to wait. Just as I lower myself onto the couch in the sitting room, my phone chimes.

Sterling: Come out.

How romantic.

Yelling my goodbye to Rose, I stride out of the door to see all four of them leaning against a dark grey Range Rover with muddy tires. And while the car may be dirty, I can't help but notice that they all look like they've just come back from a hike. Jeans, dirty shirts with... is that blood? Why am I so dressed up when they look like they've been digging someone's grave? Well, everyone except Alaric, whose grey t-shirt and jeans are spotless.

"I thought a car was picking me—"

"Get in, Harlow," Alaric growls.

His tone causes me to pause. The dress, hair, and makeup were all fun and games, but I think I'm in over my head associating with these brutes. And if that *is* blood on their shirts... what the *hell* am I doing willingly getting into the car with them?

I need to get myself out of this situation.

But... how?

"If you want us to clap for showing up looking like a goddamn princess, here you go," Theo says sarcastically, clapping loudly. "Well done."

Grinding my jaw, I look over my shoulder. The last thing I need is for Rose to see me standing here with all of them, especially in their state.

"You told me to dress nice—"

"There's been a change of plans," Gideon says, and my eyes snap to his.

It's only then that I see the knife in his hand.

What other choice do I have? If I go back into the house, it's not going to stop them from hunting me down. Or worse...

I might as well get tonight over with.

You've been through hell and back, Harlow Windsor.

You can handle one dinner with these assholes, and then you can figure out a loophole in this whole Lords of Darkness bullshit. This is just temporary.

Standing taller, I walk forward. "Lead the way, sir," I taunt, smirking as I pass Sterling.

I don't miss the way something dark passes behind his eyes.

CHAPTER 10

ALARIC

I drive away from Blackwell House quickly. Our little detour earlier is going to make us very fucking late to the dinner tonight, but it is what it is, I guess. Harlow is quiet in the back, and when I glance in the rearview mirror, I see Sterling clenching his jaw and staring out of the window. To fit everyone in, we had to set her on his lap, and I can tell he's not happy about it. It's not my fault that we're all over six-foot-three, taking up three spots for two people. Though I'm not sure if he's angry that she's on his lap, or if he likes it and just refuses to admit how goddamn beautiful she looks.

My eyes glance over her silky, straight hair. Personally, I prefer the curls, but the straight hair makes me think of how it would look hanging over her large, bare tits. And that, in turn, makes me wonder how she'd look naked, with voluptuous hips, thick, womanly thighs, a soft tummy, and fuck, those tits again. I can see the outline of them and how they fill and stretch the dress perfectly. I'm sure they'd fill my palms perfectly, too.

Is it wrong to think all of this about our only Lady? Maybe. In a thousand years, being as close as we all are... it's bound to happen. She's not the first Lady of Darkness. I imagine in our line of work, where we work under the mantra of kill or be killed, things can get passionate and heated quickly. In a way, perhaps it brought them closer—and just like our quintet, perhaps it will bring us all a little closer.

"Did you not receive the shoes I sent?" Sterling grits out, his voice low.

Harlow snorts. "I couldn't walk in those spiky things."

My lips tilt up into a smile. "You'll need to learn soon, little monster," I tell her.

Her eyes snap to me in the rearview mirror, those fierce, blue irises boring into mine from the back seat. Her makeup intensifies the blue somehow, and *fuck me*, she looks so goddamn hot. It's going to be hard to stay away from her.

"I'm fine in my boots, thank you very much."

"As a Lady, you will be expected to adhere to the dress code," I add.

I turn onto the main road, keeping my attention on where we're headed. My eyes flick to hers in the mirror, just in time to see her nostrils flare delicately.

"Let's get some things straight," she tells us confidently. Must be the New Yorker in her. She doesn't know when to shut the fuck up. "One, I will wear the dresses. This one is nice, and as long as I don't have to wear anything ridiculous, you can put me in whatever you want."

I can't help but envision her covered in my come.

"Two, I will wear whatever shoes I want. Did you know that every single muscle in your body relies on your feet? They are the foundation of movement, so I have to be comfortable. Three, I will read what I want to read. If you're going to make me join this dumbass order, I will need to decompress. Especially since it seems like you all fought off a pack of wolves and barely lived to tell the tale before picking me up. If you mess with my Kindle library one more time, I will cut you."

Feisty little one.

I can't help the smile that breaks out on my face.

"It wasn't a pack of wolves. It was a fucking rapist, and his body is in the trunk," Gideon says nonchalantly, playing with his knife and looking out of the passenger seat window.

I watch Harlow in the mirror for her reaction. Her throat bobs, and then she flattens her palms on her thighs before turning around to verify Gideon's statement.

"Holy fuck," she whispers, turning back around and squeezing her eyes shut. "Holy fuck," she repeats, louder this time. "I'm an idiot. You're going to kill me, aren't you? You're going to kill me, and I just got in the car with you, and oh my God, did you all kill my father?" she asks, her face white.

I furrow my brows. She fumbles for something in her purse, but I can't see what it is.

"Harlow," Theo says from the other back seat. "Calm dow–"

"Oh my God, that's a dead body," she says quickly. Her breathing is way too erratic. I find Theo's eyes in the rearview mirror, nodding once as I pull off to the side of the road. My eyes flick between the shoulder of the road and the mirror. "You guys... killed him. Bullet through the head if I'm not mistaken." I see her pop a pill, but before I can ask her about it, she continues her tirade. "I'm in a car with murderers–" She squeaks in pain just as Theo plunges the syringe into her thigh before pulling it out a second later. At least he was quick and injected her before she noticed.

"What the fuck did you just do?" she yells. Rearing her fist back, she punches Theo square in the nose.

Because he wasn't expecting that, he doesn't stop her, and then Sterling clamps his hands around her arms, keeping her thrashing body still as her angry eyes find mine in the mirror. Gideon just laughs quietly to himself.

"What... did... you..." she trails off, and her eyes go hazy as her body begins to slow. "Mother... fuckers..." she whispers, just before she completely slumps over, losing control of every muscle in her body, even her vocal cords. She's still conscious and awake, but she won't be able to speak or move for a solid hour.

"Much quieter now," Gideon chimes.

I scowl as I make my way back down the country road to the barn. It's still light out, so we're going to need to wait to burn the body. But we also need to get the body out of the car, too. We've never been stopped by the police with a body in the car, and today was not going to be the first day that happened. Especially since the resounding mess and cleanup of killing more people would be tiresome.

Parking in the back, away from the road, I climb out of the car and open the back door. Harlow glares at me silently as I pick her up and slump her limp body over my shoulder. Lightly smacking her ass, I smile as we walk inside. I can only *imagine* how much she hates me right this very second. In fact, I can feel the vitriol rolling off her.

"It's your lucky day, Harlow. You get to meet your ancestors."

CHAPTER 11

Harlow

I can't scream. It's like something invisible is clogging up my throat, making my muscles and limbs completely numb. I'm in a twilight state, awake, feeling everything, but just... numb. Completely numb.

I wish I could fight back. I'd bite off one of Alaric's fingers for touching my ass like that.

Like he fucking owns me.

Bastard.

Maybe my way out of this mess would be to just kill them all and spend the rest of my life in jail. It'd be better than spending it with them.

And Theo—I could kill him with my bare hands for using that syringe against me. How did they expect I was going to react to a dead fucking body in the trunk? How could they possibly be surprised I would start to hyperventilate? There's a reason I have to take two anti-anxiety pills every day. I'm not like them; I've never been around a dead body before.

Besides my mom.

Alaric sets me down in a chair gently. I slump over, trying to scream again. He ties some rope around my waist and my shoulders to hoist me up as if I'm in a child's seat. *Prick.* I want to look around, but I can't move my neck. We're in an old barn—cross-hatched beams and stone walls give it away. But it's also been restored because the windows are new and thick.

Probably soundproofed, I realize.

The only thing in front of me is a pile of wood. My stomach churns with nausea, my lunch threatening to come back up as I realize what they intend to do—burn the body.

The four of them are talking quietly a few feet away from me. God, I wish I could tell them how *fucked* this whole situation is. It doesn't help that I feel like I'm choking on my saliva, and my mouth is filled with a horrid, bitter taste. *From whatever they injected into me.* My heart races despite being numb. I guess they didn't give me the good stuff to calm me down, because it feels like my rushing pulse is going to make my blood vessels burst. My head throbs and my breathing gets more ragged. Am I choking? Am I *dying?* My throat burns, as if I've been screaming, even though I can't. My skin tingles. Like it's crawling with insects. But I can't move, can't speak.

The pill I just took isn't working.

That same panicked feeling from inside the car begins to fill me with a sense of doom. Except this time, I can't yell, or cry, or do anything except feel it all. Tears stream down my face as my heart pounds against my ribs. Everything feels so heavy, and my body vibrates with nerves.

Sterling walks over and unties me. I try to scream again, but I can't. *Obviously.* He carries me over his shoulder to what looks like a side room, and then he sets me down on my feet, which don't hold me up. Theo comes to my other side, and together, they hold me up underneath my arms. Alaric walks in and flicks on the light. My scream is silent, my throat constricting as the hairs on the back of my neck raise. I can't even close my eyes, which means I am forced to stare at the shelf of skulls. And I know in my gut that these are real human skulls. Bile works up my esophagus at the sheer number in here.

At least fifty.

Maybe more.

Alaric stalks over to the skull farthest to the right, picking it up and admiring it. "I've always been fascinated with death, Harlow. Always loved holding a fresh, warm skull in my hands. A person is guaranteed two major life events—birth, and death. Being the person who initiated the second event..." He smiles, his eyes narrowing on my own. "It's an honor." Holding the skull out in front of him, he cocks his head. *Oh, so he's a psychotic killer. Cool beans.* "I guess we should probably be honest with you now that you can't scream," he says slowly, and my gut tells me I already know what he's about to say.

"We killed your father," he admits slowly, and the air suddenly feels so heavy, so poignant, that it stills. *I knew it.* Somewhere deep inside, I knew they were responsible. A stroke? *Please.* It was a weak excuse from the get-go. "We're not going to kill you, little monster," he adds, his voice way too fucking amused for this conversation. "In case that's what you're thinking. Unless you betray us like he did, and then I'll have no problem slitting your pretty little throat."

Fuck.

I try to move, but I can't. I'm still stuck under the grip of whatever the fuck they injected me with.

"Lesson number one: our order is sacred. You will learn to trust us more than you trust yourself. You will learn to obey our commands because we do not work alone. We are a hive mind, one breath away from being able to read each other's thoughts and emotions. There is no relationship closer than this one. So, if one of us breaks the covenant, we can all vote to eliminate them."

My throat feels like it's closing. I can't stop looking at the skull in his hand. My father's skull. These guys are *sick*. Twisted. Demented. Legitimate psychopaths.

"You said you needed more time to decide," Alaric continues, setting my father's skull back on the shelf.

It's then that I realize... these aren't random skulls.

It's your lucky day, Harlow. You get to meet your ancestors.

My stomach rolls again.

It's not just my father—it's all the Lords and Ladies of Darkness.

"But I'm afraid your time is up. We need to know tonight because you've already seen too much. You've been privy to a lot of confidential information." Walking up to me, he sneers. "Blink once if you don't accept our invitation to join the Lords of Darkness as a Lady. Blink twice if you do."

I feel my eyes twitch with the effort to keep from blinking. He tilts his head and rubs his mouth with his hand. Fuck, if he wasn't a complete psycho, I'd say that move was hot. My eyes burn, and I feel a fresh tear drip down my right cheek. If I say no, I am condemning Archie. If I say yes...

This is my life now.

For now—until I figure out how to get myself the fuck out of this situation.

And not a second longer.

I would not entertain the idea of leaving everything behind. Gemma, NYU, Brooklyn, New York pizza... it was my *home*. This place would *never* be my home. My bloodline would haunt me for a little while, until I found a way out. I'm the only heir to take the place in this order besides Archie.

And I would do all of this for Archie.

I would put myself through this, temporarily, for Archie. Big sisters are supposed to protect their younger siblings. It's a cardinal rule. Archie is just a baby. So small, so innocent. I could never let anything happen to him.

I blink once as another tear streams down. And then I blink again as that tear drops onto the stone floor.

"Good girl," Alaric growls, coming closer and taking my chin roughly between his index finger and thumb. "Good fucking girl," he repeats, and despite my hatred for him, I feel my heart skip a beat at the heat in his eyes. He looks behind me. "Get the strike ready, Gideon."

My panic returns with those four words. Theo and Sterling carry me back to the main room of the barn, sitting me down in the chair and tying me up again. A flurry of movement happens around me, and in the next minute, Alaric is sitting down at a small, folding table next to me. He opens an old wooden box, placing a clean towel down and setting out a bunch of tools I don't recognize. My eyes slide to Sterling and Theo, who are now moving the body to the top of the wood.

Please, God, I don't want to see that.

"Harlow," Alaric says, his voice sending shivers down my spine. I'm now able to move my neck the tiniest bit so that I'm looking at him. I can wiggle my toes and fingers again, just barely. But it's enough to have some autonomy. Not like it matters. If I fight back, they'll kill me and place my skull up on that decrepit shelf. I'd probably break a record for the shortest stint in this fucked up order. "I'm going to point to places on your body, and you're going to blink twice to tell me where you want me to brand you."

Brand you.

Oh my God.

He shows me his left forearm, running his finger over the raised, shiny scar that's in a skull and crown outline.

"Back when the Lords of Darkness was founded, the people in our order used a branding strike, like what you'd use for livestock. Unlike tattoos, brands cannot be removed. They are permanent. They signify ownership, or in your case, a rite of passage. To become a Lady of Darkness is to bear our mark. It's painful, but we see enduring the pain as a means to an end, allowing us to enter a more heightened state of awareness." He leans forward, spreading his legs as he looks at me. "Like I said, it's painful. We've all been through it. I will use sanitary equipment and your skin will be sterilized. It entails heating up a stainless-steel wand and placing it on your skin for several seconds. Now, in this day and age, there are other methods for branding—electrosurgery, electrocautery, and moxibustion, but we prefer to use what our ancestors used. And, it gives us all a more uniform mark."

How the hell am I going to get out of this? He wants to brand *me?*

Holy fuck, I need to get my head straight and run far away from these guys. They're not going to let me go—I can already tell they'll chase me to the ends of the earth to find me. I was joking earlier when I said I might need to kill them... but if they continue to act like we're one big happy family, maybe that'll make it easier for me.

Lull them into a false sense of closeness.

Get them to trust me.

And then, I'll strike.

My brain is spinning with ideas, but I don't have time to ruminate on any of them right now. All I need to do in this moment is pretend I'm game for all of this fucked up shit.

If I can survive what I've survived, I can handle a few days with these psychos.

Alaric pulls out a long, black wand. *Fuck me, maybe not.* My insides turn to jelly. On one end is a handle, and on the other end is the outline of a skull and crown.

"There have been different iterations of the mark over the years. This particular wand goes back to Victorian times." Cocking his head, he begins to twirl it around. "It will cause third-degree burns, but we'll make sure it's taken care of. During the branding process, you may feel faint, have difficulty breathing, or even pass out."

My eyes flick to Sterling, who sheds his shirt, showing his right bicep. *Right.* I remember that from last night. Theo pulls his shirt up to reveal the brand right in the middle of his chest. I want to wince, but I can't. Gideon saunters up to me, unbuttoning his jeans. My tongue seems to swell as he unzips himself, pulling his pants down a few inches. I can't miss the outline of his thick cock. It's hanging to the right, and my mouth goes dry. If he's this big soft... *Jesus.* Only then do my eyes wander to his lower right hip, where the skull is branded just above a light brown patch of hair.

"Harlow," Alaric says, snapping me out of my daze. Moving my neck is difficult, but I can do it if I concentrate. I look back at him slowly. "You can choose where we brand you. We've all chosen places that can be hidden by a suit, and my suggestion would be to find a place you can cover up easily. There are a lot of people who wish to hunt us down and can identify us by our mark/brand. It's important and symbolic for us, but it's also a death sentence. Do you understand?"

I'm fucked no matter what, basically.

I blink multiple times just to throw him off.

"It's wearing off," he says to no one in particular. Looking back at me, he leans forward on his chair, placing his hands on his knees as he spreads his legs. "Are you going to be a good girl, or do you need us to give you another dose of the tranquilizer?"

I bare my teeth as much as I can. "Fuck... you..." I say, slurring my words.

He clucks his tongue, nodding at Theo. "Then we'll have to do this the hard way."

I don't look away from him as Theo injects another needle into my thigh. It hardly even stings. What the fuck does he expect? It's not like I sought them all out to join this order. They *forced* me into this whole thing. If they wanted to drug me for this, fine, but there was nothing in our agreement about enjoying this whole ordeal.

Theo takes the wand over to the fireplace in the corner. Alaric kneels in front of me, and my eyes find his. I send every ounce of hatred into my gaze, and his perfect lips tilt up as Alaric's hand comes up my legs.

"How about here?" he asks, his warm palm resting on my inner thigh. *Pig.* "Blink once for no, twice for yes, little monster."

I blink once, and his hand roves to the crease where my leg meets my hip. His touch sends a shiver across my skin, and I can feel my nipples harden instantly. *No, no, no.* His eyes drag up slowly, and he tilts his head slightly as he squeezes the flesh at my hip.

"Here?"

I blink once.

I want him to stop, but I also want him to keep going. The dichotomy of hating him but liking his touch makes me feel dirty. His hand roves up to my belly button, and then it goes right between my breasts. His gaze catches on my nipples, and he snaps his eyes to mine. He gives me a knowing, heated look.

"Here?"

One blink.

His hand moves over my nipple, and everything inside of me fires to life. If I wasn't drugged, I'm pretty sure I would've shuddered at his touch. Running a finger down my arm, he stops on my bicep.

"Here?"

One blink.

I don't even *know* where I want this stupid brand. I just don't want him to stop touching me.

His finger trails up the inside of my arm, down my right side, until he gets to the top of my ribs.

"If you don't choose a place soon, I'm going to choose one for you," Alaric murmurs.

I blink once.

Twice.

He cocks his head. "Interesting placement. Supposed to be painful."

Well... fuck. I did not know that.

He tugs my dress down delicately, his finger working the thin strap down my shoulder. I can't move, can't warn him that the light material is going to fall right down and expose my breast. I can't even look down, but I can tell when it happens, because my right nipple begins to tingle, the tip feeling suddenly cold. That and the way Alaric's eyes wander down, darkening ever so slightly.

"You have perfect tits, Harlow," he says softly. "I can't wait to suck and bite those nipples one day soon."

Everything goes cold at his words. *Like hell he would.*

He moves my right arm so that it hangs in front of my chest, covering my exposed breast and giving him access to the spot above my ribs. Disinfecting my skin for what feels like forever, he snaps on rubber gloves and leans forward.

"Ready?" Alaric asks, even though he knows I can't answer him verbally. Theo walks up to us, the branding wand bright orange on the end. Alaric takes it and looks back at me, a dark glint in his already-black eyes. "On the count of three," he says slowly.

Oh, fuck.

Fuck, fuck, fuck.

"One."

Without another warning, he places the wand on my skin.

Jesus Christ on a cracker!

I can't breathe, scream, or cry, but I know my face is bright red from the pain. Tears stream down my face, and *holy fucking shit this hurts*. It's a flashing kind of pain—visceral and strong, the kind of pain that would knock me over if I were standing. Every muscle tries to go taut against the drugs, tries to move and fight back, but it's futile.

"Sorry, baby. I lied about counting."

If I could punch him, I would. My skin is drenched in sweat, and the room sways before me. The nausea gets worse. How will I vomit if I can't move? *Oh, God. I can smell my burning flesh.* More tears stream down my face, and it feels as if my eyes are going to pop out of their sockets.

"I'm done. Blink twice if you're okay."

I blink twice immediately, pulling every ounce of resolve I have to stay resolute. It still feels like he's branding me. The searing pain is lasting, so potent that I can taste the vomit in my throat.

I hear the other guys go in and out of the barn, then Sterling's grabbing my hair and forcing me to look up at him. At one point or another, he must've changed into a suit, because instead of his bloody grey t-shirt, he's now wearing a dark blue suit and tie.

"You look so good bearing our mark, little monster." He drops my head as Alaric cleans up. Every few minutes, he asks me if I'm okay, and I dutifully blink twice.

Did my mom know about all of this? Is this why my father never married her?

In a weird way, maybe he was protecting her—protecting me.

But then, what about Archie? Surely, he must've known I would never let that happen.

The pain eventually subsides enough to give me some semblance of relief, and I start to get drowsy. Coming down from an anxiety attack always leaves me feeling exhausted, and this—this was on par with what happened to me at sixteen.

I never wanted to feel *this* again, and yet here I am.

My body begins to shut down, their voices droning on in the background. I know it's my mind's way of keeping me safe. I don't want to feel anything anymore. I don't want to go back to *that place* again. I fought for so long, saw so many therapists, and tried so many different medications before I found the one that worked for me.

Panic disorder and psychosis.

That was the diagnosis.

Everything that happened that night in our apartment. The reason for my mother's death. It triggered the longest and worst psychotic episode of my life. I hallucinated, in a state of complete psychosis for months.

It was *terrifying*.

And here I am again, in a situation that could very well end my life, with men who *murdered* my father.

I would *not* go back there.

I would *not* go back to that dark place, *ever again*.

They could show up in my bedroom, brand me, or worse. I would stay strong. I had the backing of my medication to keep me steady.

I had eighteen months of growth and strength behind me.

I'd pulled myself out of a dark place once, and I could do it again.

I would show them I was fine—that I could handle this.

Alaric lifts my chin with his index finger, his brows pinched as he watches me.

"Harlow," he mutters. "Blink twice if you're okay."

I hardly have the energy. And the injection seems to have worn off some, because I'm able to hold myself up straighter as he cleans the brand, applying salve and putting a clear bandage over it.

I stare right into his eyes as he bandages me, pulling my dress back up.

I'm going to be okay. I *have* to be. They're going to rue the day they decided to make me a Lady of Darkness.

And I'm going to make sure they all burn in hell.

So yes, I'm more than okay.

Never been better, asshole, I think as I blink twice. *You'll regret ever touching me.*

CHAPTER 12

Gideon

"Is she okay?" I ask Alaric, who is disinfecting the table.

He glances over at Harlow, who is staring straight ahead indifferently. "She's fine."

I button my collar, tying a knot in my tie and lacing it through. Alaric puts everything away as Sterling and Theo walk into the barn, freshly dressed.

"Car's washed," Theo says. "Nick was able to get us some new mats for the trunk so we can burn these," he adds, tossing the folded mat I know is still soaked with blood on top of the body. "Are we doing this now?" he asks, gesturing to the pile of wood.

I shake my head. "We're already an hour late for dinner. Let's do it when we get back later. You should get dressed," I tell Alaric, and he nods before retreating into one of the rooms. Glancing down at Harlow, I pull a syringe from my pocket, kneeling in front of her. "This is the antidote to the tranquilizer we gave you," I tell her, and her eyes bore into mine. "If you're a good girl, you can have it. Do you understand?"

She blinks twice, and I smile as I uncap the needle. Pulling her dress up over her knee, my fingers graze her soft-as-sin skin. I smile when I notice the goosebumps that rise at my touch, and I snap my eyes up to hers as I slam the needle into her fleshy thigh. She hardly even reacts, just watches me with defiance and resentment. My cock hardens ever so slightly at the way she lifts her chin, at the way her brows begin to furrow as the tranquilizer wears off.

She's so fucking strong and she doesn't even realize it.

Slowly, she comes back to life. Little movements at first, and then she clears her throat and looks around at all of us.

Like a lioness observing her surroundings, waiting to attack.

"Well, that's one way to initiate someone," she says, anger tinging her words. "I hope that the next time I have a panic attack, I'm not tranquilized like a fucking animal," she snarls. "Otherwise, this arrangement is never going to work for me."

"A panic attack?" I ask.

Her eyes snap to mine. "Yes. A panic attack." Her words are clear, firmly stated. But I don't miss the way she swallows, the way she balls her hands.

I normally have a heart of steel. I joke around so that I don't feel too much. My father made sure I was never on the receiving end of his love. He thought it would soften me. So I keep my armor up. *Always*. But seeing Harlow's throat bob like that, seeing the way her angry expression falls for just a second... something akin to guilt washes over me.

And I'm not sure I like feeling vulnerable like this, so I push it all away.

I stand. "Let's get going. We have an important dinner to get to."

Harlow rises from the chair. She's wobbly for a second, but then she rights herself, wincing as her arm grazes the side of her body. Grabbing her jacket, she shrugs it on, freeing her hair in one fell swoop. Cocking her head and looking at me, she holds her arms out.

"Lead the way."

I don't know what I expected when we picked her up earlier. For one, our entire day had been derailed. The man we were after made a run for it, so we had to hunt him down. *Literally*. He ditched his car and ran into the forest thirty miles from here, and we had to trek through goddamn mud to get to him. So while our target has been taken care of, we still must make an appearance tonight. I half expected Harlow to put up a bigger fight—perhaps to cry or complain. But she just looks right at me, waiting and ready. Like we didn't just fucking tranquilize and brand her.

Alaric walks out right then, wearing his signature black suit. His hair is slicked back, and he's adjusting his tie as his eyes sweep over the room.

"Very nice," he says, holding his arm out for Harlow.

She doesn't take it at first, and I see Alaric's gaze darken for a second. Something passes between them, and to my surprise, she steps forward and links her arm with his.

"Don't we make a nice quintet," he comments, smirking.

After I lock up, we all head to the freshly washed car. Normally, we'd have a car pick us up, but since we're already running late, I know Alaric doesn't want any extra attention on us. The plan is to park nearby and enter through the back, like we've been there the entire time. Sterling grumbles something about Harlow sitting on his lap for the drive, so I pull her onto mine as we begin the drive.

She's stiff, sitting upright and as far away from me as possible.

"You can relax," I murmur, running a finger down her leg.

She smacks my hand away. "Don't you fucking touch me," she growls.

I smirk, and Theo chuckles from the passenger seat. "You won't be saying that for long."

"Fuck off," she adds, her voice shaking with anger.

Oh, I like how our little monster fights back so fiercely. I bet she's a tiger in bed.

"I suggest you do yourself a favor and stop fighting us. This will all be easier if you accept your new position as the fifth limb of this order."

That shuts her up.

"Too late to turn back now," Theo says from the front seat. "You're ours now, little monster."

I feel the way her body tenses at his words. "He's right," I add. "Our network is known all over the world, and I can guarantee, if you run away tomorrow, there will be someone ready to blow your head off the instant you leave if they ever see the mark on your skin. You'll have a target on your head for the rest of your life. And if you think we're rough with you, you have no idea what else is out there."

She's quiet for the rest of the drive.

CHAPTER 13

Harlow

You're ours now, little monster.
Five words that will forever give me nightmares. Five words that should solidify my role in all of this, but instead, give me the motivation to come up with a plan. Their warning about the brand is something I never considered, but if I can stay alive and free, I'll wear a goddamn turtleneck every damn day for the rest of my life. I'll do whatever it takes to get out of this.

They think I'm spending the drive worrying and afraid, but really, I'm plotting.

The first thing I need to do is get them to trust me. This won't work if they don't, and if they get even the tiniest whiff of betrayal, they'll have no problem eliminating me.

Just like they eliminated my father.

The second thing is to figure a way out of this. Whether it entails running away to a place they could never find Cecelia, Archie, and me, or... ensuring they can't run after us *at all*.

It's the only choice that makes sense.

Kill, or be killed.

Third, I had to make everyone else in my life believe that I chose this in the meantime. That means I'll have to commit to this full force. There could be no hesitating, no denying anything. If it means I have to lie to Gemma, so be it. She will understand, and hopefully, this whole thing will blow over before we start at NYU in the fall.

I have to save Archie. But by doing that, it would mean sacrificing myself, giving myself over to these monsters for a few weeks. Earning their trust.

Befriending them. Doing bad things. Killing people and not being able to have a say over anything I did until they were six feet under.

I'd sold my soul to four devils, but eventually, I would steal it right back from them.

The adrenaline rush from being branded is gone, and now my whole right side is throbbing. My throat is sore from trying to scream, and I need water. I'm starving, and I have to pee. Everything hurts from fighting the tranquilizer, from being manhandled for the last two hours. As we pull into a dark, covered parking lot, my nerves get the best of me again, and a knot forms in my stomach.

"Listen closely," Sterling says slowly, leaning over to whisper into my ear. His warm breath on my skin causes my whole body to spark with unexpected and unwelcome pleasure. "We will not be letting you out of our sight tonight. You're still a flight risk, and quite frankly, I don't trust you. You will stay with us. We will accompany you everywhere, and you are not to speak a single word to anyone. Do you understand?"

"Okay, sir," I grumble.

Alaric pulls into a spot, and I throw the door open before the others can get out. Alaric, Gideon, and Theo begin to walk ahead. I stay back a couple of feet, and then suddenly Sterling pulls me back into his body. For someone so moody and brooding, he sure loves to manhandle me.

"What did I tell you about calling me sir?" Sterling snarls.

My lips curl up all on their own. "Sorry. *Sir*."

In one swift movement, he throws me against the door of the car, pinning me to the cool metal.

"Do not call me sir unless you accept everything that comes with that word."

"Which is?" I taunt, quirking my brow. He only pins me down even harder.

"You, on your knees, obeying every command I give you."

"I'd rather rot in hell," I tell him.

Grabbing the hair at the nape of my neck, he pulls my head back, making my spine arch in an unnatural way.

"I didn't say you'd have a choice."

I swallow. I'm not sexually inexperienced, per se. I'm an average teen from Brooklyn. I've slept with a few guys, and I have a few kinks of my own. But right now? My whole body throbs with an intense kind of longing I've never experienced. I *like* the idea of pushing back with Sterling—with all of them. It's dangerous and stupid, but I can't help it. Something innate wants to fight back.

And I want them to punish me for it.

"Okay," I tell him, my voice softer than I'd like it to be.

He releases me. It takes me several seconds to right myself, fix my tear-stained makeup, and smooth my ruffled hair, but I follow him to where the guys are standing, waiting for me. Standing up tall, I look each of them in the eyes.

"Well? Let's get this over with." I head toward the exit, smiling when I hear them follow me out.

We end up a couple of blocks away, and I'm grateful I decided to forego the heels. We must be somewhere in central London, because there are tall buildings and lots of black taxis on the street. People in suits pass us, and I try not to complain at the way all four of them are walking extremely fast. I'm a good foot shorter than all of them, and I practically have to jog to keep up. Arriving at a nondescript white door, Alaric turns the handle and pushes it open, ushering us all in.

We're in some kind of back entrance, and Alaric steers us forward. "If anyone asks, we've been here since six," he says, his voice low. He runs his hands over his hair and straightens his tie.

"What time is it?" I ask. It's just starting to get dark, but I know we were at the barn for at least an hour–maybe more. And the drive...

"Half-past seven," he answers. "Dinner is at eight, so luckily, we should be able to blend right in."

"And what sort of dinner is this?" I ask.

"An important one," Sterling responds.

One of them wraps an arm around my waist, and I look up to see Theo grinning down at me.

I don't trust him. He looks too nice, which means he's probably just the opposite.

"Be a good girl and keep me company tonight," he says, his white-blonde hair falling in over his forehead.

I ignore the way he smells like fresh rain, and how his warm hand on my waist causes me to relax.

Alaric opens another door at the end of the hallway, slipping inside first. I can hear voices, low music, and glasses clinking. Gideon goes next, followed by Sterling. Theo tugs me back when I go to open it.

"Give them a minute," he says slowly. "They're making sure there are no threats present."

I swallow. "And if there are?"

He leans down, his breath grazing my ear. "Then we get the fuck out of here."

I stare at the plain white door before us. "Do people in there know who you are?"

"The important ones do. Publicly facing, we are just your average English nobility. And we will introduce you as such."

"But I'm not. My parents were never married."

Theo pulls something out of his suit jacket. "Are you sure?" he asks, handing me a thick sheet of paper about the size of a greeting card.

I glance down at the writing, squinting. It's almost too dark to read in here, but as my eyes adjust to the formal text, they widen.

"What the hell is this?" I seethe. *"Certified Copy of an Entry of Marriage?!"*

"You're welcome, Lady Blackwell," Theo says, grabbing the paper back and tucking it back into his suit.

"Who the hell did you marry me off to?"

Theo turns to face me fully. "As much as I'd love to officially make you my wife, Harlow, I'm afraid your reading abilities are quite lacking. This is a certificate between your mother and your father. Therefore, you are officially Lady Blackwell."

I clench my jaw. "But they never got married."

Theo grabs the handle. "I think you underestimate just how much power we have."

And then he swings the door open, pulling us both into the crowded dining room without another word of explanation.

CHAPTER 14

STERLING

Theo and Harlow walk through the sea of people, her arm linked with his. Something dark and possessive runs through me at the sight, but I shake it off quickly.

She's not only mine.

She belongs to all of us.

Being a Lord of Darkness means we don't take sides. We are one, moving, singular unit. A slithering, black mass that breathes, sleeps, eats, and fucks together. She wouldn't be the first woman we all shared. The only difference would be that she's one of us—so we would need to cherish her. Revere her. *Worship* her.

People look in Harlow's direction curiously. I feel my jaw feather when my eyes travel down to her feet—where her black boots poke out of the golden fabric. As much as I wanted to see her in those four-inch heels, she still looks fucking gorgeous. The boots and leather jacket give her an edge, and I know everyone is wondering who she is, and why she's here with us.

People in certain circles know of the Lords of Darkness. Not just because of what we do, but because we predate every other single organized crime group. It's sort of like being the oldest kid at a sleepover. We're experienced, and we have our extensive history to back us up. The people in this room look up to us.

If anyone even thinks of betraying us, we have the entire world at our fingertips.

They respect and fear us.

And right now, everyone is curious about our newest member.

My eyes scan the crowd of people. Everyone is dressed in formal wear, and the low lighting hides the dark corners of the room—where I'm sure deals are being made in private. Tonight, we're here as a gesture of good faith for the new leader of Acadia, the largest crime ring in Montenegro. The man is in the center of the room. Dark hair, olive skin, tall… he's holding a martini glass. He's young—can't be older than twenty-five. And from what we've been digging up on him the last few days… he's wholly unprepared to do this job. But I know better than to get close to him. There are hundreds of people who want his job, and who will stop at nothing to get it.

He won't last the year.

When you're in a position like ours, you must be tough. *Hard*. No remorse, no pity, no emotion.

I would serve our brotherhood with everything I had, even if it meant I left bodies in my wake.

"Here," Alaric says, handing me a G&T as he sips his whiskey.

I stir my drink, eyeing the crowd. "What do you think?" I ask.

"About what?" Alaric leans against the wall next to me.

"Acadia," I say, watching the young man as his eyes find Harlow.

We're both silent, watching what happens next. Like two predators protecting our prey. We almost have her, and anyone or anything that gets in the way of that will be incinerated.

Theo is chatting with someone I don't know, and Harlow is looking around with a scowl on her face. Her arms are at her sides, and the new Acadian leader, Armin, saunters over to her. I grip the glass in my hands tightly, fingertips white as he reaches out and touches her shoulder.

I'm one second away from shattering my glass.

"He's about to have his fucking eyes gouged out," Alaric drawls, barely restrained rage tinging his words. "Motherfucker has a death wish, doesn't he?"

We push off the wall together, striding over to where Theo and Harlow are standing. Gideon must've noticed, too, because he approaches from behind.

"Armin," I say brusquely. "Thank you for inviting us tonight." He pulls his eyes from Harlow and looks right at me. I see the realization dawn on his face.

"Sterling," he says quickly, holding a hand out.

I just stare at it, taking a sip of my drink instead. "Enjoying the view?" I ask.

His face pales.

I give him until the end of the month before someone offs him.

"I…" he stutters, holding his hands up. "Apologies, Lord Beauchamp. I thought she was here with Lord Wolf."

Harlow looks at all of us with a pinched expression, but before she can intervene and get in the middle of our pissing match, Theo steps forward.

"She is. I am pleased to introduce you to Lady Blackwell."

Armin's face pales further. He looks at Alaric. "Enjoy your night."

Just as he's about to turn, I reach out and grab his hand. To anyone else, it looks like a friendly gesture, but I bend down and whisper my veiled threat. "You look at her like that one more time, and you won't have the eyes to do so again. Got it?"

He clenches his jaw tightly, but then he pulls away and gives me a tight smile before walking away.

I look over at Harlow and she's watching me with disgust. "You sicken me," she says quickly, crossing her arms. "You're all pigs." She twists out of Theo's grasp, walking to the bar.

Theo's eyes narrow. "Should I—"

I hold a hand up. "Let her be. But do not let her talk to anyone."

"Shouldn't she be with us at all times?" Gideon asks.

I watch as Harlow leans forward, ass out, wiggling it a couple of times as she looks over her shoulder at me. What a defiant little brat.

I roll my tongue inside my cheek as I look at Gideon. "There's no harm in giving her a small sliver of freedom before she's chained to us for the rest of her life."

"You're a lot nicer than me," Alaric mutters.

"She'll have it hard enough later tonight," I tell him.

Because tonight will be her first initiation task.

CHAPTER 15

HARLOW

I push the food around my plate as Alaric, Gideon, Sterling, and Theo make small talk with the other three people at the table, one of which is the man from earlier. Armin is his name, and he's seated to my left.

He's handsome, with short, dark hair and light brown eyes. I don't recognize his accent; it sounds Russian, but not quite. I know the dinner tonight is in his honor, because he wears a gold ring on his finger with a symbol that matches the centerpiece at every table. Knowing the circles the *Lords* play in, he must be bratva, or some kind of nefarious organization.

And yes, I only know that term from my mafia romance books.

I always found those scenarios sexy—a brooding mafia man who forces the main female character to marry him, and then they fall in love amid violence and angst.

Is that the scenario I'm currently in? Being paraded around in my fancy dress on the arms of four of the most dangerous men in the world, against my will? If so, why aren't I doing more to stop it?

Maybe I shouldn't be looking too deep into those questions.

I'm not sure I'll like the answer.

"Do you not like the food?" Armin asks. "It is Njegusi prosciutto. Very common in Montenegro."

I glance up at the guys, paying special attention to Alaric seated next to me, but none of them have noticed Armin speaking to me.

I give him a quick smile. "I'm just not very hungry tonight," I say, keeping my voice low. Taking a sip of my water, I look back over at Armin.

"Is that where you're from?" I ask, so curious about everything.

I'm also trying to be polite. I have no idea how these dinners are supposed to go, and one wrong move could mean Armin here kidnaps me or something.

I've definitely read too many mafia books.

He nods. "Yes." Patting his lips with his napkin, he places a large hand on my thigh.

My eyes nearly bulge out of my head. If the guys catch him touching me...

"You are a very beautiful woman," he says, smirking.

I give him a forced smile. "Those will be your last words if you're not careful."

Removing his hand, he winks at me. "I hope my last words are something I'm whispering into your ear in my bed. A woman of your caliber, and the leader of Acadia... we could be explosive together."

Oh. He went there.

I clear my throat just as Alaric turns to face me fully. "Harlow, I'm feeling thirsty. Please get me a whiskey from the bar. Straight. And none of the house shit. Macallan."

I whip my head in his direction, narrowing my eyes. "I'm not your servant."

His dark gaze bores into mine. "It wasn't a question."

Pushing away from the table, I look at Armin quickly before turning and walking toward the bar. When I look back at the table, Alaric is laughing with Armin, but the way Gideon, Sterling, and Theo are glaring at Armin sends shivers down my spine.

Facing the bartender, I tell him Alaric's order. I watch as he grabs the bottle, measuring out exactly one drink's worth and pouring it gently into a cut crystal glass. It takes all of thirty seconds, but when I thank him and begin my walk back to the table, Alaric and Armin are gone.

I set Alaric's drink at his place and sit down in my seat, leaning back slightly.

"Where did they go?" I ask Theo.

He doesn't answer, and instead, Gideon watches me with an amused expression. "Eat, Harlow," he commands.

"I'm not hungry," I tell him.

"You're going to need your strength later," he adds.

I want to take my fork and stab the top of his splayed palm, but instead, I take three giant bites, keeping my eyes locked on his as I do.

"It seems you need an etiquette lesson," he says, placing his napkin on the table.

"You're probably right. Maybe you could send me to school for bad girls who read smut and don't know proper table manners. Better yet, make sure to enroll me in a course on how to withstand getting tranquilized and branded."

His jaw ticks, but he doesn't say anything.

I take another large bite just to spite him. A few bites later, I lean back and place a hand on my stomach. I'm still nauseous from earlier–from what I witnessed. But I will admit, I feel better now that I've eaten.

We are served dessert shortly after that, and when we finish, everyone stands and begins to mingle once again.

"They've been gone for a long time," I tell Gideon as he, Sterling, and Theo lead me away from the table.

Again, no answer.

Theo puts a hand on the small of my back, leading me to the back of the opulent dining room. I stop walking, crossing my arms as the three of them turn to face me.

"Are we done? Where are we going? And where did Alaric and Armin go?"

"We're leaving now, Harlow," Sterling says gruffly. Reaching out to grab my arm, I pull away even farther.

"No. You're not telling me something. And if I'm going to be *one of you*, then I at least deserve the truth."

Sterling's jaw ticks as he looks between Gideon and Theo. Finally, he shrugs.

"It's too risky to tell you in here, but we can tell you once we're in the car," he says, his voice even.

Nodding, I follow them out and back into the garage. To my surprise, the dark grey Range Rover is waiting for us, with Alaric behind the wheel. I climb into the passenger seat before any of them can say anything. The second the door closes, Alaric speeds off and out into the night. I barely have a chance to pull my seatbelt over my lap before he's twisting us around and making the tires screech.

"Jesus," I mutter. "Let me guess. Armin's body is in the trunk, and that's why we had to make a run for it?"

"She's learning," Gideon says from the back. "I'm so proud."

Scowling at Alaric, I take in his clenched jaw and white knuckles wrapped around the leather steering wheel.

"So, you killed him because it was his dinner? Or... what? Clearly, I'm not understanding," I add, trying to keep my voice from shaking.

Fuck. Two dead bodies in one day?

Just breathe, Harlow.

"He touched you," Alaric growls.

My whole body stiffens, and I swear I can hear the blood whooshing in my ears. "For a second!" I yell, my voice shrill. "Are you really that possessive that you fucking *murdered* a man because he touched my leg?"

He doesn't answer.

I turn back to face the other guys. "And you're all okay with this?" I ask, placing my shaking hands flat on my thighs.

Gideon snorts. "Alaric has a temper. Armin knew this. Therefore, he will reap the consequences."

I grind my jaw. "A temper is slamming doors and stomping feet. *Not* homicide," I grit out.

"He's weak," Sterling adds. "He would've been killed by someone else eventually. And we have a lot of sensitive information pertaining to him. All I can say is, don't feel too bad for the guy."

I open and close my mouth, looking at Theo. "And you? What do you have to say about all of this?"

He leans forward over the center console to where I'm twisted around facing the back seat. Before I can process what's happening, he holds a knife to the skin at my neck.

"You still seem to think you're the one in control of this order before your reign has even begun," he growls. I swallow as my breathing turns ragged. Until this very moment, he was the nicer one. "We don't answer to you yet. We all agreed to eliminate Armin together. Once you've been properly trained, we will include you in those discussions, because none of us were lying when we said you are one of us now. You. Are. One. Of. Us, Harlow. But tonight? You are here to learn, to observe. You do not question our authority. Do you understand?"

I glare at him as my lips part. "I understand."

Theo retreats with his knife, and I turn back around to face the front, arms crossed. I'm scowling ahead as Alaric merges onto a road that I know will take us out of London. It starts to hit me then, what they've done. First, that they killed my father. Second, that they somehow got past the security system at Blackwell House to show up in my room uninvited last night. Third, that they killed the first guy, injected me with a tranquilizer, and branded me against my will. Fourth, that they murdered Armin. For *touching* me.

I glance sidelong at Alaric, studying the way the light reflects against his cheekbones, his five o'clock shadow making the lower half of his face look darker, more menacing. They killed my father—who was a member of their order. What in the ever-loving fuck did he do to piss these guys off, and what would stop them from killing me if I misbehaved? And here I was, talking back and acting like a brat.

I roll my bottom lip between my teeth as I stare out of the window. Alaric turns the news on, and the BBC reporter drones about something I don't understand. His accent, and the fact that we're driving on a dark highway, in a country that doesn't feel like home, with a body in the trunk...

What.

The.

Fuck.

My eyes begin to prick with tears, and I turn to face the window fully so that Alaric can't see the way a teardrop just fell down my face. Or the way I'm holding in a sniffle. My stomach balls up tightly, and I pull my knees up to my chest and rest my cheek on them. Earlier today, I thought I could survive this until I found a way out of it. But now? It all feels like too much.

"Harlow," Alaric says sternly. "Look at me."

I refuse, keeping my face turned toward the window. "I don't want to talk to you," I tell him, and my voice gives me away. It's thick and wrought with emotion.

They're all quiet for the rest of the hour drive back to Blackwell, thankfully. Pulling up to the same barn as last time, I stay seated until Sterling opens the door and reaches a hand out. I stare at him for a few seconds, looking between the rings on his fingers and his mean expression.

"Inside, let's go."

I take his hand without saying anything, and he drops it the instant I'm standing on both feet. Following him and the other guys inside, I stop walking when I see Armin sitting up in a chair, facing the front door of the barn. His brown eyes lock onto mine, and his mouth is taped shut.

Not dead.

One hundred percent alive.

"I thought..." I trail off. Alaric begins to tie Armin to the same chair I sat in earlier tonight for the tattoo.

Theo shows me the syringe from his pocket, and my stomach rolls. They tranquilized him, too.

"What are you going to do with him?" I ask. The second the words leave my mouth, I want to take them back. *Stupid question.* Of course they're going to kill him.

"We are not going to do anything," Gideon says from across the barn. He's flicking his knife open and closed. "You are." I stop moving. Stop *breathing* at his words. My heart hammers against my ribs as I look back at Armin. "Consider it your first initiation task. Kill him or fail."

I can only gape at him for what feels like a full minute before responding. "Fail?"

Gideon pushes off the wall and stalks over to me. Sterling and Theo are hunched over a makeshift desk in the corner, looking at something on a laptop, but Theo's eyes snap up to mine. I glance back at Gideon.

"Eliminated, killed... whatever you want to call it, little monster. You forget that you're disposable. We have another perfectly good heir waiting for us. Right now, you need to show us that you are up to this task. Two things make you a true Lady of Darkness. One is our mark, which you already have. The second is your first kill."

I swallow the bile creeping up my throat. "I can't kill him."

Alaric finishes tying him up and looks at me. Reaching down to grab what I thought was a stick, he raises it up and brings the sword down on Armin's wrist, completely severing his hand. I jump backwards right into Gideon's chest as the entire barn goes silent for a second–that is, until Armin begins to roar behind the tape over his mouth, his face going red as he bucks against his ties.

I close my eyes, unable to get the vision of his severed hand out of my mind. Bile works up my esophagus, and I bend forward, dry heaving until someone grabs me and pulls me up. When I open my eyes, I see Alaric staring down at me. Armin is still thrashing in his chair, but I don't have the balls to look at his arm or what I'm sure is a giant puddle of blood beneath him.

"Harlow," Alaric says, commanding me to look at him by grabbing my jaw. The room sways a bit, and for a second, he looks worried. "Harlow," he says again, his voice stern. "Look at me, Harlow." I blink rapidly, suddenly feeling faint and like I'm both going to pass out and vomit. One of Alaric's arms comes under mine, hoisting me up. "He's a bad man," Alaric grits out. "I know this all makes us seem like the villain, but fuck, he rapes *children.* Do you understand what I'm saying? Acadia is known for trafficking children. And Armin here? He gets his pick of whoever he wants to take advantage of. Most of the girls he chooses are under the age of twelve."

I close my eyes again as I digest his words. *What the fuck have I gotten myself into?* Resting my cheek against Alaric's chest, I can hear his heartbeat. To my surprise, his other hand comes to the small of my back, and he gently pulls me tightly against him. Despite how terrified I feel, and despite how fucked up this all is, it feels good to be held by him.

What the hell is wrong with me?

"Let me repeat that," Alaric murmurs into my ear. "The man in that chair is a sick fuck. He touched you, and he deserves every ounce of pain that he's feeling. When you kill him, you will be removing a rapist from this world. A pedophile."

I swallow as I turn to look at Armin. His head is thrown back, and he's crying softly. Cheeks wet, growing pale, and I realize he's going to die whether I kill him or not.

"I can't kill him," I say again. "I'm sorry. If that means I failed, if that means you kill me, I can't do it," I say, my voice breaking. Pulling away, I look up into Alaric's face. "I killed a spider once, accidentally. I stepped on it, and I cried for an hour. And one time, I was driving upstate and hit a deer. It ran away, luckily, but I haven't driven in the dark since. My mom—" I choke on my words, and one of my hands comes to my neck. "I couldn't even look at my mother," I tell him softly. His brows furrow at my words, and I continue. "I like to think I'm strong, but tonight..." I trail off, sniffling. "I can't kill him," I repeat, my voice resolute. "Maybe one day. But not tonight. Ease me into it. *Please,*" I beg, my eyes watering.

I think of the night my mom died. Of the way my heart pounded in my chest and felt like it was going to explode. The sheer terror of being violated...

I lived in that nightmare for nearly three months.

Alaric's dark eyes sweep over mine. Licking his plush, pink lips, he takes a finger and runs it down the side of my face.

"Kill him, little monster," he whispers.

I set my jaw. "I can't."

"Can't? Or won't?"

I try pulling away, but he only holds me tighter. For a second, I think he's going to let me off the hook. That he's going to take pity on me, forget about what he ordered me to do. But I must've forgotten who I was with, and whose shoulder I was crying on. He is a brutal Lord–they all are. There will be no mercy with them, and it will do me good to remember that. They are never going to grant me anything. If I run, they'd chase me. If I say no, they'd force me.

Which is exactly why, right here and right now, I know in my heart that I have to kill them.

And I will.

I'd rather rot than join their psychotic order.

"Fine," I growl, pulling out of his grip. This time, he lets me go.

Get it over with, Harlow. Don't let them win.

I grab the discarded sword, not daring to look Armin in the eyes as I lift it up. It's much heavier than I thought it would be, but I manage to hold it up, aiming the tip at his chest. Gideon walks over and rips the tape off Armin's mouth, and his dark, crazed eyes find mine.

"You're not going to kill me," Armin sneers, looking me up and down. "You're a joke to this order, and soon these men will figure that out. We sell girls like you—young, fuckable girls who make me rich," he adds, and my blood boils with every word. "You may be a whore, but you're not a murderer."

I bare my teeth, stepping closer.

"Do it," Alaric says from behind me.

"You won't do it," Armin taunts.

"Shut the fuck up," I tell him, taking another step closer.

"What a dirty mouth you have. I'd get ten grand for that mouth, you know. Letting the buyer fuck your throat until you learn that a woman's place is in the hou—"

I roar as I step forward, shoving the sword into his chest. His eyes widen a bit as he looks up at me, surprise written all over his face. I quickly pull the sword out.

I'm not a murderer, but I wouldn't stand here and listen to him underestimate me.

The sword clatters to the ground, and Alaric pulls me into his chest as blood soaks Armin's shirt, dribbling out of his mouth.

"Nice work, Harlow."

I pull away from him and stalk to the corner, where I proceed to vomit up everything I ate for dinner.

CHAPTER 16

THEO

Gideon and Alaric start the fire, and Sterling begins the process of removing Armin's cell phone—it had already been de-chipped so that no one could track him here. We'd felt him up for any other evidence of trackers, but the idiot only had his phone. Acadia would appoint a new leader soon, and hopefully this time, it wouldn't be someone so young and stupid, with repulsive tendencies. I walk over to Harlow, who is sitting on the stone ground, shivering uncontrollably.

"Hey," I say, taking a seat next to her. "You did good," I add.

"Fuck off," she bites back.

I look over at her, and her lips are pale and cracked, eyes bloodshot. Her hair, which had been nice and silky earlier, is now frizzy and curled from the humid air.

"The first one is always the hardest," I tell her, trying to keep my voice even.

"Leave me alone, Theo," she retorts, turning to face away from me.

I study the back of her head, and the way her hands clasp her knees so tightly that her fingertips are white.

"Were you and your father close?" I ask, looking at the fire Gideon is tending. Two bodies tonight. Double the trouble for Harlow.

"What?" She snaps her gaze to me. "Why?"

I shrug. "Just wondering. I know this is all a lot to take in."

She snorts. "Twenty-four hours ago, my life was completely different. I thought I'd stay here for a couple of days, and then go back to my real life in New York. I have a scholarship to NYU. That's going down the drain. I miss my best friend, Gemma," she adds, her voice breaking. "We had our whole freshman year planned out, but now..." Sniffing, her blue eyes find mine.

Alaric is going to punish me for what I'm about to say but fuck it. She's had one loss after another tonight. Her life, her future, her innocence. Maybe she deserves a win.

"She can come visit," I say slowly. "This life is not meant to be isolating. The four of us have other friends. Other interests."

"Yeah, right," she snaps back.

"I like reading. Classics," I add, smirking.

She looks at me and gives me a wan smile. "So I've discovered."

"Alaric likes to clean. He also likes fancy cars. Gideon likes weapons of all kinds—he can tell you every single type of knife that exists. And Sterling... his proclivities are a little more X-rated."

"How did you do it?"

I look down at her. "Do what?"

She shrugs. "How did you walk away from your real life?"

"It's not like you must go into hiding, Harlow. This is a job. An important one. But like I said, we've never felt like we were giving anything up."

Looking down at the stone ground, she's quiet for a few seconds before responding. "Yeah, but you grew up in Blackwell. You're English. Your roots are here. Mine are in New York."

I scoot a few inches closer. "I hate to break it to you, baby, but your roots are here, too. I know you want to fight against that Blackwell ancestry, but that royal blood runs through your veins just as much as it runs through ours." I look at the others, who are dragging the bodies on top of the fire after treating the wood. "I know this is a lot. I know this life is different. But I think you'll find, sooner rather than later, that your blood calls to ours, because we've all been bred to do this. The thing about bloodlines is that they're irrefutable."

She swallows, swiping the mascara caking below her thick lashes. "Great. I come from a line of murderers." I can't help but smile as she continues. "I can't see it yet. I still want to hate you all." Something about her words sounds insincere, but I brush it off. Tonight was intense, and she needs time.

"Want to?" I tease, nudging her shoulder with mine.

Her expression sours. "I *do* hate you."

Smiling, I watch as Alaric lights a cigarette with a match, inhaling deeply before discarding the lit match in front of him. The whole pile of wood and flesh goes up in flames, and Harlow jumps back a bit as the fire dances in her blue eyes.

"You won't hate us for very long," I murmur, leaning in close. "I promise."

She pulls away petulantly, resting her chin on her knees as the barn begins to smoke. We've installed a state-of-the-art chimney in the center of the roof, with induction fans pulling the smoke up and out. Still, the barn tends to smell like a campfire during our burnings.

"I'm sure I'll get used to all of this too, won't I?" she asks, her tone morose.

"It's possible. Or it's possible that every death will feel this way for you. Maybe less of a shock next time, but no one asked you not to feel. We're not robots. We're human; we feel things, and that's the beauty of life, isn't it? You live, you learn, you work, you fuck, you die."

"I guess," she mumbles. "I just wish I could've chosen this life like you guys did."

I stare at her for a second, thinking maybe I misheard her. "Do you really think we chose this life? That we all woke up one day and decided to become Lords of Darkness?" I don't mean for my delivery to be as curt as it is, but I want to get my point across. "I had no idea this order even existed. I was studying theater in sixth form, planning on attending Guildhall School of Music and Drama."

She visibly perks up. "Really?"

"Yes. Alaric planned to start his own business, Gideon wanted to apprentice with a blacksmith, and Sterling was interested in law."

She opens and closes her mouth, furrowing her brows for a second before turning to face me.

"Don't you feel like you're missing out?"

"No. I mean, I miss acting, but I get to act every damn day. You like art? Paint the damn walls of the barn. We don't give a fuck. You find a way to incorporate the things you love into this lifestyle. It's possible. You'll see."

Harlow pulls her lower lip between her teeth, looking back down at the floor as she plays with the beads on her dress. I glance over at Alaric, and he cocks his head in question as he takes another drag of his cigarette.

We all had to sacrifice something by becoming a Lord of Darkness. We all had to give up everything we'd ever known, and it was scary as fuck. Had our fathers not been murdered by Charles, we might've had some time to live a regular life before being conscripted.

I'd never forget the day he sat us all down, just as I'm sure she'd never forget last night—when we showed up unannounced in her bedroom and flipped her entire life upside down.

I stand up, holding a hand out for Harlow. She turns to look at it, a skeptical expression hardening her pretty face. But then she takes it, and I pull her up into my body. Gripping her slender arms, my cock twitches as I lean down and graze her ear with my lips.

"Let's get you home before Rose has a heart attack."

CHAPTER 17

Harlow

The guys drop me off after the bodies are done burning, and we're all quiet in the car. I climb out and slam the door closed before any of them can say anything, and then I slip quietly inside Blackwell House, making sure not to wake Rose or any of the other household workers. I'm cold and shivering, and as I shut myself in my bedroom, I sigh and rub my face with my hands. Quickly stepping out of my jacket and shoes, I shed the dress, which is now filthy and has splatters of Armin's blood decorating the gold. I try not to wince as the material grazes the new brand—and the bandage—on the side of my ribs. Before I forget, I pop an anti-anxiety pill into my mouth and swallow.

I walk to the shower and turn it on, looking at myself in the mirror. I don't *look* like someone who just killed another person. I look like a normal eighteen-year-old. Twisting around, I take in the brand for the first time. My skin is bright pink and angry looking under the bandage. I was instructed to keep the plastic bandage on for a few days, as tempting as it is to remove it.

Climbing into the shower, I stand under the water, wincing a bit as the warmth glides down the outside of the bandage. I stay there for what feels like hours, itching to wash the entire last day from my skin, but I know it's futile. Nothing will scrub the knowledge that I killed someone off my conscience.

As I lean forward to lower my face under the stream, I remember what the guys said about Armin. How he was a pedophile, a rapist. Maybe the fact that he's not terrorizing the world is a good thing. Washing my face, hair, and body, I sit on the edge of the shower, pulling my knees to my chest. I leave the brand alone, unsure of how to clean it. At least I don't feel anxious anymore. I just feel numb. Today was a whirlwind, and I need time to process everything.

I need to come up with a solid plan on how I'm going to kill them.

Shutting the water off, I dry my body and brush my teeth before combing through the tangles in my hair. Once I'm done, I open the bathroom door, only to be greeted by Alaric sitting on the edge of my bed.

"What the fuck!" I screech, grabbing my towel and pulling it around me quickly. There's no chance he didn't just see me naked, though. I was in my birthday suit because how the hell was I supposed to know he'd be in my goddamn bedroom?! "You can't just waltz in here whenever you want," I say, my voice shrill.

Alaric just scowls at me, arms crossed. "I just wanted to make sure you were okay after tonight. Also, I need to treat that," he says, looking at where the towel is loosely draped over the aching burn.

That startles me. "Why do you care?" Walking over to my dresser, I grab a pair of sweats and a baggy t-shirt. When I turn around, he's standing a few inches from me. I take a step away from him, but he steps forward, following me.

"Why wouldn't I care?"

I scoff. "Because I'm your prisoner—"

He places two hands on my shoulders. "I'm not your enemy, Harlow." Gently shoving me backward against the dresser, he takes another step forward. "We're all in this hell together, little monster. It is my job to guide you. To help you."

He runs a warm finger down the side of my face, and I angle it away from his touch, nostrils flaring. But I can't help the way my skin pebbles, or the way my stomach bottoms out when I look back up into his intense gaze. His dark curls are mussed up, and his smooth face is now donning a hint of dark scruff. I look away again from his all-seeing eyes.

"Let me change," I say quickly, pushing past him and closing the bathroom door behind me.

Taking a few steadying breaths, I step into the baggy pajamas and hang my towel on the hook behind the door. When I walk back into the bedroom, Alaric is sitting on the bed again, this time with a leather pouch in his hands.

"Sit," he says, gesturing to the spot on the bed next to him. I hesitate long enough for him to sigh heavily, his posture sagging a bit. "Otherwise, your burn will get infected." My feet stay planted as I study him, still in his three-piece suit, feet clad in shiny leather shoes. His full red lips part slightly as he considers his next words. "Please," he says, his eyes finding mine from beneath his dark lashes.

God, he really is beautiful.
Beautiful and deadly...

With a huff, I sit down on the bed next to him, leaning forward. His fingers lift my shirt, folding it up so that it stays put. I watch as he removes the bandage and then rummages through the pouch. Using a cotton swab, he brushes healing ointment over the sensitive area. It feels nice, and I try not to moan as his fingers graze my skin. I don't want to admit how much I like this—him taking care of me—so I shove my feelings down and ignore them.

When he's done with the ointment, he places another clear bandage over the entire brand, lowering my shirt when he's done. Walking to the bathroom, he washes his hands, using my hand towel when he's done. Something about seeing his towering frame in my bathroom makes my stomach flip-flop with butterflies, and I crawl into bed, pulling the covers over my lower half.

Alaric walks back in and cleans everything up, setting the leather pouch on the chaise lounge by the window. To my surprise, he steps out of his shoes and dress jacket, folding the latter neatly over the back of one of the sitting chairs. Then, he removes his tie, keeping his dark eyes on mine as he works it loose, pulling it through his collar slowly. Laying it delicately on the back of the same chair, he slowly sits down, spreading his legs as one arm hangs between them, with the other propped up on his knee, holding his chin up.

I mean, if that isn't the sexiest thing I've seen in a while, I don't know what is.

Clearing my throat, I lean back against the old headboard. "You're staying?"

Honestly, why am I surprised?

Alaric leans back, unbuttoning the top few buttons of his shirt. My mouth goes dry when I see the dark hair curling just under the fabric. *Billionaire Daddy, indeed.* I shake the thought free as his lips tilt up into a menacing smile.

"Unless you'd rather I crawl into bed with you."

Yes. No!

"Okay," I answer, my voice unsure. "Make yourself at home, I guess."

He watches me, and I watch him, both stuck in this odd, awkward silence. I mean, on the bright side, having him here *does* distract me from the throbbing pain of the burn, and the nausea that threatens to crawl up my throat whenever I think of what I did to Armin. Adjusting myself in the bed, I hiss with pain when my shirt rubs against the wound.

Alaric jumps up, rummaging through his leather pouch. I try not to smile when he comes to me with two pills.

"These will help with the pain. I'll get you some water," he says, going into the bathroom again to fill up one of the crystal glasses.

When he brings it back, I take the pills and drink the whole glass of water, handing it back to him. He switches off all the lights except for the one on the other side of the bed.

"If you can, lay on your other side tonight," he says, his voice almost gentle as he sets the glass down on the bedside table.

And then, surprising me for the second time tonight, he rounds the bed and throws the covers open, climbing in beside me.

I suddenly feel drowsy, and I don't have anything left in me to barb or fight back against him being in bed with me. Lying down like he instructed, I get myself comfortable facing away from him. My eyes grow heavy, and I feel him reach over me for my kindle.

"Shall I read to you?" he asks, unlocking it with a swipe of his finger.

"Okay."

And then I proceed to fall asleep to the sound of Alaric's voice reading me some of the filthiest, most blasphemous smut.

CHAPTER 18

Harlow

The trees have heartbeats.
At least, that's what it looks like. I squint so that I can see the bark easier through the darkness, and it's like the trunks are all pulsing. When I take a step closer, it feels as though my throat is closing, so I wrap both hands around my neck, and that's when I realize the heartbeat isn't coming from the trees. It's coming from me.
I stop walking as my pulse roars in my ears—whoosh, whoosh, whoosh. My chest aches as my knees begin to wobble, and suddenly, the ground turns to mud, and I feel my feet sinking.
Suddenly, I'm back in my old apartment. The one I haven't seen since that night. A sob escapes my throat as my heart pulses faster. When I look down, my ankles are covered in thick, black tar, and I can't run. My stomach drops as I realize I'm not alone, and the sense of impending doom makes a cold sweat break out all over my skin. I try calling for help, but nothing comes out, and when I reach up, I feel thick, black tar covering my mouth. I try to spit it out, but it just grows and multiplies, flowing up into the roof of my mouth and making me choke and gag until I'm on all fours.
"Well, aren't you a pretty young thing?"
His voice is clear as day, despite only hearing it the one time.
I feel him move behind me, and when I look down, it's not tar anymore.
It's blood.
And my mother's body is a few feet away, the multiple stab wounds gushing with blood.
I try to scream again, but now the blood is working down my throat, clawing down my esophagus until I'm retching. Cold hands come to my backside, patting me tenderly even though I know he's going to force himself on me.

Again.

No, no, no.

The loud thumping of my heart is the only thing I can hear, and it gets louder, faster. The world begins to spin as the tar sucks me under, and I feel it flow into my nostrils as the world goes dark...

"Harlow."

I sit up in my bed, and the first thing I notice is that the room is swaying from side to side. Alaric is in front of me, gripping my shoulders and shaking me as my eyes wander to Gideon, Sterling, and Theo at the foot of my bed. Something's not right. I feel incredibly dizzy, and I'm seeing double of all of them. I hear myself giggle at the thought of *eight* of them being in my room. *God, can you imagine?* It must still be dark out, because now Theo is pacing back and forth in front of the open window, talking to someone on the phone.

"I didn't know," Alaric says quickly, walking over to where I set my purse down. "Fuck! Harlow, where do you keep your pills?"

My head lolls as I look over at him. Why is he asking about my pills?

I move my hand over something wet, and when I look down, I realize it's vomit. Did I vomit? Why did I vomit?

"Klonopin," Alaric says, holding my pill bottle up to the light and reading it off to Theo. "Take twice a day. With or without food. May be used on an as-needed basis, but not to exceed three doses—" He looks at me. "How many did you take today, Harlow?"

I open my mouth to speak, but it still feels like it's still full of blood.

"What did you give her?" Theo asks, looking at Alaric. He's still speaking to someone on the phone.

"Oxycodone," Alaric says, his face pale as he rubs it with his hand. "She was in pain, and I had some left over from my procedure, so I thought she'd get a good night's sleep. I had no idea..." he trails off. "Fuck."

Theo relays the message to whoever he's talking to, and I hear the words Klonopin and Oxycodone, risks of concomitant use of opioids and benzos, self-medicating pain, anxiety, chronic confusion, vomiting, slow reflexes, death...

Sterling walks over to me and places both palms on my cheeks. I can feel the cool metal of his gold rings on my hot skin. I snap my eyes to him, and the room spins as I try to focus on his deep blue eyes.

"Look at me," Sterling says, his voice low and commanding. Somehow, the tone cuts through the fog enough for me to swallow. "Tell me how many Klonopin you took today."

I swallow again, and Gideon brings me a glass of water. I take it and drink slowly.

"I don't know," I slur. My tongue feels like it weighs a thousand pounds.

"Give me a number."

I roll my tongue along the inside of my cheek. Everything tastes bitter, and my stomach is rolling with nausea. It hits me then that I must've been the one to vomit.

"Three," I tell him, mumbling. "I think."

"How many Oxy's did you give her?" Theo asks.

"Two," Alaric answers, running his hand through his hair.

"And what happened next?" Theo asks, looking at Alaric.

Alaric shrugs. "I tucked her in, began to read to her, and she fell asleep instantly. Then, about thirty minutes later, she started making this weird gagging sound, so I rolled her over to her side, and she vomited. I couldn't wake her after that. Not until you guys got here."

My eyes flit between all of them. They're talking about me? I squeeze my eyes shut as the room sways again, and as Sterling lets my face go, I fall over like I've had way too much to drink.

"Shit, Harlow," Sterling says, pulling me back up and cupping my face, and I swear his expression is worried.

"I'm so tired," I tell him, my voice whiny.

I see Theo hang up the phone, and he looks between the guys. "Kitt suggests we call an ambulance," he says slowly. "But the only problem is, they'll see the burn and make assumptions."

"I'm not calling an ambulance. Is Kitt on his way here, or is he just going to give us useless advice?" Sterling growls, squeezing my cheeks as my eyes start to close. "Stay awake, Harlow."

"He's on his way, but he's a good twenty minutes out. She's conscious again, which is a good sign, but we need to keep her awake."

"I am awake," I say, my tongue dry and feeling like sandpaper suddenly.

"Come on, let's get her to the car," Gideon says, wrapping an arm underneath me and placing another arm under my knees. "We can meet him halfway, at the barn."

He quietly moves me down the dark hallway, walking nimbly down the stairs. We make it outside, and the nighttime chill causes me to shiver instantly. I hear the other guys behind me, and someone opens the door, placing me in the middle back seat. I feel myself falling over just as someone shoves me upright on the other side, and a second later, Gideon and Sterling are on either side of me. Theo is driving, and Alaric is in the passenger seat.

"Don't go to sleep," Alaric instructs.

"But I'm just so... tired..."

I feel my head loll to one side as we go, and the next thing I know, everything goes black.

CHAPTER 19

❦

Alaric

Fuck, fuck, fuck.
 Theo careens us down the country roads in Blackwell, toward the barn where Theo told Kitt to meet us a second ago. Harlow is unconscious again, but she's still breathing, and she still has a heartbeat, so that's a good sign. If I must rip her open and pump her heart with my hands, I'll do it. If I must break her ribs with compressions, I'll do it. The dark possessiveness surrounding her surprises me, and until tonight, I didn't really care if she lived or died. But now, seeing the way her small body is flopping around the back seat, the way her eyes roll into the back of her head, the way her skin is *so* deathly pale...
 Initiating her into our order as a Lady of Darkness messed with my emotions. Watching her as she took our iron brand the way she did, as she killed the Acadian monster, as she went with whatever we threw at her... she's taken everything in stride, and if that's not proof that she belongs with us, I'm not sure what is. She may not believe it yet, but I know there's Blackwell blood running through her veins. And as much as I loathed Charles at the end for betraying us, I see a lot of our fellow brother in Harlow.
 The iron-clad will. The strength. The sense of humor. The vulnerability. Everything we loved about having Charles as a fellow Lord... we now have in Harlow. In a way, Charles was like a father figure. I'm still reeling from his betrayal, because I know none of us would do that to the others.
 I wasn't thinking when I gave her the oxycodone—I just wanted her to sleep deeply, to relax. I had no idea it would interact with her anti-anxiety meds.
 She looked so tired earlier. Falling asleep facing away from me, I watched her breathing even out, as her hands uncurled, as the tiny wrinkle between her

brows relaxed. All I wanted was for her to have a dreamless sleep, to rest her body, to heal the burn on her right side. But I fucked it all up, and now none of us are sure if she'll live or die.

Theo pulls us up to the barn a minute later, and I see headlights in the distance, which means Kitt must be close. Because of our profession, we have our own doctors at our disposal. Kitt specializes in chemical issues—poison, overdoses, that sort of thing—as an emergency room doctor. We pay him a hefty sum to keep quiet and to help us when needed.

I climb out once we've parked, helping Gideon and Sterling with Harlow's body. Sterling hoists her up in his arms, walking her into the barn. Kitt follows us a few seconds later.

"Boys," he says, looking at all of us with a stern expression. He's older—in his late fifties—and he looks at Harlow with a pitying expression. To the outside eye, it looks as though she's overdosed on purpose, so I don't blame him.

"She lost consciousness again a few minutes ago," I tell him, and we set her down on the stone floor.

Kitt sets a medical bag down and rummages through it, finally pulling a syringe out. "This is Naloxone," he says, his voice serious. "It will reverse the effects of the opioids in her system. I can see her breathing is slowing just since I've arrived," he adds, his brown eyes sweeping over her body. "Her coloring is pallid, and soon, she will stop breathing." He lifts one of Harlow's hands. "See her fingernails? They're turning purple." He inserts a fresh needle into a glass vial, pulling the liquid up into the syringe before he flicks it.

Then, Kitt plunges the needle into her thigh, injecting the antidote straight through her clothes.

"This will wear off in an hour," Kitt says, discarding the used needle into a sterile container. "I'll stay nearby to make sure she's okay for a couple of hours. She may need another dose."

Harlow begins to stir, groaning as she curls up and rolls to her side, vomiting.

I look at Kitt. "We didn't know she was taking Klonopin," I tell him.

Harlow pulls her knees to her chest and begins to cry in her sleep. I swallow and ball my fists.

"Klonopin is hardcore stuff," he says softly, placing a hand on the top of her head. I resist the urge to snarl at him for that. "Anxiety is painfully debilitating. If she's taking two doses every day, it must mean she's battling demons that would send us all screaming." Looking at me, he stands. "I'll be out in my car to give you all some privacy."

I stand with him, shaking his hand. "Thank you again, mate," I tell him.

Kitt just nods before he grabs his bag and leaves. I look at Theo, who releases a heavy breath. Sterling walks over to the other side of the barn, and I know he's processing everything in his own way. Gideon is seated next to Harlow, flicking his knife open and closed.

I crouch down and brush her hair out of her face. "Harlow, can you hear us?"

She moans, reaching up and wiping her mouth before her eyes flutter open. "What happened?" she asks, her voice raspy.

I hang my head a bit as I clear my throat. "Turns out, the pain meds I gave you interacted with the anxiety medication you take," I tell her.

She squints, finally cracking a small smile. "If you wanted to kill me, you could've just said so."

I huff a laugh, and I see the guys visibly relax at her words. "Glad you're feeling better, little monster," I murmur.

CHAPTER 20

HARLOW

I wake up in my bed with a throbbing headache. Hissing with pain, I sit up and squint as I look around. Why the hell is it so bright in here, and why do I feel like I got run over by a train? I place my arm over my eyes as I stand up, swaying a bit as I walk to the curtains, pulling them closed. The spot where they branded me aches, but I ignore that for now. Turning back to the bed, I yelp when I notice Alaric sleeping in the chair by the door. He sits up and rubs his face with his hands.

"Harlow."

I cross my arms. "What the hell happened? Why do I feel so crappy?" Snippets of last night flash through my mind—the barn, a man with a halo of dark hair, being placed into a car, something about Theo and a phone—but that's it. It feels fragmented, like I was drugged or something. I grind my jaw. "Did you drug me?" I ask, taking a step back.

Alaric's lips twitch with a smile. "Not intentionally. You don't remember?"

I shake my head. "Not really. Just bits and pieces."

He nods, standing up and brushing himself off, like he's dirty—which he's not. In fact, he looks just as crisp as he did at dinner. The only evidence that time has passed is the dark shadow on the bottom half of his face, and the fact that his hair looks as though he's been running his hand through it all night.

"The pain medication I gave you before bed interacted with the anxiety medication you take. You lost consciousness, and we had to inject you with something called Naloxone, to reverse the effects."

Am I imagining it, or does he look a bit sheepish? "Okay," I say, unsure of how to respond to that. "That makes sense, I guess."

I turn and walk to the bathroom, my mind spinning with what he told me. I'm just about to close the door behind me when Alaric speaks.

"Why are you taking the Klonopin?"

I go still. His voice isn't accusatory—instead, it's almost... gentle. Inquiring.

"Does it matter?"

I hear him walk over to me, and I twist around just before he stops inches from my body. "It does matter, Harlow. Things like this are good to know so that if something happens to you, we know how to treat you. Or if something goes awry, we know exactly what to tell the doctors when they're giving you medication for something that could save your life."

I swallow as I look into his black eyes. He sounds genuinely concerned. "I take it for anxiety and panic disorder." He only stares at me, so I sigh and continue. "I have crippling panic attacks. I've also been officially diagnosed with psychosis, but it's usually triggered by something. It doesn't normally happen out of the blue."

He's quiet as I finish. "Anxiety," he repeats. "And is Klonopin all you're taking for your anxiety?"

I shake my head. "No. I mean, right now, yes. It seems to work. But I also have a prescription for Zoloft and Ativan." I flick my eyes up to his again. "Is there anything else you'd like to know about my medical history?"

His nostrils flare as he places a hand on the wall next to my head. "What other medications are you taking?"

Trying not to roll my eyes, I tell him. "I have a vitamin D deficiency, so I get an infusion every few months. Other than that, there's obviously ibuprofen for headaches and period cramps, but that's all."

His eyes darken slightly. "Your periods are painful?" he asks.

"I'm pretty sure they're painful for most women, Alaric."

He leans forward a bit, his abdomen inches from mine. I can feel the heat radiating off him. "And what about birth control?"

I swallow. "I have an implant," I tell him, showing him my arm and placing a finger on the inside of my bicep. IUDs scared me—I was in no way letting someone shove a copper device up there, and I wasn't good at remembering to take the pill, so this was the next best thing.

He reaches forward with his free hand, tracing the spot where they inserted the implant a couple of years ago. My skin pebbles at his touch, and I try not to gasp as the calloused tip of his index finger finds my jaw, running an invisible line down my neck.

"That's good to know," he says, his voice deeper. His finger goes back up to the implant. I know he can feel the outline—I can feel it, so I'm sure he can, too. A shiver goes down my spine when I look up into his darkening expression, and he rakes a nail over the small scar they made when they implanted it, like he wants to claw it out. "I'm glad you're okay, Harlow."

I don't say anything as he pushes off from the wall and walks over to the chair he was sleeping in. Grabbing his tie, he wraps it around his neck and begins to make a knot. I watch, mesmerized. I never knew I had a thing about male hands and ties, but Alaric is making me rethink everything I thought I knew about these men.

Just the fact that he's here—that he stayed the night, that he's concerned... it feels nice. *Almost.*

"Get dressed. We're training in twenty minutes."

"Training?" I ask, trying to keep myself from whining.

"Yes, training. There are certain things you must know—certain things you must be able to do—to be a Lady of Darkness."

"Okay..." I trail off.

"Sterling has sent up some clothes for you to wear, since we know you don't have many clothes here."

I grind my jaw. *Of course he did.* "Fine. I'll be down in twenty minutes."

Alaric shoots me a look I can't decipher as he opens my door and walks out, leaving me feeling both nervous and... anticipatory.

I'm going to kill them, and I need to figure out how the hell I'm going to do it.

But first, I need a shower and a large cup of coffee.

☙❧

Ten minutes later, I'm scowling at the pink exercise outfit Sterling sent up. Pink leggings and a matching long-line sports bra, complete with white and pink running shoes. He even thought of a headband, socks, and a matching thong. *Charming.* I pull it all on, holding up my end of the deal. I told them I'd wear whatever they wanted me to, and these shoes are at least comfortable looking, unlike the heels from last night. It takes a little while to get the bra on, considering the bandage, but I ignore it, assuming Alaric will tend to it later. The bra is perfect, leaving a piece of loose fabric over the burn itself rather than rubbing against it. Pulling my curly hair into a high ponytail, I swipe on some sunscreen and chapstick, opting to leave my face bare in case they're planning on making me sweat.

God, I hope not.

What kind of fuckery are they going to have me do today?

Luckily, no one is waiting downstairs, so I push my way into the kitchen, where Rose is hunched over a pot of something that smells incredible.

"Hi," I tell her, and she jumps as I pour myself some coffee from the coffeemaker in the corner. Adding a bit of milk and sugar, I lean against the counter and take a sip, watching as she places the spatula on the side of the stove and turns to face me.

"Miss Windsor! You scared me." She laughs, fanning her face. "How was your date last night?"

It takes me a second to remember the lie I told her. "It was really fun," I fib. *Yes, because killing someone was fun.* "He took me to dinner. It was an early night." I check my phone, wincing when I realize it's nearly noon. "Had a bit of a lie in," I add.

She smirks at me, her lips pulling to one side. "Mmmhmm," she hums. "I'm glad you had a good time with Lord Cross."

Sipping my coffee, I nod. "I did. I think I might go out for a walk," I tell her, placing my nearly empty mug in the sink next to me. "I'm not sure when I'll be back..." I trail off. I don't want her to worry about me.

Her lips twist again. "Okay, not a problem. Tell Lord Cross I said hi." Her eyes sweep over my face, and she returns to whatever she's making. "Dinner is at six if you're back in time," she adds. "Beef stew."

My mouth waters. "That sounds amazing."

"And if you're hungry, I made some croissants this morning. They're in the basket over on the counter."

"Oooh, thank you," I say, quickly snatching two as my stomach grumbles gratefully. "See you later, Rose!" I turn and walk out of the kitchen.

"Goodbye!" she calls after me, and I check my phone as I head to the door.

It took me twenty-four minutes to get ready, which isn't bad. Stuffing my mouth with a fresh croissant, I moan as the buttery pastry practically melts in my mouth. I open the front door, only to see a black sports car awaiting me in the driveway, Gideon in the front seat. I stop mid-step as he grins at me.

"You're lucky it wasn't Sterling picking you up. He's a stickler for punctuality."

"Where are we going?" I ask, opening the passenger door and getting in just as I shove the rest of the first croissant into my mouth. Gideon snatches the second one from my hand, taking a large bite. "Hey!"

"Sharing is caring, baby. And you'll see when we get there."

He hands the half-eaten croissant back to me just as the car lurches forward, and I barely have time to buckle myself in before he's careening down the road.

Well, this should be fun.

CHAPTER 21

HARLOW

"You've got to be kidding me."

I look around the luxurious gymnasium, with shiny, state-of-the-art equipment, high ceilings, treadmills, spinning bikes, rowing machines, and three doors at the back that I'm positive don't hold anything fun. Gawking, I look at where Sterling is lying on a bench, lifting a long bar with weights on the end. He's not wearing anything but shorts, his chest and subsequent muscles glistening with sweat. I try not to stare as my eyes flick to Alaric, who is standing in the corner, dressed in a suit, texting on his phone. Theo is jogging on one of the treadmills, earbuds in his ears as he chats with someone.

"Not what you expected, baby?" Gideon asks, walking over to where I'm standing, wrapping an arm around my shoulders.

I shove his arm off. "No. By training, I thought you meant like... knife throwing. I don't exercise. In fact, I'm allergic to it."

Gideon snorts. "Well, today is the start of your formal physical training." I scowl at him as he gestures for me to follow him. "It's important that we all maintain physical agility as Lords of Darkness. As a Lady, you won't be exempt from our rigorous regimen."

"No, I don't think you understand. I tried running once and threw up. I like to go on walks, but that's about it. My body is not built for this. I'm the kind of person who likes to garden and leisurely rides my bike to stay active"

"Harlow, you don't have a choice," Gideon says, the side of his lips tilting up into an almost-smile. His dark blonde hair is pulled into his signature low bun, and his blue eyes bore into mine as he turns to face me. "I promise to make it worth your while," he adds, wiggling his brows. My stomach betrays me by swooping down low as he rolls his bottom lip between his teeth.

"Yeah? Because I'm not doing that," I declare, pointing at the treadmills.

Gideon takes my purse and sweatshirt, setting them down on the floor by the entrance. It's nearly as big as a public gym, but I assume that the guys own this place, and use it only for themselves. We're a little bit outside of the city in this warehouse, and it's the perfect place to hone those sculpted bods, I suppose. Grabbing my hand, Gideon drags me over to the spin bikes.

"You said you like to ride a bike, yeah?"

I frown at the weird-looking bike. "Yes, but... you're not going anywhere on these. It's boring. Why would someone torture themselves by riding a stationary bike?"

His lips twitch. "One of the most important things we can do is cardio. It gives us endurance in all aspects of this job, and it means we can outrun our enemies."

I nod like I'm not dreading doing *any* of this. "I understand that part. But what I'm trying to tell you is that I'm not an athletic person."

"Jesus fuck," Theo says, shoving his earbuds into his pocket and stalking over to us. I yelp as he picks me up and carries me to one of the treadmills. Setting me down on the already-moving belt, I grab onto the sides. "Walk, Harlow." He forms a barrier at the back of the treadmill, and I have no option other than to move my feet or fall flat on my face.

"So you're going to force me to run?" I ask, glancing down at the numbers that don't mean anything to me. I swing my arms as keep a fast pace.

"You're walking now, aren't you?" Theo says, eyes twinkling. "You don't have to run a marathon today, but you will run a mile."

"A mile?!" I squawk. I see Alaric chuckle from the corner of the room. "Oh, I'm sorry, Billionaire Daddy. Are you going to join us in this physical torture, or are you afraid of getting your pretty little suit dirty?"

"Ooooh," Gideon calls from next to me. "She called you out, man."

Alaric pushes off from the wall, pocketing his phone. Maybe it's the way he's giving me an angry stare, or maybe I'm already out of breath, but I swear I can't breathe when he looks at me like that.

"You want me to join you?" he asks, walking up to the treadmill I'm using. "Sterling, why don't you join us over here?"

I hear Sterling drop the bar of weights onto the rack and sit up, and *holy God, he is* cut *to the max...*

He saunters over to us, his cheeks sucked in, which only accentuates his beautiful face. He gives me a curt nod before taking up the treadmill next to me. It's then that I realize there are five of everything—five treadmills, five spin bikes, five rowing machines... this is *their* gym, but not only that, this is where my father worked out, too. Something about that makes me continue walking, filled with purpose.

If he did it, so would I.

Would he be proud to see me here? It was no secret I had daddy issues. Even though we weren't close, I always wonder *what if*.

What if we had been close?

Would he have told me about all of this?

I swallow the emotion building up inside of me, and I reach down and push the button to speed up the belt.

"Don't go too hard, too fast," Sterling warns, looking over at me as he begins an easy jog.

I look over at him as I power walk, his taut body not giggling in the slightest as he quickens his pace. Alaric reaches into a bag sitting next to a nearby machine, removing his shoes and suit quickly. Gideon and Theo take the treadmills to the right of Sterling. I watch as Alaric strips down to his grey boxer briefs, and to distract myself, I push the button to go even faster, moving into a slow jog.

I don't need to fixate on the fact that I can see the outline of his thick cock.

"This isn't so bad," I say as Alaric steps into exercise shorts. Next, he pulls on running shoes, coming up to the treadmill to my left. "I'm probably close to a mile, right?" I ask, huffing as I try to breathe evenly.

Alaric looks over at my dashboard, smirking. "0.1 miles, actually."

I groan as I speed up. "Okay. I can do this."

They all chuckle as I struggle to run. I feel both lightheaded and dizzy, but also... strong. Oddly euphoric. I can feel the sweat dripping down my cleavage, down my back... at least I know I'm hydrated. I still feel a bit queasy from what happened last night, but the croissant helped, and I'm sure sweating all the drugs out of my system will help even more. All four of them match my speed, and none of them look like they're dying—which is what I'm sure I look like. I'm practically gasping for air, and I stop running, placing my feet on the edges of the treadmill, away from the belt. Pressing the stop button, I hunch over and try to catch my breath.

"How far now?"

"A quarter of a mile," Sterling says from next to me. "Keep running, Harlow."

I snort. "I feel like I'm going to pass out."

He looks over at me. "Then lower your pace until you can maintain it."

"I'm done," I say, shrugging. "I told you, I'm not—"

"Get. Your. Ass. Back. On. The. Treadmill," Sterling grits out. "Don't stop until I tell you to."

His commanding tone makes me huff, but I do as he says, pushing it to a speed where I'm just barely jogging.

His jaw ticks as he looks at my dash and then back at me. "Good girl."

My mouth drops open, but he looks forward again, concentrating on his own run and ignoring me. I watch the numbers tick by one by one, slowly dying. Though going at this speed, it's not as hard as when I was sprinting. I'm sure I look like one of those old men who walk-jog early in the morning, but fuck it. They want me to run a mile? This is how I'm going to do it.

I finally get to a mile, slowing down to walk as I catch my breath. My bra is soaked, and my hairline is damp. Gideon hands me an ice-cold water, and I sip it, feeling my body cooling down.

"Good job," he says, taking a sip from his bottle. "Tomorrow, we will try a mile and a quarter."

"Tomorrow?" I ask, already dreading it. "Do you guys run every day?"

"No," Alaric answers. "Sometimes we row, or bike. And then we have strength-training days, too."

"Sterling likes yoga," Theo chimes in, laughing. "He'd love to teach you his tantric shit."

"How far do you all run on running days?" I ask, ignoring what Theo just told me, and the way it makes my clit throb with curiosity and desire.

"Between five and ten miles," Sterling answers. Turning his green eyes to mine, he cocks his head. "We'll get you there."

It's then that I notice his rings are gone. "You're not wearing your rings," I tell him.

He clenches his jaw as he sips his water. "They don't really work for lifting weights."

"What do they mean?" I ask. I hear Theo whistle behind him, and I look between them. "What?"

"You asked a forbidden question," Theo jokes. "Don't ask about the rings."

"But I thought we were all supposed to be close. No secrets and all that shit," I add, scowling at Sterling.

His nostrils flare as his eyes bore into mine. "They represent the people I've killed."

I go still. "You've only killed ten people?"

He shakes his head, frowning. "They represent the ones that stick with me. The ones that give me nightmares. The ones whose blood felt corroded and wrong."

"Oh, well, that makes sense," I answer quietly. Holding eye contact for a few more seconds, I feel his gaze burn into mine, and something about it makes me want to comfort him. To make him feel good. Like he's a big, fucked up rain cloud and I'm the sunshine.

Keep your head in the game, Harlow. These guys are your enemy.

"Alright, enough questions," Alaric says, wiping his face with a towel even though he doesn't look like he's sweating. "Onto the weight machines."

I snap my gaze to his. "You mean we're not done with exercising?"

He chuckles, his tongue rolling around the inside of his cheek. "Done? Little monster, we still have an hour left, *at least*," he says, beckoning me over to a scary-looking machine. "Come on. Show us what we're working with."

I step off the treadmill.

I hate them. And I should resent them for making me do all of this. Because that's what they're doing—they're forcing me into this life. They have been, since the night of my father's funeral. But for whatever reason, being around them... it makes me feel alive. And more than that, something about them makes me feel welcome. They make me feel like one of them, because I am. And I shouldn't *want* to be around them, but I do. I like the excitement, the adrenaline. It's addicting.

It's fucked up, I know.

Which is why I turn my brain off, going into autopilot. I can't get close to them, or my plan will never work.

Do as they say for a few weeks, and then take them out.

That is the plan.

CHAPTER 22

GIDEON

After I drop Harlow back at her house, I meet the guys at the office. We're all still in our workout clothes since we all received the same threatening text from Acadia, and that needs to be dealt with as soon as possible. Theo is already hard at work on his computer, and Sterling is helping him with something over his shoulder. Alaric is on the phone, and as I walk over with coffees for everyone, he puts the phone on speaker.

"They've gotten the authorities involved," the person says, and I recognize the voice as Kurtz, one of our spies in Russia. "Some of the Acadian members are headed to London later today, and they're going to review the security footage."

"That means nothing. Theo already scrubbed it," Alaric answers, sounding bored.

"Of course, my Lord. However, there are eyewitnesses that saw you two leave together."

Alaric's jaw feathers. "Okay. So we find someone else to pin this on."

"What about his phone?" Kurtz asks.

"We have it," Alaric answers.

"Good. We can edit the chip data to show texts from a burner phone."

"Let's do that," Alaric answers.

"I didn't realize Armin was a target," Kurtz says, typing something on his end.

Alaric's eyes find mine. "He wasn't. But he touched something that wasn't his."

The double entendre goes right over Kurtz's head, and they continue their conversation for a few more minutes as I sip my coffee. I flick my switchblade open and closed, focusing on the heavy metal weapon in my palm.

"So, what's the plan?" Sterling asks, walking over to me.

"Kurtz is taking care of Armin's phone. Looks like killing him was a lot messier than we realized."

It was true. When we made our kills, it was usually after weeks of thorough planning, ensuring no loose ends that would lead back to us. Our first target yesterday was supposed to be attending the dinner, and somehow, he got tipped off that we were going to be there, so he fled. We hunted him down and killed him, but because we'd already planned on killing him anyway, there was nothing more to do.

We'd sent his wife a suicide note, and his car is abandoned on the side of the road now.

No one would ask questions, and his wife wouldn't be digging too deeply, seeing as she could now openly be with her lover.

"Once the authorities get into Armin's hotel room, they'll be able to access his cellphone data, which we will have, of course, altered to show threatening texts from a burner phone."

"Who are we pinning it on?" he asks.

I shrug. "Does it matter? We could take any of these children out with a flick of our wrist. We're being polite by cooperating. Charles would've just had everyone in Acadia murdered. Problem solved."

Sterling snorts. "Maybe that's why he had so many enemies, and why he was so easily swayed. Because he acted with emotions."

"Seems like his daughter inherited that tendency," I add, thinking of Harlow last night—of how pained she looked after killing Armin. "But unlike Charles, I don't think Harlow has it in her to betray us."

Sterling is quiet for a moment. When I look over at him, he's staring straight ahead. "I wouldn't be so sure. We all saw how easily she killed Armin last night."

"Yeah, but she hesitated," I tell him.

His green eyes pierce into mine, and he cocks his head. "I think Harlow has a lot of demons we don't know about."

Theo walks over as Alaric finishes up his call with Kurtz. "Alright, we're all good to go with the phone. I'm uploading the chip data as we speak, so Kurtz will mess with it and send it back to us, and we can then pop the new data into his phone, all before lunch."

I pocket my knife and rub my mouth. "Maybe we should all agree on a target before it happens next time," I mumble, looking at Alaric, who is busy texting someone—probably Kurtz.

"You would've done the exact same thing," Theo laments, shoving my shoulder.

"Knock it off. This is serious. Acadia is big, and they won't stop until they find all the answers. Even if we edit the chip data, there were still eyewitnesses. This could all very easily get out of control."

Alaric walks over and sighs. "All good. One of us has to get back to London to plant the phone in his room."

I shake my head. "You realize that if anyone saw him using it, the phone is useless, right?"

Alaric waves his hand in the air. "Armin had a bit too much to drink at dinner last night. He started to feel funny, so he headed back to his hotel room on the sixth floor. The cameras will back this up because Kurtz is a genius with CCTV. He got dizzy, hit his head, dropped his phone, and was last seen taking the service elevator down to the parking garage, where he was shoved into an unidentified car. Presumably the same people who poisoned him at dinner."

I tilt my head and narrow my eyes. "Fuck. You're a goddamn genius."

Alaric shrugs. "Now, what are we going to do about Harlow?"

"What do you mean?" Theo asks.

He steps over to the window, pacing in front of it. "She's too soft. Too vulnerable. We must toughen her up. Think about the things Charles did to us when we were being initiated into the order... we need to get her on our level, and fast."

Sterling clears his throat. "Aside from physically training her everyday, what else did you have in mind? Do I even want to know?"

Alaric looks at Theo, who nods once and begins to speak. "I finally got ahold of her medical files, as well as the police report from the night her mother died. It was a burglary by a man who is still on the loose. He killed her mother and then he raped Harlow."

My blood cools. "He got away?" I ask, nearly growling. I look over at Sterling, and his expression is downright murderous, nostrils flaring, hands flexed at his sides. "How the fuck did he get away?"

Theo shrugs. "No idea. After he fled, it took Harlow seven hours to call the police."

"Fuck," Sterling mumbles, rubbing his face with his hands.

"I listened to the 9-1-1 call. Having been previously diagnosed with anxiety, she managed it without medication. But she also had undiagnosed psychosis, and this trauma triggered a psychotic episode. She was sent to a psychiatric hospital for three months to get the psychosis under control. She likely remembers very little of this period of her life. And that 9-1-1 call? She sounded completely incoherent. The notes on the police report show that she'd lost touch with reality, and for the first forty-eight hours, they suspected Harlow had killed her mother."

I'm biting the inside of my cheeks so hard that I draw blood. "Jesus fuck." Alaric and Theo share another look, like they want to say something, but they're not sure how. "What?"

"We saw how vulnerable she was last night. We saw how one action could create a cascade of events, compromising us. Kitt isn't going to narc, but someone else could," Theo says slowly. "I've been digging deeper into her medical records, and she's been experiencing PTSD flashbacks periodically since it happened. Since he was never caught, she has these visions where he finds her again—vivid ones. And because she was living with her friend in Brooklyn in order to finish high school, she didn't have access to quality therapy, and I'm concerned that puts us all at a disadvantage. What she needed was a qualified therapist, but she didn't have that. Psychologically, she's as high risk as we can possibly get."

I look at Alaric, who picks an invisible thread off his shoulder. "You're worried she's going to snap," I say slowly. He nods. "What can we do to ensure that doesn't happen?"

Alaric takes a step forward. "I'm not quite sure we need to avoid it. I think we just need to speed it up."

Sterling goes still, as do I. "You're suggesting we trigger a psychotic episode?"

Theo nods. "We need to break her before we can rebuild and make her whole again. This isn't about triggering her; it's about teaching her how to overcome her triggers. You've heard of Eye Movement Desensitization and Reprocessing (EMDR) therapy?"

I nod, not sure I like where this is going.

"It was initially developed for the treatment of post-traumatic stress disorder."

"Okay, fine. Say we do this. How long does it take?" I ask.

Theo looks at Alaric again. "It's usually recommended at least once a week. But for severe cases... it can be conducted on consecutive days."

"Can be?" Sterling asks.

"Harlow had a disturbing experience that continues to cause distress because the memory was not adequately processed. This puts us *all* at risk. When those memories are triggered, those disturbing elements are experienced. Imagine if we put Harlow in a situation that triggers something, and she has another psychotic episode?"

"And you think your method will work for her to overcome her trauma?" I ask.

Theo nods. "We will focus directly on the memory. Recreate the scenario if we need to. If it works, it will change the way the memory is stored in her brain, which will reduce any problematic symptoms."

I sigh, rubbing the bridge of my nose. "I want to say this is fucked up, but I'm sure you've done your research on why it needs to happen this way," I say slowly. If nothing else, I trust my brothers more than I trust myself. If this is the method Theo and Alaric want to utilize, then so be it. They never do anything for no reason. And trusting them completely is pivotal for our order.

"It's for her own good," Alaric says, rubbing his mouth. "And the stability of our order."

"When do we start?" Sterling asks. "And how will this work?"

Alaric shrugs. "We can start today if you want. The sooner, the better. As for how... I'm not sure. I'm not a psychiatrist, but I can ask around. There are methods for doing these things so that she won't experience more trauma..."

"But...?" I ask, crossing my arms.

Alaric sighs. "We don't have the luxury of time. We need to break her, and quickly. And I'm not going to be nice about it."

CHAPTER 23

Harlow

I can barely move my arms. Every single muscle is throbbing, and my burn stings with the slightest movement. Alaric cleaned it before I got dropped back off at home, so I leave it bandaged up while I take a quick shower. Once I'm done, I change into some fresh clothes and head into the kitchen to make myself a sandwich. I don't see Rose anywhere—she must be in another area of the house—but she left me some food in the fridge. I'm just walking into the dining room when I run smack into Sterling.

"Um, hi?" I say, glaring at him as I take a step back. My sandwich was precariously close to falling on the ground, which, at this level of hunger, would've been a goddamn travesty. I look around, concerned Rose is going to see him and start asking the questions I don't want to give answers for. "Are you here to bombard me with more exercise? Because I must tell you, making this sandwich was so much harder with my noodle arms."

Sterling just watches me with arms crossed.

"Okay, I'm going to go eat now," I tell him, walking toward the dining room. When I turn the corner, I see Alaric, Gideon, and Theo sitting at the table.

All three of them are wearing black—and they're each holding a gun.

Icy cold fear skitters down my spine, and I nearly drop my plate. "Um..." I say slowly, setting my sandwich down on the table carefully. "I don't think Rose will appreciate th—"

"Rose isn't here," Alaric says, his voice cold and smooth. Gone are the jokesters from earlier. Gone is the man from last night, the one who cleaned my brand and read to me. Before me are heartless killers.

The Lords of Darkness.

"Yeah, she has a daughter in Essex, and a couple of hours ago, her daughter had a burglary attempt. So, Rose has left, and the rest of the staff is off today."

I feel fear sliding down my body. Imagining the home invasion, imagining Rose and her daughter dealing with the kinds of men who break into homes...

I squeeze my eyes shut and take a deep breath.

You are safe here.

He can't find you in England.

You are safe here.

Opening my eyes, all four of them are staring at me. I was so afraid of him for so long—of the nameless man who violated me.

But four of the most dangerous men in the world are currently sitting right here in my dining room.

Fucking *great*.

I should fear them. I should be running away screaming. But I wouldn't let someone do that to me again, and I will find a way out of this. The man who hurt me will pay, and so will the *Lords*.

"What do you want?" I ask Alaric. "Am I allowed to at least eat my fucking sandwich?"

"Go ahead," Gideon says, gesturing for me to sit.

I do, placing a napkin in my lap as I take hold of the sandwich. Eating slowly to avoid whatever the fuck they have in store for me, I don't make eye contact. Instead, choosing to look down at the table. When I'm finished, I push my plate away and cross my arms, resting them on my stomach as I lean back.

Every interaction with them has been unpleasant, so I'm sure they're not going to tell me to have a nice day. They think they've trapped me, given me no option but to comply and live out this life with them. Guns, murders, fancy dinners... *no, thank you.*

They couldn't be more wrong about me.

I sit up straighter and clear my throat. "Well? Cat's got your tongue? Why are you sitting in my dining room, guns blazing?"

I look over at Gideon, who has one hand on the gun, the other on his switchblade, which he's obsessively flicking open and closed. Something about the way his hands move, his long fingers curling around the metal... it's sort of mesmerizing. Just as I'm about to repeat my question, Alaric sighs and points his gun at Gideon, firing once.

I scream and cover my ears as Gideon looks at Alaric, wide-eyed. That's when I see dark red blood begin to seep through Gideon's sweater, right in the middle of the chest.

I whirl to face Alaric fully. "What the fuck? You just shot him!"

Alaric cocks his head and glowers at me. "And?" He holds his gun and cocks it again, pointing it straight at me. "You're next, little monster. Run."

My breathing turns ragged as I flick my eyes between Gideon, Alaric, Sterling, and Theo. Alaric is still pointing the gun at me, and Gideon is now slumped over his chair, grunting. Sterling and Theo just look pissed, but not at Alaric.

At *me*.

"Fuck," Gideon whispers, clutching his chest and glaring at Alaric. "Is this about Charles?"

My blood cools. "My dad?" I whisper, standing quickly. It doesn't take a genius to realize they're talking about my father. Wracking my brain, I remember how they said they could eliminate members as they see fit. So... why are they eliminating Gideon? It's hard to think with a gun pointed at my head.

Alaric stares at me with loathing as he continues to point the gun right at my head. "Your father betrayed us. So did Gideon. Now, like I said before, you can stand there and take it, or you can run."

Everything inside of me turns to ice.

That's what he said—my rapist.

You just going to stand there and take it?

I open and close my mouth as my hands tremble. Gideon's eyes begin to droop.

"Run," he says, blood dribbling out of his mouth.

So I run like hell, sending the chair backwards as I jump up. I twist around and hear Alaric, Sterling, and Theo jump up, and a sob escapes me when I get to the front door.

It's locked.

Panic floods me when I try it again, and when I turn around, Alaric is standing there with the gun.

"Oh, my bad. Door's locked." His voice is cold, cruel—what the *hell*?!

I pull on it as hard as I can, and I debate kicking it down. But this is no hollow American door. It's a sturdy, centuries-old, solid oak door. I twist around as Alaric takes another step toward me.

"If you're going to kill me, just do it," I tell him, hoping my voice isn't shaking as much as the rest of my body.

Alaric tilts his head and looks at me, those dark curls falling over his forehead.

Beautiful and deadly.

Isn't that what I said about him last night? It couldn't be more true right now.

"I'm feeling charitable today, so I'll give you a head start. How about thirty seconds?"

I bare my teeth. "What, so you can play with your prey before you kill it?"

One corner of his mouth tilts up. "Ready, set... go."

I don't ask any more questions, afraid of delaying my time advantage. I run past him and up the stairs. It's a big house. There are hundreds of hiding places. And maybe I can jump out of my window or something.

I blindly run the opposite direction of my room, toward my father's suite. My heart is pounding so hard that I feel like it might explode. Once inside his bedroom, I close the door and rush to his window. He has a terrace, so there must be some way to get down onto the ground floor—

I pull on the window, but it's also locked somehow. Turning the old brass nob, I fiddle with it, shaking it in case it's stuck. But it doesn't budge.

"Fuck!" I scream, walking to his wardrobe and throwing it open. I find a shoehorn, and I chuck it as hard as I can against the glass door. It bounces back. I lift my foot and try to kick at the glass, but to no avail. "Come on," I growl, my breathing ragged.

I can't let them hurt me.
I refuse to be here again.
Taking a steadying breath, I look around.

Fine. They think they can try to kill me? After everything—after the show of solidarity last night—fine. I'll ruminate on why later. Right now, I need to get the upper hand.

I grab the shoehorn and slam it against the glass mirror on my father's dressing table. It shatters—so much so, that I have to duck.

I shake myself off and pick up a shard big enough to act as a large knife. Holding it in my hands, I exit his bedroom and take the stairs up to the servant's quarters.

"Where, oh where, is my little monster?" Alaric's voice sounds from the stairwell below me.

Fuck. What the fuck is going on?

"Come out, come out, wherever you are," Theo says, his low voice dark and menacing. "You can hide, but we will search this house from top to bottom until we find you. And once we do..."

Another sob escapes my throat as I stumble up the stairs two at a time. The same kind of panic from that night—the one that makes me feel shaky and hot—creeps up my spine.

I should've run that first night.

I should've figured a way out.

I make my way up to the third story, and my hands are shaking so much that I can barely open one of the random doors.

Fitting myself inside a linen closet, I stand there and wait, glass held up high. They think they can kill me?

Ha. I'll kill them first.

Watch.

Me.

CHAPTER 24

STERLING

I find her a minute after she breaks the mirror.

When I open the closet I know she's hiding in—thanks to Theo's hidden cameras—she's gasping behind one of the shelves, one hand in her armpits as she pants, half bent over. The other hand is holding a cute little shard of glass. Her cheeks are stained with tears, but the instant she sees me, she lifts her chin and spreads her legs. *Fuck, she's so fucking beautiful.* What I'd give to see those large, slightly parted red lips around my cock... and those denim blue eyes locked onto mine as I coat the back of her throat with my come.

She glares at me with daggers in her eyes, sending all her hatred into that gaze, but it only spurs on the dirty thoughts I'm having about her—about wrapping my hand around her neck as I pound into her from behind, like a predator.

Pressing her face into the stone floor.

Stretching her tight pussy.

My cock twitches at the thought.

She's still gasping, still trying to catch her breath from the adrenaline of running from us.

"This is why we suggest exercising," I tell her. "So that your enemies can't outrun you."

She bares her teeth at me as she takes up a fighting stance, arms in front of her.

Such a strong little monster.

"You're my enemy now? What the hell happened to all that crap about brotherhood and trusting each other?" Her eyes begin to fill with tears, but she blinks them away. "You just killed Gideon," she whispers. "I knew you were all psychopaths, but I didn't realize you'd just kill one of your own like that. Don't you have any integrity?"

I smile as I walk toward her in the small space. She lets out a tiny gasp that makes my cock twitch.

"Did we scare you?" I ask, taking another step closer.

"N-no," she stutters. Then she stands up a bit straighter as outrage flashes across her face. "Wait... why are you asking if you scared me?" she asks, though I can see the wheels turning.

"Gideon is fine. He's currently washing up in the powder room downstairs."

Her mouth opens. Closes. Opens again. "He—but Alaric shot him—"

I take the last step before I'm right in front of her. "Bulletproof vest and fake blood, baby."

Her eyes flash with fury and her whole body tenses. She makes the mistake of rearing the hand with the shard back slightly, so when she starts to plunge it forward, I've anticipated it. Grabbing her wrist and squeezing, she drops the shard. It clatters to the ground as her chest rises and falls with rapid, frustrated breaths.

"You tricked me," she growls. "You chased me. You threatened me with a gun," she adds, blinking away more tears. "You *lied* to me—"

I grip her shoulders with my hands and twist her around, shoving her against the wall as I push my body into the back of hers. *Fuck, she feels good here, beneath me.* She turns her head and looks at me over her shoulder.

"Yes, we tricked you. Did it work?" I ask, my cock already rock hard in my pants. She smells like fucking heaven—floral, mixed with something spicy, like cinnamon.

"You don't scare me," she mumbles, anger lacing her words.

One of my hands goes up to her damp hair, and I fist the soft, thick curls I've wanted to touch since I saw that picture of her. I pull her neck back, and she does her best not to show the fear I know is flooding her veins.

"You sure?" I ask, running my nose over her neck. My other hand roves down the side of her curvy body, settling on her stomach as I roughly pull her into me so that she can feel how hard she makes me. "I'd give anything to sink my cock inside your pussy, Harlow."

She lets out the tiniest of gasps. "You're all talk," she says, voice shaking. "You want me so badly? Have at it, sir."

Fuck. She did not *just call me sir.*

I tug on her hair, the sound of her whimper sending a thrill down my shaft. Does she like this? How is that possible? We were supposed to break her.

Not turn her on.

"I don't have your consent," I tell her.

She gives me an evil little laugh. "Wouldn't be the first time."

White-hot anger floods through me, and I grind my jaw as I pull her against me again. *Hard.*

"Then tell me to stop," I say to her, my hand roving up her jumper, and *fuck me*, she's not wearing a bra. "Fuck, Harlow," I say, my voice cracking as my finger grazes her peaked nipple. She gasps again, but she doesn't seem scared. I swear, I feel her ass grind against my cock ever so slightly. "You like this?" I growl into her ear.

She doesn't say anything, so I twist her nipple slightly between my index finger and thumb. Then, I pinch it—hard.

Crying out, she doesn't sound like she's in pain.

She sounds aroused.

Growling, I unconsciously grind against her again. I can feel the damp spot in my pants from my precome just from being this close to her, palming her perfectly sized tits... what I wouldn't give to suck on these perfect nipples.

"What about this?" I ask, moving my hand down. "I still don't have your consent." She's trembling in my arms as I graze the waistband of her sweatpants. "Tell me to stop," I say, so turned on that I can barely concentrate.

My fingers dip lower, through soft curls at the apex of her thighs. Two fingers rove lower, and I find her clit wet, ready, and waiting. The noise coming out of me sounds like a low growl mixed with a moan as I spread her with my fingers. She mewls in my arms, and when I tug her hair back to look down at her, her mouth's parted, and her eyes are closed.

My little monster likes this, even if she won't admit it.

"Giving me the silent treatment won't help your case," I tell her. "It only makes me want to punish you."

She moans—outright *moans*—for me.

I'm fighting the dominant beast inside of me with everything I have right now.

But maybe she should meet her monster sooner.

After all, Alaric is convinced we should try to break her as soon as possible. Maybe this is one way to do it. My cock would certainly be happy with that outcome.

I pull away from her even though my hands are itching to make her come around my fingers. "On your knees."

She turns around to face me, and *fuck*, I wasn't ready for the heady way she's looking at me. Darkened eyes, parted lips, rosy cheeks...

Then she does the most goddamn beautiful thing I've ever seen. She drops to her knees and gives me a defiant look.

"You think making me suck your cock will scare me?" she says, reaching forward for my belt buckle.

Fuck... me...

"Is it working?" I ask, her small, deft hands freeing my throbbing length.

"No," she says caustically. Her blue eyes find mine, and she tilts her head slightly as she licks her lips. It's then that I realize I'm not making her do anything—not really. *She* does *like this.* "You have no idea what I've been through, Sterling," she growls, and that same fury from this morning returns when I think of how someone else violated her. "Sucking you off? Easy."

My jaw ticks as the tip of my cock leaks with more precome. Harlow stares at it before turning her eyes back to me, flicking her tongue against the bead of wetness. Her warm tongue makes me moan, and I grab onto the shelves to hold myself steady as she opens her mouth, taking me in fully.

Oh fuck, oh fuck...

Her cheeks hollow out as she sucks my cock like a champ. Taking me into the back of her throat, she doesn't even gag as she holds me there... and swallows.

"Fuck, Harlow," I whisper, as my whole body jerks with how good it feels. How the muscles in her mouth and throat milk me from base to tip. "Yes, baby. Take it all."

She does it again.

"Play with my balls," I tell her, my voice hoarse.

Her hands cup my balls dutifully, and I realize... she likes being told what to do.

Free the monster.

"Let me fuck your mouth," I tell her.

She stills, placing both hands on her knees, and looks up at me with an expectant expression. Rolling her tongue over the head of my cock, I twitch at the sight of her mouth full of me, thinking about how fucking good she'd look with a mouth full of my come.

I move into her mouth farther and farther, placing a hand on her throat as I go. She sputters as I get in deep, her eyes watering as I continue going to the hilt. Once I'm all the way in, her complexion grows a bit red, so I ease up, letting her breath.

And fuck, seeing my cock settled in the back of her throat... it's so fucking hot.

I go harder and faster this time, not giving her the time to recover as I fuck her throat deep. Her teeth graze the base of my cock, and it only spurs me on. She makes a gagging sound but doesn't lose her composure. *Good girl.* Saliva dribbles onto the floor, and tears begin to stream down her cheeks, but *fuck me,* she doesn't make a move to relent.

So I keep going, keep pushing. I can feel my orgasm beginning in the base of my spine, electrifying my cock and balls. I feel them tighten, feel my cock harden and bob as I pull out. *Not yet.* I'm not done with her. She gasps a bit, but all she does is wipe her mouth with the cuff of her jumper. Looking up at me with wide, hooded eyes, I place a hand on her head.

"Stay," I tell her.

Taking a few steps back, I can see how hard her nipples are, poking through the thick material of her grey jumper. Opening the door of the linen closet, I pull my pants up and look around the hallway. The others must've suspected what we were doing in here because the hallway is empty. Turning back to face Harlow, I see her sitting with her palms on her knees, waiting for her next command.

Fuck me. She's such a good fucking girl.

"Crawl," I command, hanging my arms on the door frame.

She narrows her eyes for a fraction of a second, but then she drops down to her hands, crawling slowly toward me. I take a step back as she gets closer, her eyes piercing into mine.

"Into the hallway," I direct her, pointing behind me. I watch as she crawls obediently to the middle of the hallway with no complaints. She sits up and places her palms on her knees again, head forward.

Fuck.

This is dangerous.

"Now what?" she asks.

Marching over to her, I grab her jaw and gaze down at her. "Did I say you could speak?"

Her lips thin as she pulls out of my grip, head forward.

"Take your jumper off," I tell her. She doesn't even hesitate. Pulling her jumper up, she throws it off to the side and resumes her position. Walking over, I stand in front of her. "Take my cock out and stand taller on your knees," I growl.

She does both, reaching for my buckle again. My pants are soaked from all the precome she's drawn from me. From being so close to exploding inside of her throat. Freeing my cock, she sits up on her knees so that my shaft is right between her full breasts. I rub my leaking cock over both nipples, and I don't miss the way she hisses and arches her back.

"Press them together with your hands," I tell her. "Lace your fingers so that I can fuck your tits."

Looking up at me, she does as I say, pressing her large breasts together and lacing her fingers, creating a hollow space just for me. I snake my cock between the soft skin, moaning as I start to fuck her tits slowly.

"Fuck, you have the most perfect tits, Harlow," I rasp, quickening my pace. I thrust forward slightly; it should rock her, but she holds steady as I brutally fuck them. My release comes on quite suddenly, the telltale tingling starting in my balls and making my cock turn to steel. I pull out and she closes her eyes, opening her mouth.

Jesus fucking fuck.

I spray her mouth and face with my release, my cock throbbing intensely in my hands as I spill all my seed. I twitch as the last of it leaves my body, and when I look down at Harlow, she looks... *beautiful.* Her brows are furrowed slightly, but she's composed and waiting. I reach out and take a bit of come from her lip with my index finger, inserting it into her mouth.

She has the fucking audacity to suck, hollowing her cheeks again as she cleans the come off my finger. It makes my cock bounce just remembering how it felt to be inside of that hot, soft mouth of hers.

Taking a step back, I relish in the way she's covered in my seed. It's all over her mouth, chin, and tits—and *fuck me.* I pull my phone out and take a picture... and she fucking lets me.

When I put it away, I look back at her. "Let me clean you up." Walking into the nearest bathroom, I find a face towel, running it under warm water before I walk back to Harlow, wiping her clean. After, she just stands and pulls her jumper back on.

"Why are we in the hallway?" she asks, looking around.

I chuckle. "I was just giving my brothers a good show. Say hi," I add, pointing to the ceiling lamp.

Harlow snaps her eyes up to the old brass fixture. "You put a camera up here?"

"Theo did. That first night. We can see everything. Well, except for that linen closet. And we don't have cameras in the bathrooms, of course."

Her jaw tenses. "So, did I pass?"

I turn to face her as I buckle myself back up. "Pass?"

She shrugs. "You guys did all of this for a reason. So, did I pass the test?"

I smirk as I walk over to her, pulling her into me. "You did exceedingly well, Harlow. But we're far from done."

CHAPTER 25

HARLOW

I follow Sterling downstairs, wishing I still had that shard of glass so that I could plunge it into his neck.
Jesus.
Maybe I am a psychopath like them.
It would explain how fucking turned on I just got, even though it was *so* morally degrading. Why did I like it? Was it because I knew he'd stop if I said no? Toeing the line of consent like that, with my past... it could've been a nightmare, but instead, I find myself soaked between my legs for him. And I *liked* submitting to him. I still plan on killing all of them, don't get me wrong. I have to. This cannot be my life from now on, and I refuse to give in to any of it. So yes, I would gladly stab Sterling right now—all of them—for that show they just performed for me.
They think they can one-up me? What was the point? To scare me? Well, it didn't work. Not really. Sterling's massive cock got in the way.
And it really was massive—thick, veiny, with a dark pink head. It was the kind of cock women dreamt about, the kind of cock that dildos were molded after. *Screw him and his big, perfect cock.*
Gritting my teeth together, I find the other guys sitting around the dining room table, laughing.
Laughing.
My nostrils flare and heat flashes through my body as I rush forward, rearing my hand back to hit Alaric. But he grabs my wrist before I can do anything, instead, pulling me onto his lap. I squirm and grunt, trying to get away, but he holds me close as I kick out.

"Calm your tits, Harlow," he murmurs, and I hear Gideon guffaw from the other side of the table.

I whirl my head to him. "You," I seethe, panting.

"Me," Gideon chirps, grinning, which accentuates his scruff. "Surprise," he says, running a hand through his messy, dirty blonde hair before leaning forward and pinning me with a contemplative gaze. "Oscar-worthy performance, was it not?"

Killing them would feel so fucking good.

"Fuck you," I growl. "I wish he'd actually killed you."

Gideon snaps his switchblade back into its holder, smiling up at me. *Asshole.*

"Pretty words for a pretty girl," he murmurs. "You don't mean that, do you?"

Of course I do, but I can't give them any reason to suspect my true motives.

Softening my expression, I clear my throat and take a deep breath. "I didn't know," I say meekly, putting on a show. "I was scared."

I slowly turn my gaze to Sterling, and he's watching me with narrowed eyes. If any of them are onto me, it's him. I have to keep my eyes open around him.

"Nah, we'd never kill him," Theo says from behind a computer. He's always on his phone, or his computer, and I cock my head as I look over at him.

"Why are you always on your computer? What are you doing?" I ask, relaxing my body a bit on Alaric's lap. His hand comes around to my thigh, resting there, and I can't help but admit I like the way he always touches me. Like a possessive boyfriend.

Ew. Knock it off, Harlow.

Theo smirks, putting two hands behind his neck and leaning back. "Secret things."

I pout. "I thought we didn't have secrets as Lords."

He sighs, coming back to a regular seated position. "You really want to know?" I look at him, deadpan, and he doesn't say anything more as he turns the computer so that I can see it.

My cheeks flush instantly as I realize what he's doing, and who he's watching. Not from embarrassment either, but something else. Something raw, and primal. They were watching Sterling titty fuck me. What were they saying while they watched us? Did they like it? *God, why does that turn me on a little bit?*

I squirm in Alaric's lap as I make a noise of disgust. "You guys are pigs. Where else do you have cameras?"

Theo shrugs. "That's for us to know. Once this becomes your house, you can choose to take them out. For now, they stay, so that we can keep an eye on you."

"Why?" I pry. "If I run, you'll just hunt me down."

He levels a cold gaze in my direction. Theo may outwardly seem like a golden retriever, but a part of me knows he's also really fucking deadly. They all are. Once again, I have to wonder how the hell I'm going to get out from under their steel vise grip.

"You're a flight risk. I'll come to trust you in time, but while we're training you, the cameras stay."

I cross my arms and pretend to sulk.

You'll come to trust me... but it will be to your detriment.

"You say when this becomes my house... what do you mean?"

Gideon scowls down at his knife, rubbing his chest for a second before he turns his gaze to me. "Each Lord—or Lady—has their own house to manage. This one is yours, passed down through the years. It comes with the territory of being a Lady of Darkness."

I stiffen at his words. "But this is Cecelia's house now."

Theo clears his throat. "Technically, this house belongs to you now. We've submitted the necessary paperwork, and it will transfer over into your name sometime today."

"No. I wouldn't think of kicking Cecelia and Archie out. This is their home—"

Alaric squeezes my thigh. "Harlow."

I twist around to face him. How could he possibly be okay with this? Then again, they just staged a fucking murder right here in this very room. It's not like they have morals. They're all cruel, cold-hearted monsters.

"So, to suit your needs, you're just kicking a fresh widow out of her home, as well as her young child—"

"Just trust us," Alaric growls. "Cecelia is perfectly content in the Cotswolds with her parents. I highly doubt she will ever come back here willingly."

Something in his tone sounds harsh and hostile, but before I can ask questions, Theo closes his computer and stands.

"The authorities have Armin's phone," he announces. "We're in the clear."

I gape at him. "Armin?" *Oh, right. The guy I killed last night...*

"We've tweaked his cell phone data so no one suspects us," Alaric says from under me. His hand roves up my thigh slightly. "Our crime of passion had consequences, but we're taking care of it."

I should feel sick, violated. They kidnapped him because he talked to me, because of *one* touch. And then they made me kill him.

You're not going to kill me. You're a joke to this order, and soon these men will figure that out.

I grit my teeth as I remember Armin's words. "So... what? That's that? Onto the next victim?"

Alaric pulls me into his chest roughly, wrapping both of his arms around me so that I can't move. His lips graze my ear, and I hate how my skin pebbles with goosebumps at his touch. At the feel of his warm breath.

"The minute you stop thinking of them as victims, the better. In nearly a thousand years, we've never killed an innocent person. Think about that." I shiver at his words, and he continues. "We're meticulous. We do not make mistakes. We serve the underbelly of this country, eliminating our enemies one by one. That's why our order was started, and that's why we've lasted this long." His teeth sink into the cartilage of my ear, and I visibly tremble as my whole body lights up at his touch. He bites me—hard. I cry out, yet I can't help but squirm in his lap. *Fuck, that felt* good.

"Remember those skulls in the barn? Your ancestors. *My* ancestors. I think you fail to realize just how powerful we are—and just how much our blood flows different from others."

I try not to snort. "You sound like you have a God complex."

I feel Alaric smile against the skin of my neck, and he squeezes me tighter against him. "We are your gods, little monster. And you are ours."

Well... fuck me.

I shake off the way his words affect me, pulling out of his grasp. I look at Sterling and Gideon, who are watching me with dark, amused expressions. Theo is sitting with his hands clasped in front of him on the table.

"Fine," I say quickly, frowning. "Let's do this, then."

Sterling cocks his head. "Full throttle?"

I begin to sweat. I know what he's implying. I know what all of this is. They're testing me. Today was just a taste. I know that. They truly are monsters, and I know I have a lot worse coming my way.

"I dare you," I tell him.

Theo, Gideon, and Sterling all give me murderous smiles. "You're going to wish you never said that," Alaric taunts.

I don't say anything as I get up off his lap, walking away as I flip them off over my shoulder.

They think they're going to try to break me, but they don't know how broken I already am.

And I'm going to beat them at their own game.

CHAPTER 26

Theo

We give Harlow the rest of the day off. After she leaves the dining room, the four of us clean up our mess as quickly as possible, leaving no trace of our presence. I drove all of us here together, so we climb into my black Mercedes G-class. The guys are quiet as I turn on some music, and a Jaxson Gamble song comes on. Turning it up, I think about the process we're about to endure with Harlow—the things we have planned for her over the next couple of weeks.

Alaric and I discussed having her ready to join as a true Lady of Darkness in six weeks. It's going to take intensive physical and mental training—the latter of which will intensify over the course of this week with what we have in store for her. But if all goes to plan, she will be ready in six weeks—and people all over the world will fear our new Lady just as much as they fear the four of us.

I drop the guys off at the office, where their cars are in the car park. We make tentative plans for tomorrow, and I ensure everything is set for our final mental test this week. The wheels are in motion. I just have to hope Harlow sees past the cruelty—how we're just trying to make her unbreakable.

I make my way home after that, taking the main road around Blackwell and up the hill, which houses Wolf Manor. None of us spend a ton of time in our houses, as we prefer our office. But the houses hold a sort of reverence, a bit of a history reminder. I park and walk in, saying hello to Brenda, my house manager. Unlike Charles, who was the most old-fashioned out of all of us, Brenda doesn't wear a uniform. She doesn't even live here full-time. None of us have full-time staff. Brenda's job—which I pay her very generously for—is to ensure things like the plants are watered, groceries are stocked, house is cleaned, bills are paid, and correspondence is responded to.

Charles, on the other hand, has a full-time, live-in household of staff. There's Rose, the housekeeper. Then there's his personal secretary, who lives in London. And then there's Teddy, the chef. They were both away earlier today, and that's why Harlow and Sterling had a bit of fun. I smirk when I remember how uncomfortably turned on we all got watching them. The four of us have never been with each other sexually, but it's not like the opportunity has never arisen. We've shared women before—and it was hot as fucking hell. I wouldn't say no to that, I don't think. None of us are shy about our sexuality, and we're so close.

Closer than brothers.

Their pleasure is my pleasure.

I set my keys and laptop on the table in the foyer. I don't hear Brenda, so she must be outside in the small garden, or upstairs vacuuming. Walking into the kitchen, I grab one of the pre-cooked lunches I made myself earlier this week. Grilled chicken, brown rice, vegetables. It's not the most exciting meal, but it gives me hours of energy, and for our jobs, we must ensure our bodies are at max performance.

Eating quickly, I wash up and grab an energy bar before heading upstairs. A quick shower wank sounds delightful. Ever since I saw just how well Harlow took Sterling's cock between her tits, her hooded eyes looking up at him obediently, my cock has felt heavy, throbbing with the urge to spray my come everywhere while I think of her sucking my cock.

I take the stairs two at a time, and I'm so distracted by the idea of Harlow's cherry red lips around my shaft that I barely notice the way my office door is hanging off its hinges.

I stop in my stride, reaching into my inside suit pocket for the mini Glock I always keep on me—the one I scared Harlow with earlier. I also quickly press a button on my smart watch, which will alert the guys that I need backup. As I creep slowly toward the office, I keep my footsteps quiet. Gliding along the wall, my finger stays on the trigger as I kick the door open. The office is empty, except for—

Fuck.

Brenda's lifeless body lies on the floor, a pool of blood beneath her staining the white carpet.

I don't lower my gun, though. Instead, I turn around and scout the entire house, not finding anyone here. Walking back to the front, I see tire tracks in the dirt path leading to the main road. Quickly snapping a picture, I spin around when I hear Alaric's car pull through my front gate. He speeds up to where I'm standing, lowering his window.

"What the fuck happened?" Alaric asks.

I sigh. "Someone killed Brenda."

Alaric's cold expression softens. "Fuck. Sorry, mate. Any idea who did it?"

I shake my head, dumbfounded. My security system is state-of-the-art. No one would be able to break in without me knowing. I hadn't been checking my own cameras, though. I'd been too distracted by the cameras in Blackwell House, too focused on a certain Lady to even check in on my own property.

"Someone must've been invited in," I say, running a hand through my hair and as I pocket my Glock. Pulling my phone out, I swipe through the security alerts I have set for all our houses. *Nothing—except for a few deliveries.* Some motherfucker rang the doorbell with a fake package, and then he—or she—fucking killed Brenda.

"I'll tell the others," Alaric says quickly, pulling his phone out and shooting a quick text message to everyone.

I look down at the screen, seeing that he also alerted Harlow.

"Should we send someone there for tonight?"

Alaric shrugs. "I can have one of our guys sit watch at the house. I think we need to let Harlow process everything without the fear of a real home invasion on the horizon."

I smirk. "'That's a far cry from our plan this morning."

Alaric scowls. "This is different. Our plan is on *our* terms. We can protect her when she's with us. When we're testing her. But this is someone else's doing, and if they go after her, I will disembowel them alive."

I snort. "I see."

Alaric closes his window and parks in front of my house. I follow him, and we head inside to start cleaning the mess. Gideon and Sterling arrive a few minutes later, and then Alaric's cleanup crew arrives. I head downstairs and open my laptop, scouring the surveillance footage. There are a couple of delivery men, but they're all shown leaving. Though I'm positive that one of them—and I can't identify either of them because of their hats—came in and killed Brenda before leaving. Which means…

Someone *fucking* spliced my feed.

When I'm done, I find Gideon leaning against the wall with his switchblade, and Sterling is making phone calls to our security team. Alaric is sitting on the couch, looking exhausted.

"We've been compromised," I tell them.

CHAPTER 27

HARLOW

I am reading my smutty novel on my kindle, ignoring how hot and bothered I still feel from the unmentionable escapade with Sterling, when my phone chimes. I hold it up and stare at the text chain for a few seconds before I register what they're saying.

Alaric: Theo's house manager was found dead a few minutes ago. Stay put, and don't answer the door for anyone.

I squint at the screen, taking in the words as yet another newfound fear creeps down my spine. *Great.* Sighing, I set my phone back down on the bed beside me. Is this my life now? Break-ins, murders, sick, twisted games of hide and seek... I turn my kindle off and sit up. I can either sit here and ignore the fact that these psychos have basically quarantined me here in England, or I can do something about it. I told myself I would find a way out of this, so that's exactly what I need to do.

I'd left my computer in New York, so I pick my phone back up and do a quick google search in an incognito browser.

Easiest way to kill a man.

How can I kill someone and get away with it?

Craziest murder stories where the murderer got away...

Fuck. I don't care if I go to jail at this point, because that would be better than the alternative. But I'll do my best not to get caught.

I'll have to make it look like an accident, or a suicide. But how? How could I sneak my intentions past four brutal killers?

Alaric: Security has been dispatched to all five houses and the office building.

Sterling: Stay where you are, Harlow.

Sitting up, I stare at the texts from the guys. They're sharing sensitive information with me. That has to mean something.

Me: I'm just in bed reading my book. I have nowhere to go.

Theo: The priest book?

Frowning, I type a response.

Me: Yes.

Theo: Mmm. I bet you're still wet from earlier, too. Huh, little monster? Thinking about Sterling's cock pumping in between your perfect tits?

His words cause a white-hot bolt of electricity to flash through me. I can still feel the way Sterling used his spit to lube me up, how it felt to have him drive himself against my soft breasts and laced fingers. How *hard* he got just before he came all over my face.

Me: You wish.

Sterling: Focus. We have someone targeting us. This is serious.

Alaric: If you're all hot and bothered, you could always touch yourself, Harlow.

I swallow and stare at the screen as my clit throbs. *Damn them.*

Me: I'd rather rot in hell.

Sterling: How did this go from a security breach to a discussion about wanking?

Theo: You're one to talk, Mr. Titty.

I snort, smiling as I read their responses.

No.

I can't get attached. I can't find camaraderie with them. They are my enemy.

Me: I'm going back to my book now. Goodnight.

I set my phone down, but their words are still wrapped around the recesses of my mind. I squeeze my eyes shut, willing my body to calm down, willing myself to focus on the task at hand.

I could do all the internet searches in the world, but it wouldn't give me any answers specific to my situation. I would need to strike and kill them when they least expect it. And it would have to be something that doesn't incriminate me. Four Lords of Darkness... and me.

I lie down and pull the duvet over myself. It's only five, but I'm exhausted. Maybe I'll take a nap and then eat dinner with Rose. *If* she was back, that is. I roll to my side, determined to sleep, but sleep doesn't come. I throw the duvet off again, and then I walk around the room, trying to find the hidden camera I know Theo placed in here. I check under the tables, the lamps, the lights—everything. Every single surface is inspected, even the Teddy bear on my dresser from when I was a child. I tear it open, looking for the camera, but come up short. It's just stuffing.

"Where are you?" I mutter, as I look around the room. "Maybe they're bluffing," I tell myself. There's nothing in here; I've looked everywhere.

I climb back into bed, feeling relieved yet skeptical. But my traitorous pussy won't leave me alone, and I squeeze my legs together and try, and fail, to get the image of Sterling's cock out of my mind. It was just so pretty. And perfect. The idea of him fucking me with that thing... a shiver works down my body, and I feel my cheeks heat when I imagine what he'd do, the commanding way he'd boss me around. I took a kink quiz a few months ago, and it turns out, I enjoy submitting. I also enjoy knowing that people are watching me.

And then it occurs to me... the sooner they think I've given into their whims, the sooner I can execute my plan and go back to my real life in New York.

I'll need to lure them in, make them feel like I'm a part of their order. If I was playing that part, what would I do right now?

If you're all hot and bothered, you could always touch yourself, Harlow.

Smiling, I power my kindle up again, suddenly feeling a flush of heat rush through me at the thought of what I'm about to do. A normal person would not be so turned on right now, but my stomach flutters in the best way as I throw the duvet off me, spreading my legs so that my heels are together. *Might as well give them a front-row view.* I pretend to be casual about it, reading as I rest my hand on the patch of bare skin between my sweatshirt and sweatpants.

I can already feel how wet I am, and my clit aches and throbs, begging to be touched. It doesn't hurt that the scene I'm reading is one of the filthiest things I've ever read. Rolling my lower lip between my teeth, I part my lips as my hand dips lower, underneath my waistband.

Give them a show, Harlow.

As I move my waistband down past my hips, pulling my sweatpants off completely, I have to hide my smile. Kicking them to the side, I resume my position spread eagle, knowing they can see me. That they can see everything.

Why is this so hot? What is wrong with me?

I pretend to keep reading, biting my lower lip and moaning a little as I insert one finger inside of myself, swirling the wetness around the entire area.

I'm sure they're going crazy right now. I can only imagine what they're doing... something important, most likely, and then they see me...

I moan, but it's not fake. My wetness isn't fake, either. None of it is because my pussy is a whore for these men.

Maybe it's because of what happened to me, or maybe this feels good *despite* what happened to me. All I know is I am enjoying this, and I won't have to fake a single thing.

I squeeze my eyes shut as my finger begins to circle my engorged clit, and this time, I don't hold back. Crying out, I arch my back as a gasp leaves my lips.

"Oh God," I whimper. "Please, Alaric."

CHAPTER 28

Alaric

I'm on my way back to my house when texts from the guys begin to chime in my car system. I swipe the dashboard screen, having my voice command read them as I drive through Blackwell Village. It's a chain between the four of us.

Theo: Holy shit. Open the security app. NOW.
Sterling: Why? Did you find your guy?
Gideon: Fuck. Me. BRB.

I frown at the dashboard, wondering if it's worth pulling over for whatever it is they're talking about.

Theo: If that isn't the most perfect pussy I've ever seen...

I instantly veer over onto one of the small country roads. It's just past sunset, so I put my hazards on and pull my phone from inside my pants pocket. Opening the security app Theo installed on our phones a couple of years ago, I flick through the different feeds, wondering what the hell they're talking about.

The next feed is Harlow's bedroom, and at first, I think I might be seeing things. She's lying on her bed, legs spread, playing with herself.

Thank fuck for Theo and his hidden HD cameras.

I can see everything perfectly clearly. I can even see how fucking wet she is, glistening from the top of her black curls and down the sides of her thighs. My cock is straining so hard in my trousers, it's almost painful. I lean back and unzip, freeing myself and beginning to stroke it. Reaching up and spitting into my hand, I watch our little monster pleasure herself.

Gideon: Turn the volume up. Trust me.

I do as he says, and a second later, Harlow's whimpers sound loudly in my car speakers. I stroke myself faster, squeezing the head of my cock and rubbing the

124

precome all around. Harlow arches her back and spreads her legs even farther. I don't know where Theo hid the camera—a tiny, microscopic thing—but the view right above her is perfect. She throws her head back and moans again, the sound spurring me on.

She takes her other hand and spreads her pussy lips apart, her silky skin dripping wet as we get a full-frontal view. Using her middle finger and her thumb, she keeps herself spread for us as she inserts her index finger, and her other hand continues to work her clit. I fuck my hand harder, forming a tighter vise around my pulsing cock. I'm leaking so much goddamn precome, I know I'm going to soak myself when I finish. Gripping the handle on the top of the car, I brace myself as I work my cock faster in my hands, imagining I'm fucking Harlow's tight little pussy instead.

I harden even more, growing thick and rigid as I imagine the others stroking themselves, too. I've never gone there—never fully admitted it—but imagining them pleasuring themselves to the same image as me, perhaps even joining in on the fun *with* me... it's hot as hell.

That's something I'll have to explore another day.

Harlow's hand works in a quick rhythm, her right hand moving back and forth over her clit, and her left hand pumping all three fingers inside of herself. One leg comes up even farther, and I can see the way her toes curl, the way her mouth parts, the way her abdominal muscles contract as her orgasm crests. She gasps, crying out loudly as she slows her hand movements, her whole body twitching with her potent release. I groan when I see a small stream leak between her fingers, soaking her bed. I watch in awe as it pulses out of her as she comes.

Fuck me. She's a squirter. My fucking kryptonite.

I roar, fucking my hand hard and fast, tightening my grip so that I can barely get between my fingers. The skin on my cock is pulled tight as I work myself close to my release, and then I hold my hand still at the base of my cock as my fingers grip my balls tightly.

"Oh, fuck," I say, my voice hoarse.

And then I come—*so fucking hard*. My cock bows, curving ever so slightly as it bobs, large spurts of come shooting onto my shirt, reaching my chest. My own toes curl when I hiss, grinding my teeth as my body vibrates with each eruption. Finally, my seeping cock slows. I'm trembling, nearly breaking the handle off my car because I'm gripping it so hard.

Fuck.

I'm panting as I clean myself up quickly. I look at my phone, seeing Harlow gone from her bed, leaving a very visible wet spot behind.

I bet I could make her come harder, I think. *She'd come for days if I had my way with her.*

My softening cock is already hard again when I think about that, but I don't have time to continue wanking. Zipping myself back up, I turn my car around and continue driving home.

I chuckle when the texts start coming in again, knowing full well what we were all doing.

Theo: I'm going to need new trousers after that.
Sterling: New shower tiles for me. They'll never recover from that onslaught.

I send a voice command text back.

Me: I just wanked in my car. How's that for unhinged?
Theo: Nice. Gideon is quiet. You okay, man?

A few minutes pass before we get his response.

Gideon: I had to wank twice. Once all over my bed, humping a pillow like I was thirteen again. And again when I went to go shower. My cock still won't go down.
Theo: She's like our own version of Viagra.
Sterling: We need to be careful...
Gideon: I will gladly sacrifice myself to our worst enemies as long as I get to fuck that pussy raw.
Sterling: You're proving my point. She can't become a distraction.
Me: Whatever you say, Mr. Titty.
Theo: lol
Gideon: I think we can all agree we'd like to fuck her. Nothing wrong with that.
Sterling: Until it backfires.
Me: I call dibs next.
Theo: Second.
Gideon: Fuck you both. We can each take a hole and call it a day.
Sterling: :-/

By the time I get home, my cock is straining against my pants again when I think of all four of us fucking our little monster at once.

Maybe Sterling is right.

Maybe she is a distraction.

We need to be careful, or everything could very easily blow up in our faces.

CHAPTER 29

Harlow

Rose doesn't come back that night, but Teddy, the cook, knocks on my door around seven for dinner. He's not as chatty as Rose, but he's nice, and he serves me the beef stew she made earlier. I request that he joins me, and he does, which takes my mind off everything.

Was it only just this morning that I did everything at the gym? That the guys staged Gideon's murder?

Time is flying, and yet, it's passing so slowly.

The stew is delicious, and he serves me some gelato for dessert. Apparently, Rose is staying the night with her daughter, who is justifiably spooked.

I would make them pay for that.

When I'm done, I offer to help Teddy with the dishes, but he shoos me away. I walk upstairs, feeling groggy, and finally pick my phone back up. I have a few texts from the guys that I don't read, and three texts from Gemma.

Gemma: I'm so excited to see you tomorrow! Am I still picking you up? Send me your flight info, xoxo.

Gemma: Also, I haven't reached out because I know you're busy and grieving. But just know that I love and miss you.

Gemma: (In case I don't tell you enough)

My eyes prick with tears. I'd completely forgotten that I was supposed to leave tomorrow. In another life, I would've spent the last three days mourning my father, taking in the quaint village, and getting to know my heritage a little bit.

It's your lucky day, Harlow. You get to meet your ancestors.

Instead, I was drugged, branded, forced to become a murderer–despite

Armin's monstrous tendencies, that's what I was now—and then tormented both physically and mentally. They're holding me captive, and if I don't get out soon, I'm worried I'll never find a way to leave.

I decide now's not the time to unload everything onto Gemma, so I send her a short text explaining everything.

Me: I love and miss you too. I forgot to tell you; I think I'm going to stay for a couple of weeks. I will let you know once I have a return ticket rebooked.

While I wait for her response, I cancel my plane ticket, but I vow to rebook it soon.

Gemma: Are you doing okay?

Me: Yeah! Totally good. I just want to spend some more time with Archie, you know?

Gemma: Okay... I just know how much you were dreading it. I'm glad you've had a change of heart, though. I think it'll be good for you to stay for a couple of weeks.

Gemma: But that's ALL, you hear me? ;) Promise me you'll come home, and you won't, like, fall in love with a Duke.

If only she knew...

Me: I promise. Two weeks. I'll call you soon. Love you!

Gemma: Love you too, boo.

I stare at my phone, relieved I bought myself two weeks. Now I just need to figure out how I'm going to kill the Lords of Darkness.

Sighing, I lie down in my bed and stare at the ceiling. I'm feeling restless, sleepy from the intense orgasm I gave myself earlier, and *so* physically sore. I can't think about what I did without blushing. Did they even see it? And why do I hope that they did? I pick up my phone, flicking to the unread texts from them, wondering if they'll mention it.

Sterling: Be ready at half seven tomorrow. Gym clothes. Prepare to sweat.

Theo: Fuck, I love workout clothes on women.

Alaric: Don't leave the house tonight, Harlow.

I chew on the inside of my cheek. None of them mentioned the show they may or may not have witnessed. A pang of disappointment flashes through me. It was a good show, and I came so hard I saw stars. If they missed it, oh well. Their loss.

Alaric's text gives me an idea, though. But I have to be quick if I'm going to do this. Grabbing my phone—which I power off, in case they can track me—my boots, and my backpack of supplies, I open my bedroom door and rush down the stairs. I throw my boots on and sling my backpack on my back before opening the front door, closing it behind me as I jog away.

It's dark out now, and the village is quiet as I take the winding country road downhill into Blackwell Village. It's busier here, with people spilling out of the pubs and couples out for a nice dinner. There are a few families carrying screaming toddlers toward the public parking lot, but other than that, I blend in. I go left into a side alley, following the narrow pathway slightly wider than my body. I make another left into an empty courtyard, and then I look around to make sure I'm alone.

Dropping my backpack onto the cobblestoned ground, I pull my supplies out and begin to work, the idea coming to me suddenly. I finish up by painting a set of handcuffs, and a quick rose garden underneath the phrase.

Everything's Coming Up Roses.

Except, for an 'O' on Roses, I've used one of the cuffs on the handcuffs. Taking my stencil out, I paint my name—**MONSTER**—and snap a quick picture for Instagram.

Ha. That's going to drive them crazy.

Packing my things up, I grab my backpack and turn around.

My heart jumps into my throat when I see Alaric leaning against the opposite wall in the courtyard, his body hidden by the shadow cast by the streetlight. He's smoking a cigarette, and the light glows when he inhales.

Fuck, when did he get here?

He throws the still-lit cigarette onto the cobblestone and claps slowly, pushing off the brick wall. "Nice work," he says, cocking his head as he admires it. "But I am a little disappointed you defied my orders to stay home."

I lift my chin and stand a little straighter. "I wanted to work off some creative energy," I tell him unapologetically.

Alaric takes a few steps forward, his face coming into the light fully. I gasp when I see the unfiltered rage, like inky darkness bubbling just under the surface of his skin. He snaps his dark eyes to me.

"I was on my way to tend to your burn, and what do I see? Our little monster sneaking out. So I followed you by foot—you're entirely unaware of your surroundings, just so you know—and I've been standing against that wall for twenty minutes."

I swallow when I look up at him. "Okay. Sorry?"

His jaw feathers as he studies me. "What if it wasn't me? What if the security guard—who has been taken care of for his negligence, by the way—hadn't seen an intruder? What if someone cornered you back here and repeated the actions of the man who broke into your home eighteen months ago?"

Fear skitters down my limbs. "How do you know about that?" I ask, my voice hard.

Alaric takes another step forward. "I know everything, Harlow. I've seen your medical records. Your school records. Every public picture ever taken of you. I've scoured your social media, your contacts, your reading history, your browser history—"

"What?" I ask, nearly unable to breathe. If they saw my internet searches from earlier today, I'm fucked. Shaking my head, I try to control my hammering heart. "My medical records..." I trail off.

"Yes. I've seen it all."

Does it scare you? I want to ask.

"There is nothing you could do to push me away, Harlow," he adds, his voice gentler now. Softer, somehow. My heart continues to hammer, though now it's for an entirely different reason. "When you defy me, it puts us all in danger," he adds. "You're lucky it was me following you and not someone from Acadia."

Wonderful.

I open and close my fists. "Because I killed their leader?"

He takes another step closer. "Because you're a Lady of Darkness."

They say it takes hearing something repeatedly to believe it, and there must be some truth to that, because right now, him saying that, him being *worried* about me... it makes me feel less alone. For a split second, I consider staying here with them—fighting bad guys, being a badass killing machine and running my father's household. I imagine the five of us together, and not just in a professional manner, either. My stomach flutters when I think of being with all of them at once, giving into that carnal desire we all seem to feel...

No.

I can't give in.

I can't abandon my life—and Gemma—for a few men I met literally three days ago.

I promised Gemma I'd come home in two weeks, so I would. She's been my best friend since I was eight. There's no way I'd choose this life over her.

Hoes over bros and all of that.

In two weeks, I'll have to come up with a way to kill them—and a way to get back to my *real* life.

"It won't happen again," I tell Alaric, sounding as apologetic as I can muster.

"You don't mean that," he says, his lips quirking up in the corners ever so slightly. It's only then that I realize he's in casual wear—black running pants, white sneakers, and a black hooded sweatshirt. Even in these clothes, he looks polished and put together, as always. His shoes are glaringly white, and I have to suppress a smile at the thought of him cleaning his shoes every time he leaves the house—something he probably does. "But one day soon, you will learn to obey us. Our order only works when we're all actively participating." Taking a step forward, he tugs on my sweatshirt, bringing me flush with his body. The scent of cigarette smoke and vanilla waft through the air. It's *intoxicating*.

He's so much larger than me, so sturdy and strong. I bite my lower lip as he places a finger underneath my chin. That same warm feeling from earlier returns, and like last time, I push it away. Getting close to them, harboring any warm feelings toward *any* of them, will just make things messier in the end.

"I love the painting, little monster. Very tongue-in-cheek. But next time, do not defy my orders," he growls.

I don't say anything as he leads us away.

CHAPTER 30

H‍ARLOW

I walk down Flatbush Avenue, looking down at my phone and checking my Instagram messages. It's fucking freezing out, and the sidewalks are icy, so I hurry home as quickly as possible. My breath turns into an icy mist with each exhale, and by the time I round the corner of Bergen Street, my fingers are too cold to use my phone. Tossing it somewhere deep in my purse, I walk into the five-story apartment building where I live with my mom. A blast of warm air greets me in the lobby, and I sigh loudly in relief, taking the elevator up to the fifth story. It clangs and jerks, and I begin to sweat as it slows on the top story. That's the thing about New York winters. The outside temperature will ice you to your bones, but the instant you get inside, you sweat profusely.

I dig around for my keys, fumbling a bit with my still-frozen fingers. Finally pulling them out, I place the key in the lock. Before I turn it, the door opens inward, and I quickly realize why. The door is already open. Taking a step back, I stare at the door for a second before I push it cautiously.

"Mom?" I call out. I step inside quietly, my heart racing. Maybe she just forgot to close it when she came in? "Hello? Mom? You home?" I scour my brain, thinking of the last conversation we had this morning. She was on the first shift today, so she should've been home at four. It was now almost nine. I'd gone straight from school to Gemma's, but I don't remember her checking in when she got home. "Hello?"

I set my purse down on the island, reaching inside for my phone just in case—

Cold awareness snakes up the back of my neck. Before I can react, a deep, raspy voice speaks from behind me.

"Well, well, well... what do we have here?"

My insides liquify, and my heart lurches as I twist around. I barely get a glimpse of the intruder before he shoves me forward and pulls me close. But I can see he's balding, with pale, pinkish skin, rotting teeth, and light blue eyes.

"W-where's my mom?" I ask, trying to figure out how I'm going to call the cops with a gun pressed to the back of my neck. He presses it harder, and I look down. I don't know what compels me to look—nothing moves or catches my eyes. But it's like my subconscious is guiding me, and I scream when I see my mother's unmoving shoes sticking out from behind the island.

The intruder's free hand comes around and cups my mouth roughly. I try to bite him, but I can't get the right angle. I can't fight back; he has me held against him so that I can't move. I can't even kick back and get his shins because we're pressed up against the counter.

"Well, aren't you a pretty young thing?"

"Let me go!" I scream into his hand.

"How old are you, little one?" he asks, his voice cruel.

"Sixteen," I muffle, gagging on the taste of his skin.

"Mmm," he says, and I feel his nose brush the back of my hair. "So young. A virgin?" he asks, and I don't answer, but that must spur him on, because he lets out an evil laugh that turns my blood cold.

My mom.

He killed my mom.

And now, he's about to kill me, too.

He lets go of my mouth, and I release a bloodcurdling scream. Pressing me harder against the counter, I hear him unbuckle his belt.

No.

No.

No.

I attempt to kick back with as much force as possible, but it's futile. My hands are free, but I can't do anything with him behind me.

With the gun at the base of my skull, he presses it harder, cocking it. I stop crying, stop breathing, as he leans down and fumbles with my skirt and tights.

I don't even fight it. I'm not going to win.

He killed my mom.

He's going to rape me, and then he's probably going to kill me.

A single tear falls down my cheeks at the thought of not saying goodbye to Gemma.

I can't even muster any anger or grief about my mom—everything feels subdued, somehow.

I feel my whole body shutting down, my five senses dulling. My body is protecting me.

This isn't real.

He killed my mom.

He killed my mom.

He killed my mom.

No, he didn't.

This isn't real.

None of it is real. I squeeze my eyes shut, using all the conviction I can muster.

It's just a dream—a terrible dream.

This isn't real.

The last thing I see is his icy-blue eyes. And the last thing I hear before everything goes black is my own blood-curdling wail, and his dark, menacing laughter.

I sit up, gasping for air. Reaching up, I can feel that my cheeks are wet, and my whole body is drenched in sweat. It's early morning—the sky is a pale pink outside of my window.

Just a flashback.
Breathe, Harlow.
He can't find you here.

My fists curl around the sheets as I begin to sob, my whole body wracked with shaking, unabating grief.

He killed her.

Everything hurts even more today from the exercise yesterday, so crying feels awful. My core muscles clench and that makes me cry even harder, because *fuck, it hurts so goddamn much.* Tears spring from my eyes as I pull my knees to my chest, letting it all out.

I don't care if I wake anyone up.

I don't care that snot is mixing with tears, or that this position hurts the back of my legs.

He killed her.

If only I could find him. If only I could show that what he did to me just made me stronger.

I don't remember much from that night. I was told he raped me, but I have no memory of it. The doctors told me it would come back in pieces over time, but it hasn't yet. *Thank God.* But I do remember everything leading up to it, and I vaguely remember the police officers laying a sheet over my mother's body and handing another one to me before everything went black again.

Psychosis.

The event had triggered a psychotic break for me, and I have no recollection of being taken to the hospital, followed by the in-patient psychiatric unit. He'd broken me completely—had stolen something so pivotal from me, had violated and hurt me... and my body couldn't take it. My mind couldn't take it, especially combined with losing my mom.

I lost three months of my life to that psychiatric hospital. When I emerged out of my psychotic state, I was confused. I had to relearn everything that had happened. Gemma and her family took me in, and I recovered quite quickly, bouncing back to my old self as soon as I was physically able to. Then, doctors were stunned, but my recovery wasn't perfect.

I take a few steadying breaths as I let the overwhelming sadness and pain of that night roll through me. I don't push it away anymore. I embrace the pain because it's the pain that allows me to grow.

It's the pain that makes me stronger.

Wiping my cheeks, I look around for Alaric, but he must've left. After he'd found me in that alleyway last night, we'd walked home, and he'd quickly cleaned my burn. And, same as the night before—minus the Oxycontin—he read to me as I fell asleep.

I hate to admit how much I like him being here, how much I already feel myself counting on his presence. It would only become a distraction, so I vowed to put my head down today and get through whatever bullshit the Lords of Darkness were planning on throwing my way. I don't have much control over any of this, so the least I can do was fucking survive. *That* I can do.

Checking my phone, I see that it's nearly seven in the morning. I see an unmarked bag on my dressing table. One of them must have delivered it. If I've learned one thing about the Lords, it's that the air around them moved to accommodate their power. It was endless—they could do anything, be anyone, cover any bullshit up and make it look like an accident. The air moved for *them* in a way I'd never seen. They carried themselves within the confidence of gods, and maybe they were in a way.

A silly little security system—especially when Theo was such a tech whiz—would not deter them.

I change quickly into the outfit Sterling no doubt picked out for me. It's purple, but the leggings and sports bra have a wet, shiny feel to them. Like yesterday's workout clothes, they fit like a glove. My burn still aches today, but the fabric of my bra doesn't irritate the bandage. I decide to taunt Sterling a little bit, pulling my hair back into a French braid. I wash my face and brush my teeth, ignoring the way my stomach sours at the thought of what they have in store for me.

You are safe here.
He can't find you in England.
You are safe here.

I take a deep breath, placing my palms on the edge of the sink and leaning forward to look at myself. My uptilted eyes look tired, but I suppose that's what happens when I have four powerful men trying to break me. Their game yesterday definitely triggered something, but I'm a lot stronger than they think. Getting through this without having a psychotic episode... I can do that.

Grabbing my hoodie and phone, I walk downstairs and head to the kitchen. It's empty, and I have a few minutes, so I make myself some toast with peanut butter, and grab a banana as well. It may not be what I want to eat, but I know it'll help fuel the grueling workout ahead. *See? Growth.* Besides, in a couple of weeks, I could eat whatever the hell I wanted, because they'd all be dead. Grinning, I eat my breakfast slowly, leaning against the counter as I chew.

Speaking of... I wasn't sure how to go about it. It would have to be a last-minute decision, playing it by ear. Or it would have to be somewhat premeditated. But how the hell could I keep that information to myself, when they know everything about me? If only I could bake them poisonous cookies or something.

Ooooh. I like the idea.

But then, how would I dispose of the bodies? Maybe I could bring them to the barn and then it would accidentally go up in flames, killing everyone inside?

It's an idea.

I wipe my hands on a towel, grabbing my still-hot mug of coffee and checking my phone. It's a minute past seven-thirty, but I decide to enjoy my coffee instead of rushing around to their every whim. What did they say that first day? I was one of them? Well, okay then. I deserve to enjoy this coffee for five minutes. That's the least they could do. I lift the mug up and a car horn sounds loudly from the front of the house.

Bastards.

Gulping the rest of my life-giving liquid, I head out, pulling my hood over my head as I close the door behind me and climb into a black Mercedes G-class wagon. Theo grins at me from the driver's seat. Pulling the door shut, I buckle myself in.

"Good morning, beautiful," Theo says, his deep voice the scariest of them all, because I know what kind of monster he's hiding behind that smile.

"Fuck off," I mutter, looking out of the window as we drive away.

"Not a morning person?" he asks.

I ignore him, content with feeling sorry for myself and sulking the entire way to the gym. Just as we pull up, I go to open my door, when Theo reaches out for my other hand and tugs me into the center console.

"We see everything, Harlow," he says, his voice a threatening purr. "Don't try to outsmart us. We see everything—every Google search, every page you read, every move you make in your room," he adds, and I swear his voice gets lower when he says that.

"You saw me last night?" I ask, turning to face him. His cerulean eyes bore into mine with such intensity that my stomach swoops low and I have to clench my legs together.

"We saw you. All of us."

The corner of my mouth twitches at the thought. "And?"

Something dark passes behind his irises, making my clit throb. "I fucked my hand hard, imagining it was your hot little cunt," he murmurs.

Dear God.

I narrow my eyes and try to pull away, but he has a death grip on me. "You are ours, little monster. Now, next week, next year... don't try to run away, because we will chase you to the ends of this earth."

Well, fuck.

I swallow, giving him a small smile. "I'm not going anywhere," I tell him, ignoring the way my clit pulses with the heat of his hand.

His white-blond hair is slicked back slightly, the creases in his forehead making him seem innocent. But I know, deep down, they all have black hearts.

Nothing good can come from getting close to any of them.

"Good," he says smoothly. "I would hate for you to find out what happens to those who betray their brethren."

I hold eye contact for another beat, and then I pull away. He lets me go this time, and I climb out of the door and stalk to the gym.

He's just trying to scare me, but I won't be deterred.

I wasn't lying when I said I wasn't going anywhere.

I'll be here, concocting a plan to take them *all* down.

CHAPTER 31

Gideon

I flick my knife open and closed as I sit on the ground, knees bent and legs spread, watching Harlow massacre her mile and a quarter run. I narrow my eyes when I watch her speed up, her skin already flushed and glistening. The others are also keeping a watchful eye on her, their gazes flicking to where she's jogging with nearly perfect form—and with zero complaints—every couple of minutes. My workout is done, so I'm cooling off with some water as I try to assess what the hell is going through her mind today.

There has been no sass, no talking back. She climbed onto the treadmill and began her run without any direction. She said hi to all of us when she entered, but it was as though the entire gym was covered in a rain cloud. Her energy is dark today, and I want to know why. I pocket my switchblade, standing up and walking over to the treadmill next to her. Alaric is spotting Sterling on the bench, and Theo is doing one of his intensive spin classes, so I'm the only one who can pry her open.

Because that's exactly what I intend to do.

I push the speed button, moving into a brisk jog next to her. "How're you feeling, Harlow?" She doesn't answer me, only scowling down at the screen of the treadmill as she runs. "Your form is better today," I add, hoping encouragement will do the trick. But she just continues to run, panting and moving her arms as her eyes look down at the screen. The crease on her forehead deepens. I look down at her feet, my eyes then moving up to her ass. Fuck, her ass is amazing. Round, fleshy... something I could sink my teeth into. "Try engaging your core," I tell her, hoping it's a helpful hint.

She jabs a finger down on the stop button, slowing down as she turns to face me. Her breathing is ragged, and she glares at me as her chest heaves up and down, her nipples peaked and hard beneath her sports bra.

"What do you want, Gideon?" she asks, sounding indifferent. "I'm trying to run. Trying to do the thing you guys asked of me. Just... leave me alone."

Facing forward again, she continues her run, speeding up to the same pace she was before—and continuing to ignore me.

I end my jog, seeing as she's not going to give me an inch while she's working out. Walking over to where Alaric is helping Sterling with his bench press, I lean against the machine and rub my mouth.

"What crawled up her ass today?" I ask.

Alaric chuckles. "She wasn't too happy that I caught her out past her curfew last night," he jokes.

I look over at where Harlow is jogging, steadfast. "Something else is going on."

"Theo scoured her search history. There were a few hits about how to kill a man, how to kill someone and get away with it..." Sterling says, grunting as he lifts 380 pounds. The dude is a fucking beast.

"That's cute," I reply, looking back over at Harlow. "Think she's seriously going to try to kill us?"

"Might be fun to let her try," Alaric muses, following my gaze to where Harlow is slowing down her run a bit. Probably losing steam. Building up to a casual five miles takes time—and we like to be half-marathon ready at all times, so she'll need to work up to thirteen miles.

"What's the plan for today?" I ask, taking a sip of water.

"Yesterday wasn't enough," Alaric says, helping Sterling sit up. They both look over at Harlow at the same time I do. "We attempted to break down her defenses, but we didn't even penetrate the outer layer of her skin."

"Sterling penetrated her tits," I joke.

He glares at me as he sips his water. "Fuck off, man."

"So, what then? Try something worse?"

Alaric narrows his eyes as Harlow looks over at all of us, her blue eyes searing, fists curling as she slows down to a walk.

"Done," she yells across the gym, holding her chin up high.

I look back at Alaric and Sterling. "We need to recreate her worst nightmare."

Sterling stands up, stretching his chest as Alaric frowns at me. "You mean..." he trails off.

I nod. "If anyone can find him, it's Theo."

The three of us look back at Harlow, who steps down from the machine and turns to face us.

And then she raises both hands, flipping us off before heading over to the spin bikes.

"I can't wait to watch her break, piece by piece," I growl.

She looks so pretty when she cries...

CHAPTER 32

HARLOW

I thought yesterday was difficult, but today, I can barely move. After I finished a ten-minute climb ride on the bike, I had Sterling show me how to bench press. I could only lift eighty pounds. I know I'll need to work my way up eventually, but it doesn't really matter, because I wasn't going to invest in this life. I couldn't. I kept my head down, like I said, and I got through the grueling thirty minutes of body weight exercises on the mat. Afterward, Theo drove me home and made small talk, but I only gave him one-word answers.

Rose is home when I walk through the door, and I see her dusting something on the foyer table as I close the door behind me.

She raises an eyebrow. "Hello, Miss Windsor," she says, giving me a mirthful smile. "Or, should I say, Lady Blackwell?" My heart stutters for a beat before she walks over with a large envelope. I open it, pulling out the deed to the manor, with my new, official name on it. *Lady Harlow May Windsor, of Blackwell.* I don't know what to say, or how to process the fact that this is now my house. I know Theo said he filed the requisite paperwork the night of the dinner, but I have no idea what this means going forward.

"What about Cecelia and Archie?" I ask, unsure of how much Rose knows, or how I'm going to explain all of this to her.

She shrugs. "You are welcome to invite them back here to live. I'm not sure she will want to leave the Cotswolds, though. I spoke to her this morning, and she seems to be very comfortable there with her parents. Running this house by herself was always a daunting prospect, and her father is... very overprotective."

I open and close my mouth. How did Theo pull it off and make it look realistic? Before I can ask, she points to the packet of papers in my hand.

"Your father's personal secretary stopped by this morning with some paperwork explaining that there was a clause in your father's will. Apparently, he and your mother had secretly eloped before you were born, only divorcing after you were born, and thereby making you Lady of Blackwell. He's already informed Cecelia, and from what I understand, she's relieved about the prospect of not inheriting the house."

"Does she keep her title?"

Rose sighs, placing her hands on her hips. "She has voluntarily given up her title at the advice of her father. She let me know just this morning, and the decision was made before the clause in your father's will was brought to light. She never wanted it. She loved your father, but she's happy for you to take over."

Oh.

I look at Rose, and she looks at me. *God, now I'm the Lady of the House, and I'm her employer. How the hell am I going to do all of this?*

"Randolph, your father's secretary, will be in touch this week sometime to go over everything with you."

Of course.

"Okay," I say, feeling lightheaded with this new information.

"I made a cake to celebrate," Rose adds, her cheeks going rosy.

I smile. "Thank you, Rose. I think I need to go lie down," I tell her.

"Then I'll have a piece delivered to your room," she answers, taking her duster and going back to cleaning the table. "And I still want to know how the date went with Lord Cross. I saw Lord Wolf drive you home... have you had a change of heart?"

Oh, God.

I shake my head. "No, we're just friends." What else can I even tell her?!

"Whatever you say, Lady Blackwell."

It suddenly sinks in fully. I am now officially the new Lady of the House.

༺༻

I end up taking a three-hour nap after my shower, and when I wake up, I am wholly disoriented. It takes me several minutes to remember where I am, and by the time I do, I sit up and rub my eyes, feeling depressed about everything. Rose must've brought some cake up, because two squares of Victoria sponge cake sit on a porcelain plate, with plastic draped over the top delicately. How the hell does she manage to make cling wrap look fancy?

Once I devour the cakes with my hands like a heathen, I decide to get dressed and wander around the manor. Now that it's mine officially, I want to see what I'm working with.

How did I go from a struggling art student to a 'Lady' in possession of an entire manor? Like, how does that even happen?

I pull on my dark green dress, closing my eyes when I think of the message I received on Instagram that second day here.

That green really brings out the golden hue of your skin. I want to lick that skin from head to toe.

Tugging on my black boots and a loose, black cardigan, I wander down the hallway and peek into every room. There are nine bedrooms, not including mine, and at the very end of the hallway is the master suite. Looking around, I enter what was once my father's suite.

There's a reception room with couches and a casual table by the window. Then there's a large fireplace, and a door leading to his bedroom. I pull it open, taking in the massive bedroom. Aside from yesterday, when I'd broken the dressing table mirror—which had been miraculously cleaned up and replaced by the *Lords*—I'd only been in this room a few times as a child. The sheer size of it is still stunning. There's a four-poster bed, dark green accents, and dark wood furniture.

I meander out of the room, walking down the grand staircase and through the ground floor. Sitting back down in my father's office, I look around. What would I even do in here? Plan my murders? Organize my weapons? Apparently, the Lords already have an office somewhere in the village. Even if I did manage to get out from underneath the Lord's grip... I'd still have this manor to contend with. *Fuck*.

I lean back in the leather office chair, thinking.

The manor was an easy fix. I could keep it as an inheritance gift, but live in New York part of the time while Rose takes care of it. Okay, easy peasy. I just needed a way out of their grip. How the hell was I going to do that, though?

Theo's warning earlier sent chills crawling down my spine. They knew I'd been snooping around the internet, so I have to get smart. Pulling my phone out of the pocket of my cardigan, I text our group.

Me: Need to run into town for some things. Just a heads up, I will be back later.
Sterling: What things?
Me: Period things.

There's a minute of silence, and I smile when I think of how uncomfortable they must be.

Alaric: Do you think we're stupid, Harlow?

My mouth drops open, my pulse picking up as I reread his words.

Alaric: Did you forget we have access to your period tracking app?

Fuck. My period isn't due for two weeks. I know that, and now they know that. *Think, Harlow. Think!* If my period is due in two weeks, that means I'm ovulating, which means...

Me: Did you know that sometimes women spot when they ovulate? I need supplies for that.

Ha! Take that, assholes.

Sterling: One of us will accompany you.
Me: Joy.
Gideon: Pick you up in half an hour, sugar tits.

I groan and slam my phone face down on the desk. Fine. They wanted to come with me? They couldn't possibly watch me every single second, could they? I'd figure out a way to obtain information about how to kill them without being monitored.

It was my only option at this point.

CHAPTER 33

STERLING

The flight to New York takes just over six hours. I spend the time working, following up on any of the leads we have going for the men we're hunting. A big part of our job is going after our competition. We usually keep to ourselves, as long as other people keep to themselves. England is ours, but that doesn't mean we don't get involved with other networks from time to time. And there's always someone who thinks they can take us down, which means we must put them in their place.

Like Acadia.

The other big part of our job is managing the drugs and weapons trade, and though we have people for that, Gideon and I oversee all communication as well as cash flow.

I land just as Gideon confirms he's picked up Harlow from her house. I'm not quite sure what she has up her sleeve. I still don't trust her fully, but I do think it's cute that she's trying so hard to defy us.

I can't wait to give her a taste of what life could be like with us. And not just the unsavory parts, but the other parts—the ways we could worship her, the ways in which we'd drive pleasure into her. She was ours, body and soul, and we would have *all* of her.

My cock hardens when I think of yesterday, of how good she was, kneeling for me. A natural submissive, hidden in a tough exterior. She is perfect—everything about her is perfect. From the way she sucked my cock, to the way her soft tits milked me dry, to her gorgeous body and face. It's like someone created my biggest wet dream and made her mine.

Because she was mine now. Ours. She was *ours* to keep.

I was going to make sure she knew she was ours as soon as I was back in Blackwell.

There's a car waiting for me, and I exit the private jet, climbing into the backseat. The driver is our normal contact for this area, and his people have already located our target. *Good.*

I was delighted to meet the bastard who hurt our little monster.

We bypass the city, driving upstate for an hour. Greg, the driver, gives me the details on our guy. Harrison Smith, forty-eight, convicted in the past on drug and burglary charges but released ten years ago after spending seven years in prison. He's currently living upstate in a trailer by himself, so he's easy pickings.

Finding him was difficult. Theo's been looking since we found out about Harlow. The cops hardly did any reconnaissance after her rape. She was in such a disoriented state because of her psychosis; they didn't bother tracking the guy down. I could kill everyone involved just for that fact alone. Still, they neglected to check the cameras on the building. By the time Harlow came around, the camera footage had apparently been wiped completely. The authorities took that and basically gave up, citing it as an unfortunate event.

I *would* kill them one day for that.

Theo was able to track it down, though. Turns out, Harlow's building kept backups for three years—something the authorities also neglected to check for. From there, it was a piece of cake. We had a face in one frame, and Theo ran it through his system, coming up with a match in less than a minute. I even found the bastard's credit card bill, and he'd purchased a ride on the metro an hour before killing Harlow's mother.

Pulling up to a line of trailers, the driver parks in front of number five.

Lucky number five.

I take that as a good sign.

"Ready?" I ask, pulling my gun out of my bag. I screw on a silencer, and then I pull my mask on. I know Greg's already covered the license plates, and for something like this, dealing with a man who may or may not be connected to the wrong people, we must practice caution.

"Ready," Greg says, pulling his mask on.

They're not black ski masks. In fact, at first glance, they look like real faces. They're just not *our* faces.

Opening the door, we pocket our guns and casually walk up to the door. I ring the doorbell once, waiting. I shove my hand in my back pocket, ready to end this motherfucker. But I know he deserves to be tortured, deserves the worst that's coming to him.

A man opens the door. *Bingo.* He's almost as tall as me, with muscles and a graying beard.

"Excuse me," I ask in an American accent. "I was visiting a friend and left my headlights on. Is it possible to use your truck to jumpstart my car?"

Harrison hesitates for a second, taking in my mask. He backs up slightly, and I take a step forward.

"Get the fuck out of here," he says, moving to close the door.

I place my foot in front of it to stop it, pulling my gun out and pointing it at him. The blood drains from his face, and his icy-blue eyes widen with fear.

"That won't be happening," I say, grinning underneath my mask. *God, I wish I could blow his brains out.*

"I said, get the fuck out of h—"

I cock my gun, aiming it right at his forehead. "Get in the fucking car, Harrison, or I will kill you."

"Is this about the money? I promise, I'll pay it next week—"

"I don't give a flying fuck about some money," I growl, placing the tip of the gun against his forehead.

"What is this about, then?" he asks, his voice shaking.

I cock my head and pull my mask off. He doesn't know me, of course, but I want him to feel how much vitriol I'm about to funnel into my next sentence.

"This is about touching what's not fucking yours. About taking someone's innocence and violating them. Don't worry, though. I'm not going to kill you."

"You aren't?" he asks, sounding almost relieved. How laughable.

"No. But she is."

CHAPTER 34

Harlow

Gideon is quiet as we drive into Blackwell village. It's not far, only about a mile, so we're there in a couple of minutes. He parks in the parking lot just opposite of the main square. I open the door right as he stops, but he reaches a hand out and grabs hold of the front of my dress. I squeak in surprise.

"If you try anything funny, little monster, you will be punished."

"Get your hands off of me," I growl, shoving him away and opening the door. I manage to make it out and across the square before he catches up to me, linking his arm with mine. I glare up at him, ignoring how good he looks in his tight jeans, black boots, white shirt, and black blazer. "Might be easier if you peed on me," I grit out.

Gideon chuckles. "We never said we weren't possessive."

"You don't say? It's not like you killed a man for touching me or anything."

"Did we kill him? I recall a different outcome."

I try to pull out of his grip as we get closer to the drugstore on the edge of town, but he only squeezes me tighter against him.

"Let me go," I tell him, looking up at him with a pleading expression. "Please. I'm not going anywhere. I just don't want to be watched while I peruse the tampon aisle."

His blue eyes bore into mine, and his nostrils flare slightly as he lets me go. "I'm trusting you, Harlow." *You shouldn't.* "Fuck around and find out just how much we'd punish you." He glares at me before leaning against the building and pulling his phone out. Conversation over. I take in his muscular form for a second. *How is it fair that he looks this good all the time?*

I walk inside before he changes his mind, glancing over my shoulder every

145

two seconds. I make a beeline for the women's products section, and then I take a deep, calming breath. *Think, Harlow.* What do I need to get information? What would be useful? The internet, but I can't use my phone... my eyes wander to the back of the store. There are a few pay as you go phones lining the back wall, and I grab a random box of tampons and pantyliners as I look back over my shoulder. Both the cashiers aren't paying attention, so I swipe one of the phones off the rack and slide it into my purse.

Shoplifting and murder, all in one week...

I pay for the tampons, using the cash I took out when I arrived at the airport. The cashier absentmindedly asks me if I want a bag, and I say no, grabbing the two small boxes and placing them on top of everything else in my purse to hide my phone. Just as I turn around to walk out, one of the cashiers calls out for me.

"Miss?"

I freeze, my blood turning cold.

Shit, shit, shit. If Gideon catches me stealing a phone, I'll never hear the end of it. They killed my father. They have proven they have no mercy. Chances are, I've poked the bear too many times and they'll eliminate me to make things easier.

Heart racing, I turn back to face the cashier. *They make it seem so easy, too. They'd make it look like an accident, and there would be news articles about the tragic deaths of father and daughter in the same two weeks.* I swallow and walk back to the register.

"You forgot your receipt," the cashier says, handing me the receipt.

I let out a long exhale. "Oh. Thanks."

Stuffing it into my purse, I exit the drugstore, walking right up to Gideon.

"Get your things?" he asks, looking me up and down slowly. The way his eyes study me like that, like he can see right through me...

I ignore my flushed cheeks and nod.

"Yep."

"Hungry?" he asks, gesturing to the pub on the corner.

"No."

"Well, I am. Come on."

Linking arms with me once again, he drags me to the front of the pub. All I want to do is go home and make a plan, but I guess that'll have to wait. We enter through the doorway, taking the small table by the window. If I didn't hate my circumstances so much, I might find this pub charming. It's cozy and inviting, with plush couches in each of the rooms, as well as working fireplaces. It's not cold today, but the weather has cooled considerably, so it feels nice to sit next to an open fire. Large, dark beams line the ceiling, and the walls are slightly slanted, which means this pub is freaking *old*. Even the iron sconces on the wall look dusty and ancient.

"The Lords have been coming here for over five hundred years," Gideon mutters, running a hand through his dark blonde hair. It's pulled back into a low bun, but the front pieces are loose. How can a psychopath look so good? How is that fair? That's what he is—what they all are. I took a psychology class at Berkeley Carroll, and I remember our teacher telling us the difference between a sociopath and a psychopath. Sociopaths have a tiny morsel of empathy—a struggling, weak conscience. Psychopaths, on the other hand, have no conscience. No remorse or sympathy.

At worst, they're cold, calculating killers.
Master manipulators.
They don't fear consequences.

I remember that part—remember thinking of my rapist.

Shuddering, I look up at Gideon, who is leaning back in his chair and looking at me with a heated gaze. Why am I so physically affected by them? They should be revolting. Their behavior should terrify and disgust me. But for some reason, there's an edge of curiosity. I'm intrigued, and I hate myself for it. Maybe it's some sort of last-ditch effort to get to know my father better. He was a Lord, so a small part of me feels a kinship with the other Lords. I could analyze it for years, but right now, I have to stick to the basics.

They are evil.

I have to kill them.

And I have to get away.

"I did a bit of research this morning," Gideon continues. "Apparently, over the years, there have only been four Ladies of Darkness."

I scowl. "That doesn't surprise me."

"The last one was in 1882. She died when she was twenty-two, just four years after joining the order. Stabbed by an enemy while walking down the street."

Jesus.

I open my mouth to respond, but he stands up, walking to the bar a few feet away. "Two lagers, please, as well as two fish and chips," he tells the blonde bartender. I open my mouth to protest, but he holds up a hand to silence me. *Bastard.* "Ketchup on the side, as well as tartar sauce."

"Yes, my Lord." She bats her lashes and places a manicured hand on his. "It's been ages since I've seen one of you in here."

Jealousy festers inside of me as I watch her squeeze his hand once, smiling seductively and ignoring me completely.

"It has been a while. How have you been?" Gideon asks, his voice... alluring. Soft like velvet.

What the hell? Is he seriously flirting with her right in front of me? Also, why *do I* care?

"I've been well, thanks. I hope it isn't months before I see you again," she adds, popping a hip and walking away.

I glare at the back of her head as she goes, and when Gideon sits back down across from me, he's grinning.

"What?" I ask, crossing my arms.

"You're an open book, Harlow. You can't hide anything from me." Reaching into his pocket, he pulls out his switchblade. "For example, I know you're jealous right now."

I press my lips together before responding. "You wish."

His eyes glint with something dark and menacing as he leans forward. "What if I told you she used to suck my cock in the back alley?"

My stomach bottoms out. I'm both turned on and appalled. And yes, jealous. I don't know why. I don't enjoy having this reaction. He's allowed to do whatever he wants with other people.

"I don't care," I tell him.

"She was okay," he purrs, leaning back and looking out of the window. Dropping his voice, he snaps his eyes back to me. "But like the rest of them, she wasn't enough."

The waitress walks back just at that moment, smiling at Gideon as she sets our beers down. I take a few large sips, grateful that the drinking age is eighteen here. I have a feeling I'll need some alcohol for this conversation.

"She couldn't handle us," he adds, sipping his beer.

"Us?" I ask, suddenly feeling hot.

Gideon's lips lift ever so slightly as his eyes find mine. "We like to share," he growls.

Jesus.

I take three more large sips of beer. "Sounds lovely," I say sarcastically.

Gideon takes another sip of beer, and then leans his large frame forward across the table. My stomach does a somersault as he subtly licks his lower lip, dragging his blue eyes down to my mouth.

"But you," he purrs, rolling his tongue around the inside of his cheek. He's close enough that I can see the details of the blonde and grey scruff on his face, as well as the gold flecks in his eyes. "You like to play just as much as we do, don't you, Harlow?" I have to squeeze my thighs to get rid of the throbbing. I don't know how to answer that, so I just stay silent. *No. Yes. Gods, yes.* "Your little show last night proved that."

My cheeks redden, and I start to lean away from him. But he reaches out and grips both of my hands, pulling me close enough that the table jams into my ribs.

"What exactly did it prove?" I ask as my heart pounds against my ribs.

"You like being pursued. You like being watched. You like being told what to do in bed." I swallow, and the sound is audible. Gideon notices, and he cocks his head as he tugs me impossibly closer. "Your pussy is perfect, by the way. I've been hard all day because I can't stop thinking about how hard you came, and how I wished I was inside of your tight cunt when you did. I came three times thinking about how much better it would feel to fill you up with all my come."

Holy.

Fucking.

Hell.

My whole body flushes at his words, and I can feel my chest and neck reddening. It happens sometimes when I'm anxious or excited. He looks down at my neck and then snaps his eyes back to me. My chest is rising and falling rapidly. His words had the effect he was looking for, but so what?

"Next time, I want to be between your legs, lapping everything up. I want to taste your come, I want to drink your blood, I want to chain you to my bed forever. I've never been more affected by a person before."

Something stutters in my chest at his words.

No. No. No. Don't fall for the psychopath.

I clear my throat. "That won't be happening," I say quickly, pulling out of his grasp. He doesn't let me go, though. His hands squeeze around mine, and I can't help but like the way his large, warm fingers feel against my cool ones. How even just his presence is nice sometimes, like a big, hulking bodyguard. As crazy as it sounds, I now know they'd kill for me, and would never let anything happen to me. That has to count for something.

Still, it's too little too late.

I need out of this life, this order, and there's only one way to go about that.

"I wouldn't be so sure," Gideon purrs, and before I can respond, the waitress brings our food over. Lucky for me, he dismisses her quickly, his eyes watching me as I look down at my food. "Eat," he commands.

And I do. Because as much as I hate to admit it, I like being told what to do.

Damn him, too, because my stomach growls appreciatively. *Guess I am hungry.*

We finish quickly, and he pays for the check, his black AmEx clicking heavily against the card reader machine as he does. Once we're outside, he tugs me into his side. The wind has picked up, and it's starting to mist. I remember this from my summers here. It could be hot one day, and cold and rainy the next. I let Gideon protect me from the elements. I let him open my door and drive me home. In a way, it's nice not thinking for a change.

When we pull up to Blackwell House, he turns the car off and faces me. The windows fog up instantly from the rain, and something about being in here, with him, makes me feel hot all over again.

"You should take the day to do some life admin," he says, sounding glum.

I snort. "What the hell is life admin?"

He tilts his head. "It's what we call paperwork in England. Bills, follow-ups, and in your case, a meeting with your father's personal secretary."

I swallow. *Shit.* I'd forgotten about that. "Why?"

He looks out of the front window, even though we can't see anything through the fog. His jaw ticks as he turns to face me again. This time, his expression seems sad.

"This job is dangerous. You should figure all your shit out in case the worst happens."

Fuck. Is he hinting that they're going to kill me? "Okay?"

He sighs, running his hand through his messy hair. "You have an estate, a house, and a half-brother who all rely on you."

"What about Cecelia?"

He pauses, opening his mouth like he's going to say something, but then he changes his mind. A few seconds go by before he answers.

"Cecelia will always be protected by her family." He looks at me and continues. "Being a Lady of Darkness means there is always a target on your back. Don't be like the last Lady. Her estate ended up in auction, and her family fell into disrepair. It took eighteen years before this house came back to the Blackwell family."

I stiffen. "This house?"

He rubs his lips. "Her name was Helena. Lady Helena Blackwell."

My mind sputters with questions, but before I can ask any of them, Gideon gets out of the car, walking around to my side. Opening my door, he holds his hand out.

"Do you guys have your shit together?" I ask, taking his hand as he shields us with his umbrella. How *gentlemanly*.

"Yes. Chances are, we won't see forty, so we've had our shit together for years. If one of us falls, the others have protections in place."

Won't see forty? I don't like how that sounds. Not because I care about them... but because it just doesn't seem fair. They were thrust into this life just as much as I was. Forty is less than a decade away for all of them.

"And if I fall?" I ask, wondering what my death would mean.

Gideon's eyes glaze with something contemplative. We're standing just outside of Blackwell House, and the rain is coming down heavily, pelting the black umbrella Gideon has propped over our heads. It feels very gothic, standing here with a man like him as it pours rain all around us, the backdrop of the stately Blackwell House blocking the grey sky.

Talking about death, of course.

"We'd lay our lives down for you, Harlow. In time, you'll feel the same way about us."

I swallow. They'd sacrifice themselves for... me?

Chances are, we won't see forty.

Why does that thought make me so uncomfortable? After all, I'm the one buying a cheap phone to google murder tactics.

"It never hurts to be prepared," Gideon says, his voice a low murmur. "Helena Blackwell was your ancestor. She was only four years older than you." Reaching out, he places a finger under my chin, directing my gaze straight up into his. "I haven't known you very long, Lady Harlow Windsor, but if something happened to you, I could never forgive myself."

Even if I betray you?

Before I can respond, he lowers his hand and dips his head—almost like he's bowing. "Get your affairs in order. That way, should anything happen, the people you love will be protected. Some of us don't have any family to protect."

He leads me to the door and opens it for me so that I'm out of the rain. Then he turns and walks away, his boots crunching in the wet gravel. I watch him shake the umbrella off before getting into the car and driving off. Despite my hesitation earlier... I *liked* being with him. I like being with all of them. Somehow, they're managing to break through my hardened shell of a heart, making me feel *sorry* for them.

But I can't let that happen.

Reaching into my purse, I feel for the box containing the burner phone. I should feel vindictive, gleeful that I found a way to get around their watchful eyes. But instead, I hesitate for a second. Staring into the house I now own—the house owned by my father, and every ancestor before me—I feel a strange tug to finish what they started. The Lords insist on protecting their country. They work to rid the world of bad people. Who's to say I don't want that, too? Maybe it runs in my blood, through my veins. Maybe I'm not so different.

Maybe I've been a Lady of Darkness all my life without even realizing it.

CHAPTER 35

Theo

I wipe this asshole's phone clean, gathering every morsel of data. He's not a very interesting guy—sort of sad, when you think about it. Spends a few days in the city every month, mugging and burglarizing to pay for his sad shack of a house. A rap sheet taller than him. A shady past with some lowly gangs. There are thousands of guys like him all over the world—guys who don't have any soul. They need money to survive, but nothing excites them anymore—nothing sets their souls on fire. They're hardened criminals, shut down emotionally from their time in prison. It's almost anticlimactic to torture guys like this because they have nothing to live for. They just take the beating, unfeeling.

I'd rather burn in hell for eternity than end up like this guy.

Alaric is quiet, smoking a cigarette in the corner of the barn, watching Harrison with narrowed eyes. Of all of us, Alaric is the most revenge-driven, the most passionate. It's gotten him in trouble countless times—like a few nights ago, with Armin. He hides a lot underneath his pretty exterior—a fucked up childhood, a suicidal mother who took her own life, and a cruel father. He may look refined to the untrained eye, but all of us know he's hiding some very dark, harrowing memories.

It's just a matter of time before they surface in a black flame of fury, engulfing everyone around him.

Gideon is sitting in the chair facing Harrison, his knife splayed in his palm. He's been acting funny all day—quieter than normal. Angrier. Sterling is behind Harrison, tying Harrison's hands up in a zip tie before moving on to his ankles. He's not gentle about it, either. I can see where the plastic zip tie is cutting into Harrison's hands, the blood trickling down his wrist and onto his sweatpants.

Good. He's a sick fuck, just like the rest of them.

I am going to enjoy hurting him before our little monster finishes him off.

Alaric walks over to Harrison, placing the lit end of his cigarette right in the middle of his chest. Harrison screams as it burns, but Alaric doesn't flinch. Even as Harrison bucks against the ties, Alaric looks almost bored. When he's finished, he walks over to me.

"Fuck him up. Make it hurt. But leave him strong enough to give Harlow a proper fight."

I nod as he walks away, and then I begin to sort through the data from Harrison's cell phone. He doesn't appear to be involved with any of our rivals. I suspected as much—if he had, he would've been living like a king. There is money to be had in certain crime rings, the Lords included. But he's working alone. Probably thought he was better off because of it.

Gideon leans forward, sneering at Harrison. The bastard has the audacity to spit in Gideon's face, and before I can tell him not to, Gideon takes his knife and begins to saw Harrison's pinky off.

Sterling slaps a piece of duct tape over Harrison's mouth to keep him from screaming, and Gideon continues to saw away at the flesh and bone. It takes a couple of minutes, and finally, his pinky finger falls away. I close my laptop and walk over to the blubbering mess of a man. I imagine how much he must've enjoyed fucking our little monster, taking her virginity against her will when she was just sixteen.

He may be pathetic, but I intend to hurt him thoroughly before we introduce him to his worst nightmare. Grabbing the probe I plugged in earlier, I kneel before Harrison and take his injured hand. The gaping wound where his pinky used to be is dribbling blood, and I take the thin cautery probe and press it against the wound. Harrison screams and thrashes. I can't imagine the pain of cauterizing a fresh wound without any sedatives. Pressing harder, I wait until it stops bleeding. The smell is foul, and I have to breathe through my mouth. Not an ideal situation, but we don't want him bleeding out or getting infected before the fun begins.

Harrison looks at me with pleading eyes. I can see some of his fight is already gone. *Weakling*.

"I think you're going to like what we have in store for you," I tell him, setting the probe down and crouching in front of him. His blue eyes bore into mine with vitriol, and I imagine those same eyes terrorizing our little monster.

It's one thing when we do it in a controlled environment. I know none of us could ever truly hurt her, and even what we have planned has been organized and thought out by me and Alaric. Exposure therapy—and the chance to fight back against the person who hurt her. It would hopefully be enough to break her down, wade through the web of memories clinging to the recesses of her mind. To make her as strong as us, she needs to be completely open, and we needed to clear her trauma in order for us to keep her safe.

This is going to be her chance to do that.

Some might find it fucked up, but we aren't known for our morally sound methods.

But this guy? The one before me? I could rip his heart straight out of his chest for what he did to her.

Our little monster is going to get her happy ending.

She just can't see it yet.

CHAPTER 36

HARLOW

I spend the rest of the afternoon going through the files I neglected my second day here, organizing his office into something I can hopefully use for myself. Around five, there's a delivery—a new computer, naturally. I open the crisp white box, unveiling the pristine laptop. Opening it, I see that it's already been programmed for me. The backdrop is a simple skull and crown pattern.

Of course.

I email my father's personal secretary and introduce myself. I have no idea if this is how these things work, or if it's usually more formal. I'm sure there's going to be a lot I'll have to learn, even if I do end up going back to New York. A small part of me is toying with staying, living here and making this my life. Maybe Gemma could visit, maybe I could find an art class to take on the side...

That is, until six o'clock rolls around, and a large delivery is brought into the house. Rose is in the kitchen helping Teddy with dinner, but the movers bring in several boxes of my things.

Somehow, the *Lords* got ahold of my personal belongings in New York.

No way. No fucking way. Not going to happen. Stomping upstairs and into my room, I grab my purse and take it into the bathroom with me. Sterling said there aren't cameras in the bathroom, so this is where I need to be. Before I power on the burner phone, I furiously type out a text to the group on my regular phone.

Me: You guys sure are full of yourselves.
Alaric: You're welcome for the computer.
Me: You can't just erase my life in New York! I have friends there. A future. Now it's just... gone.

Sterling: Your life is here now.
Grinding my teeth together, I let out a frustrated cry as my fingers fumble with the burner phone. It powers on, and I activate the sim card, then in about two minutes, I have unmonitored access to a web browser. I don't connect to the Wi-Fi, instead using the data from the phone.

Just in case.

How do I obtain arsenic?

Article after article show up, the most interesting one about vintage fly paper and how they are riddled with arsenic. I even found a guide for how to soak that fly paper in water and extract the arsenic to use however I need to. Googling again for how to obtain old fly paper, I see that it's still for sale on eBay. Before I can even think about the repercussions, I order two strips, hoping it's enough. I even use PayPal, the account that used to be connected to my mom. *Hopefully*, they won't think to check her account, too.

Bookmarking the site about how to soak the fly paper once it's delivered—hopefully tomorrow, as the seller is in the UK—I hide the box and the phone way back in one of my bathroom drawers.

My hands are shaking by the time I head back into my bedroom, so I sit down on my bed and form a plan. I can figure out how to bake the arsenic into some cookies, bring them with me next time I go to the barn... and then what? Burn their bodies? I shift uncomfortably. This whole thing is so fucked up. Also, a small part of me is dreading this—of watching them die, knowing I betrayed them. What would happen to the order? Would it collapse? If I take them out, would I be hunted forever, like Alaric seems to think?

I can't think about that right now. Looking around at all my things, I'm hit with another wave of anger. Someone broke into my storage unit—*someone broke into my bedroom at Gemma's house*—and removed my things. They're making it harder and harder for me to leave. Like true predators, they're going to immobilize me—*trap* me here with them.

Hell fucking no.

I lie down on my bed to calm down, grabbing my kindle. When I open it, I see more books have been added to my library.

The Art of War

The Secret World: A History of Intelligence

I groan, deleting them instantly. *No, thank you.* Pulling up a new romance book about a grumpy, hot boss, I settle into my bed and relax, reading for a few minutes before Rose comes to collect me for dinner. It's just me tonight—I haven't heard from the *Lords*—so I eat my meal alone. Working out in the mornings has really increased my appetite, because I eat every bite of my roast dinner, as well as two servings of lemon posset for dessert.

I fall asleep quickly a couple of hours later, and I must admit, the silence on their end is slightly concerning. I'm under no false pretenses that they're giving me some time because it might benefit me. I'm sure they're just preparing for battle, gathering everything they need for my next "test." I have a feeling I failed the last one. Can't win them all.

Still... it makes me nervous for what's coming.

CHAPTER 37

Harlow

I wake up just after six with a pounding heart and the sense that someone's here with me. It doesn't take me long to find Alaric leaning against my dresser, watching me like a dark god of night. Pulling the covers up to my chin, I sit up and frown at him. He's dressed in a full suit, black jacket, and trousers that fit him like a glove, and shiny leather shoes that match his leather watch. His hair is slicked back, the curls gathered on top making him seem younger, somehow.

He's not the god of night.

He's the god of death.

"Wow, a full suit at six in the morning. What's the occasion?"

"We have a long day planned, so I figured I'd come take you to work out early. Also, I was working last night, so I need to change the dressing on your burn."

"You mean from where you branded me like a cow?"

He scowls, his jaw twitching. "Either way, it needs changing."

He stalks closer, carrying that same leather pouch from a few nights ago. "What else do you keep in there besides restricted drugs and tools to clean the victims you torture?"

I guess I woke up and decided murder was on the menu today, because surely, he's going to kill me for being such a brat.

I can't read his expression as he digs through his pouch, pulling out some gauze. I lean forward, letting the duvet fall onto my lap. I'm only wearing a thin t-shirt, with no underwear. I didn't think that through.

"Take your shirt off, please."

I pull my shirt over my head, delighting in the way his eyes travel immediately to my chest. Wrapping my arms around myself, I lean forward as he sits down next to me, removing the old bandage.

"It's healing beautifully," he murmurs. The way his breath feathers across my skin makes my skin pebble. He must notice, because he drags his other hand to my back, running a calloused finger down my spine. "You respond to our touch beautifully, too."

"Is that what you tell all the other women?" I ask, thinking of lunch with Gideon yesterday, and how fired up I got when he flirted with the waitress.

"Women... and men," Alaric answers.

I swallow. Looking up at him, his dark eyes bore into mine. "Have you and the guys ever..." I trail off.

"No. But we've shared women before."

God. Imagine being shared by all of them? Four, large, dangerous men... I close my eyes to get rid of that erotic image and what it does to my clit.

"Have you ever been with more than one man?" Alaric asks, using a cotton swab to cover my burn with fresh antibiotic ointment.

"No."

He frowns as he places a new bandage over my burn, and then he hands me my shirt back. I stare at it in his hands. Maybe it's because I'm imagining them all sharing me, or maybe it's because the idea of fucking another man–or being fucked by another man–does something to me. Why do they turn me on so much? What is it about them that seems to ignite something between my legs every time?

Something passes behind his eyes, and he drops my shirt onto the floor. My heart hammers against my ribs as I stand, completely naked, before him.

"What are you doing, Harlow?" he growls, hooded eyes on mine, which is a feat, I'm sure. "Get dressed."

I smirk. "I need to shower first." And then I say something I've never said before. "Want to watch?"

I didn't realize until the other night how much I liked exhibitionism. How hot it made me to know that someone was watching me.

"Harlow," Alaric repeats, and this time, his voice is stern, commanding.

"I'm very dirty," I add, rolling my lower lip between my teeth as I run my hands up my abdomen, coming to my breasts and squeezing.

His eyes drink me in hungrily, and *fuck*, this is so much fun. Alaric is so polished all the time–perfect hair, perfect suit. I want to peel away those smooth layers to see what kind of filth he's hiding underneath it all.

Something tells me I'll be pleasantly surprised when he lets his guard down. And I want to experience it.

Plus... they don't have long, do they? Might as well make them feel good before I kill them.

Jesus. Did I just think that?

"What are you doing?" he asks. His hard expression and clenched fists tell me everything I need to know. He's *so* close to snapping.

"I'm just showering, Alaric. Calm your tits."

I give him a coy smile before I saunter to the bathroom, making sure to sway my hips as I go. I don't check to see if he's following me. I *know* he is. Turning the shower on, I glance over my shoulder and grin when I see him leaning against the bathroom door with one arm hanging above his head. His eyes don't leave mine. Lucky for me, there's no door, as the shower is quite large.

Stepping into the waterfall stream, I begin my routine of washing my hair, going slowly, and popping a hip to show more of my curves. I rinse the shampoo out, making sure to face him as I lean my head back. I grab some conditioner and run it through my curly strands. When I look up again, Alaric is glaring at me.

And—*fuck*. I can see the outline of his cock, the large, curved shaft pressing against the zipper of his trousers.

Because I chose to die today, I squirt some soap into my hand, washing my chest, making sure to moan as I pinch my nipples. Working down, I wash between my legs, throwing my head back and groaning. When I'm done, I notice how hard Alaric is gripping the top frame of the door—his fingertips are white, and his other hand is opening and closing into a fist.

"I can't quite get myself clean," I taunt.

Oh my God, Harlow. What are you doing?

"Can you help me?" And then I do something that makes my cheeks burn as I do. I bend over, watching him over my shoulder as he gets a full view of my ass.

He pushes off the wall and stalks over, his hands in his pockets. Cocking his head, he looks at me furiously. "Spread your cheeks, little monster. Let me see all of you."

And fuck, if it was anyone else—anyone other than *him*—I might balk, hesitate, change my mind. Instead, I do exactly as he ordered. For him.

He groans, leaning back a little to see *everything*.

"I'm sorry," he growls, looking at me with blackened pupils.

I release my hands, standing up a bit taller as my brows furrow. "For what?"

"For what I'm about to do to you." He places his phone, keys, and wallet on the bathroom counter, slowly taking his watch off as well. There's a low, reverberating sound coming from his chest as he steps forward, into the shower.

I gasp as one hand comes around my neck, and then he presses my back against the wall of the shower, forcefully. The water rains down on him, soaking his white shirt and black jacket. It runs down his face and ruins his neat hair, making it hang over his forehead in dripping tendrils. He looks completely unhinged, inside my shower in his full suit. Losing that much control *because of me*.

"You still think you're calling the shots, don't you, baby?" I can hardly breathe with his hand around my neck. I don't move, though. I can't. I'm both terrified and *on fucking fire*. His other hand comes to my chest, and he cups my right breast, pinching my nipple so hard that my back arches, and I cry out in a mixture of pain and pleasure. Choking me harder, he moves his hand down to the apex of my thighs. He growls when he finds me slick for him, sliding a finger between my slit before bringing it back up to his mouth, tasting me.

He groans, and his eyes do a funny flutter that makes my stomach swoop low. "You're not in charge. We are. If I want your pussy to taste like apple pie instead of strawberries, I'll do it," he growls, nudging his jaw at the strawberry scented soap I was just using. "If I want to spend my entire day between your legs, I'll do it. If I want to fuck your tight little ass, I'll do it," he grits out, his voice menacing and low.

He loosens his grip just enough for me to take a deep breath—and to talk back. "I have more power than you realize," I seethe, reaching a hand out and placing it over his chest. I can feel how fast his heart is beating, how erratic his pulse is. *All for me.* "You're the one who got in the shower fully clothed."

Baring his teeth, he shoves me against the wall again. My head smacks against the tile, and I groan when he inserts two fingers into my pussy. I cry out as I clench around him. His large fingers stretch me, and despite my throbbing skull, I find myself wanting *more*. He works his arm, penetrating me with a strong pump, and my mouth drops open.

"Do you like being a fucking brat? I think you want me to make your pussy scream, don't you, little monster?"

I don't even know what to say to that, which is good because at just that moment, he curves his fingers just so, massaging the spot that makes my knees buckle.

"Oh God," I whimper.

"What have I told you about God, Harlow?"

My eyes shutter closed, my whole body igniting underneath his touch. It feels so fucking good that I start to ride his hand.

"I don't know," I whisper, and his grip tightens around my neck.

I gasp for air, my pussy simultaneously clenching around his thick fingers. He moves them roughly inside of me, and he might as well be a skilled puppeteer with how he's working me, how he's making me feel things I've never felt. It's like he knows my body better than I do.

"*We* are your gods," he murmurs, licking my lower lip before he bites it. *We are your gods, little monster. And you are ours.* I taste blood and moan, my legs beginning to shake underneath him. He's still gripping my neck, but he relents a little bit, pulling away from me a few inches. "And?"

"And what?" I ask, my voice a low rasp.

"Say it."

We are your gods, little monster. And you are ours.

Everything is throbbing with delicious need, and he scissors his fingers as I try to respond. My legs tremble, barely holding myself up. He looks so possessed—his wet hair hanging down, water dripping off the tip of his nose, the white shirt clinging to his muscled chest as he pulls his lower lip between his teeth...

Jesus Christ.

"I am yours," I say, my voice hoarse.

"You're such a good girl, Harlow," he murmurs, his free hand running from my neck to my engorged clit, where he clamps it between two fingers, squeezing. It's both painful and delightful, and I cry out as pleasure skitters down my spine.

I buck my hips, trying to get him to go faster, go harder, when he suddenly pulls his hand out.

"What the hell?" I ask, sounding much whinier than I intended.

Alaric doesn't answer, instead spinning me around so that I'm facing the marble shower wall. *Oh.* I hear his zipper, the way he's grunting, the sound of a belt buckle falling away...

"I want to feel you squeeze my cock when you come," he growls, pushing me against the stone. He knocks my knees apart so that I'm spread wide, and then I feel the head of his thick cock against my entrance. Despite my earlier hesitation, I want him. I want it all. I both hate myself and hate him for making me want this so badly.

"Fuck me, Alaric," I tell him, working my ass into a little shimmy.

He grabs a fistful of my hair, jerking my head back. "Stay still. This will hurt."

Good.

I don't say it out loud, but I think it. Make it hurt—erase every single thing my rapist took from me. Between Alaric's tight hold on my hair, and the way his cock enters me, stretching me beyond what I ever thought was possible, tears begin to spring from my eyes. I'm not sure why, but it happens. I can feel how my body gives into him fully, and I gasp when he pushes through the barrier, pushes through to the hilt, absolutely filling me. I'll be sore tomorrow and riddled with bruises.

Good. I want to be.

I want this, and therein lies the difference between what happened to me and what's happening now.

"God, Harlow," he growls, speaking into my hair as he pulls out slowly before driving back in. "You're so fucking tight."

I whimper as he pulls out again slowly before pounding back into me—over, and over, and over. Crying out, my nails scrape down the stone, and I feel my body accommodate him, feel myself fluttering around his thick shaft. My eyes roll into the back of my head as he continues his onslaught, and I move back onto his cock so that he drives into me harder. The pleasure begins to build inside my core, snaking down my limbs and spine in full-body tingles. My knees are actively shaking as he grunts and groans behind me.

"You like this cock, little monster?"

I don't answer, and he tugs my hair harder, jerking my neck so that my back is arched to the brink. I can see him looking down at me, and the vision is... *God...* he looks otherworldly. His muscled forearm is gripping my long hair, and he's breathing heavily as he moves in and out of me, making my pussy contract around him more with every thrust.

"Answer me," he mutters.

Everything coils tightly inside of me, and I know I'm seconds away from having the most powerful orgasm of my life.

"Yes," I whisper, my voice sounding pained.

"Imagine all of us giving you this much pleasure at once," he grits out, snarling down at me as water drips down his face from above and onto my forehead. "Imagine two of us in your pussy at once," he growls, driving into me so deeply that my whole body practically levitates. *I can imagine it—how they would stretch me and fill me so completely.* "Imagine one of us between your legs right now, licking you up and down your slit, lapping up the come you're about to spray all over my cock."

Jesus fuck.

My cries of pleasure mount. He doesn't stop or slow down. "Imagine watching as one of us fucks the other, making eye contact as we all come at the same time," he adds, letting my hair go as he holds my body closer to him. "That's what you could have, Harlow. That's what we *will* have. Sharing you. Worshiping you. Blinding you with pleasure."

I lose myself at the thought of them together, of us being a unit like that. I gasp as my orgasm begins, my muscles uncoiling delightfully slowly, the pulses of lightening hot pleasure working through my whole body. It's a cataclysmic event, and I cry out, convulsing in his arms as wave after wave hits me. He continues to pound into me as my pussy grips him tightly.

I can never go back.

He didn't just fuck me—he stole my soul, and he'll never willingly give it back.

"That's it, baby. I can feel you gushing," he growls. "Now I'm going to fill you up with my come—practice for the main event," he says, his voice hoarse and uneven.

I'm still trying to catch my breath. "The main event?"

His hand comes to my arm, right to where my birth control implant is. "One day you'll be so full of our come that we'll put a baby in your belly."

"Hell no," I say, still quivering from the aftershocks.

"We are the Lords of Darkness, little monster. Our royal lineage *will* continue. So yes, one day, we will fill you one after the other, over, and over and over, until we have five little heirs."

I gasp as he hardens inside of me, his cock turning to steel before it bows and curves, stretching me in a different way, filling me so completely that my eyes roll back into my head again.

Despite his horrifying declaration, I find myself gripping him again, wanting more, wanting everything he's telling me. My second orgasm comes out of nowhere, and I scream at the same time Alaric roars. He spills his seed inside of me, hips jerking. His come fills me until I'm full, our mixed releases gushing out and sliding down my thighs. He makes the hottest sounds I've ever heard as he finishes.

I wanted to see him come undone, and he did.

He completely unraveled because of *me*.

I'm still holding on to the wall for dear life, my knees weak. Then I feel him twitch behind me as he pulls out, letting out a long, slow breath.

"I could live inside your pussy, Harlow. Burrow deep, inhaling your intoxicating scent for the rest of my life and die a happy man," Alaric says. He twists me around and kisses me, his still-leaking cock pressed against my stomach as his hands come to the sides of my face. His kiss is both punishing and gentle, passionate and soft. He kisses me with reverence, like all of this was natural.

Like it was the best fucking thing that's ever happened to him.

I pull back, looking up into his dark eyes. "I should get dressed," I say, pulling out of his grip. He doesn't let go, and one corner of his mouth tilts up.

"You're not going anywhere, little monster. I'm not done with you."

CHAPTER 38

ALARIC

I delight in the way Harlow looks both scared and aroused as I pull her out of the shower with me. She thinks one quick shower fuck is enough to satiate me? She's never been more wrong, and my cock is already hard again as I take in her curvy, soft body spread before me on the bed. She's still soaking wet, and as I push her legs apart, I see my come still leaking out of her. The creamy white liquid looks so good against her flushed, swollen flesh, but my instincts want to push it back inside.

One day.

One day, I'll cut that implant out and delight in filling her with my seed.

All four of us, one after the other.

She'll be so full of our come, she won't be able to think straight.

I feel like a man who's been starved for too long, with his prey laid bare before him in the most tantalizing position. Grunting, I take my wet clothes off, leaving them in a pile on the floor.

I don't care about anything other than eating her pussy until she's crying, until she's begging and trembling and gushing with another load. Until she's so sore that she thinks of me every time she moves, and the others know from my marks that I got to fuck her first. A strange, satisfying sort of possessiveness courses through me at that thought, and I stroke my hard-as-sin cock as I walk up to her.

"See what you do to me?" I ask, loving the way her eyes widen at seeing my cock up close for the first time. "I'm hard again, so ready to fill you up. But first, I want to see what that bratty little mouth can do."

Her eyes darken, and I fucking *love* the way her lower lip rolls between her teeth as she watches me hungrily.

"How do you want me?" she asks, playing with her nipples.

Fuck. I could watch her all fucking day long. Everything about her is perfect. She's like sin incarnate, made for me by the devil himself.

"On your back. Come to the edge of the bed so that I can fuck your mouth."

Her lips part as she takes in what I'm asking her, but she does as I say, scooting down the bed so that her head is hanging off the edge. I groan as I walk up, and she opens her mouth wide as I place the tip of my cock against her tongue.

"How deep can I go?" I ask her, rubbing my precome along her red, swollen lower lip.

"As deep as you can," she answers, her voice husky.

Fuck.

I position myself on top of her, and then I bend my knees and move my hips so that my shaft slides down her tongue. She takes me so well, allowing me into her throat as she jerks with surprise. Gagging once, she squeezes her eyes shut as tears leak from the corners. *God, she looks so beautiful with her mouth full of my cock.* I go deeper, and she doesn't react, only moving her eyes up to mine. *Daring* me to go deeper.

So I do. I pull out, and then I fuck her mouth with abandon, driving into the back of her throat, angling my curved cock so that it goes straight down, so deep her front teeth graze my balls. She sputters but quickly recovers, more tears leaking out of her eyes. But she doesn't complain. Instead, she plays with her tits, rolling her nipples as she squeezes her thighs together.

When we first met her, I never would've pegged her as the type of girl to let me fuck her throat like this, the kind of girl who enjoyed mixing pain with pleasure. But as she moves one hand down to her clit, spreading her lips and rubbing her nub vigorously, I realize how wrong I was—and how fucking *dirty* she is.

I continue my assault on her mouth, moaning as the hand playing with her nipples comes up and grips my balls—tightly. A lightning bolt of pleasure spears through me. I cry out, and my cock grows impossibly hard as her warm, wet mouth brings me close to another orgasm. I can feel my balls tightening in her hand, so I pull out quickly.

One day, I'll watch as she swallows every drop of my come.

But today, I want to fuck every hole she has.

"On your stomach," I tell her, spreading her cheeks wide so that I have a full view of her ass. Spitting into my hand, I rub two fingers against her tight pucker.

"Alaric—"

"Want me to stop?" I ask, taunting her.

She's quiet for a few seconds. "No. I don't want you to stop."

I add more spit, making sure she's lubed up before I place a thumb against her entrance. "Relax, Harlow."

She takes a deep breath, and I see her visibly sag so that she's fully lying on the bed. I pull her hips up to me so that I can get my other hand down to her clit. Spreading her pussy lips, I begin to rub, and I moan when I feel just how goddamn wet she is. I push my thumb into her ass, and she gasps, but her pussy contracts at the invasion.

"You like that, don't you?" I murmur. I fuck her with my thumb for a few seconds, ensuring she's nice and ready, and then I grab her hips and pull them up to my cock. "This is going to hurt. But then you will come so hard, you'll see fucking stars. Do you understand?"

"Yes," she whispers.

I nudge the head of my length against her ass, and then I slowly push in. *God.* Her pussy was so incredibly tight, but this? I barely fit. It's like a soft, warm vise has my cock in a goddamn chokehold. I work my way in a few millimeters at a time, and when I look down at Harlow, I see her fists gripping the fabric of her duvet, and the small sounds she makes every time I move in deeper are making me insane with need.

"Fuck," I say, my voice shaky. Using my other hand, I flick her clit, moaning when her pussy flutters on the other side of the thin barrier. "You're squeezing me so tight." I fill her fully, and then I pull out before slowly driving back in again.

"Oh, God," she moans, and her voice is so low, so sultry, I know I won't last longer than a minute or two. I'm going to explode so hard inside of her. "Play with my clit harder," she begs, and I groan at the way she knows what she wants. I move my hand against her swollen clit, rubbing it as she writhes underneath me. "Yes," she hisses. "Fuck, I'm going to come, Alaric."

Her voice is like music to my ears. I move my hand faster as I push into her ass again, and each time it's like trying to get through a thick, tight wall, compressing my cock and milking me so delightfully.

"Come for me, little monster. Milk me dry."

She cries out, her whole body shaking underneath me. Her little mewls and the way her ass grips me with every contraction spurs on my orgasm, and I groan loudly as my cock throbs inside of her. I'm so deep inside, and *fuck, it feels fucking perfect here inside her ass.* I growl as we both come down from our climaxes. Slowly pulling out, my come dribbles out and onto the bed. Harlow collapses onto her stomach, panting. I lie down next to her as my cock still twitches, searching for her pussy all over again.

"I've never..." she trails off.

I reach over and brush the wet hair from her face. "I know. I'm honored to be your first."

"That was..." She closes her eyes as her chest rises and falls rapidly.

Something primal in me delights in the fact that I've rendered her speechless. "Me too," I tell her.

She opens her eyes and scowls at me. "Right. Like I'm supposed to believe someone like you has never had incredible sex. You are sex incarnate."

I huff a laugh. "Am I?"

Her cheeks redden as she looks at me, her eyes wandering down my bare chest. "Yeah, I mean, you're hot. All of you are too hot for your own good."

I smile as I snuggle closer. "Mmm. What did you think of me the first time you saw me?" I ask.

She giggles. "I thought you were a control freak."

I bend down and kiss her, nibbling on her lower lip again. Pulling away, I look down into her eyes.

"I am."

"I know," she answers, her voice soft.

"So you fancy all of us, then?" I ask, moving over to her ear, sucking and biting her soft lobe.

She moans. "I never said that."

"Would you let all of us fuck your ass like that, one after the other?"

She hesitates for just long enough for me to know her answer would be *yes*. Why does that thought make me hard again? Haven't I had enough?

"No. I don't—no," she repeats, sitting up. "I'm getting dressed. Stop cuddling me. You're distracting when you're nice."

"And when I'm not nice?" I ask, my voice a low purr.

She looks over her shoulder at me as she walks into the bathroom, narrowing her eyes.

I can still remember how she screamed my name just a few minutes ago when I was punishing her.

Following her, I glance down at my phone to see the screen lighting up with a text.

Theo: Change of plans. Come to Crowne now. And bring Harlow.

CHAPTER 39

HARLOW

After using the toilet and cleaning myself up with another shower, I walk into the bedroom to see Alaric wearing a fresh suit.

"How did you—" My mouth snaps closed when his eyes look up from his gold cufflinks, finding my eyes. I know those cufflinks. I'd seen my father wear them several times. "That's my father's suit."

"It is."

I take in the suit, and how it seems to fit him well enough. The pants aren't as fitted, and Alaric's shoulders are too wide for the jacket, but for the most part, it works.

"Since I ruined my suit," he adds, dark eyes boring into mine. My pussy literally shivers when he looks at me like that. "This is just to get me to our office. I have a change of clothes there."

"Your office?" I ask, holding the towel tighter around my chest.

"Yes."

Swallowing, I look at the workout clothes on my dresser. A new pair—this time, dark red leggings and a matching bra. The material is glittery. Where the hell is Sterling finding these clothes? His choice in colors is interesting, too.

"We're not going to the gym?" I ask, sounding hopeful.

"Not today."

Something about the way he says that makes my heated skin cool, and once he's done pulling my father's shoes on, he adjusts his tie and looks at me expectantly.

"I'll wait downstairs," he says, his demeanor completely different from what it was earlier. For a minute, his hard, exterior shell had cracked, and he'd smiled–been romantic, even. It was... nice. Confusing. Terrifying.

He walks out, and I pull on the workout clothes. At least they're comfortable. I braid my wet hair into two thick French braids that hang down my back. Even the shoes are comfortable and cushioning, but really... how many pairs of workout shoes does one person need? I'm going to need to have a conversation with Sterling.

It doesn't matter, because in two weeks, you'll be done with this life.

My heart lurches when I think that, but I quickly push the thought away.

I apply sunscreen and grab a cardigan, walking out of my bedroom. Rose is vacuuming the hallway–*because of course she is*. Giving me a wry smile, she continues her work without saying anything. *Great.* I give her a smile as I walk down the stairs, finding Alaric leaning against the edge of the staircase.

Seeing him here, in this house–*my* house–knowing what we just did... my stomach erupts with butterflies.

Knock it off.

I can't get attached. I can't develop feelings for any of them. My plan will work as long as I can separate them from my emotions–separate the sex from any traitorous feelings.

I can do that.

Right?

"Let's go," Alaric says, walking ahead of me to the front door.

"Wait," I tell him, halting. "What the hell happened between up there and–this," I say, gesturing to his rigid posture.

I see it then, the way his eyes soften slightly, the way his hard expression drops from his handsome face. He's fighting his feelings just like I am. But why? I have my reasons. But why is he fighting against himself?

Alaric walks up to where I'm standing. The cold expression wins out, and he looks down at me with dark eyes and a menacing scowl.

"I fucked you, Harlow. That's it."

I stifle the hurt his words cause me. The hurt–and the anger. I hate games, and right now, I don't know what games he's playing.

"You're such a coward," I tell him, baring my teeth.

"Harlow, just stop. You don't understand."

Turning around, he walks away, opening the door and not even bothering to hold it open. I follow him out like a sad puppy dog. *Fine.* He wants to play games? Pretend we didn't share something up there? I can do that. He's right. We had sex. That's it. Getting close to him won't do me any favors.

I climb into the grey Range Rover, and he speeds off before I can even get my seatbelt on.

"You'll do well to remember, little monster, that we are trained killers. We may fuck like rabbits, but anything beyond that is a threat to our order."

I swallow and pull my cardigan tighter. "Yeah. Got it."

"You are a Lady of Darkness, Harlow. You need to learn how to separate sex and love."

Love.

I most definitely do not *love* him.

"Thanks for the explanation," I tell him, my tone harsh. "You don't have to tell me that love isn't involved. I'm not a child."

"I know you're not a child," Alaric answers.

"I could never love you," I add, turning to face the window.

We don't speak for the rest of the drive into town. He pulls into a parking garage, and my stomach swoops when I see three other luxury cars lined up next to the entrance to the building.

Crowne Tower.

"Let's go," Alaric says, again walking ahead of me.

Fuck this. And fuck him.

I wrap my arms around myself as we head through a narrow passageway, and onto the main street of Blackwell Village. Alaric swipes a card, and the ancient iron door creaks open. He gestures for me to walk down the stairs into what looks like a basement. I hesitate, looking down into the darkness.

Alaric must notice my trepidation, because he comes up behind me, moving one of my braids off my shoulder as he whispers into my ear.

"We have a surprise for you."

My whole body breaks into a cold sweat. "A deadly surprise?" I ask, trying to keep my voice lighthearted.

He chuckles, but his laugh sounds monstrous. Whatever is down there... That's why he's in such a weird mood. I can feel the excitement, the darkened energy, radiating off his skin.

"Think of it as a gift. And no, not a deadly surprise. Not for you, anyway."

"Okay, because if you're just planning on killing me—"

"We're not going to kill you unless you betray us." Alaric's hand wraps around my braid, tugging my head back. "Next time I fuck you senseless, you should wear these, so I have something to grab onto." I involuntarily whimper at his words, and he laughs again. "Go down the stairs, Harlow."

I swallow as he lets me go, walking down the winding, stone staircase. His words cause my stomach to coil with dread. *We're not going to kill you unless you betray us.* I try not to think about the vintage fly paper that's supposed to be delivered tomorrow—about the ways I plan to take them all down. Is that still the plan? Am I still going to go through with it?

I don't have time to think about it right now. I'm intrigued by the surprise he's promising... though I can't imagine what it could be. Step after step, we head down, and the temperature plummets the farther we get into the stone dungeon. I pull my cardigan tighter around me. My hand gripping the iron railing begins to sweat, and I take a few steadying breaths. Finally, I enter a large underground chamber. Gideon, Sterling, and Theo are all standing around, and there's a door open to a large cell in the back, though I can't see who or what is inside.

Before I can ask what's going on, Alaric nudges me forward. "It'll be better if you have the element of surprise."

"What?" I ask, and he continues to push me into the cell. "Are you locking me up?" I ask, my voice shrill.

I should've killed them sooner.

Closing the door and locking me inside, I twist back around to where they're all watching me.

"What the fuck?"

Sterling comes over to where I'm standing. His boots make a clicking noise against the flagstone floor. My heart races when I look around, noticing a man with a bag over his head in the corner, unmoving.

"Do you remember what I told you about my rings, Harlow?" My body goes still, and his green eyes are twinkling with something I'm sure I'm not going to like the sound of. I don't answer, and he continues. "Rarely, the kills stay with me. That's what these rings are for—to honor those people. But most of the time, each kill we make is satisfying. Eliminating the scum from this fucked up world. Making it a tiny bit better, one person at a time. I *like* killing them, baby." He laughs, the sound dark and menacing. "Enjoy every minute of it."

I swallow audibly. "So, what? You want me to kill whoever is under that hood?" I ask, trying to sound strong. Trying to sound resolute. It was easy to forget *this* part of the job with all the exercise and shower sex. But deep down, these guys are murderers. Cold-blooded brutes with no soul.

And they expect me to be one of them.

Sterling chuckles. "No, darling. I want you to do more than kill this man. I want you to *make it hurt*, and I want you to *make him pay* for what he did to you."

I freeze. My blood turns to ice in my veins, and I look at the man again, closer this time. My hands shake as they drop to my sides.

"I told you about my rings—about the people we killed for this job, about the souls who haunt me at night, who visit me in my dreams. These rings are for them. But the man here? I've never wanted to kill someone so badly," he growls, his voice ominous.

I look up at the others, and they're all just as murderous as Sterling. But... there's no way. This can't be... *him*. Can it? How did they find him? How did they have time to bring him here? I twist around, panic flooding my veins.

They didn't just bring him here.

They locked me up with him.

A sob escapes my throat when I realize what they've done. "No," I whisper, backing up. "There's no way," I add, my voice breaking.

"Take the bag off of his head and find out for yourself," Theo says, his light blue eyes shining in the dim light. "Feel the anger. Let it fuel you. Get the revenge we know you crave."

You are safe here.
He can't find you in England.
You are safe here.
Except... these assholes brought him to England.
They brought him to me, and now he's here.
He's right in front of me.

My heart hammers in my chest as I take a step forward. Then another. The man is still breathing, and my eyes adjust to the dark cell so that I get a clear view of his bloodied clothes. His dirty fingernails, and the three stumps where fingers should be. Stepping forward, I discard my cardigan in case he lunges for me, which is entirely possible, seeing as these fucking *Lords* didn't even tie him up.

"How am I supposed to kill him?" I ask, looking over my shoulder. The guys just watch me with dark expressions. "With my hands? He's a solid foot taller than me. It's a death sentence," I add, trying not to freak the fuck out.

This is *so* fucked up. Beyond fucked up. If the test the other day didn't trigger me... this will. Will they stop him if he hurts me? Or will they watch with glee as he...

No.

I can't think about that.

My vision blurs with tears just as a scraping sound pierces the air, and before I can move, the guy in the cell leaps forward, knocking me down and pulling the bag off his face. I cry out when my back hits the stone floor, the air leaving my chest. I can't cry, can't scream, as those blue eyes glare down into mine once again.

No.
No.
No.
This is a dream.
This isn't happening.

I gasp for air as my lungs recover, and then I let out an ear-piercing scream.

"Hello again," he says, leering down at me. "I remember you."

"Get off of me!" I scream, trying to shove him off. Pure, cold panic fills me, and black spots cloud my vision.

I can't breathe.

I can't think.

How could they *do* this?

What kind of fucked up test is this? Kill or be killed?

"You sick motherfuckers," I shout, as the man brings his hands to my neck. "I hate you. I hate you all!" I screech, kicking the guy off me with a force that surprises me. He must be weak. I remember how strong he used to be. He stumbles back, and I use that time to stand up and circle him.

"What do you wish you had done back then, Harlow?" Sterling says, his voice nearby, taunting me. I don't look, though. Instead, I watch as my rapist bares his teeth, following my circle with anger written all over his face. I hear something slide on the stone floor, hitting my foot. "Punish him for what he did to you. Make a statement. Make it *count*."

I quickly reach down and grab what he slid to me, grabbing a knife with a white handle. It's old, so unlike the shiny, new knives Gideon likes to play with. I grip it in my right hand as tears run down my face. I can't help it. Hiccupping, I hold my knife-wielding hand up in front of my face.

"This knife is our initiation knife," Alaric says from somewhere outside of the cell. "By using this knife, you are taking a blood oath. You are officially ours. *Kill him.*"

"This is so fucking twisted," I growl, tears springing from my eyes. "You guys want to watch him fight me? Is this some sort of sick game to you?" I'm full on crying now, my body shaking as I circle the man.

"Little monster," Theo says, and I hear him walk up to the cell door. "This is not for us. It's for you."

"Fuck you," I seethe. "Don't condescend to me. Am I supposed to believe this is all *for me*? Am I supposed to believe this isn't for *your* enjoyment?!"

"You're right," Theo says slowly. "We will enjoy watching you slaughter him."

I barely have time to register his words before the man lunges forward again. This time, I'm prepared, and I jump out of the way. He stumbles a bit, and I use that half a second to kick him in the groin. I'm still gripping the knife, should I need it. He falls to his knees. Suddenly, my whole body, my whole being, hums with deep-rooted rage. I wipe my cheeks and kick him again–harder. These shoes have a thick sole, and I barely feel anything as he falls to the ground.

Wiping my face again, I stand over him. "You are not going to win this time," I tell him, my voice hoarse. "You killed my mother. You raped me!" I scream, spit flying as the anger only grows stronger. He tries to move, and I kick him again– this time, in the face. "You *ruined my life*," I cry out, sobbing. "And now, I'm going to enjoy watching the light leave your eyes," I growl, kicking him in the face again.

And again.

I fall to my knees, bringing the knife up and then down into his abdomen.

Over, and over.

I smell the blood before I see it, and when I look down, his nose is bleeding, and he's moaning in pain. I crouch in front of him.

"You're pathetic. How old are you? Fifty? And yet you find power in hurting little girls? Why?" I croak, needing an answer. "Why us?"

"Your mom killed my wife," he says, his voice weak. "My wife died of cancer five years ago. And your mom was the one to unplug her, even though I begged her not to." He begins to cry, and I scowl down at him.

I remember that.

I remember how affected my mother was, how she came home crying.

"Your wife was dead," I tell him. "Your wife was already dead."

"And *your mother* killed her."

"Don't let him talk his way out of this," Sterling says from behind me. I snarl as I look at him. "Sometimes I make mistakes. That's what these rings represent. But some people don't feel that same remorse. Some people have rotting, feted souls, Harlow. They wreak havoc on the world. They do not make it a better place." I look at him with tear-stained cheeks. *How can he not see he's one of them?* "They release their darkness into innocents. Killing. Raping. Stealing. Almost everyone has a closet full of skeletons, little monster. But it's what you do with those skeletons–what you do with that anger–that dictates your character."

I look back down at the man before me. Somehow, knowing his motivation– albeit a weak one–puts everything into perspective. The weight of my mother's murder lifts from my shoulders, and I walk back over to the man, who is now shaking like a leaf.

It wasn't just some unfair, random crime. She didn't die for nothing—*he* killed her. There was a reason, and that's all I need to know.

"I'm not going to apologize for killing you," I tell him. "Because you don't deserve an apology for what you did to my mother. For what you did to *me*."

One day soon, I'll channel this same anger and kill the Lords of Darkness.

At least now I proved to myself that I could do it.

"Please," he begs, but I feel nothing but the rush of revenge. "Please don't kill me."

"I remember asking you not to rape me, too. And look where that got me," I growl, sinking the knife down into his chest again. "This is for me," I say, using all the force I have inside of me to stab him repeatedly. "And this," I add, stabbing him again, "Is for my mom."

He goes still, his last breath leaving his chest before blood begins to pour out of him. I'm trembling so violently I can barely stumble back, and I hear the click of the cell open. Theo is the first to wrap his arms around me, followed by Gideon. Suddenly, all four of them have me wrapped up between them, and I feel... dizzy. Crazy. Strong. Resilient.

But not because of them.

Because of *me*.

"Get away from me," I growl at them, pushing them away.

"You did beautifully, baby," Alaric says, running his hand down my back.

"Oh, fuck off!" I scream.

I can barely hold myself up, and then I feel Theo's hands on my face as he gazes down at me.

"There's a reason we brought him here, little monster." I'm so upset that I'm still shaking beneath his touch. I need to funnel this fury for when I kill them. "We needed you to face your biggest fear. It was for the safety of the order. And you did it. You killed him. You took back the power he always held over you, and you used it to remove an evil man from this world."

I shove him away, my anger making me strong. He stumbles back, a look of mild surprise on his face. I'm still holding the knife, and I grip it harder.

"We're not sorry for doing it," Sterling murmurs. "One day, you'll see why we had to."

"All the physical fitness and scare tactics do nothing against our true demons, Harlow," Gideon says. "We all entered this order with baggage. And we all overcame that baggage. You conquered your worst fear. Let that sink in."

"No," I growl. *I would make them pay for this.* "It wasn't up to you!" They all look at me, and *God, I am seething.* "This wasn't something I overcame. Stop congratulating me," I hiss. "You forced me to do this. You talk so much shit about ridding the world of evil, and you just put me in a cage with my rapist! Do you not see how fucked up that is?" I cry, my voice breaking. "You're all hypocrites. You're just as terrible and sick as the pieces of shit you hunt."

Theo steps forward. "Harlow—"

"Don't touch me."

I conquered my worst fear against my will.

I conquered my worst fear because of them.

"You may have had good intentions, but this was beyond fucked up. You can't always be in charge. You can't always dictate my life like this. This wasn't your decision to make. Trapping me with my rapist..." I trail off, looking at all of them with disgust. Luckily, they all seem slightly remorseful. "Facilitating something like this was *my* call. I will never forgive any of you," I tell them. "And now I want to go home."

If I stay, this will be my life. Sick games, twisted men, so much blood and gore. If I go, if I follow through with my plan, I will be free.

From this man, and from the Lords.

So, fuck this.

I choose freedom.

CHAPTER 40

GIDEON.

I drive Harlow home, torn between wanting to console her and wanting to push her harder. I think our experiment worked–I *hope* it worked. She's sitting in the passenger seat, facing the window. We haven't spoken a word since we got into my car, and as we drive up the winding road to her house, I resist the urge to place my hand on her thigh.

I'm pretty sure she'd bite it off if I tried.

I remember being initiated, and how fucked up everything seemed. I was thrust into this from a life of dinner parties, suits, and luxury. Sure, I still had all those things, but now murder, blood, and espionage accompanied those things– tainting them. This would be a big adjustment for Harlow, and she'd have to face the music soon, whether she wanted to or not.

She was a Lady of Darkness, and there was no going back now.

I pull through the iron gate of Blackwell House, coming to a stop just outside the front door. Turning to face Harlow, I can see how pale she is, how red her eyes are from crying. And I *hate* it. I hate what we had to do to her.

And that's saying a lot, because sometimes I wonder if I was born without a heart.

"Do you want me to come inside with y–"

"No." She sniffs and then pushes her door open.

Maybe we went too far. Maybe we pushed her too hard. She walks to the front door and closes it behind her without looking back at me.

I pull my phone out and text the guys.

Me: She's home now.
Sterling: Theo, keep an eye on her.

Theo: You really think she'd run now? Did you see how far her eyes rolled back into her skull earlier?

My cock twitches as I think about watching her with Alaric earlier. I wanted to join in, wanted to let her sit on my face as she came.

Sterling: You all think very highly of yourselves, don't you?

Alaric: You tell us, Mr. Titty.

Sterling: And what does that make you?

Theo: How about Flycheeks McGee?

I grin.

Me: Mr. McGee for short.

Alaric: You're all hilarious.

Sterling: How about we get back to murdering bad guys and saving the world one rapist at a time?

Alaric: Speaking of... I'll have my guys clean up the evidence in the dungeon.

Theo: By far my favorite use of those prison cells.

Sterling: Get back to work. All of you.

I smile as I drive away. Once I park and walk into St. Claire Manor, I check the camera app to see what Harlow is doing. I don't see her in her room, instead, she's in the kitchen. Squinting at the screen, I see her begin to mix something in a bowl. *Huh.*

Setting my keys and wallet down, I look at the video feed again. "What are you up to, little monster?"

Something tells me we'll find out soon enough.

CHAPTER 41

Harlow

Thank the universe for overnight shipping.

Finding basic instructions on the burner phone for the arsenic was easy—soak the fly paper in water, and that water now becomes arsenic-infused water. *Easy peasy.* It was simple enough to grab a large bowl of water and bring it into my bathroom. I let them soak for a few minutes, until the vintage fly paper was saturated. And then I very carefully carried that bowl of water down the stairs, disguised in a laundry hamper, of course. Rose and Teddy are nowhere to be seen, fortunately, and I quickly add the water into the brownie mix I find in the cabinet.

The article I found says this stuff is very powerful, and to be careful handling it, so I make sure to wear Rose's thick rubber gloves the entire time. When the mix is finished, I butter a pan and spread the thick batter around, placing it into the oven.

And then I walk around to the back of the house, disposing of the bowls I used, covered with a bag of trash. *Just in case.* To the naked eye, it would look as though I was simply baking brownies. They'd have to be able to piece everything together, and while they're smart, they're not that smart. *At least, I hope so.* Rose flits in while the brownies are baking, but I tell her they're for Alaric, and she leaves me alone after that, winking.

I'll need to come up with an alibi—or some way to ensure I wasn't convicted of my crimes. But first... I needed them to die.

No more bullshit.

No more tests.

It's time for them to meet their maker.

I push down any warm feelings I may have developed for them—any kind words they may have muttered to me.

I need to eliminate them.

Once the brownies are done, I place foil over the top of the pan and carry them to my room, ensuring I grab a towel to set them down on. I'll also need to figure out a way to get the guys to eat them—some sob story where they'd take pity on me and ingest them without question. Because obviously this was only going to work if they all ate them at the same time—and *hopefully*—they'll all lose consciousness before they realize what's happening.

Arsenic is funny that way, though. It works quickly and efficiently, and my hope was that by the time it takes effect, they'll be too inebriated to retaliate.

Still, I should have a backup plan.

Looking around the kitchen, I find the knife rack, grabbing a small paring knife. It was silly to think the Lords could be defeated by the same instrument used to cut an apple, but I needed something small and lethal. I could tease them, lure them in if needed, and then I'd strike.

To make it believable, I'll need to play it cool. Make it seem like brownies were a thing I liked to do. Suddenly, I had an idea. Grabbing my real phone, I google brownie recipes—several of them, so Theo notices when he looks through my browser history. Then, I go on Instagram, reposting an old piece of art I did near the Brooklyn bridge. It's an image of a woman with angel wings and red eyes, getting fed a piece of cake by a man's hand. The caption is, *Half angel, half demon*. At the time, it was ironic—a demon woman on her knees for a man. It was supposed to show the dichotomy of femininity, but right now, it'll serve another purpose.

Reposting the image, I make the caption: *Anyone else bake when they're stressed?*

To make the point crystal clear, I even download a couple of small-town romance books with bakeries as the setting. Hopefully, this will work.

This is my only way out of this mess.

※

I spend the rest of the day helping Rose catalog Cecelia's items in the house, packing them up to send to the Cotswolds. Just like Rose and the guys suspected, she has no desire to come back to Blackwell House, and she even sends me a nice text telling me she'll be back soon to visit with Archie, and that I'm welcome in the Cotswolds any time. Around two, her things are packed and loaded into the moving truck, and by three, I look around at what used to be my father's house.

What now is *my* house.

Whatever happened with the guys doesn't matter. I would still be Lady Blackwell, and this place would still be mine. A week ago, that thought would've sent me screaming, but now? A lot has happened, and I'm a new person. A *different* person. I owe it to my father to take care of Rose and Teddy, to look after Archie, to look after the house that has been in our family for centuries.

I eat a quick dinner around six, retiring to my room shortly after.

I read for a couple of hours before I fall asleep, my eyes trained on the pan of brownies I plan to use tomorrow.

Tomorrow.

I'll be free and clear of every nightmare tomorrow.

CHAPTER 42

Sterling

I pick Harlow up at half past seven, and she walks out of the house wearing the white shorts and sports bra set I sent her. It's made of faux leather material, and with her hair pulled into a high ponytail, she looks like a sexy unicorn. She's carrying something wrapped in foil, as well as a large bag, and when she gets in, I stare down at the foil wrapped pan.

"Did you make me some mince and mash?" I joke.

She snorts. "I don't even know what that is."

"Think of it as a British casserole. Ground meat in a gravy with mashed potatoes."

"Hmm, I'm afraid it's not that. I made brownies for you all yesterday."

I glance down at the pan and back up at her face—which is indifferent and... expectant. She clears her throat.

"I just... I was thinking... I wanted to do something nice for you guys. I think I overreacted yesterday. I was angry, but after I calmed down and got a good night's sleep, I realized you were all right. I'm glad I killed my rapist. I feel strong, and worthy of being in this order."

I narrow my eyes. "Really?"

She scoffs as she buckles herself in. "Fine. You don't have to eat them." I reach for the pan, but she slaps my hand away. "Not now, you heathen. *After* we workout. I also brought some candles," she adds, shaking her bag. The sound of wax pillar candles clacking together permeates the air.

"Candles?"

She shrugs. "I thought you could show me some of your yoga stuff. They use candles... right?" she asks, twirling her hair.

180

Something is off about her today, but I can't put my finger on it. She's hiding something. "Sure. Yeah. We can use the candles if you want."

She smiles. I stare at her suspiciously before driving away.

"So, you guys all mentioned how my father betrayed your fathers, and that's why you were made Lords so young," she starts. "But are your mothers still alive?" She turns to face me.

I shake my head. "Two are dead, two are alive. Mine died just after I was born. Alaric's mother took her own life when he was eleven, Gideon's mother divorced his father and now lives in rural Scotland, and Theo's mother is too busy traveling to remember she has a son."

Her brows knit together. "I'm sorry."

I shrug. "My father raised me. I turned out okay. And Alaric had a line of matronly nannies to run to after his mom died. So, we survived."

She swallows. "Will you guys have to marry? To carry on the lineage of the Lords?"

"We need to produce an heir."

She squirms in her seat. "Will I need to produce an heir, too?"

I rub my mouth with one hand, trying not to smile as my other hand steers us to the gym. "You will. The Blackwell bloodline must go on."

She lets out a giggle. I sneak a peek at her, surprised by her lightheartedness. "You sound like King Henry VIII." She sighs. "Okay, fine. But what if I can't produce an heir? What if none of us produces heirs? What happens?"

"Well, then the Lords of Darkness would fall. For good."

We're both quiet until I pull up to the front of the gym. "Has that ever happened? You say the Lords of Darkness have been ruling for almost a thousand years, and in all that time, no one has dealt with infertility, or had a child die before they can produce an heir? I find that hard to believe."

I pull the parking brake, turning the engine of my car off. "Well, I'm sure over the years there have been some... unsavory methods for producing heirs. But no, for the most part, the order has progressed as it should. A few times, a niece, nephew, or sibling has taken the place of a Lord, but yes. For a thousand years, we've been breeding murder machines."

I like the way her chest flushes then, and her dark blue eyes flick up my arms and down my body, like she's drinking me in.

"Any more questions?" I ask. Her nostrils flare at my insinuation, so I reach out for her hand, taking it in mine. "What I mean is, we are your family now. You are a part of this order. Whatever questions you have, we will answer to the best of our ability."

She presses her lips together, and I swear she wants to say something, but doesn't. Instead, she climbs out of the car and heads inside the gym.

What the hell is up with her?

I follow her, and she sets her things by the door, grabbing water and heading to the treadmill. She quickly jumps on, starting at a fast walk and waving to the other guys, who are also watching her suspiciously. All three of them walk over to me as she moves into a jog, staring down at the dashboard of the treadmill with full concentration.

"What'd you do to her?" Alaric jokes, his skin still flushed and sweaty from his workout.

"I didn't do anything," I tell him, and we're all quiet as Harlow looks over at all of us—and *smiles*. "She's hiding something," I add, taking a sip of water. "Any news about the intruder?" I ask, referring to the person living in Theo's house.

Theo grunts. "Not yet. But I have a feeling it's tied to Acadia."

I turn to face him. "Acadia?"

He shrugs. "They've been suspicious since Armin disappeared. That's how long we suspect the person's been living up there. Plus, we found a book of Montenegrin poems."

I bite the inside of my cheek, thinking. "But why would they be spying on you? Why kill Brenda?"

"No idea. I guess we'll have to wait and find the guy."

We all finish our workouts, and I show Harlow the yoga studio. We do a few easy poses with the candles she brought, and then she walks over to the pan, unwrapping it and coming back over to where we're seated on the mats.

"I baked brownies," she tells them, holding the pan out.

My eyes find hers, and she gives me a large, uncharacteristic smile.

I would've believed her good intentions, would've taken a brownie without hesitation had her hand not been shaking so much.

"Brownies?" Alaric asks, staring into the pan and narrowing his eyes. "You bake brownies?"

I look at Alaric, and his nostrils flare just enough for me to know that the others are just as suspicious.

I sense all three guys watching me as I stand up, reaching into the pan and pulling one out. There's no way she was about to do what I think she was about to do, is there? I bring the baked treat to my nose, inhaling the cocoa scent.

Again, had I not been trained in espionage and a Lord of fucking Darkness, I would not have smelled the subtle hint of garlic wafting from the brownie she so kindly made us. We spent weeks training our senses to be mindful of certain poisons and gasses. I'd know the smell of cyanide and arsenic anywhere. Cyanide smells like bitter almonds, and arsenic smells a bit like garlic. But only when cooked. *Like in brownies.* Looking down at the square, I place it back in the pan, laughing.

I love the way her face pales, and I have to check the anger beginning to boil to the surface. My temper is not my friend, but right now, I'm fucking furious.

"It's interesting," I say, just as Harlow's grip on the pan tightens. "Most arsenic is undetectable to the senses since it has no smell or taste. But when arsenic is heated, it passes directly from a solid state to a gas and gives off a distinctive garlic odor."

Her whole body is trembling now, and the guys come up behind me as I take the pan from her.

"Sterling—"

Before she can give us any excuses, I throw the pan against the wall behind her. She screams and covers her head, and my nostrils flare when I see the hatred in her eyes.

"You were going to poison us," Theo says from next to me.

"With arsenic," I say slowly. "How the fuck did you get ahold of arsenic?"

Her lip quivers once before she takes a step back. I clench my fists at my sides, and when I glance at Alaric, he just looks… sad. Gideon is playing with his knife, looking just like he did the night we killed Charles.

Betrayed. Hurt. Confused.

Again.

I look between my brothers, trying to gauge how to proceed. On the one hand, I know we could and should kill her for this. After all, we killed her father for a similar transgression.

"Vintage fly paper."

I shake my head as I rub my mouth. "You want us dead?"

Her eyes begin to water, and she opens and closes her mouth. I look again at Alaric, and he nods once. It's all the confirmation I need.

I walk over to where the brownies are, grabbing one and holding it up in the air.

"Easy enough," I tell Harlow, who is now actively crying. Out of fear or remorse, I'm not sure. It doesn't matter. "You went through all the trouble," I tell her, my voice shaking with fury. "So, fuck it. Kill me. Kill us all."

I glare at her as she shakes her head without saying anything.

"One word, and I'll eat it," I threaten, still holding the brownie. "Let's end the order now, while there are no more heirs to continue," I add, my voice hoarse. "I'm calling for a vote," I drawl, looking at Alaric, Gideon, and Theo. "All in favor of eliminating ourselves?"

They all look sad now—even Theo.

And they're all just as crazy as me because they raise their fucking hands.

I'd eat this and die at her feet if she so wished. If she *actually* hates us as much as she thinks she does. And I know the others would, too.

I would do anything for her, which is why her betrayal stings so much.

"Four votes," I tell her, smiling like a maniac.

"Sterling, don't," she begs, reaching out for me.

I take a step back. "The Lords of Darkness will end tonight. The lineage will not continue. You will go into hiding. One thousand years, and it ends tonight."

She sobs again. I like hearing her cry. I *want* to hurt her.

Just like she hurt me. Just like she hurt all of us.

"I can't do it," she says softly. "I changed my mind."

"Too late," I growl, shoving the entire brownie into my mouth. She cries out, lunging forward, but Theo holds her back. Alaric retrieves the pan and hands Gideon and Theo a brownie, and they all eat just as quickly as I did. "You wanted to kill us?" I ask, chewing. Throwing my hands out to the side in surrender, I glare at her as I swallow. "You got your fucking wish."

To be continued…

LADY OF DARKNESS
BOOK TWO

AUTHOR'S NOTE

This is book two in a dark reverse harem romance series. It is advised to read the books in order. Lady of Darkness does not end on a cliffhanger, and there is a HEA. Please note: this book is dark. You will love the heroes, and then you will hate them before you love them again. If you're looking for villains who eventually turn good, that doesn't happen in this book. They are the antithesis to a romantic hero in every way. Please proceed with caution.

For a complete list of triggers, please visit my website here:

www.authoramandarichardson.com/triggers

For my readers. Thanks for loving the Lords so much already.

Such as we are made of, such we be.

William Shakespeare

PROLOGUE

ALARIC
   Fourteen Years Ago

I lean against the brick wall of Cross Manor, taking a drag of my cigarette as people in black pass me by. Black suits, black dresses, black fascinators, my house is awash in a sea of black. A few of the funeral attendees stop and offer their condolences, but it doesn't feel genuine. Their pitying smiles are fake. The way their hands grasp mine tightly, patting gently—all fake. When your family is as notorious as mine, people tend to be afraid, to keep their distance. Their words are as insincere as their simpering smiles, and I hate them all for it. They're only here because the circumstances surrounding my father's death are making people morbidly curious.

A gas leak.

As if a gas leak could take down one of the most powerful and cruelest men in England.

Tempest Cross is his name—*was* his name.

People revered him, and subsequently, me. It was just the two of us after my mother took her own life seven years ago, and I'd lived those years in fear of the man being buried today.

I was glad he was dead, because it meant I could focus on starting my own business after university.

It meant that my real life could start without the hovering scowl of disapproval.

Pushing off the wall, I stub the cigarette out with my dress shoe. The wake is over, and the committal is just wrapping up. I spy Gideon St. Claire, Sterling Beauchamp, and Theodore Wolf near the back. I don't know them well, though we all went to school together and our fathers were close. This is the fourth funeral in five days. Our fathers passed away in the same accident, and the entire country is abuzz with gossip. I give them all a sincere smile before finding my way to Cecelia Crawford, the daughter of one of my father's biggest rivals, though I couldn't tell you why. He hated the Crawfords for reasons unknown. Her family lives in the Cotswolds, and she's a few months younger than me. She's pretty, but she's not my type. Her parents stand next to her, along with Charles Blackwell on her other side. I feel the eyes of Charles boring into the back of my skull.

Twisting around to look at him, he smiles sympathetically.

I don't like him, nor do I trust him.

I'm not exactly sure what kind of bullshit my dad was wrapped up in, but I know it involved Charles–and Cecelia's family.

I shift uncomfortably as the committal finally ends, and people begin to scatter. Mary, my housekeeper, offered to host a celebration of life party at Cross Manor after the funeral, but I declined. The manor was mine now. As the Lord of the house, the last thing I wanted was people snooping around *my* home. I wanted peace and quiet. I wanted my own space, to find myself outside of my father's tight grip. I had dreams and aspirations, and nothing was going to stand in my way now.

Once everyone is gone, I head inside, where Mary is talking with Charles Blackwell.

What the hell is he still doing here?

Gideon, Sterling, and Theodore are all sitting at the dining room table, looking just as confused as I feel.

"Can I help you with something?" I ask Charles.

What I *really* want is for people to leave me the fuck alone.

Mary quickly disappears into the kitchen, and Charles turns around to face me. He's ten years older than the four of us, but you'd never guess it by looking at him. He's tall, fit, and clean shaven.

A snake in a suit.

He grabs five glasses from the bar, setting one down in front of each of us.

God, if this is some kind of heroic gesture now that we're all fatherless, I'm going to be sick.

I stay standing, unsure of what this is all about. Pouring us each a finger of whiskey, he gestures for me to sit. Narrowing my eyes as I do, I wait impatiently for the bullshit. Because that's all this is. Every single person, all of the pomp and circumstance in this whole damn community is a *farce*. I couldn't wait to be free of it.

I glance at the others, but they all seem as uncomfortable as me.

"Boys," Charles says, taking a sip of whiskey. We all do the same, and I try not to wince as it burns going down my throat. "Or shall I say... men." None of us says anything, and he just chuckles. "It's the dawn of a new era. You're all the Lords of your houses–the five most noble houses in England." Charles's dark blue eyes pin me to the spot. "Your fathers are dead, which means you are the new heirs to your estates."

"And what does that mean?" Gideon snaps, leaning forward. "Is there a reason you're telling us this while Tempest Cross is still warm in the ground?"

I've always liked Gideon. He gives zero shits. A small part of me wishes I could be more like him.

Charles swirls his whiskey and finishes it, setting the glass down. "You have so much to learn, and so little time to learn it."

"How scintillating," Theodore drawls, pouring himself another glass. "Are you going to cut to the chase, or are we going to be subjected to more of whatever nonsense this is?"

I like Theo, too. In a way, I wish we'd all been closer. As they sit here beside me, I realize we probably have much more in common than we think.

"Learn what?" Sterling asks, leaning back, narrowing his green eyes. He's holding the glass of whiskey with such a tight grip that his fingertips are white. I also take note of the fact that he hasn't had a single sip.

"How to kill without being killed," Charles says casually. "How to command the world."

I snort. "Do you really think English nobility has the power to command the world? No one cares about us. Not really," I retort.

Charles's smile doesn't waver. Instead, he just cocks his head and gives me a withering look. "I'm not speaking of your English nobility," he says slowly. "I'm speaking to you as the new Lords of Darkness."

CHAPTER 1

Harlow
One Week Ago

"The Lords of Darkness will end tonight. The lineage will not continue. You will go into hiding. One thousand years, and it ends tonight."
"I can't do it," I tell him. "I changed my mind."
Please don't do it.
"Too late," he growls.
And then he shoves the entire damn brownie into his mouth.
I scream. Cry. Thrash. Someone holds me back—I think it's Theo. If Sterling eats those brownies, he *will* die. And I can't let that happen.
To my horror, the other guys eat a brownie in the blink of an eye, and I scream again. My throat stings from the force of my crying, and my face is wet with tears.
"You wanted to kill us?" Sterling asks. He throws his hands out to the side, swallowing and giving me a look of hate mixed with melancholy. "You got your fucking wish."
I gasp as I sit up from my bed, one hand around my throat as panic fills me. The entire scene from earlier tonight drags through my mind slowly, each detail imprinted in my memory.
The horror as they all ate the brownies.
The screams I realized were mine.
The way Alaric calmly watched me with a pointed, challenging gaze.
Wasn't he scared?
Wasn't he afraid of dying?
The confusion when nothing happened, and the subsequent explanation.
I remember Theo walking over to me, crossing his arms. His normally blue

eyes were darker, more expressive. As he scowled down at me, his jaw feathered. He was angry, but there was also something else behind his eyes.

Hurt.

Confusion.

Disbelief.

I think it was the disbelief that killed me. They trusted me, and here I was plotting their death.

"Did you know that certain populations possess something called the AS3MT gene, Harlow?" Theo drawls, licking his fingers. "It's rare, but our bloodline carries it, likely because we built up a tolerance to arsenic over centuries. Tiny doses over many years... starting from the first year of being initiated."

I swallow. Of fucking *course they have a tolerance to* fucking *poison.*

I take a deep, calming breath as the rest of the night plays out before my eyes.

It was the silence—the pure, unadulterated hurt and fury on their faces—that sent me into a tailspin of nightmares tonight.

None of them said anything after that.

Sterling threw the pan away, and the guys packed up their things at the gym. Without a word, Gideon grabbed my arm and dragged me to his car.

I tried to talk, but every time, he would tell me I'm on *thin fucking ice.* Whatever the hell that meant. I felt like I was being scolded, like a little girl who got caught lying.

It was humiliating.

He dropped me off and sped away, and I'd been licking my traitorous wounds ever since.

Throwing the covers off with a huff, I walk downstairs for a glass of water. My throat still feels raw from screaming—from crying.

I drink an entire glass before setting it down. Looking out of the dark window, I don't see anything. But I know they're watching. If not outside, then somewhere in this kitchen.

Always watching.

It's only four in the morning, but I don't feel tired anymore. I make my way to my father's study, pulling my cardigan tighter around me as I sit down in his chair.

I tried so hard to fight it—to fight this life, this part of me. But the longer I stay, and the more I get to know the order, the more I realize this life is beginning to sink its claws into me, one day at a time. Scribbling on his fancy notepad, I tear the first few pages of notes off. It's just places and numbers—complete gibberish. I tear the pages one at a time, and then, six pages in, I see my name. My heart skips a beat as my eyes scan my father's handwriting. His normally neat scrawl is sloppy, like he was in a rush when he wrote it. I glance at the date—a month ago.

Right before he died.

Harlow,

I don't know if you'll read this, or even if you'll see this. If you are reading these words, it's because I'm gone. I want to say this before it's too late, so please, listen closely.

If the Lords have found you, go with them.
If you are scared, don't be.
You can trust them. Know that I'd never lead you astray.
They may seem hard around the edges, but this kind of life is hard for all of us, as you may one day come to find out. They are your brethren, and with them, you will find a true connection unlike anything you've ever known before.
Don't let that connection go.
I made many mistakes, and I regret them every day. If I could erase my mistakes, I would. Whatever they say about me after I'm gone... it's true.
I was selfish, power-hungry, and I thought I was better than my best friends.
Please don't be like me.
One last thing... it is an honor to be a Lady of Darkness. Use that honor wisely.
You have a big heart—just like your mother. Which is why I haven't written a letter for Archie. Do with that information what you will, but I think you can come to your own conclusions.
Take care of Archie.
Take care of Cecelia, as she had no part in all of this. Trust me on this one—it's important. Cecelia is innocent.
Take care of the Lords. They need you just as much as you need them.
Love,
Charles, your father

I don't realize I'm crying until a teardrop splatters onto the paper. Swiping at my cheeks, I take the letter and fold it up. Leaning back in the desk chair, I look up at the ceiling, willing myself to stop being such an emotional mess.

He knew they were going to kill him. He thought he deserved it. He probably did, though I still don't know what the betrayal was.

Can't have been worse than mine.

Why didn't the other Lords know about me? I suppose it was easy to hide my mother and I away, to keep me locked up in this house every summer when he was working.

And they wouldn't have felt the need to check after Archie was born. Why would they? My father had likely never mentioned me in order to keep me safe.

After a few minutes, I calm myself down and head back upstairs, where I proceed to ignore the letter, my father's betrayal, and that damn pan of brownies. Pulling my Kindle into bed, I begin to read one of my romance books. My throat stings when I think of Alaric and how he would lie down in his suit.

Like he cared.

Because he did. He did care. And I threw it all away by trying to kill them.

I squeeze my eyes shut and take a few more calming breaths. There's a hollowness in my chest, an aching emptiness since reading that letter.

I was selfish, power-hungry, and I thought I was better than my best friends.
Please don't be like me.

For the first time since his death... I think I miss my dad.

CHAPTER 2

Harlow
Present

I stare out of my window as the rain begins to slide down the glass in thick rivulets. Thunder booms from nearby, and the sky lights up every few seconds with lightning. I've always loved summer storms, and here, they're even more beautiful, lighting up the green, rolling hills, and old, stone fences. If I squint, it's as if no time has passed, as if this entire community has been existing with the storms for centuries, bending to its whims. I quickly change into my all-black workout outfit, courtesy of Sterling, and pull on my white sneakers.

If he wasn't a Lord of Darkness, he could definitely start a leisurewear fashion line.

I grab a raincoat from the hallway wardrobe—probably Cecelia's—and then I head downstairs for a quick cup of coffee and a freshly baked croissant. Rose is putzing around a large pot, probably making some sort of stew for dinner. I smile and tell her that I'll be out with Alaric—which is still my go-to excuse—and then I head out to the front door, where a dark grey Range Rover awaits me. Stopping midstep, I take a deep breath before walking up to the passenger door and pulling it open.

Alaric is waiting for me in the driver's seat, staring straight ahead and gripping the steering wheel with both hands.

"Hi," I say quickly, closing the door and buckling myself in.

He doesn't respond, not that I expect him to.

Ever since the *incident* last week, none of them have spoken more than two words to me. They spend their mornings bossing me around in the gym, and my afternoons are filled with learning about the Lords of Darkness. And it's not a *brief* history, either. They all make sure I retain every minute detail of every single Lord in the order since 1066.

Next week, we move on to lessons about espionage.

It's grueling, but it means that by the time they drop me off for dinner at six, I'm so exhausted that I barely have time to think about how I tried and failed to kill them—and how they're punishing me for it.

Gone are the jokes and the camaraderie. They're teaching me what they need to teach me out of obligation rather than pleasure, and I can tell they're still fuming. None of them can even look me in the eye.

Which is fine. I guess I deserve it. But it makes for boring days, and I hate myself for admitting that I miss them.

I miss how they'd laugh with me.

I miss how Alaric would show up in my bedroom.

I miss how Sterling would taunt me, and how Gideon would joke with me.

I miss Theo's smile.

It unnerves me that I miss them, the men who stole me from my real life and vowed to make it hurt in the process. I shouldn't feel anything for them, but I can't deny the hurt and loneliness of the past week.

The worst thing is, I wish they'd unleash themselves.

I *wish* they'd get their anger out. I want them to hurt me. I want to see them feel *something* other than cold indifference. I want to get any sort of reaction out of them, because right now, they're robots.

At least when they were monsters, I knew what to expect. Right now, I have no idea what's around the corner. No idea when that dam will break.

One thing I know for sure is... that fury is coming, and it's coming soon.

I just don't know how, or when.

And that fact *terrifies* me.

I look over at Alaric as he drives to the gym. His face has some extra scruff today, which is unlike him. He looks tired—*weary*. Clenching his jaw, he quickly glances over at me before turning back to the road.

This is a totally fucked up situation.

I should be mad at *them*.

They put me in a room with my rapist, and I was forced to kill him.

Just thinking about that day makes my blood turn cold.

And yet, I feel bad for doing what I did, for lacing those brownies with arsenic.

I was desperate.

I fought back.

And I lost.

I just didn't expect to keep paying for it a week later.

Once Alaric pulls into the gym and parks, I follow him inside the large warehouse and find the other guys already working out.

I can't help but drool a little as Theo does pull-ups effortlessly, his taut, muscled skin glistening with sweat. His light blue eyes sweep over me briefly before he resumes staring at the wall in front of him. I try not to stare at the way his corded arms work his body upward, how his muscles curve and twist as he does twenty more. Flicking my eyes to Sterling, I watch as he jogs casually on one of the treadmills. When his green eyes find mine, something dark passes behind them before he goes back to ignoring me, his fists clenched. Gideon is on one of the spin bikes, concentrating on the screen as he breathes. His hair is unbound and falls to his shoulders, held away from his face by a headband. I've never seen him with his hair down, but I like it. He ignores me completely, so I find my way to the treadmills to get my least favorite part of the workout out of the way.

At least I'm up to two miles now, and I don't feel like a weakling anymore.

Over the last two weeks, I've noticed my endurance increasing, tiny muscles beginning to form on my arms, stomach, and legs. Nothing substantial to anyone but me, but still, it makes me feel like I'm working toward something.

Like this is all for some greater good.

I start off slow, increasing my speed until I find my preferred pace. Sterling looks over at me, and when I look at him, he snaps his eyes away.

Fine.

Be mad.

It doesn't bother me.

Grinding my jaw, I increase my speed.

I can do this.

I don't need their friendship.

All I have to do is survive and get through this, and then maybe one day, they'll forgive me.

When I'm finished, I drink some water and stretch. The guys are all huddled in the corner, and I glance over to where they're standing every few minutes as I cool down. I don't like the hushed murmurs, so I try to ignore it—along with the hurt feeling of being left out. I think that's why all of this sucks so much. They encouraged me to become a Lady of Darkness, told me that we'd all be close and there wouldn't be any secrets between us. And yet, I still haven't been privy to any sensitive information. I assume it's because I'm not fully trained, but I know they're also keeping things from me out of spite.

I didn't just hurt myself the day I tried to kill them.

I hurt *them*.

It's like a giant, gaping chasm has formed between me and the guys, and now, things are cold and awkward. But hopefully not irreparable.

I regret what I did, but I'm ready to move on. Only they're still licking their wounds.

Just as I'm about to stand up, Alaric walks over to me and reaches a hand out. I take it skeptically, knowing their whispers and this peace offering are somehow related. Still, feeling how easily he pulls me up with his large, warm hand makes me happy.

Maybe they're *finally* ready to forgive me.

"Grab another water. We're going on a walk."

"A walk?"

"Sorry, I forgot you Americans call it something else. We're going hiking."

He frowns down at me and gives me a withering look before turning away and heading toward the front door.

Okay, maybe not.

CHAPTER 3

HARLOW

Alaric drives us all to the edge of town, near Blackwell Cemetery. I'm in the passenger seat. There's been no attempt to position me on anyone's lap. In fact, they've barely touched me since that day. Whatever they thought they desired in me is gone... extinguished.

It's probably better this way.

It's still raining, and I'm glad I thought of grabbing a rain jacket this morning. Alaric parks on the side of the road, and we all walk in single file for a few minutes, skirting the edge of Oxbridge Forest. I haven't been over this way in years, but I know we're on the southeast part of Blackwell, near Beauchamp House. When I look behind me at Sterling, I see he's focused straight ahead. Pulling my hood up and my jacket tighter, I follow Alaric into the dark woods.

"Where are we going?" I ask, and none of them attempt to answer me.

Great.

We continue further and further, until we reach what looks like the beginning of an upwards path. There are hills in Blackwell, but the hills here are nothing compared to places like upstate New York. They're softer, more rolling. Still, we wind upwards for what feels like hours, zigzagging up what looks like a bunny hill, but what feels like Mt. Everest. My legs begin to burn, and I empty the entire second water bottle before we reach the top. The guys trek on as if this is a piece of cake, and I'm nearly gasping for air trying to keep up.

"Are we almost there?" I ask between pants.

"Not even close," Theo grumbles from the front of the group.

I resist the urge to whimper.

A few minutes later, they turn left, veering through the woods at a steep incline. I take back everything I ever thought I knew about the terrain in Blackwell. Maybe there is a mountain somewhere. I vow to look next time I'm in town.

"What about now?" I ask, trying really hard to keep the whine out of my voice.

I will *not* break down because of a small mountain climb.

He says nothing.

No answer, no acknowledgment that they heard me.

I continue on, even after I begin to see stars, even as my mouth dries out completely and I've shed all clothes except my sports bra and leggings. The tiny hairs at the base of my neck are sticking to my skin, and my legs shake with every step. I refuse to show weakness, and even as they all slow down and we reach what I assume is the top, I can't catch my breath.

"Fifty sit-ups," Alaric says, looking at me with his hands on his hips. He has his shirt off, and if I wasn't actively dying, I might be admiring how his shorts hang over his visible bulge.

"What?" I ask, still wheezing.

"You heard me."

I look down, and it's only mud and rocks. "Here? In the mud?" Alaric crosses his arms and waits, not answering me. "Is this how it's going to be from now on?" I ask, the wobble in my voice evident. "Punishing me? Pushing me like this, day in and day out? What's the point? I said I was sorry…"

He cocks his head and sucks in his cheeks. "We'll punish you for however long we see fit. And I'm not going to ask you again. Fifty sit-ups."

I choke back a sob as I get down onto the ground, wincing as the small pebbles dig into my back and the cold, gritty mud seeps into my pores. It hurts, and five sit-ups in, I grab my jacket to put underneath me. By number thirty, my whole body is trembling.

By number forty, I feel like I'm going to throw up.

I get to fifty only by screaming, and then I roll over and vomit up every ounce of water I've had today.

When I sit up, I wipe my mouth with the back of my hand. Everything hurts, and I'm starting to feel dizzy.

"Fifty push-ups," Gideon says, and I swing around to look at him.

"I can't," I tell him, no longer caring if I sound pathetic. The rain is pouring down on me now, and I'm completely soaked. We all are.

"Can't? Or won't?"

I feel my lower lip crack as I look between all of them. "You want to punish me? Fine. But you can't push me past my breaking point and expect my body to cooperate. I'm not a puppet. I can only do so much," I add, my voice breaking on the last word.

"Fifty push-ups," Gideon says, giving me a monstrous smile. "You say you're not a puppet, but you forget that we can command you however we please."

I grind my teeth together. "To an extent. I am tired. I physically cannot do it, Gideon."

"My Lord," he growls.

My eyes widen. "What?"

"You will address me as *My Lord*."

Despite being hot and sweaty, my blood cools at his words—at the cool indifference in his tone. And yet... his eyes travel down my body as he tilts his head, assessing me. The way his hungry eyes take me in makes my whole body tingle.

I can't keep up with how I feel around them, and apparently, neither can my libido.

Gideon walks over to me and grabs my wrist, tugging me into his hard, wet body. He smells like earth and sweat, and something about seeing his hair unbound and wild, about being in nature with him—a goddamn psychopath—it makes my knees weak, my core molten, despite my mind screaming to get away.

"You have to earn our trust back, Harlow. Don't you think for one second that we're ever going to forgive and forget what you did, little monster." I whimper as he reaches up and tugs my wet ponytail back with his other hand, exposing my neck. "Your punishment is under *my* jurisdiction. It is *my* decision. Not yours. With your betrayal, you have lost your autonomy. So you will do as I say, act as I please, and submit to me—*to us*—fully. Am I making myself clear?"

"Yes," I whisper.

He tugs harder. "Yes, what?"

I hate him. I hate him, and I am still so angry about everything. Him bossing me around like this sparks the fury that's been boiling underneath the surface.

He grips my hair tighter, and I groan, my scalp stinging. *Why do I like this and hate this at the same time?*

"Yes, my Lord." Gideon lets me go, and I stumble forward. I look at all of them defiantly. "Funny how I have to earn *your* trust back. How easily you all forget that you lost mine the second you put me in a cage with my rapist." I swear I see all of their hard expressions falter for just a second.

I drop to my knees and place my hands in the mud. I do twenty push-ups before taking a short break, and my arms shake by the time I get to thirty. It's extra effort trying to keep my palms from sliding around in the mud. Alaric and Sterling walk over to the edge of the outlook a few yards away. Sterling is on the phone, and I'm guessing some issue cropped up with Acadia again. I've heard them talking about it.

I don't care.

At thirty-five, my arms give up completely, and I fall onto my stomach.

Theo mounts me, grabbing my hair and pulling my neck back. My eyes find Gideon's. They're glinted, and he licks his lips as he watches us. "I only counted thirty-five. Get up and do fifteen more," he growls, pushing me down into the dirt.

"I can't."

Fuck you.

Suddenly, he flips me over and takes my wrists, pressing them down in the mud above my head. I thrash against him as anger blazes in his expression. He scowls down at me and knocks my legs apart with his knee, settling himself between them. I am *covered* in mud. Head to toe. Lowering himself, he thrusts against me.

His hard cock presses against my clit, and I bite back a whimper.

"Do you think those boring lessons and grueling mornings at the gym are the only things we can do to you, little monster?" he asks, bending down so that his mouth is near my ear. "Not even close. The things we could do would make your nightmares scream. You think this is bad?" I grunt in response, ignoring my throbbing, traitorous clit. "Or did you forget that we own you?"

"I thought we were all equals?" I ask, trying to get away.

He chuckles. It's that same dark chuckle that makes me break out into a cold sweat, that sends ice skittering down my spine. And yet, when he thrusts against me with his cock once more, fire explodes inside of me, and I moan.

"We were equals," he growls, licking the side of my neck. "But then you fucked us over, didn't you?"

I cry out, pleasure exploding inside of me as he thrusts against me again. The friction hurts a little because of our damp clothes, but it also feels... incredible. I hate myself for liking it. For *craving* it.

"You psychopaths locked me in a cage with my rapist," I hiss, pushing against him. "What did you expect? You deserved it," I bite back.

When he thrusts this time, I actually see stars.

"Did we? Because all I saw were men so intent on helping you that they got carried away. You tried to *kill* us," he grits out with another thrust.

I can't help it, I cry out this time. "This doesn't feel like punishment," I say, taunting him as I roll my hips against his shaft.

He roars in anger, and the sky suddenly unleashes. Thick raindrops pelt down on top of us as Theo stares at me. Except, it's not a man behind those eyes.

It's a beast–a predator.

"Do not disobey me, Harlow," he murmurs, reaching lower and pulling my leggings down slightly so that he can get his hand inside. "Do not taunt me. Do not *play the game* unless you're ready to play by *my* rules."

I gasp when his hand comes between my legs, spreading my pussy as I grind against him. He rubs two fingers against my clit, and I groan as he roughly inserts a third finger inside of me. I feel Gideon kneel behind me, can see him in my peripheral vision. *Gods... two of them. Both of them.*

At the same time.

Yes.

"This pussy... is ours," he growls. He looks up at Gideon, and something passes between them. I feel wet instantly just thinking about them together.

The rain cools my heated, flushed skin. Gideon's hands run through my hair, and I feel him move above me, unsheathing his massive cock. He strokes it just above my face.

"Technically, it's theirs, too," I say breathlessly, looking over at Alaric and Sterling. Sterling is too busy talking on the phone, but Alaric's eyes glimmer with something dark and heated as he watches the three of us. Heat flares across my skin and down my limbs, pooling in my core and making my pussy contract and flutter around his fingers.

"Yeah? So if we all want to pump your pussy full of our come, that's fine with you?"

God, yes.

"If we want to take turns fucking you so hard that you see stars, that's fine with you?"

Yes, please.

"Even if we make it hurt?"

Especially if it hurts.

I don't answer out loud, and he works his hand harder. The pebbles and grit underneath me dig into my back, and I know I'm covered in sweat and mud. Still, there's something so primal about the way he's fucking me with his hand, right out in the open in the pouring rain. I moan and gyrate against his touch, and he pinches my swollen clit. *Hard.*

Gideon rubs the edge of his cock against my lips, and I open for him without hesitation, sticking my tongue out.

He takes advantage, lowering himself so that he's fucking my mouth upside down. The way his hips move, pushing past my teeth into the back of my throat...

I gag, crying out as Theo pinches my clit again.

"Do not mistake this as something for your enjoyment," Theo growls. "This is for me. For us. This is us taking what we want."

A wet piece of white-blond hair falls in front of his face. I look back at Gideon, at the way he has his lower lip between his teeth, how his hair is dripping wet onto his bare chest...

Fuck.

I close my eyes and arch my back, my throat full of Gideon's shaft. What they don't understand is that *I* want this, too.

Even if it hurts.

Gideon pulls out and readjusts, and I take the time to make a snarky comment.

"If it was for your enjoyment, wouldn't you be fucking me?" I ask, keeping my eyes on Theo.

I hear the rip before I feel the rain against my pelvis. Theo removes his hand from inside of me and unsheathes his cock from his shorts. Placing it against my slit, he slides it between the wetness pooling there. I buck my hips as he moves again, not penetrating me, but positioning himself perfectly enveloped in my folds. When he thrusts upward, he hits my clit, and I see stars.

Gideon pushes into my mouth again, and I swallow him as much as I can.

Theo's precome laces with my arousal, and beads of sweet precome from Gideon's cock drip down my throat. Everything about this is downright dirty. As Theo presses down harder, I moan around Gideon's thickness. Looking up at Theo, his icy blue eyes are locked onto my face, and his jaw is tight as he thrusts again.

This doesn't even remotely resemble lovemaking.

This is them punishing me in a whole new way, and I already know they're going to leave me bereft and wanting. *That* is their revenge. Giving me enough to beg for more, but not granting that wish.

Gideon pulls away before thrusting back along my wetness slowly. It's torture. The next time he does it, I speak.

"Fuck me. Please. Both of you." I hate how desperate I sound, but I need one of them inside of me. I need to feel one of them on top of me, stretching me.

Theo raises himself enough to place a hand around my neck, glaring down at me with pure hatred.

He's *hate fucking* me.

Instead of answering me, he growls as he closes his hand around my throat, using his other hand to hold himself up. I choke as he drives between my slit harder, faster. Gideon moves behind him, stroking himself hard and fast as he glares at me from behind Theo. I can't make any sounds thanks to Theo's tight hold, but my whole body goes taut as his cock begins to spurt onto my stomach. Working my hips, I try to chase my climax, but he pulls away before I have the chance. I am *so* close–three more seconds, and I would've fallen over the edge. Instead, he stands up as I gasp for air, pulling his shorts up and leaving me on the ground, like a discarded doll.

"Hey!" I don't bother cleaning up. He ripped my leggings straight down the seam, so I grab the raincoat and quickly wrap it around my waist to hold them up.

Bastard.

Gideon watches me as I hold back a sob, jabbing a finger into Theo's chest.

"What the *hell*?!" I ask, trying to keep my voice from shaking.

Theo looks down at my finger and then grabs my wrist, squeezing tight. Pulling me into his soaking wet body, he bends down and purrs into my ear.

"What's wrong, little monster? Is your needy clit throbbing?"

"Fuck you," I growl, trying to pull away. I hear Gideon laugh behind me, and the next thing I know, Gideon is spinning me around and pushing me down to my knees. My skin cries out as the pebbles dig into my flesh.

"What did we tell you?" Gideon asks, his voice firm and soft all at once. "This is your punishment."

I choke back a sob. "I told you I was sorry–"

"Saying sorry isn't going to cut it. I'm pissed off. Fucking livid. Because I trusted you, and you broke that trust."

I look up at him, and even through the pouring rain, I can see the emotion passing over his expression. But a second later, it's gone, replaced by that cruel indifference.

"Finish what you started," he demands, pushing his rock-hard cock back into my mouth.

I hollow my cheeks and use both hands, rotating between soft and hard, fast and slow. He groans loudly as my hand moves to his balls, and I feel them tighten instantly.

"Swallow," he grits out.

I smile against his taut shaft as he comes. *He fucking wishes.*

His come fills my mouth as he groans, and he jerks as the last of it leaves his body. I pull away, and then I spit his come onto the dirt, making eye contact the entire time.

Pure wrath and ire cross his face, and he growls as he grabs me by the jaw, lifting me up. I cry out in pain as he tries to force my mouth open.

"What the fuck did you just do?" he seethes. I glare back at him as my chest rises and falls. "Open your mouth."

I keep my jaw closed, but he forces it open and then he spits inside of it.

He *spits* in my mouth.

"You will swallow me today, little monster. One way or another." Shoving me away, he walks over to Alaric and Sterling, who are watching with humorless expressions.

I spit it out and wipe my mouth with the back of my hand.

"Bastard."

He ignores me, because of course.

I begin to shake as my body fully cools, and I wrap my arms around myself. Alaric mutters something to the guys, and they all follow him down the mountain. I stay up there for a few minutes by myself, holding in the dam of tears that want to spring free.

Not because I didn't come, or because they're punishing me, or because Gideon spit in my mouth.

But because I *hurt* them.

And that means at some point, I meant something to them.

These men—these four brooding, savage men—they *cared* about me enough to be hurt by my betrayal.

They cared enough about me to *almost* die. To eat those brownies, to tempt fate.

I remember what they said that first night, the night that changed everything.

Don't be scared, little monster. You've just inherited a whole goddamn family. Your blood runs black, just like ours.

They accepted me from day one. Considered me family, from day one.

They'd have to get through us first, little monster. And that's sure as fuck never going to happen once you're officially ours.

Protecting me from day one.

Of course they're hurt.

I took their trust and killed it.

Now, I'd have to earn it back.

One way or another.

CHAPTER 4

Harlow

Later that afternoon, I'm trying not to fall asleep during a PowerPoint about rival crime syndicates, when the name Crawford comes up. I sit up straighter as the family tree appears, and to my surprise, Cecelia's name and picture are on the screen. I read the information provided, feeling my stomach drop as it sinks in.

The Crawford Family dates back to 1200 A.D. They currently reside in a small village in the Cotswolds, with George Crawford, the current leader of the Crawford empire. Since its founding, the Crawfords have been attempting to undermine the Lords of Darkness in every way possible. Most recently, George Crawford set up a marriage between Cecelia, his eldest daughter, and the late Charles Blackwell, previously one of the Lords of Darkness. It is thought that George and Charles were secretly working together, with Charles feeding sensitive information to George for several years before his unfortunate death.

"What the fuck?" I whisper, looking around the small room.

His unfortunate death.

I'm watching these boring presentations in a room off of their office, so I stand up and march outside, finding all four of them working on computers. It makes me pause for a second, because right now, they look so ordinary–simply men in suits, working on their computers.

I clear my throat.

"How come no one told me about Cecelia?"

Alaric cracks his knuckles. "It wasn't pertinent for you to know at the time."

"Is that why you told me she wouldn't fight me for the title and house? Because her father..."

I trail off, remembering something Rose said a couple of weeks ago.

Running this house by herself was always a daunting prospect, and her father is... very overprotective.

Theo laughs. "George Crawford would never let his daughter reside in the house of a Lord of Darkness. Once Charles died, she went right back to her family, because her being in Blackwell was of no use to her father anymore. He's still licking his wounds now that their informant—your father—is dead. Their access to our information was severed."

I open and close my mouth, trying to digest everything he's telling me. "Does Cecelia know?"

Gideon shakes his head. "No. She never knew she was just a pawn in their game."

My father's words from his letter filter back into my mind.

I made many mistakes, and I regret them every day. If I could erase my mistakes, I would. Whatever they say about me after I'm gone... it's true.

I was selfish, power-hungry, and I thought I was better than my best friends.

Please don't be like me.

"What does this mean about Archie?"

"George already has an heir, Cecelia's older brother, plus or minus a few nephews, so Archie was never a target. If you'd walked away from the Lords, Archie would've become a Lord of Darkness, just like we said he would. George would not have fought us on it."

I sit down on the couch next to Alaric's desk. "Was my mother..." I trail off, swallowing.

The truth is, ever since I found out about the Lords, I wondered if my mother ever knew. If she ever suspected what my father was a part of, or what kind of bloodline she was carrying forward.

"No," Alaric says slowly. "Your mother and father were young and in love. She knew him before he was a Lord."

I nod. I vaguely remember my grandfather, and that he died when I was really little. "So, Cecelia's family was working with my father, but Cecelia didn't know about it?"

Alaric clears his throat. "Yes. And neither did we, until a few weeks ago. He kept everything very cleverly hidden." His eyes rove over my face. "He kept a lot of things very cleverly hidden."

I look down at my boots, trying to understand. "But why would he do that? Why feed information to the Crawford family, going against you and every ancestor we ever had? Why ruin something almost a thousand years old?"

Gideon shrugs from his position in front of me. "We don't know the reason. Stupidity, greed, or a blind desperation for power... who knows. But for now, the Crawfords have backed off. We handed Cecelia back unharmed—something we didn't have to do, mind you—and George knows she will be our first target if he decides to go after us."

"I had to scrub our servers, delete any sensitive information, and transfer it to a new server," Theo interjects. "He basically had every single piece of information funneling to the Crawfords—every email, every target, every text. I'm surprised they didn't kill us. They had many opportunities. Instead, they studied us, which is even more disconcerting. We were vulnerable as hell, but I learned my lesson. We now all have to approve any new contacts to the system, and our entire infrastructure is visible to all of us. The comings and goings, *everything*. Any changes require a 30-character password from each of us." His icy blue eyes bore into mine. "It's impossible to penetrate now—more secure than the U.S. government."

I swallow. "That's good."

"If anyone tries to betray us, I will be the first to know." He cocks his head as he peers at me from over the computer.

I snap my gaze to Sterling, who is watching me from the corner of the office. "So, what? We just move on knowing my father was working with the Crawfords, but not knowing why?"

Sterling pushes off from the wall, and I shrink back as he comes to stop a foot away from me. Looking up at him, I hate how sexy he looks when he's all commanding and pissed off.

"There are a lot of people we'd like to kill, Harlow. Hundreds. *Thousands*. But we do not, because it would disrupt the order of the world. Charles may have been working with the Crawfords, but he paid the consequences of that betrayal with his life. Now, we move on, and deal with our real enemy."

"You mean Acadia," I say slowly. Theo grumbles something from behind his computer, but none of them answer me. Sterling walks back over to his desk, and Alaric and Gideon are looking at something on Gideon's phone. "You know, you have to tell me eventually. Whether you like it or not, I am a part of this order."

They all go still, and Alaric glares over at me. His black eyes are emotionless and cold. "Is that so? Because last time I checked, you were ready to do just about anything to get away from us."

Touché.

I roll my bottom lip between my teeth, placing my palms underneath my bare thighs. I'm wearing jean shorts and a baggy t-shirt tonight. There's supposed to be a heatwave tomorrow, and the weather is already hot and muggy. I can't keep up with the English weather fluctuations in the summer.

"I just mean, withholding information from me isn't going to help anyone. Maybe I can offer a fresh perspective," I tell them, my voice perky.

I'm met with four identical scowls.

"We will begin to share information with you once we feel the time is right. Let's get you trained, and then we can talk."

I visibly sag, pouting. "Fine. But if they try to kidnap me or something, knowing more about them might be helpful."

Theo snorts from his place at the desk. "You sure think highly of yourself, don't you, little monster?"

Standing up, I walk back to the small classroom they have set up for me. "I don't know how many times I can say I'm sorry before my tongue falls off," I tell them all before heading back inside the dark room.

Around six, Sterling drops me off at home, driving off before I'm even inside.

They can't stay mad at me forever.

I just have to remind myself of that.

I do regret what I did—mostly because I was caught, but that's neither here nor there. Truly, I don't know how I would've felt if they had died—if the poison had worked, and they had sacrificed themselves like that. What was my plan? Four dead bodies that weighed nearly twice as much as me... was I just going to light the place on fire and call it a day?

I ball my fists uncomfortably as I walk around the perimeter of Blackwell House. Pulling my phone out, I sigh and dial Gemma's number. It's time to tell her as much as I can—and to sort my life in New York. Just thinking about going back, after everything I've been through, seems strange. I'm a different person now, and going back to that life doesn't quite feel right.

And neither does this life with four angry Lords.

"Oh my God, finally," Gemma says quickly, speaking in a hushed tone. "I've been meaning to talk to you for *over a week*."

I laugh. "I'm sorry. I've been... busy."

I hear a door close on the other line. "I have so much to tell you."

Smiling, I sit on one of the benches in the rose garden. "Me too."

"Okay, you go first. Tell me everything."

I take a deep breath. Here goes nothing... "Well... I met someone. And... I think I'm going to stay here. At least for a few months. Sort out my dad's house. Figure out my life."

She shrieks on the other end. "What! You met someone? Who is he? Is he a Duke?"

"No, but he is a Lord." *Just not the kind of Lord you're used to...*

"Oh my God. Okay, well, I am sad you're not coming back. But wait, didn't your dad have a wife and a kid?"

Yeah... about that...

"Cecelia and Archie have decided to stay with her family for a while. Which leaves the house in my possession. I can't just leave it, you know?"

She sighs. "Damn. I get it. I don't like it, but I get it. What about NYU?"

"I don't know... I guess I can look into going to college here? Maybe taking a gap year?"

"Won't you lose your scholarship?"

I'm quiet for a few seconds. *Shit.* I didn't even think of that. Damn the *Lords*.

"I honestly haven't thought that far ahead, Gem. I'm taking it day by day." I'm not even lying about that.

"Okay. We're going to come back to this. Now, tell me about this mysterious Lord."

I almost say *which one*, but I stop myself just in time. "He's older. Lives in Blackwell. I like him... a lot."

She squeals. "I can't wait to meet him."

Will that ever happen? Theo mentioned that was a possibility the first night. It's a question for another day...

"Your turn," I say quickly, changing the subject.

LADY OF DARKNESS

I hear her move somewhere else, possibly somewhere quieter. "I met someone, too. His name is Luka, and he's from a place... hold on a sec, I need to pronounce it correctly. Monte... Montenegro?"

My blood turns to ice as she giggles on the other line. "What?" I ask, barely a whisper.

"I know. I hadn't heard of it either. I actually met him outside of our building. He was taking photos of the building for work—at least that's what he said—and we started talking... I told him about you, and how you were in England, and then he took me out to lunch, and well... I think I'm in love, Harlow."

No.

No.

No.

It couldn't possibly be someone from Acadia, could it?

"You told him about me?"

She laughs. "Well, yeah. He was there the day those crazy movers were boxing up your stuff. Which, by the way, was not cool. A warning would've been nice."

My head begins to spin. "Right, the movers..."

The day the *Lords* sent my stuff to Blackwell House. They'd packed everything up at Gemma's house and moved it to Blackwell House without my permission. The thought still makes my blood boil.

"Gemma, please be careful. It sounds like you hardly know the guy."

She scoffs. "I mean, the same could be said for you, bestie."

"You're right. Just... call me if you need anything. Keep your head on straight."

"I promise I will. You too. Talk soon, okay?"

"Okay. Love you."

We hang up, and I stare at my phone for a few seconds before moving into action. I text the guys.

Me: Is there someone named Luca, or Luka, who works for Acadia?
Alaric: Why?
Me: Because I think he's going after my best friend, Gemma.
Theo: Luka Jovovic. 24. Confirmed member of Acadia.

My heart beats wildly against my ribs. *That was fast,* but of course, Theo has the world at his fingertips.

Me: He's in New York with Gemma. I think he was looking for me. She met him taking pictures outside of her building.
Theo: One sec. Let me search his travel history. He's on my suspect list for Brenda's murder. He'd been in London that same day.

I swallow.

God, what the hell have I gotten myself into?

It was one thing to sacrifice myself—to subject myself to this life. But Gemma? She's innocent, and her parents are almost never around. She's young and vulnerable, and I hate myself for putting her in danger.

Gideon: The timing would match up.
Theo: Yup. Confirmed. He caught an evening flight from London to

215

NYC the same day we found Brenda's body. Which means he was in NYC the next day.

Me: That's the day you boxed up my stuff, and the day he met Gemma.

Me: Oh God. We have to keep her safe. What if they kill her?!

Sterling: Relax, Harlow. We'll take care of it.

Me: Just keep her safe. Please.

Theo: I'll keep a close eye on him. Four of my guys are on their way to Gemma's flat. In disguise, of course.

Alaric: We'll keep her safe, little monster.

Me: Thank you.

I set my phone down and look around the rose garden. They'll protect her. They'll keep her safe. Everything is going to be okay. If there's one thing I know is true, it's that they are powerful, and they can call on hundreds—or thousands—of people to do their bidding.

Please, let Gemma be safe.

Standing up, I look up at Blackwell House, ornate and grand against the deep blue sky. I love how late it stays light here in the summer—as a kid, it meant I could play outside longer. Stretching my legs, I begin the short walk back to the house when a man appears from behind one of the rose hedges.

Panic fills me as he saunters closer, an overcoat flowing behind him. His dark hair is coiffed perfectly—longer on top, shaved on the sides. He has golden skin and black eyes. He's frowning, and he's also huge. I stiffen, trying to remember what the guys taught me about self-defense. But before I can even process what's happening, another man appears to my right, also wearing a dark overcoat.

"Who are you?" I ask, my voice higher than I intended. I hold my fists up.

The first man chuckles. "Ah, I figured you'd already guessed. After all, weren't you just talking about me?"

Luka.

I open my mouth to scream, but the second guy wraps an arm around me and presses a cloth to my mouth. I inhale once, smelling something ether-like and sweet, before everything goes black.

CHAPTER 5

Sterling

I set my phone down, rubbing my eyes and turning to face the guys. We've been at the office since Harlow's frantic texts about an hour ago, working on locating Luka Jovovic. His trail went dark earlier today, likely as a precaution. He's well-connected. There's a good chance he knows, or at least suspects, we are keeping tabs on him. Still, I don't like not knowing where he is, especially with Harlow's friend so vulnerable. Our guys just arrived at her flat, and they've confirmed she's safe and sound. I open up the security app to check on Harlow, but I don't see her anywhere.

"Is she still in the rose garden?" I ask, squinting at the back camera. The video feed cuts off near the brass gate, and we saw her go in, but she never came out.

"Guessing so," Alaric mumbles. "Her phone record shows she was on the phone with Gemma."

I pull up her phone record on my computer. "Yeah, but that call ended over an hour ago."

"Check the location," Theo murmurs. "She's still there. Probably just sulking."

"I wonder why," I bite back.

Theo snorts. "She deserved every damn thing we subjected her to today."

"Even your cock?" Gideon interjects.

Theo glares at him. "You're one to talk, you bastard."

I can't help but smile. I pull out my phone and text her, which is unlike me. But something is worrying my mind a bit... the fact that both Harlow and Luka have gone silent at the same time.

Me: Can confirm that Gemma is safe. We won't let her out of our sight.

Alaric walks over to me and stares down at his phone. "Why would she just be sitting out there? It's nearly sunset, and she's never done that." He dials her number, scowling at the wall as it rings and rings. He hangs up. "She didn't answer."

"Fuck," I murmur, trying her from my phone. "Honestly, these two probably scared her off," I accuse, narrowing my eyes in Gideon's direction.

It goes to voicemail, and I stand up. "Alright. Let's go make sure she's okay."

Theo and Gideon aren't smiling anymore, and we all high-tail it to Blackwell House in Alaric's car.

None of us say anything. We're all imagining the worst. I know I am. Because of our jobs, we encounter serial killers, crime lords, and the biggest drug dealers in the world. These are the people associated with us.

If she's gone...

Anyone could have her. *Anyone.* All it takes is three seconds, and we know Acadia is adept at splicing security feeds because of Brenda's murder. We've been distracted trying to find Luka. Something could've easily slipped past us. My heart races with possibilities.

If anyone hurts her, I will not stop until they're all piles of ash.

I vow to keep a closer eye on her, to put more safeguards, to implement more safety protocols. We've had a slew of security guards at her house, but a security guard is nothing compared to some of the most highly trained criminals in the world.

We recruited her as a Lady—a fifth, vital leg of our order—and yet, something could've happened to her. *Because* of us.

My throat swells and I ball my fists.

Once we drive through the gate of Blackwell House, we all sprint to the back garden. Harlow's phone is laying face down in the dirt, and a small, white cloth sits a few feet away. I pick it up and sniff, rearing my head back when I realize what it is.

"Chloroform," I growl, fisting the material in my hand. It's only then that I see the 'A' monogrammed on the cloth. As if her captors want us to know who took her. Turning to face the guys, I bare my teeth. My pulse is pounding in my ears, the rushing sound making everything seem faint. *They fucking have her.*

Without a word, I grab the nearest planter, ripping it from the ground and smashing the white ceramic pot against the dirt ground. The shards explode, but none of the guys shrink back. In fact, their expressions are just as murderous as mine.

Acadia.
They took her.
They took what's ours.

"Fuck!" I scream as we all quickly make our way back to Alaric's car. I punch the side of it, not caring about anything. I'd burn this car for her. I'd do anything for her—for any of the guys, really.

We were all a team.

LADY OF DARKNESS

A quintet.

And now she's gone.

We weren't keeping a close enough eye on her, and now she's gone.

The guilt hurts the most, followed by unadulterated fury.

"If they hurt her, I will rip their heads off myself," Theo grits out.

"They know better than to fuck with us," Alaric growls. "They're going to use her as a bargaining chip," he adds, speeding down the road to Theo's house.

Theo will find them. I'm confident of that fact.

But what will they have done to her?

Acadia especially—the motherfucking kings of human trafficking.

If they wanted to make her disappear, I have no doubt they could find a way. That's the thing with their sick industry. They take people and turn them into new people—*hidden* people.

Hopefully Alaric is right and they wouldn't think of fucking with us.

"If they so much as touch her," Gideon starts, his voice deep and menacing. "I will cut them from head to toe. I will take their entire network down, one person at a time. With my bare hands."

"That's a given," I snarl. "They fucked with the wrong men."

We let one of our rivals take our little monster. My nostrils flare and my throat stings when I think of what we subjected her to today.

We punished her, rode her so hard, and now... she's gone.

I'm sure she's terrified.

And she probably doesn't even think we'll come after her.

She's wrong, of course.

We'd rip the world apart to find her—one human sack of Acadian shit at a time.

"We'll find her," Alaric assures me as we make eye contact in the rearview mirror. His voice is calm, but it's tinged with unease. Still, his eyes bore into mine. He's the only one who can sense when I'm about to go feral. And right now, I don't even feel where my knuckles are bleeding, or how my wrist is slashed from a shard of the planter. There's blood all over my arm and on my trousers, but I don't care.

I would cleave the world in half to get back to her, because right now, her betrayal doesn't matter. She is one of *us*. And you do not fuck with the Lords of Darkness.

"We have to. We have no choice," I tell him, my voice guttural. "There are about to be a lot of fucking dead bodies."

CHAPTER 6

Theo

I rub my eyes and lean back in my chair, sighing. I keep replaying the texts from Harlow.

He's in New York with Gemma. I think he was looking for me. She met him taking pictures outside of her building.
Oh God. We have to keep her safe. What if they kill her?!
Just keep her safe. Please.

Gemma was never the target. Harlow was.

We've heard nothing.

The trail for Luka Jovovic is cold, and my spy for Acadia is dead.

This wasn't a flash, spur-of-the-moment kidnapping. It was a well thought-out plan, probably in the works since we killed Armin.

I now have no doubt they knew it was us all along.

Somehow, somewhere, we fucked up, and we exposed ourselves.

Luka meeting Gemma wasn't a coincidence—he planned it as a diversion. He wanted to make Harlow believe he would hurt Gemma, so that we used our resources to protect her. Then, he planned to strike, taking Harlow when we were looking the other way.

I'm now fully convinced it was Luka who killed Brenda.

They've been after us for weeks, it seems. Tearing down the walls I so expertly put up.

Not good enough. I wasn't good enough to figure it out.
They still got her.

Acadia was prepared to fight us, to take us on. Vengeance for killing their leader, or perhaps just for power. They were foolish for doing so–everyone knows not to fuck with us. But I suppose they snapped when we killed Armin, especially for seemingly no reason. I'd be pissed off, too.

Did they know she killed him? Likely not, unless she tells them.

Fuck, I hope she's okay.

I refresh my server, scanning the long lines of text and numbers. I've been trying to hack into Acadia for a few weeks, and just recently made progress getting into their email system. The problem is, they hardly ever email; instead opting to text with burner phones they changed out every week. It was nearly impossible to hack those.

They're smarter than I originally thought.

Every few years, someone attempts to fuck with us. Someone, somewhere–usually a newer order–tries to take us down.

One thousand years.

We have one *thousand* years of history behind us.

One thousand years of winning the war.

It always fails, and we continue our reign as the oldest and most powerful crime syndicate in the world. Most of that power resides in respect. Respect for our order, for what we do, for *who* we are.

I can't wait to show Acadia who they're fucking around with, because I plan to make it hurt for every single one of them.

An email comes through their server, located in their deleted files. I download it before they can scrub it, which they do. They read emails, and then they delete them permanently seconds later. Grabbing the file, I open it up and smile when I realize what it is. A one-way plane ticket for Luka Jovovic, and his wife, Sofia Jovovic. London to Podgorica, Montenegro's capital. Though I know they're probably headed to nearby Cetinje, the historical, cultural center of the capital, and the home base for Acadia.

Me: Got them. 23:55 Heathrow to Podgorica.

Gideon and Sterling have already pre-empted their moves, and they're on their way to Montenegro in our private plane. I stayed back in Blackwell with Alaric, who is keeping watch over the cameras in the various houses in case Acadia attempts any more shit. I upped the security for all of us, which included activating the trackers we all have inserted just under the skin in our arms. If *any* of us move past the boundaries I have set up–accounting for the flight Gideon and Sterling are currently on–I'll know immediately. We've had them for years, but tonight is the first time we feel the need to use them.

We'd have to put the tracker in Harlow once we got her back.

I was sure as fuck never going to let something like this happen again.

Alaric: I booked us on the 05:40 to Podgorica.

Me: That's nearly seven hours away.

Alaric: We could take the other jet, but two private jets coming into Podgorica airspace might alert them that we're on our way. I'm sure the air traffic controllers have already been paid off–if not before, then definitely after tonight. They know they hit a vein by taking her, and they know we're coming after her.

Alaric and I don't always agree, but he does usually offer a differing perspective, and right now, I know he's right. In fact, I have a new idea.

Me: Sterling, where are you guys?

Sterling: Somewhere over Italy.

Me: Tell the pilot to land at Dubrovnik. We'll drive across the border to Podgorica.

Dubrovnik—a Croatian city about two and a half hours away—is a better meeting point.

I don't trust Acadia, and I certainly don't want to get caught within their territory. Croatia is a bordering country, and they won't think to look for us there.

Sterling: Will do. Should be another hour or two.

Me: Alaric and I will head out shortly and meet you in Dubrovnik.

I pack my computer up, placing my three external hard drives in my briefcase. Even while I'm traveling, I make sure to take everything with me. You never know when you'll need your full setup.

Running a hand through my hair, I walk down to the car park and get into my car. Alaric will meet me at my house, and then we'll head out to the airport.

Two hours later, Alaric and I are pulling up to the side of our second jet. I relay our destination to the pilot as we walk aboard, and then I set everything up on the mahogany table. Alaric pours us two whiskeys, handing one to me as he sits down in his perfectly ironed suit.

"Sterling and Gideon are waiting for us. We should arrive in Dubrovnik just as Harlow and Luka land in Podgorica."

I growl, grinding my jaw. "They're going to pay for this."

Alaric sneers before looking out of the window, shooting his entire drink before slamming it down on the table.

"If I could intercept the plane and throw Luka out of the door, I would."

I grunt my approval, and we take off a few minutes later.

My computer dings with new information, and as I pull up the image before me, my mouth goes dry. I had an algorithm going across all cameras in Heathrow. They're surprisingly easy to hack. Running it in tandem with my face scanning program, it alerts me whenever a camera picks Harlow up. Low and behold...

It's a security image of Harlow and Luka. She's wearing sunglasses and a white sweater, and he's somehow fastened a short, red bob on her head. But it's her, and she looks completely out of it. His arm is around her shoulders, holding her up. Luka, on the other hand, is wearing a casual hoodie and jeans.

I nearly snap my computer in half.

Showing Alaric the image from airport security, his jaw ticks and he looks away. The night Armin touched Harlow was nothing compared to this. Acadia was going to rue the day they decided to fuck with us. Alaric wouldn't sleep until they were all being burned alive, or whatever massacre he has planned for them.

Charles would've killed Acadia quickly and thoroughly, but I know Alaric is going to make it hurt.

We would get her back.

Even if it meant we had to incinerate the whole damn capital of Montenegro.

CHAPTER 7

Harlow

The piece of tape over my mouth wakes me up. It's pulling the skin around my lips. I snap my eyes open as my heart begins to race. Thrashing against the bed I'm chained to, I scream, but the tape mutes it. I study my surroundings. A nicely decorated, ornate bedroom. A large window overlooking a city I don't recognize—with bars, of course—so that I can't escape. Furniture made of black wood. Thick carpets lining the tiled floors. Blinking rapidly, I try to hold back the tears.

Where the hell am I, and why am I tied up?

As I wrack my brain for clues, I only find hazy flashes. I was talking to Gemma about Luka. Then I texted the guys. Did I go inside next? What happened? Whoever did this obviously drugged me, because I can't remember a damn thing, and my head is pounding. My mouth feels dry—almost like I've been asleep for a long time.

I pull against the handcuffs on my wrists and ankles. Looking down, I notice I'm not in my clothes. I have a pair of baggy jeans and a fuzzy white sweater. *These aren't my clothes.* I'm also wearing white boots that aren't mine. My scalp itches, and I can see red hair hanging down the side of my face from my peripheral. Swallowing, I attempt to quell my panic.

At least with the guys, I knew we were equals. At the end of the day, it was in their best interest to keep me alive.

A tear slips down my cheek. I take a few steadying breaths through my nose and try to remember what happened.

I was talking to Gemma.

She told me about Luka.

I texted the guys...

I close my eyes, piecing everything together. It's like wading through tar. My mind feels sluggish and my whole body aches.

What happened next?

Where am I?

How long have I been asleep?

The bedroom door opens, and a man swaggers inside. He smirks as he walks up to me, wearing a crisp all-white suit. His dark hair is slicked back, and his brown eyes swim with wickedness and mirth. My stomach drops when I see the gold ring on his finger.

The same one Armin was wearing the night of the dinner—the night I killed him.

Acadia.

"Hello, Harlow. Or shall I call you by your full title, Lady Blackwell?" He reaches forward and rips the tape off of my mouth. It stings like hell, but I keep my face neutral. My eyes water as I take deep breaths.

Will the guys come after me? Do they know I've been taken?

It would be so much easier if they just let Acadia have me. *Especially* after what I did to them. I wouldn't blame them if they left me here to rot.

"Where am I?" I growl, pulling against the chains. My throat is dry, and my voice is hoarse as I speak.

He smiles and looks down at his watch, making a tsking sound. "I think you can guess where we are."

"Montenegro," I tell him.

Fuck, I don't even know where that is on a map.

"Do you know where that is?" The man laughs, and my silence is my only answer. "Stupid girl."

My stomach is in knots when I remember—when everything slams back into me.

Gemma.

New York.

Luka Jovovich, that must be who this man is. The new leader of Acadia.

"Where is Gemma?" I ask, my voice shaking.

"She's safe at home, but I have two of my guys watching her. I think you and your Lords underestimated us. We killed your men instantly, and now she's unguarded. So you will do as I say, or we will hurt her, yes?"

His accent is light, but as I thrash and look around, I realize I'm in enemy territory.

And they have access to Gemma.

"What do you want?" I ask. Everything hurts—every muscle, every joint. I can tell by my foggy vision and the way my bladder is screaming for release that I've been chained up for a while. Maybe a day, or more.

"Your cooperation," Luka says slowly, assessing me with his cold eyes. "We've been working for years to take down the notorious Lords of Darkness. They are our biggest rival. When you killed Armin, it gave us the push we didn't know we needed. We had a reason to go after you, and we set the plan in motion."

LADY OF DARKNESS

I swallow as my heart beats in my chest. When *you* killed Armin. Do they know it was me, specifically? *Don't say anything. Don't incriminate yourself.*

Luka continues. "This is our chance. The Lords have weakened themselves with their love for you. Capturing Armin was a mistake—one they could've avoided, had it not been for you. So it was easy. I found out what mattered the most to *you*. My dear Gemma." He holds out his phone and hits a button, and to my horror, Gemma answers. Luka holds a hand to his lips, telling me to be quiet.

"Hi, baby," Gemma says sleepily.

It's her, though. I'd recognize her voice anywhere. Tears prick at my eyes. If I say anything, if I shout or call out to her, Luka will hurt her.

"Sweetheart, did I wake you?" Luka purrs.

"It's fine. I was dreaming about you anyway," she responds.

No, Gemma! Get away from him!

I begin to cry, and Luka holds his finger to his lips again, glaring at me. "I just wanted to call and say hello. I miss you so very much."

"When will you be home?" she asks sweetly.

I've never wished for the gift of telepathy more than at this moment.

"In a few days. It just depends if the problem we encountered becomes a bigger issue or not. If it cooperates, I should be home by Friday."

"Okay, baby. Let's hope it cooperates, then. I love you."

Love? Seriously, Gem?!

"I love you too, sweetheart. Talk soon."

Pushing a button, he pockets his phone and gives me a smug look. "So?" Luka asks, his voice smooth and confident.

"If you hurt her, I will kill you," I grit out.

He tilts his head and steps closer to me, trailing a hand down my leg. I shake at his touch, recoiling as much as I can. He just chuckles, roving his finger to the space between my thighs.

"I could have fun with you two," he adds, his expression dark. "If you don't cooperate, I mean. She has no idea about this life of yours, yes? It might be fun to bring her here. To show her what a murderous little bitch you've become."

Okay, so he does know I killed Armin. That's not great.

I bare my teeth at him. If I could kick him in the nuts, I would. Smash his face in.

I thought I hated the Lords...

I was wrong.

This hate goes so much deeper.

"You keep saying I need to cooperate, but I don't know what you mean."

He walks around to the foot of the bed, contemplating his answer for a few seconds. "The Lords will come for you. They are already on their way, as a matter of fact."

My heart twists at his words, and something akin to hope fills me.

I thought for sure they wouldn't bother, but they're on their way.

They're coming for me.

I close my eyes as more tears threaten to spill out from the inner corners.

We'd lay our lives down for you, Harlow. In time, you'll feel the same way about us.

225

Gideon's words from last week float through my mind.

"And?" I snap back, letting the tears fall freely now.

Luka's eyes narrow as he continues. "Let them find you. Let them come here. But it will be a trap, one to lure them in. We will kill them, and you will join Acadia. Or not," he adds with a sickening smile. "If you choose not to, we can always kill you."

I sniff.

"So... are you going to cooperate, or not?"

Fuck, fuck, fuck.

Once the Lords are here, they will burn this entire building to the ground. For now, I need to pretend—*again*. I need to figure out a way out of this.

I need to make it believable.

Again.

Pretend, pretend, pretend.

Isn't that what this job is all about?

I just need to buy myself more time.

"Why would I do that?"

Luka grins. "You have to choose. Save Gemma or save the Lords."

"That's an easy answer. I will always choose Gemma," I tell him. It's not a lie, but I hope it doesn't come to that. Hopefully, I won't need to choose.

"Then you will do as I say. Otherwise, Gemma will be killed."

"And if I cooperate? You'll leave Gemma alone?"

He smiles, brushing a finger along his lips and leering down at me. "Yes. I will leave her alone for good. But you..." he purrs, his eyes skirting down my body. "You will be mine."

Please, God, let the Lords take this vile man down.

My lip wobbles as I nod. *I can lie. I can do this. I can buy myself—and the Lords—time.*

He's lying, but they're on their way here.

I can lie, too.

"Okay. I'm in."

CHAPTER 8

GIDEON

Sometimes, I really fucking love my job. Today is one of those days, despite our circumstances. The guards of the Acadian compound nearly shit their pants when they see the four of us stalk up with no warning. We have a... reputation. And they are more than willing to sell us information to save their lives.

I kill them anyway for being a part of this whole fucked up plan.

For helping to *take* what was ours.

No one here deserves our mercy.

We have an entire van of ammo—and weapons only certain militaries have access to.

And I am ready to burn the entire place down.

Raze it to the fucking ground.

But she isn't here. We'd killed at least fifty guards for nothing, and our little monster isn't even here.

No one knows anything about her or her whereabouts.

Theo goes out of his mind, and Alaric holds his gun out, ready to kill. Sterling has his hand wrapped around a grenade. He isn't fucking around, and neither am I. When we get back to our car, we're all silent for a minute or two. Finally, Theo breaks the silence. He's looking at something on his phone.

"She could be in any of their safehouses," he says, showing us a map with at least fifty dots scattered across the country. "I suspected this one because it's their home base, but clearly I was wrong."

Alaric's jaw ticks, and I know he's pissed.

"Then let's start with the first one on the list," I suggest.

"These are only the known safehouses. There might be others," he adds, shaking his head in frustration.

I sigh. Leaning back, I rub my lips. "Then we go door to fucking door on every house in this whole goddamn city. This whole goddamn country."

Theo starts the car, and we head out to the first safe house.

I grind my jaw as I think of the worst-case scenario. "What if she's—"

"Don't," Sterling growls. "Don't you fucking utter those words."

CHAPTER 9

Harlow

My imprisonment is more like a hotel stay, but with locked windows and doors, of course. I spend the next hour inspecting the bedroom, searching for any clues or ways I can communicate with the Lords. Even if I could... would they even want to find me? I'm under no false pretenses that they want or need to rescue me. They may very well leave me here to rot. A thousand years of history... and I've only been a part of it for a few weeks. They have Archie. And there's the fact that I tried to poison them last week.

It would be easier to call it a loss.

I don't have any special abilities, or secret information.

And even though they seemed to like me before I tried to kill them... was I really going to sway four of the most powerful men in the world? They were smart and practical.

Why risk their lives for me, when I proved to them *seven days ago* that I didn't care about them *at all?*

I take a long, hot shower, trying not to think of the future and what mine might look like now. When I'm done, I walk back into the bedroom to find a pair of silk pajamas on the bed. Taking a deep breath, I pull them on quickly—just in case there are cameras in here. The bathroom is full of assorted products, so I spend some time applying serums and lotions, brushing my hair out, and staring at myself in the mirror.

They certainly aren't treating me like a captive. I don't plan on letting my guard down, but it is strange how well they're treating me, especially seeing that I am a Lady of Darkness.

Their sworn enemy.

I climb into bed and look around. None of my personal belongings are here—no phone, no purse, no clothes. Someone must've changed me at a certain point. Either before we arrived in Montenegro, or after we got here. That thought leaves a bitter taste in my mouth. What the hell are their intentions? Why aren't they treating me like a captive? Are they just luring me in, waiting until I become comfortable, waiting to spring?

Unease coils in my belly when I hear heavy footsteps outside of my door. Luka throws it open, followed by a man who instantly makes me nervous. He's smaller than Luka, thinner. Shaved black hair, eyes that are so deep-set and black that they look bottomless. He smiles, and one of his teeth is made of gold. I look at Luka—anywhere but at that man.

"Harlow," Luka purrs. "I see you've made yourself at home."

I don't say anything. Instead, I just glare at them and cross my arms.

"Do you remember what I said about cooperating?" Luka adds.

I swallow the bile beginning to crawl up my throat.

"Yes. Why do you ask?" My voice comes out higher than I intended.

Luka smirks. "This is our biggest client. One of the richest men in the world. He has... offered us a significant amount of money for one night with you. Consider tonight a test."

My stomach bottoms out, and I break into a cold sweat. Suddenly, Alaric's words from the night I killed Armin float into my mind.

Acadia is known for trafficking children. And Armin here? He gets his pick of whoever he wants to take advantage of. Most of the girls he chooses are under the age of twelve.

Acadia's specialty is human trafficking, and I'm the new, exciting product for these monsters.

That's what I am.

That's what this is.

They don't care that I'm their rival, because to them, I am no better than chattel. I am their slave, in every way. They know it, too.

Why didn't I see it sooner?

I squeeze my eyes shut as Armin's words come back to me.

"We sell girls like you—young, fuckable girls who make me rich."

"That wasn't a part of the deal," I grind out, trying to keep myself from shaking. I could really use some of my medication right now. I haven't taken it in days. Fuck the Lords for distracting me, and fuck Acadia for capturing me. "You said all I had to do was lure the Lords here and you would kill them. That Gemma would go free."

"That's correct. And what did I say about you? What will become of you, Harlow?"

My heart stutters. "I will be yours," I tell him, my eyes pricking with tears.

"Exactly. You will be mine. I can cut off your fingers," he adds, sneering. "I can dye your hair, make you do a thousand jumping jacks in the morning, and I can most certainly sell you to our biggest client," he finishes, baring his teeth.

I couldn't wait to see his corpse rot.

I hold my chin up high, and Luka nudges the man forward. "Say hello to Savo. Your newest client. If you're nice to him, he won't hurt you."

My lips tremble as Luka saunters away and closes the door behind him, leaving me with Savo—with this man who looks like he eats puppies for breakfast. There are tattoos scattered along his neck, and I can tell by the shiny watch and shoes that he's disgustingly rich.

"I'm not having sex with you," I tell him defiantly. "I'm on my period."

He grins, taking a step closer.

No.

I would *not* let this happen again. My hands shake as I move away from him, scooting to the back of the bed.

"I don't think you have a choice, angel." His voice is deep and grating, like metal scraping against cement. "You're mine tonight, and right now, I want a taste of that sweet pussy."

My face screws up at the thought. "No."

"You think a little blood scares me? Most of them bleed, angel. You're no different. I like the blood. It reminds me of innocence."

What.

The.

Fuck.

I scurry out of the bedroom and into the bathroom. I hear him behind me, but I close and lock the door before he can get to me.

"Take your time," Savo says, his voice cruel. "I'll be out here. Waiting for that pussy. Don't take too long, though, or I'll have to break the door in. Savo gets mad when he has to wait."

I rush over to the frosted window, trying to unlatch it, but it's sealed shut. Looking around, I don't see anything I can use to break it, so I look back at the window and clench my jaw.

Here goes nothing.

Rearing my arm back, I punch through the glass, screaming as some of it embeds into my knuckles.

"It's a long way to fall, angel. I wouldn't run if I were you, unless you want to be roadkill," Savo growls from the other side of the bathroom door.

A sob breaks free from my chest when I hear him toying with the lock. I look out of the hole I made, holding my bloody hand close to my chest. My sobs get louder when I realize I'm several stories up, probably seven or eight. Too high to jump, and nothing to climb onto. *Fuck.* I get dizzy as I look down onto the empty street.

I have nowhere to go.

And there's no one here to save me but myself.

I walk over to the sink and clean my hand carefully, rinsing the blood away. It drips onto the porcelain sink, and I use the fancy soap to clean the cuts before dabbing it dry with one of the fresh towels. Swallowing roughly, I look at myself in the mirror. My dark hair is still wet, slicked back behind my ears from my shower. I lift my shirt, looking at the brand on the side of my body that's now almost completely healed. The edges are raised and pink, and something akin to pride fills me. My abdomen is also looking leaner, as are my arms and legs. I feel physically strong for the first time in my life.

Luka can't just sell me to the highest bidder, like I'm his property.

I am a goddamn *Lady of Darkness*.

I was going to kill this motherfucker, and everyone in this building. I just had to figure out how.

Leaning against the counter, I take a deep, steadying breath. Savo continues to work the door, but I have a couple of minutes to think. I push aside the panic as much as I can. He must have a phone, so I can use that to dial Gemma. I can tell her to call Rose, who will call one of the guys.

It could work. I just need to get to his phone. Most men keep it on them, so I need to immobilize him somehow. I doubt he'll let me tie him up, but...

This has to work.

I throw the door open, and Savo openly leers at me. "Hello, angel. Change your mind?"

I could do this. For them, I would do this. For Gemma, and for the guys.

If the Lords have found you, go with them.

If you are scared, don't be.

You can trust them.

My father's words from his letter flit through my mind.

The Lords did find me, but I threw it all away because I thought I knew better.

And now, I was about to prove to them that I was worthy of their order—worthy of *our* order.

They would find me again.

I just had to trust them.

"No, but I guess I have no choice," I tell him, willing my voice to stay strong.

His resounding grin makes my stomach churn. But not for long.

CHAPTER 10

Alaric

Harlow wasn't in the first three houses, but we would find her.

Even if we're up for five days straight.

Even if bodies littered the ground.

We would find her and bring her *home*.

I smooth my suit as we wait in the car outside of safehouse number four. It's the penthouse suite in downtown Podgorica. It's not a huge city—at least not compared to London or New York. And it's nearly empty now, seeing as it's the middle of the night.

I make sure I'm all set—with the hidden knife inside of my watch, as well as the gun in the back of my waistband. I also have a backup gun strapped to my ankle. Theo has his entire computer set up in the car, and we are all wired with microphones. Our plan is for Sterling and I to go inside, scout the place, and if we find her, Theo and Gideon are under direct orders to kill everyone inside, except for women and children, who would go to one of our safehouses in Croatia.

Luka and the rest of Acadia most certainly know we are coming after Harlow. By taking her, they'd declared war, and the three safehouses we'd just raided had probably raised some kind of silent alarm. Because of that, we are most likely going to enter into a trap. We agreed early on that we wouldn't let Luka fuck with us. We'd get Harlow, and we'd get out. She might fight us, because Luka had probably threatened Gemma if she didn't.

It's war tactics 101. We basically wrote the manual for this shit. Every once in a while, someone thinks they're so novel, so tricky. But we always come out on top.

We are the ones who came up with this shit.

We are the ones who *invented* every single resource these guys use.

Tonight would be no different.

Sterling and I climb out of the car, hands on the guns tucked into the back of our belts. We walk into the lobby of the building, and several men twist around with guns, but they're dead in a matter of seconds. Blind rage is fueling me, and my thirst for murder is as high as it's ever been.

Thanks to Theo, he opens up the elevator without the requisite keycard. We take it all the way to the top, and I look over at Sterling as we grab our guns, aiming them forward. Surely there will be more guards once the door opens.

We always err on the side of caution, waiting for the worst scenario. When the doors slide open, Luka is standing there with his hands in his pockets, grinning.

My finger hovers over the trigger.

He stole Harlow. I should kill him. But I resist. Instead, I aim my gun at his skull as my pulse whooshes in my ears.

I will fucking rip his heart out.

"Where is she?" I growl, feeling my blood begin to boil with the pent-up rage that's barely restrained inside of me. My teeth are so clenched that they could crack at any second. I flick my eyes to Sterling for a millisecond, and he looks just as furious.

By now, Theo will have seen and heard Luka, and he and Gideon will be on their way up the stairs. I hold my arm with the gun steady.

"You mean the whore you call a Lady?" Luka barks out. Something low and deep begins to rumble in Sterling's chest. "She's fucking one of my clients right now."

Sterling cocks his gun, but I shake my head, signaling for him to stand down.

"You're lying."

Luka laughs. "I'll show you. We have cameras. Everyone's enjoying the show." Looking at Sterling, I see him compose himself and give Luka a cold, indifferent stare. We can't show our hand too soon. We can't show weakness. I stand up taller and mask my face into neutral indifference.

I want to blow his fucking brains out, but I need to think rationally.

I need to think with my mind, not my heart.

"Oh, and if either of you attempt to hurt me, there are about forty men on the roof waiting to kill you and your two friends who just walked into the lobby."

Fuck.

We're obviously not the only ones who are wired and connected to a larger network. Luka is either way more equipped than we thought... or... he's bluffing.

It's likely the former.

This is Acadia, and they are powerful.

Just not as powerful as *us*.

"Come on. I'll show you. Your little slut will ride anything with a cock."

He turns and walks away, and I am *so close* to shooting him in the back. I can't, though. I don't want to put Harlow in any danger. This isn't our normal mission where we take down the bad guy at first glance. It's a goddamn rescue mission, and one fuck up could mean a bullet in Harlow's head.

I'd burn the world down before that happened, so I have to get my emotions in check.

Theo and Gideon are on their way up the stairs. They'd take out any threats, and Sterling would help me find Harlow.

We have this planned.

We do things like this all the time.

We know what we're doing.

Luka stops at one of the doors in the hallway, opening it up. Two security guards are looking at the multiple screen setup. My mouth goes dry when I realize what they're watching.

Harlow is topless, standing next to a tall, thin man. He's leering down at her, and she smiles as she reaches out and unbuckles his belt. I hear Sterling mutter something under his breath. I can tell by the way her smile doesn't reach her eyes that she's faking it. And while I want to chop this prick's cock off for touching her, I am *so proud* that my little monster has become a master manipulator.

Pride fills me, and my chest swells.

"*I'd heard rumors about the men in Montenegro,*" Harlow purrs on the camera feed. She cups his groin, and he moans. "*I'm used to English men, you see.*"

"She's really very skilled," Luka says, his voice raspy. "Savo is one of our wealthiest clients. When he caught word that we had an actual *Lady of Darkness*..." Luka chuckles, and I grip the metal gun so hard I'm afraid I might bend it. "Milos, why don't you zoom in a bit?" One of the guards clicks a button, and the camera zooms in on Harlow. She's smiling demurely, and then she takes her pants off, throwing them to the side as she pushes Savo onto the bed, wearing only a thong. "Tell me... how does it feel to know she's a whore for any powerful man? That you're not special?"

The deep, rumbling coming from Sterling continues. The primal, alpha part of me wants to kill everyone in this room, and then put a bullet through Savo's head while I carry Harlow out on my shoulders like an ape. But the intellectual, highly trained crime lord in me knows this is all an illusion. Harlow would never willingly fuck some random guy unless she needed something from him.

That's the thing with trust.

You throw caution to the wind, putting your trust in another person, hoping they catch it.

Because when they do... there is nothing more beautiful.

Which means... she trusts us. She must. She wouldn't willingly put herself in this position unless she knew we were going to incinerate everyone around us.

I saw the remorse written all over her face after she gave us those brownies. All last week, she would look at us expectantly, waiting for our approval. So, yes. To the naked eye, it looks like she's about to fuck that prick on the screen. But I know, deep down, that she's doing it for a reason.

She's doing it because she trusts us to save her.

Which... *fuck*.

I swallow as emotion claws up my throat.

Our beautiful, intelligent, cunning, gorgeous little monster.

My job now is to play along. If it means getting to her, *showing* her that we're here, that she was right to trust us...

I have to get to her.

If that means killing Luka, so be it.

The low-volume updates in my earpiece give me a boost of confidence. Theo and Gideon are already finished taking out the men upstairs. Their grunted updates are all the motivation I need.

Acadia underestimated us.

People always do.

Chuckling deeply, I lower my gun. "She can fuck whoever she wants, however she wants."

Luka's brown eyes widen slightly with something akin to surprise. "You're just going to let your woman fuck another man?"

I smirk. "I don't own her, Luka. Unlike Acadia, the Lords do not shackle their women." I look at Sterling, and his green eyes flare. I know from working with him for twelve years that he heard the update in his earpiece, too. "Unlike Acadia, our women fuck us willingly."

There's a split second where Luka's smile falters, but before he can act, Sterling shoots the two security guards in the back of the head and points his gun at Luka.

"You have about ten seconds to take us to her room."

Luka sneers at us, holding his hands up in surrender. "You just made a deadly mistake, my Lords. Like I said, I have forty men on the roof waiting to kill you."

Theo and Gideon suddenly shove through the door of the security room. They're both bloody yet composed, and there's a gun in each of their hands.

I shake my head and stare at Luka, who's now white as a sheet. "You obviously know nothing of our capabilities if you think the four of us can't take down your whole goddamn network, including those fools on the roof. In *minutes*," I hiss. "It wasn't even all four. It was two. *Think about that,*" I sneer. "Think about the fact that *half* of my order just took your entire defense down in *minutes.* And I'll torch this whole building if I have to."

Cocking my gun, I point it straight at his face before looking at Theo and Gideon. I tilt my head slightly, which for us means *take care of the other distractions*. Sterling and I will find her, and Theo and Gideon will make sure we don't encounter anyone else on our way out.

It's simple.

We've practiced.

We could do this in our sleep.

"Now, take us to her, or I'll put two fucking bullets straight through your eye sockets."

CHAPTER 11

Harlow

Savo reaches up from where I'm straddling him on the bed and cups one of my breasts, and I have to swallow repeatedly to keep the vomit from creeping up my throat.

"Nice round tits," Savo purrs, squeezing them roughly. "My tits," he adds, leering up at me. "At least for tonight."

I will myself to stay still, to not tremble on top of him and give everything away.

Not yours. Not ever.

The Lords have already claimed me, and once they find out Savo touched me...

They are going to smear what's left of him across the floor.

"Such perfect nipples," Savo continues, rolling one of them between two fingers.

I resist the urge to close my eyes, or better yet, to clock him in the face.

I just need to immobilize him somehow, distract him enough to knock him out and grab his phone.

"Thanks," I mutter awkwardly.

This is *so* demeaning in every way.

With the guys, I felt like they were doing it for my pleasure. I felt a connection with them. I *liked* giving them pleasure, because even though I was angry, we were all connected in a fucked up way.

But this? It makes me sick.

I grind up and down his pants, rolling my hips. I'm naked except for my thong. I didn't want to touch him, didn't want to have any unnecessary contact with him. He groans, throwing his head back.

"You like that?" I purr, moving quicker.

He grunts and spasms. Is he coming already?

His body shudders underneath me, and his eyes roll into the back of his head. *Yep, he definitely just came.*

Now's my chance.

As he twitches underneath me, I move my thigh and slide my hand into his front pocket, securing his phone. Quickly holding it up to his face, it unlocks. His eyes stare at me with a confused expression for half a second before I bring my other elbow up and then shove it down onto his face. He groans, and both of his hands go up to his nose as it gushes blood. I scramble off of him and run to the other side of the room.

"What the fuck are you doing?" he yells, sitting up. My hands shake as I attempt to dial Gemma. *Faster, go faster!* Everything slows down, and my mind whirls. "You make Savo mad," Savo mutters darkly, pinching his nose as he stalks toward me.

Fuck. My hand is shaking too hard, and I keep pressing the wrong button. *Stupid fat fingers! Stupid international numbers!*

"You make Savo *very* mad," he growls, and in half a second, he's in front of me. His black eyes narrow slightly as he bares his teeth at me.

My thumb just presses down on the green dial button when he lunges forward, grabbing the phone and ending the call. *Fuck, fuck, fuck!*

Pocketing his phone, he looks up and sneers at me, his expression purely homicidal.

Here we go.

This is it.

This is how I'm going to die.

Even if the guys are on their way, they're going to be too late.

I pissed off the wrong man, and now he would spend the night hurting me, making me pay. If Savo doesn't kill me for this, Luka certainly will.

And Gemma.

They would hurt Gemma.

I stifle a whimper at the thought.

My whole body trembles as he lunges for me, and his body collides with mine as I cry out. At the same time, there's a loud crack. At first, I think he must've pushed me so hard that my body damaged the wall–

Then the bedroom door *shatters* into pieces a few feet away.

Savo jumps back and I cover my head as pieces of wood fly past us, and then I nearly sob with relief when I see Alaric and Sterling standing at the threshold. Alaric's eyes skim over me briefly, but then they snap to Savo.

Sterling's eyes don't leave mine as he slowly walks inside, and then his eyes survey the room quickly, taking in the bed, my nearly naked body, Savo's unbuttoned pants...

"Did you touch her?" Alaric demands, stalking into the room with heavy footsteps and a gun pointed right at Savo's head.

Savo smirks, holding his hands up, but he doesn't answer Alaric.

Alaric *does not* like that.

I scream as a bullet rips through his skull. Blood splatters everywhere, and I'm shaking as Alaric lowers his weapon, looking at me. Savo crumples to the ground a few feet away, the dark red stain of blood spreading quickly across the tiled floor.

Sterling stalks over to me, stopping a few inches away. Reaching out, he places a hand on my cheek. I'm still trembling, still processing.

Even now, even weeks later, a death is a death.

I will never get used to this, to the sheer power they possess.

The ability to simply end an entire life in a heartbeat with no qualms.

He opens his mouth to speak, and at the same time, I hear a zipping sound. To my horror, Sterling stumbles forward, clutching his chest.

I scream.

My eyes dart behind him. *Luka.* He points his gun at Alaric next. *Where are Gideon and Theo?* Sterling is on his knees before me, and I look down at him. He grimaces as blood begins to bloom across his white shirt.

Luka shot him in the back.

"I told you I'd show you where she was," Luka says slowly. "Though of course, now I will have to kill all of you."

Alaric has his gun pointed at Luka, and Luka has his gun pointed at *me*.

He circles the three of us—four, if you count Savo. As he looks down at Savo's lifeless body, he clucks his tongue. "What a shame. He was always the highest bidder." Looking at Alaric, he shoots quickly and without hesitation. Alaric stumbles back. *Why didn't Alaric act quicker? He was pointing his gun! Fire the gun!*

I see the bullet tear a hole in Alaric's suit jacket, his eyes widening.

I know he's quicker than that! Why didn't he move?

"Every empire falls eventually, doesn't it?" Luka says cruelly.

I hear someone scream, and I realize a second later that the sound is coming from my own mouth.

"You just lost me a lot of money, Lord Cross," Luka says angrily. He snaps his eyes to me. "Come with me, or I will have Gemma killed."

I'm in too much shock to cry. My eyes look at Alaric and Sterling, and I notice the seeping red liquid growing on Sterling's shirt, dripping down Alaric's hand as he clutches his chest. I glance between them, unsure of what to do. Alaric's dark eyes bore into mine, but he doesn't move. Doesn't say anything. I can't tell if he's in shock, or if he's trying to tell me something.

Why isn't he saying anything?

If the Lords have found you, go with them.

If you are scared, don't be.

You can trust them.

Sterling falls to his knees. His eyes find mine, but he doesn't say a word. *Why?*

They killed Savo immediately, but they aren't going after Luka.

They are trying to tell me something, but what is it?

You can trust them.

239

You can trust them.
You can trust them.
I look at Luka. "You shot them."
Glancing back over at Alaric, he licks his lips. It's like they're waiting for me to do something.

The memory snaps into place, and I remember when they tricked me a few weeks ago, pretending to kill Gideon to scare me. *Bulletproof vest and fake blood, baby.* They'd used tools then to pretend, to fake Gideon's death.

Alaric's eyes find mine.

They're wearing vests, and it's fake blood. They *must* be faking it.

Now I just have to play *with* them.

I smile. "I'm glad you shot them." Looking at Luka, I grab my pajamas from next to the bed, pulling them on quickly. Standing taller, I turn to face him. "You better keep your end of the bargain," I mumble.

Luka grins. "I promise that Gemma is safe."

Casting one more quick glance over at the guys, I give them a look of indifference before I follow Luka out of the room.

Please be right.
Please be right.

We walk down a dark hallway, and a warm breeze flutters through the air. This whole house is so impersonal—beige and bland, as grand as it is. I much prefer the dark, edgy vibes in England. Luka places an arm around my shoulders as he leads us further away.

"Idiots. Not so powerful now, are they?"

I laugh, but my stomach churns with nausea.

Please be okay.

"I knew they'd be thinking with their cocks and want to find you first. My men followed them inside. The other two are probably already dead," he says, chuckling as we get to another one of the bedrooms.

Gideon and Theo.

I swallow as Luka closes the door. He walks over to me and kisses me on the cheek. I have to keep stiff as a board to keep from recoiling.

"You did beautifully," he purrs. One of his hands comes to my hair, and he brushes it back. I try not to gag. "You want power, don't you, darling?"

I want your fucking hands off of me.

I nod, and he smiles. If his personality wasn't so fucking repulsive, I might find him handsome. I can see why Gemma fell for him so quickly.

"The rest of our life begins now, Harlow. With the Lords dead, we can rule the world together." His other hand comes to my mouth, and my nostrils flare at his touch. "Unless, of course, Lord Cross and Lord Beauchamp aren't actually dead, and you mean to deceive me."

Wait, what?!

I open my mouth to scream as he pins me to the edge of his bed. Fighting against him, I use my knees, but he holds my hands behind me—the telltale feel of cold metal clamping around my wrists.

As I try to scream again, Luka shoves the tip of a gun inside of my mouth, prying my jaw open.

I whimper and shake. *How the fuck could he tell?*

"Let's get one thing straight," he growls. "You may think your order is all powerful, all present, all mighty. You may call yourselves gods, but I'll tell you what I told your little fuck buddies earlier: every empire eventually falls."

I'm trembling as he removes the gun from my mouth. The acrid taste of gunpowder and metal makes me retch. Luka slams me face down onto the bed, and I scream again when he pulls my pants down from my hips.

"Your men are going to die. I told them I had forty men, but it's really over two hundred. They may be well-trained, but they are still human, their flesh still able to be torn apart by hundreds of machine guns," he murmurs. "We'll shoot them in the head to be sure this time."

Tears fall down my cheeks as he spreads my ass.

Please.

Please.

Don't let this happen again.

Let them be okay.

Let this be over.

I hear him spit into his palm, and I squeeze my eyes shut. My whole body is shaking underneath him, and he shoves my hands away. I feel him shift behind me, and then–

Boom.

I hear an explosion nearby, jolting beneath him, ears ringing.

Luka stiffens.

Boom.

Another one. The bed shakes, and Luka climbs off.

"What the–"

The bedroom door flies open. The smell of gunpowder and burnt wood hits my nostrils instantly. I turn my head to the side, and Theo and Gideon are standing in the doorway, looking absolutely fucking murderous.

Relief washes over me, and I see Theo's eyes move from Luka to me–prone on the bed, pants at my ankles, my hands cuffed. A low growl emanates from his chest, and he looks at Luka before he cocks his gun and his head at the same time, pointing the gun straight at him as he strolls into the bedroom.

"How did you get in here?" Luka asks.

"Your order has always underestimated us," Theo says, his voice low as he ignores Luka's question. "And right now, I'm *fucking furious* that you touched someone that wasn't yours." He shoots Luka before anyone can react. Luka screams and falls to his knees. Blood spurts from his hand. "I'm going to put one bullet somewhere on your body for every fucking time you touched our woman."

My stomach swoops down low at his words–at his claim.

Our woman.

"I didn't–"

The sound of a shot fills the air, and Luka screams again. Both hands are bloodied now.

Gideon walks up to Theo and whispers something in his ear. Theo smirks, and then he twists around, shooting the window. It shatters, and I flinch from my place on the bed.

"Your men are dead," Theo says, his voice eerily quiet. "We killed all two-hundred and twelve of them."

"Impossible," Luka sneers, baring his teeth.

Gideon marches over to Luka, placing his gun against Luka's skull. "I'd be happy to show you their bloodied bodies. There was a fucking massacre up there." His voice is smooth like velvet. It feels like a warm balm against my skin.

Four men killed over two hundred men.

They're powerful, immensely *skilled*. They truly are at the top of the food chain.

Luka was wrong.

The Lords *are* Gods.

Gideon and Theo grab Luka by his arms and drag him to the open window. The Lords are so much bigger, their presence so much more powerful. Luka looks like a child next to them.

"I want you to think about touching what's not yours the entire way down. Goodbye, Luka. How did you phrase it? Oh, right. Every empire eventually falls," Theo growls, shoving Luka forward and out of the window.

Just like that, he's gone.

I breathe a sigh of relief. Gideon rushes over to me, pulling me to a standing position and then into his arms. My body begins to shake as I cry, as I inhale his familiar scent. I feel Theo come behind me, and he tries to loosen the handcuffs.

"Fuck, we don't have the key."

Panic rises in my throat. "Shoot them off," I beg, twisting around to face him. "I need them off. Please."

Gideon runs a hand through my hair and down the back of my neck, and his eyes scan my face and neck for any injuries.

"Did he hurt you?" Gideon asks, almost in a whisper.

I shake my head. "No. He hadn't..." I trail off, stepping out of my pants. My shirt is long enough to cover me, though I don't really care being around them.

"Hold your hands to the side, little monster," Theo murmurs from behind me.

I hold them up, pulling them apart as much as I can as Theo aims his gun at them. The chain is taut. "Do it. *Please*."

Gideon's arm snakes around my waist. He leans down and whispers, "Alaric can find a key—"

"I want them off. Now."

Because as strong as I felt for part of tonight, when Luka had me on the bed, it was just a reminder of my past. Of that loss of power, of that loss of control.

That past haunted me for over a year.

And I refuse to be shackled to that past for another second.

Theo aims his gun and shoots. I flinch as my hands snap apart, as I feel the reverberation of the bullet rip through the metal and sever the chain. My knees buckle, and Theo catches me just before I fall.

He pulls me into his warm body as tears leak from my eyes. Not out of sadness, or because I was scared, I realize.

But because they're safe.

"What did I tell you?" Theo whispers, running a hand down the back of my head. "We would've burned the world to the ground to find you. I told you that the first night—if you tried to run, we would find you."

I smile against his chest as I dry my eyes. "Are Alaric and Sterling okay?"

Gideon chuckles from next to me. "They're fine. We're all wired, so I can hear everything they're saying. They're just cleaning up the mess."

Two-hundred and twelve armed, dangerous men.

And my Lords just took them down in mere *minutes*.

"What about Gemma?"

"She's safe. One of my guys confirmed he has eyes on her 24/7. He's the best in his field. I'd trust him with my life."

I nod and walk over to the window. Luka's body—and a puddle of blood—are splayed out at odd angles on the sidewalk below us. Because it's so late, no one is out, but soon, someone will discover him. Shivering, I walk back toward Gideon and Theo.

Theo kneels in front of me, and I can barely breathe. "We thought you were dead," he murmurs. I'm still shaking with adrenaline. It must be at least two in the morning, and yet I feel wide awake.

They saved me.

They care about me.

"I figured you guys wouldn't bother after what I did," I tell him honestly.

Gideon walks up behind me, and my breathing stutters when I realize we're a foot away from the open, shattered window. He knocks my legs apart as his lips graze the back of my neck. I groan despite myself, because it feels *so good* to be touched by them.

"Wouldn't bother?" Gideon growls. "You really think we *wouldn't bother* saving you?"

I moan as he reaches a hand underneath my shirt and fingers my panties, ripping them off in one fell swoop.

Theo's face nuzzles between my legs, and his hands grip my ass firmly, pulling me closer. I moan, and my knees buckle as his tongue languidly sweeps up my slit.

"Now that we have you back, we're not ever letting you go," Theo murmurs, his breath hot against my clit.

Gideon continues to kiss my neck. "We're going to fuck you in front of this window—to show the world just how powerful we are together. Just how beautiful you are when you come," he says. "Scream loud, little monster. I want the entire city to know we'd kill them all to get you back."

CHAPTER 12

HARLOW

I run my fingers through Theo's white-blond hair, gripping it tightly as his tongue sweeps down my slit. The way he's licking me, it's as if he's a starving man who hasn't eaten in days. He groans as he swirls and flicks his tongue against my nub, diving it deep inside of me as his nails dig into my flesh. I throw my head back against Gideon's chest, and Gideon's hands slowly wrap around me and begin to unbutton my shirt as he places soft kisses on my neck.

It feels wrong—to be doing this here with dead bodies everywhere.

But it's also hot as hell.

Maybe it's the adrenaline, or the fact that we're in enemy territory, but I can't help the shiver that works down my spine, or the way my eyes flutter closed for a second with every touch.

I have no doubt that the rest of Acadia—or what's left of them—is after us, so our time is limited. We should leave, get out of here as fast as possible, but Theo and Gideon are moving their hands and pulling at my flesh without pause, acting like they can't help themselves. Like they're possessed. It terrifies me and turns me on all at once, and my heart is still hammering from what almost happened.

I groan as Theo inserts one thick finger inside of me. They're both covered in blood, but I don't fucking care. If anything, it adds to everything. It makes everything so much more real.

Blood was shed—for me.

They really did tear the world apart.

For me.

My knees buckle beneath me as I contract around his touch, feeling as if a maelstrom of fire is burning brightly throughout my nerve endings. Gideon pulls my shirt off in one swift tug, and then his warm hands are wrapping back around me and cupping my breasts as his teeth nip my ear.

"Oh God," I cry as Theo inserts another finger.

"So fucking wet," Theo grunts, working his hand quicker as his tongue flicks around my swollen clit. "Such a naughty little monster. You like it when your men massacre an entire organization for you?"

God, fuck yes.

I gasp as Gideon pinches my nipples simultaneously. "I think she does," Gideon purrs against me, then sucks a toe-curling kiss onto my neck. "I think our Lady fucking *loves* it."

"Good," Theo says as he removes his fingers, looking up at me with a wet chin.

God.

I want to take a mental picture of Theodore Wolf on his knees, mouth wet with my arousal.

It's almost disconcerting seeing someone so powerful, so cunning, eager to dive back in and give *me* pleasure.

Especially after what they did.

Coming to Montenegro to save me.

Killing Luka and Savo.

Wiping Acadia off the map in mere seconds.

I tried to kill them a week ago, and they organized a goddamn rescue mission for me in return.

"On the bed, Harlow," Gideon murmurs, pushing me forward.

I walk over as both he and Theo unzip themselves. Relaxing back onto my elbows, I spread my legs for them as they begin to stroke themselves a few feet away, and *fuck*...

"You've shared a girl before?" I ask, running a finger down between legs and giving them a show.

"Of course we have," Theo bites back, taking a step closer.

"Have you ever been with each other?" They both stop and give each other a *look*. I sit up and grin. "Tell me more."

Gideon smirks. "I'm bisexual. The guys know. And I've fucked men before. But never the other Lords."

Frowning, I slump back down. "I was hoping for a different answer."

"What do *you* want, little monster?" Theo asks.

I shrug. "I don't know. I want to see you guys together."

They look at each other and then back at me. "In what way?" Gideon questions.

"I think she wants you to blow me, Lord St. Claire," Theo taunts, and Gideon narrows his eyes.

"You want me to suck your cock?"

Theo shrugs. "A mouth is a mouth. Give me what you've got."

Before I can interject, Gideon drops to his knees and pulls Theo forward by his hips. The resounding hiss that escapes Theo's mouth when Gideon swallows him is... wet dream inducing. I move my finger to my clit quickly as I lie back and watch them, as Theo juts his hips forward and grabs onto Gideon's hair. Wetness pools between my legs, and I moan as I move my hand faster.

"Fuck," Theo grunts, looking down at Gideon.

And when Gideon looks up at Theo, when he reaches up and begins to play with his balls as he moves his mouth up and down Theo's shaft, I nearly explode in a glittering storm of pleasure.

I take another mental picture—of Gideon on his knees for Theo.

Theo's curved cock moves in and out, and he makes hissing noises every time Gideon moves down on his shaft. His eyes are hooded and dark, and he grips Gideon's hair harder. Just when I think it can't get any hotter, Gideon uses his free hand to begin stroking his leaking cock, drops of precum stringing down onto the tile. He pumps his hand quickly while using his other hand to glide along Theo's shaft, and his mouth expertly hollows with every drive forward.

I moan again, closing my eyes as my impending orgasm begins, but before I reach that peak, Theo is flipping me over onto my stomach, and knocking my knees apart. I gasp as he comes behind me, his hard, wet shaft rubbing along my ass.

"Did I say you could come without us?" he snarls, grabbing my hair.

A second later, I feel Gideon on the other side of the bed. Theo directs me over to him, and then Gideon is grabbing my face before his lips are on mine. His tongue laps at mine, and my stomach swoops as his mouth possesses me wholly. He groans and fists my hair, and I realize with a start that I don't think any of them have ever kissed me—not really. Not like this. And I need so much more of it. I moan as Gideon bites my lower lip, then runs his fingers through my hair, his hand gripping the nape of my neck to keep me close. Theo comes up behind me and rocks his cock against my ass again, moving my hair off my shoulder and placing multiple delicate kisses there.

It's the dichotomy of sweet and brutal—the punishing commands mixed with gentle kisses—that makes me nearly implode with warm, sweet arousal.

"Ride me," Gideon whispers.

He lies down—still in his full, bloodied suit—and I move my legs to straddle him. I feel Theo's fingers grazing my back as I lower myself closer to sit on Gideon's cock. It's large, thick, and wet, still leaking with precome, and I certainly don't need any lubricant. Slowly, I lower myself until he enters me fully, inch by inch as he stretches me.

"Fuck me," Gideon growls, jutting his hips upward as he pushes the rest of the way inside of me.

I gasp. "Oh, my God," I whisper, my breath stuttering.

I can barely accommodate his girth, and it stings at first. He stays still, deep inside of me as his hands grip the flesh at my hips.

"Fuck, Harlow," he says, his hoarse voice uneven.

I've never seen any of them lose their composure, but right now, Gideon looks like he's completely unraveling before my eyes.

The burning sensation gives way to a satisfying fullness, and I rock my hips slightly against him.

He grips me harder. "I'm so fucking close to coming, little monster," he warns. "You're so fucking tight, and you feel too fucking good."

Theo murmurs something unintelligible behind me. I hear him spit into his hand, and then my body freezes when I realize what he's about to do. He places a hand on my ass. I look back at him—at the man with white-blond hair, the one who could bring down the world with his knowledge and power—and I wait for him to enter me.

"Good girl," Theo growls, placing the thick head of his cock against my back entrance. I cry out as he pushes in slowly, and *God,* I've never felt this full. "Breathe, little monster."

They both stay still, and I'm utterly and completely at their mercy. Theo's hands rove up and down my back before they reach around and begin to circle my aching clit. My body convulses at the light touch, and I feel everything inside of me contract around them.

"Fuck," Gideon groans, rubbing his mouth with one hand. "Fuck, this feels too fucking good. I can feel your pussy squeezing me, Harlow."

"Me too," Theo adds, moving his hand quicker against my swollen cunt.

"Oh fuck, yes," I moan, propping myself over Gideon as he moves inside of me. Slapping my ass, Theo grunts in approval. I rock my hips just slightly, just enough to give me more friction, to feel them press even deeper. Theo begins to move, using two fingers to slide on either side of my clit.

It feels... *out of this world.*

I can already tell I'm going to shoot off when I come.

Theo circles his fingers against my clit, pinching it roughly and working it between two fingers.

"Oh my God," I cry out, squeezing my eyes shut.

"I'll suck everyone's cock if it means I get to fuck you after," Gideon growls, pounding into me now. "Look at me, Harlow." He speeds up, holding on to my hips for leverage as he drives into me full force.

I feel like I'm being torn in half—in the best possible way.

My pussy contracts around Gideon, and Theo's fingers move in just the right way...

They start to fuck me in sync—so that I'm being impaled by both cocks at once.

I whimper, my hands turning to fists on Gideon's chest.

"Fuck yes," Gideon roars. When I move my hips to match their thrusts, he throws his head back. "Come for me, little monster. Soak me with it and milk me with that pretty little cunt of yours."

"Don't stop. Oh my God," I repeat. My body turns to liquid fire as everything begins to tingle. There's a deep pressure building rapidly in my core, stronger than I've ever felt. It doesn't hurt—it just feels... explosive. Overwhelming. Powerful. Like a volcano waiting to erupt.

"Don't hold back," Theo commands, biting my shoulder. "I want you to watch yourself come all over me."

His words release the dam building inside of me, and I scream as wave after wave of my climax bursts through me. My limbs lock as my voice turns feral. My eyes cross and roll. I feel myself reject both of them, spraying Gideon's shirt as I writhe and pant on top of him, empty and wanting.

I'm still twitching as Theo slams back into my ass, just as Gideon uses my arousal to slide easily back into my pussy.

"Fuck, that was so fucking hot," Gideon snarls as his eyes lock onto my blurry gaze. "Now I'm going to fill you up with my come."

His cock hardens, then he roars and stills, his cock pulsing inside of me.

"I'm going to come," Theo says, his voice thick. "Oh fuck, I'm coming."

I feel him harden inside my ass before he cries out, using his nails to dig into my flesh. He convulses a few times before he stops with a groan. We're all panting when he finishes.

"Holy fuck," Gideon whispers, rubbing his face. "You came all over my suit."

Theo pulls out slowly, as does Gideon, and I collapse onto the bed as they both work to clean everything up.

"That was…"

Theo procures a wet washcloth and cleans me from top to bottom, murmuring something as he places a kiss on my stomach.

"One day, I'm going to fill you with so much seed that you'll have my baby in your belly."

His words cause my chest to ache with longing.

"Not if I get there first," Gideon growls, dabbing himself where I soaked him. He sniffs the towel he's using and smiles. "Best fucking smell on the planet."

CHAPTER 13

ALARIC

Sterling and I walk around the penthouse three times to check for any stragglers. We'd killed them all—the entire team on the roof, waiting to raid the place while we were here. It wasn't easy, and I know I stink of blood, sweat, piss, and tears. It doesn't bode well for me that I did not bring a clean suit to change into. It's like I can feel every morsel of dirt on me, and I can't fucking wait to scrub the Acadian filth off of my skin.

I hate getting dirty, but sometimes, our jobs call for it. Tonight, we used as much tactical gear as we could—grenades, AK-47s, everything with a high output. That shit gets messy really quickly.

Sterling stretches his shoulders and cracks his neck. That wasn't an easy mission, but it also wasn't the hardest. We all spend two weeks every year retraining ourselves with the most powerful militaries in the world. They didn't fuck around, and some of the obstacle courses they put us through were ten times harder than tonight.

But we needed to be ridden hard, by the best of the best. That was how we stayed on top.

That was how we *won* every damn time.

My knuckles are bleeding from throwing punches, and Sterling has a fat lip and a split eyebrow. We walk over body after body, kicking them to ensure they're dead. Twice now we've come across someone moaning in pain, so I put them out of their misery, though not a single one of them deserves it.

Two hundred and twelve.

Well, two hundred and twenty-two, if you include Luka, Savo, the two men in the camera room, the two guards manning the staircase to the roof, and the four guards in the lobby of the building.

It was easy—almost too easy.

I know Acadia's order is small, but I don't think we got them all. In fact, I'm sure we'll be hearing from someone very soon. It will just serve as a reminder to stay vigilant.

Once we located them… they were as good as dead.

"Coast is clear," Sterling says, shoving a body with his foot. The man groans, and his fingers twitch.

Sterling cocks his gun and shoots him in the face.

"Think they're done fucking?" I ask, kicking another body as we make our way toward the staircase.

Sterling chuckles. "Sounds like it."

The idiots had forgotten they're wired, and we could hear every dirty word they spoke to Harlow—and every sound she made as they pleasured her.

It certainly made cleaning up our mess much more fun than it normally was.

"We should get out of here," Sterling adds, and I nod.

"Yeah. Let's go find them and leave."

When we arrive in the bedroom, Harlow, Theo, and Gideon are getting themselves cleaned up and dressed. Harlow is wearing a set of silk pajamas that instantly makes me want to rip them off of her, and the guys are wiping everything down—as we do. Sterling and I were just doing the same thing upstairs and on the roof. We used unidentifiable bullets and grenades, and then we cleaned every door handle and surface we passed. I know Theo will grab the security footage on our way out too.

"Have fun?" I ask Theo sardonically.

He just grins. "Always."

My eyes skate to Harlow's, and to my surprise, her cheeks redden. Walking over to her, I know I look like a goddamn angel of death with all of the gore. Using my bloodied index finger, I place it under her chin and study her face.

"What's wrong, little monster?"

She opens and closes her mouth. Her eyes flick to where Theo and Gideon are standing before landing back on mine.

"If you're wondering whether I'm mad that you fucked them, you don't have to worry. We can learn to share."

She looks relieved, wrapping her fingers around my wrist. Leaning closer, I feel my cock twitch in my pants, growing impossibly steely, as her breath flutters over my neck.

"Sharing is caring," she murmurs, before flicking her tongue to the finger resting on her chin.

I hardly breathe as she takes it—blood, dirt, and all—pulling it into her mouth.

"We should go," Sterling growls from behind us, breaking the moment.

Harlow pulls away and winks at me.

I'm stunned—too stunned to speak, really. She gets kidnapped, doesn't see me for a day, and when she does, it's like someone gave her an aphrodisiac.

Before she gets too far, I grab her arm and tug her into me. "Consider this a taste, a warm up, to the main event."

"Which is?" she asks, breathless.

I smirk, subtly grinding against her. "Exactly what I promised you that day in the shower. All of us at once. Sharing you. Worshiping you. Blinding you with pleasure."

Her breathing turns ragged. I twist away from her as Theo and Gideon finish sweeping the room for evidence. Once we're all done, we walk into the elevator, climbing into the car.

"I want to go home," Harlow murmurs as she snuggles up against Sterling's chest.

"Sleep, little monster. You're safe now," he says, stroking her hair.

I realize then that we're all relaxed because we're *complete*.

Our quintet.

The four Lords... and their Lady.

CHAPTER 14

HARLOW

I wake up to someone carrying me across a tarmac, and panic starts to flood my veins. Everything comes crashing back—the kidnapping, Savo, Luka, the guys recusing me, Luka falling to his death, Alaric looking like he walked straight out of a war zone...

Panicked, I begin to flail.

"Shh," a familiar voice says. *Sterling.* "I've got you, baby. You're safe now. I'm never going to let someone hurt you again."

My wildly beating heart calms a bit as he walks up the steps of a private jet, carrying me effortlessly. Once inside, he sets me down on a large, luxurious white leather window seat near the front of the plane, scowling down at me.

"Better?" he asks.

I nod. "Yeah. I just fell asleep, and I thought..." I look up at him, my eyes stinging with emotion.

Two weeks ago, *they* were monsters. Now, they're my saviors. I want them, I like being around them, and most importantly, I trust them. With everything I have.

And I can't tell if that's my body's way of coping with all I've been through, or if they truly deserve it. All I know is, seeing Sterling, seeing Alaric, and knowing they took down this organization *for me*... it makes me feel all warm and fuzzy, even though I know it's fucked up. This whole situation is fucked up, but I need to learn to adapt, because it's my life now.

Whether I like it or not, these men are my life now.

"You're having a hard time deciphering between good and evil," he answers, spreading his legs and crossing his arms. "It's understandable."

With a rough swallow, I shrug. "I guess. I'm going to regret saying this but... Acadia was worse."

Sterling's resounding smile is pure wickedness. "Don't be so sure, little monster."

He turns and sits down next to Gideon, across the aisle from me.

Theo is on his computer on the couch. Gideon is playing with his butterfly knife, flicking it open and closed as he and Sterling exchange low murmurs. I glance over at Alaric, who is speaking to the pilot. He turns his head, and his brown eyes find mine. They narrow slightly, one corner of his lips tilting up as they rake over my body.

His promise from earlier sends shivers through me, and I feel hot and cold at the same time. As the plane begins to back up, he saunters over to where I'm seated, his arms above his head as he uses the overhead cabin space for leverage.

"You okay?" he asks, staring down at me with an expression I can't place.

I nod. "Yeah. Why do you ask?"

He smirks, which only enhances his sharp cheekbones. He'd managed to wash his skin, but his suit is still caked in blood.

He might prefer to be clean, but... I liked him dirty.

He must notice my appraisal because he sits down in the seat next to me. "Buckle up. We're about to take off."

I hear Sterling and Gideon buckle themselves in, and Theo closes his computer, walking over to a spare seat in the back.

Probably to do some more reconnaissance.

The pilot dims the lights, and we're plunged into a startling darkness. I close my eyes and grip the edges of the seat dividers. I've always hated flying—getting to England took a lot of convincing on my part. I should've been fine with it, considering I'd been flying since I was five. There was no reason to hate it as much as I did. Still, as the engine fires up and the telltale vibrations begin, I squeeze my eyes shut and take a few steadying breaths. Once we lift off, the force flattens me against the seat, and I break out into a cold sweat.

I *really* wish I had my medication with me.

"Breathe, Harlow," Alaric murmurs, his hand coming to rest on top of mine.

"I hate flying," I tell him shakily, trying to distract myself.

"I can see that."

I hear clinking glass, and before I open my eyes, something cold rests on my thigh.

"Drink."

Looking down at the crystal tumbler, it's filled with what smells like whiskey. I don't hesitate, shooting it back and wincing as the burning sensation slowly crawls down my esophagus.

"Fuck," I say glumly, holding the glass out for more. Alaric procures the bottle from somewhere on the other side of his seat, pouring me the same amount. I shoot this one, too. "Jesus." Coughing, I rub my chest.

Alaric smiles as he takes my glass. "Take it easy. That should help."

I nod as I stare out of the window. I'm quiet for a minute as we level out. "How did you know where I was?"

Alaric places his hand on mine again as we hit a patch of turbulence going through a cloud. "Theo hacked into their email system. We saw Luka had booked you a ticket to Podgorica, but we didn't want to alert Montenegrin airspace that we were coming after you, so we landed in Dubrovnik, Croatia. Then we drove and just started going down the list of Acadian safehouses."

"You have a list?"

He nods. "There were about fifty possibilities. We got lucky on the fourth house."

"I see." My head is spinning from the whiskey, and I'm both tired and anxious. This information making me somewhat uneasy. "What if I'd been in house number fifty?" I ask slowly, my voice quiet.

I can't see Alaric's face that well because of the dim light, but I see the way his expression changes—the way it softens at my question.

They're so hard, so severe, that it always takes my breath away when they act like normal human beings.

"Then there would've been forty-nine piles of ash behind us," he answers, his voice rough and low. That answer has my stomach fluttering and thighs clenching. If we weren't in the air, I'd be in his lap in the next second.

His hand moves from my hand to my thigh, lightly brushing the silk fabric of my pajamas. At his touch, a moan catches in my throat. His eyes are so black when they meet mine, and I can see the way he's breathing quickly, the way he pulls his lower lip between his teeth as his brows furrow in concentration and restraint. The seatbelt sign switches off, indicating that we've hit 10,000 feet, and I'm suddenly so hot, so flushed from his attention.

I hear him snap our seatbelts off, and then he stands quickly, grabbing me under the arms and pulling me out of my seat.

"What are you—"

He drops me onto the couch and places a palm over my mouth. "I thought you were dead, Harlow. Let me feast. Let me get that fear out of my fucking system."

I gasp as he tugs my pants down. I don't have time to say another word before his tongue is on me, sliding up and down my slit. He's already sending me into a frenzy with how sensitive I am from earlier. My hips buck against his face when he sucks on my clit, and a long, wanton moan escapes my lips as he looks up at me with a smirk.

"That's a good girl," Sterling says, coming behind Alaric.

"Fuck yes," Alaric murmurs, his breath warm between my legs. "I can still taste their come on you, and it's fucking incredible mixed with your juices, baby."

"Let me taste," Sterling demands, kneeling next to Alaric.

I whimper as Alaric pulls back, letting Sterling eat me next. His tongue is cooler, harder—an entirely different feel than Alaric's. My head falls back as Sterling flicks his tongue against my swollen clit, slurping as he goes. The sound is so erotic, I feel my core clench around nothing.

"Mmm," Sterling moans. "Our come tastes so good on you, little monster."

Moaning in response, the couch sags on either side of me. My eyes flutter closed, and I arch my back as Sterling continues his onslaught. Gideon and Theo take my hands, pinning me down on the couch as they pepper my face and neck with kisses.

Is this what it's like to be worshiped?

The plane shakes a bit as it hits a wind shear, and my stomach bottoms out. It only intensifies the feeling of Sterling's tongue takes over again, sliding up and down my slit. It's enough friction to make it feel good, but not enough friction to come. I try to move against his mouth, but he holds me still.

"Not yet, Harlow. I want to be inside of you when you come."

Okay, then.

I look over at Gideon, who is still holding his knife in one hand. His hooded eyes follow my line of vision, and he grins.

"You want to have some real fun, baby?" he asks, moving the knife to my chest.

The cold metal makes my skin pebble with goosebumps. He works down to where my pajama shirt collar meets the skin of my neck, sliding the blade against the silk and cutting through it. *Too easily.* The sound of the blade slicing through the fabric makes me tremble with anticipation.

Theo leans down and begins to suck on my exposed nipple as Sterling unzips his pants, stroking his rock-hard cock. I stare down at it, at the thick, taut skin with veins running to his pink head. *God, I love his cock. I love all their cocks, to be honest.*

"I know I should be a good boy and share," Sterling growls, pulling my hips to the edge of the couch. He kneels and sweeps my legs over his shoulders. "But right now, I need you all to myself." Without warning, he impales me. And I scream.

"God," I moan, fisting the fabric of Gideon's shirt next to me. "*Yes.*"

Sterling pushes in deeper, inch by inch, stretching me to the brim. In this position, he can go *so fucking deep.* I gasp as he slides all the way in, and then out. Slowly. So fucking slowly.

Alaric is behind him, running a hand over his back. My pussy contracts around Sterling's cock when I see Alaric unbutton his pants.

"Beauchamp," Alaric growls.

Sterling smirks at me. "You want him to fuck me while I fuck you, baby?"

"Fuck yes," I hiss.

Is that a real question? Am I dreaming?

Theo and Gideon work my tits. Theo sits up on his knees next to me, unsheathing himself. He begins to stroke himself just as Gideon does the same. They're pleasuring themselves on either side of my body, watching as Sterling slowly drives in and out of me. He starts to move quicker, and then begins fucking me with zero abandon, thrusting into me hard and fast, over and over. His thick cock hits that sweet spot inside of me every single time, pulling sounds from my chest that I barely recognize.

"Oh my God," I whimper, feeling my toes curl with my impending orgasm. "I'm going to–"

Sterling pulls out, and I let out a cry of frustration, lowering my legs.

"Not yet," he says, his voice low and commanding. He grits his jaw, and I see Alaric spit into his hand as he moves directly behind Sterling.

"Ready?" Alaric asks him.

Sterling pins me with a heated gaze and nods. "Fuck yes."

Alaric moves into Sterling slowly, and Sterling's hiss of pleasure sends a shock wave of electricity through me. His head drops back, and Alaric's hand comes gently around his neck.

Oh, God.

I moan when Sterling's cock drips precome, twitching as Alaric penetrates him.

"Fuck," Alaric growls.

I don't want to look away—I can't look away. Especially as Sterling's green eyes flutter closed, and his mouth drops open.

"Holy shit," he murmurs. When he snaps his eyes open, boring into mine, they're darker. "Spread your legs, Harlow. I'm ready to come. And you will too."

I nod eagerly as Sterling maneuvers himself over to me, sliding into my throbbing pussy. He groans as he grips my ankles, his fingers digging into my skin.

"Fuck, this feels so fucking good," he murmurs. As he drives into me, Alaric drives into his ass. I can feel his cock curve and harden with every thrust of Alaric's hips, and *fuck,* it's too much.

I look to my left at Gideon, and then at Theo to my right. They're watching this all unfold, and they stroke themselves quicker and faster to match every thrust.

"Fuck her harder," Theo tells Sterling. "I want to spray my come all over her bouncing tits."

The mouths on these men...

"Open your mouth, Harlow," Gideon says, moving closer.

I look up at him and smile, opening my mouth and sticking my tongue out. He groans as his body begins to convulse. Fisting his cock roughly, ropes of come pulse out, hitting my tongue. I moan at the taste, looking up at him through my lashes, and he clenches his jaw as his cock continues to throb.

"Fuck," he whispers, finishing. Leaning down, he kisses me, swirling his tongue in my mouth and tasting himself. "Fuck, Harlow. That's my girl."

Pride fills me at his praise, and I turn to look at Theo. He's baring his teeth and groaning as he quickens the pace of his hand.

"I'm going to come," he says, his voice frayed and uneven. "Fuuuuck," he growls, stopping his hand altogether as his cock bows and curves. He empties himself all over my chest, shaking as the last of it leaves his body.

Seeing them—seeing all four of them fucking and coming—I cry out as Sterling fucks me hard and fast again. I'm slick underneath him, and he's hard as a rock. Alaric groans behind him, and our eyes meet for a second, jolting me.

God, yes.

"I'm close," I tell him, my voice high and squeaky.

Sterling gives me a wicked smile. "Be a good fucking girl and come all over my cock, baby."

Jesus.

It feels like he's fucking my soul right out of my body.

"Come on, little monster," Alaric growls. "I'm so fucking close. I want us all to come together."

Sterling grunts. "Fuck yes. Come on, baby. Let me feel that pussy squeeze my cock until there's nothing left."

His words cause my eyes to roll back as my climax unleashes. I soar into oblivion, gripping him tightly, feeling my orgasm surge out of me and onto Sterling's chest. It keeps going, the torrent of pleasure making me jolt and shake beneath them. A shrill moan climbs out of my throat, and stars overtake my vision. I am burning up, my nerves tingling more with every pump of their hips.

"Fuck yeah, Harlow," he says, his fingers clawing Sterling as he empties inside of him with a roar.

Sterling looks completely unhinged as he lets go—as he groans and grows impossibly hard inside of me. His cock tightens as he stills, and I feel it curve up inside of me. We both look down as a loud, intense howl leaves his chest. His hands are gripping my hips as he shakes and shivers above me, spilling the last of his seed with a gasp.

"Holy shit," he says softly, looking down at me as Alaric pulls out of him.

Sterling pulls out of me next, and in a flurry of movement, all four guys begin to clean up. There are hot washcloths running down my chest, between my legs... it feels exquisite, especially since I am so fucking tired after that.

"Use the restroom," Sterling says gently. He helps me up, pulling me into his large body.

"You're not the boss of me," I say sleepily.

His green eyes look down into mine, and something flashes behind them at my disobedience.

"Actually, I am. Whether you like it or not."

I smirk up at him. I love playing with his dominant side. One day, I'd push him hard enough to unleash on me fully. My whole body shivers at the thought.

"Yes, sir."

He growls as I walk to the airplane restroom.

CHAPTER 15

Sterling
Ten Years Ago

"Kneel," I tell my sub, gripping her jaw so tight that she squirms. She obeys, resting her palms on her thighs like a good girl. "Suck my cock." Her brown eyes look up at me through her lashes, and she smirks as she unbuttons my pants. I hiss as she fists my shaft, and my body twitches as she takes me into her mouth. "Fuck," I say, holding on to the wall for support.

I come in three minutes, and she swallows me effortlessly. When she's finished, she smacks her lips and stands up.

"Did I say you could stand?" I snarl, willing my voice to sound angry.

She gives me a sardonic smile. "The scene is over, Lord Beauchamp."

"The fuck it is," I growl. Just as I reach out for her, she grabs my wrist and squeezes. The firm grip sends a cloud of dominance over me. Dropping to my knees without thinking, she stands over me and laughs.

"That was good. But you need to *own* it. *You* are the Dom. There should be no hesitation, no second guessing. Your sub will be watching you. Judging you. I certainly was."

I grind my jaw in shame as I place my palms on my thighs. "Very well."

To my surprise, Diana kneels down in front of me and takes my hands. "There's a reason you came to me. A reason you sought me out, and came all the way to Amsterdam to learn under me. You're not my normal client, Sterling, but one day, you will be just as renowned as me. You just have to believe in yourself. Practice. Find a good sub who will let you."

I nod. I still haven't told her that I'm having second thoughts.

When I came to her last year, I thought I was a sub–I thought I wanted to be dominated. So, I sought out the most elite dominatrix Europe had to offer.

It became clear very quickly that I was no natural submissive.

Diana noticed, too, and she was nice enough to offer to train me. Being a switch, she can easily flit between dominant and submissive. Me... not so much.

Being defied–being told what to do–drove me mad.

Still, I wanted to be the best. I wanted to *learn* from the best. So we continued to see each other every month. I continued to endure the humiliation, the shame, the submissiveness that never, ever came easily.

In between sessions, I practiced. Mostly in the BDSM clubs in London. Sometimes I'd pick up women at bars, or on a job. The power I held was an aphrodisiac for most people, men included.

I hadn't exactly explored *that* part of my sexuality yet, but I did know that I liked fucking men just as much as women.

I say goodbye to Diana and walk through the red-light district smoking a cigarette. I should quit, but smoking in Europe feels so natural. The streets were meant to be wandered with a cigarette braced between two fingers.

My phone vibrates, and I glance at the name on the screen.

"Hey," I say, stubbing my cigarette out as I look out across one of the many canals.

"We have a... situation," Alaric drawls on the other end.

I sigh. Every time I come to Amsterdam, I'm called away early for my job. As a Lord of Darkness, our jobs don't stop. We never take holidays or sick days. I'm burnt the fuck out.

"I'll fly home tonight." I try to keep the contempt out of my voice.

"Yeah. Get here quickly. Charles says it's urgent."

It's always fucking urgent.

"Got it," I tell him.

"Have a nice time?" he asks, his voice sounding amused.

"Learning a lot."

"That's good."

The guys know about my proclivities. They've been in the same room while I've shagged women (and men). They understand my need to dominate, so they don't judge me, and they don't ask questions. I spend most of my free time at the alt clubs in London, and they're fine with it.

"See you at Wolf Manor in a couple of hours," Alaric adds. "Tell Diana we say hello."

He hangs up, and I pocket my phone. Running my hand through my hair, I lean against the bridge for a minute.

Being twenty-two and a part of the world's most dangerous crime syndicate is exhausting. I feel thirty. Forty, some days. The responsibility of the world rests on my shoulders. The others don't seem to feel as bitter as I do. They've taken to Charles like he's their goddamn father figure, but he and I haven't gotten as close.

Alaric, Gideon, and Theo don't seem to resent this life as much as I do. Most days I hate it, but there's nothing I can do to change it. When my father died in the gas leak, I was orphaned, then shucked into this life without even being asked.

We all were.

And I hated everything and everyone because of it.

Two giggling Dutch girls pass me. I clear my throat as they turn to smile at me. Curving a finger, I beckon them over, and they giggle some more before they decide to come talk to me.

Diana says I need to practice my dominance? I can do that.

I can squeeze in one more fuck before I head back to Blackwell.

Fuck it. Fuck the Lords. Fuck my job, and fuck Charles Blackwell for ever sitting us down that day after Duke Cross died.

Fuck everything.

CHAPTER 16

HARLOW

We get back to Blackwell just as the sun begins to rise over the horizon. They don't take me home, though. Instead, we pull up to a manor bigger than Blackwell House. It's ornately decorated. Rose bushes lining the perimeter, a manicured lawn, and a stone path that winds to the back of the house. The grey stone contrasts against the black door, but the gold accents make it feel welcoming rather than foreboding.

"Welcome to Wolf Manor," Theo says, packing his computer up as our car arrives.

"Shouldn't I get back home so that Rose doesn't call the authorities?"

Theo smirks. "Baby, we are the authorities. And no. Alaric let her know that you were on a weekend trip with him. You're staying with me tonight."

I ignore the way those words give me butterflies.

"Apparently, she's still under the impression that I'm courting you," Alaric growls, sounding displeased.

"You sound angry about that." Gideon chuckles from his seat.

"He's right, though," I interject. "She's going to figure out soon that it's not just Alaric."

"And?" Sterling asks, opening the door for us to climb out. "What will you tell her?"

I shrug, feeling brazen. "I'll say you all gave me no choice when you essentially kidnapped me and made me join the order."

Everyone but Sterling laughs. His eyes pin me to my seat. "You sure like being mouthy, don't you?"

My cheeks flame, but not with embarrassment. It's his tone of voice. The dominant one. It gets me wet every single time.

"Better get used to it," I chirp, climbing out of the car.

Luckily, the driver was given instructions to bring me some clothes when we landed, seeing as Gideon sliced my pajama shirt to shreds. It must've been Sterling who gave the order, because I'm now donning faux leather leggings with a moto design down the sides and a white cropped t-shirt. He even thought of socks and white sneakers.

"Do you coordinate our outfits?" I ask, looking at his bloody, white dress shirt and black pants.

I swear I see the hint of a smile tug at the corners of his lips as we walk toward the front entrance of Wolf Manor.

"Not exactly," he says, his voice all serious and growly.

"You could start your own fashion brand with these clothes," I add. "You're a fan of leggings, aren't you?"

His jaw twitches as we enter Theo's house. I look around quickly, noting the dark furniture and white accents. It looks nothing like Blackwell House. It's large and airy, modern and neat. The stairs and floor are made of shiny, flawless marble. There are no gilded portraits hanging on the walls, Victorian furniture, and I don't see a single patch of floral wallpaper. I'm so distracted that I hardly notice when Sterling tugs me into his side, speaking into my ear in a low murmur.

"I'm a fan of you wearing whatever the fuck I tell you to wear. It makes my cock so hard to watch you walk around in my clothes."

My knees buckle at his words. I *should* be insulted. The feminist in me is screaming. But fuck... the way he commands me and speaks to me like that... it's really fucking hot.

I open my mouth to retort, but before I can be a smartass, he lets me go. "Sleep. You need rest."

I cross my arms as he makes his way to the back of the house. "I assumed we'd be at the gym this morning."

His green eyes find mine, and my stomach bottoms out as they scan up and down my body. "I think you've had enough exercise today, don't you think? Go to bed, Harlow."

I'm still pouting when Alaric, Gideon, and Theo walk through the front door.

"Upstairs. Sleep," Alaric says, snapping his fingers.

I gawk at him. I can't help the tug of exhaustion creeping through my bones, though.

"I'll show you to my room," Theo says, walking past me and up the wide marble staircase.

I try not to stare at his ass on the walk up, or the way his large hands run through his white hair. As we go up another flight of stairs, I have a realization. A month ago, two flights of stairs would've winded me. But today... I'm not even out of breath.

He pushes a white door open, and inside is the most badass bedroom room

I've ever seen. First of all... there's a fucking *lap pool* by the large window. The ceiling is high and vaulted, and made of some kind of light wood. The bed is on the floor, and though the white bedding is neat and crisp, it feels cozy. There are plants in every corner and hanging above his bed. There's no door to the bathroom—it's just open, showcasing a modern, sleek countertop and a large, open shower room. There's also a door that I suspect is a sauna.

It completely juxtaposes the old exterior of the house.

"I love your house," I tell him, looking around at the black accents in awe.

He shrugs. "I completely renovated it after my father died. My mother flung herself into her travels, leaving me the house. It was way too fucking stuffy back then."

I wrap my arms around myself. I'm so tired, but it's so rare to get one-on-one time with Theo. He's always working, always plotting and thinking one step ahead. I want to get to know him. I want to see beyond the endlessly intelligent, lethal exterior he portrays.

"Are you and your mother close?"

He shakes his head. "Not really. She calls me every couple of months out of obligation. She's currently living in Kenya with her Kenyan boyfriend, who is thirty years younger than her," he says, rolling his eyes. "I met him once, and he's head over heels for her. I had to do my due diligence to see if he was legitimate, and he is. I'm happy she's happy."

"Does she know..." I trail off.

"No. She never had any idea about my father or the Lords. There's no rule saying it must be kept secret, but most of us prefer to keep it under wraps."

I nod. "That makes sense."

"You should get some rest, Harlow," he murmurs, looking at me with those captivating light blue eyes.

My throat constricts when I think of being all alone.

I know they're here. I know they'll never let anything like that happen to me again. But still... it's not my bedroom, or my house, or my clothes. I don't even have my phone to check on Gemma. The guys assured me she's fine, but Luka is dead. I don't know how much she'll ever know about his death, if anything. I should be there for her.

My eyes flick around the room, and I resist the urge to beg him to stay.

I don't really want to be alone.

I open my mouth to ask when he steps forward, lifting a hand and brushing a piece of hair out of my face.

"What can I do to get you to relax?" His voice is *so* gentle. I bite my lower lip to keep from crying.

These men... they're so tough on the outside. It's like a hard, protective shell. But they're also not afraid to let that exterior fall around me.

And I fucking love seeing what's inside, what's underneath that hard shell.

"Will you stay with me? I know you're probably busy killing people and tracking the remaining Acadian members down—"

Bending down, he takes my chin between his index finger and thumb. When his lips brush against mine, I relax instantly. He pulls back to look into my eyes.

"The only place I need to be is here."

My eyes prick with tears as I nod and walk over to the bed, kicking my shoes off before climbing in. Theo follows me, discarding his suit jacket on the floor. He's not like Alaric, who would rather die than have wrinkled clothing. I smile at the thought.

"What's so funny?" Theo asks, climbing into behind me and pulling my body against his.

"I was just thinking about how you're going to give Alaric an aneurysm with the way you just threw your jacket on the floor."

He chuckles as his lips graze my ear. "Give him some slack. He lost his mother when he was young, and his father was a control freak. He had Lottie, his nanny, but she left right before his father died. I think he fought so hard for so long to be different from his father, but genetics are wild, and he ended up being a control freak anyway."

"I see." I snuggle up my behind to him, feeling his hard shaft pressing into my ass. *Oh.* I move my ass against his cock, but he just growls and squeezes my shoulder.

"Don't do that," he snarls. "Unless you want me to fuck you all day long."

"And what if I do?"

He sighs. "You need sleep, little monster. Sleep, and then I'll fuck you."

I smile as my eyes begin to drift closed. "Promise?"

I feel him nod. "Always."

CHAPTER 17

THEO

Once Harlow falls into a deep sleep, I carefully climb out of bed and pull my tie off, discarding it on the floor. Glancing down, I realize with a pang that Brenda is dead. There's no one to pick up after me anymore. Sighing, I grab the clothes and place them in the bag for dry cleaning. I suppose I'll have to find another house manager at some point. I glance back at Harlow one last time before shutting the door and walking down the stairs in my socks.

I'm so fucking tired, but I have so much work to do. If I die early, it'll be because I don't get enough sleep.

The guys are all hanging out in my kitchen.

"Sure, help yourselves," I joke, walking to the refrigerator and grabbing a bottle of sparkling water.

Gideon snorts. "I haven't eaten since before we knew Harlow was missing."

"Same," Alaric says.

"You want to borrow some clothes?" I ask him. He must be going out of his mind wearing a dirty suit.

"Please."

I nod and walk to my utility room, where I grab a shirt and shorts for him to wear. Tossing the clothes to him, I point to the bathroom off of the kitchen.

"You can shower in there."

He grins. "You've read my mind."

As he walks away, I stare down at the floor for a few seconds.

"You look knackered," Gideon says, eyeing me up and down.

I shrug. "It was a long couple of days."

"You should sleep," Sterling says from his place at the breakfast bar. He's eating some oatmeal, while Gideon is digging into a bag of crisps.

"I don't have time to sleep."

They're both quiet after that. There's no arguing. This job isn't easy, and it sure as hell doesn't stop. I already spend an hour every morning catching up on what I missed while I got my nightly four hours of sleep.

Like I said, I was probably going to die prematurely because of it.

After I finish my leftover roast dinner—something I ordered in, because again, Brenda was dead—I clear my throat and take a sip of water.

"We missed a few of them."

Sterling stills. "Acadia?"

I nod. "They fled after the first safehouse raid. They're currently regrouping somewhere in Poland. They've overhauled their entire system, and I can't locate them."

"Fuck," Gideon sighs, looking just as exhausted as I feel. "How many?"

"Twenty or thirty. It's hard to tell. They're in hiding and I can't get a good read on them."

"Oooh, that must really bother you," Gideon teases. "Imagine *not* being able to track our enemies' every move like you usually do?"

I smirk, but my chest is tightening at the thought. "It's a terrible feeling."

Gideon laughs and places a hand on my shoulder. "We'll find them. And then we'll kill them."

I clench my teeth. "I'm worried they're going to go after Harlow."

There it is. The reason I've been so tense since we rescued her. The thing eating at me, making me feel enraged and anxious all at once.

"She stays with us until they're taken care of, then."

I nod. "She stays here. I have the best security system. In fact, I think we should all stay here. I don't trust Acadia. They have a lot of allies who would love to see us dead. They've got nothing to lose, so they might come after us hard and fast out of anger and vengeance."

Alaric walks into the kitchen and grabs a water bottle from the fridge. "Who might come after us?"

"Acadia," I tell him.

He raises his eyebrows. "They can certainly try."

I sigh and run both hands through my hair. I need a shower. I also need to sleep. "We said that a week ago. Look where it got us."

"Theo thinks we should all stay here until it blows over."

Alaric nods. "That's fine."

"I call dibs on Harlow," Gideon says, grinning at Sterling.

Gideon is the ultimate brat, and it irritates Sterling to no end.

"Fuck off," Alaric murmurs, shoving Gideon playfully.

While the guys fight over Harlow, my phone chimes, and I squint down at it, wondering if I'm reading the email notification correctly.

"Interesting." I look up at the other guys, my brow furrowing. "Acadia is coming on strong. We've been invited to dinner at The Sage Club in London tonight."

Gideon snorts. "And here I was thinking they'd play hard to get."

I scowl down at my phone. What the hell is their angle?

"Do we trust them enough to go?" Alaric asks, looking just as unsettled as I feel.

I shrug. "There's only one way to find out."

CHAPTER 18

Harlow

I wake up to the afternoon sun shining in through Theo's window. Everything hurts—either from Luka handling me roughly or the guys handling me even rougher. I squeeze my legs together and smile, stretching slowly before climbing out of bed. Last night—or this morning, technically—was incredible. My stomach swoops low when I think of what we did in the private jet, the mind-numbing pleasure I experienced. I walk over to the large, floor-to-ceiling window, which looks out onto a large green space. The grass is endless, sloping slowly downward to what I know is Blackwell Village below us.

I use the bathroom and shower, changing into a pair of oversized sweatpants and a t-shirt. I'm swimming in them—they must be Theo's—but they're soft and cozy. Plus, they smell like him. As I pad downstairs, I listen for the guys. It's completely quiet while I slowly peruse the beautiful, daunting house known as Wolf Manor. Everything is so modern and elegant. There's even a goddamn library. The room is *full* of books, lined perfectly on pristine white shelves. I reach out and run my finger along the spine of an old book, and a feeling of warm nostalgia washes over me. This room is gorgeous. Further down is an old, ornate mirror with desilvering around the edges. Looking at my reflection in the aged glass, I gasp when I see Theo leaning against the door at the back of the room.

"How long have you been there?" I ask. My heart is beating wildly in my chest at the sight of him.

He's wearing grey jeans and a black sweater. He's so composed, always so put together. Even his hair looks perfectly coiffed.

His cerulean eyes twinkle as he cocks his head. "A while."

My stomach does that stupid swooping thing again that feels like butterflies going wild in my guts.

"Are you hungry?" he asks, his voice low.

"A little. Are the other guys here?"

He shakes his head, pushing off of the door. "They went to their houses to grab some things. We're all going to stay here until Acadia blows over."

"I guess that makes sense."

My nerves are fried, and being in his presence alone doesn't help. It only sets them on fire all over again.

"They'll be back soon. We have a dinner event in London tonight."

I perk up at that. Since the day I tried poisoning them, I hoped they'd start including me in real work. If this is going to be my full-time job, surely I'd be doing more than exercising and reading war tactic books.

"With who?" I ask.

"Acadia."

My face pales. "Seriously?!"

He nods, his expression unmoving. "Dead serious."

"They want to have dinner with us after what they did?" I add, my voice shrill.

"I'm not sure what their motive is."

I scoff with a rapid shake of my head. "It's probably a trap."

"No, I think it's genuine. I suspect they either want to call a truce, or strike a deal."

A chill works through my body. "What kind of deal?"

Theo takes another step forward. "In this business, we sometimes have to appease our enemies by forming an alliance."

"They tried to kill me, Theo."

He nods again, this time looking annoyed. "I know. And I want to burn them all to the ground for it."

"So, why don't you?"

Whew, when the hell did I become a cold-hearted murderer?

Theo's lips twitch, as if he's trying not to smile. "Because we can't just go around killing everyone who tries to kill us. There'd be no one left."

I clench my fists tighter as he stalks closer. "I don't trust them."

When he's a few inches away from me, he reaches a hand out and places it underneath my chin, tilting it up.

"I will ensure you stay safe, little monster."

I swallow. "Not—not just me. You guys, too."

He gives me a monstrous smile. "Catching feelings for us, Lady Blackwell?"

"No, I–"

Before I can finish my useless denial, he lowers his face and brushes my lips with his. It's so sweet, so gentle... he pulls away slightly, but I reach up and place a hand behind his head, pulling his mouth to mine again.

He groans and moves us backward a step, shoving me into the bookshelf. A couple of books fall, and I gasp in relief as his hands roam underneath my t-shirt, palming my breasts.

"God, Harlow," Theo says, his voice husky. "I want to take my time working down your body, tasting and teasing every single part of you. I don't want to share. I want to bury myself deep inside of you so that you have nowhere to go. No way to escape. You are *mine*," he growls. "For right now, at least."

I moan as his fingers twist my nipples gently. "Then do it."

He pulls back and tugs my t-shirt over my head. I stay still as he kneels, pulling my sweatpants down slowly. As he stands back up, his hands travel with him up my legs, making me shiver. Fully bare before him, I step out of my pants as he removes his sweater. My heart thumps wildly as he unbuckles his jeans, and my mouth goes dry when I see how big and hard he is. Then he's removing his black boxers, standing naked in front of me. It's like someone carved him from stone. He's not chiseled and sharp like Alaric and Sterling, or pumped full of muscle like Gideon. It's as if someone honed him with air and water versus a chisel. His large arm muscles contract as he pumps his cock and smirks down at me.

"Like what you see?"

It's the first time I've seen any of them completely naked. There's a certain vulnerability to it. I swallow thickly. He truly is beautiful.

"It's okay," I tease, smiling.

He growls and pushes me against the shelves, and he places his lips roughly on mine, using his tongue to part my mouth. As I moan into him, my hands grasp at his shoulders, unable to get myself close enough for him to consume me completely.

Just over a week ago, I was plotting their demise. But now, all I want is him. All I want is *all of them*.

"Fuck, Harlow," he hisses, lips an inch from mine. I can feel his hard shaft on my hip, as well as the arousal already accumulating on the head of his cock.

Wetness pools between my legs with every swipe of his tongue against mine, every caress of his calloused fingers against my hot, feverish skin. In one quick movement, he hoists me up, and I wrap my legs around his waist, breathing heavily. He glides his cock between the lips of my pussy, lowering my hips until I groan.

"Are you going to tease me again?" I ask, pulling away from our kiss and scowling.

His wicked grin sends a shock wave through my body, and he nudges my opening with his cock, teasing me with my wetness. It's so thick, it almost looks fake.

"Of course," he mutters, and then he drives into me with zero warning. I cry out, nails digging into him and legs tightening around his waist. His size is painful as he stretches me, but it also feels electrifying. "I wouldn't have it any other way."

"Bastard," I grit out with a laugh that's quickly cut off by his movements.

He pounds into me. The slapping sound reverberates around the large room, and it shakes the bookcase. More books fall beside us, but I don't care. His hands grab onto my ass and bring me down on his cock, hard and fast. I gasp, throwing my head back, writhing against him.

"Fuck," I whimper. "Yes." I grind my hips as much as I can on top of him, grabbing the shelf above my head for leverage. Lifting myself slightly, I roll along his shaft.

"Mmm," Theo moans. "Yes, baby. You're a needy little monster, aren't you?" he growls.

"Only if you're done punishing me," I bite back.

He frowns as a piece of white-blond hair falls over his forehead. His jaw tenses in concentration as he pounds into me with abandon.

"Can't I fuck you and punish you at the same time?" he asks, reaching up with one hand and wrapping his fingers around my neck. "Can't I make you gasp for air as your tight cunt pulses around my cock?"

I let out a squeak as he squeezes tighter. "Yes," I gasp.

My spine scrapes against the bookshelf as he holds me in place. I rock my hips onto his hard cock, and he groans, the sound low and guttural. Keeping me pinned, he drives into me, taking total control of my pleasure.

"Good. Get ready, Harlow. I'm going to fill you so full of my come that you'll be feeling me leak down your thighs for days."

I begin to shake as he slows, angling himself against my inner wall as one hand keeps hold of my neck.

Oh, God.

I moan in frustration, needing the friction. I am *so fucking close*. Every muscle inside of me is bound up tightly, waiting to unravel in a tidal wave of pleasure.

"Harder?" he asks, slamming into me.

I cry out. "Yes. And deeper."

He impales me then, moving his hand from my throat to grip my other hip. As he slams me down on his shaft, my eyes roll into the back of my head. He is filling me so completely, so perfectly. His balls slap against my ass with every thrust, and I feel him deep in my abdomen as my climax crests.

"Yes, Harlow." He stops moving, letting me ride his cock. "You're going to make me come."

I scream and dig my nails into Theo's back as my hips rock and slide against him. Pleasure zaps through me strong and quick, and I can feel myself contract around his thick length as my muscles convulse and my nails draw blood. Streams of my own come gush out of me, causing our joining to sound wet and filthy. I shudder as the last of it leaves my body. I'm still moving against him when I feel his cock harden even more. It pulses into me, jets of come hitting my cervix as he hisses and bellows.

I shudder as Theo thrusts one more time, jerking into me and groaning. I hold on to the bookshelf as we both stare at each other, panting. My legs are still around his waist, and he's still inside of me.

"Fuck," he says, gripping my ass. His cock is still twitching inside of me, and he smiles. "I don't think I'll ever get enough of you."

"Well, you have me for life. You all made damn sure of that fact," I say in jest, but the words feel heavy somehow.

He brushes my damp hair off of my face, placing a gentle kiss on my neck. "Fuck yeah, we did."

"I'm still convinced this is Stockholm Syndrome," I tell him, rolling my eyes.

He pulls away and looks at me with a serious expression. "Darling, if this were Stockholm Syndrome, you wouldn't be coming so hard and begging me to fill you up."

To my surprise, he's still hard, and he thrusts up into me again.

I feel a gush of fluid leave me, but Theo just uses that for extra lube. I'm sore, but the way he's looking at me with that unhinged expression...

"I don't think that's true," I say, my voice hoarse as I instinctually move against him, already craving another release.

He thrusts. I gasp.

"You like us. You may even be falling in love with us."

I stiffen at his words, but he continues to drive into me. I don't even have a good retort for that, because it's the last thing I expected him to say.

"And if I am?" My voice is quiet.

I don't love them, of course. But I'm curious to see what he'd say, how he'd react.

"You don't have to be coy, little monster," he murmurs. "I don't *have you* for the rest of my life. You *are* the rest of my life. You have a permanent place in my soul. Is that clear?"

His words stun me, and I stare into his blue eyes before I bring my lips to his, ignoring the way I feel light and happy all of a sudden.

CHAPTER 19

GIDEON

Adjusting my tie, I study myself in the mirror. I've pulled my hair back but kept my Converse on. Formal on the top, party on the bottom. My hand slides over the butterfly knife in my pocket, ensuring it's still there. I grab my jacket and my weekend bag, since I'll be staying at Theo's house for a couple of days. I'm the only one without a house manager or housekeeper, though I do have a professional cleaning service come into St. Claire House twice a week. Still, shit piles up, and I grimace when I glance over at the piles of mail and various packages sitting on the dining room table.

Out of the four guys, I am the least organized.

Rough around the edges, like a raw diamond. But when I polish myself up... I smile into the mirror before locking my place behind me. Setting my bag and jacket in the passenger seat, I climb into the driver's seat of my black Maserati Granturismo. This thing drives like sex feels–smooth, pleasurable, and it just gets better the longer I have it. My hands grip the wheel as I speed down the country road to Theo's house.

My phone rings, so I pick it up with my car Bluetooth. I can see it's my mother calling.

"Hi, Mum."

"Hello, Gideon. Just checking up on my favorite son."

I smile. "I'm your only son."

"I'm teasing you. How are the guys?"

"They're fine. Same old."

There's a beat of silence before she continues. I know this will be the *real*

273

reason she called. Since she knows about my job and the Lords—she's the only parent who does—she often calls because she's worried. It's sort of funny to hear how much she berates my dead father for leaving me with such an important legacy.

"I heard about Charles. I'm so sorry to hear about his untimely death."

Before we killed him, we all agreed that the four of us—now five—would be the only ones to know the real cause of Charles Blackwell's demise.

"Yeah. It was quite shocking. He was so young."

"Yes. He was." She pauses. "I worry about you, Gideon. The stress of that job can't be good for you, and Charles was only ten years older than you—"

"Mum, I'm fine. I promise."

She clucks her tongue on the other end. "And who will replace him, then?"

I swallow uncomfortably. It's one thing to plan your psychotic schemes involving an eighteen-year-old woman with the other three Lords... it's an entirely different thing to tell your mother about it.

"Charles had a daughter, so she will be taking his place."

"Oh?" Her voice perks up. I know exactly what she's going to say next. "Is she pretty?"

I laugh. "She's fucking gorgeous, Mum."

I swear, I can hear her smiling on the other end of the line. "Well, you must bring her to visit me soon."

"Okay, I'll try. I have to go, Mum. Love you."

We hang up, and I'm still smiling as I pull up to Theo's house.

My mother and I were very close growing up. She'd left my father and moved to northern Scotland when I was a lad, so it was my father who was the default parent. Still, she came to visit often, and I went up to hers every summer. I don't blame her for leaving him. Maxwell St. Claire was a prick, and a part of me is glad Charles killed him. Even so, he was hardly ever home. My childhood was normal. Sheltered, even. I was a happy child... until Charles showed up that day in Cross Manor.

We all rebelled in our own ways. I was studying under a blacksmith when he conscripted me, so weapons were always an interest of mine. After I joined the Lords... that interest in weapons became a lot more dangerous. I took seminars with the Russian military, spent weeks with the U.S. Army, and learned all I could from the top weapons specialists in the world.

I pull my knife out of my pocket. It's a butterfly knife—a type of folding pocketknife that originated in the Philippines. It has two handles that counter-rotate around the blade in a way that, when closed, the blade is concealed. A small latch holds the handles together, and mine is nearly worn down from overuse.

I made my very first kill with this knife, and I intend to make my last with it, too.

I carry it as a way out—a scapegoat if things should go wrong. I know my veins and arteries, and I know how to nick them just so for the least amount of pain.

Hopefully, it will never come to that.

I hop out of the car and grab my things, looking up at Wolf Manor for a few seconds before I pocket my knife and walk inside.

CHAPTER 20

Harlow

"Seriously? My breasts are going to spill out of this thing," I groan, looking at myself in the wardrobe mirror in Theo's room. The guys are all dressed. They're just waiting on me now. Our car will be arriving in ten minutes for dinner in London with Acadia.

"We had a deal," Sterling says, standing behind me. His fingers graze my straps, and the reflection of his eyes bore into mine. The other three guys are sitting on Theo's bed several feet away. "You could wear your boots, but you had to wear the dress I picked out. Weren't those the terms you laid out for us that very first night?"

I frown. "Don't get me wrong, I love the dress. But I'm going to flash someone if I move."

It's true—the dress is incredible, as are the professional stylists that Theo called in. They didn't do as much as the first night. In fact, my hair is hanging down in loose waves, and my makeup is minimal—save for the dark red lipstick they applied. And the dress? It's truly gorgeous. Long, black, and glittering, the sleeves are sheer and the bodice is fitted. It loosens around my hips and cascades over my body like a pool of black, inky water. But the cut? It's so deep, the V is nearly to my belly button.

"I also think my hair should be up," I murmur, angling my head to the right and then the left. "What do you think?" I ask Sterling.

"Mmm," he says, his front brushing up against my back as he runs his hands through my hair. His fingers are warm, and I groan when he begins tugging it around.

"What are you doing?" I ask, nearly breathless with pleasure.

He doesn't answer me. His eyes are focused on the top of my head as he pulls and tugs. Moving lower, his fingers graze my neck before Gideon hands him a clear band. My body erupts in goosebumps when I realize... he just freaking braided my hair into a French braid.

Why the hell is that so hot?

"How do you know how to braid hair?" I ask him, my voice husky.

And damn him... because the braid suits the dress and my makeup perfectly.

"I've braided a lot of hair," he mutters, one corner of his lips tilting up. "My subs liked it."

Something raw and primal swoops through my core at his words.

"I see."

"And for the dress," he adds, reaching over to the dresser. "I had this sent over." He hands it to me.

"Double-sided tape?"

He shrugs. "It should help hold the fabric in place."

Huh. He certainly thinks of everything.

I add a couple of pieces to the inside of the dress, and he's right. It stays.

"How do you know all of this? Why are you so good at picking out clothes and dressing women?"

He takes a step back and places his hands in his trouser pockets. "Because I like control, Harlow. Because I like to dress my subs and control what they wear, what they eat, how they walk, and who they talk to. Some dominants only want dominance in the bedroom. I want it *all the time.*"

He growls the last three words, and my pulse spikes. "So, am I your submissive, then?"

Something dark comes over his expression. "If you want to be."

That would have to be something I consider. I definitely wanted to explore the Dom/sub dynamic with him one day soon. Before I can respond, Alaric walks over to us.

"The car is here," he says, smiling as he bends down to kiss me. "You look beautiful. A true Lady of Darkness."

He twists me around so that I can study myself in the mirror. Gideon and Theo walk over, standing behind Alaric, Sterling, and I. Goosebumps claw up and down my skin, making it tingle. The five of us dressed up and together like this... I nearly lose my breath at the sight. I remembered seeing them at the back of my father's funeral, but right now, they seem ten times more deadly. Back then, I referred to them as the four horsemen of death. But right now... the five of us look straight out of the underworld.

Four demons and their newest monster.

CHAPTER 21

ALARIC

We make our way to the car—a Cadillac Escalade that has been retrofitted to look like a limousine inside. Harlow climbs in first, followed by the rest of us. The driver speaks to Theo before we set off, and once we do, the lights are dimmed and are replaced with low, red lighting.

I reach over to the small mahogany bar and pour us all a finger of whiskey. Handing the crystal tumblers out, we're all quiet as we drink. The air is thick with anticipation, but the whiskey helps ease our nerves. Pouring a second round, we all clink glasses before setting them down.

"I think it comes as no surprise that Acadia is going to want Harlow in exchange for peace," I tell them, looking at Harlow.

She stiffens, and her face pales at my words. "Why? What's so special about me?"

Everything.

"They want the only thing we're not willing to give up," I growl. Looking around at the other guys, at Harlow—*they* are my entire life. Whether they know it or not.

Acadia will rot in hell for eternity for trying to take what's mine.

"And they know it, too," Theo says glumly from his seat. "In asking for you, they will be starting a war."

"Why not just kill them?" she asks, looking between us, her question spoken with such dark naivety it has me holding back a smirk. It also turns me on.

"Because the dinner will be flecked with traps. If we shoot, they will have someone in hiding waiting to stab us in the back. We are walking into their lair—we are giving up our power."

She furrows her brows. "Why?"

I sigh. "Because we're going to make them think they can take you again."

A frown immediately transforms her face. "Really? I don't want to—"

I reach forward and grab her by her arms, pulling her onto my lap. Wrapping my arms around her, I smile when I realize she's not even trying to pull away.

"There are a lot of things we must do in this business, little monster. Espionage is a huge aspect of being a Lord—or *Lady*—of Darkness. We have to pretend, play the game, make them think they're on top."

"He's not wrong," Sterling says, studying something on his phone with a serious expression.

She relaxes further, sinking into my body. She smells so fucking delightful—like roses.

"But at what cost? I'm just supposed to go with them and hope you can find me again before they try to—"

I lurch forward and sink my teeth into her neck. "No one is ever going to take you from us again. You. Are. *Ours*."

She groans and writhes in my arms, moving her ass along my erection. "Am I? Because it feels like I'm just a pawn in your egotistical, male-centric war." There's a bite, an edge, to her voice that makes me stiffen.

"You truly think that?" I ask, my hands roving down her breasts and stomach, coming to her thighs.

"We're headed to a dinner where I'm supposed to pretend to be okay with becoming Acadia's whore. How long do I have to act this time? How long until my four knights in shining armor come to save me? I'll be at their beck and call until you decide—"

"Baby," I murmur, interrupting her. "You're misunderstanding. There won't be any knights in shining armor coming for you. Because you're going to save yourself."

She gasps, and at the same time, I reach forward to the hem of her dress, hiking it up so that I have access to her panties. She squirms as I brush two fingers against the wet fabric. It feels... oddly slick. I quickly push inside to find her completely bare.

"Oh, little monster," I groan. "What have you done?"

She turns her neck to look up at me, her eyes hooded and dark. "I had Theo's people... wax something other than my eyebrows."

My cock jerks when I think of spreading her legs and lapping everything up—before I plunge into her smooth, bare cunt.

"Our little monster is such a tease," Gideon murmurs as he flicks his knife open and closed.

I chuckle. "Indeed."

"Let's get her wired up," Theo says, pulling his laptop open.

"Wired up?" she asks, her voice still husky from the way I'm trailing my fingers up and down her slit.

"I told you we were walking into the lion's lair... now we just need to make sure you come out on top."

"Do I kill them?" she asks, shaking slightly as I part her lips. I groan again when I feel how goddamn drenched she is, how she's dripping onto my fingers. What I wouldn't give to shove my cock into her pussy.

Later tonight, I would do just that.

"No, Harlow. You don't have to kill them. You just have to blow them to pieces."

She lets out another tiny gasp. "How?"

I reach into my suit pocket, producing a tiny remote control. It's small enough to insert inside of Harlow. It also happens to be the one place they won't check right away if they feel her up for weapons after we hand her over.

That thought makes me feel so goddamn sick and homicidal.

"I'm going to place this inside of you," I tell her, moving the round remote control to her opening. "You're going to press the button when we tell you to, and then you will have thirty seconds to get out of the building."

"What building?" she asks, once I move it up inside of her and secure it. She doesn't even flinch.

"The restaurant. Are you ready to play?"

She nods. "Yes."

I kiss her temple. "Good. Let's do this. For once and for all."

CHAPTER 22

Harlow

Once we arrive in London, our car takes us to a nondescript parking garage. There's a large black van waiting for us, and I follow the guys out of the Escalade and into the van. I gasp when I look around. There are several computers and screens, flashing buttons, and a switchboard of electronics on one wall. Theo says hello to the man setting everything up, whose name is Monty.

I swear, Theo knows everyone.

They explained what's going to happen tonight, and how they're going to make it seem as real as possible.

Of course, Theo's guys have already scoped the restaurant out, and it's crawling with Acadian members. He set up explosives all over the building. One trigger will ignite them all, and it should kill everyone inside.

Of course, being central London, it will ultimately be disguised as a faulty gas line.

They counted thirty-six total members here tonight. The last remnants of the organization. They're utilizing every single member to make this deal. We already know they want me, so when they propose peace in exchange for me, I'm supposed to throw a fit—cry, scream, yell my head off to make it seem realistic. I need to act surprised, betrayed, and then the guys will leave—presuming things go according to plan. There's no doubt in our minds that they'll check me for weapons, which I won't have, and then drag me to the back. They will want to secure me inside their vehicle as soon as possible. I will then pretend to get sick—Alaric will ensure he doses me with something that will make me vomit.

After using the bathroom, I'm supposed to press the button, and then escape through the small trap door that already exists in the bathroom stall furthest from the door.

It's complicated, but also easy.

I just have to make them believe the guys sold me out.

I have to act distraught.

So distraught that I get sick.

"I'll be listening to every word," Monty says. "We'll be able to see you and hear you. Once you press the button, Harlow, we will count to thirty and detonate. Make sure you're out of the building."

I nod.

"If anything goes awry," Theo says to me, holding my face in his hands, "we will go in there with guns. But that's our backup plan. Stick with the explosives. It ensures we eliminate every single Acadian member. I have set the bombs up to maximize casualties. The building will implode and kill everyone who wasn't peppered with the initial blast."

I nod, swallowing my nerves as he releases me.

Monty hands the four guys four gold rings. "These are charged and ready to go. It will vibrate just before detonation, okay?"

The rings all have skulls with crowns on them. He turns and hands me a smaller version of theirs—with diamonds outlining the skull and crown. Different, more feminine... but still powerful as fuck.

"These have hidden cameras as well as microphones," Monty explains. "We can see and hear you. He reaches into one of the metal drawers and pulls out a small metal device that looks like a tiny toothpick. "This is your tracker, Harlow."

I look at Theo. "A tracker?"

Theo nods. "We all have them. I still kick myself that you didn't have yours inserted before Acadia kidnapped you."

"Right arm, please," Monty says. Grimacing, he holds out a large needle. "The tracker goes in here, and I insert it just under your skin."

"Okay. Like my birth control implant."

Monty nods, and I wince as he rolls my sleeve up, swipes my skin with an antibiotic wipe, and places the tracker. It barely bleeds, and in thirty seconds, I'm done.

The guys test the microphones and cameras, and once we're sure everything is set, Alaric throws the door open.

"Alright. Let's kill these motherfuckers."

CHAPTER 23

Sterling

The Escalade drops us off in front of The Sage Club in Shoreditch a few minutes later. When the guys get out of the car, I stay back with Harlow. We're making sure there are no traps near the door or anyone waiting to jump us. Luckily, it's clear, so we head inside just as Harlow downs the drug that will cause her to vomit in about thirty minutes. The restaurant—which is a fine-dining establishment—is closed to the public for the evening. All tables except for one are empty. I feel Harlow stiffen next to me as we greet the two seated Acadian members politely. Jurgen and Kristoff are the two men here with us, though I know from Theo's intelligence that there are several men waiting in the kitchen, the roof, and the other dining room.

We all take a seat at the round table. Harlow between me and Alaric.

"Gentlemen," Jurgen says as a server places a bottle of red wine in the center. It appears sealed, but I don't trust a single fucking person in his organization. "I hope you don't mind that we ordered wine for the table."

"Not at all," Alaric says, watching the server as he unscrews the cork and pours all seven of us a small glass. Alaric holds his glass up. "You go first, since you ordered it. It's a lovely bottle of wine. A 2000 Château Lafite Rothschild... very nice."

Jurgen smiles. "Of course." He holds the glass up to his nose and sniffs. Taking a small sip, he nods. "Perfect." Dismissing the waiter, he sets his glass down and leans forward.

Harlow goes to take a sip of the wine, but I grab her wrist subtly, shaking my head once.

I still don't trust them. She is not to eat or drink anything unless I say it's safe.

"Gentlemen," Alaric starts, sighing. "Why are we here? Let's call a truce and move on. We do our thing, you do yours. Our territories hardly ever overlap. I'm tired of fighting."

Kristoff slams his fist on the table, and Harlow jumps. "You killed Luka. You killed Armin. And now you ask for *peace?*" he sneers, spitting.

"Kristoff," Jurgen murmurs, placing his hand on top of Kristoff's. He turns to face Alaric. "Kristoff is right. It's very easy to ask for peace when you have killed so many of our men."

Alaric leans back in his seat. Picking at a fleck of dust on his shoulder, he clasps his hands together on his chest and shrugs.

"What is it that you want, then? We're here. We're willing to negotiate."

Jurgen's eyes flash to Harlow, and I tamp down the possessive, predatory growl that wants to erupt from my chest.

She is ours.

Alaric's nostrils flare as he leans forward. "She is a Lady of Darkness. I'm afraid she's not for sale, just in the same way that Kristoff is not for sale," he adds, baring his teeth at Kristoff.

"Okay, let me rephrase that," Jurgen says slowly, grinning. "We take Harlow with us, or you all die here tonight."

We all sit up straight and my pulse pounds angrily in my ears.

She is ours.

Theo glares at Jurgen, as does Gideon.

Harlow crosses her arms. "No."

I let out a long sigh. "What are the terms?" I ask Jurgen, and her head whips to me with a pointed glare.

He shrugs. "We just want her. And then we will leave you alone for good."

Yeah fucking right. We all knew Acadia was too stupid to walk away. As long as they existed, they'd try to kill us. If not today, then soon. Their idiocy knows no bounds, and they'd keep trying as long as they were alive.

She is ours.

If we'd known that weeks ago with Armin, we would've done something about it.

For the purposes of our plan, I nod, like I'm considering. "For good?" I ask, leaning forward.

Jurgen nods. "We will have you escorted out ourselves, and we will never bother you again."

I pretend to debate it. I look between Alaric, Theo, Gideon, and Harlow, who scoffs and stands up, throwing her napkin down on the table.

"Are you seriously considering this?" she asks, her voice shrill. Her cheeks are flushed, and *fuck me*, she's doing such a good fucking job.

She's a true Lady of Darkness tonight.

She is ours.

I grab her wrist as her eyes narrow. She tries pulling out of my grasp, but I tug her back down and into my lap.

"You've been nothing but a problem since the day we initiated you," I growl. "If we have to choose you or peace for our order... we have to think long term." I bite her earlobe, and the moan that escapes her lips isn't fake. She likes pain—that's really fucking good to know. Even here in front of our enemies, she's distracting as fuck. "Our order is a thousand years old. You've been with us for a few weeks. I'm sorry, Harlow. We have to let you go and cut our losses."

I glance at Alaric, who looks both pleased and horrified at the same time. "I told you, she's not for sale," he growls. He's playing his part very well, too. His voice has less conviction.

"It is up to you," Jurgen says simply. "But there is only one way you're walking out of here alive tonight. And that's without her."

She is ours.

Alaric leans forward, glaring at Jurgen. "We have men waiting just outside."

Jurgen mimics Alaric's murderous expression, clasping his hands together on the table. "As do we. It's your call. Risk your lives, or let her go."

Alaric pretends to consider as Harlow sits tensed on my lap. He pinches the bridge of his nose and releases a pained sigh.

"Do you promise not to hurt her?" Alaric asks, his voice tight.

"No, no, no," Harlow begs, thrashing against me.

"She's feisty," I grit out, holding her still with my arms. "Be prepared."

She is ours.

Jurgen and Kristoff grin as Jurgen stands, holding a hand out for her.

"No," she says quickly, her breaths becoming rapid with panic. "I'm not going anywhere with you."

"Take her," I tell Jurgen. "She's going to put up a fight."

Jurgen reaches for Harlow, and she flinches when his hand gets near.

I'm suddenly feeling downright murderous. It reminds me of the first night, of how she flinched away from our touch.

She doesn't do that with us anymore.

She is ours.

Jurgen grabs Harlow roughly and pulls her into a standing position. "We'll take good care of you," he says gruffly, using his hands to feel her up. We made sure she was free of weapons tonight. One of them darts into the cut of her dress, and she gasps when he squeezes her left breast. "Mmm, these are... magnificent. We're going to have fun with you, Lady Blackwell."

I'm gripping the edge of the seat so hard, I'm afraid I might shatter into pieces. By the looks on Gideon, Alaric, and Theo's faces... they all feel the same way. But a second later, we will our expressions and body language into neutrality. If Jurgen knows how much we care about her...

She is ours.

"Thank you for your cooperation, my Lords," he taunts, wrapping his free arm around Harlow's waist.

Alaric stands abruptly, his expression one of cool indifference. "If this is all you wanted, we'll be on our way." He smooths the lapels of his jacket and waits impatiently.

He's the most possessive of the bunch.

The fact that he's not even looking at Harlow... the control it must take for him to appear unfazed...

I admire the hell out of him.

"We will take very good care of her," Jurgen says smugly, lying through his teeth.

Alaric's expression doesn't falter, and he doesn't look at Harlow.

"Kristoff, please escort the Lords out of the building."

Theo's jaw rolls as he stands, looking at Jurgen, but he doesn't say anything either. None of us do. If we show our hand too early, everything will go awry.

Theo cocks his head. "I wish I could say it was a pleasure," he grits out.

Gideon stands next, his dark blue eyes glittering with rage. Like Alaric and I, though, he stays quiet.

I can say for certain that we've undergone much more complex missions in the past, but this is the first time for all of us that the stakes are so high. I'm a second away from blowing our entire cover just so we don't have to watch Jurgen's fingers maim our little monster.

She is ours.

Harlow sobs, and real tears fall from her eyes. "Please don't leave me with them." She thrashes against Jurgen. "I promise to be better."

Gideon walks over to her and kisses her gently on the lips. His lips form a thin line as he shrugs.

"Sorry, baby. Sometimes life's not fair. We have to maintain our order over everything else."

"I am a part of your fucking order!" she screams, her eyes black with fury.

I shake my head and smirk. "You were. We'll find someone else. You're not worth the trouble."

Turning, I walk away with Kristoff and Alaric. Theo and Gideon follow us closely. I move my hand to the gun tucked against my back, watching as Alaric does the same thing. Kristoff pushes the door open, walking through it before us, strutting onto the sidewalk like a man who just won the war.

I nearly laugh.

Cardinal rule number one: Never turn your back on your enemy.

As the restaurant doors close behind us, Kristoff chuckles and begins to turn around.

Alaric shoots him in the head before he can say a word. My eyes scan the area, but it's clear of people. Thanks to the silencer and special bullet, there's no noise and hardly any splatter. Still, since we're in a public area, Alaric places a cap over his head and hoists him up, like he's carrying a friend who passed out at the pub. One block later, we all clamber into Monty's van.

Monty doesn't bat an eye as he clicks through to the camera on Harlow's hand. There's movement, but we can't make anything out.

"Turn the volume up," I order Monty.

He does, and we're all silent as we wait for Harlow to complete the mission.

Our Lady is about to take everyone the fuck out.

She is ours.

CHAPTER 24

Harlow

I have to curl my fists at my sides to keep my hands from shaking. The guys are gone, and now it's just me and this vile man.

Jurgen.

Why are these Acadian members all so awful?

My stomach tugs with nausea, and I know the medicine Alaric gave me is working. I pretend to cry as Jurgen gestures for me to sit.

"Now that the filth has taken itself out, we should enjoy our meal. Drink." He holds his wine glass up, and I do the same with shaky hands. Tears are falling down my cheeks as I pretend to sip, but the liquid doesn't touch my lips.

"You will pay for this," I grit out, glaring at him. I know my mascara is running down my cheeks, and I attempt to make my hands shake even more.

Pretend, pretend, pretend.

He huffs a laugh as he chews a piece of bread. "Yes, yes. Luka mentioned you were all talk. You can threaten me all you want. At the end of the day, we both know your Lords sold you to me. They care about their lives more than yours. How does it feel to be betrayed like that?" he asks, his voice cruel.

"Fuck you," I hiss. My stomach rolls again, and I lean forward. If I'm going to make this all believable, I need him to think I'm distraught. "I can't believe this is happening," I say quietly, my gaze drifting down. Gripping the edge of the table, I inhale deeply as my eyes flutter closed. "Oh God. I think I'm going to be sick."

It's not a lie. My stomach lurches, and I gag.

Jurgen jumps up. "Fuck," he snarls. Grabbing my elbow as I gag again, he quickly drags me toward the back. "Get yourself under control," he hisses, shoving me into the women's restroom. "And don't even *think* of fleeing. I'll be waiting for you right here. Disgusting," he mutters as I retch loudly.

I fall into the bathroom from the force of his push, clawing my way up to hands and knees as I vomit all over the tiled floor. It's intense—I continue vomiting, making sure I'm loud about it. My whole body is trembling as I finish, and all I want to do is lie down on the floor until my stomach settles. But I can't. I have a job to do.

Standing up with shaky legs, I make my way to the sink, splashing water on my face. I look at myself in the mirror. Mascara is smeared all over my face, skin flushed and blotchy, eyes glassy and irritated. My hair has come out of my braid partially, and I look crazed. Smiling, I dry my face and walk into the stall closest to the wall. Feeling around, my fingers catch on a latch hidden behind the ornate wallpaper. I scrape the paper away and lift.

A door appears.

It's small, and I have to open it slowly because it's tearing the paper at the same time.

"Almost done?"

Jurgen's voice booms through the bathroom.

I nearly jump.

"Just using the toilet." I take a deep, calming breath.

"You have one minute," he barks.

And you have thirty seconds, you bastard.

I place one foot on the toilet as I reach inside of myself and remove the remote control. My thumb shakes over the button.

Lifting my hand with the ring up, I whisper.

"Okay. Ready to detonate. Thirty-second warning."

My ring vibrates once.

I press the button and then I creep through the hidden doorway, pulling it closed behind me and counting the seconds in my head.

Twenty seconds.

Hopefully, if Jurgen bursts into the bathroom before the bomb detonates, he won't see the door at first.

Fifteen seconds.

My ring vibrates intensely.

Slowly hunching over as I walk through the dark passageway, I keep moving until I see a door at the end of the long hallway. I squint my eyes and reach out, feeling a handle, twisting the knob. It's locked, and my heart sinks.

Ten seconds.

I pound against it, screaming. "It's locked!" I have no idea if they're on the other side of it or not.

Eight seconds.

My breathing catches as I begin to panic. It's so overwhelming that I can feel my vision cloud, my pulse skyrocket, and my skin tingle. My hands sweat as I press my body into the door over and over, sobbing as I go.

Six seconds.

"Help me!" I scream. I look behind me, and the door to the bathroom is only fifteen feet away. A blast that carries through the bathroom will surely reach me.

I have set the bombs up to maximize casualties. The building will implode and kill everyone who wasn't peppered with the initial blast.

My heart hammers so wildly against my chest, I can hardly catch my breath. This can't be happening.

My ring vibrates again—a warning.

Five.

It vibrates again. Indicating the five second countdown.

Four.

I look around once more, deciding that I may as well be ducking if I'm going to get hit with a blast. *If* I survive, as there's probably a bomb in here too in case Jurgen decided to come after me.

Three.

The ring vibrates again. My mind spins with hopelessness, and I fall to my knees, covering my head.

Two.

Someone shouts behind me, and I feel a pair of hands grab my arms roughly, pulling me to the side just as the ground shakes underneath me. Falling, I land on a body, looking down to see Alaric gripping me. His eyes flash with something I can't decipher, and then—

One.

A loud, quaking, all-consuming boom envelopes us just as Alaric pins his body over mine, shielding me completely. I scream as I feel his body twitch on top of mine, but then I don't hear anything. Only a ear-piercing, ringing noise.

"Alaric," I shout, looking around. I can't hear myself say his name, but I know I do. There's smoke, rubble, and dust everywhere. It smells like gunpowder and burning wood. As I try to take a breath, I cough, looking up at Alaric. My heart stills as I realize he's unconscious.

"Alaric!"

I try to shove him off of my body, but my arms are still weak and shaky from not only vomiting viciously, but from having a panic attack. One that I'm still deep in the trenches of as I begin to hyperventilate, sobbing as I scream, trying to push him off so that I can help him.

So that I can *fix* him.

"Alaric," I cry. "Please don't die."

I reach up and check his pulse, and I feel it flutter beneath my finger. I need to get out from under him so that I can get help—so that I can save him.

A second later, someone lifts him up. I see Theo and Sterling wrap their arms underneath his shoulders, dragging him to a nearby van. Gideon rushes over to me and pulls me up, but my knees wobble, and I stumble.

He says something that I can't make out, his hands reaching for me and inspecting my face, my chest, my shoulders. Once he determines I'm okay, he says something else, but I still can't hear him.

"The bomb... Alaric—" I mutter. The ringing in my ears gets worse when I speak. Gideon shouts something that sounds like it's coming from a mile away, when he's really right beside me. "He... Alaric, he—"

Gideon picks me up, hoisting me up with an arm under my knees and another behind my back, walking us back to the van quickly. When he sets me down on one of the seats, I stare at Alaric, horrified.

I vaguely hear the sound of a door slamming shut as renewed tears prick at my eyes.

Alaric is slumped over across from me, and he's dripping with blood. His shirt and jacket are in tatters. He's still unconscious, and I see his chest rising and falling rapidly.

The ringing begins to subside, but as it does, a pounding takes its place. I reach up and touch my forehead, and when I pull my fingers away, they're covered in blood.

"Fuck," Gideon hisses as we drive away from the scene. He runs his fingers through his hair and looks around wildly. "Well, *that* did not go according to plan."

Theo pins him with a glare. "You think?"

"Why the fuck was the door locked?" Sterling growls. "Did Acadia know about that passageway?"

"I highly doubt it," Theo hisses. "No one had been in that passage for *years*. When I laid those bombs *myself* just hours ago, the dust on the floor was thick from years of disuse."

The van parks, and Monty climbs into the back with us. He jiggles the mouse on the main computer.

"Let me pull up the footage," he murmurs, clicking through security images.

Everyone is quiet except for me. My breathing is ragged, still panicked from the blast. "Is he... will he—" I look at Alaric, my stomach clenching.

"He'll be fine," Gideon says quickly. "We're taking him to our doctor in London right now." His eyes sweep over my face. "He should look at your gash, too."

Relief washes over me, and he must sense that I'm about to have a full-on breakdown, because he comes to sit next to me.

"Shh," he whispers, pulling me into his side gently. "You did your job beautifully. Alaric will be okay. I'm so proud of you. So fucking proud," he adds, his voice catching as he holds me close.

I cry quietly for a few seconds, feeling better in his arms.

"We thought we lost you," Sterling growls from across the van. "We thought... we didn't have time to think. Alaric ran out and shot the lock off, and then—" He looks away, rubbing his mouth. "A second later, and you both would've been dead. He pulled you within *feet* of the perimeter of the building. Any closer, and the wall of the building would've come down on top of the both of you."

I swallow and let out a shaky breath. Just as I open my mouth to respond, Monty clears his throat.

"I think I found out what happened," he murmurs, turning his screen to face all of us. I watch in horror as Jurgen walks into the frame of the video feed, using his key to lock the side door I was meant to come out of. He turns slowly, looking directly into the camera lens, and then he grins as he holds two middle fingers up before walking away.

"Bastard. Fucking bastard. It must've been right before we arrived," Theo says, his voice tainted with fury. "I checked the door when I laid the bombs. Fucking bastard," he hisses, closing his eyes. "He was ensuring he locked us in there like termites."

My stomach drops. "Are we sure they're all dead?" I ask tentatively. "If they knew what our plan was..."

"They didn't know," Theo growls, leaning forward. "They were probably just covering their tracks in case we decided to run with you at dinner. But we—unexpectedly—agreed to their terms. They didn't need to kill us. They're dead. I'll have my guys confirm later. We are looking for thirty-six men. If there are less than that... well, then I guess I'm going to have to hunt the rest down myself," he adds, his menacing voice gritty and low. His blue eyes lock onto mine. "I thought you were going to die, Harlow."

I swallow and nod. My head is still pounding. "I thought so, too."

"I was never going to let that fucking happen," Alaric croaks, but then inhales sharply as he stirs. "Fuck, everything fucking hurts." He winces, squeezing his eyes shut.

I nearly sob with relief, leaping forward and colliding with his body. He just chuckles softly and looks down at me. One of his eyes is swollen shut, and his face is peppered with tiny gashes.

"I'm here, baby. We're alive. We won."

CHAPTER 25

Theo

We pull up to Kitt's large, terraced townhouse in Marylebone. I help the guys move Harlow inside, and then we all hoist Alaric and carefully drag him up the steps to Kitt's front door. The door opens and Kitt stares down at us, an exasperated look on his face. His eyes flick over to Harlow, and he suddenly looks like such a father figure. Straightening up, he crosses his arms and scowls at me.

"What the hell have you guys been doing to this poor woman?"

I chuckle. *If only he knew.*

"First an accidental overdose a few weeks ago, and now..." he trails off, helping us all inside.

I quickly jog back down the stairs and pass Monty his payment. He grins when I hand him the bag. Fifty-thousand dollars per job, that's our agreement. I'd pay him ten times that if he asked.

"Thanks, man," he mutters. "You have my number for next time."

"I added an extra five-hundred quid for cleanup," I reply, grimacing as I look around the blood-stained van. "Be safe."

I close the door and tap the roof of the van as he drives away.

So many people think we're pure monsters. Killing machines with no heart or empathy. I can be. I can put the Lords mask on and kill without remorse. We all can. But when it comes to the *good* parts of this life—making connections, helping others, having a reliable support network that makes it all possible—that's what makes this life worth living.

That's what makes this job bearable.

I watch Monty turn the corner, and then I jog up the stairs to Kitt's house.

He's already treating Alaric, cutting his jacket and shirt off slowly. Harlow is sitting down next to him, holding his hand as Kitt inspects the gashes.

"You have glass and concrete imbedded in your skin," Kitt mumbles. His hands move to Alaric's head. "You don't appear to have a concussion, and I suspect you don't have blast lung, either."

Harlow pales. "Blast lung?"

Kitt nods. "It's when an explosive shock wave passes through the thorax and penetrates the lung tissue." He turns to face her. "You have a piece of glass embedded in your forehead, but it's a minor wound."

I sag with relief. "So, nothing fatal?"

Kitt shakes his head. "I don't think so. Let's get both of them hooked up and check their vitals. Alaric lost consciousness from the blunt force trauma, so I'll have to check for internal bleeding, but otherwise, they should both make full recoveries." He looks down at Alaric. "You saved her life. You should be proud."

Alaric's eyes find Harlow's, and he squeezes her hand.

A few minutes later, after Kitt cleans Harlow up and gives her a couple of dissolvable stitches, she walks over to me.

"So? Are they dead?" Her voice is low, and I turn my head to face her.

"They are. My men confirmed it a couple of minutes ago. Thirty-six bodies."

She nods, her face hard and angry. "What about the staff?"

I shake my head. "They were all Acadia."

She swallows. "Good. I'm—I'm glad they're dead. I'm glad this nightmare is over."

"Me too."

"I'm just glad it worked. I was convinced Jurgen was going to follow me into the bathroom, and I'd never get a chance to detonate the bomb."

I smirk. "I was pretty certain he would leave you alone." She looks at me questioningly. I can't help the wicked grin that spreads across my face. "My specialty is in finding what makes others tick, little monster. It's why Rose left to go help her daughter with the break-in, why we threatened and chased you. I knew burglaries were your trigger. And when we put you in that cage with Harrison, I knew it would cause something to snap inside of you. Something pivotal for your growth as a Lady."

She scowls up at me, and I continue.

"I do the same with all of our targets. Armin's weakness was little girls. Luka's weakness was his arrogance. Savo's weakness was his sex addiction. And Jurgen? He had emetophobia. An extreme fear of vomiting. Seeing vomit, watching other people vomit..." I chuckle. "We had to utilize his weakness somehow, and we couldn't have him following you into the bathroom."

As she stares at me, it's with a mix of shock, adoration, and horror. "You guys really are psychopaths," she mutters.

I place an arm around her shoulders, pulling her tight into my chest. "I never claimed we weren't."

She scoffs. "I suppose that's true."

"So... your first real mission was mostly a success. How does it feel?"

Her lips quirk to one side, pondering. I brush a piece of hair off of her forehead delicately, and her dark blue eyes find mine. As I look her over this up close, I notice her lipstick is still fully intact, and aside from her wild hair and large bandage on her forehead, I'd say she walked away unscathed. Hopefully she believes in herself enough to realize how vital she is—how well she did tonight, despite the complications.

We couldn't have done it without her.

"It feels... good," she concludes, smiling. "I feel strong. I feel like we did the right thing."

"Good," I murmur, kissing the top of her head and closing my eyes. "You should also feel proud, Harlow."

She stiffens for a second before relaxing. "Proud? Yeah, I guess."

"With time, you will come to find pride in this order. It will guide you. It will heal you. Give it time."

She nods against my chest. "And until then?"

I smile. "Just keep being a badass. We'll teach you everything else."

CHAPTER 26

H<small>ARLOW</small>

A couple of hours later, the Escalade picks us up. Alaric is fine, with no internal injuries. Just the many small cuts all over his body. It's fully dark now, and the weather has turned cold. I shiver as I walk down the front step of Kitt's house. Someone tugs me back as the guys descend down the stairs. I twist to find Kitt looking down at me with a worried expression.

"Here's my card," he says, handing me a white card containing only a phone number. "Take care of yourself. Don't let them boss you around."

I can't help but snort as I pocket his card. "Thanks, Kitt. But I think you've got it confused. *I* boss *them* around."

He grins. "Glad to hear it." It's obvious he wants to say more as he opens and closes his mouth a couple of times. I look at him expectantly. He's older, probably sixty or so. He has that wholesome, fatherly persona about him that makes me feel comfortable in his presence. Seeming to change his mind, he smiles again and waves me off. "It's cold out. Get in the car before I have to treat hypothermia, too."

I say goodbye and do exactly that. Sterling is holding the door open for me, and his hand snaps out, grabbing my wrist before I go inside.

"What did he say to you?" he asks, his voice laced with possession.

I roll my eyes. "He just told me to take care of myself and not to let you guys boss me around."

Sterling pushes me gently against the side of the Escalade. "Is that all?"

"God," I hiss, pushing him off of me. "You're like a dog who has to piss all over his belongings, aren't you?"

His lips twitch. I know I should be angry, but having them there—having Sterling be so protective and intense—it feels good.

"You don't have to be jealous about every single person I talk to," I add, trying to pull away from him.

He grips me even tighter, pinning me against the car with his body. His green eyes find mine, boring somewhere deep down into my soul as he rolls his jaw.

"Don't I?" he asks, his voice unusually quiet. "Armin. Luka. Savo. Jurgen. The list goes on, Harlow. Men who wanted to *hurt* you." My breath catches as he traces a calloused finger down the side of my jaw. He looks crazed—but also worried, angry, powerful. "Every single one of them tried to hurt you." His voice quiets even further. "You—you almost died tonight, Harlow."

My jaw clenches as I stare into his eyes. London traffic bypasses us, the sounds of groups of people laughing, glasses clinking, and crosswalks beeping meet my ears. But I can't look away from Sterling. I can't break this moment, because it's so heart wrenching and rare.

I want to retort. I want to tell him that a few days ago, I was still being punished by them. Pinned down and edged, physically exhausted, emotionally tormented. But I don't. Because I can tell by his expression that he's done treating me that way. The anger is gone, replaced with unwavering guilt and... a frenzy of hunger and possession. He's like a dragon—fiery, dominant, hoarding things that are precious to him. It's the only way he knows how to... be with me.

"I almost died. But I didn't," I tell him quietly.

His chest rises and falls like he doesn't believe me. As he grips my face with both hands, his nostrils flare slightly.

"Never again. Never. Again," he growls.

I nod as my heart stutters in my chest. "Okay."

"Forgive me if I'm being an arsehole about Kitt," he adds. "I just... I can't almost lose you again. Do you understand?"

My mouth flickers with a smile. "Yes, sir."

He growls. "Get in the car, Harlow."

"Yes, sir," I taunt.

I *love* the way his eyes nearly glow with something—not anger, but... wildness.

I climb into the Escalade behind Alaric, who winces every time he moves. He won't admit it, but I know the blast hurt him. I'm sure he'll be back and blue all over tomorrow. I take the seat next to him, gently pulling him close so that his head is on my chest. Closing my eyes, I wrap my arms around him.

None of us talk the entire way back to Blackwell.

❦

The car drops us all off at Theo's house. I suppose it makes sense, since all of our stuff is there. I don't have the energy to argue. The exhaustion set in on the way home, and my whole body aches from being tense. Once I'm upstairs, I immediately shower. I want all traces of Acadia gone from my body. I carefully wash my face while trying to avoid the gash on my forehead. Once I'm done, I slip into a pair of sweatpants and a sweatshirt. The weather has cooled significantly, so I also pull on some thick socks. Though it does feel funny to be wearing them in July.

July 15th.

I check my phone, ensuring the date is right.

This was the day I was supposed to move into the apartment with Gemma.

Has it really been almost six weeks since I arrived here? It feels like it's been longer, but it also feels like yesterday in the weirdest way. I brush my damp hair back and then I go downstairs in search of food. When I get down there, I don't expect the sight before me.

Alaric is sitting on one of the stools, icing his swollen eye. Gideon is next to him, flicking his knife open and closed. Sterling and Theo are... cooking.

They've all showered and changed, too. Even Theo. He must've showered in another room. They're all donning casual pants and t-shirts. Theo is stirring something on the stove, and Sterling is mixing a salad on the island. They all look so *normal*. My throat constricts as I watch them all from my spot in the doorway. Sterling moves around Theo effortlessly, like he's aware of his every move. Gideon pats Alaric's shoulder softly, and Alaric gives him a grimace. Theo glances up and asks Gideon to grab the salt, but Sterling already has it in his hand and passes it to Theo.

It's like watching an orchestrated dance. Like watching groups of atoms shift around each other as though they all belong to one single soul.

They're all *so* close. I knew that—I'd seen it before. But this... the way they could just... exist in each other's presence without speaking, without saying anything... it illustrates how close they really are.

I clear my throat and walk into the kitchen fully.

"That smells delicious." I head over to where Theo is stirring.

"Don't get your hopes up. I can't really cook, but I wanted to try."

Glancing into the pot, I smirk. "Is that... soup?" I ask hopefully.

He nods. I smile as his brows knit together in concern. I realize then that he's probably never had to cook for himself before.

"Chicken soup. Gideon helped me. There's bread, and salad..." he trails off, looking down at me. "What?"

I laugh at his confused expression. "Nothing. It looks great." As I sit down next to Gideon, I reach out for his knife. "What's the deal with this?" I ask, running my finger along the smooth steel. The feeling gives me goosebumps.

"It's the beginning and the end," Gideon murmurs, staring longingly down at the hunk of metal.

My lips twitch. I look at Alaric, and he's leaning against the counter, eyes closed.

"You know, I had nicknames for you all the first time I saw you," I tell them. I don't know why I want to tell them, but I do. They all just seem so... drained from today. Maybe they could use a laugh. Their shields are down. It's like seeing the person behind your favorite Disney character. Vulnerable. Tired. Exposed to the elements. I realize with a start that they're probably like this a lot more than they're like the murdering, villainous monsters they portray themselves as.

"Alaric is Billionaire Daddy," I start, and his eyes quirk open as he frowns.

"Very funny," he mutters.

I place a hand over Gideon's knife. "Your nickname is Trouble," I tell him.

He cocks his head. "So apt of you."

I snap my gaze to Sterling. "Yours is Mr. Grumpy."

The other guys laugh, even Alaric. Sterling just scowls at me from over the salad bowl as he finishes up.

I look at Theo last. He's leaning against the counter, watching me with faint amusement. "Yours is Murder Puppy."

His smile is lopsided as he shrugs. "You might be onto something."

"Want to know yours?" Alaric asks, leaning close to me. I realize then that he's either drunk or high. His one good eye is dilated, and his words are slightly slurred. As my gaze shifts to the counter, I notice the empty whiskey glass in front of him. He's probably had four or five refills, if his glassy eyes are any indication.

Shivers creep down my spine as he studies my face. It's like he can see everything inside of me.

"Beautiful. Smart. Cunning. Bratty," he adds, furrowing his brows. "Lady of Darkness. Future mother of my children. Mine."

With each passing word, my stomach flutters with nervous longing. "Are you drunk?" I ask him quietly.

He shrugs, but the motion makes him wince. "Perhaps." Reaching out slowly, he grits his jaw as he grabs my right arm. His thumb caresses the *exact* spot of my birth control implant. "I wasn't lying when I said I was going to cut this out of you one day and put a baby inside of you."

His eyes flick up and down my face before pinning me with a heated gaze.

I don't say anything. The thought both excites and terrifies me.

The power.

The possession.

The claiming of my body.

I dread it, yet I want it.

I also remember what Gideon once said about heirs. Now that I've chosen this life, I would have to produce a Blackwell heir at some point. I wasn't sure when that point would be, but it would come. Probably soon, if Alaric's dark gaze is any indication.

I pull away from him and smirk. "Just because you're all old men doesn't mean I want to be tied down by a baby anytime soon." Alaric opens his mouth to argue, but I hold a hand up to silence him. He looks both impressed and irritated that I'm putting my foot down. "I won't hear any arguments about this. You've already given me no choice but to become a Lady of Darkness. I won't give up my bodily autonomy at the same time." Alaric frowns but listens intently, and I continue. "One day. One day, when the time comes, I will... produce an heir."

Just saying it puts a metallic tang in my mouth.

I'm only eighteen. *Definitely* not ready for a baby.

"Dinner is ready," Theo interrupts, grinning.

"What's so funny?" I ask, realizing they're all laughing and shaking their heads.

Theo shrugs. "I think it's cute that you think you have any say over this."

My stomach bottoms out.

Today reminded me how much I care about these men. How much they mean to me. Screaming at Alaric to get up... I was devastated.

Doing normal things like wearing casual clothes and cooking dinner may humanize them briefly.

But right now? When they say things like that? I'm reminded of the *other* side of them. The one that takes up more space. Not aristocratic Lords. But the *Lords of Darkness.*

Something akin to fear slithers down my spine, and I sit up straight. This is one point I was not willing to compromise on.

"Four years," I tell them. "I get four years of not having to worry that you'll do something to get me pregnant."

Alaric turns to face me. His brown eyes are pure black. "And after that?"

I throw my hands up. "We can figure it out then. Do we have a deal?" They all nod reluctantly. "I need a verbal agreement."

Theo checks his phone and cocks his head. "Deal. You have fourteen-hundred and sixty days."

I scoff. "You did *not* just count the days."

He grins, his white teeth flashing. "Fourteen-hundred and fifty-nine now. Clock just struck midnight."

CHAPTER 27

GIDEON

Alaric, Theo, Sterling, and I all take guest bedrooms while Harlow sleeps in Theo's bedroom. I can't sleep. The fucking day keeps playing back in my mind. From Jurgen and Kristoff at dinner, to hearing Harlow tell us she pressed the detonation button, to thinking she was going to die in that goddamn building...

I sit up and run my hand through my hair before pulling it back into a low bun. Sighing, I grab my shirt and joggers, heading downstairs for a bit. Just as I'm pulling my second arm through my sleeve, I look up and see Harlow seated on a couch in the library, reading on her Kindle.

"Can't sleep?" I ask, taking a seat next to her.

She shrugs. "Too much adrenaline for one day. Plus, my stomach still feels funny from whatever Alaric gave me."

I nod, rubbing my eyes before pulling her into my chest. Whatever resistance she once had around us is gone. I can feel it in the way she doesn't fight back, like the cells in her body are drawn to mine. She curls up to my side as I kiss the top of her head. Fisting her shirt, I lift her slightly so that she's eye to eye with me.

"You did an amazing thing today," I murmur, gazing at the cute little cut on her forehead.

Her lip wobbles slightly. "I know. But I still feel like a murderer. They teach you in school that violence is not the answer—"

I place a finger over her red lips. "*They* are not *us*. We live by different rules."

She nods. "No, I know that. And I was so eager to do it in the moment. But it still feels..." Sighing, she looks away. "I still feel tainted. Like every death corrodes my soul a little bit." Turning her dark blue eyes toward me, she looks at me through her lashes. "When does that feeling ever go away?"

I'm quiet for a minute before answering. "It doesn't ever go away. But that's okay, because it means we still have a conscience. It means there's a soul left to corrode. Sometimes, I worry this job eats away at everything good in this world. Like it flays my soul with tiny, irreparable cuts, and eventually, it'll just fall away and I'll be left hollow and numb to everything around me. But that hasn't happened yet."

"That's why Sterling wears his rings, isn't it?" she asks quietly.

I nod. "It's easy for me. I have my mom. Theo has his security system." She laughs, and I continue. "Alaric has his sense of control. Sterling didn't have a mother growing up. He didn't have a tether to his childhood once he joined the order. His mother was dead. His father was dead. He needed something to cling to that *feeling* of life being worth it. He's all or nothing. And because of that, he took all of this the hardest."

"Really?"

"Yeah. He was always flying to different corners of Europe, drowning in sex and dominance. I thought he was going to off himself. He thought he could outrun it."

"Like me," she replies quietly.

I smile. "Sterling never tried to kill us, little monster."

She smirks, but I can see the regret in her eyes. Her emotions are always so easy to read, but maybe that's just because of how deep our feelings for her run. We can all sense what she wants, what she needs, before she has to say a thing. And it's becoming the same way with us. She's getting to know us so quickly; it's remarkable. "I said I was sorry—"

I bend down and place my lips against hers, stopping her from apologizing again. It's not necessary. Her soft lips move against mine, and as I part them with my tongue, she welcomes me with a moan. I growl and flip her onto her back in one breath, and she gasps as I hover over her, using my elbows to prop me up.

"Gideon—"

I move down and pull her sweatpants past her hips in one quick motion.

"Gideon, stop," she murmurs.

I stiffen, looking down at her bare pussy. When my eyes track back up to hers, she blushes.

"I'm—I started my period earlier."

"So?" As my eyes meet hers again, my hands rove down her waist and graze her mound. "You think I fucking care about a little bit of blood?" Wrapping my finger around her tampon string, I tug it out gently and discard it into the nearby trashcan.

She gasps. "You can't—you just—"

Her words break off as I kiss her neck, working my way down to her tits. Lifting her jumper up, I bite down on her left nipple. She arches her back and moans, but still, she's got more to say.

"We should put a towel down or some—"

I scoot back and spread her legs, hoping to take away any more fretting as I spit into my hand as I look down at her. *Fuck.* She's so fucking perfect. Hard, purple nipples. An ass to grab onto. Mesmerizing eyes. A mess of dark curls flowing around her, swollen, pink lips, and the prettiest fucking pussy I've ever seen. Ever since she said that she waxed it earlier, I've been dying to see it up close.

As I rub my wet fingers against her clit, she lets out a tiny gasp, her hips bucking to meet my touch.

"Gideon—"

I place my other hand over her mouth. "It's just blood. Unless you're in pain?" I question, pulling my hand away.

She shakes her head. "No. No, I–don't stop," she says breathlessly.

Smiling at that, I scissor my fingers gently over her swollen bud. She jerks every time I move them, like the feeling is too intense. I lighten my touch so that I'm barely grazing her clit with my fingers, and I notice the wetness leaking from her pussy with every twitch of her body.

"That... that feels..." She gasps when I add more spit, drawing soft, slow circles around her clit. "Better there than in my mouth."

A deep chuckle reverberates through my chest. "That was fucking hot," I admit. "Your disobedience, the way you glared at me as you wiped your lips."

She rolls her eyes just as I slip a finger into her tight pussy, letting out a low howl of pleasure.

My cock throbs painfully as I watch her hands move up to her tits, massaging her nipples as I work her pussy. She lets her legs fall completely open, no longer feeling self-conscious, and I look down at the way her pussy grips my finger tightly, the way it leaks with blood and arousal.

Her lips part and her eyes flutter closed as I curve my finger up, feeling for the spongy spot I know will make her scream my name. I massage it for a few seconds before adding my index finger. She moans and writhes when I add my thumb to her clit.

I'm so hard, I might actually bust a nut just watching her come undone before me.

"Do you like this, Harlow?" I ask gruffly, biting my lower lip as I impale her with my hand. There's already so much blood all over my fingers, but it only spurs me on more.

She squeezes her eyes shut as I massage the spot inside of her, gently circling her clit with my thumb at the same time. Her mouth drops open, and I feel her tight cunt pulse around me.

Jesus.

I rock my hips against nothing, needing friction, needing something. My cock is hard as steel, and I utilize the band of my sweatpants to move my cock against it ever so slightly.

"I–I–" she gasps.

"Say it," I grit out roughly. "Tell me you love it."

She lets out a long, sexy as fuck moan as she rolls her hips against my hand, asking for more.

"I fucking love it," she hisses, looking me in the eyes as my cock throbs for her.

God. One breath of air against the head of my shaft, and I'll fucking lose it all over her stomach.

"Be a good girl and come on my hand," I growl.

She nods, looking almost scared. "It's—it's so intense."

I curve my fingers more, moving them up and down her G-spot. My thumb presses down on her clit as I go, then I add a third finger. She bucks her hips, the shiver going from her core and radiating out to her limbs.

"Fuck, Gideon, what are you doing to me…"

I work my hand harder. Faster. The filthy sounds of her blood and arousal echo around us in the large room louder than her moans. She begins to keen as I massage all three fingers against her wall. Shaking roughly, her body suddenly stiffens, and her pussy grips me tight.

"Oh, God!" she screams. "Oh, fuck, I'm going to—"

I roar as she spasms. She rejects my fingers, and a stream of come soaks me. Growling, I watch her continue to pulse with pleasure as my thumb works her nub. My own release explodes in my joggers, and I squeeze my eyes shut as my cock spasms and twitches, soaking the front of them. I grip her thigh and hiss as the last of it leaves my body. When I look down, she's watching me with wide eyes.

"Did you just—" She snaps her mouth closed. "I mean, it's fine if you did, I was just wondering."

I give her a sly smile. "That's never happened to me before."

She rolls her bottom lip between her teeth. "Well, I guess I should be flattered, then."

Looking down at the mess of blood and come, I unsheathe my still-twitching cock, gripping it tightly as I stroke it, keeping myself hard. "You most definitely should be flattered," I tell her.

She looks between us and gasps. "It looks like a crime scene."

I cock my head and smile. "Damn right it does. Now, spread your legs."

"I should clean it—"

"Leave it," I growl, glaring down at her. Knocking her knees apart, I tease the head of my cock against her entrance. "Like I said before, a little blood doesn't scare me. And now I want it all on my cock."

CHAPTER 28

HARLOW

After Gideon fucks me—twice, I might add—we lazily make our way to Theo's room to sleep. He quickly cleans me up and I fall asleep to the beat of his heart as he hugs me close to his chest. When I wake up a few hours later, he's still fully asleep—facing me on the other side of the bed. I reach over and brush a piece of dark blonde hair from his forehead. His hand shoots out and grabs my wrist instinctively.

"Morning," he says, his voice deep and rumbling.

"Morning."

I roll over and walk to the bathroom, looking over my shoulder as I go. After brushing my teeth and washing my face, I pull Theo's robe around myself and head back into the bedroom. Gideon is still there, as are Alaric, Sterling, and Theo.

"Well, well, well," Theo drawls. "Did you guys fuck in my bed?"

I give him a simpering smile as I shake my head. "No. Just the couch in the library."

"Sorry about the mess," Gideon adds, giving them a cocky smile as he places his hands behind his head. The covers are over his lap, but he's shirtless. His muscles contract and ripple with every movement as his blue eyes find mine.

My cheeks flame. *God, I'd forgotten the mess.* Blood and... bodily fluids. Gideon said they'd take care of it. But still, I somehow feel shameful about my period.

"Yeah, sorry, there was a lot of blood."

Alaric walks forward. He's wearing a white t-shirt and black sweatpants that cling to his narrow hips. His eye looks better today—not swollen anymore, but still black and blue. My stomach does a somersault at the sight. He looks like even more of a badass now.

He saved your life.

"Are you on your period?" he asks, eyeing me up and down as he stalks even closer.

I nod, swallowing. "Yep. Blood. Everywhere."

He chuckles. "That's cute."

"What is?"

"That you think a little blood is going to scare us off when we kill people for a living."

I open and close my mouth. "I–it was–"

He steps right in front of me and places a finger over my lips. "You don't need to be ashamed of it."

I shake my head. "I'm not."

He tilts his head and looks at me, a dark curl falling over his forehead as he rolls his bottom lip between his teeth.

"Are you sure? Because you deleted your period tracking app once we mentioned we had access to it."

My mouth twitches. "Yeah, well, it's *weird* that you can access that."

He reaches out and grips my chin gently between two fingers. "Why? We have access to every other aspect of your life. Why not this one?"

My cheeks redden even further. "I don't know."

"Do you remember what we said when you first joined the order, little monster?" he murmurs. "The night I showed you the wall of ancestors?"

My skin pebbles. My hand goes to my ribs instinctively, running over the healed brand. It feels like that was ages ago, but it wasn't. Only a few weeks. I was convinced my life was over that night. I was *terrified*. But now, my life feels full. Exciting.

"I told you that our order is sacred. That you will learn to trust us more than you trust yourself. You will learn to obey our commands, because we do not work alone. I think the phrase I used was... *one breath away from being able to read each other's minds*."

I pull away from him. "I remember."

"There is no relationship closer than this one," Theo says from the other side of the room. Gideon is still smirking as he lounges on the bed. Sterling is watching us all with a clenched jaw.

"Not even marriage?" I ask, crossing my arms.

Alaric chuckles. The sound is dark and deep, and it grates down my spine one vertebra at a time.

"Marriage is a piece of paper and a silly vow. This?" He presses himself against me, and I gasp when I feel his hardness against my hip. "This is divine. Eternal. It transcends everything else, Harlow."

Goosebumps claw up my skin at his words. He reaches behind me and places two hands on my ass, gripping me firmly as he thrusts into me again.

A flash of heat works through me at the animal-like way he's handling me. At his darkened pupils and ravenous expression.

I open my mouth to reply with a snarky retort when Theo's phone chimes loudly.

I flick my eyes over to where he's scowling down at his phone—or one of them, at least. I've come to discover they each have multiple phones for different purposes.

"What?" I ask, taking a step back from Alaric.

Theo sighs. "Cecelia just showed up at Blackwell House."

I stare at him. "So? She did live there for several years."

He runs his hands through his hair as he looks at me. "The security guard is getting a verbal lashing from her. Looks like she might have found out about the deal between Charles and her father."

Oh.

"Shit," I whisper.

I quickly change into jeans and a dark grey sweater, pulling my hair half up and slipping into my boots. Alaric drives us to Blackwell House, and I hop out as we stop near the front door.

The guys follow me.

"What are you doing?" I ask, twisting around as they walk up the front step. All of them changed into jeans and shirts, looking deathly and casual all at once.

"This is as much our problem as it is yours," Alaric growls, grabbing my hands and tugging me backward. "If she knows about the deal your fathers made, she might blame you. She will most certainly blame us for corrupting you."

I swallow. I didn't think about that. *God, does she know they killed my father?* I don't have time to consider any of it, because just then, the door swings open.

Cecelia gasps when she sees me with them. Her eyes widen, and her lower lip wobbles.

"Not you too," she cries, hiccupping.

I walk inside with the guys without saying anything.

Gideon shuts the door as Cecelia backs up a few steps, crossing her arms. "Rose is at the market. Archie's napping upstairs," she says, her tone cold. "He really wanted to see you." She levels me with a petulant gaze.

"Cecelia..." I trail off, unsure where to start. *How much does she know?*

She stands up a bit taller. She's exactly how I remembered her—small, and maybe slightly frail from grief, but spunky in a way that makes me wish we were friends.

"Come inside. I'll get the tea and biscuits." Twisting around, she stalks toward the kitchen.

I look back at the guys. "Tea?"

Theo snorts. "Welcome to England."

I shake my head. "She doesn't even seem mad."

Sterling shrugs. "We're a reserved bunch. Give her a few minutes and a hot cuppa."

We all sit down at the dining room table at my house. Cecelia places a platter consisting of different kinds of cookies as well as a teapot, mugs and saucers, spoons, milk, and sugar.

"I suppose you should be the one getting everyone tea, Harlow," she says. Her nostrils flare slightly when she looks at me. "Apologies. I meant Lady Blackwell."

"I told them you're welcome to keep your title—"

Shaking her head, she sits down as her lip wobbles again. "I don't want the title. I don't want any of this. I just wanted Charles, and now he's—he's—"

She begins to cry, placing a napkin over her face. Theo is seated next to her, and beside her tiny frame, he seems huge.

"I know it's been an adjustment," he says softly, patting her on the shoulder.

She snorts and glares at him with tear-stained eyes. "Please. Like you weren't in on the whole thing."

Theo furrows his brows. "Actually, we weren't. We didn't know Charles was working with your father until after his death."

I find Alaric watching me, and his eyes bore into mine as if to say, *stay quiet*.

Cecelia sniffs. "Really?"

Theo nods. "It would've been a massive betrayal to us." He pauses, considering his words. "It *was* a massive betrayal to us."

His expression shifts just slightly, and I can see the hurt written all over his features. But in one blink, it's gone.

Her eyes widen, and she looks around at the other guys before her eyes land on me. "What about you, Harlow? Did you have any idea?"

I shake my head. "None. Not until the day of the funeral."

Cecelia sits up straighter. "Okay. I believe you." She gives me a wan smile. "Obviously, I'd like to stay here for a few weeks. My father and I... are not on speaking terms."

My lip twitches with a smile. "This is just as much your home as it is mine. You're always welcome."

She nods once. "Very well. Now..." She looks at Alaric when she says that, jutting her chin forward. "Tell me everything."

CHAPTER 29

Alaric

"How much do you want to know?" I ask Cecelia.

She sighs. "I don't know, Alaric. Humor me. Whatever I need to know, I suppose."

She's most comfortable with me out of the guys. We'd been close acquaintances growing up. We were never friends, per se, but the consistency with which she's been in my life... I still remember my father's funeral. I still remember how she seemed to be the only person who didn't look at me with that sad, pitiful smile.

"Well, obviously, we worked with your father," I say carefully. "Our line of work is... very similar to your father's."

She scoffs. "I figured. I don't need or want any details."

I look over at Harlow, and she's sipping her tea and watching me with an amused expression. I try not to smile.

Brat.

"Charles knew your father before we were introduced to him. They'd made the deal... just before our fathers died."

Cecelia nods slowly. "Did their death have anything to do with Charles or my father?"

I shrug. *Yes. Completely.* I can't tell her that, though. "It doesn't matter. The point is, Charles tricked us just as much as he tricked you. I'm sorry you found out this way."

She puckers her cheeks and shrugs. "It's all water under the bridge without Charles."

"He loved you," I add, remembering how young he seemed when he'd been courting her. "Truly. Unequivocally."

Cecelia's eyes begin to water, and she wipes underneath her lashes as she sniffs. "I know. What we had was real. Despite my piggish father." She turns her gaze to Harlow. "And what about you? How do you fit into all of this?"

Harlow stiffens. I nod, giving her a small smile.

"Um... I'm taking over for him. There are... we do... it's complicated. But the job requires a blood relative to do it."

Cecelia stares at her. "A blood relative?"

Harlow nods. "Like I said, it's complicated. If you truly want to know everything—"

"I don't," Cecelia says quickly.

Harlow chews on the inside of her cheek. "Archie would've been the next heir if I hadn't stepped up."

Cecelia's face pales. She turns and glares at me. "You will never touch him."

I nod. "I know that. Harlow is a perfectly capable heir. She took his place after only knowing him for a couple of days."

Harlow shrugs. "He's my brother." She looks at Cecelia and smiles. "We're family now, right?"

Cecelia starts to cry again. Harlow goes and sits down next to her, rubbing her back and consoling her. They hug, and Harlow seems... peaceful. Maybe this whole ordeal is a good thing. Maybe Harlow needs Cecelia, just like Cecelia needs Harlow.

I hear Theo hiss as he glares at his phone.

"Fuck, what now?" I ask, glancing down at the screen.

"It's Harlow's friend, Gemma," he murmurs, so that only I can hear. "She just bought a one-way ticket to London."

I sigh, closing my eyes and running a hand through my hair. "When does she arrive?"

"Tonight," he says.

We both look over at Harlow, who is holding Cecelia's hand while laughing.

"When should we tell her?" I ask.

"Soon. One thing at a time."

CHAPTER 30

Harlow

Theo pulls me off to the side after I'm done talking to Cecelia. I can tell by his expression that more shit has hit the fan.

"What is it?" I ask, my voice tinged with worry.

What else could go wrong?!

"Gemma is on her way to London," he tells me, his voice low. "The security personnel I had watching over her flat told me she left in a hurry."

"Fuck," I mutter, shaking my head. "She's probably distraught about Luka. They were *in love*." My nose wrinkles at the thought.

Theo's lips curve upward. "What's wrong with being in love?" he asks, smirking.

"It's just... so soon. She only met him a few weeks ago!" That has his smile broadening. "What?"

"You don't think it's possible to fall in love that quickly?" His icy blue eyes are twinkling with mirth, and my heart thrums against my ribs as he places a hand over my head, essentially pinning me against the wall behind me.

I shake my head. "No. I mean, I'm not a total grinch, but I know from experience that it takes more than love to sustain a relationship."

My voice catches, and I swallow as Theo furrows his brows. "You mean because of your parents?"

I nod hesitantly. "Yeah. Gemma's parents are always traveling together, but they never speak to each other. I think they're only together for her. And for me, since they sort of took me in after my mom died."

Theo continues to look at me, and I have to turn my gaze to his shirt. It feels like he can see right through me.

"And my mom... she pined for my dad for most of my life. I saw how devastated she was when he met Cecelia. And he did love my mom. I know he did. I could tell. But she wasn't enough for him."

Theo narrows his eyes as he runs a finger down my jaw. "Are you worried we'll abandon you, little monster?"

I scrunch my nose up. "No. I just... no. This is about Gemma. Not me."

He smiles and drops his hand. "I think it's beautiful seeing two people in love."

My stomach dips at his words, sending a cascade of butterflies through my core. These men are so contradictory to what I thought they would be. They're not afraid to feel, not afraid to tell me how they feel, or what they're thinking. Most men are mercurial, mysterious... but not them. They know how dark and deadly they can be, but they don't mask their true emotions. I've never had to play games with them. And I knew I would never need to guess where they stood with me.

"Luka was a murderer," I add, changing the subject. "What should I tell her when she gets here?"

"It's up to you. Like we told you before, whatever you decide to share with people is up to you. To the general public, we are Lords and Ladies, but our close friends and family have every right to know. It's not like our presence is a secret to our enemies."

I twist my lips to the side. "Okay. I'll figure it out. When does her plane land?"

I spend the day at the gym with the guys, and then I help Cecelia with Archie's dinner and bath. In between chasing a giggling toddler and eating his leftover fish sticks, I try to imagine this life in six months, a year, five years. Maybe Cecelia will still be here, or maybe I'll be living in this house alone, just like my father, and his father, and his father...

Truthfully, it doesn't scare me anymore. I can still take art classes here. I'll insist on retaining that part of myself. And if the accountant was correct, I also inherited a shit ton of money when my father died, which means I can fly Gemma out any time I want to.

I was so afraid of giving in to this life, but it pulled me in completely, and now, it feels like home. *This* feels like my life.

And I'm okay with that.

Around ten, I see headlights appear outside. Cecelia and Archie are already in bed, so I told them they could meet Gemma tomorrow. Theo promised me he'd send a driver to pick Gemma up. I can't wait to hear all about how *that* went down, since I'm sure she probably thought she was being kidnapped. When I swing the front door open, I don't expect the tear-stained cheeks or red lips. Gemma wobbles inside, and then she drops her bags and wraps her arms around me as she sobs.

When she's done crying, she pulls away and looks at me with bloodshot eyes. "I think Luka ghosted me."

I don't have the heart to tell her the truth. A part of me wants to come clean about everything, but the other part wants to protect her—wants to keep her and New York separate from this life. If another one of our enemies finds her...

It's safer to keep her separate.

I whisk her inside and make her a cup of tea. When we sit down in the living room, she looks around for the first time.

"Holy shit. You weren't joking that your dad was some kind of..." she trails off.

"He was a Duke. And apparently, since my parents were married in secret, I am now Lady Blackwell."

Her large, brown eyes widen as she sniffs. "For real? Like, all of this is yours?"

I nod. "Jesus. It's like the goddamn Princess Diaries."

"Not quite," I mutter.

There's way more murder, espionage, and violence, but okay.

She levels me with her no bullshit gaze. "So, you're staying here?"

I nod again. "I just... I'm not..."

I don't know how to explain my situation without giving everything away. One day, I'll tell her. But not today. She's still heartbroken over Luka.

"I really like it here," I conclude.

Her eyes narrow as they scan me. "Well, England suits you. You look great." She reaches over and pokes my arm. "Have you been working out?"

I shrug. "I've been going on walks and doing push-ups and stuff."

Gemma rears her head back. "Really? But you hate exer—" She grins. "Oh. He exercises, doesn't he?"

My cheeks redden. "Who?"

"The guy you told me about. The Lord!"

How do I tell her there's more than one?

"Yeah, I mean, he's showing me how to run and lift weights."

She cackles. "I never thought I'd see the day. Harlow Windsor running for fun. I still remember the time Coach Rampor made you run a mile in ninth grade. You nearly shit your pants."

I laugh. "That's not true."

She leans back and sips her tea. "How did you know I was coming?"

Her question startles me. "What do you mean?"

Setting her cup down, she looks at me again, but this time, her face is serious. "There was a weird driver waiting for me at the airport. I didn't let you know that I was on my way. Luka is... gone... so it couldn't have been his doing." She looks around before her eyes find mine again. "So how did you know?"

Fuck.

I didn't think about that, but of course she would have questions. Screw Theo and his technological meddling.

"Umm..."

Do I tell her everything? Or do I lie?

"I'll start at the beginning," I say slowly. It's better to come clean now. "My father was... special. He was a Duke, but he also had special jobs that he did with four other guys. Now that he's dead, I have to take over."

Her face pales. "What the fuck, Harlow? What do you mean, you *have* to take over?" Her eyes widen as she looks around. "Do you need me to call the police?" she whispers.

I laugh. "No. It's sort of like a special military unit," I explain. "Anyway, I agreed. *Mostly* on my own accord, though that took some time. The guys–the Lords–they're the ones I was telling you about–"

"*Lords?* As in multiple Lords?"

I bite my lower lip and wring my hands together. "Yes. Four of them."

Her mouth drops open as she grins. "Okay, now I can see why you wanted to stay."

"Anyway, they have... ways... of tracking people. They knew how important you were to me, so they knew you were coming to London."

She looks flabbergasted. "How?"

"They have their ways."

She opens and closes her mouth, narrowing her eyes. "Okay. I see. I don't need to know anything else."

"But–"

She holds her hand up. "Nope. It's a secret and mysterious job. That's all I need to know."

She looks around, her expression unsure.

Please don't ask about Luka.
Please don't ask about Luka.
Please don't ask about Luka.

"Is it safe?" she asks after a minute, her voice fraught with emotion.

I shrug. "The guys ensure I'm always safe."

She nods, swiping a stray tear away. "Okay. I'd like to meet them."

My mouth drops open. "Really?"

"Yes. I need to meet the men who convinced my best friend to try running for fun."

We both laugh before we talk some more. She tells me about Luka, crying a couple of times while I offer her advice about getting over him. After an hour, I bring her into the kitchen and make her eat, and then around midnight, we crawl into bed together. Gemma passes out instantly.

It reminds me so much of when my mother died, of having her curl around me and make me feel safe. Tonight, I curl around her.

Perhaps there is a way to have both. To be a Lady of Darkness while also keeping my friends and family.

And that thought makes me smile as I drift off to sleep.

CHAPTER 31

STERLING

We spend the next few days going hard on Harlow in the gym. We've eased up on the educational part of our training so that she can spend time with Gemma, Cecelia, and Archie. We hardly see her except at the gym, but she seems happier. She smiles more. A big part of this job, especially at first, is getting used to it. And for us, this is how most days unfold. Gym, work, sleep. Our targets are still out there, but it's been a slow week, so there's no harm in giving Harlow some space.

A week after Gemma arrived, we got a last-minute call that one of our targets was on the move, so we picked her up from her house and brought her to London. It was an easy job—a small crime ring based in Argentina. Their leader was visiting family in London. He wasn't a good guy; he hid drugs in children's toys and was a part of the larger drug ring.

Most of their profit was made from forcing children to be dealers.

One day, we'd find everyone in that fucking ring and take them out.

Harlow hardly flinched when she pulled the trigger on the sniper. I'd been behind her on top of the building, showing her how to use it and how to aim correctly. I nearly got distracted by her scent and the way she ground her ass into me. But she did it with our help. She killed him while he was texting on his balcony. Afterward, as we dismantled our station, she was solemn.

"Is this it?" she asks, watching as Theo puts the sniper back in its case. We rarely get to use it, but when we do... it gives me a certain thrill.

"Is what it, baby?" I ask, pulling her into my side.

"Running ten miles in the morning, killing men at night?" Her eyes are misty as she curls her arms around herself.

I smirk. "And what exactly are you missing?"

She turns to face me, her cheeks tinged with pink. "I don't know. Something... else. Something to make me forget this part of my day."

She walks away, and I don't answer her.

But I think I have an idea.

As we make our way back to the car, I pull her back. "We're not going home right away."

Her eyes glaze over slightly as her throat bobs. Then she nods hopefully. "Okay."

"The Rose," I tell Alaric, who is waiting for us to join them in the black car.

"Right now?"

"Right now."

The drive to The Rose Hotel is short and tense. I don't miss the way Harlow fidgets with her necklace. It's not like we haven't all fucked her individually—we have. In between sets at the gym. Before yoga. During yoga. Late at night, when one of us sneaks into her house. But they've all been short, lust-filled quickies.

Right now, I need her on her knees.

I need to savor her.

And I want to watch as we all give her pleasure, as we make her forget the kills.

The car drops us off and we walk through the large, black gates of the grand central hotel.

"This is beautiful," she says, looking around.

"It's ours," I tell her, and she twists around to face me.

"Ours?"

I nod. "Queen Victoria left it to the Lords in 1842." Her mouth drops open, and I continue. "The entire top three floors make up our London Suite. Ten bedrooms, eight bathrooms. The best view of the London skyline," I add, weaving my fingers through hers.

"And the queen just... gifted it to the Lords?" she asks suspiciously.

My lips twitch with the faintest smile. "We helped her take care of a problem the crown was having."

Rolling her eyes, she pulls her hand out of mine. "I'm sure."

"There are clues about the Lords everywhere," I tell her, giving a small nod of acknowledgment to the doorman. Using my key, I open the elevator for all five of us. "In books, movies, the bible, museums, artifacts—"

"The bible?"

"Yes," Theo interjects. "Sterling has done all the research, so he knows more than me. We show up in the most random places. Once, an ancestor of ours was on the currency. You can look up the coin. It's a mystery, as no one could ever figure out who was on it."

"Ah, a gift from Henry VII," Alaric adds.

Harlow's jaw drops as we climb to the twentieth floor. "Wow. That's pretty incredible."

The doors spring open a second later, and we all walk out into the expansive suite. Harlow stops and does a full 360. Her eyes are wide when she turns to face me.

"You've got to be kidding me."

CHAPTER 32

Harlow

It's the most beautiful place I've ever seen. I'm not sure if I can even call it a hotel, as it seems like a massive house instead. The foyer is made of pure marble. The shiny white floors and walls are immaculate. There's an ornate table off to the side with a massive bouquet of fresh peonies, which happens to be my favorite flower. The ceilings must be at least twenty feet high. A beaded chandelier hangs over us, and as my eyes scan the rest of the suite, I can't help but gape.

There's a formal living room to the left, decorated with striped black and white carpets and tan leather furniture. The lower half of the wall is made up of dark wood, and there's a fire going in the massive fireplace. Two leather chesterfields face each other and between them is a gilded marble and wood coffee table.

Further down is what I assume to be the kitchen, though I can only make out the white marble counters and the dark green cabinets.

To my right is a dining room, which is decorated with dark wood and patterned turquoise wallpaper. The chairs are all striped black and white, and more fresh peonies sit in the middle of the eighteen-seat table.

I wrap my arms around myself as I take it all in. I'm wearing jeans and a black sweater with my combat boots. Tonight wasn't a fancy job; it just required comfort since we were on the roof of a building a couple of blocks away from our target. The guys are all wearing suits, so at least they look like they fit in here. I twirl around to find Gideon holding a glass of whiskey out to me. I hadn't even seen the wet bar situated in the living room.

"Thanks," I tell him, sipping it slowly.

My nerves are on fire. Aside from the night they killed Luka, and the subsequent airplane ride back to England, all five of us haven't been together like this since then. In *this* way. Just thinking about it, about the way we were all so connected... my chest begins to flush.

Alaric walks over to me and wraps an arm around my shoulder, directing me to one of the Chesterfield sofas.

"Relax," he whispers, his breath skirting down the skin behind my ear.

"I am relaxed," I lie, sitting down petulantly.

They all sit down—Alaric and Gideon on either side of me, and Theo and Sterling across from us. The fire snaps and crackles, filling the silence. I look anywhere but into their eyes, instead focusing on the spines of the books on the bookshelf.

"Your training is complete," Alaric muses from next to me.

I stiffen. "Really? Already? But, I still have the other slideshows—"

"You're ready," Gideon says from my right side. "The slides will always be there."

I press my lips together. "I don't feel ready. I didn't even know how to use a sniper rifle."

"But you did it," Alaric says. "You are running five miles. Soon, it'll be the requisite ten miles. You've been trained on weaponry, our history, and our future targets. Theo will get you up to speed on the technology aspect. However, today we received last-minute information about a target and *you* eliminated him."

I fill with pride. "I mean, I guess—"

"Learn to take a compliment, Harlow," Alaric growls, his large hand gripping my thigh. It sends shivers down my spine when he squeezes it. "Let's toast."

I hold my glass up as all four guys hold theirs up.

"To Harlow," Sterling drawls. "Our Lady of Darkness."

My throat catches as I finally meet their eyes. They're all watching me with darkened expressions, and I realize that tonight is a turning point for them. And for me. It's *acceptance*. It's the union of five souls merging into one. After tonight, I'm in it for good. This is my life. And they're all waiting for me to change my mind.

Waiting for me to betray them again.

"To being your Lady," I say slowly. I look at Alaric as I sip, and then I set my glass down and lean back against the couch. "Now what?"

Alaric downs his drink quickly and places it on the side table. Then he reaches into his coat pocket and pulls out a gun.

"Want to play a little game?"

My breathing catches when I look at the weapon. Small. Black. *Lethal.*

"What kind of game?" When I gaze up into his eyes, he's staring at me with dark amusement.

Cocking his head, he leans forward and gestures to the gun with his hand. "Pick it up."

My heart races as I reach forward, holding it in my hands delicately. They've trained me on how to handle a gun properly, how to shoot, how to pop the safety on and off... but as I place it in my lap, I have a feeling their idea of a "game" is a lot more sinister.

Because as much as I want to believe these men are normal... they're not.

Even if they rescue me.

Even if they cuddle with me.

Even if they build me up to make me stronger.

At the end of the day, they're monsters in suits. And by being here with them, so am I.

Love and respect don't mean everything is perfect, all of the time. It means you love and respect someone *despite* their flaws.

They have blood on their hands, but I still trust them.

I still *crave* the excitement something like this brings.

Because even though I like to think I'm different... I'm not.

I'm just like them.

And this is how I'll prove it.

"Pick up the gun and hold it to your head, Harlow," Alaric murmurs.

I take a slow, steady breath as I do what he says. When the barrel is pressing against my temple, Alaric bites his lower lip as he begins to remove his tie.

"Good girl," he says, his voice low. "Now, pull the trigger."

CHAPTER 33

Theo

Harlow's hand shakes as she stares at Alaric, wide-eyed.

"Is it loaded?" she asks.

He stands up and begins to unbutton his shirt. For some reason, I think of when he fucked Sterling on the plane, and my cock twitches.

I've never been attracted to the other guys like that. Before Harlow, we shared women, but we never crossed that line. We made sure of it. However, with her, it feels... like we're all officially connected.

"Scared?" Alaric asks, discarding his jacket and shirt neatly on the back of the couch. After kicking off his shoes, he places one knee on either side of her hips. She gasps as she looks into his eyes.

"No. I'm not scared." Her hands shake even more as her finger tightens on the trigger. It clicks, and she sags in relief. "Asshole," she whispers, setting the gun down before springing forward and wrapping her arms around Alaric's neck.

Pulling him down, she kisses him fiercely.

Something about seeing Alaric straddle her, about seeing their bodies move against each other...

Gideon and Sterling both look like they're about to pounce as well.

I stand up and walk over to the gun, kneeling in front of where Alaric and Harlow are sitting on the couch.

"You like danger, don't you, little monster?" I smile as I drag the gun down her calf.

Alaric climbs off of her and tugs her jeans off. And then she's pulling her sweater and bra over her head before her hooded eyes find mine.

"I like real danger. I bet that gun isn't even loaded." She gives me a challenging smile.

After I knock her legs apart with my hands and scoot between her legs, I cock my head and move the gun over her bare skin. She shivers.

"Is that so?" I ask, narrowing my eyes.

Her golden skin pebbles as I hold it up to the ceiling and pull the trigger. It fires, and a bullet cracks through the plaster. Harlow screams and looks at me in horror.

"I could've killed myself before!"

"You think we were playing around?" I chuckle, delighting in the way she shrinks back. She likes fear... and I like scaring her. "We don't play games, Harlow. We don't half ass anything. Of course it's loaded. Now, spread your legs wider and do what I say."

Her legs shake as she pulls them apart. Being on my knees, I get a fantastic view of her bare pussy. Growling, I reach up and palm her perfect tits with my free hand.

"I'm going to ask the same question," I murmur, running the gun down her abdomen slowly. "You like danger, don't you?"

She nods. "Yes."

I place the barrel against her opening. She's nearly convulsing.

"One slip of my hand," I tell her, nudging the barrel inside.

My finger doesn't leave the trigger.

"Oh, God," she whimpers.

"God?" I ask, rolling my jaw. "God isn't the one fucking you with a gun."

She closes her eyes, but the shaking doesn't stop. I see the beads of sweat across her forehead as I shove the gun deeper inside of her. With every movement, she whimpers, and I can't tell if it's from fear or from being turned on.

I feel Sterling move behind me, his hand on my shoulder. "Push it in deeper," he tells me.

I push the barrel all the way in and angle it so that it's massaging her G-spot.

"Oh, fuck," she moans as Gideon places his palm over her clit and begins to move it against her.

"Good girl," Alaric murmurs as she grinds her hips. "You fought against this life for so long." He leans over and kisses her neck.

Gideon uses one arm to palm her tits, and the other one to play with her clit. He spreads her pussy and begins doing circles around her bud, teasing her to the brink.

"But you're just like us," Alaric adds, looking at her as though he's trying to memorize the way her brows are furrowed, the way her mouth is parted. She's breathing so raggedly that her tits bounce with every sharp inhale. "You *crave* the fear. You need it. Imagine going back to your life in New York?" He pauses to bite her lower lip, dragging it between his teeth. Harlow moans in response. "Imagine meeting a guy who brings you back to his small apartment. Imagine lying down and fucking him on your back, with no regard for your pleasure."

She whimpers as I pull the gun out, setting it down on the floor. I insert two fingers inside of her in its place and she bucks against my arm.

"You would never know this kind of pleasure," Alaric says, dragging his index finger and thumb over her nipple before he pinches it.

She spasms and cries out. "Fuck!"

"You'd probably get married and move to the suburbs," he growls, and I know we all feel the heat of possession in those words. Like hell I'd let her marry and fuck someone other than us. "Pop out a couple of kids. Join an MLM. Then what? Next thing you know, you're sixty and you've never experienced your true destiny."

I slow my hand inside of her, delighting in the way she's so fucking wet and tight for me.

"Harder," she whines.

I look at Gideon, and he nods. Removing my hand, I stand up and start to undress.

"Please don't stop," she begs, looking at me with a face filled with desperation.

Gideon stops working her clit, and then her eyes flash with irritation.

"Don't worry, baby," I purr. "You get both of us at once now."

CHAPTER 34

Harlow

I still feel high from the adrenaline of having the gun inside of me, and blood is whooshing past my ears as Theo and Gideon undress in front of me.

"How do you want to do this, baby?" Alaric murmurs, his hand running down my neck.

My skin pebbles at his touch. It feels like all of my nerves are on fire, like the faintest touch will bring me the utmost pleasure. Must be the fear they think I love so much.

"I want to watch the two of you together."

Alaric chuckles. "Okay. You pick."

My eyes flick between the four of them. It's like I'm a kid at a candy shop. How will I ever choose?

I'm just about to open my mouth when Alaric grabs his tie. "I have a better idea."

He pulls me up and drags me to the bedroom. It's just as beautiful as the other rooms. A massive, black, four-poster bed with a white linen duvet, striped carpet, and black leather furniture. It feels luxurious and a bit menacing, too.

Just like them.

I hear the three others follow us into the bedroom as Alaric shoves me down onto the bed. He's shirtless, and his hair is all messed up from where I was running my fingers through it earlier. He looks *wild*. Straddling me, he pulls each of my arms up to the top of the bed, looping the tie around my wrists and securing it around a knob in the middle of the bed frame. It's like I'm wearing handcuffs. His heavy weight presses into me as he climbs off and smiles.

"I could get out of this if I wanted to," I taunt, shaking my wrists to prove a point. "They're flimsy," I add, and his nostrils flare.

"I wouldn't test my patience tonight, little monster. I have all night to feast on you, and I'm going to use every single second wisely. You'll do well to remember that provoking us will only make us want to punish you harder."

A chill goes down my spine. I swallow and nod as my core clenches with anticipation. I don't even need to prove that I'm turned on. They can all see how wet I am, how his words make me needy for him. For all of them.

"You wanted to watch us together," Alaric murmurs, his voice low. He unbuckles his belt slowly as his black eyes pin me to the center of the bed. "You can watch, but you can't touch."

My heart hammers against my ribs, and my nipples tighten as I watch him kick his underwear off, freeing his massive cock.

My lips part as he walks over to Theo, grabs the back of his head, and pulls him in for a kiss. Theo looks surprised at first. He stiffens, hesitating as his hands come up into the air. Alaric pulls back and grins at me.

"Watch us. All four of us."

My mouth drops all the way open when Alaric begins to untie Theo's tie, pulling it through his collar slowly. Theo says something to Alaric that I can't decipher, and a second later, he's shoving his pants off. Alaric helps him remove his shirt, and the way Alaric touches him, the way Theo's eyes narrow slightly with arousal as they watch Alaric tug his boxers off...

I cross my legs and squeeze as Theo and Alaric begin to kiss, fully naked. *Gods.*

Then, Gideon and Sterling start to undress.

"You ready to suck my cock, St. Claire?" Sterling asks Gideon.

Gideon smirks. "I give great head. Or so I've been told."

"Yeah?" Sterling asks. "Prove it."

Fuck.

Me.

I glance back over at Alaric and Theo. Alaric's hands are on Theo's ass as he pulls Theo's cock against his own. Theo's hands are on Alaric's face as they kiss. They're both pressing and bucking their hips against each other.

I moan.

Both cocks are hard and tight, and my legs squeeze harder as Alaric spits into his hand and lubes both of them up. Theo hisses when Alaric's hand comes around both of their cocks, and then they continue grinding into each other as their gazes meet with palpable hunger. They're both moving frantically, and my clit is pulsing so hard, it hurts. I feel wetness slide between my thighs as I buck my own hips in search of a release.

I don't think I've ever seen anything hotter than this.

Alaric looks over at me as he moves against Theo's cock, thrusting upward against his shaft.

"How wet are you, Harlow?"

I lick my lips. "I wish I could tell you, but my hands are tied up."

Alaric growls as he pulls Theo's face to his, biting his lower lip. "Hmm. Seems she still wants to be a brat. I guess that means I'll have to make you come, Wolf."

"You better fucking make me come," Theo growls, kissing Alaric back.

His ass contracts with every thrust, and *God, I am going to combust soon.* This is too hot, too much, and I need release.

I move my hips and my legs so that I'm squeezing as tight as I can. My eyes flick to Gideon and Sterling. They're nearly naked now, and Gideon unsheathes himself as he drops to his knees.

As he takes Sterling's cock deep into his mouth, Sterling groans. I remember how it danced and bobbed the instant it hit the back of my throat, the sweet and salty taste of his precome.

Gideon looks up at Sterling with a darkened expression, and Sterling fists Gideon's bun, using it to his advantage as he pushes deeper into his mouth.

"Fuck," Sterling hisses, baring his teeth as he moves quicker. "You do give good head, St. Claire."

I can't take it anymore. I begin to whimper as I work my legs back and forth, humping the air.

"You like that?" Sterling asks me, the corner of his lips quirking up as he drives into Gideon's mouth. "You remember what it was like to suck this cock, don't you?"

I moan and nod. "Yes," I whisper, but it sounds pathetic.

"Do you want to watch me pump all my come down his throat?"

"Yes," I whisper, repeating myself quickly. "Yes, God, yes."

"Fuck," Theo says, his voice ragged. I look over just as he groans. "I'm going to come, Cross."

Alaric ups his tempo. "Me too." He turns to face me as he moves quicker. "Watch us, baby."

He grunts with every thrust as Theo roars, chasing his release. Alaric's cock tightens as his come erupts against Theo's stomach, and then Theo's head drops back as his cock curves toward his body, twitching with fountains of his come. They don't stop. They both move faster as they hiss and pant and growl. Ropes of semen spill all over the floor, and they stay still for a few seconds as their cocks spasm against each other one last time.

Theo turns to look at me as he pants. "Enjoy the show? Are you ready for us next?"

All I do is whimper. I can see how soaked the bed is underneath me.

"She's so fucking ready," Sterling grits out.

Gideon is stroking his own shaft hard and fast as Sterling fucks his mouth. My nipples are so taut that they're burning, and if having an orgasm without touch were possible, this would be the time it would happen to me. I can't undulating my hips and squeezing my legs. I'm too wet, though, and it just adds to the pressure building in my swollen clit. Everything is tingling with anticipation—my skin, my nerves, my flesh. Even my mind. I can't get the image of Alaric and Theo fucking each other like that out of my mine—how hard they came—

I moan as I look back at Sterling, just as he's roaring and bucking his hips. Gideon's throat contracts, swallowing every drop of Sterling's seed. Then only seconds later, Gideon moans and his come surges out in quick, long streams all over the carpet.

God, I need release.

Even just the feel of the silk sheets against the backs of my legs and ass sends waves of pleasure skittering down my spine. I never knew arousal could be a form of torture, but I'm throbbing so hard that I don't doubt how effective it is.

When they're both done, Sterling pulls out of Gideon's mouth.

His eyes are nearly black as he strokes his wet cock, walking over to where I'm lying down. He reaches out and unties me.

"If you touch yourself, I'll make sure you don't come tonight."

His words terrify me. I'd never sleep. I need this release more than I need air right now.

"Please," I beg, my fists curling at my sides as I wait for him to give me directions. Theo, Alaric, and Gideon are cleaning up a few feet away. "Please, Sterling."

He cocks his head as he climbs into the bed, knocking my knees apart. "Is that how you ask?"

I swallow. "Please, *sir*."

He narrows his eyes and hollows his cheeks as he nods once. "Good girl. Now you can have your reward."

I nearly cry with relief as he climbs between my legs. Every brush of his skin against mine makes little gasps leave my lips. I am *on fire*. I'm sure my pupils are pure black. I'd fuck anything with a cock at this point.

"Please, sir," I beg again.

Sterling chuckles. "So impatient." He grabs my legs and pulls them over his shoulders. I move my hips up toward his mouth, but his nails dig into my thigh as he presses me down. "*So* impatient," he growls, letting out a low groan when he sees how wet I am.

Lowering his head, my eyes flutter closed in anticipation, but he doesn't touch my clit. Instead, he bites the inside of my thigh.

"Please, sir. Please," I beg again, like an idiot.

He stills, biting my flesh harder in retaliation.

I groan, the sound slipping from my lips as my hips thrash.

But he just continues to nibble the flesh on my thighs, never getting close to my clit. His tongue sweeps down the skin on my leg and I hiss.

I.

Am.

Burning.

Just when I think he'll alleviate this ache, Sterling places a soft kiss a couple of inches above my clit. His scruff *barely* brushes the sensitive bundle of nerves. I keen, moving against his chin involuntarily, but he just holds me down and grips me harder. His breath fans against my clit, the warmth making me cry out.

"You're so wound up, little monster," he murmurs, his breath hot against my throbbing nub.

He bites down on my clit gently, and I hiss as fireworks explode inside of me. Pulling back slightly, his tongue sweeps up my slit, pressing against my clit. *Fuck.* My eyes roll so far back into my head that I can practically see behind me. A low moan escapes my lips, and my body stiffens—already on the precipice of a climax. The feeling that overcomes me is delicious—slow, sweet, intense. I'm gasping for air as he pulls away.

"Don't stop," I whisper, my voice fragmented and husky. Everything feels ten times more sensitive, and I've never needed to come so badly in my life.

"You're so fucking wet," Sterling says, his green eyes boring into mine from between my legs.

"Keep going," I whine. "Please."

Narrowing his eyes, he adjusts my legs around his ears, and then he lurches forward and suctions his mouth to my mound. I nearly fly off the bed as his tongue presses hard against my nub and flicks up and down slowly. I scream his name and fist the sheets.

"Fuck! Shit! Oh, God!"

"Mmm," he breathes, his voice sending vibrations through my skin and into my soul. "Yes, baby. You're gushing for me."

I arch my back as he sweeps his tongue up and down, and up and down once more. Slowly. So, so slowly. Gripping the back of his head, I lift my ass slightly, needing the friction. I roll my hips against his mouth, and he punishes me by clamping down on my swollen, tortured clit.

"Good girls wait their turn," he murmurs.

I hate him.

I'm shaking so hard that I'm not sure if it's the nerves, my arousal, or my impending climax. With every sweep of his tongue, I get closer. The pressure builds, and I'm almost scared to come—scared to see what will happen. Everything inside of me aches. I feel like I'm on the precipice of something big, like a tidal wave is about to crash through me. The clawing sensation is almost like I need to pee, but a thousand times more intense.

It also feels *in-fucking-credible.*

I open my mouth to scream when he inserts two fingers—deep and hard. The tug of him stretching me so quickly sends me flying over the edge, and I can feel his fingers curl inside of me as I begin to come.

"Fuck yes," Sterling growls. "You're squeezing my fingers so hard, little monster. Imagine how fucking good it will feel to have you wring my cock dry."

I moan and thrash as stars explode in my vision.

It feels catastrophic.

Everything unleashes, and I scream again as my body rejects him. Sterling roars as I buck my hips, feeling a steady stream of come pour out of me. Wave after wave of the most mind-bending pleasure wracks through my body. I am weightless, tethered only to this orgasm, to his tongue, to his fingers.

I swear to God, my soul leaves my body.

"That's a good fucking girl," Sterling says, his face wet.

I tremble as I come down from my climax, totally spent. My body feels like it just got electrocuted, and I lie limp on the bed for what feels like minutes—but

I'm sure it's just seconds. When I look up at Sterling, he brushes a piece of hair out of my eyes.

"You're so fucking beautiful when you come."

CHAPTER 35

Gideon

My cock never went down after I came all over Sterling's feet. How could it? I've never been attracted to my brothers like this before, never thought we'd all get a chance to have each other, but Harlow makes everything possible. She opens us up and makes us re-evaluate ourselves and what we enjoy. Two months ago, I would've laughed at the idea of Sterling letting me suck his cock. I was always down for some action–I like everyone, regardless of gender–but he seemed straight as an arrow. Harlow, though... she's awoken something in us.

We are closer now, in *every* way.

And watching Harlow fall apart under Sterling's mouth... it was one of the most beautiful things I'd ever seen.

I stroke my shaft as I climb onto the bed. Harlow looks at me with a half-dazed expression. She's still shaking, still soaked from her orgasm. I can't help but chuckle.

"Did you know that you're a squirter?" I ask, lying down next to her as I stroke her arm with my free hand.

She shakes her head. "No. Until you guys–until I–" She bites her lower lip. "I didn't realize it would happen every time."

I grin. "It's nothing to be embarrassed about, baby." Her dark blue eyes land on mine, and she seems so young and vulnerable all of a sudden. It hits me that while I was off fucking anything with a hole, she was still in school. She was growing up. I pull her closer to me and kiss the top of her head. "It's a good thing. It means you're not faking it."

She snorts. "I could never fake it. I just didn't know it was a real thing."

I make a humming sound in the back of my throat as she turns to face me.

"Oh, it's real. And it feels so fucking good for us, too. Feeling your pussy flutter around our cocks, squeezing out our come..." Her mouth parts, eyes darkening. "Are you ready for round two?"

She nods, answering without pause. "Yes."

Smiling, I sit up and look at the guys. Like me, despite coming only a few minutes ago, they are all already hard again. My cock twitches.

"Okay. Trust us, Harlow. I need you to get up on your knees and face the foot of the bed." She swallows nervously, but does as I say. I can't help but notice the pink flush across her chest, and the way she licks her lips. I lie down and pat the bed on either side of me. "Okay, now face away from me and straddle me." She pauses and looks at the other guys. "Unless you'd rather we fuck you one after the other," I growl.

"No. I want–I want all of you."

She climbs on top of me, and my cock is only inches from her pussy. "Good." Alaric walks over to the bed, climbing onto it so that he's facing Harlow.

"Can–I want both of you," she says bashfully.

I smile wickedly. "That's the plan, little monster."

She nods once and leans her back into my chest. I prop her up underneath her arms.

"It might hurt at first," Alaric says, his voice low. He looks at me with a heated expression.

"You've done this before?" she asks, looking over her shoulder at me.

I nod. "A few times. Now, sit on my cock and lean back."

She lowers herself, angling my aching shaft right at her entrance. Before she can finish, I thrust up and enter her and, *holy fuck, it feels absolutely incredible.* I hiss as I slide into her tight, warm heat, feeling the way she grips me as she moans out loud.

"Fuck, Harlow," I say, my voice hoarse. "You feel so fucking good." I pull out slowly and push back in, and each time she whimpers. "Spread your legs." I reach under her to grab her thighs. She's resting her back on me fully, but Alaric needs access.

"You look so fucking gorgeous with Gideon's cock inside of you," he growls, lining his cock up at her entrance. Theo and Sterling climb onto the bed.

"Where do you want us?" Theo asks, his blue eyes hooded and dark. The tip of his cock is still leaking, and my length pulses when I think of how vigorously he fucked Alaric earlier.

What the hell is Harlow doing to our order?

She's turning us into sex-crazed animals.

"I want to taste both of you," she whimpers as I slam into her.

Theo and Sterling climb on either side of us, and they position their cocks to line up with her mouth. She flicks her tongue out and they both groan when they rub their precome all over her lips.

Fuck.

"Deep breath," Alaric purrs, setting his cock on top of mine. He spits, lubing everything up, though we don't really need lube with how wet she is from her orgasm. As he tries to push in slowly, I feel Harlow tense up.

LADY OF DARKNESS

"Relax," I tell her softly as I spread her legs wider.

Alaric slowly begins to circle her clit with his thumb, and her head falls back onto my chest.

"Fuck," she cries out. Alaric pushes in, and *fucking hell*, it feels so goddamn incredible. I feel when her opening stretches, the way it snaps closed around us as he drives in slowly, the taut skin of his shaft sliding against mine.

I groan. "Jesus Christ."

Harlow lets out gasps with every inch Alaric moves inside of her. She's damp with sweat, and her hands are fisted at my sides. I move against Alaric, and we make eye contact. Something white-hot passes through my body, tightening my shaft and balls. This is so epically hot. Seeing my friends lose their goddamn minds to her pussy, to the feel of us all together...

Why the hell did we wait so long to do this?

"Open your mouth, Harlow," Sterling orders.

She does, and both he and Theo pop their cocks between her lips.

"Fuck," Alaric breathes, his voice shaky and uneven. "If you could fucking see how fucking beautiful you are double-stuffed with our cocks, little monster," he growls, working his hips forward. "Your pussy stretched so wide, your mouth so full... you're going to be so fucking full of our seed, it'll leak out for days."

She moans, the sound muffled around Theo and Sterling. Alaric and I find a good rhythm, and we both thrust into her at the same time. She screams and her body tightens as she gags. Theo and Sterling relent a bit, pulling out from her mouth as spit falls down her chin in strings. She looks over her shoulder at me and bares her teeth.

"Fuck!" she cries out as we move quicker. Deeper. *Harder*.

Alaric works his thumb faster against her swollen nub. "You like it when we stretch you, little monster?"

She nods vigorously, reaching out and wrapping her arms around his neck. They kiss and Alaric moves slower as I pound into them.

"Fuck, St. Claire," Alaric rasps around Harlow's mouth. "Your cock grinding against mine is going to make me come."

"Oh fuck yes," Harlow begs, leaning back again and opening her mouth for Sterling and Theo.

They pop into her mouth, and she moans and rolls her hips. The noises she's making get louder, more intense, and I can feel the way her pussy is lightly squeezing mine in anticipation.

It's too much for me. I roar loudly as my cock begins to pulse, and Alaric's growl of pleasure sends my orgasm shooting up into Harlow. My balls pull up and my cock tightens as I spill my come inside of her.

"I can feel you fucking coming," Alaric says, looking at me like he's right on the edge. He reaches down and takes my hands before throwing his head back. His cock curves and Harlow screams his name as she comes around him, spraying her come everywhere as she milks every last drop of semen from his pulsing shaft.

"Fuck," I murmur, rubbing my face as Alaric pulls out. Harlow is still twitching when I slide my cock out of her.

"Our turn," Sterling growls.

I move to the side as Sterling flips her onto her back. She groans as he plunges two fingers inside of her.

"Just pushing the come back in," he says, smirking. Then, he punches his cock into her and begins to fuck her, one leg over his shoulder.

"Oh fuck, oh fuck," she says, whining. "How is it possible that I feel like coming again?"

"Because the head of my cock is hitting your G-spot," Sterling says. "Come for me, little monster. Squeeze me dry."

Harlow stiffens and arches her back. "Oh my God," she whispers. "Oh my God, I'm—"

She begins to convulse, and Sterling hisses as he pulls nearly all the way out as she rejects him. Her pussy contracts as she sprays his chest, her toes curled at his neck.

I watch, mesmerized, as his cock quivers inside of her, filling her even more. His fingers are white where he's gripping her hips, and then he slows. They're both panting.

My cock leaks even more come—or precome. I don't even know at this point. It feels like we all took triple doses of Viagra. I've never stayed hard for this long, especially after spilling two loads.

"Wolf, plug her up," Sterling says, pulling out quickly.

Theo doesn't waste any time. He drives into her, spreading her legs wide as he pulls her hips onto his shaft with each thrust.

Harlow's eyes roll into the back of her head.

"Yeah?" he asks her, baring his teeth. "Just because I'm the last doesn't mean I'm not going to make you scream my name."

Harlow whimpers, and her eyes flutter closed.

"Look at me," Theo says, working himself faster. She's so full of our come that the sounds of Theo fucking her will forever be embedded in my mind. The way her pussy spills our come all over Theo's cock, the way it leaks down between her ass cheeks...

Jesus.

"Look at me as I fill you to the brim," he growls.

She meets every thrust, moving her hips against his shaft, milking it completely. "Oh God, Theo," she keens.

"You like taking our come like this?"

"Yes," she hisses, and she reaches up to play with her nipples. "I fucking love it," she growls, sounding more feral by the second.

Theo plunges into her harder, his balls slapping her with each thrust as he goes all the way in. Her tits bounce and her head hits the wooden bed frame.

"What else do you love?" Theo asks, his pace unforgiving as he moves even harder.

She's going to break in half from the force of it.

"Oh God, oh my fucking God." She lets out a deep moan as Theo reaches down and flicks her clit.

"I told you. You like this. You like to fuck us until your pussy is raw. You like the fear, and the danger," he growls.

"Yes, I fucking love all of it," she says, her voice faraway and breathy. "Oh God," she cries out.

"Say. It," Theo commands, placing one hand around her neck as he works his hips flush against hers, pressing as deep as he can and making her gasp. "Who do you love?"

"You!" she screams. "I fucking love all of you, okay?"

Theo chuckles, and then he pinches her clit just as she rejects his cock. She sprays his chest and bucks her hips as her eyes move to the back of her head. All of her muscles spasm as she comes down from her orgasm. Theo pulls her back onto his cock as he spills into her silently. His mouth drops open as he finishes, his body jerking. Staring down at her, he stops moving.

"Fuck, baby," he says, running a hand through his blond hair. He pulls out slowly, looking down. "Hold our come in," he murmurs, pressing the creamy white liquid back inside of her.

"Why?" she asks, giving him a teasing smile.

Theo smirks, his free hand grazing her breasts. "Because I fucking love seeing you so full of our come," he says, his hand moving down to her stomach. "I fucking delight in the idea of making new heirs with you, Harlow."

She blushes. "You have a while before that happens."

He cocks his head, plunging a third finger inside of her so that no more semen spills out. "Do I?"

Her lips part as he rubs the come all over her lips. It begins to gush out, and she whimpers when his fingers—wet with our come—begin to slowly play with her swollen, pink clit.

"Four years," he murmurs, bending down and licking her clean.

My cock bobs. *Jesus, Wolf.*

"You have four years until we put a baby in your belly. Until this," he says slowly, as more come seeps out, "is the real deal."

"And if I say no?" she asks, her voice husky.

He tilts his head and gives her a dark smile. "Don't make us cut that implant out sooner."

Her lips twitch. "You wouldn't dare."

Theo laughs. "Then you don't know us very well, little monster."

CHAPTER 36

Harlow

After the guys clean me up, we exit the suite and make our way back to Blackwell. I toy with the idea of staying in London overnight, but Gemma is still staying with me, and I told her I'd be home late. My body is sore and tender, and my nerves are completely shot from the teasing and pounding—*literal* pounding. I can't think about it for too long, otherwise I have to squeeze my legs together and take a few calming breaths.

I told them I loved them.

God, it's crazy what I'll do for an orgasm.

It wasn't real... was it?

I glance at all of them—at Alaric and Gideon on their phones. At Theo with his laptop. At Sterling, who is looking out of the window as we drive out of London.

Do I really love them?

Sterling looks over at me, and something in my throat catches when he smiles. My stomach drops, and everything begins to tingle.

I remember how scared I was when Alaric saved me from the bomb. I remember how much I regretted baking those brownies. I remember how their expressions were a mix of anger and hurt—and how uncomfortable it made me to see them so wounded afterward.

But does that all equate to love? I've never been in love before. It's a powerful word, especially when it comes to the Lords.

I fucking love all of you, okay?

My cheeks heat when I think about how easily I caved. How natural it felt, how *good* it felt to admit it.

Maybe I do love them. Maybe not. But I will, one day soon. You can't have this kind of connection—this kind of tether between souls—without love. I think of what Alaric said a week ago.

Marriage is a piece of paper and a silly vow. This? This is divine. Eternal. It transcends everything else, Harlow.

When we get to Blackwell House, Alaric walks me to the door. It feels really fucking cute when he grabs my hand and pulls me close, leaning down and kissing me on the tip of the nose before saying goodnight.

I look up into his eyes, into the eyes of the man I maybe love.

Dangerous.

Murderer.

Sensual.

Caring.

Witty.

Ruthless.

All of his truths wrapped up into one. The good and the bad. The psychopath and the aristocrat. Two sides of one coin, both able to make me feel things I never even thought were possible. I swallow as he walks away, waving back at me. The lump in my throat is bigger now, and I open my front door and walk inside. When it's shut and locked, I sigh and lean against the heavy wood barrier. I rub my chest and close my eyes, sighing again, when someone clears their throat.

Not some*one*. Two people.

Cecelia and Gemma.

They're both sitting on the couch in the living room, staring at me.

"Hi," I say softly, suddenly overcome with all of the emotions from the past few weeks. I hardly ever cry, but right now... it doesn't stop.

Gemma rushes forward and pulls me onto the couch with her. Cecelia pours me some tea from the pot they've been sharing, and Gemma–bless her–knows to add sugar and milk. She stirs it around and hands it to me.

"I've been told that British people offer tea when you're sad," she says matter-of-factly, smiling at Cecelia.

I swipe under my eyes as I sniff, trying to compose myself. "I'm not sad. Just overwhelmed."

They look between each other as Gemma rubs my back. "We also have cookies."

"Biscuits," Cecelia corrects, smirking.

We all laugh.

I take a few sips of tea, feeling so much better already. Both of them are looking at me expectantly, and I don't even know where to start. I just shake my head and set my teacup down on the saucer.

"I think... I think I love them," I say glumly.

"That's usually a good thing, right?" Gemma asks.

"Not always," Cecelia adds.

I notice then that they're both wearing pajamas. "You're both up late."

Cecelia shrugs. "Archie woke up, and once I settled him back down, I couldn't go back to sleep." She gestures at the baby monitor on the coffee table. "Gemma was down here reading, and we got to talking."

I nod. "That's nice."

"I was telling her about Luka," Gemma says.

"And we've concluded he's an arsehole," Cecelia interjects, looking at Gemma pointedly.

Gemma shrugs. "He's an arsehole."

I smile. "You should stay. Here, I mean."

Gemma rolls her lower lip between her teeth and sighs. "I wish I could. But classes start soon, and I have to find another apartment to rent, since my roomie is abandoning me."

I grimace. "I'm sorry."

Gemma's brown eyes study my face for a minute before she responds. "It's okay. I see now what you mean—about this being your calling. You sparkle more here than you ever did in New York. It's like you came alive," she adds, shaking her head. "I'll miss you, but now that you're rich, you can fly me out every Christmas."

I snort. Pulling her into a hug, I don't let go for several seconds. "Always. You're always welcome." As I look over at Cecelia, I add, "You're always welcome, too. I know this is officially my house now, but it was your home for five years. You can stay if you want to."

Cecelia gives me a warm smile and takes my hand. "That's very kind of you. But I think..." she trails off, furrowing her brows. "I think I need to carve out a place of my own. I was so close to my family growing up, and then Charles and I started dating, and I went from one house to the next without really thinking about what *I* wanted."

"Have you talked to your father?" I ask her gently.

She shakes her head. "No. I can't forgive him, Harlow. Not after everything he did. And... I'm so mad at Charles. I know what we had was real—so whether or not he did it because he loved me, I don't know." She looks at me with watery eyes. "I always had a crush on him, you know."

"Really?"

Cecelia nods. "Our families go way back, and I'd seen him around when I was in secondary school. He was older, of course. And then when I was twenty-seven, we both attended a party at some swanky nightclub, and he confessed he'd always loved me. But now I'm left questioning if it was real, or if my father orchestrated the whole thing."

I nod. "I'm sorry. I can't imagine how that must feel."

She leans back into the sofa, and Gemma sighs. "Men," Gemma mumbles. "They reel you in, play games, and then they disappear... or die."

Gemma winces apologetically, and Cecelia giggles. "It's true." The lines around her face aren't as deep as when I arrived in England. She seemed so sad then, so distraught. Frail. But now... she seems stronger. More sure of herself. Whatever sadness she was carrying around has been replaced by anger at her family. It might not be the healthiest coping mechanism, but I know it's probably the best thing for her.

"What about you?" Cecelia asks, taking a bite of a shortbread biscuit. Her green eyes bore into mine, and I swallow once before answering.

"What about me?"

Gemma barks a laugh. "You walked through the door like Cinderella after the ball. Your cheeks are flushed, and your hair is... it's seen better days, which probably means you had crazy sex tonight."

My lips twitch with a smile as my hands go up to my hair. "What's wrong with my hair?"

Gemma wrinkles her nose. "It's just-fucked hair."

Cecelia snorts as my cheeks redden.

"It is not!"

"Okay, whatever you say. So you weren't having sex?" she teases.

I suck in my cheeks. "I plead the fifth."

"Please tell me it was with all four of them," Gemma begs, taking my hands. "Please. Tell me it was all of them at once. A massive, hot guy orgy."

I nearly double over with laughter. "I'll never tell."

"That means it was," Cecelia interjects, her pinky out, as she sips her tea.

When I'm done laughing, I shrug and cross my arms. "It all feels like a lot. I got so wrapped up in them—in this life. New York seems like a lifetime ago."

"But that's how it happens," Gemma says gently. "Life goes on. Sometimes things are unplanned, but those often end up being the best surprises."

An hour later, we all head upstairs. I take a long shower and get changed for bed. As I'm sitting in the dark with my phone, my finger hovers over the group text chain with the guys.

I don't even know what I want to say, but my fingers move of their own accord.

Me: I meant what I said earlier. Just in case any of you were on the edge of your seats, waiting.

A few seconds later, they all reply back.

Alaric: I know, baby. See you tomorrow.

Gideon: Night, sugartits.

I can't help the large grin that breaks out across my face.

Sterling: Get some rest xx

Theo: Unless you want to spread those glorious legs and show us how that smutty monster book makes you feel.

I frown and flip my room off, hoping he can see me on the camera.

Theo: You're getting spanked tomorrow for that, little monster.

I'm smiling as I fall asleep reading my monster smut.

This life... it isn't so bad.

At least I know it'll never be boring.

CHAPTER 37

ALARIC

I finish my whiskey and set it down next to the sink. The summer weather has been fluctuating between hot and cold, and when I look out of my window into the large field beyond Cross Manor, I can make out the mist covering the green grass. I walk into my office and open my laptop, making sure Cecelia's new deed is all settled. When she told me this morning that she wanted to find her own place, I offered to buy it for her. Outside of her family, she doesn't have any money, and she would need a safe, secure home for her and Archie.

I didn't trust George Crawford, her father.

She found the place last week, and we'd been secretly working on the offer for the owners. I offered cash for a quick sale, and the deed should transfer to her name tomorrow. It's a five-bedroom cottage on the other side of Blackwell, near the barn. I looked for a place that was close and central, seeing as she wants Archie to get to know Harlow. I think it's too small, but she seems to love it.

I pull up the next surprise, flicking through the pictures of the warehouse space. It's in a neighboring village, which I don't love, but... it's perfect for Harlow's studio. It's an old, abandoned factory from the 1700s. Originally a wool mill, it's been abandoned for 150 years. Seeing as it also comes with one hundred and fifty acres of land, it's not cheap. I figured Harlow could use it for her runs, since she's taken to them quite well. I've already been in contact with a landscaper to flush the trails out for her. I'm also meeting with a contractor next week to discuss refurbishing the factory into a large studio with plenty of space for her to work.

Sighing, I close my laptop and pinch the bridge of my nose.

It's been a fucking crazy whirlwind since the night we killed Charles and found out about Harlow. The emotions running through me—the fury, the kindling of lust, the worry, the contempt, the love... it's like she came into our order and turned everything upside down. I smile when I think of tonight. When I think of how hot and bothered she got watching me with Theo. How hot *I* got being with Theo. I'd never explored that part of me sexually. I'd participated in orgies before, but nothing like this.

It's like she came in, dropped a match, and lit everything on fire with her presence.

As I walk upstairs, I begin to unfasten my tie, slipping it off and hanging it neatly over the back of my desk chair. I place my jacket in the bag meant for dry cleaning, and then I undress fully, hopping into my large stone shower for a quick wash. The entire time, I think of Harlow—and the guys. I've never thought about them like that before, but suddenly, it makes perfect sense.

Closer than brothers.

Closing my eyes, I place an arm on the wall. The other begins to stroke my shaft slowly. I think back to how it felt being inside of Harlow at the same time as Gideon. How exquisite and cataclysmic it was. To be close to someone in spirit, and then move into the physical realm like that...

I fist my cock harder, using soap to lube it up as I throw my head back.

I should be spent. Two orgasms in a row. Instead, my need gnaws at the base of my spine as if I haven't come in days.

That's what she does to me—to us.

I come quick and fast, pelting the stone wall with jets of hot come. I watch as it washes down the drain, panting as my chest heaves up and down.

She burned our entire order to the ground slowly. Not with poison, like she intended, but with something deeper. Something fundamentally vivid and powerful. She ripped us open day by day until we became the kind of men who had to nut twice a day. The kind of men who would murder hundreds of people to get her back. Thousands of people, if we needed to. *Millions.* I'd never been in love, but our little monster had burrowed so far into my heart that I couldn't breathe when I thought of losing her again.

We wanted so badly to break her, but *she* broke *us*.

I would make sure I spent the rest of my life proving our worth to her.

CHAPTER 38

Harlow
Ten Weeks Later

I hang up my FaceTime call with Gemma as I walk down the stairs of Blackwell House. Looking around, I smile. Rose and Teddy have been helping me renovate. I've kept most of my dad's things, but I've also gifted a lot of it to Cecelia for her new house. Then there's the more valuable or sentimental family heirlooms, which I've set aside in storage for now, replacing them with things I brought in from local vendors in New York—modern furniture, abstract art... things that bring a little bit of Brooklyn into this old, stuffy manor. I've even taken over one wall in the living room and painted a mural. Four skeletons with crowns, kneeling before a skeleton with long, curly hair—and a crown.

I smile when I pass it.

The guys *love* it, because of course they do.

I made it for them.

Gemma is settling in well at NYU. It's nearly Halloween, and she's making new friends every day. Cecelia and Archie come over three days a week so I can hang out with Archie while Cecelia goes to Pilates. She's all moved into her new house across town, and it's picturesque and quaint as fuck. It even has a thatched roof.

"I'm not sure about this," Rose says slowly, looking at the sculpture I had brought in from one of my favorite artists in New York.

It's two bodies entwined, and they're very clearly engaged in some graphic sex.

I smirk. "It's art," I counter. "You don't have to be sure about it."

Rose huffs and walks away, shaking her head as she continues dusting the furniture.

She no longer lives here, only coming in three days a week to clean and help me with the redecorating. Teddy only comes once a week to help prep some food for the week. They both live permanently with their families now. I even tripled their salaries so that they can buy nice places of their own if they so wish.

It feels nice to throw the old traditions away and start my own. After all, this is my domain now. My house, my rules. My eyes flick to the window that used to overlook the rose garden, but I recently replaced it with a state-of-the-art jungle gym for Archie. Considering my mother always hated roses, it feels like a good way to honor her.

This house works for me now, but who knows about the future? Plus, some of the things I'm putting aside are irreplaceable. Old tapestries from the 1400s, gorgeous Victorian furniture, some of the art… it doesn't really fit my style, but I feel obligated to keep it. The sense of responsibility of honoring my ancestors as the last Blackwell descendant—aside from Archie—is heavy. It weighs on me a lot. But I'm here. I'm a Lady of Darkness, and I'm carving a space for myself in this life.

I'm making it work for me, and that's all I can really do.

I round the dining room, having opted to keep everything the same in here. One day, I might do a complete overhaul, but for now, I like the idea of keeping some things familiar for Archie.

After making myself some coffee, I head into my office and check my email. We don't receive emails very often, and things are encrypted or in code—something Theo is teaching me how to decipher. He's also teaching me most of what he knows about computers, security, and servers. I'm finding that I have a natural proficiency for hacking, as well as espionage—two things I've utilized more often than I expected to.

It's been a busy autumn, that's for sure.

George Crawford has backed off some, and he respects Cecelia's need for independence. We are still monitoring the Crawford family for any wrongdoings, but so far, they've stayed in their lane. It's a lot of monitoring. Most of the other, smaller crime orders and syndicates—even the various mafias and mobs around the world—orbit around us. I know more about the cartel and the Irish mafia—the latter being so close to England by proximity—than I ever anticipated. The guys were right. I've seen people blanch when they find out I'm a Lady of Darkness. Our reputation precedes us, and our reputation has a stronghold over the entire world.

It has been wild to witness firsthand.

Theo sends me an email—another required reading list. It's full of nonfiction and classic books. A lot of them are pertinent to the job, but I don't appreciate the gusto with which he tries to interfere in my reading material. I roll my eyes as I filter it into the inbox folder marked 'In Case I'm Lobotomized'.

He doesn't think it's very funny.

My phone chimes and I smirk as I pick it up.

Theo: You can keep adding my emails to your cheeky little folder, but that doesn't mean I'll ever stop trying to continue your literary education.

Me: My *literary education* is just fine, thank you.

Theo: I don't understand how someone gets through life without reading Ulysses. It's such a phenomenal piece of writing.

Me: You're right. I feel bereft without it.

Theo: Mmm. Now you're just being a brat on purpose.

Me: Maybe I am.

Giggling, I set my phone down and pull my cardigan tightly around myself. The weather has fully transitioned, and Sterling made it his mission to take me shopping in London a few weeks ago. I now have a closet full of designer clothes that make me feel like a badass for the colder weather. As I sip my coffee, I stare out at the forest beyond the window of my father's office. It's serene here, peaceful. I smile as I finish my coffee quickly, walking back into the kitchen as Rose flits around, taking something out of the oven.

"Smells good," I say, inhaling deeply.

"Thanks," she replies cheerfully as she wipes her hands on her jeans. I banished the uniforms for everyone once I took over completely, and it makes me happy to see Rose in her own clothes. She's sort of stepped into the role of my surrogate mother. She spends her two free days a week watching Archie. It's like we have a little commune going on here. Between me and the guys, Rose, Teddy, and Cecelia... it all sort of does feel like one big, extended family. Especially since I host dinner for everyone every Sunday. "I'm making brownies for the boys."

My lips twitch. "Oh?"

She nods. "I figured you could bring them over to Lord Cross's house later."

I narrow my eyes. "How'd you know about that?"

Alaric was keeping a secret from me—that much I could ascertain. He'd texted me earlier saying he was going to pick me up around four. I'd checked our joint work calendar, but there was nothing, and he was acting really cagey when I asked him what we were doing. Normally, they add everything to the calendar, so I'm always aware of what the day holds. But not today.

"He asked me to make sure you were ready to be picked up just before four. I figured he could enjoy some home-baked brownies for whatever he has planned."

I flatten my lips. *The irony...*

"Okay. I can bring them when he picks me up. Thanks, Rose."

She pops some foil over the pan and pats it. "Give it thirty minutes to cool." Her eyes wander up and down my romper and cardigan. "Is that what you're wearing? What if he pops the question?"

I huff a laugh. "I highly doubt that, Rose. I've only known him for a few months!"

Still, I go upstairs and change into black pants and a dark green silk blouse. It feels casual, yet fancy enough if needed. I still refuse most footwear, so I pull on my trusty pair of leather Converse before fixing my hair and applying a thin layer of makeup. Five minutes before four, I head downstairs and grab the brownies from the counter.

"Thanks again, Rose!"

"Good luck tonight," she yells from somewhere in the dining room.

I try not to roll my eyes as I grab my coat hanging by the front door. It's soft and luxurious, made of cashmere. It also cost as much as my rent in New York would've per month. Sterling's proclivity for luxury is truly unmatched, but I can't complain. I like it. And it *is* very warm, especially for tonight, since it's in the forties already with the spitting kind of rain.

Grabbing an umbrella, I rush to the dark grey Range Rover waiting by the front door. It takes a bit of finagling to climb in with a pan of brownies and an open umbrella, but I manage to figure it out. When I close the door, I turn to face Alaric.

"Hi," I say breathlessly.

"I was going to come get you at the door," he says sternly, furrowing his brows. "You don't always need to be so stubborn. I could've held the door open for you."

I shrug. "It's fine. I wouldn't want you to ruin your suit," I retort, my eyes running over the clean lines of his dark grey suit. Most of the others spend their days in more casual clothes, but not Alaric.

He clicks his tongue before he dips his head down and kisses me softly on my lips. He tastes like peppermint and cigarettes, and I can't help the soft moan that escapes me.

"Hi," he murmurs, a warm finger grazing the side of my cheek.

"So, what's this surprise?" I ask, smiling as he pulls out of the driveway.

His lips twitch. "You'll see. What's in the pan?"

I have to cover my mouth with my hand to keep from smiling. "Rose made brownies."

"Oh?" He turns to face me for a second, his lips pulled up into a mischievous smile. "Poisonous brownies?"

I scoff. "I knew you were going to have something to say about it."

He laughs—a rich, booming sound. I hardly ever get to hear it, but when I do, it's glorious.

"Can you blame me, little monster? Come on." Placing a hand on my thigh, he squeezes lightly. My whole body shivers at his touch.

"It would be the perfect murder, though," I muse. I look over at him, and he gives me a lopsided smile as I continue. "Attempt to murder you all once, get forgiveness and make you feel safe, and then try again a few months later. Genius."

He chuckles. "It is genius."

"You'd never see it coming," I add, opening the foil to show him Rose's perfectly baked brownies.

"You're right. I wouldn't. We all trust you fully now."

"To your detriment." He laughs as he pulls onto a side road. I look around. "Where the hell are you taking me, Cross?"

They all call each other by their last names, so sometimes, I find myself doing the same thing to remind them that I am one of them.

"Patience, Windsor."

I cross my arms as we make our way out of town on the narrow country lane. My palms sweat as Alaric takes the turns at 60mph, with no regard that someone could be coming around the narrow bend. Driving in England is not for the faint of heart. Even though I know I'll need to drive here at some point, I am not looking forward to it.

He pulls down a dirt driveway. There are trees on either side, and the rain begins to pour as we drive up to a massive brick building. It's similar to the barn—what I've crudely coined the *Bloodshed Barn*. Except, this place is bigger. Prettier, somehow. There's a large red door and flowers all around the perimeter. It looks like there's a forest beyond the warehouse, too. Large factory windows made of black metal dot the exterior of the building.

"What is this?" I ask, looking over at Alaric as he parks.

"I'll show you." He exits the car and walks around to open my door, popping an umbrella for me.

I set the brownies on the dashboard and climb out, walking to the large red door by his side. He holds out an old skeleton key and gestures for me to take it.

"What is this?" I ask, already suspicious. Taking the key, I place it in the old brass lock. After a click, I push the door open, stiffening when I see what's inside.

Theo, Gideon, and Sterling are all standing in front of what looks like stacks of shelves, but as I take a step inside, I realize it's not shelves.

It's row after row of massive brick walls several feet tall by several feet wide. Row, after row, after row. Beyond that is a wall *full* of spray paint—*hundreds* of cans in all different colors. There are oversized tables with stencils and thin, plastic boards for me to make my own stencils, an industrial sink, and a wall with a couple of aprons and masks hung up. Looking up, I see state-of-the-art ventilation fans whirring. I flick my eyes to the guys as my throat closes up.

"Is this..." I trail off, turning to face Alaric.

He's leaning against the door. "Surprise."

"Welcome to your new studio," Theo says, walking over to where I'm standing. The other guys follow suit.

"There's even a running trail out back. Alaric brought in a landscaper in case you'd like to do your runs outside. The loop is five miles, but there are over a hundred acres out there to do with what you want."

I stare at him, shaking my head in shock. "A hundred acres? For me?"

Sterling nods. "This is all for you. Maybe you could build a new house. Open up a B&B. Build a theme park. It's all yours. We'd give you the fucking world if we could, little monster. Maybe we will one day."

My eyes prick with tears as my eyes sweep over the studio a second time. The light is incredible because of the massive windows, and it's so open and airy that I instantly feel inspired.

"This doesn't replace your street art," Alaric purrs, wrapping an arm around my side. His fingers sink into my flesh. "But we know you had to give up a prestigious scholarship to stay here, and we wanted to make it up to you. Paint here or out on the street. We don't give a fuck. We just want you to be happy."

I swallow my emotion, just barely. On my third glance around, I notice the corner on the right set up with an easel and paints, as well as notebooks for sketching. They thought of everything.

"If there's anything else you need, we can bring it in," Gideon adds.

I open and close my mouth. "Can–can I–" I point to the back wall.

"It's yours," Alaric says. "You don't need to ask permission."

I make my way to the back wall and pick up a can of black paint. Placing it down on the table, I inspect the stencils. I sort through them, grabbing a few for what I need. Then I go to the nearest wall and begin to work. My mind is spinning with ideas, and my hands don't stop moving for almost an hour. At some point, one of the guys places a mask over my face for safety, but they stand back and watch as I perfect my creation. Pulling my mask off, it hangs at my side as I turn to face the guys.

"What do you think?" I ask, feeling breathless with excitement. "Do you like it?"

Alaric cocks his head and smiles. "Did it ever matter if we liked it, Harlow? The question is, do *you* like it?"

I look back at the painting. It's a black anatomical heart cut evenly into five sections.

If it all ends in fire, then we will all burn together.

"I do like it," I say, pulling my phone out of my pocket and snapping a picture for my Instagram.

"Would you still do it without your fans?" Gideon asks, walking up to the wall and inspecting the paint. He turns to face me with a scrutinizing expression.

I shrug, thinking it over for a moment. "Probably. It became my solace after my mom died."

He nods and comes closer to me, pulling me in for a kiss. "Then that's all that matters."

My heart stutters in my chest as I grab the back of his head and pull him in for another kiss. He moans into my mouth as he grinds himself against me, and that's all it takes for me to unbuckle his belt.

"Are we doing this here?" he asks smugly.

"Shut up," I hiss, pressing his body against the wall with the art.

"I don't want to mess it up–"

"It's fine. I can make another one. I have the space now."

His eyes darken as he unbuttons my shirt, pulling it down my arms. Then he kneels, taking my shoes and pants off before hoisting me up and twisting me around so that my back is against the wet paint.

We're all going to be covered in black after this.

I groan and bite his lip when I feel one of the other guys kiss my neck. Pulling away from Gideon, I turn my head to face Sterling on my right. He bends down and kisses me as Gideon lines his cock up against my underwear. He swipes it to the side and enters me in one thrust. I gasp against Sterling's mouth, looking at Theo on my left.

My mouth drops open when his tongue slides down my cleavage, and then, with his bare teeth, he tears my bra off and sucks my left nipple into his mouth.

Crying out, I roll my hips against Gideon's cock. He maneuvers us so that his back is to the painting, and I feel Alaric come up behind me.

"Do you like it?" he asks, nipping the back of my neck as his hand trails down my back.

I moan as Gideon grips my hips tighter, slamming me down on his cock. "I do. I love it."

He makes a low, satisfied sound as he spits into his hand and rubs it all around the entrance to my ass.

"Good, baby." He presses his cock against my back entrance, and I hiss as he pushes in slowly. "Deep breath. Count to three."

"One," I whisper, and before I'm even done saying the word, he pumps into me in one quick jerk.

I gasp, the feeling of being full of Gideon and Alaric at the same time exquisite, just like it always is.

"Liar," I grit out, my eyes rolling into the back of my head.

He chuckles. "Feel good?"

I let out a deep moan. "God, yes."

Gideon takes two fingers and rubs my clit gently between them. When I spasm in his arms, he groans.

"I just felt your tight little pussy quiver around me, baby. You like that?" he growls, quickening his pace as he drives into me.

"Our little monster likes two of us at a time, I think," Alaric says, brushing my hair away as he bites the space between my shoulder and neck. I throw my head back against his chest as the pressure builds in every single muscle. My core tightens and contracts around both Gideon and Alaric, and then Gideon flicks my swollen clit once. It's just enough fire to send me over the edge.

I scream as my hips jerk, making Alaric hiss with his release. Gideon roars as they both stretch me wider with their tightening cocks. Stars dance in my vision as euphoria floods me, my pussy fluttering around Gideon with the aftershocks.

"Yes, Harlow," he says, his voice hoarse as he shakes. Alaric's hands come around to my chest as he finishes pulsing into my ass.

"Fuck," I mumble, looking over my shoulder to see Theo and Sterling waiting eagerly.

That's the hard part about all of this—sometimes people get left out.

It just means more rounds for me, and you won't ever find me complaining about that.

Gideon sets me down and I feel both him and Alaric's seed drip down my thighs as I walk to Theo and Sterling.

They're both leaning against the wall, their hard cocks straining against their pants.

"How—"

Before I can finish asking my question, Sterling drops to his knees. He kisses me on my stomach as he moves lower, lying down on the stone floor.

"Sit on my face, Harlow."

LADY OF DARKNESS

A flash of electricity shoots through me as I straddle him, and he grabs my hips and pulls me forward.

"Let me lick that sweet pussy." He lowers me down onto his face before I can respond, and I whimper as his wide tongue begins to lap at me.

Jesus.

His stubble is rough against me, but it also increases the pleasure. I move my hips back and forth as his tongue darts into my opening, cleaning up Gideon's come.

Theo stands in front of me, reaching down and running a hand through my hair as I moan.

I unbuckle his jeans with shaking hands, taking the head of his cock into my mouth with gusto.

"Fuck," he hisses. His cock bounces against the roof of my mouth as I play with his balls. "Keep going, baby."

I move my mouth up and down his shaft, stroking his length with one hand, and cupping his balls with the other. He jerks when I hollow my cheeks, moaning against his tight skin as Sterling flicks his tongue hard and fast against my clit.

"That's it," Theo purrs, gripping my hair harder as he starts to fuck my mouth.

With a deep groan, He impales my throat. I gag a few times, but I squeeze my eyes shut as he plunges his hips forward. I open as wide as I can, taking him into the back of my throat as flashes of another orgasm work from my core, tingling through my limbs. He fists my hair tighter, driving into my throat relentlessly as Sterling brings me to the precipice. I jerk my hips as he flattens his tongue against my engorged bud, and suddenly I'm spiraling down into an intense release. One that has me moaning and whimpering around Theo's length. Sterling moves his tongue up and down my entire slit languidly as I jerk and tremble above, never stopping.

"Swallow my come," Theo commands, which only spurs me on. I continue riding Sterling's face as Theo's cock bobs inside of me. I feel his balls tighten and then he pulls me all the way onto his cock, holding me there as he empties himself. I groan and gag as another orgasm flares through me unexpectedly.

My toes curl and I grip Theo's ass as I ride wave after wave of my climax on Sterling's face. I swallow every hot jet of come Theo shoots down my throat, and when he finishes, he leans down and kisses the top of my head.

I lick my lips as Sterling moves me down his body, lining the head of his cock up with my entrance before he pulls me down onto him roughly.

I cry out and arch my back as he slams into me.

"It's so fucking hot to make you come while you're blowing Wolf," he growls. The force of his hands moving me on top of him creates a slapping sound, and I roll my hips every time he pulls me down so that he gets maximum friction. "Oh, fuck yes," he says, his voice low and rough. "Come on, baby." He works himself faster as I whimper. "Come for me one more time. I want to feel your pussy ripple around my cock as I stuff you full of my seed."

"Fuck yes," I whisper, grabbing his hands for leverage as I lace my fingers with his.

I move my hips as the sounds get wetter, and then he thrusts up to meet my movements. Spiraling into another orgasm, my whole body pulses with pleasure. I feel Sterling hold me down on his cock as he spills inside of me, and my eyes flutter closed as he finishes. I'm panting when his hands rove up to my stomach, carefully caressing me.

"Jesus Christ," he says, using one hand to rub his face. The other grips onto my flesh like he doesn't want to let go. "Sex with you is like an addiction."

I take a steadying breath before I feel Alaric help me up. "You think one orgasm is addicting? Try four," I retort.

Alaric pats my bare ass as he lifts one of my legs and cleans me up with a warm rag.

"Poor you," he murmurs, discarding the cloth and wrapping a large towel around my body. "The heating is on the fritz," he explains. "I don't want you to be cold."

It's then that I realize we're all covered with black paint. It's on my legs, my arms, and probably my hair. Gideon is wiping himself with a towel, and the others have it all over their hands and faces.

"That's one way to break in my new studio," I say, smiling as I watch them.

It suddenly hits me—the words Sterling spoke to me the first night we met.

Don't be scared, little monster. You've just inherited a whole goddamn family. Your blood runs black, just like ours. Welcome to the Lords of Darkness, Lady Blackwell.

I swallow as emotion after emotion overwhelms me.

Love.

Longing.

Adoration.

I pull the towel tighter around myself, willing myself not to cry, not to get all sentimental about the metaphor of us all *actually* being covered in black paint.

"It's a good thing I had the foresight to install a shower," Alaric muses, walking over to a door near the back wall. He unbuttons his shirt and cocks his head as he places the stained shirt neatly over one of the tables. "Care to clean up with me?" His eyes rove to the others, and we all follow him into the bathroom.

There's a massive shower with flagstone floors and stone walls. It's new, which means he had it renovated, just like the rest of the studio. As he takes a handful of shampoo and begins to work it through my hair, I feel Sterling soaping up my body from behind.

"Thank you," I say quietly, looking up into Alaric's eyes before glancing at the others. "For this. For all of it. For everything."

Gideon chuckles as he runs a bar of soap over his body. "Are you still glad we broke into your room that night?"

My lips pull to the side. "I mean, you could've been nicer about it, I guess."

Theo laughs. "Oh yeah? How? Waltz into your bedroom and sing you a song?"

I smile. "No. I don't regret how it happened. You obviously won."

Taking the bar of soap, I walk over to Sterling, lathering his chest as I gaze into his eyes.

His hand comes around my wrist, and I drop the soap on the ground. There's such intensity burning in green eyes as they stare into mine that my pulse speeds up.

"We always win, little monster."

EPILOGUE, PART ONE

Alaric
Four Years Later

I steeple my hands in front of me on the table. The guys are seated on my side of the large conference table, and Harlow across from us. Her eyes narrow into a withering gaze as she leans back and crosses her legs, her black heels tapping against one of the legs of the table. London crawls with people below us, and the floor-to-ceiling windows overlook the river Thames. Tucking her hair behind one ear, she clasps her hands together and makes eye contact with all of us before flicking her dark blue eyes back to me.

"Is there a reason you've called me into this room?" she asks, her tone sardonic and annoyed all at once.

Theo lets out a whoosh of air as he leans back. "I think you know exactly why we're here, little monster."

He slides a piece of paper across the table. She leans forward, and her eyes scan the drafted contract he came up with months ago in anticipation of this day. Her expression goes from slightly irritated to *really fucking aggravated* in about two seconds flat, and her golden skin pales before turning pink. We've provoked her, but we knew exactly what we were doing by bringing her here. She clears her throat and crosses her arms as her eyes bore into Theo's. I see her jaw tick as she cocks her head and waits for him to continue.

"Did you have a chance to read over the terms?" he asks, rolling his tongue around the inside of his cheek.

"I did. And I don't agree with them."

Theo's eyes narrow as he glances over at me. I am pressing my lips together to keep from smiling.

"Which part?" he asks smoothly.

She scoffs. "Please. This is so ridiculous. I can't believe you hired out an entire penthouse conference room for this bullshit pomp and circumstance. I also can't believe you *remember* one dumb thing I said four years ago—"

"Dumb?" I ask quietly, my voice nearly a whisper. "You think the continuation of the Lords of Darkness is dumb, Harlow?"

She rolls her eyes. *There she is.* "Of course it's dumb! You brought me here, to London, and now you want me to sign some crazy contract about surrogates and sperm donors," she hisses. Her eyes flick to the paper again. "Oh, sorry, I read that part wrong. I'm to agree to that *after* we produce an heir not intended for Lordship? Am I reading that right?"

"You are," Theo retorts, one side of his lips quirking up.

She slides the paper back to him. "I'm not interested in the proposal you've outlined here." Her gaze is hard and cold as she assesses Theo, and I press my fingers together a bit harder to distract myself from smiling.

God, she's fucking sexy when she's negotiating.

There's a reason every single crime syndicate out there fears the Lady. She's ruthless, and she's carved herself quite the reputation in our world.

We trained her to be as good as us.

But she ended up being better at everything.

Even Theo's computer skills, which disturbs him to no end.

She places her palm flat on the table and drums her nails along the shiny mahogany. Her posture remains rigid and composed—she doesn't falter once.

We've trained her well, but she was the one who took it one step beyond and became a legend in her own right.

"This is not a choice," Theo murmurs, his voice low and rough.

"Oh? Is that so? Would you be the one carrying a baby for nine months and pushing it out of your vagina?" Theo smiles, and it makes Harlow see red. I hear Gideon mutter *"here we go"* while Sterling hides his laugh behind a cough. "That's very easy for you to say. No choice, my ass," she growls, reaching over and grabbing the piece of paper before tearing it in half.

"Harlow," I growl, leaning over the table. "You agreed. You set the terms."

She barks a laugh. "Yeah, four years ago. I can't believe you remembered the exact fucking date I uttered those stupid words." Her neck is still slightly flushed, and I see the telltale sign of her thighs squeezing together.

Interesting. Is my little monster aroused?

Standing up, I straighten my tie as I walk around to her side of the table. I see the way her chest rises and falls rapidly as I approach, like watching me prowl toward her still sends a shiver down her spine. As it should. Even four years in, we could still surprise her, still romance the fucking hell out of her.

We could still scare the living daylights out of her, too.

I go behind her chair and place a hand on her shoulder. As I do, her skin jumps so subtly that I probably wouldn't have felt it had I not been touching her. Swiveling her around to face me, I give her a monstrous smile before I bend my knees and crouch down in front of her.

"If you didn't agree to the terms, then why did you schedule an appointment with Kitt to remove your birth control implant next week?"

She gasps as I reach out and wrap my fingers around her bicep. "How the hell did you know about that?"

I chuckle, grazing the implant just under her skin. "There's nothing we don't know, baby. Haven't you learned that about us by now?"

Her brows pinch together. "I–I didn't want to tell you right away. They say you need to wait. It can take a few months."

"Actually," Theo interjects, smirking. "A new study that analyzed data from nearly 18,000 women found that fertility returned quickest in patients who had used intrauterine devices or implants. Your fertile window begins tomorrow, and we certainly know how to use a knife, don't we, boys?"

Her eyes widen as she looks between us. "Seriously? How do you know my cycle better than I do?" Before any of us can respond, she closes her eyes and holds her hand out. "Listen. I don't have a problem with trying for a baby. You know how much I've loved being around Archie. But..." She swallows, opening her eyes as they turn glassy. "I don't want surrogates. I don't want random strangers as sperm donors."

"Harlow, you know that logistically we can't have five true blood siblings as heirs. It wouldn't make sense, and it would complicate the delicate lineages we've carved out over the years. We'll each submit a sperm sample and we'll select only women who understands what the futures of their children will hold. We can all have as many babies together as we want, but the Lords will live on in strangers."

She blinks and looks me dead in the eye. "That's the thing. That's my issue." She pauses and swallows again. "I don't think I want the Lords of Darkness to continue *at all*."

EPILOGUE, PART TWO

Harlow

I take a deep breath as my statement settles over all four of them. Alaric's eyes narrow ever so slightly, and when I avert my eyes to look at the others, they all seem just as dumbfounded as Alaric. When I look back at him, I try to hide the emotion in my voice as I continue. As I explain what's been keeping me up at night for months now.

"I vowed to become a Lady of Darkness because I didn't want to subject Archie to this life. You all remember that. How could I possibly know that five innocent children—children we *chose* to bring into the world, mind you—would live this kind of life? The danger, the notoriety... they'd never be able to do what they wanted. I got lucky. I fell into this easily. Who's to say they will?"

Alaric looks stunned, and I use his silence to keep talking.

"Furthermore, if we have kids, we're basically lifting them up and keeping them away from that danger, which gives them an unfair advantage." Sniffing once, I sit up taller and will my face into the cold indifference I'm so used to portraying. "I agree that you can knock me up as soon as you want, however many times as I see fit. But... I think the Lords should die with us."

They all shift uncomfortably as they consider my words. It's not crazy by any means. I've been thinking this through for months. *Years.* How could we ever feel right training an eighteen-year-old, knowing we brought it upon them to live this life? Sure, it paid well, but I'd been shot, stabbed, and nearly killed dozens of times. It isn't safe. That's a fact. I'd want better for these stranger babies.

Another thought clangs through my mind when I think of everything I've been through.

"If we decide to have a baby, we have to give all of this up. We can't have both."

"Are you fucking serious?" Theo asks, his good humor from earlier replaced with disgruntled confusion. "You don't just walk away from this life, Harlow."

I jut my chin out and cross my arms. "What if I'm shot while pregnant?"

That shuts them up. Theo whips his gaze to Alaric, who reaches out and places his large, warm hands on my thighs. I hate how his touch makes me shiver with desire, even when we're having a serious conversation such as this.

"What if we have a child and they take him or her like Acadia took me? What if something happens to them? I'll be out of commission for weeks after the birth, and you'll be down one person."

Gideon's jaw feathers as he runs a hand over his mouth. His hair has silver strands in it now, and he cut it short, like Sterling's, a few years ago. In fact, they're all starting to go a bit grey, which I guess is what happens when you're thirty-six years old.

"We could hire a replacement," he suggests, wincing.

"Fuck no," Alaric says, glaring at him. "I'm not having this conversation right now." He turns to face me again. "We can't just walk away, little monster. We all took an oath. To serve and protect until the next generation takes over."

I nod. "I know that. I love this job, don't get me wrong. But having a baby was always this abstract thing. When I really think about it, I'm... I'm not sure I could handle something bad happening."

My voice breaks on the last word, and Alaric squeezes my thighs as he leans forward to kiss me.

"Nothing is ever guaranteed, though. Even if we weren't the Lords of Darkness, we could get hit by a car walking down the street."

"He's right," Sterling murmurs. "My mum died because of complications during my birth. No one expected or planned that." He walks around to my side of the table. "Like Alaric said, nothing is guaranteed. You know that. Doing this job... you must know that, because it hits you in the face every single day."

I look at all four of them—at the faint crinkles around Alaric's eyes, the silver strands in Gideon's hair, the lines around Theo's mouth, and Sterling's dark circles. This life has taken a toll on all of us. It's turned me into someone people whisper about at dinner parties—someone who makes headlines in gossip magazines. I've clung to my art like a life raft, but even that is sort of falling to the wayside.

This life—this job—it takes, and it takes, and it takes. I'm exhausted. I love it, but I'm exhausted.

"I will get pregnant tomorrow if you promise me one thing."

Alaric's eyes swim with mirth. "Okay, shoot."

I swallow. "I'm not asking you to give this up. But when we all die, the Lords die with us. Our kids will not inherit this."

Sterling rolls his jaw. "How the hell are we going to keep the world together, then?"

I shrug. "We have plenty of time to figure it out. I don't want our future children subjected to *any* of this," I growl, my emotions getting the better of me.

I hold my hand out. "So, I agree to your terms, as long as you agree to mine. No surrogates. No sperm donors. And the Lords of Darkness die with us."

They all hesitate for several seconds as my heart beats wildly in my chest.

Please say yes.

Please say yes.

Please say yes.

"Deal," Alaric growls, taking my hand.

The other guys lay their hands on top of ours, and I've never been more relieved in my entire life.

EPILOGUE, PART THREE

THEO

Harlow tosses and turns in our gigantic bed, and I roll over to face her. Checking my watch, I see that it's nearly midnight.

Fucking close enough.

The other guys are asleep, and my cock won't stay down.

Four years.

She promised we could knock her up in four years.

Not counting the leap year, because I'm impatient as fuck, that lands us on tomorrow's date.

Harlow lets out a low moan as she writhes and rolls her hips. Is she dreaming about us? Her nipples harden as she turns over onto her back, completely naked. She's so goddamn beautiful when she sleeps. Long, dark hair spilling around her face, bronzed skin, full lips... I could watch her like this for hours.

I prop myself up on my elbows and glance around. These fuckers are conked out. Now that we all share my home, we usually sleep together in my Alaskan king bed. My finger trails up her bare leg, and she moans in her sleep again. I sit up and position myself between her legs, knocking them apart gently, so that I don't wake her. I fist my aching cock as I look down at her–at the way her dark curls gather near the apex of her thigh, at the way her flesh is so perfect, soft, and round.

I let out a low groan as she pulls one knee to the side in her sleep, baring herself to me.

Her pussy is glistening and wet. She's having a fucking sex dream. Her hands fist the sheets as she rolls her hips again. I bend down and lick up her slit, and she moans loudly, trying to fuck my face and chase her pleasure in her sleep. When I lick down this time, she jerks.

Her body responds to me even unconsciously.

I lap up the wetness gathering between the soft lips of her pussy, flicking my tongue against her already swelling bud.

My hand works my shaft faster, harder, as I continue to eat her up in her sleep.

She's unabashedly moaning now, crying out without restraint as I continue my onslaught. Her whole body trembles and shudders with every movement, and the skin on her chest and neck turns pink. Her head moves from side to side as she licks her lips and cries out again when I go back in, using my tongue to dive into her tight cunt. I feel her grip it, feel the fluttering sensation I've come to discover is her orgasm cresting. Pulling away, I move myself up and place the head of my cock at her entrance.

She's still asleep, and a small part of me feels like maybe I should stop.

But then her hands come to my ass, and she pulls me up into her.

"Yes, Theo," she whimpers.

I look down at her, and her eyes are fully open now. Gasping, I drive into her all the way, so hard that her head hits the headboard.

"Oh my God," she mewls, scrunching her face up as her pussy quivers around my hard-as-sin cock before it clamps down, spurring me into my own orgasm. "Oh fuck, Theo," she murmurs, her words barely intelligible. She contracts so firmly around me that my orgasm shoots off, and I bite her neck as we pulse together. Panting, I kiss her gently as I move slowly inside of her.

"That's a nice way to wake up," she whispers, wrapping her arms around my neck.

I smile. "I couldn't help it. You were having a sex dream and making these noises..." I trail off. "Plus, it's past midnight."

Understanding dawns on her face as I grin and pull out of her.

Alaric stirs from next to her, and he rubs his eyes as he scowls at me. "Did you just fuck her while we were all asleep?"

I climb off the bed and walk to the bedside table.

The guys all stir from the noise, and I grab Gideon's knife before walking back to where Harlow is lying, still leaking with my come.

"Happy October 28th, little monster."

"Theo," she warns, looking between me and the knife.

"You promised," I growl, placing the knife against her bicep. I can feel the implant just underneath her skin. It would only take a tiny cut to remove it.

Harlow's eyes are hooded as she looks down at where the knife presses against her skin.

The others are silent, watching as she turns back to face me. Her dark hair is fanned all around her face, and her chest is still flushed from when she came.

"Do it," she whispers, her voice husky. "Cut it out of me."

"Let me," Gideon interrupts, crawling over to us. His cock is rigid and firm as he takes the knife from my hand. "Never pick my knife up like that again, Wolf," he threatens. His eyes run down my body, and I shiver involuntarily when they come back up to my face. He turns to Harlow and places the tip of his knife against the implant. "Breathe, baby."

She takes a deep breath as he slices into her skin. Blood immediately seeps onto the bed, but none of us care.

This feels too important to care.

Gideon squeezes her flesh, and the plastic implant pops out slightly. He grabs it and pulls it out, taking one look at it before tossing it over his shoulder. Harlow's chest is heaving up and down as she stares at him.

"Buckle up, little monster," he murmurs, mounting her. Pressing his cock into her entrance, he hisses as he penetrates her. "I'm going to fuck a baby into you."

"Yes, please," Harlow whimpers.

Gideon quickens his pace, grabbing her thighs and spreading them wide. "You sure? Because we're not coming back from this. I can stuff you full of my come, or..." he trails off, cocking his head.

"Yes. I want it. I want all of it." She turns to look at us. "With all of you."

EPILOGUE, PART FOUR

Sterling

Gideon drives into Harlow as she looks up at him with bared teeth.

"Yes," she whimpers, throwing her head back. "Oh fuck."

"You want my come?" he asks, slamming into her.

I'm fisting my cock quickly as I watch, waiting my turn.

"Yes!" she screams, rejecting him as her own come leaks out in soft fountains onto the sheets.

"Fucking hell," he grits out, coming in a matter of seconds once he's back inside of her. He drives in deep and roars as he comes. "Fuck, fuck, yes, baby," he hisses. "I want every drop of my come to stay inside of your perfect pussy." Groaning, he finishes.

"I want Sterling next," she says, looking at me with a darkened expression.

Don't mind if I fucking do.

Gideon pulls out of her, and I crawl over. Reaching down, I drag her down to the foot of the bed and flip her over so that I can fuck her doggy style.

Fuck, I want to bust a nut inside of her and fill her with my seed.

I didn't even realize how compelled I felt to impregnate her until now. Until I knew for certain her implant is out of the picture.

I am going to fuck her bare and raw.

Pulling her ass up, I admire the creamy white come leaking out between her folds. Before it drips out, I push it back in with my cock.

"Can't waste any," I murmur, grabbing her hair as I fuck her.

Her tight pussy grips onto mine as she cries out with pleasure.

"Such a good fucking girl," I tell her, my other hand coming around to her neck. I close my eyes and pound into her, inhaling sharply when I feel her ripple around me. Pulling out, I slowly push into her again.

I can see Alaric and Theo fisting their cocks on the bed next to her. *Fuck yes.*

As I continue slowly thrusting into her inch by inch, I revel in the way her dripping wet, tight pussy grabs onto me every time I fill her to the hilt. I slap her ass—hard—loving the way each slap elicits her pussy to feather against me.

"Holy shit, Sterling," she whimpers, crying out. I feel her quiver around my hard-as-fuck shaft. "Oh, fuck. I'm going to—"

She grips onto my cock and contracts around me. I lose myself inside of her. Feeling her soak the bed underneath her sends me over the edge. I grunt and explode in a frenzy of pleasure, my body convulsing as I finish filling her.

I pull out instinctually, but just as I see my come begin to seep out, I use a finger to plug her back up. She's *so* fucking wet—so *fucking* full of our come.

Her heavy-lidded eyes find Alaric's.

"Cross, you're next. Or should I say, Billionaire *Daddy*."

EPILOGUE, PART FIVE

Harlow

Sterling continues swirling his finger into my pussy and all around my slit, making a mess of their come as it slides down my thighs and drips onto the bed.

Alaric comes behind me, pressing me down onto the bed as he knocks my legs apart.

I love this. I fucking love being with all of them like this.

I feel him spread my ass cheeks playfully. "Sterling made your ass all red," he says, his voice amused and possessed all at once. He pulls my hips up slightly and lets out a low growl.

"Look at my good girl," he purrs, slowly sinking inside of me. It feels exquisite. "Your tight little pussy is so good at keeping our come in, isn't it?"

I whimper as he presses me down into the mattress and uses his knees to spread my legs wider.

"Jesus Christ, Harlow. You're so wet and full. And I'm going to flood you with more come. You ready?"

I nod. "Yes, please," I beg him, moving my hips as my orgasm creeps down my spine.

With just one more grind, I moan as my climax fires through me. In this position, I can't reject him, and the feeling is... it's too much. I buck my hips, trying to lessen the intensity, the strength of it so overpowering, I can't even scream. It skitters across my skin and gives me instant goosebumps. I gasp and pant and flail as I soak the bed underneath me.

"Fuck, yes, baby," Alaric murmurs. He stops thrusting, and I can feel his cock begin to curve as he shoots his come inside of me.

Everything leaks out of me when he finishes. It slides down between my legs. Pulling out, he spreads my thighs and looks down at me.

"Should we let Theo have another turn?" he asks.

I smirk and look over at Theo. "Only if he can get it up."

Theo growls, his cock already hard because of how he'd been pumping it from watching all of us.

"Is that a challenge, little monster?"

He hoists my hips up and over his shoulders. "Get ready to be stuffed again. And by the way, I'm keeping you up here for twenty minutes after I fire hose my come into you."

I stifle a laugh. "Why?"

He cocks his head as he swirls his cock against my entrance. Groaning, he pushes inside me slowly, and my eyes roll into the back of my head from the angle.

"Because you're going to keep our come inside of your pussy for as long as possible to ensure our seed takes root."

EPILOGUE, FINAL PART

Harlow
Five Years Later

I squint at my computer screen, trying to decipher my target's motive.

What the hell are they doing in London?

Flagging the questionable text, I send it to Theo. Sometimes these things just need a second set of eyes.

I grab my glasses and pull them on. *Much better.* Trashing every email that doesn't immediately get responded to—and then filing the rest away into our secure filing system—I shut my computer just as Archie and Edith wander into my office.

"Mummy," Edith chirps, holding a flower out in her hand. "Look what Archie found for me! A rose!"

I twist around in my chair and bend down to look at the dark red rosebud in Edith's hand. "A rose? Where did you find a rose?"

Archie shrugs. He's so tall now, and I swear he grows an inch every day. "Near the playground." His voice cracks, and my heart lurches when I realize his voice is starting to break.

I look down at Edith and smile at my daughter. Her dark brown eyes bore into mine with such intensity that I can't help but chuckle slightly. She's so much like Alaric—always pristine, always slightly grouchy, and her eyes, curly dark hair, and skin tone are a dead ringer for him.

"You know, before you were born, there used to be a big rose garden out there. It's probably from that."

She scrunches up her nose. At four, she's so inquisitive, so curious and interested in everything.

"But we haven't watered it. How can it still be there?"

I shrug. "Sometimes, especially when things are very strong-willed, they defy all odds."

"I didn't know the playground used to be a rose garden," Archie says, scratching his head. "How long ago?"

I furrow my brows as I think. "About nine years ago?"

"Interesting." He turns to face Edith. "I'm going to go find Mum. See you later, Edie."

He gives me a small smile before retreating upstairs.

Edith is still holding the rose, a perfectly pristine bud that hasn't bloomed yet.

"Did you plant the rose garden?" Edith asks, crawling up into my lap.

Now that she's four, wanting to climb into my lap is getting rarer by the day. I squeeze her tight as I smell the top of her head, soaking it all in while she's still little.

"No. My father did."

"Who was your father?"

I smirk. "His name was Charles. Same as Archie's father. Remember?"

Edith shakes her head. She's quiet for a minute. "Where is he?"

I shrug. "He was... he got sick, and he died of something called a stroke, Edie."

She turns to face me. "Will my dads die?"

I chew on the inside of my cheek as I look down at her. "Not for a long time, sweetheart."

Just then, Alaric saunters into the office. Edith jumps off of my lap and into his arms. They're basically twins. I watch as he pets the back of her hair and gives her a kiss on her nose.

"I hear you found a rose by the playground," he murmurs.

I nod. "Resilient fuck-freaking plant," I correct myself.

We have to watch our language around Edie. She's a parrot at school.

"I think I like roses," she says slowly, admiring the bud in her palm.

Alaric sets her down, and she wanders off into the living area. I hear Rose ask her a question about the rose as I turn to face Alaric.

"So?" I ask, taking my glasses off. "How did it go?"

Alaric smirks as he leans against the door frame. "Contracts are signed. The deal is done."

I release a breath I didn't know I was holding. "For real this time?"

He nods. "Gideon is... inducting them as we speak."

I smile. "I assume no tranquilizers were needed."

He saunters over to me. "No. because unlike our little monster, the new Lords—or whatever they will call themselves—actually know how to listen."

I wrinkle my nose. "I've never been a very good listener."

Pulling me up into his body, he kisses the top of my head before wrapping his arms around me. I inhale the scent of cologne and peppermint. Long gone are the days of him smelling like cigarettes. He quit before Edith was born.

Pulling away, he grips my shoulders as he looks down at me. At forty-one, his face is still young, but I'm acutely aware of the fact that he's nearly my father's age when they killed him. His dark hair is speckled with grey, and the lines in his forehead have deepened. Still, despite that, the man has aged like fine fucking wine. And his suits... they're still impeccable.

"When do they... when does it..." I trail off, pulling my lower lip between my teeth.

"Six months. It gives them time to train. Time to learn everything we have to teach them."

I nod, releasing another sigh. "I can't believe... I'm just so happy."

"Me too," he murmurs, pulling me against him again as he hugs me. "You have no idea how fucking happy I am."

Later that night, I turn over to face Sterling. He's still awake, reading something on his phone with his glasses resting on the bridge of his nose. We all wear glasses now—it's pretty hilarious in the morning when we're all groping for five different pairs.

"Can't sleep?" I ask him.

"I'm awake, too," Gideon says from my other side.

"Be quiet," Theo murmurs from the end of the bed.

"Shh." Alaric sits up. "Go to sleep. Edith's football match is at eight."

"Bloody hell," Gideon whines, placing a hand over his face. "Why the fuck do they start so fucking early?"

I smile. "To torture the parents."

We're all quiet for a few minutes. I know why. Today was monumental. Today, five people—three men, two women—signed contracts to take over for the Lords of Darkness. They won't inherit the name, of course. That was my clause, that the 'Lords of Darkness' die with us. The bloodlines will return to normal—no more crime rings, no more syndicates, no more history. They will choose a new name, and form a new history.

And Edith would never be conscripted.

These people were all admirers of ours, too—they *wanted* to do this. That was Sterling's clause. We had to find people who would enjoy the hell out of it.

Which meant that in six months' time, we would be free of it.

And they would continue without us.

Alaric's only clause was that we needed time to train them. He was right all those years ago. The world would fall apart without us. But who said it had to be us? Why not another group, under another name, with no dark history under their belts?

"It feels too good to be true," I say quietly.

None of them answer right away. The moon shines through Theo's bedroom window, casting pearly, luminescent light onto the wide mattress. After I joined the order officially, we all moved in with Theo and never left. It feels the most serene, the most like *our* home. We still have our respective homes—and Cecelia still has her cottage with Archie, though they're here most days of the week.

Gemma is currently getting her master's degree in Psychology, and she spends every Christmas in snowy England with us.

Edith is... she's the fucking light of my life.

I've never loved so intensely before, and never been so in awe of the men in this bed. They're such good fathers. We never did a DNA test, but we all know she's Alaric's.

Theo is still bitter, seeing as he'd doubled his chances the night we conceived.

In a year or two, I'd consider having another baby. I've already told them that once this all settles down, we can try for a couple more. I enjoy being a mom.

And I suppose I'll need something to occupy all of my free time.

Gideon shifts next to me. "No. Not for me. We put in our time. We paid for it with blood, sweat, and tears. We've earned this. Don't you agree?"

"I fucking agree," Sterling interjects. "You know I love you guys, but I'm... excited for the future for the first time in my adult life."

"Me too," Alaric mumbles.

"Me three," Theo adds.

I nod. "Yeah. Freedom will be nice."

"You sound sad," Alaric asks me.

"No. I'm not sad. But I'd resigned myself to this life a long time ago. I had to. I had to do it to survive mentally," I add. I'm still taking medication for my anxiety daily, but luckily, it seems to be in check. Thank God for modern medicine. "So now that I know my future is open again... it's sort of terrifying."

"We can find something else to pass the time," Gideon suggests.

I scowl at him as we lock eyes. "Like what?"

"The world is our oyster. We can do whatever the fuck we want now."

The thought is both terrifying and exhilarating.

"Yeah, that's true." I look at Gideon again. "What will you do with all of your free time?"

His pupils twinkle with mischief. "Well, after I fuck you... I guess we'll have to figure that out together, won't we?"

The End

PRINCES OF SIN
BOOK THREE

AUTHOR'S NOTE

Welcome back to Blackwell, England, little reader.

If you're new to this world, I suggest going back to Lords of Darkness and starting there. However, it is not a necessity, so I'll provide a very brief summary of the order and the world below.

Situated between London and Oxford, Blackwell is a fictitious English village. It's filled with aristocracy–most notably four Lords and a Lady. They are *actual* English nobility with titles and manors and all sorts of connections.

The Lords of Darkness is an ancient, underground order/secret society. Think of them as half-mafia, half-Illuminati. The Lords are unhinged and have very questionable morals. Everyone is afraid of them. Everyone bows to them. Before the events of **this** book, a fifth member came along: the first Lady of Darkness in over a century. Lords of Darkness and Lady of Darkness tell their story, which is why I encourage you to read them first to get the best overview of them, their personalities, and the order. However, should you just want a taste of darkness, you're in the right place.

Princes of Sin is a spin-off. The Lords have decided to step down and make way for a new generation. Previously ruled by blood and lineage, the Lords decided to start fresh and choose people who *wanted* to do this, instead of forcing someone into the order because of their birthright.

Hence... the Princes of Sin was born.

The first rule of the order: *never betray your brethren...*

TRIGGERS

For a complete list of triggers, please visit my website here:

www.authoramandarichardson.com/triggers

For my why choose readers.
You changed my life, and this book is a love letter to you.

The Lords are back...

Vengeance is in my heart, death in my hand, blood and revenge are hammering in my head.

William Shakespeare

PART I

PROLOGUE

CHARLOTTE
Ten Years Ago

Everything comes back into focus, and the cool air makes my skin pebble. My heart is racing, but I can't remember why. Curling my hands, whatever's coating them is sticky, and the smell... I retch as the sickeningly sweet, metallic scent takes over my other senses. I glance down at myself and my heart thumps heavily in my chest as I realize what the smell is.

As I realize what's on my hands.
No, what's *all* over me.
Blood.
I inhale sharply and look around frantically, trying to orient myself. My chest heaves as my eyes flick over the familiar wallpaper of the second story hallway–as they skim over the bloody footprints and smears all over the wall.
Blood.
Wiggling my toes, that same sticky feeling makes me gag once again, and my eyes prick with overwhelmed, panicked tears.
Blood.
"Mum? Dad?" I call out into the large house. My voice gets swallowed up, so I repeat myself–louder this time.
Nothing.
Why am I covered in blood?
I close my eyes briefly as I begin walking toward their bedroom. My throat feels raw–like I've been screaming. Something heavy settles deep inside of me, and it takes me a few seconds to realize it's dread. It's not a feeling I'm accustomed to, except for when I get an exam result back or Mum wants to have

379

another one of her sex talks. I'm fortunate that I've lived a privileged life, but this? This is an all-consuming dread like I've never experienced before.

I swallow and walk slower, and when I reach their door, I lift a trembling hand to their door handle. Dark red blood coats the brass handle, and I let out a choked sob as I turn it.

The smell hits me before anything, and I start to shake so hard that my teeth are chattering. That sweet, iron-rich smell—

The room is still dark. Their curtains are pulled closed, so I feel along the wall for the light switch while trying to calm my racing heart. Taking a deep breath, I flip the switch, and then—

I fall to my knees.

Blood.

So much blood.

It's everywhere—on the walls, all over the curtains, on the floor—

Mum and Dad are splayed awkwardly on the floor, right next to Helga, our housekeeper. My eyes sweep over the rest of the room, and then I see Bruno sitting in one of the chairs.

With a hole in his head.

My stomach rolls as I squeeze my eyes shut.

This is all a dream.

This has to be a dream.

Please let this be a bad dream.

The smell, though... it's so potent.

My cheeks are wet with tears, but I'm shaking too much to move, so I just stay on my knees and cry, unsure of what to do. Unsure of where all of these feelings should go. I'm breaking in half, and for a second I wonder if it's possible to die from heartache. My chest aches, my throat burns, and the smell of blood is all around me—

"There you are," someone says, and I jump up, startled. Spinning around, I see a man in a suit watching me with narrowed eyes. His hands are covered in blood, and I see a gun sticking out of the waistband of his trousers.

He killed them.

He killed my parents.

He killed Helga.

He killed Bruno.

"I've been looking for you, Ms. Banks. Please follow me and I'll escort you away from the crime scene—"

I growl as I rush forward, shoving him against the doorframe with all of my strength. To my surprise, he falls backward with a startled expression. The sound of his skull cracking against the wood paneling should be nauseating, but knowing I can *hurt* him feels so good. I drag my nails down the sides of his neck, drawing blood as I scream. He's so much bigger than me, but my rage is all-encompassing.

He killed them.

He killed them.

He killed them.

I'm crying and screaming when his hands grip my wrists and drag them down, away from his neck. I kick and thrash against him but someone pulls me away.

"Calm down," another man says, wrapping his arms around me.

I twist and shove my elbow into his ribs, but he preempts my move and holds me tighter.

"What happened?" a third man asks, his heavy footsteps causing my pulse to quicken.

"She woke up and walked in on us," the first man says. "Ran out of the room, and when I was calling cleanup, she came back in and started freaking out."

"Fuck," the second guy says, his hands flexing as they pull my flailing body even tighter.

"Who are you?" I scream.

The man behind me chuckles. "Your worst nightmare."

"That's not an answer!"

He laughs some more, as if this is the funniest thing in the world. "I am Lord Alaric Cross."

Lord? He's a Lord?

And where have I heard that name before?

"Just do it," the third man says. "No witnesses."

I fight harder, bucking against the man that holds me, but a hand comes to my mouth before I can scream.

I gnaw at his flesh, trying to bite him as my legs thrash and kick.

"Deep breath," the man holding me growls. "It'll hurt more if you fight it."

My eyes go wide and I try to shake my head and scream as something pinches me in my neck—a sharp prick that makes my eyes water.

"What'd you give her?"

"Some pentobarbital and my own cocktail of other things to make it painless," the man murmurs. "Ten minutes to death, give or take."

My skin begins to tingle, and just as the panic rises up my throat, it dissipates, and my whole body goes limp. In a flurry of movement, the man holding me loosens his grip and the first man grabs me and hoists me over his shoulders.

"Now," one of the men says.

I hear a match strike before a whoosh fills my ears, and the dry heat of a flame licks my face and arms.

I'm carried down the hallway, body limp, and then down the stairs. The man who's carrying me is quick and sure on his feet.

A second later, he lays me down on the floor of the foyer with more care than I would've expected. He kneels over me with a resigned expression. His green eyes bore into mine, and I try to speak, but the muscles in my mouth won't work.

"Sorry about this, kid. The medication will kick in soon and it'll feel like falling asleep." It seems like he wants to say more, but his furrowed brows and concerned expression don't make me feel any better about the situation.

He stands as black spots fill my vision, as my body gets heavy, as my heartbeat slows.

My head lolls to the side, and the last thing I see is a pair of shiny, black shoes walking away from me.

<hr />

Smoke.

I can't breathe.

Gasping, I sit up as black smoke swirls around me, as orange flames envelop the wooden foyer table. Despite feeling sore and heavy, I stand up and pull the front door open, coughing as I cover my mouth with my hand.

That's when I notice the blood.

Looking down, a sob cleaves through my chest at the sight of my bloodied pajamas, hands, and feet.

Mum and Dad.

I look back at the house, staggering backward as a window shatters above me and flames escape the structure.

Those men—they killed my parents.

They tried to kill me, but for whatever reason, it didn't work.

I scan the premises frantically, looking for any sign of them, but there's nothing.

Just me, alone, standing in front of my house as a fire burns through everything in my life.

Every memory.

Every piece of clothing, picture, and piece of art.

Every sheet of music I composed.

Every room I laughed in with Dad, every bed I slept tucked in Mum's arms.

Gone.

What about Cocoa, our dog? Did she escape? She must've…

Without thinking, I walk around the perimeter of our country estate to the separate garden house. It's locked, so I rear my foot back–

Wait.

The voice in my head is my own yet it still surprises me. I'm trembling so hard, teeth chattering, that I can barely stand straight, let alone think straight.

I am Lord Alaric Cross.

The name clangs through me, and I realize where I've heard that name before. Just yesterday I'd walked in on my parents arguing—something they rarely did. My father was sitting at his desk, head in his hands, and my mum was leaning against the bookshelf.

"They're going to know," my father had said, his voice resigned.

"Darling, we don't know that," my mum had replied, sounding exasperated.

"Lord Alaric Cross has been watching me for years. Trust me. They know."

"The Lords of Darkness are a scourge on this earth. We have to trust that our people will take care of it before it becomes an issue."

I'd heard that name before—heard the rumors in boarding school.

The Lords of Darkness.

Monsters. Murderers. Working for only themselves, with a deadly agenda.

They killed my parents, but why?
And where am I supposed to go now?

I take a step back from the garden house. If they find out I'm alive, they will come after me. If the official report notices that the garden house was broken into...

My chest heaves as I cry, head dropping in despair.

I can't leave any evidence.

I can't leave *any* trail for them to find me.

And I have nowhere to go.

The vast emptiness of that thought causes me to drop onto the ground and wrap my arms around my knees. The only thing I can do is watch as my home burns to the ground, along with every person I've ever loved.

Nowhere to go.

Nowhere.

The various aunts and uncles I have scattered throughout the country won't work, either. That'll be the first place they look. All of my options aren't *actually* options, because I know enough about them to know they will hunt me to the ends of the earth if they know I survived this.

All for simply being a witness to my parents' murder.

The grief morphs into anger as the night drags on. The warm, June air is hardly comforting. I can't stop shivering, and it's not until I hear sirens that I stand up and walk into the forest beyond the estate. I don't stop crying as the fire engine stops in front of my house—as several men unwind a hose and begin to attempt to put out the flames. But from my vantage point—from the way the angry flames are spilling out of all of the windows—there's no way one hose will be enough to touch this fire.

There's a loud groaning sound, and the firefighters shout to each other as the house collapses in on itself. Four stories are flattened in an instant, sending a large plume of dark grey smoke into the sky. Another fire truck arrives, and by the time the third arrives, I can't watch any more. I turn and walk into the forest, knowing that in fifteen or so miles, I will meet one of the country roads.

And from there...

I have no idea.

All I know is that I have to get away, have to lay low for a few weeks.

Sniffling and keeping my chin up, I walk forward, knowing that with every step, I'm shedding my old self one piece at a time.

I've never been more grateful for the warm summer weather, and my feet start to ache as I walk over the pebbled dirt. Focusing on my breathing, I know I'm safe. I push down the thoughts about my parents—about how *lifeless* they looked—

I can't think about that.

I have to keep moving forward.

A couple of hours later, I come up to a small, country house. Walking slowly, I hide behind the foliage as I walk around the perimeter. There are no cars, and all of the curtains are drawn despite it being midday. *Empty.* My lips are cracked, and my throat is aching for water. I should also wash myself off, if possible, in case I encounter someone.

Keep a low profile.

My eyes sweep over the outside of the house, and I don't see a camera or security system.

Walking to one of the back windows, I stand back and ascertain the size. It's small enough to hopefully be unlocked, since it appears to be a bathroom window. I twist my shirt around and use a clean spot to lift the sash window, letting out a sob when it gives way and slides up. Shimmying into the bathroom, I'm met with my reflection for the first time.

Blood.

Everywhere.

I do what I need to do—gulping water from the sink and then stepping into the large shower. I wash the blood from my hair and body, shampooing everything—every crevice, every inch of my skin, watching as it slides down the drain. Using one of the towels on the towel rack, I dry myself and then use it to dry the shower completely.

I set it in a pile next to my clothes, and then I go through the cabinets for anything useful.

Scissors.

Hair bleach.

Before I can change my mind, I begin cutting my long, brown hair as tears stream down my face. When it's a short pixie-style cut, I open the box of bleach with shaking hands, mixing the ingredients quickly.

While I let it sit on my head, I flush all of my hair down the toilet, bit by bit.

And when I rinse the bleach out, I hardly recognize myself.

Wrapping the towel around myself, I quickly walk into one of the bedrooms. I can't take anything that will be noticed, so I soak my clothes in the sink, scrubbing the blood out of my pajamas as much as I can. I find a pair of old boots with caked on mud in the back of the bedroom wardrobe, so I pull those on, hoping the owners don't notice and don't report anything. They're about five sizes too big, but I don't have any other choice.

When I get back to the bathroom, I replace the used towel with a fresh one, and add the bleach products to the pile of things I'll need to burn. Gathering it all into my arms, I throw it out the window before hoisting myself out after it.

And then I run—as fast as I can in the boots.

I'm crying.

Hungry.

Shaking.

I have no idea where I'm going to go, but I do know one thing...

One day, I am going to make the Lords pay.

I am going to kill them all for what they did, for everything they took from me.

And I'm going to enjoy every single fucking second of it.

CHAPTER 1

Lachlan
Present

I lift the brass skull and crown knocker and rap it against the door three times. Standing back, I smooth my trousers and run a hand through my hair. The sun is beating against the back of my neck relentlessly, so I place one hand there, massaging the sore muscles just as light footsteps sound on the other side of the door. When it opens, I'm surprised to find a little girl with long, black hair looking up at me.

"Hello," I tell her, brows furrowed. "Am I at the right house?"

She shrugs. "Are you looking for Mum or one of my dads?"

"Any adult is fine," I say, skeptical.

"Who are you?" she asks confidently.

This kid can't be older than five, and yet the intensity of her stare makes me clear my throat before speaking.

"Lachlan Weir."

She wrinkles her nose. "Never heard of you."

"Edie! Who's at the door?" a female voice with an American accent calls from the stairs, and I see a young woman come up behind the little girl. "Oh! I was expecting you tomorrow," she says, her large blue eyes boring into mine.

I had nowhere else to go.

"That's okay," she says quickly, seeing my hesitation. "Come in. I'll make some coffee."

I step inside as the little girl skips away, and the woman turns to face me. Taking her casual clothes and curly hair in fully, it takes me a moment to realize I'm staring at *the* Lady of Darkness.

Lady Harlow Windsor.

"Right, first things first. The guys might make you call them the Lords, but you can just call me Harlow," she says, matter-of-factly. Her eyes skim over my face and neck before she crosses her arms. "You must be Lachlan?"

I open and close my mouth, suddenly realizing the little girl must be her daughter.

Their daughter.

"That's me," I say slowly, holding a hand out.

Harlow takes it, her grip firm. Her face is bare of makeup, and she just seems so much more... normal than I expected.

This is the deadliest person in the world? She can't be more than five foot three, and she looks more like a Uni student than a deadly assassin in her oversized jumper and baggy jeans.

"Come on. I can make you coffee, and Rose made some sandwiches earlier. We can talk and get to know each other."

She turns and walks away, and I have no choice but to set my bag down and follow her. The house is... brighter than I would've imagined. The white curtains are pulled away from all the windows. The way the light bounces off the fabric illuminates all the dark crevices of the old house. Modern art with colorful paint strokes, lighter-colored furniture, and pops of color everywhere. It's not like I have experience with posh houses but I guess I always thought they'd be stuffy and dark, filled to the brim with dark wood and gilded paintings of royal ancestors.

Once we reach the kitchen, Harlow walks over to a fancy looking machine. "So? Coffee, tea...?"

"Do you have anything a bit stronger?"

She smirks. "Of course. I'm sure Alaric won't mind if I get you a bit of his favorite whiskey."

She walks past me, and I hear the tinkling of glasses coming from what I presume is a dining room.

"Come on. We can get started while we wait for the others."

I walk into a formal dining room, surprised to see paperwork already set up at five of the places. I stand behind one of the chairs, not wanting to sit until I'm told. Harlow sets a glass tumbler full of amber liquid in front of me before sitting down at the head of the table, hands clasped together.

I take a seat next to her.

"So..." she says slowly, eyes narrowing slightly. "Your scores were the highest out of all the people we tested. And yet... you didn't even finish secondary school."

"Ah. Diving right into it, then," I joke, reaching for the tumbler and relishing in the smooth burn all the way down my throat. I haven't had a drink in... *five years.*

Harlow watches me expectantly.

"What, exactly, do you want to know? Being who you are, I can assume that you already know everything there is to know about me."

"I do. But I want to hear it from your mouth."

"Alright. The reason I didn't finish school is because I went to prison. Twice, actually, because I violated my parole and they sent me back. While I was there, I spent my days with books. I taught myself advanced maths and science. I read all the classic literature, and I have all the important historical dates memorized."

Harlow's lips twitch, and she leans forward slightly. Her dark blue eyes feel like they're taking hold of my very soul, and as they narrow, I suddenly understand why she's so good at her job.

"You're not seriously telling me that you learned how to assemble a handmade bomb in prison, are you?"

I purse my lips. "Not exactly. I learned... all of that... when I got out."

What I don't say is that being a quiet kid growing up, I was never the type to fuck off at school. Despite not finishing, I was a good student, and I enjoyed learning. One of my social workers growing up had called me gifted, but of course, being a foster kid, I was never able to see that through.

That thirst for knowledge carried into adulthood. For everything wrong with the prison system, I was fortunate enough to be placed in one that had books.

And I'd read every single one of them.

She arches a brow. "You got out eighteen months ago."

"I'm a fast learner."

"Look, you don't have to convince me. We've already chosen you to carry on our legacy. This isn't an interview. I was just expressing how impressed I was with your scores."

Pride flushes through me, and I grimace as I take another sip of the posh whiskey. "Thank you." I watch as Harlow shuffles through some paperwork—presumably everything she needs to know about us. "Will I get to meet the other Lords and Ladies today?"

Truth be told, it's the thing I'm most looking forward to. Having grown up in the system, I never had a solid foundation. Foster brothers and sisters were as common as neighbors—a dime a dozen. It wasn't until prison that I knew what camaraderie even was, and when I left... I floundered.

The whole *one breathing unit* thing about the Lords of Darkness appeals to me more than I want to let on. Meeting the four other people has been at the top of my mind since I found out I'd been selected.

"Tomorrow," Harlow says quickly. "But I can tell you more about them if you want?"

"Sure," I say, trying to keep my voice casual.

Harlow gives me a coy smile as she sits up straighter. "Okay. You're our top scorer, which means you've been assigned as the leader. That may change after you've all been trained, but as of now, you will have that extra responsibility on your shoulders."

"That's fine."

"The second highest score is from a young woman named Astern Hackbolt. I'm actually very interested in learning more about her, because she doesn't have much of a history other than a reputation as a dark web hacker. The third highest score is a woman named Quinn Taylor. Top of her class at Oxford, she's now a Criminology professor at Cambridge. The fourth and fifth members are brothers from Denmark." She huffs a little laugh. "Crown *Princes*, to be exact."

My eyebrows shoot up. "Sounds like we have a healthy gamut of personalities and backgrounds, then."

"We sure do," Harlow says, agreeing. "Do you have any questions?" she asks.

How many people will I have to kill before I forget her face?

"I don't think so," I say slowly. "The job description is pretty explanatory."

"Okay, great, I just wanted to meet you before the official orientation tomorrow. I know you've met the guys already, so I only thought it fair that you meet me, too."

I stand up, finish my drink, and dip my chin politely. "Thanks for having me."

"Of course. Everyone will be here tomorrow for orientation, but would you rather meet the two brothers now? I believe they're staying in London tonight, and I could have the driver take you back to their house."

I don't want to sound too eager, so I shrug. "Sure."

"You can bond with them before meeting Astern and Quinn tomorrow." She stands and walks me back to the door. "Enjoy your last night of freedom, Lachlan. And welcome to the Lords of Darkness."

CHAPTER 2

Astern

I should *not* have had that fourth drink.

The room sways a bit as the music pounds into the ground, pulsing up my legs and into my body. I close my eyes and try to imagine that I'm somewhere else and *not* at a crowded bar in SoHo. I could get lost in the music—how it all blends together and comes apart. I can pick out the bass, the rhythm, and the melody. For me, music is like breathing. I find the beat instantly, and my blood sings with the itch to play. To *create*.

"Let's dance?" Quinn asks, already pulling me onto the dance floor. "Come on."

I groan as I follow her to the center of the dance floor, feeling my body move to the bass without thinking. I always seek out the bass. The low tenor that's at the back of every song. Subtle, low, deep... it calls to me.

Well, it used to call to me.

Before everything happened...

Though I haven't played piano in over ten years, I still feel the pull of certain music—certain songs—almost like my body is possessed beyond my control.

It's the only time I can fully let myself go—the only time I let myself remember how my life used to be.

I glance over at Quinn, and her short, curly hair bounces as she moves, as her body twists and twirls. She looks incredible in her white linen shorts with a tie waist, paired with a black leather cropped top. The strappy sandals affixed to her feet make her legs look a mile long. *So* different from me in every way, including the fact that unlike me, she has her life together. If this doesn't work out, she has a career to fall back on.

If this doesn't work out for me...

Then everything I've worked for will be for nothing.

The amount of pressure is staggering.

"Do you think they're twins?" she asks, murmuring into my ear and pointing at two guys off to the side of the dance floor.

I glance over at the two men—tall, muscular, with dirty blond hair. They're both looking around uncomfortably, sipping from their beers as their heads bob to the music.

"You should go say hi. They look cute."

I snort. "I highly doubt two fit guys like that would want—"

"Stop spewing that bloody self-deprecating bullshit. You're a fucking ten. Small, tight body, pretty face, gorgeous, long hair... if you didn't spend all of your time with your nose behind a screen, you might actually begin to figure that out yourself."

I've known Quinn for less than twenty-four hours, and already she's managed to summarize my life better than I have.

"Go say hi to them. They look a little bit lost and may need a bed to sleep in tonight."

"Fuck off," I tell her, holding my empty glass up to her. "I'm getting another one."

"You sure? Our first day is tomorrow."

"I know. I need the liquid courage."

I twist away from Quinn and walk over to the bar, setting my pint down. Just as I lift my hand to get the bartender's attention, I feel strong hands pull me out of the way as my glass falls onto the floor and shatters everywhere.

"Careful, pet," a man growls in my ear.

Yanking myself free of his grip, I twist around and lock eyes with one of the most beautiful men I've ever seen. Dark hair that's longer on top. It's parted at the side, revealing gorgeous tattoos that flow up his neck to the back of his skull, and down beneath the black collar of his shirt. His face is so perfect I want to weep. Sharp cheekbones, angular jawline, and pale, blue eyes. He's tall—nearly a head taller than me, and slim. Yet, the sleeves of the black dress shirt he's wearing are rolled to his elbows—showcasing muscular, corded arms full of tattoos.

"Um—thanks," I mutter, taking another step back. When I glance behind me, someone's already cleaning the glass up. I can only imagine how it would've felt to have it shatter all over my open-toed foot.

My savior smirks, shoving his hands in his pockets. Tipping his head at me once, he turns and walks away, and I'm left staring at his backside, flabbergasted.

I rarely find random men attractive. While I can appreciate the finer specimens, I generally need some sort of connection to feel attracted to a bloke. But that guy was... everything I never knew I wanted, wrapped up in one dark, tattooed fantasy.

Careful, pet.

Once I procure another drink, I nearly roll my eyes when I see Quinn dancing with the blond twins.

I close my eyes and sip my drink as I let my body sway to the music. Quinn dressed me tonight, so I'm wearing a tight, black dress that is several inches too short and silver, strappy heels that bring me up to a respectable height. *Same color as your hair,* she insisted, referring to my prematurely white-grey locks. These shoes are harder to dance in than my normal choice of trainers, but they work for tonight. Once my drink is done, Quinn snatches it from my hand and smirks at me.

"Want to dance with my new friends?"

I have to actively try not to roll my eyes at her. Instead, I give the twins a small smile.

"Hi."

"I'm Max," says the first, stepping forward.

I get my first good glimpse at him up close, and *good God* this bar must attract the hottest males that London has to offer. He's tall with golden blond hair that curls around his ears. He's wearing thick-framed glasses and his light grey t-shirt is entirely too tight–showing off all the impressive muscles that contract and undulate as he runs a hand through his hair. He's clad in distressed jeans that hug his sinfully muscular thighs. His eyes are a darker green shade, and his skin is the same shade as spun gold. When he smiles, the straight, white teeth are only further whitened by the black lights.

I purposely don't introduce myself. The more people who don't know my name, the better.

"This is my brother, Otto."

My eyes flick to Otto, and it's like I'm looking at a slimmer, more flirty version of Max. Where Max looks like a CEO, Otto seems like his golden retriever younger brother. Despite also being clean-shaven, his hair is shorter, and he's wearing a blazer without a shirt, showcasing just how fit he is. Paired with the dark grey trousers... he's exactly the kind of fuckboy I attempt to stay away from.

"Hi," I tell them, waving awkwardly. I know my fifth drink is *really* going to my head when I begin to envision what it would be like to dance with both of them–to be caught between both hard bodies, to feel surrounded by their good looks despite being so different from each other. It's almost dizzying.

"And this is our new friend, Lachlan," Max adds, gesturing over his shoulder.

My eyes snap up to the dark-haired figure behind Otto–the same one who saved me from the glass just a few moments ago.

Fuck. I am indeed in trouble now.

Lachlan's eyes penetrate mine as his lips tilt up into a cocky smirk. "And what's your name, pet?"

I smirk and shake my head. "That information is earned."

"That's alright. I think I like my nickname better," he purrs. "Dance with me."

Before I can mull over his words, he pulls me closer and begins to dance with me. Gasping, my hands come up to his neck as his hands grip my hips firmly. Up close, his tattoos are mesmerizing–a honeycomb pattern affixed to every surface of skin up the back of his neck and behind his ears. He has several piercings dotted along his earlobes, and his eyes land on my face, taking in my septum piercing. His icy blue eyes hold me captive, and when they're done perusing my face, he gives me a lopsided smile.

I'm so dizzy and lightheaded that I feel high, and one of my favorite songs begins to play just as Otto and Max dance on either side of me. I'm surrounded by hot men. It almost feels like a dream until I hear Quinn cackling from a few feet away.

"Alright, I'm going to let you enjoy this. Don't leave without telling me."

She's gone before I can protest, but then Lachlan's fingers are digging into my flesh, and Otto is pulling me back against his body as Max runs a hand behind my neck, lifting the hair from my sweaty neck and pressing his lips to the hot skin underneath my ear. I close my eyes, letting myself feel the sensation of being pinned between not one guy, but three. Their hands are all over me—in a respectful way, that is—and we all move easily together.

I almost wish they weren't being so respectful.

When the next song starts, I feel Otto pull me closer to his chest, and my mouth drops open when I feel the hardness at my lower back. Something about this—the noisy, busy bar, lost in a sea of people as the strobe lights make me feel like I'm dreaming—is highly erotic. Lachlan moves his thigh between my legs, and I throw my head back against Otto's broad chest. Raising my arms above my head, I move against them—and the tiny bit of friction against Lachlan's muscular thigh is enough for me to pull my lower lip between my teeth and moan.

Max runs his hands along my stomach, and I feel Otto move over so that they're both behind me. I feel him wrap an arm around my waist, tugging me against his body as we undulate against the music. Every few seconds, my eyes lock with Lachlan's, and he looks both turned on and cocky as fuck. The duality of seeing the way his eyes have grown dark, mixed with the way his smile is slightly lopsided... I let my head fall back against Otto's chest as I sway my hips against him.

Max's lips brush against my ear as he tugs me ever closer. "We're just a few blocks away. Come home with us tonight?"

My body heats up at his words. I look up at Lachlan through hooded eyes, and he cocks his head.

"What do you say? We can continue the party at our flat... no pressure. Just dancing. Your friend can come, too."

I glance behind them, only to see Quinn grinding against a tall, redheaded man. Lachlan takes my hand and backs up half a step, bringing my palm to his lips and kissing me gently. *Holy hell.*

"Come home with us."

Us.

Plural.

I look over my shoulder at Max and Otto briefly. I've never been a one-night stand type of girl. Between university and my job, I just never had the time—and though the opportunity had presented itself a few times before, I'd never been tempted.

Until now.

Otto's hand snakes around my waist. I inhale sharply as my nerves come to life and pleasure skitters down my spine at the contact.

"I can't," I whisper. "I'm starting a new job tomorrow, and I have to be up early."

"Please," Otto says, his voice a low murmur. "One drink. I'll even schedule your Uber home so that we have an end time if that makes you more comfortable."

Warning bells are going off all over the place, and if I wasn't trained in highly specialized martial arts, it would be an automatic 'no.' But for whatever reason, they seem to need this as much as I do.

A release.

One night before my life changes forever.

Lachlan pulls me against his body. His arms wrap around my waist, and I suddenly feel like I'm on fire. I've never had this kind of reaction to anyone before. Bending down, his lips graze my temple.

"When's the last time you did something spontaneous, pet?"

And damn him, because I'm seriously considering it.

This is *crazy*. Like, *'this-is-how-she-got-murdered'* insane.

I shouldn't do this. I don't know anything about them other than their names. They could be murderers or psychopaths. There's no telling what kinds of skeletons could be in their closets—and what kinds of things I'd be subjected to if I were to go home with them.

Then again, I highly doubt they expect me to be armed with not one but two knives—one in my handbag and one inside a secret pocket of my bra.

The more I think about it, the more I realize that Lachlan is right. After tomorrow, everything will change for me. My new job is not a normal job. Highly secretive and important, it will require all of my brain power both physically and mentally. I'd accepted the job knowing that it would completely take over my life.

Becoming a Lady of Darkness... it's not for the faint of heart.

The screening process was rigorous as hell, but somehow, I scored the second highest in a vast sea of applicants. I hadn't met any of the other members beside Quinn, but that would change tomorrow.

I'd start the process of becoming death incarnate—feared, revered, and formidable.

After tomorrow, people in certain circles might certainly know who *I* was.

The new me, at least.

Tonight was likely my last night of anonymity.

It was now or never.

The opportunity to give into temptation just once is too tempting to pass up.

"One drink," I tell them, holding one finger up for emphasis.

Lachlan smirks. "One drink. I promise."

CHAPTER 3

Otto

The mystery girls follow us back to my flat, whispering with her friend the entire way. The redheaded man is with the dark-haired one, which is just as well. She didn't seem interested in us—not like the little, silver one.

Something about her is so fucking enticing.

And it's not just her fiery blue eyes and silver hair, either. There's something beguiling about the way she holds herself. It's like she's always on the offensive, always looking for an exit. It makes me want to take care of her, to make her feel good. I don't pity her, but a beautiful woman like that should not spend her life afraid of everything. And if I can change that, why not?

Max and Lachlan chat up ahead of me as we walk through SoHo. We're not far from the club, and once we arrive in front of an old townhouse, I pull my keys out and walk up to the door. Everyone follows me inside and I flick the lights on.

"Wow," the silver mystery girl says, looking around. "You *live* here?" she asks. Her eyes immediately flit up to the camera by the door before those eyes float over Max's high-tech, state-of-the-art security system on the wall.

Interesting that she would check for that first.

"It was our parents' house," I answer, as if that explains everything.

Silver mystery girl sets her handbag down on the marble entry table, and I try not to smirk as she admires the modern art, the pristine expensive-looking furniture, and colorful rugs in the living room.

"And *who* exactly are you?" the other mystery girl asks, looking around with her arms crossed. She quirks a dark brow at me before pursing her lips.

"Drinks?" Max calls out from the living room.

We all follow him into the room off to the right of the foyer, and I study the silver mystery girl as her eyes skirt over the old-style swords hung up above the fireplace and the ornate, gilded art.

She swings around and looks at Lachlan. "Do you live here, too?"

He shakes his head. "I fucking wish. But no, I just met Max and Otto tonight."

I wink at him when he looks at me with a dark, moody expression before turning away. He's so broody, and if it weren't for the silver minx in our presence, I might be interested in figuring out exactly how wound up he is. Then again, Max made me promise I wouldn't come onto the other Lords, which is no fucking fun at all.

Max pours everyone some wine, saving the silver minx for last.

"How presumptuous of you," she tells him, eyes boring into his.

A spark of heat flares through me at the thought of watching the mystery girl with my brother.

"I wagered a guess," he murmurs. "Was I wrong to assume?"

She takes a sip and nods once. "You got lucky this time."

"Is that a threat?" he teases.

I snap my fingers and music begins to play instantly, breaking up the tension. "We're here to dance and have fun. *Not* to argue."

Max claps and the lights dim. "There."

"Where's Quinn?" mystery girl asks, platinum hair cascading down her back as she looks at me over her shoulder.

Max smirks as he sits down on one of the couches. "She's in the kitchen admiring the stand mixer with her date. I invited them to join our activities, but they declined. I believe they're now... preoccupied."

Silver minx quickly finishes her wine a few seconds later and hands the glass to Lachlan. "Thank you for the drink. I should probably grab Quinn and head back home now."

"Stay. For a little bit," I add, giving her a flirtatious smile. I know I shouldn't be a cocky arsehole, but I have yet to be turned down when utilizing this smile.

Her expression oscillates between caution and intrigue, and when I cock my head to the side and smile wider, I can see the fight leave her body.

"I suppose I could stay for one more—"

I'm already stepping forward and leaning down to kiss her before she can finish her sentence.

Everything erupts in a maelstrom of fire and ice—nerves skirting the surface of my skin as my hands wrap around her waist. When she moans, I grin against her lips as my tongue pries her mouth open. She feels so fucking good in my arms—and she smells like heaven.

I need this.

We *all* need this—at least, Max, Lachlan, and I do.

"Stay," I repeat once I pull away a couple of inches.

"Why?" she asks, fisting my shirt and pulling me closer. The move makes me chuckle. She wants this just as bad as we do, so I give her a taste of what she could have when I angle my pelvis into her stomach.

She gasps at my hardening cock. Her pupils bloom black, so I lean down to kiss her again. Her little hands come under my shirt, the feel of them hot on my skin, and she tastes like red wine. I kiss her harder and one of my hands moves to the back of her head, grabbing her hair and pulling slightly. Moaning, her mouth drops open just as my mouth trails little kisses along her exposed neck and collarbone.

"Because you want this just as much as we do."

We.

Plural.

As I say it, I feel Max and Lachlan's eyes on me.

"You should stay," Max adds.

Lachlan doesn't say anything, but if he's not experienced in the art of orgies, I am more than happy to show him the way. The air is fraught with possibility, heavy and thick with tension. I have no idea *why* mystery girl needs this so badly, but I know why the three of us do.

My fist tightens around her soft, fine hair, eliciting a louder moan from her.

Fuck.

I have a beautiful woman in my arms, and I'm already mourning the months and years I might have to abstain. Not because sex is prohibited as a Lord of Darkness, but because life is about to get really fucking crazy, and I might not have the time.

But her... this...

I will miss casual sex more than anything else.

Mystery girl shivers as my brother's hands come to the back of her thighs, knocking them apart. He runs a hand down the inside of her thigh, and I hold her tighter as he leans into her.

"See what you could have? The three of us worshiping you. Just for tonight."

"Okay," she agrees.

"Let's go upstairs," I tell her, uncurling my hand from her hair and tugging her toward the door of the living room.

"I should tell Quinn—"

The instant the words leave her mouth, I hear a low, distant moan.

"Never mind," she adds, shaking her head and laughing.

Her smile lights up her face, and I vow to get her to smile again before the night is through.

"Like we said, Quinn is... otherwise occupied," Max murmurs from behind us.

"Okay, wait. I have *never* done anything like this," she starts, looking at me with wide eyes.

"I can't say the same," I tease, running a hand down her cheek. "But I can say this: whatever it is that we're both running from is going to find us as soon as the sun is up. We only have tonight."

"He's right," Max drawls, eyes finding mine.

There's nothing I love more than sharing a woman with him, and as my eyes move over to Lachlan's, he gives me a cautious look.

"Are you ready?" I ask him, knowing that my words are taunting him.

"All of us?" he asks, eyes narrowing when I smirk back at him.

"Of course. Unless you're afraid."

His entire resolve changes, and *fuck* it's hot when he stands up straight and glowers. "Who said I was afraid?" he asks, challenging me.

Marching forward, he scoops mystery girl up and hoists her over his shoulder before taking the stairs two at a time.

"Stop pushing his boundaries," Max drawls under his breath as we follow the giggling minx and her brooding, mysterious savior. "Not everyone grew up in and out of brothels."

"I'll have you know that they were not brothels. They were respectable establishments with fine young women and men."

Max rolls his eyes. "All I'm saying is, don't scare away one of the Lords before we've even begun."

I snort. "You think a foursome—and maybe a dash of anilingus—is going to deter him? I don't think so. He needs this just as much as we do."

CHAPTER 4

Astern

I must've pleased some God in a former life, because this fate is more than I could ever ask for. Growing up, I was not an overly sexual person. I kept to myself, focused on piano and being a nice, respectable young lady—until everything went to shit and my whole world burned down.
Literally.
After that, I kept my head down. I'm no virginal soul by any means, but this? With Lachlan kneeling before me as he slips my heels off, to Max behind me, unzipping my dress, and Otto, staring at me while he removes his t-shirt... the sinful things I could do to the contracting muscles on his abdomen alone are... *fuck.* Those tiny divots on either side of his lower stomach will be the death of me.
Before I can study his body too closely, Lachlan stands up and pushes me back against the large bed. I fall just as Lachlan tugs my dress down, leaving me in my bra and knickers on a bed with three strange men. Three *hot* as fuck strange men. My stomach flips as all three of them come closer, watching me like predators. Lachlan starts to remove his shirt at the same time as Max, but I shake my head.
"Keep them on," I whisper before I can think.
Max's eyebrows shoot up, his green eyes twinkling as he leaves his white t-shirt affixed to his muscles.
"Want me to put mine back on?" Otto asks, holding it up.
I nod. "I like—" I bite my bottom lip as my cheeks bloom with color.
Lachlan crawls on top of me, pushing my legs apart with his knee. Looking

down at me, I realize just how beautiful he is in normal light. They all are. I *have to* be dreaming.

"You need to tell us what you want, darling. We're not mind readers."

Should I tell them what I like, even if some people find it weird? I'll never see them again, so it's not like it matters. I might as well enjoy this last moment of freedom as much as I can.

"I like it when the men are fully dressed," I tell them quietly. "And I also like to be called names."

I hardly know these guys, and yet here I am, spilling all of my dirtiest fantasies to them—things like a bit of violence, a bit of pain, and a hell of a lot of degradation.

Lachlan's lips twitch as he slowly moves to remove my underwear. He pauses for a second once I'm bared to him, his finger brushing the apex of my thigh and my core gently before he discards them off to the side.

"You want us to fuck you fully clothed? Like you're a harlot?"

I whimper, and Lachlan's eyes darken at the sound.

"Like that?" His voice is a purr, and he reaches his hand to the front clasp of my bra, snapping it open in one fell swoop.

My knife—

The heavy thud as it falls to the ground causes me to stop breathing for a second, but none of them seem to notice that I'm armed with a weapon.

Lachlan's hand trails down my bare stomach, coming to the soft, dark curls between my thighs. Slowly—so torturously slowly—he slides a finger through my folds and then brings it back up in front of his face. "You're so fucking wet, pet." And then he brings his finger to his mouth, sucking on it slowly. "So fucking sweet," he adds. He pushes deep inside of me and curves his finger so that it massages the inner wall I can never reach on my own.

I feel the bed dip behind me as I arch into Lachlan's hand. Otto is hovering over me, hands on my shoulders. "I am going to watch Lachlan and my brother fuck you while you suck my cock," he growls.

I mewl out loud, arching my back. The commanding tone—the way he gives me no choice...

In the deepest recesses of my mind, I've always been turned on by bullies—by the mean, commanding men who call their lovers names. I've always been attracted to men who can dominate women in bed. Though I've never actually been in a relationship like that, the thought of Max, Lachlan, and Otto fucking me with their clothes on—while calling me names—just might be the most exhilarating sexual experience I'll ever have.

"Yes," I whisper. "Please."

"Our little pet is begging for it," Lachlan murmurs, spreading my legs wider as he removes his finger. "I think we should make her beg harder." He moves back to the floor and pulls my legs to the edge of the bed, kneeling on his knees until his face is lined up with my core.

And then his tongue begins to flick against my swollen bud.

"Oh God," I groan, bucking my hips into his mouth. I see white and my eyes roll back as he slowly licks me from top to bottom and back up again.

"Look how wet our little slut is," Max says from behind Lachlan. "That's it. Get her nice and wet for us."

The filthy mouths on these men...

I moan again as Lachlan adds his finger back into me. "She's so fucking wet," he says against my core. "Her cunt is begging to be fucked."

"Please," I whisper again.

I hear a belt unbuckling, and Otto hovers above me—his cock huge and hard above my face. His shaft is a soft pink, and he strokes himself above my face as my mouth waters for him.

"Be a good girl and take my cock down your pretty, little throat."

I moan as Lachlan's tongue flicks against my clit, and my mouth pops open as if commanded by a puppeteer. Tilting my head backward so that he has a better angle, Otto slides the head of his cock against my tongue, and I taste the precum already dripping off the end. Moaning, I close my mouth around him and suck *hard*.

"Fucking hell," Otto hisses, bucking his hips. "Yes, darling. You take my cock so fucking well."

I open my mouth as he begins to make small movements into my mouth—fucking it as I tense around Lachlan's finger. He adds another finger and I nearly buck off the bed.

"Good girl," Lachlan murmurs. "Don't come yet. I'm going to fuck you into this bed in a minute and I want to feel you shatter around me."

God...

I have to be dreaming.

Otto quickens his movements as Lachlan stands up. I can't see him with my head tilted back, but I hear him make a popping, sucking sound. *Tasting me.* My eyes flutter closed as he spreads my legs even wider. I'm completely exposed and wide open for him.

"This might hurt a bit, pet."

I moan, unable to speak with Otto's cock in my mouth. Just then, Otto removes his shaft and pushes my head up with one hand.

"Watch."

My eyes flick to Max, who is behind Lachlan, watching me like I'm a meal he's about to devour.

That's it. Get her nice and wet for us.

My eyes move over to Lachlan, and when I see him unzip himself, I tense.

"That's not going to fit—"

"Oh, I'll make it fit," Lachlan says, smirking. "I warned you. This might sting."

He rocks his hips closer, placing the edge of his monster cock against my entrance as he brings my knees to my chest. My skin begins to pebble with nerves. It's *massive*. The size of a forearm. And it's *thick*.

"Breathe, darling," he murmurs, pushing into me. I feel myself stiffen, like my body knows it's about to be intruded upon. Like I said, I'm not a virgin, but I've never taken someone of that size before. "Breathe," Lachlan repeats. He pushes in slowly, and my mouth drops open, feeling the way he stretches me. It stings, and yet... it feels fucking fantastic.

"Go slow," I beg him.

He gives me a monstrous smile. "I will. At first," he adds, his words dark and menacing.

Pushing in further, he gets about halfway in before pulling out again.

"Fuck, your cunt is taking my cock so well. The last woman I tried to fuck gave up."

The thought sends a heady, hot rush of adrenaline through me. "I can handle it," I tell him, my voice low and husky.

"I know you can," he says softly. "Watch."

So I do. I watch as the head of his cock—more purple than Otto's—presses against my swollen cunt. And then it disappears as he pushes into me. It feels better this time. Incredible, even. He slides in easier, and he gets three quarters of the way before he pulls back out again. Giving me a mischievous smile, he isn't so gentle the third time—and his hips rock forward all the way, until I'm gasping and my cunt is pulsing around him.

"Fuck," he hisses.

"You feel so—" I start to tell him how good he feels, but then he pulls out and drives back into me. Like he promised, it isn't slow, and it isn't gentle.

I scream as his thumb begins to work my aching clit. In and out he goes, until my head dips back and I open my mouth for Otto, needing to feel his cock inside of my mouth. Otto pushes past my teeth until he's fucking my mouth properly—making me gag as Lachlan fucks me into the bed... just like he said he would.

Everything inside of me tenses up. I'm like a coil, ready to spring. I can feel the way my muscles are pulling taut, feel the power behind the impending orgasm. It's almost scary—the pressure and the feel of the way Lachlan's cock fills me so completely.

I'm worried I might be ruined forever.

Fisting the sheets on the bed, I open my mouth wider as Otto pistons into my mouth between my teeth.

Fuck...

"That's it, baby," he growls. "Are you going to be a good little whore and swallow my cum?"

I nod against his hands, and he instantly stiffens inside of me.

It's too much—the feel of Otto's cock bobbing inside of my mouth, the taste of his cum as it shoots down my throat... he places a hand on my throat and roars as he continues coming.

"Fuck," he says, his voice low and hoarse. "I'm halfway down your throat, darling. Such a good, little harlot."

When he removes himself from my mouth, I look up at Lachlan—and he's watching me with something dark and possessed.

"Come inside of me," I beg him. "I'm on birth control."

He growls. "I almost wish you weren't, pet." He shifts our bodies so that he's all the way on top of me, using his hips to fuck me. I wrap my legs around his waist, using the heels of my feet to pull him in deeper. He groans. "I like the idea of filling you with my cum. And then having Max push it inside even deeper."

I moan as he slams into me, feeling my core begin to contract around his cock.

"Come for me, little minx."

My body is *so* close—and Lachlan uses his thumb on my clit, pressing down firmly. I whimper as he slides in and out, feeling the way the bed rocks with every movement. Looking up into his blue eyes, something dark passes behind them as he bares his teeth.

"*Now*," he commands.

I shatter around him. Screaming his name, my nails dig into the flesh at his back as I feel myself clench around him over and over. He stills, coming with me, a roar leaving his chest as I shake underneath him. Toes still curled, I feel myself go boneless as we finish, and Lachlan peppers my face and neck with little kisses.

So filthy between the sheets, and so sweet when it's over... I could get used to this.

Except I won't, because tomorrow we'll all go our separate ways.

Before I have a chance to recover, he pulls out of me. Just as quickly as he pulled out, Max is grabbing my legs and flipping me over onto my stomach. For someone who looks so innocent, he's rough with me—fingers digging into the flesh at my hips, hands coming to my hair and pulling my neck back.

"My turn," he growls, and I feel him press himself inside of me before Lachlan's cum can even begin to spill out. He groans, going still once he's inside of me. "Fuck. Your cunt feels like velvet, and you're so fucking wet."

"You're welcome," I hear Lachlan mutter.

My body heats at his words—at the implications of having all three of them inside of me. Max lets go of my hair and pulls my hips back onto his cock with both hands. I cry out at the angle. He's more curved than Lachlan, and the head of his cock hits the perfect spot inside of me.

"If you want to be properly fucked, you come to me, little minx," Max mutters. He slams in and out of me, harder than Lachlan was, *rougher* with a raw, animalistic edge. His nails nearly pierce my skin as he tugs me onto his cock with every thrust, and I have to lay my chest down on the bed to find purchase—to grip onto something, because he's about to fuck me into the headboard.

"Yes," I moan, my cheek pressed into the soft sheets. "Harder."

He slaps my ass—*hard*. Again. And again. After the fourth slap, he reaches around and adds two fingers, sliding them to either side of my clit. It's just enough friction along the swollen bud to send me over the edge.

I come around his cock, and he nearly impales me with force, grunting as he comes inside of me. I feel him pulse into me with every wave of my orgasm, as if I'm drawing his climax out, and the thought has my mouth dropping open, my nerves tingling, and my whole body convulsing. When he's finished, he places a hand on the small of my back before running it down to my ass and running a soothing, circular motion over the area he slapped just moments ago.

"So beautiful when you come, darling," Max says, sliding out of me. I go to sit up, but his hand stays on my back and he clicks his tongue. "Keep that pretty, little ass in the air, pet. We want to see our cum drip out of you."

I am half-horrified, half turned on.

But I stay, completely exposed to them as my body quivers from exertion. I feel Lachlan come to one side, and Otto on the other as they run their fingers along my skin, brushing my hair out of my sweaty face. Max continues to rub my hips and ass.

"Good girl," he murmurs. I feel something slide down my legs as he pats my ass cheek softly. "Our cum looks so good leaking down your creamy thighs, but I think I prefer it deep inside of you."

His words cause me to shiver, but then he pats my ass again, and I take that as an indication that I can sit up now. When I do, they're all zipping up their trousers and watching me carefully.

"That was..." I trail off, holding a sheet up to cover myself. My eyes glance to the clock on the side table, and my eyes nearly bulge out. "Oh, fuck. It's nearly four in the morning," I groan, standing quickly.

Snatching my dress, I pull it on without bothering to find my bra or panties. Slipping into my heels, I give them all a soft smile—but they're watching me like predators.

My skin tingles as Otto speaks, and before I can protest, he grabs a piece of paper and a pen, writing something down. "We're going to need to see you again, darling. Here's my number." His darkened pupils regard me, and I take the scrap of paper from his hand. "Don't lose it."

I nod and open the bedroom door. "Thank you for tonight."

Quickly slipping through the door, I walk down the stairs.

"Quinn!" I hiss. "Let's go!"

Quinn saunters out of the kitchen looking thoroughly fucked—probably similar to me, in fact. Her eyes widen at my appearance, but she nods as we walk over to the marble entryway table, grabbing our handbags.

"Hold on, did you—"

"*Not now*," I hiss. "It's four in the bloody morning. We need to get back to the hotel."

"Yeah, let's get the hell out of here," she mumbles, straightening her top.

As I reach for the front door, I glance back up at the stairway. My skin prickles when I see Lachlan, Otto, and Max watching me from the second story.

I don't have time for them—for any of this.

Tomorrow, my life will not be my own.

I take the piece of paper that Otto handed me and set it on the table.

And I swear to god, when I look back up at them, I can see the way Otto's eyes darken as I take a step away.

It's almost... *menacing*.

I glance around the posh townhouse, my eyes flicking to the swords and furniture that scream *old money*, wondering what the hell I'd gotten myself mixed up with.

Who I'd gotten mixed up with.

AMANDA RICHARDSON

I'd just had a one-night stand with three strangers.
Thank fucking God I'd never have to see them again.

CHAPTER 5

MAX

"What are the chances we can use our newfound profession to track her down?" Otto muses, holding a tumbler of something alcoholic as I brush my teeth.

"Only you would join the Lords of Darkness so that you could fuck more people," I mumble, spitting the toothpaste out.

I've changed into pajama bottoms and a t-shirt, and unlike me, Otto is wearing a dark purple, velvet dressing gown as if it's not almost five in the morning.

"It *is* a very prestigious occupation," he adds, tilting his head. "If I'm going to put myself in danger every single day, I think I should at least have the opportunity to fuck people whenever I want to."

After I rinse my mouth out, I turn to face him. "You should get some sleep. We have to be up in an hour."

"Sleeping is for boring people. Like Lachlan."

I snort. "Well, then let me politely request that you get the fuck out of my room."

"Such a mean big brother," Otto whines. "But fine. Maybe I'll go see if the other Lord is asleep yet."

Sighing, I climb into bed. "Leave him alone."

"Speaking of... what *do* we think of him?"

I shrug as I set my phone down on the wireless charger. "Christ, it's been a few hours, Ot. I don't know him well enough to form an opinion."

"He seems... repressed," Otto replies, looking at the wall with a faraway look.

"No," I tell him automatically. "Just because you think someone is fit does not mean you can attempt to change their sexuality. The world doesn't work that way."

He pouts as he stands up. "Fine. I just—"

A knock at the door startles both of us, and Otto's raised brows make me roll my eyes. "Come in," I call out.

Lachlan steps into the room, looking between Otto and me. "Sorry, am I interrupting?"

Otto mumbles something that sounds a lot like *you could never interrupt us*, but I shake my head.

"No. Just getting ready to go to sleep," I tell him.

"Right." Lachlan rubs the back of his neck and looks at me. "Look, I just want to be sure there's no weirdness between us after..."

"After our foursome?" Otto offers, smirking as he takes another sip of his drink. "I'd sure hope not, because I expect we'll all be sharing lots of holes and cocks in the coming years and decades."

"I don't do... cock," Lachlan mutters, shaking his head as if he's not sure what to make of my rakish brother. "And I've also never shared a woman before, so I don't know how this all should work—"

"Relax," I tell him. "It's fine. Otto and I have shared a few women over the years. Obviously we're not into incest but if the occasion arises, we've enjoyed taking turns."

"This job is important to me," Lachlan says, his voice taking on a serious note. "I don't want to jeopardize anything."

"The only time you jeopardized anything is when you said you don't do cock," Otto says. "It's a shame, really..."

Lachlan's eyes get harder as they rove over to my brother. "I meant it. I'm not a—" He stops speaking, pressing his lips together.

He doesn't need to say it.

We all know what he meant.

Otto stands up and walks over to Lachlan. He may seem innocent with his flirting and extravagant personality, but he's taken men twice his size down with one well-placed punch. He's lovable but deadly, and my jaw tenses as I watch Lachlan size him up.

"Men like you are all the same," he snarls, now toe to toe with Lachlan. I didn't realize that Otto is nearly the same height as him—the surly, tatted man carries himself with threats and swagger, making him seem bigger. "A tough exterior, moody personality, and insecurities that run a mile deep. You think you're different just because your life was tough? I think not. We're all carrying the burdens of our past, and we all have skeletons in our closet. We're in this thing together now, and I see you for what you are."

Lachlan's brows shoot up. I highly doubt he expected the menacing attitude to come from my fun-loving brother, and I can only smile as Lachlan takes a step back.

"He's right," I say. "There's a reason we all scored so high. There's a reason they chose us. Let's act like the fucking professionals they expect us to be."

"Exactly," Otto says, taking a step back. "And if that happens to be group sex every once in a while—"

Lachlan mutters *fuck off* before turning around and walking out the door.

"He's talkative," Otto observes, closing my door and crossing his arms.

"Can you blame him? You scolded him within an inch of his life."

"He deserved it," Otto mumbles, good mood forgotten. "Anyway, I need my beauty rest now. See you in an hour."

I wave him off before turning the light out and taking my glasses off.

It doesn't seem like it now, but I know that when tomorrow comes, our lives will never be the same again.

CHAPTER 6

Astern

The morning comes entirely too soon—probably because Quinn and I crawled into our hotel beds at half past four. After getting back, we'd both taken showers and passed the fuck out. I could still use ten more hours of sleep, but it's not like I'm not used to being sleep deprived. And when my alarm finally goes off at seven, Quinn is hovering over the side of my bed with a takeaway cup of hotel coffee and a bagel.

"I love you," I mumble, taking them from her as I sit up.

"You slept with him, didn't you?" she asks, her eyes gleaming with mischief. "You looked like you were properly shagged."

"Which 'him' are you referring to?" I ask, taking large bites of the bagel.

Her mouth pops open. "You cheeky trollop! Do tell," she says, sitting down on the end of the bed. I open and close my mouth, unsure how much of it was real. My head is still swirling with alcohol and lack of sleep.

"I had sex with all of them. At once."

"Good for you," she says quickly. "I shagged the tall redhead and his cock was the size of a pencil, so I'm not jealous at all."

We both burst out laughing, and despite only knowing her for a day, I have a feeling that Quinn and I are going to be fast friends.

At half past seven, we carry our overnight bags into the lobby, waiting for the car that Alaric Cross promised would show up to collect us. Lord Alaric *bloody*

Cross. The name sent shivers down my spine—as it did for most people who knew about the Lords.

However, it caused me anxiety for an entirely different reason.

My new job is part-intelligence, part-computer science, and part-espionage. The Lords of Darkness have been modernized over the last few years, so instead of the ritualistic rites and blood oaths of the middle ages, it's now modern and technological. And I'm taking over that entire branch—something Lord Theodore Wolf had been doing before me.

Surveillance and security are my specialties. Over the last few years, I'd acquired a double master's degree in Criminology and Computer Science with a bachelor's degree in Music History. Even though I hadn't played in over a decade, I still enjoyed learning about classical music. And before getting this job, I'd begun master level classes in Arabic, Spanish, and French. Most recently, I worked freelance as a computer hacker for insidious people on the dark web.

As I recall the thorough interview process, I remember Lord Wolf commenting that I was likely *over*qualified.

That's because I've spent ten years trying to get here.

There would be six months of training first. Our belongings had already been sent to the manor we'd all be staying at to get to know each other and begin training—a grueling process, from what I'd heard. Fortunately, I had Quinn. And luck was on our side because I still ran five miles every day, meaning the physical aspect should be a breeze. The mental gymnastics would be interesting, but I hoped that my dedication would see me through it. *It had to.*

I could do this.

I wouldn't let my parents down.

A black car pulls up to the curb, and Quinn gives me an excited smirk before she opens the door. We'd talked a bit yesterday on the way to the club, bonding over our shared Criminology backgrounds. Together, we make a formidable pair.

Ruthless. Hard-working. Smart. Capable.

When I sit down, I wince slightly, and Quinn snorts as we start the hour drive to Blackwell. She berates me with questions, and I give her answers, growing hot all over again at the way they all commanded me, at the way they called me *pet* and *darling* and *good girl.* I cross my legs and squeeze my thighs together when I recount how they wanted to watch their seed drip out, and Quinn gasps, agreeing that the whole breeding kink thing is hot. When I ask about *her* night, she tells me all about the terrible sex she had, and we laugh some more.

Recounting it makes me regret leaving Otto's number on the foyer table. Then again, I don't have time to get involved in whatever last night was.

I need to see last night for what it was: a last hurrah before my life turns into complete chaos.

As we pull up to an old house on the outskirts of Blackwell, Quinn lets out a low whistle. *Thorn Manor.* It's enormous—at least four stories, wide, with arched windows and dark red brick. It doesn't surprise me. If you're wealthy and you live in England, chances are you live in London or Blackwell. I'm sure there were numerous manors to choose from when appointing us housing.

Lord Gideon St. Claire walks out of the house, wearing a black denim jacket and dark grey trousers. His newly cut, dirty-blond hair hangs off to one side, and he quirks an eyebrow once Quinn and I exit the car.

"You two certainly look rough around the edges for your first day of training," he says, his voice somehow both intimidating and friendly at once.

"Yes, well, we're here now," Quinn says quickly. I can't recall how she knows Gideon—I remember her mentioning that they went to the same primary school at one point—so they have a less formal camaraderie. Quinn is a society girl through and through. I often wonder if she could become the next prime minister if she wanted to, and for a second, I mourn the life and the connections I could have had if everything hadn't happened the way it did when I was fifteen.

"The other guys are inside," Gideon says, nodding once in my direction as a show of greeting. "Once you've all been introduced, Sterling will escort you to the gym. I should've told you—today will be rough. Day one always is. Might've been good to get a full night's sleep, because we're going to ride you hard today," he adds, smirking.

I groan internally as we make our way inside the manor. It's gorgeous—and my mouth goes dry at the sight of the grand piano sitting inside the formal lounge. The gleaming, polished wood practically sings to me, but I keep my feet planted.

"Welcome to the Lords of Darkness, ladies. Follow me. You can meet the other initiates before training."

My whole body is sore from last night, which means exercise will feel extra hard today. But I have to do it. I have to prove myself to everyone.

Most importantly... to myself.

As Quinn, Gideon, and I round the corner, I stop walking at the sight before me.

No.

Lachlan, Max, and Otto are sitting at the dining room table, looking just as confused as I feel.

"My Lords," Gideon says, his tone mocking. "Or rather, your *majesties*," he drawls. "Please meet your Ladies of Darkness, Astern Hackbolt and Quinn Taylor." He turns to face us.

I feel the blood drain from my face as everything clicks into place.

"Ladies, please meet your Lords. Lachlan Weir, and the infamous crown princes of Denmark, Maximilian and Otto Thorn. They have kindly lent us this country house for the duration of your training, after which, you'll be able to select any of our current houses to reside in."

Quinn smiles from next to me. "Very nice to meet you," she says, her voice friendly. I can practically hear the silent squeal of laughter she's withholding. "And you two are *actual* princes?"

I'm still trying to get my bearings—still trying to process everything—when Otto nods and grins.

"We are. Though we're seventh in line, so unlikely to be crowned King unless a lot of people die. We grew up in SoHo." His lips quirk for just a second, knowing his admission will only make me feel more unsettled because I'd just left that SoHo house only a few hours ago.

Lachlan is quiet as his eyes roam over my face, and there's only one way to describe his expression: regretful.

"Hello," he says, his voice a dark purr. His eyes stay lingering on mine for a second longer than Quinn's.

Max and Otto do the same—though Otto's lips are pressed together like he's trying hard not to laugh.

We're going to need to see you again, pet.

Well, they got their fucking wish.

Gideon continues to talk, but I don't hear anything over the roaring in my ears. Quinn follows Gideon out of the dining room, but I stay—pinning my cold, narrowed eyes on Lachlan. Once Gideon is out of earshot, I cross my arms.

"Did you know?" I ask, my voice tight and unkind as I assess all three of them.

Lachlan frowns. "Of course not."

"And you two?" I ask, looking at Max and Otto.

"It's like Christmas came early," Otto says slowly, smiling.

Max looks just as disturbed as I do.

If you want to be properly fucked, you come to me, baby girl.

His words from last night clang through me. Suddenly, I realize that perhaps last night was a last hurrah for them as well—one last chance to do something crazy. I mean, what are the chances?

I hear Gideon call for us from the other room. The three of them stand, and Max walks past me with an unreadable expression.

Otto's eyes narrow, but he doesn't give any indication that he's about to tell Gideon what occurred between us last night. "What a lovely surprise," he murmurs, his voice sultry.

His finger grazes my hand as he walks by, and then he's gone.

I let my eyes wander back to Lachlan. "You should know that this job is everything to me, and I won't let *anything* get in the way of it."

He brushes past me, his arm brushing my shoulder. I gasp at the contact, at the way my whole body ignites with his touch.

I like the idea of filling you with my cum.

I narrow my eyes and open my mouth to reply, but he leaves me alone and bereft in the dining room, regretting every single impulsive decision I made last night.

Closing my eyes, I take a deep breath and follow my new co-workers into the formal living room, knowing I have to forget that last night ever happened if I'm going to survive this.

As I do, I catch Otto's eye, and he cocks his head slightly, dipping his eyes low to my throat and lingering there before snapping them back up.

Fuck.

I'm never going to survive this.

Just get through training, and then you can kill all *of them in their sleep.*

They have no idea they've just allowed a lethal viper into the Lords of Darkness.

CHAPTER 7

Lachlan

While in prison, I learned very early on how to drown out the noise. The fighting, the howling, the laughing, and the wanking—I heard it all, whether or not I wanted to. Tuning everything out became one of my specialties, and I'm positive it's one of the reasons I managed to keep my head on straight while there. I kept my focus every second of every day and kept my head down.

Which is why, as I lift weights on the bench, I'm not paying attention to Astern and Quinn whispering as they cool down on the mats.

I'm not listening to Harlow murmuring with the Lords about something.

I'm not paying attention to *anything*.

Which means when Theodore Wolf comes to sit down next to me, I don't notice until he starts to clap.

"Nearly one hundred and fifty kilograms. Well done, mate." My jaw grinds as I slowly lower it back into the holder. "Next time, ask one of us to spot you. The last thing we need is one of our new Lords having a smashed skull on the first day of training."

"I've done it by myself for years," I grunt, sitting up and taking a sip of water.

"Yes, fine. Prison isolation and all of that. Still, we're not in prison now, and you have nine people standing around that can help you."

I don't say anything as I take another sip of water.

"Meeting room in thirty seconds," Sterling Beauchamp announces to everyone in the large gymnasium.

I stand up, and Otto and Max walk past me—the former of whom turns and winks at me.

I don't try to hide the simmering growl that escapes my throat.

"The more you fight back, the more he's going to push. You understand that, right? Trust me. I've been in your shoes," Theo murmurs, following me into what looks like a classroom.

Again, I don't respond.

Last night was a mistake and unlike anything I'd ever done. I've never been one to sleep with someone without a bit of an emotional connection. Abby...

Abby used to call me demisexual.

I *couldn't* feel sexual attraction without an emotional connection.

And I have no idea what overcame me at Max and Otto's house. I'd never done anything like that before, and I'd especially never fucked anyone in front of other guys. I'd been drinking, and I guess my tolerance is not what it used to be. Plus, saying no didn't feel like an option. I *wanted* so badly to be friends with them, and it felt like a precipice of sorts. I could do it and we could bond, or I could say no and push them away forever.

And fuck me, but I couldn't resist Astern. Beautiful and mysterious... it was hard to retain my self-control.

I have to do this job well—without distractions.

I take a seat in the very last row, leaning back in the small chair as it groans under my weight. Much to my chagrin, Astern takes the seat next to me.

"Feels like Uni all over again," she murmurs.

"I wouldn't know."

Her eyes find mine as they flash with surprise. "You didn't go to Uni?"

I don't answer her, and before she can ask questions, Sterling claps his hands once.

"Right, let's just get into it. Welcome to the Lords of Darkness, ladies and gents. You're now a part of the deadliest order in the world. By the end of training, you'll be able to kill a man a hundred ways, all undetectable, while also knowing how to keep tabs on every single group or threat out in the real world. As you know, the current Lords—myself included—have decided to step down. While we've tried to keep this information private, there are now rumors that our order will fall. This has created a power vacuum in Britain and all over Europe. We have more threats today than we had even a year ago, so we're going to have to go full-force with everything immediately. Is that understood?"

Otto, Max, Astern, Quinn, and I all murmur our agreement.

"Good. We don't have time to fuck around, so if your heart isn't one-hundred percent in this, I need you to walk out of this room right now."

I look around, waiting for any of them to change their minds, but none of them do.

"Your first assignment is tonight. There's a royal ball in London, and there have been several threats against the royal family. They've asked us to keep watch." I raise my hand, and Sterling drags his eyes over to me. "Yes?"

"Who is the threat?"

"The question right now is more who *isn't* a threat. But to answer your question, it's a homegrown group of terrorists who want the royal family gone. Their official name is Citadel, and they consist of a few very dedicated extremists who don't care about innocents and want the country to be ruled by right-wing fascists."

Astern raises her hand. "How will we know who they are?"

Sterling glares at her, eyes narrowed. "Theo will be going through the active member profiles with you all today. That will be your first lesson after you've showered and cleaned up. The five of us will be accompanying you on all missions until you're fully trained, so tonight is about watching, learning, and most importantly, listening. If tonight goes well, then tomorrow we can make it official."

Quinn raises her hand. "And what does official mean?"

"Choosing your new name, and taking the brand, of course," Sterling says, giving us all a monstrous smile. "Go get cleaned up. We'll meet back here in an hour."

All five of us stand, but as we get to the door, I see Sterling bend down to Astern.

"I need to speak with you, Ms. Hackbolt."

I glance back at Astern as her eyes widen, but I don't have time to contemplate why Sterling Beauchamp needs to speak to her because Max and Otto are pushing me out of the room.

CHAPTER 8

✦

Astern

My heart pounds against my ribs as Quinn, Otto, Max, and Lachlan leave me alone in a classroom with Sterling Beauchamp. I smooth my hair down and stand up straighter, despite being more than a foot shorter than him. Once everyone's out of earshot, he leans against the brick wall of the room.

Please don't recognize me.
Please don't imagine me with dark hair.
Please don't ask too many questions.

"We've been going through everyone's references. Quinn's were fantastic, and Otto and Max seem to do well for themselves despite being Danish princes. Lachlan's were... well... his prison guards told us everything we needed to know. But you?" He pushes off the wall and walks closer. "You're a bit of a mystery, *Astern Hackbolt.*"

There's a bite to the way he says my name, and my pulse speeds up as I swallow. "My parents died in a car accident when I was a teenager. I stayed with some family friends until I went to Uni."

"And these family friends of yours... who are they?"

I clear my throat. "Like I said in my application, they've since passed away."

His eyes study my face, and I have to hope beyond belief that he doesn't see the way my heart is faltering, or the way my pulse is throbbing against my neck. I lay my hands flat on my thighs so that he can't see the way they're shaking.

"I meant what I said earlier, you know. If you're not one-hundred and ten percent on board with the Lords of Darkness, now is your only chance to walk away. Once you're initiated, there is no going back. Do you understand?"

"I understand," I tell him confidently, despite the slight quiver in my voice.

There's something in his gaze that unsettles me—that makes me feel like I'm being held under an X-ray machine and scrutinized within an inch of my life. I hold my ground, though, and stand up a bit taller as he assesses me. When he sees that I'm not going to back down, his nostrils flare and his lips go thin—like he's about to strike.

"I should also mention that betrayal warrants a slow, painful death."

Goosebumps erupt along the back of my neck. "Understood," I say firmly.

"Your hair color..." he trails off, eyes wandering over my silver hair. "It's not very often that you see a twenty-five year old woman with grey hair. Is it natural?"

The words he's speaking are more playful, but the tone in his voice is dark and threatening.

Like he's trying to catch me in a lie.

"It is," I tell him, chin high. "I had a lot of trauma as a teenager, and my hairdresser thinks the stress caused it," I answer, my voice just as hard as his.

Because of you, I think. *Because you all ruined my life and took everything from me.*

"Do you mean your parents'... car accident?"

No.

Not just that.

The homelessness.

The begging for money in Brixton.

The hunger.

Bloody hell... I was hungry for three years straight.

Despite it all—despite being utterly alone in the world, I managed to get into Uni on a full scholarship. Once I was there, I regrouped and put my all into my education, graduating with high marks and making a name for myself in the world of hacking, working on the dark web for three years until rumors began to trickle in about how the infamous *Lords of Darkness* would be hiring new Lords and Ladies.

I'd almost given up on getting my revenge.

I'd almost come to terms with my parents' brutal murders.

I had a well-paying job doing what I loved. For a couple of years, I had no desire to seek the vengeance I sought for so long.

But when the opportunity dropped into my lap, I couldn't say no.

I had no fucking desire to be a Lady.

I *only* wanted to slaughter them all for what they did.

And until now, I was sure they had no idea about my past. How could they? I died that night in the fire. That's what all the articles said.

Tragic fire kills prominent family of three in Berkshire.

It was all over the media for days—pictures of my mum, my dad, and me.

I kept my hair short and blonde when I was homeless—a vast difference from the healthy teenager with long, straight, dark brown hair.

And then, of course, it actually did turn grey.

No one ever put two and two together.

And as Sterling's eyes narrow even further, I realize that I have to play my part until I can do to him what he did to my parents.

If there's one thing I do well, it's survive.

"Yes. Their car accident," I say quickly.

"I'm very sorry for your loss," he adds, eyes pinning me to the spot. Before I can thank him, he turns and walks out of the classroom–leaving me a shaking, anxious mess.

Fuck.

Why do I feel like Sterling knows more than he's letting on? Surely, there's no way he remembers me–especially now that I'm older and my hair is completely different.

Then again, this is the Lords of Darkness we're talking about.

I should know better than anyone that they always have the upper hand.

There's a reason they always come out on top.

Now I just have to hope that I get the upper hand for long enough to take action against them.

⚜

Once I'm back at Thorn manor, I finally get to fully take in my surroundings. The house is large, and despite the stuffy architecture, the furnishings are modern and cozy. Even so, a house of this grandeur...

And it belongs to Max and Otto?

I close my eyes briefly and take a calming breath.

It's not actually *that* similar to the house I grew up in, but parts of it make my chest ache with nostalgia.

That house is gone.

My parents are dead.

I have one objective for being here, and getting sentimental won't help me.

As I walk up the stairs, I gather my resolve and strength and keep my expression neutral as I walk down the hallway. I have no idea which room is mine, so I peek inside all of the bedrooms, assuming someone took our bags up. One of the doors is cracked, and I see Quinn talking to someone on the phone. Further down the hallway, I hear Max and Otto talking, though I can't make out what they're saying. When Otto sees me passing by the door, he winks at me.

I'm a bloody idiot because the sight of it makes my stomach flop.

Lachlan's room must be the one with the closed door, so I open the slightly ajar one next to it.

The bedroom is large but not ostentatious. There's a four-poster bed, a large window overlooking the back garden, and a large wardrobe on the opposite wall. My suitcase is sitting on top of the bench at the foot of the four-poster, and after I'm done slowly walking around the bedroom, I pull the curtains closed and sit down on the bed.

Even though I look different now–even though it's been ten years, it's a habit to lock myself away behind doors, curtains, and windows.

Blend in.

Head down.

People don't ask questions when you don't present yourself as interesting.

Since we have our first lesson in less than an hour, I remove my workout clothes and grab my shower things. With my shampoo clutched to my chest, I walk to the door to my ensuite, pushing it open and yelping as Lachlan steps out of the shower.

Completely fucking naked.

My eyes can't help but wander down to his cock, which is massive even when it's soft. Before I can inspect it further, I grab a nearby towel and cover myself.

"Why are you showering in my bathroom?" I demand.

He glares at me but doesn't even try to cover himself up.

"Don't you mean *my* bathroom?" He frowns as he grabs a towel and begins drying himself off. "This bathroom is attached to my bedroom."

I glance at the slightly ajar door behind him leading to another bedroom.

Wonderful.

"Will you be done soon?" I ask, wrapping the towel tighter around myself.

Lachlan doesn't smile as his eyes rove down my body slowly, like he's drinking me in.

"I'll be done soon," he grits out.

I look between him and the glass shower door, wondering if I should save my integrity and wait my turn.

But then I think, fuck this. And fuck him.

It's my bathroom too.

His eyes widen slightly as I drop the towel onto the floor and smirk as I walk to the shower, turning it on and stepping inside.

I don't look at him as I wash myself, but my skin prickles with awareness as I lather my hair with shampoo.

When I bend over to wash my legs, I chance a look up, and what I see has me nearly gasping.

Lachlan is leaning against the bathroom vanity, arms crossed with the towel wrapped around his hips as he watches me. His cock is pressing against the white material, and his eyes aren't dark with lust or arousal.

They're menacing and furious.

It startles me. Last night, while he was more serious than Max and Otto at times, he was still nice to me. But right now? I'll be lucky if he doesn't murder me.

"What changed between last night and now?" I ask, standing up as I rinse the conditioner out of my hair.

His jaw feathers as he considers my words. The steam makes it difficult to see him clearly, but I don't miss the way his nostrils flare.

"Last night was supposed to be a casual hookup," he says, his voice low and deadly. "I never expected to see you again. I never *wanted* to see you again," he adds cruelly.

I disguise the hurt searing through my chest by releasing a quick huff of laughter.

"Well, I was surprised, too. It's not like I planned it."

I turn the shower off and step out, reaching for my towel. But when my eyes flick up to his face, I don't miss the way his eyes trail down my naked body.

And it's really hard to miss the most obvious sign of his arousal.

Instead of covering myself, I slowly begin to pat myself dry as I arch my back.

He shakes his head and looks away. "You have no fucking idea how hard I've worked for this—"

"Oh? Is that so? I don't remember reminiscing about who had it harder last night when you were deep inside of me. Because I have news for you, Lachlan Weir. My life was far from easy, and I worked my fucking arse off for this, too."

I drop the towel when I'm done, knowing that I have an advantage over him by arguing naked. His expression oscillates between fury and interest, and I smile when his eyes lock onto my chest.

"Come on. How about we call a truce?" I say, making my voice sound sweeter than normal.

I hold my hand out toward him, and when his eyes find mine again, something dark passes behind them. He reaches out like he's going to shake my hand, but instead, he pulls me into his body before pressing me against the vanity. I gasp when one hand comes to my waist, and the other wraps around my neck.

"A truce?" he growls. "This isn't fucking Girl Scouts. It's the Lords of Fucking Darkness—"

"You say that like I don't know," I rasp out, rolling my eyes. "You don't have to mansplain the Lords of Darkness to me."

Lachlan does *not* like that. His hand squeezes my neck tighter, and I hate myself for being turned on—for imagining him hoisting me onto the vanity and hate fucking me with his massive cock. Despite having a firm hold on my windpipe and being hardly able to breathe, I feel myself get wetter as arousal lances through me.

"I'm not interested in a truce. I'm interested in finding your weaknesses and exploiting them until you flounder. Because I can tell you one thing, Astern Hackbolt: I refuse to compromise this job for anyone or anything. So if you continue to tempt me, I will have to do something about it."

"Mmm, baby. Keep talking dirty to me," I say, my voice hoarse.

He bares his teeth as a low rumble sounds in his chest.

"Last night never happened. If I'd known you were going to be here, I wouldn't have touched you," he snarls.

"Why?" I ask.

The question hangs in the air, and for a split second, he looks unsure. His hand loosens its grip around my neck, but then it's replaced with something akin to disgust.

"Because you're a distraction," he growls. "A complication."

Before I can respond, he lets go and walks off without another word.

CHAPTER 9

Otto

Having a beautiful yet deadly woman sitting on my lap makes for the most arousing drive to London. Alaric Cross is driving, Quinn is in the passenger seat, Max is next to me, and Lachlan is beside him. Naturally, everyone agreed that Astern should sit on someone's lap since she is the smallest, and of course I volunteered.

So as Alaric weaves us through the countryside, I can't help but trail my hands up and down Astern's legs. And by the way she trembles on top of me, she's remembering last night just like I am.

"Stop," she whispers.

"Is that your safe word?" I ask, my voice thick as I pull her against my hard cock.

"You don't want to know my safe word," she mutters. "I don't think you could handle it."

"Do you want me to stop?" I ask, my voice low enough for only her to hear.

She doesn't respond, so I take that as a no. Smiling, I run a hand up her stomach to her chest, and then I let my hand snake underneath the beaded strap of her dress. She arches her back slightly as my thumb brushes against her tightened nipple, and when I pinch her firmly between my thumb and forefinger, she hardly reacts. Instead, she rolls her hips against me.

I use my other hand to brush her long, straight hair off her shoulder and plant a kiss against her bare skin.

Women can be so sensual—soft, forgiving, smooth... I love the idea of handling a woman and taking charge. Making them come. Watching them unravel. It's why as much as I love sleeping with men, I could never fully give up sleeping with women.

My brother wasn't wrong when he said I'd fuck anyone. It's not someone's gender that I'm attracted to.

It's the way they carry themselves.

The way they speak, and move through the world.

The way they *fuck*.

And Astern Hackbolt has her soft, little hand wrapped around my heart and my cock at the same time. Metaphorically, of course—though I endeavor to have her hand around my actual cock soon.

When I find someone that interests me, I fall hard, and I fall fast. I've had my heart broken more than a dozen times, but fortunately for me, there's always someone else to shag.

Sometimes multiple people at once.

Dubbed as Denmark's very own Casanova, I don't mind the nickname. I don't shy away from an adventure. So when Max told me about the opening within the Lords of Darkness, I thought, *why the fuck not?*

Having been raised as royals, we were already used to secrecy. We'd been trained by the best of the best, and both of us knew what kinds of evil lurked around every corner more than anyone.

I never expected to get the job, but the more I thought about it, the more it made sense. I wanted to be remembered as something other than a Prince. I wanted to make a name for myself.

"Does my pretty, little minx enjoy being edged?" I whisper into her ear as my tongue flicks against the skin of her neck.

"Fuck off," she replies.

I chuckle as I pinch her nipple harder. This makes her let out a tiny, breathless sigh.

"You think I'm done with you?"

"Does it matter if I say no?"

This makes me laugh. "Very good."

"We shouldn't," she adds.

"Why?"

"Because this is a job."

"You're right. It is a job, but it happens to be a job where any one of us could die at any point. And do you know what turns me on more than anything, darling?"

I swear I feel her heart jump at the nickname.

"What?" she asks, squirming on top of me.

"Danger."

I let my fingers fondle and circle her nipple for a few more minutes—until she's rocking her hips to get any kind of friction. My cock is leaking precum, and as I continue to subtly nibble and whisper sweet nothings into her ear, we arrive at the venue.

It's a palace just outside of the city, and a chauffeur opens our doors. Astern hops off my lap and I have to adjust myself before I get out, but when I do, she shoots me a darkened look before stalking off with Quinn.

"Subtle," Max murmurs as Lachlan walks ahead of us with Alaric.

Sterling, Theo, Gideon, and Harlow are all in a car behind us, and I hear them pull up to the valet line as we walk up to the house.

I look over my shoulder and wink at them as we're all ushered into the house. There's already a crowd of stuffy people wearing suits and gowns, drinking champagne out of crystal flutes in the foyer. Most people are standing around the formal ballroom. As I meander through the crowd with my brother, I make sure to keep an eye out for our targets without being obvious about it.

Once we get to the other side of the ballroom, I see a group of people surrounding the King—who is sitting on a chair resembling a throne. Though I've met him a few times at various head of state dinners, I'm here tonight for other reasons, and I doubt I'll have time to say hello.

"I know who you're looking for," Max says, his voice low in my ear.

I smirk. "One can hope."

"He's not here. Not after what happened last year."

Alexander Charles Reginald Mountbatten III.

He was considered a crown prince of England up until last year, when it came out that he wasn't actually related to the King at all but was instead a child born due to an affair the Queen had before she passed away.

It was all very scandalous, but it doesn't change the fact that Alexander—or Alex, for short—was my first crush.

He was also the first and only man I ever let top me.

But that was all years ago.

In the past.

He's not here, so it doesn't matter.

Besides, I'm here for important business. Not to gawk at my long lost crush.

"Too bad," I pout, thinking of the confident, tall, rakish young man I still harbored feelings for.

"Too bad for whom? Your cock or your job?"

"Very funny," I murmur, swiping a champagne flute from a passing server.

My eyes scan the people around us, and I can tell Max is doing the same thing. Our "lesson" earlier—if you could call it that—entailed studying the profiles of three prominent members of Citadel. The organization is run by a man named Charlie Hoeffler, who is supposed to make a secret appearance tonight. The threat against the crown is real, and this organization has expressed wanting to harm the royal family, so everyone is on high alert. I'm sure half of the people here are MI6 or private security that the King has hired. Still, as my eyes catch on a solo man sitting at the ornate bar, I nudge Max subtly.

"Is it me, or does that look like Target Number One with a bad dye job?"

The man is sipping what looks like water—or I suppose it could be vodka—as he types something into his phone.

Max taps his earpiece—something we're all wearing—and in a low voice, speaks to Alaric, who is listening in.

"Target Number One is at the bar. White shirt, black hair."

Max nods once and Alaric must confirm, because Max gives me a thumbs-up.

My brother and I pretend to make conversation with other guests, and out of the corner of my eyes, I see Quinn approach the bar.

Our plan—according to Sterling—would be to ensure that each of the three targets had a Lord or Lady trailing them. So it doesn't surprise me as Quinn laughs and places her hand on the man's arm. He seems charmed with her, and his eyes drag over her chest not so subtly.

"Target Number Two is moving to the back exit of the ballroom. Black suit, brown hair. He's pretending to speak on the phone," Harlow says to me through the earpiece. "The two of you need to trail him."

"Let's go," I tell Max. "Target Number Two, black suit," I say under my breath. "Back exit."

I spot the target instantly. His eyes skim back and forth briefly before he pushes one of the back doors open.

We wait a few seconds before following him, and when we do, we're met with a dark hallway.

"Comforting," Max muses.

"Target Number Three heading for the back door. Astern is taking this one. He prefers blonds," Harlow says to me.

I relay the message to Max, and as I do, a flash of jealousy works through me as I crack my neck.

"I know," Max murmurs as if he can read my mind. "But just because we had her once doesn't make her ours."

"Life's not fair," I whine, keeping my voice low and quiet.

The sound of a door closing up ahead gives us our first clue, and when we enter, I stop so suddenly that Max runs into my back.

Alexander—*Prince* Alexander—is lounging on a couch in what appears to be a formal lounge.

"Well, hello there," he muses, and my whole body goes still at the sound of his voice. He's wearing a navy suit that brings out his brown eyes. His dark scruff and the way he's loosely holding a tumbler full of amber liquid give him an unhinged look. "I know you miss me, Otto, but you could've just texted me," he adds, smirking.

Before I can respond, shouting voices sound from the hallway. Max and I step into the room and close the door quietly.

"Have you seen a man in a black suit?" I ask casually.

"He may have passed by in the hallway, but—"

The door flies open, and Harlow, Alaric, Sterling, Theo, and Gideon all walk in with Lachlan trailing at the rear.

"Where's the target?" Gideon asks, walking right up to Alex and flicking his knife open.

"Excuse you," Alex says, uncrossing his legs and sighing before he stands up. "I'll be on my way since I can't seem to find this person you're all looking for," he drawls.

"Stop," Sterling growls. To my surprise, Alex obeys. "You're not going anywhere until we locate the targets."

Alex rolls his eyes. "I can assure you that I'm innocent in whatever you think I'm a part of."

Harlow steps forward, eyes narrowed. She looks fucking fierce tonight—dark curls spilling over her shoulder. Her dark red dress matches the shade of her lipstick perfectly.

"Really?" she asks, stepping up to Alex despite being a full foot shorter. "Because I think working for Citadel makes a lot of sense for you. Bastard son. Shunned from most royal functions. Your whole life went up in flames after that exposition came out, didn't it? Why wouldn't you want revenge on the family who cut you out for something you could never control? From my viewpoint, you and Citadel probably have a lot in common."

Alex huffs a laugh. "Citadel? Aren't those the idiots who continue to threaten blowing up Buckingshire Palace?" He looks at all of us, but his eyes linger on mine for a fraction of a second longer. "Okay, I think there's been a misunderstanding—"

"Astern turned her earpiece off," Theo says, brows furrowed as he taps something on his phone.

"Fuck," Sterling says, pacing. "And Quinn?"

"Nothing from either of them now," Theo says, communicating silently with the other three Lords and Lady.

"I'll go," Sterling growls.

"No," Harlow says quickly, brows furrowed. "If you go out there, you might blow the cover. Let's give them a chance to do this alone."

"Alone?" Lachlan asks, speaking for the first time. "Two untrained people against three highly efficient terrorists?"

Harlow considers what he's saying, but before anyone else can speak up, more voices in the hallway sound through the closed door of the lounge. A few seconds later, Astern walks in with two men—looking smug and confident.

"What the hell is this—" One of them reaches for their gun, but Harlow is quick and she shoots both of them with a bullet through the skull—smack in the middle of their foreheads. It takes less than a second before they both collapse.

"Fuck," I mutter, mouth dropping open as I stare at the sole Lady of Darkness. "That was fucking amazing."

"Holy fuck. Uh," Alex says, running a hand through his dark hair. "I'm just going to go—"

"You'll stay," Alaric growls. "Until the last target is taken care of, we need you here."

Alex looks like he's going to be sick, and he looks up at me. "What the hell sort of shit have you gotten wrapped up in? You're condoning *murder* now?" I don't miss the shakiness in his voice.

"So what if I was? Does it turn you on?" I ask, smirking.

"Now's not the time for a lover's spat," Max says sternly.

Sterling disregards the conversation as well as the dead bodies, instead walking up to Astern. "Where's Quinn?"

Astern blanches. "She's not here?" she asks, her eyes scanning the room. "She was supposed to meet us here—"

"Never. Leave. Anyone. Alone," Sterling grits out, his voice menacing and low. "That was the first thing I taught you today. We all have partners for a reason, for every single mission."

"I didn't know," she says quickly, panic pacing her tone. "I'm sure she's fine—"

A loud boom and subsequent screams emit from the ballroom, and Gideon is the first out of the room. We all run out after him, but the smell of gunpowder permeates my senses as we jog down the hallway. People are running in all directions, but mostly toward the various exits along the wall of the ballroom. A cloud of smoke makes it hard to see clearly—was it a bomb?

As we get closer and more people clear out, I hear Astern let out a sob.

Amid the debris near the bar—right where we left her—is Quinn.

Or, most of Quinn.

I have to put my hand on my mouth to keep from heaving as my eyes wander over her decimated body.

There's no blood—just... bits. Of her. Everywhere.

Astern runs over to her and starts crying as she kneels down next to her.

"Oh god, we need to call 999—"

"She's gone, Astern," Max says solemnly.

We all look at Quinn's lifeless eyes, and as Astern looks up at Max, her cheeks are streaked with mascara.

"No. That's not—she's not—"

"She's gone," Alaric says slowly, kneeling down next to her.

"No. Tonight was just training. No one is *actually* supposed to die—"

"Tonight was your first mission," Sterling responds. He's a serious bloke but he seems to really dislike Astern for some reason. And that makes me dislike him. "You failed. The threat was always real, and it's no one's fault but your own if someone died on your watch."

She starts to cry harder, and I see Harlow run a hand over Sterling's face before murmuring something into his ear. Then, she turns toward Astern before crouching down to her level.

"Astern," Harlow says gently. "Let's go. Come on." Reaching down, she pulls Astern to a standing position.

"I should probably go," Alex says, looking white as a sheet.

"I don't think so," Gideon says, flicking his knife open and holding it out in front of him. "You've seen too much now."

Alex goes pale as he looks over at me and laughs uncomfortably. "I promise I'll just go back to my boring life of an outcast, bastard Prince of England who drinks too much."

"We need to kill him," Theo says, eyes lighting up with glee.

"Hold on," Harlow says slowly, looking between Quinn's body and Alexander. "Let's think this through. He grew up as a *Prince*. Despite being ostracized as a bastard, the King still cares for him and he still has access to a lot of things we've never been able to get access to. And with Citadel still out there wreaking havoc..."

"You're not seriously considering making Prince Alexander a Lord of Darkness, are you?" Theo asks incredulously.

"I'm sorry, but are you speaking about the *actual* Lords of Darkness?" Alex asks, looking between everyone. "And you're working with them?" he asks me, dark eyes unbelieving.

I shrug. "It sounded fun at the time."

"We need to vote," Harlow says quickly. "And we need to vote now before the police get here."

"I vote yes," Alaric says quickly, grabbing Harlow's hand and giving it a quick kiss.

"Me too," Sterling says, shrugging.

"Me three," Gideon says, snapping his knife shut.

"Fine," Theo says, rolling his eyes. "And you lot?"

Astern looks confused and stricken, but she nods once—as do Max, Lachlan, and me.

"Great," Harlow says, clapping her hands together. "Prince Alexander is now a Lord of Darkness."

"Don't I get a say?" Alex asks incredulously.

The sounds of sirens break through the silent and mostly empty ballroom.

"We need to go," Alaric says quickly.

CHAPTER 10

Astern

My hands are shaking as Harlow leads us out of one of the back exits, and as Sterling talks with Theo about what happened, all I can hear is the deafening silence of the ballroom after we found Quinn's body.
She's dead.
And it's my fault.
To make matters worse, Sterling continues to glare at me whenever he gets a chance, so between him and Lachlan hating me, dread begins to curdle inside of me.
Perhaps this was a bad idea.
Maybe I'm not cut out for this.
I failed the first mission, and Quinn is dead.
Someone *died* because of me.
As we get back to the car, I realize that Quinn left her handbag sitting on the passenger seat, and that causes a fresh wave of tears to leak from my eyes.
"I'm sorry about your friend," Prince Alexander says, hands in the pockets of his trousers.
I huff a laugh. Suddenly this all feels so fucking absurd. I'm walking back to the car with Prince Fucking Alexander—someone I used to drool over in those awful teen magazines. He's a couple of years older than me, and he's lived his life in the spotlight. It feels like I know him, and that thought is so surreal and ironic.
Now, he's a Lord of Darkness.
Like me.
"Thanks," I tell him glumly.

When I look up at him, he's watching me with veiled concern. His brows are furrowed, and he's frowning. Despite that, I feel my heart skip a beat.

He's so bloody handsome, and even more so in person.

We all load into the car in the same order we came, and Alexander takes the front seat.

"So, uh, where are we headed?" he asks as Alaric gets into the driver's seat.

"Blackwell," Alaric tells him, and I hardly hear him begin to explain how it all works.

How absurd for him... hiding out in one of the back rooms to now being driven away as a Lord of Darkness. That has to be a record for quickest acquisition of a new Lord in the history of the Lords.

Otto's arms come around me as we drive out of London, and I let the tears fall without bothering to wipe them away, leaning against his warm chest. I hate myself for thinking it, but his warm body is comforting. And he seems to be the only one who doesn't hate me.

Guilt claws through me, and my stomach rolls any time I think back to what happened.

It could've been me.

It *should've* been me.

Quinn was with Target Number One, and I was going after Target Number Three. He'd started walking away, and I'd followed him to the back room, leaving Quinn alone—leaving Quinn *exposed*. I *knew* not to leave her. We'd come as a pair, and we were meant to stay together. But... I panicked. And then I ran into Target Number Two, and we'd all stumbled into the room with the Lords—

I never should've left Quinn alone.

At some point, I must fall asleep, because Otto is nudging me awake a bit later. I gasp as I sit straight, looking around and realizing we're parked in front of the manor.

It all comes crashing back, and that black, inky feeling of guilt returns.

"Come on, darling. Let's go inside," Otto murmurs.

I follow them all into the manor, expecting to be able to go to bed. I can't fathom doing anything else, but everyone files into the formal dining room.

Standing by the door, I cross my arms as the nine others take a seat.

"Going forward, Astern will be shadowing missions with one of us," Alaric says, his voice indifferent.

When I look over at Sterling, he's glaring at me.

Why does he hate me so much?

"I'm sorry," I choke out.

"Despite the massive failure, we believe we have a location for Citadel's headquarters," Theo says. "My system was able to hack into the phones of the two Citadel members we killed, and their last location before the gala was a nondescript flat in Brixton."

Exhaustion rocks me, and I finally give in and take a seat next to Lachlan, who doesn't acknowledge me at all.

"Right. The initiation ceremony will take place in two days instead of tomorrow. Let's take tomorrow off," Sterling says gruffly. "Before we break up for the night, I just want to reiterate that the Lords of Darkness is nothing to play around with. If you're here for revenge or for fun," he adds, glaring at Otto, "then I expect a resignation letter from you first thing tomorrow."

I swallow as the silence buzzes around me, and as Sterling's eyes don't leave mine, the hair on the back of my neck prickles.

"I assume I get no say in this," Alexander interjects.

"You can stay or you can die," Gideon says gruffly.

"Right," Alexander says, sighing. "Very well. I should let my father know."

Gideon nods. "We'll do it."

Alexander blanches. "My sister—"

"Doesn't need to know," Harlow finishes. "We can tell the King because he knows of us, but no one else needs to know. Is that understood?"

Alexander nods. "Understood."

We're dismissed a minute later, and as Alexander stays behind to get a tour of the house, I go upstairs with Lachlan, Otto, and Max.

When we get to the top, Lachlan scowls at me before walking to his bedroom. Otto and Max hang around—probably to ensure I don't go throw myself off my balcony.

"I'm fine," I say, sniffing.

"You're not," Max replies, running a hand behind his neck. He looks uncomfortable, but I realize it's because he's worried. *About me.* "Do you want to talk about it?"

I've known these guys for twenty-four hours, but there's something comforting about knowing they're worried about me. Today was a massive failure on my part, and I want to forget about it entirely.

"Or," Otto says, cocking his head. "We don't have to talk—"

I rush forward and kiss Otto, his surprise quickly replaced by a low groan.

I don't know why I do it—maybe because I'm fucked up in the head right now.

Or maybe because I want to do anything to rid myself of the guilt eating away at me.

It doesn't matter, because I'm not thinking about Quinn as Otto drags me into his bedroom, his brother following close behind us.

I hear the door click closed as Otto runs his hands down my sides, gripping the flesh at my hips as his mouth nips at my jaw, my neck, my collarbone.

"Such a fucking whore," he mumbles, and I moan at his insult.

I need this.

Max hooks his finger under the strap of my beaded dress, doing the same with the other side. I gasp when I feel his hardness against my arse, and I'm suddenly so, so hot.

My dress falls to the floor, and Otto takes a step back as he admires me.

"Look at you," he purrs, unbuckling his pants. "My perfect, little slut. And what's this?" he asks, eyeing the holster strapped to my thigh containing a knife.

"Are you seriously asking why a woman is choosing to arm herself while working for a deadly crime syndicate?"

"Very true," Otto murmurs. "Silly me," he adds, unstrapping it and letting it fall to the floor. "Now, what would you like me to do next?"

I whimper. I can't think straight, and I don't care how it happens. I need one thing, and I'm not in the mood to be teased or make any decisions.

"Please," I say, my voice hoarse. I hope I'm conveying how I don't have the brain power to decide anything right now.

"Get on the bed," Max murmurs, pushing me forward slightly.

I do as he says, kicking my heels off and climbing onto Otto's four poster bed so that I'm on my hands and knees.

"That's it," Max says, walking over and running a large, warm hand over my arse. "You'll make such a pretty, little spit roast."

"What?"

Otto gets onto the bed and climbs over to me on his knees, and I suddenly understand what he meant by a *spit roast*. He pulls his cock out and begins to stroke it.

"You've been teasing me all night," Otto says, blue-grey eyes boring into mine as he looks down at me. A piece of hair falls over his forehead, and in that moment, I understand why good genes make a difference. I know Max and Otto come from a long line of pure-bred royals, and the way his lips are pulled into a lopsided smile makes my stomach flip upside down. *God. How can someone be that beautiful?* "Open your mouth, darling."

I do as he says, and just as he presses his cock between my teeth, I feel Max tug me backward slightly and he teases the thick head of his shaft against my core. I can hear how wet I am already, and my cheeks heat as Max growls, running his hands over my arse in smooth, slow motions.

"Mmm," he says. "Needy, are we?"

"Fuck," Otto hisses as he slides into my mouth all the way until he's settled in the back of my throat. I don't mean to gag, but he's very well-endowed. "You want to be filled by the Thorn brothers tonight, little minx?"

I moan as Max's hips jerk forward, impaling me on his cock. My eyes roll back as his hands settle around my waist.

"Such a good fucking harlot," Max says. "Someone dies and all you want is our cocks."

Surprise and grief jolt through me. I start to pull off Otto's cock but his hand moves to the back of my head and he holds me in place.

"I don't think so," he mutters, thrusting deeply into my mouth until my body is heaving and gagging violently. "You need this just as much as we do."

Panic starts to swirl inside of me. I can't breathe, and Max continues to fuck me harder, pressing Otto's cock further into the back of my throat. It's hot and scary as fuck all at once, and my skin burns with panic.

I can't breathe—I can't—

Otto pulls out and chuckles as I sputter and cough. "What the fuck," I hiss, wiping my mouth with the back of my hand. I watch as Otto studies my face and smirks, and I realize that I'm smiling.

Smiling.

Some sick and sadistic part of me *liked* what he did.

Max grabs my hair and tugs me back so that my back arches unnaturally. "I'm sorry, but did you expect this to be sweet lovemaking? Did you want us to cuddle and comfort you?"

"Fuck you," I groan as he pounds into me relentlessly.

"You already are," Max muses, his voice low and deep.

"Open your mouth, Astern," Otto commands.

My lips pull to the side, and I arch a brow in defiance as his brother fucks me.

Otto grabs my jaw with one hand. "I don't want to ask you again," he threatens.

My mouth drops open and I glare at him as he slides against my tongue. The taste of his salty precum makes me moan, and his hand gently begins to brush my hair away from my face.

"I'm getting close," Otto murmurs.

Max grunts as he rolls his hips behind me, driving into me with a forceful and steady rhythm. One of his hands comes around to my clit, and I let out a low groan around Otto's shaft when Max begins to tease me between two fingers.

"Fuck," Max rasps. "Your cunt is so fucking tight, despite being such a whore." I close my eyes as pleasure surges through me at his words. "That's it. Your pussy doesn't want to let go of my cock when I call you a whore. Is that what you are? My whore?"

"Our whore," Otto responds, thrusting into my mouth. "There you go, darling. I'm going to come—"

His cock thickens, and it begins to throb against my tongue. I make sure I swallow with each pulse as hot jets of cum slide down my throat. He moans as his fingers fist my hair, holding his cock deep inside of my throat as he finishes.

He pulls out quickly as Max grabs my hips and flips me over. He hovers over me, holding himself up with thick, sculpted muscles that stretch his dress shirt in a way that makes me circle my hips slightly, waiting for him.

"So needy," he says, smirking.

Before he can fuck me again, he spreads my legs and lowers himself to my cunt, dipping his head as his tongue slides up my slick cleft.

"You taste so fucking good," Max says, making a slurping sound.

My back arches as he continues his ministrations, and I see Otto walk around to where his brother is feasting on me. Where Max is built and has more muscles, Otto is leaner. His arms are corded, but his body reminds me of a statue. Having both of them want to be with me...

"What does she taste like?" Otto asks.

"Why don't you find out for yourself?" Max asks as he flicks his tongue against my swollen bud.

Otto drops to his knees and crawls up next to his brother, taking one of my knees and moving it even further to the side.

"I suppose we can share, brother," he says, looking up at me through dark lashes.

Oh, fuck.

"Yes, please, please—" My voice is strained, and I know I'm begging, but I don't even care. My muscles are coiled tight, ready to release, and as Max uses his tongue to get me close, Otto dips his head and sniffs loudly.

"So fucking sweet," he growls. One of his fingers slides into my cunt, and then he dips his head down to my clit and begins to suck.

My hands fly to the duvet, gripping it tightly as the two of them work together. Max's tongue is firm and flat, whereas Otto uses the tip to tease me and uses his finger to massage my inner walls.

"Oh god," I whine, lifting my hips.

"Such a spoiled, little slut," Otto mutters. "Come for us, Astern."

"Oh, fuck—"

Max's tongue presses against my clit, laving it back and forth as Otto inserts another finger.

I shatter and explode, crying out as my body convulses. Max's hands hold me down as my body jumps, and I see Otto stroking himself as I come down from the high. I'm still panting as Max stands, pulling my hips to the edge of the bed and wrapping my legs around his waist.

"My turn," he growls.

His long, blond hair is pulled back into a low bun, but a piece comes out from behind his ear. His muscles strain against his clothes, and despite being more serious than Otto, there's something gentle and caring in his gaze.

And good god... his body could make women weep.

Otto stands behind his brother as he strokes himself. "Fuck, little minx. You're going to make me come twice tonight."

"Yes," I whisper.

Max lifts my hips with his large hands and thrusts into me. *Hard.* I scream as I see white, the feeling of being full of him so soon after that mind-blowing orgasm making me feel needier than I've ever felt.

"Harder," I whimper.

"Fuck yes," Max says. "I'm not going to last very long in your tight pussy."

"Come inside of me," I beg him.

He chuckles as his left hand hikes my leg higher against my chest so that he can go deeper.

"You'd like that, wouldn't you?" he asks.

I clench around his shaft, and he roars. "Fuck, Astern—"

He goes still and his face goes slack. His body jerks as hot spikes of cum spill into me, and I don't let go even when his mouth drops open. He drops his head back, his fingers squeezing my thighs as he comes for what feels like a full minute.

"Jesus Christ," he murmurs, pulling out of me.

Otto takes his place. "Let me paint that pretty, little cunt."

My mouth drops open at the same time his mouth does, and he groans. I watch in awe as thick jets of cum spill all over my core. When he finishes, he takes a step back as he catches his breath.

Then, he drops to his knees and feeds his seed into me with his index finger, mixing it with Max's.

"Such a gorgeous sight, don't you think?" he asks Max.

I cover my face with my hands as heat flashes through me. I'm still trying to catch my breath, and I see Otto high five his brother after they put their cocks away, and then Max is walking into the bathroom for a rag to clean me up.

Otto climbs back onto the bed and pulls me into his warm, large body. "Feel better now?"

"Yes. Very."

"Good," he murmurs, sighing contentedly.

Despite how rough he was with me, I can't help but sink against his body and feel comforted. The guilt from earlier is still present, but it's dulled now, and catching my breath with Otto behind me, running his fingers through my hair gently...

I have to admit, this is very nice.

Max comes back a second later with a wet cloth. "Spread your legs, little minx."

I do as I'm told, and he cleans me up—wiping his brother's cum off me.

After disposing of the cloth, he crawls into bed and pulls my front against him so that I'm sandwiched between the two of them.

"You should use the loo in a minute, but right now, I just want you to know that you're safe. That today wasn't your fault, and it could've happened to any of us. Is that understood?"

A tear slides down my cheek, and I don't wipe it away. "Okay."

A girl could get used to this, and a small part of me wants to continue whatever this is.

But once I make my move... I'm going to have to kill them, too.

CHAPTER 11

Alexander

I'm pacing the bedroom when there's a knock on the door. Much to my chagrin, the scary man with curly, dark hair walks in and closes the door behind him. I've been around a lot of vicious people in my life as a royal. The general public was ruthless and intent on weaseling their way into our private lives, but the man before me? He's dangerous in an entirely different way. There's something serpent-like about the way he moves, and I don't trust him.

"We haven't officially met," he says slowly, holding a hand out. I look down at it, wondering about the four gold bands around his ring finger. I don't say anything, though, and he continues. "I'm Alaric Cross."

"I'd introduce myself but I can assume you know who I am," I grumble, sitting down in one of the sitting chairs.

Alaric chuckles. "I do. Everyone in Britain and the world knows of Prince Alexander." He sighs and runs a hand through his hair, but he doesn't move to sit down, and it makes me uneasy. "I just spoke to the King. He's supportive of this new endeavor of yours. He thinks it'll let you earn some respect back."

I scoff. "My father *would* be proud that I've fallen in with a notorious crime syndicate as long as it reflects well on the royal family."

Alaric cocks his head. "Am I right in presuming that you don't want to be here?"

"Fuck no, I don't want to be here," I say quickly, rubbing my mouth with a shaking hand. "Imagine trying to mind your own business and then, quite literally, being in the wrong place at the wrong time."

"Or, the right place at the right time?" he asks, smirking.

"There's no situation in which I will want to be here," I tell him honestly. "Before you lot showed up, I was content nursing my wounds in private."

"How sad," Alaric muses, walking over to the back of my chair. I sit up straighter. "Letting the media and the general public decide your life for you."

I open and close my mouth. "No one *decided*," I snap. "Very private health information containing my DNA was leaked to the press. I am not related to the King. My mother had an affair. I am no more royal than you. The media had a field day, as I'm sure you and the rest of the world remembers," I finish, running a hand through my hair.

Alaric walks back around to stand in front of me. "Actually, one of my ancestors was King Henry III in the 1200s." When I don't respond, he sighs and takes a seat in the chair across from me. "My point is, the Lords always used to operate by noble blood. However, over the last year, we've decided that the Lords deserve to make a name for themselves, regardless of birthright or nobility status. It's a chance for anyone to make a name for themselves."

"Yes, for murdering people."

Alaric huffs a laugh. "We do more than kill people, you know."

I scowl down at the carpet, considering his words. He must know I'm mulling it over, because he doesn't speak for several seconds.

"Can I offer some advice?" he asks, leaning forward.

I shrug. "Go right ahead."

"Use this opportunity."

My brows furrow. "How so?"

"You're the laughing stock of the country, no?"

Frowning, I roll my eyes. "That's a little dramatic. It'll die down soon. The next royal scandal will take its place, and I will be forgotten. Which is exactly what I hoped and planned for."

Alaric stares at me, and it's as if he can see every one of my thoughts.

"But what if you weren't forgotten? What if you one day grew to be respected? *Revered?*"

I laugh. "And you can promise me that?"

He nods. "I can. Join the Lords officially and we'll make sure no one ever dictates the story of your life again. You can prove yourself and show the world who you actually are."

"It's all very tempting," I drawl, cracking my neck. "But it also sounds like a lot of work. And I don't like hard work."

At this, Alaric's smile turns snake-like. "I don't believe that. You were top of your class. You studied law and physics, and you got top marks in all of your classes at Uni. You play rugby, football, and you regularly compete in marathons. Are you actually trying to tell me that you're not used to working hard?"

I swallow and run a hand down my face. "You've got me pegged."

"Is that a yes?"

I glare at him. "I don't really have a choice, do I?"

Alaric stands up and claps me on the shoulder. "Smart man. Take tomorrow to get your affairs in order. I've sent for your things, and they should arrive later tonight."

I stand up and cross my arms. "So, that's it? What about my sister?" I ask, thinking of Sylvie, my half-sister. A true princess—with actual royal blood. Unlike me.

And what about...

I briefly close my eyes. No point in thinking about it.

"She may visit whenever she wants to, though you'll have to come up with a story to tell her because she can't know about us."

Us.

What the fuck would I tell her? That'd I'd suddenly become friends with a random assortment of Lords and now lived with them?

I feel weary just thinking about it.

I'd have to figure it out tomorrow.

"And if I decide not to follow through with this?" I ask.

Alaric's expression grows dark. "Don't be daft. You know exactly what will happen." I clench my jaw at the unfairness of it all. "Do you believe in fate, Alexander?" I don't answer, but Alaric just tilts his head. "I do. And I don't think tonight was a coincidence at all." He smiles. "Breakfast will be served in the dining room every morning. Lunch is your responsibility, and even though everyone is taking tomorrow to grieve, we will reconvene for dinner at six sharp."

I want to kick or punch something. I want to tell him to fuck off. I want to call my driver and tell him to take me back to Buckinghshire Palace, where the man I once called my father is letting me reside.

For now, at least.

But... then what? What if he decides to kick me out? Who in their right mind would want to be reminded of their late wife's transgressions?

Will I spend my life listlessly floating through the historic halls of the palace, drinking myself into oblivion?

Will I continue pretending I don't see the articles written about me or my mother?

Will Sylvie continue pitying me and allowing me to complain to her day in and day out as she attempts to move on with her life?

I'd only hold her back.

One day, she'd get married and have children, and I wouldn't be able to whinge to her about every injustice.

One day, I'd have to move on.

Being a Lord of Darkness could be the way I move on. It could be something for *me*. I don't exactly have a choice, but maybe being thrust into a thrilling and dangerous occupation is exactly what I need.

Though, if I had my way, I would've preferred to win the lottery.

The media could go fuck themselves—I wouldn't allow them to continue printing the bullshit about me, but especially about my mother. As a Lord, perhaps I could get back at them.

Now *that* sounds like fun.

Alaric is right. I've never shied away from a challenge, so why start now?

"Okay," I tell Alaric. "I'm in."

Alaric smiles. "See you tomorrow, Your Highness." He grabs the handle of the door, and I can't help but blurt the question I've been wondering about all evening.

"Your rings..." I swallow and point to his hand, and he looks down at the four thin, gold bands. "What do they mean?"

Alaric smirks. "They're wedding bands."

A shock rolls through me. "You mean..." I think back to earlier in the night.

"Harlow joined the Lords when she was eighteen. When she was twenty-two, we all decided to let the Lords die with us, and shortly after that, we conceived our daughter, Edith."

"So you're all... together?" I ask.

Alaric nods. "Five bodies, one mind. One soul." He takes another step through the door. "Get some sleep, and we'll talk more tomorrow. Someone will bring your things up shortly."

When the door clicks closed, I sit down on the bed and fall back, groaning.

What in the actual fuck have I gotten myself into?

CHAPTER 12

Astern

I wake up feeling disoriented, and when I look around, I realize that I'm in my own bedroom—which means Max or Otto must've carried me here after I'd fallen asleep. My whole body is sore, and when I turn over in bed, I notice the light pink light of the sky peeking through the slit in my curtains.

The events of yesterday slam back through me, and dread lances through me when I think of Quinn.

I didn't know her well, but I assumed I'd know her for the rest of my life. There was so much potential there, and that budding friendship got ripped out from under me like a rug.

Because of me.
Because I hadn't followed protocol.

Now that I've had a full night's sleep, I can see the error in my ways. I see how I was in the wrong, and the mistakes I made that led to her death.

It hurts, but I've also accepted it—and I accept whatever punishment Sterling Beauchamp has planned for me.

More than anything though, I want revenge.

I want to hurt the man that hurt her—and I want Citadel to burn to the ground for taking such a beautiful light from this world.

Grinding my jaw, I walk to the bathroom and quickly brush my teeth and wash my face. When I'm finished, my whole body is antsy with nerves and fury, mixing together to form an adrenaline-fueled urge to *move*.

Slipping into leggings and a tank top, I tie my sneakers and pop my knife into my bra before heading downstairs.

The house is eerily quiet, and I tiptoe the entire way to the front door.

Once I'm outside, my chest feels like it cracks in half as I let out a quick sob. I let myself feel the grief for one minute, and then I push it to the back of my mind.

Compartmentalize...

And then I'm off.

I run up the hill behind the house, taking the narrow trail all the way to the top. My chest burns and I'm gasping for air, but moving this way is cathartic. It always has been—at least since I was fifteen. *Feeling* how strong my body is, how it pushes up the hill to the University and then back down the pavement toward Blackwell Village. My heart beats quickly inside of my rib cage, and sweat trickles down my temple, down my neck, between my breasts. My lungs expand with every inhale, and I choke back sobs with every exhale. The pink sky fades into an orange, and then that fades into a light blue, and the air is thick with humidity.

Still, I run.

And with every step, the grief and the guilt lessens.

I go until I see people beginning to walk their dogs. Until the first train comes into the station. My legs ache as I zig zag across the entire village, circling it and repeating my path twice. My mouth is dry, and as I slowly jog up the street back to Thorn Manor, I feel better.

I'm too tired to feel anything but better.

I walk the path up to the house with my hands on my hips, attempting to catch my breath. I'm sure my face is beet red, and my shirt is sticking to me with sweat. Looking down at my watch, my eyes widen when I realize I just ran twelve miles.

More than double my normal distance.

Parched, I walk straight to the kitchen and gulp down a large glass of water. It's not until I set it down that I see Prince Alexander leaning against the counter, brows raised while he reads the Times.

In dark grey sweatpants and no shirt.

My eyes track down his lean body. I'm still panting from my run, and my vision vibrates slightly when my eyes track down to the band of his sweatpants, and how his abdomen is sculpted yet soft. Unlike Max, whose muscles could cut glass, Alexander's six-pack is soft, like it's just how his body is.

These fucking royals have the best genes.

"Morning," he says, smirking as he sets the Times down.

"Morning," I answer, filling my glass back up.

"Have a nice run?" he asks.

"I did, thank you."

"Kill anyone before breakfast?"

I choke on my water and he comes around to my back, patting it gently as I cough.

"I was only joking. No need to be so dramatic," he adds, giving me an easy smile.

"Very funny. I'm afraid murder isn't on the agenda today."

Alexander laughs. "Never say never."

"How are you feeling about it all?" I ask, leaning against the opposite counter and holding my water as I cool down.

He shrugs. "I've decided to stay, if only so I don't die."

I smile. He's funny—something I didn't expect. Despite having a crush on him as a teenager, I assumed he would be buttoned up and formal like the rest of the royal family. But he's carefree and fun. In a way, I think he'll make a nice addition to our order—even if he was never meant to be here.

"Well that's good. I'm glad you're staying," I tell him honestly.

His brows furrow and he looks like he wants to ask me a question. It takes him a few seconds to form the words.

"Can I ask you something?"

"Okay," I tell him, setting my empty glass down.

"Why did you want to join the Lords of Darkness?"

I think of how I can tell him the truth without outing myself. Because for some reason, I want to tell him the truth. So I decide on a half-truth. Or, I suppose it's the full-truth—just with some of the facts omitted.

"Ten years ago, my parents were killed," I start, careful about how I word things. "And I suppose I've been trying to figure out a way to run away from that grief ever since. To ensure something like that never happens again."

All of what I'm saying is the truth.

My parents were killed.

I've been running away from grief and into the arms of vengeance.

And it would never happen again—I'd never let the Lords forget what they did.

"I'm so sorry for your loss," he says earnestly. His voice is smooth and his concern is genuine.

It causes my throat to constrict because I suppose I'm not used to people being kind.

"Thank you," I say quietly.

"I assume this..." he trails off. "The five of us will become very close. So I hope you know that you can always talk to me."

My eyes water when I look up at him, and just as I'm about to respond, Lachlan walks into the kitchen.

He stops when he sees us, and I swipe at my eyes quickly. "Morning," he grumbles, walking to the refrigerator and pulling it open. When he closes it, he sips on a green juice beverage as his eyes flick between us. "Sorry, am I interrupting something?" His voice is hard, and when we make eye contact, it feels like everything inside of me burns up.

The two of them are such a juxtaposition. Lachlan is quiet and mysterious, motivated by his desire to be here. Despite what happened between us a couple of nights ago, he's been nothing but cold and indifferent toward me.

Alexander is... different. He's warm and friendly. He doesn't take himself too seriously.

"No," Alexander says. "I was only telling Astern that we're all supposed to get very close in the coming months and that she can talk to me about anything."

Lachlan's expression sours as he presses his lips together and looks at me.

"How kind," he says slowly.

"The same goes for you, of course," Alexander says, his voice a bit lower now that he's talking to Lachlan. I can imagine that Lachlan seems intimidating to any observer.

Lachlan is quiet as he reaches for a protein bar, and once he closes the pantry, he throws me one. I catch it without fail, and then he gestures to the door.

"I'm going on a run. See you later," he says, his eyes tracking over my face for a second too long before he leaves the kitchen.

"He's nice," Alexander says sarcastically.

I huff a laugh as I look down at the protein bar he tossed me. Even when he's being grumpy, he's still looking out for me.

"He's alright," I say, smiling. "See you later, Your Highness."

"Call me Alex," he says quickly, and then he stretches, both arms behind his head.

Jesus Christ.

My eyes catch on a faded, black tattoo on the inside of his right bicep. I'd missed it earlier, and when he sees me looking, he smirks.

"Is that a Black Sabbath tattoo?" I ask, grinning.

Alex blushes and shakes his head. "It was a stupid thing I did in my youth—"

I laugh. "You are not what I expected," I mutter.

"I hope that's a good thing," he responds, brows furrowed.

"It is."

I walk out of the kitchen without another word, still laughing that the formal Prince who stood rigidly at all of the state functions when I was growing up has a tattoo.

CHAPTER 13

Max

The day passes quickly. After a quiet breakfast with Astern, Otto, Lachlan, and Alex, Harlow comes over with thick binders full of information we're supposed to study.

"I've been compiling information for years—"

"Good lord. You could kill someone with this," Otto murmurs, holding the binder up. "Wait. Is that the point? Are these murder weapons?"

Harlow laughs. "I think you'll find anything can be a murder weapon. But no, it's just everything I've thought of writing down over the last five years."

"Because of your daughter?" Alex asks, and everyone goes quiet.

Edith had made an appearance earlier to show us all her collection of black feathers—something we all found to be endearing yet not surprising. She *is* the daughter of the Lords of Darkness, and I can't envision her playing with dolls and teddy bears.

Harlow shrugs. "Yes and no. It's true that after I got pregnant with Edith, I wanted to end the Lords. And we almost did a few times." She looks down at the floor. "This job isn't easy, but it's an honor. Does that make sense?"

Alex nods. "I suppose so."

"The world needs the Lords—or whatever you decide to call yourselves. I worry if we ceased to exist altogether that a lot of deplorable people would get away with doing a lot of heinous things. We've always existed as long as Britain was a nation. We're natural predators, and without us, pests would roam the country unchecked."

Everyone is quiet as we flip through the binder. It's color-coded and organized alphabetically. I hear Otto snicker as he mutters about how organized it is, and as Harlow leaves us to study until dinner, I look up at Astern.

Her brows are pulled together as she flicks through the pages. She looks up at me and smiles, a pink blush breaking out over her cheeks.

Oh, little minx... I'm going to have fun with you.

After a few hours of lounging and reading, we're summoned for dinner in the dining room. The old Lords and Lady join us, and it's a quiet, tense affair. Once everyone finishes their pudding, Sterling Beauchamp puts his fork down on his plate and turns to face Lachlan.

"We will resume training tomorrow," he says, eyes flitting between all of us. "Followed by your formal initiation ceremony."

"And what does that entail?" Alexander asks.

"Taking the brand," Alaric says.

Alexander's eyes go wide. "I'm sorry, did you say a *brand*? Like... for cattle?"

"Yes."

Alexander swallows and nods once before Alaric stands. The other Lords follow suit, and they bid farewell before leaving the five of us alone.

None of us moves as the front door closes.

"So, who's up for an orgy?" Otto asks.

Lachlan glares at him before walking away, heading upstairs. Alexander follows suit as he shakes his head in warning.

Astern stands up and shrugs. "I got my period this morning."

Little liar.

"You think I'm scared of a little blood, darling?" Otto asks, tugging her into him and kissing her.

She pulls away. "Not tonight. Goodnight," she tells us both before walking up the stairs.

"Was it something I said?" Otto says, pouting as he dramatically drops into a chair and leans back.

I chuckle. "Keep it in your pants," I tell him before going upstairs as well. "You're coming on a bit strong."

Otto sighs. "Fine. You're all no fun."

CHAPTER 14

Astern

I hardly sleep, and when I finally doze off, my dreams are riddled with nightmares about being covered in blood. I wake up just as the sun is beginning to rise again, so like yesterday, I change into running clothes and go for a long run. It's warmer today, and the run feels harder somehow—probably from lack of sleep—yet I still manage thirteen miles.

By the time I get back to the manor, I'm famished, exhausted, and grouchy. There's no one in the kitchen, so I make myself some toast, fruit, and coffee, eating until I'm satisfied. After washing my dishes and taking a quick shower, I head downstairs with my book until the others wake up.

I'm a few chapters in when Lachlan wanders down the stairs, rubbing his eyes. He stops walking when he sees me, and his face goes from neutral to on guard in an instant.

"Morning," I tell him, admiring the black sweatpants that are hanging off his hips, and the impressive appendage that can't be hidden by the flimsy material.

Stop looking at his willy, I tell myself.

"What are you reading?" he asks, sitting down on the chair opposite me.

"It's a mafia romance. She's a mafia princess and she just cut someone's balls off for touching her."

Lachlan huffs a laugh, and I smile. It's nice to see him not frowning.

"Taking notes?" he asks, arching a brow.

"It depends," I answer, pulling my legs underneath myself. "Personally, I'd go for the hands first. Slice them off and let him wallow in misery while I carve my name into his testicles before slowly sawing them off."

"Christ. Such a violent, little thing, aren't you?"

I smile sweetly. "Only if you're mean to me."

He hangs his head and rubs the back of his neck, leaning forward between his spread legs. His white t-shirt is thin, and I can see the outline of his tattoos stretching across his broad chest before snaking down both arms. I've always been a sucker for a man with tattoos—which is why I was so attracted to him that first night. There's something broken and beautiful about Lachlan Weir, and I want to slowly unwrap him, bit by bit. Like every other woman in the world, I want to save him.

Which is a dangerous thing to want considering our current occupation and how dangerous it is for all of us.

"Listen, I wanted to apologize," he says slowly. "For what I said in the bathroom the other night."

"Which part? The part where you told me you never wanted to see me again after the night we shared, or the part where you said you were going to find my weaknesses and exploit them, all for simply existing? Perhaps it was the veiled threat of *doing* something about me if I continued to tempt you—"

"Fuck, Astern. I'm trying to say that I'm sorry."

I stand up from where I'm sitting and walk over to him. He leans back and his eyes go wide when I put one knee on either side of his waist, straddling him. Reaching into my shirt, I pluck the switchblade from my bra and press it against his neck. He lets out a ragged breath as I narrow my eyes.

"If we're going to be working together, you need to be less of an arsehole to me," I murmur, hating how I can feel him getting hard underneath me.

"Do you always carry a knife?" he asks, his voice a low purr. "Because I must say, it's fucking hot."

I press the knife harder against his throat, drawing blood. "I do. And you would too if you were small and vulnerable, living on the streets by yourself."

He swallows, his flesh pressing against the blade further in the process. "You're not vulnerable, though, are you?" he says softly. "Just look at you."

I ignore the way his words send a maelstrom of want through me—how I'm tempted to rock against his erection or bend forward to press my lips against his.

God, he's fucking beautiful.

"How about that truce I asked for?" I say softly.

"Fine, we can have a truce."

"And what do you say in return?" I taunt, smirking. "Perhaps an apology of some sort for being such a twat?"

His lips twitch. "I'm sorry. For what I said and the way I acted. If we're going to be initiated tonight, there can't be any bad blood between us."

"I agree."

I remove the knife from his throat and smile, but before I can feel too confident, he lifts me up and flips me onto my back so that he's hovering over me.

"One thing, darling," he purrs, face inches from mine as one hand comes to my neck. He certainly likes to have his hand around my neck. "Don't ever hold a knife to my throat again, or I might really have to kill you."

"Bad memories?" I ask, arching my back slightly. "Life in prison wasn't everything you ever dreamt of?"

"Careful, Astern," he growls, the sound low and guttural. He grinds his shaft against my cleft, and despite wearing jeans, I can feel how hard he is—and how perfectly he slots himself against me.

I have to bite my lower lip to keep from groaning out loud. "Or what?"

"I meant it when I said this can't happen between us again. I agreed to a truce, not a shag."

"That's fine," I say firmly, trying not to show how disappointed his words make me. "Guess I'll just have to keep shagging Otto and Max."

The hand that's wrapped around my neck tightens. "Are you really?" he asks, his expression open for half a second. But then his grumpy demeanor falls back over his sharp cheekbones and dark scruff, concealing the fact that he's truly curious.

"Would it bother you if I said yes?" His cock twitches against my core, and I smirk.

"No. You're not mine to claim, Astern Hackbolt."

Fuck. Why do I want him to?

Before I can respond, he climbs off me and stands up. "I'm going to go make coffee."

I continue laying on the couch for several seconds until he's gone, and when I stand up, I realize the space between my legs is pulsing.

Don't do it, I think—but before I can second-guess myself, I'm climbing the stairs two at a time. I knock on Otto's door a few times, and he answers it squinting and shirtless.

"Astern? Is everything—"

I rush forward and kiss him, and without a second of hesitation, he growls and pulls me into his body.

"Well good fucking morning to me," he grumbles before kicking the door closed. "To what do I owe the pleasure?"

"Not what, but who," I mumble, pulling my jumper off and unzipping my jeans. "Lachlan is a tease."

Otto barks a laugh just as I toss my jeans off to the side. "Well, then I suppose we should be extra loud then." I open my mouth to reply, but Otto rushes forward and presses me against the door. "Come on, darling. Let's give the whole house a show."

I throw my head back as he hoists me up and pushes my knickers to the side. "God," I whimper, running my hand through his white blond hair.

"There's no God in this room, Astern."

Fuck.

He presses his cock against my center, and my mouth falls open when he pushes into me.

"Hold on, love," he mutters, filling me to the hilt before pulling out slowly.

"Harder," I gasp, one hand moving down to his arse in order to hold him closer.

"So bossy," he purrs, thrusting back into me as hard as he can. The door groans under the pressure, and Otto grins. "There we go."

He does it again—and again.

The door knocks against the hinges with each movement.

My body goes taut as he takes both hands and grips my arse, sliding my slick channel up and down his cock. The pressure is intense, and my eyes begin to roll back into my head when he roars, going still. It spurs on my own climax, and I roll my hips over his cock as my body starts convulsing. He's watching me with icy grey eyes, enraptured, and I'm panting when he pulls out and lowers me to the ground.

"Feel better?" he asks, smirking as he grabs a cloth to clean us both up.

"Very."

"He'll come around," Otto murmurs, walking over to me and gently wiping up the mess between my thighs. "Lachlan, I mean."

I swallow as he gets on his knees, his long tongue sliding up my thighs as he looks up at me, as his hands grip my thighs.

"I'm not so sure," I whisper.

"He will. Because he's one of us."

"Poor Alex," I tease. "All left out—"

"Oh, Alex will come around, too. Trust me on that."

I look down at Otto as he finishes cleaning me up and pulling my knickers back in place. When he stands, he bends down and kisses me on the forehead.

"If nothing else, you have us."

He wraps his arms around me, and I stay there for several seconds, just breathing in his masculine scent—something musky and slightly smelling of tobacco, even though I don't think he smokes.

"Why?" I ask quietly.

"Why what?"

"You've been nothing but kind to me. I guess I'm just trying to ascertain why you're saying all of these nice things when you hardly know me."

Otto sighs and holds me tighter, squeezing me in a way that fills me with warmth. "It makes me sad that you've lived a life where you have to question why someone is being kind, Astern. Maybe some of us are good people. You know, underneath the brutal murder machines we're about to become."

I smile. "I can't imagine you killing anyone."

"For you, I would."

"You hardly know me."

Otto pulls away and places both hands on either side of my face. His expression is serious, and so earnest that it makes my chest ache.

"You don't feel it? This thing between us?"

I open and close my mouth. "I mean, I suppose I do—"

"I've been in love a lot, little minx. I've had lovers for every month, every season. But you're different. I don't believe in love at first sight, so don't get any ideas," he teases, smirking. "But when I saw you on that dance floor for the first time... I knew immediately that you were going to be an important person in my life."

"I wish I could trust that easily," I tell him, feeling my eyes prick with tears. "I wish I could let myself feel *something* other than hate."

His thumb swipes at a stray tear, and he tilts his head before responding. "Nothing in life is guaranteed. I don't believe in fate. We have dangerous jobs, and there's a decent chance that another one of us will die before the end of training. I've never felt the point in hiding my feelings and skirting around how someone makes me feel when it could all be taken away tomorrow."

"Where have you been all my life?" I whisper.

He bops my nose with his finger. "I'm here now, darling. I'm here now."

CHAPTER 15

LACHLAN

I can't concentrate on the treadmill because Astern is in front of me doing all sorts of yoga poses. Finishing a five-mile run is difficult while sporting a semi, but I manage. I'm just about to hop off, wiping my face with my towel, when Alexander gets onto the treadmill next to me.

"Fancy a race?" he asks, smirking.

"Not really," I grumble.

"Aw, come on."

I turn my head to glare at him. "With all due respect, I'm done and I don't *fancy* a race," I tell him, trying to keep the sneer off my face.

While I was rotting away in a jail cell, this guy was eating off gilded platters and wearing diamond-encrusted crowns. The fact that he's now one of the Lords is irksome, but as long as he keeps to himself, I won't want to pummel him too much.

Alexander sighs and comes to the front of my treadmill, bracing himself on the front of it so that his face is close to mine. Up close, his eyes aren't just brown—there are flecks of gold in them.

Fuck.

Why am I speculating about the color of Prince Alexander's eyes?

"Listen, mate. I don't exactly want to be here, but that doesn't mean we can't be friends."

I swallow before clearing my throat. "You and I have nothing in common."

He arches a brow as he cocks his head. "You sure about that?"

"Trust me," I growl, leaning closer.

"You seem keen on assuming some things about me because of my upbringing. But at the end of the day, we're in this order together. Brethren. Isn't that what we are to each other now?"

"We can work together and do our jobs. That doesn't mean we're *mates*. Is that understood?"

Alexander smirks, and the sight makes me supremely uncomfortable in ways I don't dare acknowledge.

"You see them?" he asks, nudging his jaw in the direction of the Lords. Alaric, Theo, Gideon, and Sterling are all standing on the opposite side of the gym, against the wall, and Harlow is wrapped in Theo's arms. She reaches her left hand out, and Alaric takes it in his hand. "Alaric is wearing four wedding bands—"

"Why are you telling me this? I didn't apply to be a Lord so that I could be a part of some polyamorous fuck ring. I applied to be a Lord so that I could make the world a better place. Don't get me wrong; I have nothing against polyamory. It's just not my thing."

Alexander frowns. "Is that the only reason you joined? Because I don't believe for a second that you want to make the world a better place, Lachlan Weir."

Don't I?

I joined the order to rid the world of the kinds of people who kill innocents every day.

The kinds of people who kill people like *Abby*.

He pushes off my treadmill, and I get a whiff of cinnamon and sweat. I stare at his bare back as he walks away—as he plops down next to Astern. She smiles when he offers to help her stretch, and my semi from earlier gets harder when I watch them interact.

No.

I didn't come here to fuck.

I didn't come here to fantasize about watching two other people fucking.

I came here to forget *her* face.

The last time I got romantically involved with someone, they fucking *died*.

I hop off the treadmill and stalk to the exit. I know training isn't done, but I don't want to sit around and wait for one of the other Lords to lecture me again.

I came here to make friends—to form a union with other people—*not* to fuck around—and I hate that I feel so unsettled around every single one of them.

CHAPTER 16

Astern

After we all finish training, we're instructed to go back to the manor to change. Having never been initiated into a criminal order before, I have no idea what to wear. When I'm done drying my hair and putting on makeup, I settle on a simple black dress. It's formfitting but not skintight, and it comes down to my knees. The straps are thick, and the neckline is square. I grab a dark red cardigan and slip into my black Converse before walking downstairs to meet up with everyone else.

Otto and Max are the only two ready, and they're sitting on the couch while they wait for everyone else.

God, they look good.

Otto is in a classic white Oxford shirt, black trousers, and his white-blond hair is slicked back with a bit of product. He looks handsome and lethal.

Max is wearing tan trousers and a dark blue shirt. The sleeves are rolled up, and the first two buttons near his collar are unbuttoned. His thick, black glasses frame his beautiful face, and his wavy blond hair is secured in a neat bun.

They both turn to look at me when I walk into the reception room, and Otto gives me a lopsided smile that makes my heart stutter a bit.

"I'm not particularly excited to get branded like cattle," Otto starts, his voice low. "But if it means you wear dresses like *that*," he adds, whistling.

I smile. "It's an old dress."

"Don't be modest, darling," Max offers, walking over to me. "You are beautiful."

I arch a brow as he bends down and kisses me on both cheeks before pulling away. "The two of you flatter me. What do you want?"

"Us? Want something?" Otto says, feigning outrage. "You should know by now that the only thing we want is your legs spread wide and our tongues on your cunt."

Lachlan enters the room and clears his throat. I hide my laugh in a cough as he scowls between the two brothers. Otto saunters over to him. Lachlan stiffens but doesn't move away as Otto brushes the front of his waistcoat.

I use the uncomfortable silence that follows to take in Lachlan's outfit. Light grey trousers, a black Oxford, and a matching grey waistcoat. His hair is styled like Otto's—slightly slicked back, which only makes the neck tattoos seem more prominent, somehow.

"This is nice," Otto murmurs.

Lachlan clears his throat. "Thanks. You all, uh, look good too."

"If you want to fuck us again, all you have to do is ask."

I huff a laugh as Max rolls his eyes. "Lay off it, Ot."

"I'm just trying to understand," Otto drawls, stepping into Lachlan's personal space. "You're willing to have a foursome with us before we find out about Astern, but not after? Are you truly that bad at sharing?"

Lachlan lets out a low growl. "Careful, Otto."

Otto's face gets hard. "Or what? Because to me, it seems like you've lost. Can you guess who was inside of her earlier, making her scream—"

Lachlan rears his hand back and punches Otto in the jaw. Otto hardly stumbles—instead, he just holds his arms wide as he grins. Blood begins to dribble down his right nostril.

"That's your best? A beefy guy like you should really learn to put your weight behind your punches—"

Lachlan punches him again, and this time, Otto stumbles backward. When he looks up, he's baring his bloodied teeth at Lachlan.

"I'm going to tell you right now that you're going to need to share if you want to be a part of this order," Otto grumbles, his voice hard and menacing.

He's normally so friendly—and seeing him like this, all dark and slightly unhinged...

I hate how much I love seeing it.

"Otto," I warn him. "That's enough."

He looks over at me and nods once. Giving Lachlan one last wrathful glance, he sits down on the sofa next to me. I grab a tissue from my handbag and begin to dab at his face.

"Bloody idiot," I murmur.

He smiles, and his teeth are stained red. "Your idiot."

I look up at Lachlan as I clean Otto up, and he's shaking his hand out at his side, scowling at us.

"Get over here," I tell him sternly. "Let me make sure it's not broken."

He hesitates for a second before walking over and sitting down on my other side. "Sorry," he grumbles in Otto's direction.

"Fools," I mutter.

"I'll go get everyone some water so they can cool down," Max says, glaring at his brother and Lachlan.

He exits the reception room just as I turn around and pull Lachlan's hand onto my lap. His knuckles are split, so I gently dab the blood with a new tissue. I can feel his eyes on me the entire time, and Max returns with water for everyone—handing Otto and Lachlan their own glasses before handing one to me.

"For our resident nurse," he says, smiling.

I grin when I take it. "I wouldn't have to be the resident nurse if these two would stop their pissing contest."

"I reckon we could get Lachlan into bed with us if you dressed up as a sexy nurse," Otto offers.

Lachlan glares at him, and I stand up to put the used tissues in the bin. "Right. I'm going to put these in the rubbish, and then we'll head out. No more violence," I warn, pointing at Otto and then Lachlan.

"I like it when she's bossy," Otto mumbles when I walk into the kitchen.

※

An hour later, we're all headed to an abandoned barn with Alex at the wheel of a dark grey Range Rover. I assume it's his car considering there are no registration plates, which means it's owned by the royal family. I've snagged the passenger seat—something I won easily due to Otto and Lachlan grumbling 'thank yous' to me the entire way to the car.

It's quite funny to see the three men squeeze in the back seats of the car, though—and it's a short drive.

"So, is anyone going to tell me what I missed?" Alex asks as he turns onto a winding country road.

I can't help but admire his outfit—a black tux that fits him all too well. I can only assume he's used to having suits tailored to fit his body. His hair is combed back and his scruff is neat and trim.

"Lachlan fancies Astern, Astern fancies Otto, and Otto fancies Astern *and* Lachlan," Max muses.

"Hmm," Alex says, looking serious and contemplative. "I suppose I should mention that I fancy all of you."

An ache of pleasure fills me at his words, and I realize this is everything I've ever wanted.

"Fuck," Lachlan grumbles, looking out of the window.

"Oh, and I forgot to mention that Lachlan, Max, Astern, and I all shared an incredible night together before we knew who she was, so don't let Lachlan's grumpy demeanor fool you," Otto adds.

Alex laughs and looks over at me. "That explains a lot. What in god's name have I walked into?"

"Don't pretend like you're innocent," Otto adds, placing a hand on Alex's seat.

Alex doesn't say anything, but I don't miss the way his jaw feathers. "Wait..." I say slowly, trailing off.

"Smart girl," Otto praises, his hand coming to the back of my arm. "Prince

Alexander and I have quite the history. One night when we were both eighteen, he rocked my world and fucked me like I've never been fucked before—"

"Otto," Alex growls.

I can't suppress my squeak of laughter. "Oh my god, I need to know more."

"Well, we were both born royals, so we attended a lot of boring, stuffy state dinners together. Alexander here used to eye fuck me all throughout dinner and edge me until my cock was hard enough to slice through ice. We had fun for a bit, but then he got a girlfriend and stopped being fun."

"So, you're both bi?" Lachlan asks.

Otto scoffs. "I do not place labels on my sexuality. If anything, I'm pansexual. I am attracted to people, not genders."

"Same," Alex admits, his hands gripping the wheel.

"And you?" Lachlan asks Max.

"I'm more heteroflexible. I'm not attracted to men, but I don't mind sharing women with other men," Max answers.

Lachlan is quiet as he considers Max's answer. "Interesting," is all he says.

The rest of the drive is quiet, and as everyone exits the car, I tug on Alex's arm to pull him back.

"I didn't know about you and Otto," I tell him.

Alex shrugs. "It was a long time ago."

"So you don't still..." I trail off.

Alex presses his lips together before they twist to the side. "I didn't say that. This is certainly going to be an interesting six months."

I laugh. "That's an understatement."

"I have a feeling we all have to iron out our... kinks... a bit, yes?"

When he walks off, I see Lachlan watching us with a frown.

Oh yes. We most certainly have to iron out some kinks.

CHAPTER 17

Otto

The bridge of my nose is still throbbing when the five of us all walk into the old barn. The outside is brick, but it seems a bit more modernized inside. Tall, dark beams hold up the tall ceiling, but juxtaposed against the age of the beams are new windows, doors, and cement floors. There's a single chair in the middle, and the old Lords are sitting at a table in the corner of the barn.

"Welcome," Alaric says, standing up. "Any volunteers want to go first?"

"That's it?" Lachlan asks, still pumped up with testosterone from our *sexually charged* scuffle. "You're going to brand us and send us on our way? I was envisioning something a bit more... ritualistic."

Fucking idiot.

Alaric arches a brow. "Did you? Well then... I was going to save this for after, but I suppose we can get cracking now."

My skin pebbles as the other Lords stand up. Sterling walks over to us and holds out five manila-colored folders.

"I have five folders here. Each one contains a secret you've all kept from us—from your fellow Lords. I've been working nonstop for days to gather evidence."

Astern shifts uncomfortably next to me, and Sterling continues.

"I suppose we should go into the initiation with all of the skeletons in our closets bared for all to see, don't you think?" he asks, sounding almost excited as his eyes find Astern's. "Each of you has lied. Each of you walked through that door to be initiated harboring those very lies. One thing you should know is that the Lords of Darkness do *not* tolerate liars. We do not tolerate betrayal. The consequence is death."

Everyone is quiet, and Max looks at me over his shoulder.

Fuck.

What could Sterling possibly have on us? It certainly couldn't be the one thing we've kept between us since we were eighteen… could it?

Fuck, fuck, fuck.

"Because I'm a nice guy," Sterling starts, and Harlow snorts. "I'm going to give you each the chance to *confess*. Five minutes in that chair. If you don't—or if you confess the wrong thing—I will kill you."

Astern inhales sharply. "How do we know what information you have on us?" she asks, her voice steady.

"I suppose you'll just have to confess your deepest, *darkest* secret to be sure, Astern Hackbolt."

I hear her swallow as Sterling pulls one of the folders out. "Maximillian Thorn, you're first."

Max nods once before he walks to the chair. Being his younger brother, I know all of his nervous tells—like the way he wipes his palms on his thighs, or the way he curls his hands at his side. I'll bet when he turns around, he'll have little beads of sweat along his hairline.

Don't tell them, I think, silently begging him to read my mind.

"You have five minutes," Sterling tells him.

"I only need thirty seconds," he retorts, his voice hard.

No—

"Ten years ago, my brother and I killed someone. It was an accident, and we buried the body. We couldn't be charged with murder—despite being seventh in line, our eldest brother was due to get married the next day. It would've pulled all the attention away from the nuptials, and every single person in Denmark would've hated us for taking that away from them. A royal wedding is… the event of the century. Especially since he was next in line to be King. No one else knows, and the man we hit has been officially missing since that night."

Fuck.

I break out into a cold sweat as Sterling laughs. It's not a kind laugh, either. Walking up to Max, he holds a knife with a white handle to his throat.

"No," I whisper, my voice breaking.

What else *could Sterling possibly have on him?*

The only other thing is—

Impossible.

"Let this be the first lesson," Sterling growls. "Do not *ever* undermine the Lords of Darkness. And you just spilled the wrong secret." Pressing the knife to his windpipe, I take a step forward as Astern gasps.

"I'm sorry," Max hisses, looking at me with wide eyes.

"Say goodbye, Maximilian Thorn," Sterling grits out.

CHAPTER 18

ASTERN

"Fine! Fine!" Max shouts, breathing heavily. Each exhale presses against the knife, deepening the cut on his throat.

"Don't do it," Otto growls. "Don't tell them—"

"Are you serious?" I ask, heart pounding. "If he doesn't, he'll *die—*"

"Years ago, our father—who was the Crowned King of Denmark—fell down the stairs. No one else was home, but Otto and I heard it happen. We also heard the garbled cries as he choked on his own blood. We knew what was happening. We watched him bleed out from the crack in the back of his skull. When he'd been gone for over an hour, we called an ambulance and feigned ignorance."

Otto sighs heavily and runs his hand down over his face. "It's fucking *treason—*"

"Very good," Sterling says slowly, removing the knife. "Technically, I shouldn't give you another chance, but I'm feeling nice today."

"How very kind of you," I grit out, glaring at him.

"He beat us," Max adds, his voice sounding broken. Slumping over, his wild eyes find Otto's. "He molested... all of us. For so long, I wanted nothing more than for his death. We could've saved him that day, but we watched him bleed out. If anyone were to ever find out... we'd be sent to jail for much longer than an accidental homicide."

"Well done," Sterling says, wiping his bloodied knife on his thigh. "I spent a lot of time going over the autopsy report to figure that out, I'll have you know. He died of blood loss, and the alibi you both provided to the court was flimsy. You'll need to do much better than that when you become Lords. Now, who wants to go next?"

459

Holy fuck.

I go still, and as I sneak a peek at Alex, Otto, and Lachlan, they're all looking around cautiously. Lachlan's eyes keep darting toward the exit, like he's about to make a run for it.

What the hell is he hiding?

"I'll go," Otto says, walking over to where Max is sitting. "I have nothing to hide. Well, not anymore."

Max stands up and claps Otto on the shoulder. A look passes between them, and Otto nods once in confirmation.

When Otto sits down, Sterling watches him with crossed arms.

"I have an Only Fans..." he starts. "I record myself coming and call it ASMR porn. I have over a million followers." He looks up at Sterling, who only arches a brow. Sighing, Otto shakes his head. "Fine. I sometimes frequent a gloryhole and film as I suck off strangers."

"And?" Sterling says.

"Once a month, I invite a follower over for a fuck and record it."

"Very good," Sterling says, and Otto frowns up at him before standing.

"A million followers?" Lachlan asks incredulously.

"Don't worry, pretty boy. I'll give you my username so you can check out my co...ntent," he says slowly, winking at him.

I huff a laugh. "Why am I not surprised?"

"As his brother, I am *very much* not surprised. But how'd you manage to keep this a secret from me?"

Otto shrugs. "I don't tell you everything, brother."

"Glory holes? Really?" Alex asks, arms crossed. He looks half-intrigued, half-disgusted.

Otto smirks. "You're just jealous because you know I give a good jobby."

Alex scowls as Lachlan disguises a choked laugh behind a cough.

"Next?" Sterling asks.

I'm still grinning as Alex walks over to the chair. He sits down reluctantly, slowly looking up at the folder in Sterling's hands.

"I've no idea what you have in there. All of my secrets have been unearthed. My biggest secret was always that I used to shag Otto Thorn years ago. All of my dirty laundry is out there now. Whoever leaked my DNA test has it all—they hacked into every nook and cranny of my life."

Sterling makes a tsking sound. "Hmm. Maybe you're right. Or maybe there's something you've hidden deep down in the recesses of your mind... something you haven't thought about in years. Or, *someone*."

Alex stiffens at this.

"It took me a while to figure out if you knew—if you were even aware. After all, it wouldn't be fair if I had something in here that you didn't know about. I love a good game, but that's just unfair. However, after some expert reconnaissance, I discovered that you actually *visited* this person in the States two years ago, before you were ever deemed a bastard child."

Alex's face goes white. "There's no fucking way you could possibly know about that."

"Come on, Alexander," Otto chimes. "Tell us your deep, dark secret. I'm *so* curious."

"There's no way you know—absolutely *no one* knows. I made sure. I flew coach with a hat and sunglasses, for Christ's sake. Even my *sister* doesn't know."

"Well? Are you going to confess or do I have to start carving their initials into the skin of your neck?" Alex's eyes go wide. "Don't think I won't, *Your Highness*. I've done much worse for a lot less."

My eyes flick between Alex and Sterling, who walks over to the former, knife at the ready beside him. Alex's jaw feathers as Sterling holds the knife to his throat. They stare at each other for a few tense beats, but then Sterling presses the knife into his flesh.

"One more centimeter and you're dead," Sterling murmurs.

Alex is breathing heavily now, chest puffing out with every inhale. "Fuck you—"

"Come now, let's hear it. I'll give you three seconds," Sterling grits out, taking his other hand and holding it at the back of Alex's neck. *To make it easier to slit his throat.* I don't even realize my palms are sweating until I wipe them on my dress. "One, two, thr—"

"Fine. Fucking *fine*," Alex spits out. "I slept with a woman four years ago and she became pregnant. Somewhere in Connecticut is my son, who is three years old. I have money sent to them every month, but it's untraceable—how you found out is beyond me," he adds, face flushed with anger.

Sterling removes the knife from his throat, and blood dribbles down, staining the white collar of his shirt.

"That wasn't so hard, was it?"

Alex stands up and rushes forward, placing both hands around Sterling's throat. "How *the fuck* did you find out?"

Sterling sputters but doesn't move to remove Alex's hands. "You forget, *Prince*. We are—the Lords of—Darkness," he chokes. "Our order is—older than the crown, and we outrank you—in every—way. There is *nothing* we—don't know. Do you understand?"

Alex removes his hands and takes a step back, running a hand through his hair. He's breathing heavily as he walks back over to us, not meeting any of our eyes.

He has a son?
Otto has an Only Fans?
And Max watched his abusive father—the King of Denmark—die...

My hands begin to tremble as Sterling cracks his neck and looks over at Lachlan and me.

"I'll go," Lachlan murmurs, brushing past my shoulder and walking over to the chair.

"Saving the best for last, I see," Sterling grits out, eyes twinkling with rage as Lachlan sits down. "Very well. Let's hear your confession, Lachlan Weir."

Unlike the others, Lachlan sits up straight and glowers at Sterling. The other Lords are observing from the opposite wall, and I notice Harlow holding hands with Theo. For a second, I let myself envision *that* life—being here, being with Otto, Max, Lachlan, and Alex—in *that* way.

But then I remember, I'm going to die today.

Because there's no way in *hell* they're ever going to find out about me and my past life.

CHAPTER 19

Alex

I'm still shaking when I rejoin Astern, Otto, and Max. I don't know Lachlan well but I admire how composed he looks. It's almost like he's completely unfazed by all of this, but I suppose when you spend a decade in prison, nothing bothers you anymore. I take a few steadying breaths as Sterling taps the manila folder in his hand.

"Twelve years ago, when I was sixteen, I was dating my foster sister," Lachlan begins. "We were both assigned to this family in Essex, and we lived there for four years before..." He looks down. "Anyway, this particular family had several children already. Abby was only a few months younger than me, so we sort of grew up together. Our foster brother, Jack, was wrapped up in drugs and alcohol. He'd steal from our foster parents all the time, and he was often high or drunk. He'd been kicked out of schools and he had no support... our foster parents certainly didn't give a rat's arse," he adds, almost growling.

"Anyway, Jack started sneaking into Abby's room. It went on for a couple of years, and since he was only a year older than us, he still lived at home. She'd freak out, we'd tell our foster parents, rinse and repeat. He never actually..." Lachlan trails off, brushing his nose. "He tried, but I started sleeping in Abby's room. We were already dating at that point. It felt... endless. We felt completely alone—our anger at the system and our parents... at Jack... we wanted out."

"One night, we decided to leave, but Jack overheard our plan and outed us to our foster parents. They threatened to separate Abby and me—to put me in another home. So that night, Abby and I followed Jack to his drug deal with the intent to record it and send it to the police. We wanted revenge, and he felt like the only person standing in our way. But things went awry, and Abby got stabbed. She d—she died in my arms," Lachlan finishes, his voice hoarse.

"Holy shit," Astern whispers from next to me.

I study the man sitting in the chair—the way his energy is so big, the way he seems so strong—and yet, there's a reason. My chest aches when I think of what he said in the gym.

You and I have nothing in common.

He grew up in foster homes, and I grew up a Prince.

I wish I could hug him—I wish I could tell him that while I don't understand, I'm sorry for everything he went through.

"Anyway, the ambulance was on their way, and I ended up beating the shit out of Jack. He died right next to Abby, his face smashed in. And it felt... *good*," Lachlan finishes. "I'm fucking glad he's dead. I only regret that Abby..." He swallows, his throat clicking as he looks down. "So, that's why I went to prison. It was supposed to be a life imprisonment, but they let me out because of good behavior. I went back when I violated parole last year for contacting my foster parents. Apparently, I violated the terms of my parole by doing that."

"Thank you," Sterling says, nodding once.

Lachlan stands and swipes at his nose, walking to his spot next to Max.

"Shall we?" Sterling asks, looking up at Astern with his scary, reptilian-green eyes.

Astern huffs a laugh. "You expect me to confess my deepest, darkest secret?" She walks over to Sterling and stops right in front of him. "I think not."

Holy fuck, she's a bloody idiot for defying a Lord like that.

Sterling cocks his head as he considers her. "You think you're tough? You think you'll die with respect and integrity? You think your secret will stay a secret as your body cools on the concrete beneath your feet?" he grits out cruelly.

Astern's chest rises and falls, but she doesn't back down.

In one swift movement, she does some kind of self-defense maneuver, kneeing Sterling in the balls, using her elbow to knock his chin back, and then she swipes the knife from his left hand.

I step forward ready to help her as Sterling growls and overtakes her. The folders and the papers inside scatter to the ground, and all the guys and I walk over to break up the fight.

She's feisty, indeed.

She grunts as Sterling pins her arms behind her back. "Bold move, Ms. Hackbolt."

"Come on, Astern," Lachlan says under his breath as we reach them. Her hair is messy, hanging in front of her face as she tugs and tries to pull out of Sterling's grip. "We all had to confess."

Otto kneels down and starts to collect the papers, and I quickly glance down at him. We haven't had a chance to talk about anything that happened between us all those years ago, and seeing him here, like this...

I swallow.

"You realize I could kill you for attempting to disarm me," Sterling tells her.

"Also, do you truly think any of *them* would allow you to get near me?" he asks, nodding to the old Lords, who are watching from a few feet away. Harlow, especially, looks ready to pummel Astern.

"Fuck you," Astern hisses, her voice breaking on the last word.

Sterling pushes her down to her knees. "I changed my mind. For your insolence, I'm going to have one of your *new friends* kill you." Sterling snaps his gaze to me, and then he holds a hand out. "Take it," he commands, breathing heavily. "You'll need to learn how to do this anyway."

I narrow my eyes as I look between him and Astern. "Are you serious?"

Sterling cracks his neck as he takes a step forward. "Dead serious. If you fail, I will have to kill you, too. The Lords of Darkness cannot have any weak spots."

Interestingly, Harlow covers a cough with her hand that sounds a lot like *hypocrite,* and when my eyes flick to the other Lords, they almost seem proud of the fact that I refuse to do this.

Like they're proud of the fact that we want to protect each other.

"If you won't do it, I'm sure one of the others would happily take your place. I'm not fucking around."

My skin pebbles as I look between him and the old Lords.

I don't think he's serious—I *know* he is.

Just as I step forward to tell him to fuck himself, Otto begins speaking.

"Who is Charlotte Banks?"

When I look over at him, he's looking down at one of the papers he collected from the ground.

Charlotte Banks? Wasn't she the posh girl from Berkshire who died in a house fire? It's all anyone talked about for weeks—how tragic it was, how charitable the family was. I'd given a speech on fire safety about it—it was one of my first public speeches at the ripe age of eighteen. I vaguely recall a picture of a small brunette girl standing in front of her parents...

My eyes flick to Astern, and she's deathly white.

Suddenly, it clicks into place.

"You're Charlotte Banks," I murmur.

CHAPTER 20

Astern

I can't breathe.
 I can't do *anything* but panic.
 He knows.
 He *knows*.
 I let my gaze wander over to Alaric, and his dark eyes regard me with interest. Harlow whispers something, and he nods. Theo and Gideon shift uncomfortably, and when I look back at Sterling, he's smirking.
 He's... *not mad.*
 "Let me repeat what I said earlier. We are the Lords of Darkness, and there is nothing we don't know. Did you believe you survived a lethal injection, Ms. Hackbolt? Nice play on your name, by the way. Charlotte Banks = Astern Hackbolt. It's a simplistic, amateur anagram and it was all too easy to solve. If you're going to be in this order, you'll need to do better next time."
 I stiffen. My heart pounds against my ribs, and that whole godawful night comes roaring back to the forefront of my mind.
 The blood.
 The bodies.
 The *terror*.
 "No. I did not inject you with a lethal dose that night, *Charlotte*. You woke up exactly when you were meant to, and I've been waiting for you to find us for a decade."
 "Can *someone* explain what the fuck is happening and who Charlotte Banks is?" Otto asks.
 "Go ahead," Sterling says. "Tell them. Or I will."

My thoughts are scrambled, and I realize that I've been crying. "I c—can't—"

Otto steps forward, and Sterling lets me go. The next thing I know, Otto is wrapping his arms around me.

"You can tell us. The whole point of this is to be honest with each other."

"It's better than someone drugging you and forcing you to take a brand," Harlow interjects. I pull away from Sterling and watch her as she inspects her nails. "Trust me, that wasn't fun. They did much worse, too. My point is, this is not for the faint of heart. We've been trying to tell you all that for days. I tried to kill them with poisonous brownies. They locked me in a room with my rapist. Yes, it sounds horrible, but now? I can't imagine my life without them. *That* is the bond we're hoping you all form."

Otto's hands come to my arms, and he squeezes them. "She's right. Tell us, little minx."

"What did you mean earlier?" I ask Sterling. "You said you didn't give me a lethal dose. That you've been waiting for me," I grit out, fists curling.

Sterling crosses his arms. "I gave you a fraction of the lethal dose—just enough to knock you out for a few minutes. I've never liked killing innocents—and even when it's a necessity, I always try and give them another way out, even if I can't say it outright. I saw something in you that night. You are—and still are—a fighter. It would've been a shame to snuff that out."

"And... what? You *wanted* me to be homeless? To struggle for food and money? To live my life as not only orphaned, but *alone*?"

"I hoped you'd try and find me. I hoped you'd carry that spark with you, Lottie."

Lottie.

No one has called me that in... *a decade.*

"When you walked in during the first interview, I knew you looked familiar, but I couldn't place it. It wasn't until that first day in class that it all clicked into place."

Your hair color... It's not very often that you see a twenty-five year old woman with grey hair. Is it natural?

He knew. Back then, and now.

There's no point in hiding it.

No point in running.

They've got me just where they want me.

"Ten years ago, I woke up because my parents were yelling," I start. "I was used to them arguing, but never to this extent. I ran to their room and that's when I saw them get brutally murdered with my own eyes. I'll nev—never—forget their screams. They killed my housekeeper and my house manager. I ran over to my mum and cradled her head against my chest, but the rest is foggy. I must have gone into some kind of trance because I blocked the first part of that night out for years."

I continue, voice wobbly. "When I came to, there was blood all over my hands and pajamas. Do you know how terrifying it was to see all that blood and not know where it came from?" I ask, a sob cleaving from deep inside my chest.

467

"I made it back to my parents' bedroom and had to relive everything again, but my grief was short-lived. The four guys found me."

I look at Alaric pointedly.

"I tried to fight back, but one of them was able to inject me with something and another one carried me down the stairs," I add, glancing at Sterling. "The house was on fire by this point, so I ran outside. I watched it all unfold from the forest behind my house, and I realized who was behind my parents' death. I'd heard them talking about the Lords. I'm not sure what my father was involved in, but I'd heard Alaric's name a few times. I knew I had to disappear."

"I always wondered what happened to you," Sterling murmurs, looking... impressed. "So, what happened next?"

I bark out a sarcastic laugh. "I cut my hair off and I ran. I stole and begged and—" I choke back another sob. "I was able to find a place to stay for a couple of weeks to get my feet on the ground. The man who ran the hostel was a pig, but he didn't ask for money. I saved enough to pay for a fake ID, which said I was eighteen. I made up a whole backstory as to why I never finished school, but no one asked too many questions. I took my GCSE's early and a year and a half later, I got a full scholarship to a University."

"What did he do?" Max asks. "You said the man who ran the hostel didn't want money. So what did he want?"

I look him in the eyes as I answer. "I let him touch me. Thirty minutes every night. He never made me do anything—and he stayed above my knickers. It was only for a couple of years."

"Fuck," Max hisses, running a hand over his face.

"What's his name?" Lachlan asks.

I stand up straighter and lie through my teeth. I don't have the energy for *more* revenge, so if they assume he's not around, it's better for everyone.

"He's dead now. But thanks for pretending to care."

His brows draw together in an agonized expression for half a second, and then it quickly disappears. "I do care," he says slowly. "We all care."

"That's some fucked up shit," Otto adds. "Killing her parents and leaving her to be mauled by a pedophile for two years without doing *anything*," he adds, glaring at Sterling.

"This job isn't fair. Most of the time, you're turning children into orphans or murdering someone's father. Someone's husband. Someone's *son*," Sterling growls. "I saved her life that night. I saw the fight behind her eyes—"

"What did they do? My parents, I mean?" I ask, interrupting Sterling.

He sighs before looking down at the ground. "They were bad people, Astern—"

"I didn't ask you about their character. I asked you *what they did*," I hiss.

"They knowingly funded a human trafficking ring. Your father was in financial ruin by the time we got to him, but before he pissed his money away, he donated *millions* of pounds to places aimed at trafficking. He was one of over a hundred. Your family was not special, Astern. They were one stop on a very large map of criminals who exploited people for monetary gain. I won't apologize for what we did, but I will say that I'm sorry about what happened to you."

His words are genuine, and when he looks back up at me, I swear his eyes are a bit glassy.

"You were right. I ended up staying alive somehow. I ended up graduating with top marks and securing a job as a professional hacker."

"Why did you apply if you knew they killed your parents?" Alex asks.

Fuck.

It's the one question I was hoping no one would ask, but of course, why wouldn't they?

"Revenge," I answer.

"And do you still want revenge?" Harlow asks, stepping closer. "Because if you do, let me save you the trouble of thinking you can defeat this order. You can't. You will be screaming into an empty void if you try. So you can either lay down your life for the Lords of Darkness, or you can lay down your life as a sacrifice—which means we'll kill you without a moment's notice. Your choice," she adds casually, giving me a monstrous smile.

A cool breeze runs through the barn, and goosebumps erupt along my skin. I realize with a start that Harlow purposefully presents herself as unassuming—non-threatening. But that's twice now that she's reprimanded me. Twice now that she's been scary as fuck when talking to me.

She walks up to Sterling and places a hand on his shoulder. "I should also mention that if you *ever* try to disarm or harm any of us again, I won't hesitate to slit your throat."

Swallowing, I look between her and the other Lords. They're watching me with darkened expressions—like they're unsure if I'm going to hurt them or back down.

Hurt them...

Or back down.

You can either lay down your life for the Lords of Darkness, or you can lay down your life as a sacrifice.

"I never actually considered staying," I say quietly. "I don't even know if I'd be a good Lady. I mean, look what happened to Quinn—"

"Then don't be a Lady. Pick another name," Harlow says, her voice hard.

I look back at the guys—at Otto's concerned expression. At Max's tense jaw. At Lachlan's brooding scowl. At Alex's furrowed brows.

I couldn't hurt them even if I wanted to. I couldn't hurt any of them—not anymore.

Which leaves me with one choice.

"I'll stay."

CHAPTER 21

Max

There's a murmuring of voices but I'm not paying attention. A large trunk is dragged across the concrete, and I vaguely register someone starting a fire in the corner fireplace. Metal clanking sounds through the open barn, and my eyes refuse to stray from Astern.

She was just a girl.
She had no choice, no power, no way to fight back.
Just like us...

Something about her called to me that first night in the bar. There was something... enigmatic about her—like her battles matched our own. I hadn't known at the time, but I could tell by the way she acted around us. Sure, I was attracted to her, but I also saw the depth in her expression.

Now I know why.

And I sure as fuck couldn't let her go now.

"Have you chosen a name?" Alaric asks Lachlan.

"A name?"

"For the order. You are free to choose a new name or continue using the moniker of Lords and Lady of Darkness. It's entirely up to you. The function of this order will not change, so it doesn't matter what you call yourselves."

"I feel like it'd be a missed opportunity not to call ourselves the Princes," Otto interjects. "Seeing as there are now three princes in the order."

"'Princes of Darkness' doesn't exactly have the same ring to it," I add, scowling.

"Princes of Gluttony. Princes of Lust," Otto asks, looking at Astern. "Princes of Wrath—"

"Princes of Sin," Astern says quietly. "It encompasses all of the seven sins. That's what you were going for, right?" she asks Otto. "And I can be a Princess of Sin." Her eyes are heavy as she looks between all of us. "I'm sure as fuck not going to heaven, so we may as well burn together in hell."

No one speaks for several seconds, and the sound of Astern swallowing is deafening.

"Very well," Alaric says. "You'll be branded as the Princes of Sin tonight," he says, looking between us.

"Any volunteers to go first?" Theo Wolf asks from next to the fireplace. He's holding a bright red branding iron, and he's watching all of us with a large smile.

I don't hesitate to answer. "I will."

Another deafening silence works through the barn, and I sit down in the solo chair as Theo walks over, pulling my shirt over my head.

"And where are we placing it?" he asks, cocking his head.

In another lifetime, he could've been our older brother. His white-blond hair reminds me of Otto, and he seems to have the same sort of playfulness about him. Tonight, he's wearing a white Oxford and his blond hair loose and wavy around his ears. Plus, he's a computer nerd like me. Of the five of the Lords, he's the one I'm most interested in learning from.

"Left arm," I grit out. "It's not my dominant one, so I should be fine."

"You've thought about this," he muses, standing at my left side. The iron isn't close, but I can feel the heat radiating off it. "Last chance, Mr. Thorn."

I stay quiet, and he takes that as my affirmation. The wand slowly drifts closer, and *fuck* it's already so hot—

I hiss in pain, and my body jerks slightly when it makes contact with my skin. A warbled scream echoes through the barn, and I have to squeeze my eyes shut to defer the pain somewhere else, *anywhere else*—

"All done," Theo says, kneeling next to me and using some kind of antibacterial wipe to dab at the burn.

I'm panting and sweating as Gideon walks over with some gauze and bandages. I look up and find Astern watching me with a concerned expression, and I don't look away as Gideon wraps the brand up and pats me on the shoulder.

"Good boy," he says, smirking.

I glower at him as I stand up and walk over to where my brother is standing with Astern. I nod once at Otto, telling him that I'm fine without communicating. Astern's hand comes to my neck.

"You okay?"

I give her a tight smile because my whole arm feels like it's on fire. "I'm fine, little minx."

Otto volunteers next, and I feel a bit woozy as my brother sits stoically on the chair, as if he's getting a fucking tattoo. He chooses a spot on his right shoulder blade.

Astern goes next, and she hesitates about where to put it. "Where did you put yours?" she asks Harlow.

Harlow removes her suit jacket, revealing a sparkly camisole. She pulls the side down slightly, showing off the area on the side of her ribs.

"I'll get mine there, too," Astern says resolutely. She pulls the strap of her dress down, and as Theo sears her with the brand, she grits her teeth and screams through them.

"Fuck!"

"All done, princess," he says, chuckling.

She glares at him as Gideon bandages her up.

"Next?" Alaric orders.

"Cattle, indeed," Otto murmurs to me. "They might as well have an assembly line."

"Very funny, Mr. Thorn," Alaric growls.

Lachlan goes next and hardly flinches as they brand the middle of his back. When he's finished, he just glares at everyone and resumes his position in the back of our group.

"I suppose that means it's my turn," Alex says. He lets out a long sigh. "And I suppose there's no chance I can still back out and plead bad luck?"

Theo spins the branding iron and chuckles, but it's not kind in any way. "Not a chance."

Alex cries out when he gets his brand on the underside of his right arm, but he takes it well. They clean and bandage him up.

"Bring them in," Alaric tells Sterling, who nods once.

"Bring who in?" I ask, following Alaric's gaze to the door.

"Your first kill."

CHAPTER 22

Astern

My body feels heavy, lagged down with adrenaline that's come and gone. The burning at my side is starting to throb. All I want to do is go back to the manor and go to sleep, but when Alaric drags a bound and gagged man to the center of the barn, none of us says anything. Dread fills me, causing my heart to race—like it knows not to relax. Not yet, anyway.

And I just took the mark, so not *ever*.

My life will never be the same again.

The weight of what happened tonight causes my hands to start shaking, and as the man is forced to his knees before us, Alaric removes the bag from his head, revealing a young man. He looks... familiar.

"The Lords of Darkness has two rules for initiation. One is taking the brand—and the other is making your first kill," he adds, holding a small knife with a white handle out to Alex. "Last in, first up—it's only fair. Go ahead, *Your Highness*."

My chest tightens when I see Alex's mouth drop open. "Me?"

Alaric nods.

Alex stares at the knife in Alaric's hand for a few seconds before taking the knife. "How do I..." He swallows audibly. "I've never..."

My legs move to step closer to him, but I don't know why. I'm helpless, and completely unable to help him, despite wanting to.

"I'm sure you can figure that out yourself," Alaric tells Alex.

"And if I can't?" he asks.

Alaric tilts his head in warning and shrugs.

The message is loud and clear: kill him or die.

Alex steps closer to the man, who is thrashing. "Who is he?" he asks.

"A member of Citadel. Theo was able to track him down after the ball earlier this week. He was the one who killed Quinn."

The room starts to spin, and my eyes widen as I assess the man. He had brown hair, dark eyes that night... the man before us has blond hair and blueish eyes. *A disguise,* I realize.

I vaguely recall the image of him that we'd studied. His straight nose. His pronounced brow bone. His cleft chin. Those were things we were told to track, because hair and eyes were the easiest things to change.

Of course.

"Quinn. The woman I replaced," he states.

"Yes," I whisper.

"Very well," he says, inhaling deeply and muttering something to himself. "Fuck, forgive me father—"

He lunges forward and plunges the knife in the man's neck. I jump back when the man yells, thrashing wildly. Alex holds him down, pressing the knife deeper into his neck where blood spurts out.

The man slumps forward a few seconds later—

There's *so* much blood... holy *fuck*...

Alex lets out a garbled sob as the knife clatters to the ground. He drops to his knees and places his hands over his face as he cries. It's the most gut-wrenching sound, and my throat clogs as I watch him.

This isn't right—it isn't *fair*.

The four of us all signed up for this, but Alex didn't.

I walk over to him and drop down next to him, placing a hand on his back. "Hey," I murmur.

He turns and pulls me into him, and I don't even care that I scrape my knees on the concrete, or that I know there's blood in my hair now...

I close my eyes and let Alex cry as he holds me.

"I suggest you take your fellow Prince home. Tomorrow, there will be another kill, but I think that's enough for tonight," Sterling says to the five of us.

I look up at him, and something passes over his expression.

Understanding.

Sympathy.

Respect.

I help Alex up, and Lachlan leads us to the door. I realize with a start that before tonight, we were just training. Now, we're the official Princes of Sin—and that places a clear divide between us and the old Lords.

They stay behind in the barn to clean up, but soon, one of us will have to do that job. One of us—or all of us—will have to track these people down.

Torture, kill, rinse, repeat.

The adrenaline from earlier races through me, but I tamp it down as Alex clings to me. He's not crying anymore, but as I sit next to him on the short car ride back to the manor, he doesn't let go of my hand.

And honestly, I'm not sure I want him to.

These four men are all I have now, and the heavy air around us tells me that we all know it. We're all very aware of what our futures hold, but if nothing else, we have each other.

Lachlan says goodnight, but Otto and Max follow us up to Alex's room. He's almost despondent, and my stomach drops when I wave a hand in front of him and he doesn't react.

"Can one of you run a bath?" I ask the brothers.

"On it," Otto says.

Max helps me undress Alex, careful to mind the bandage on his arm. He doesn't fight us—he only murmurs a low *thank you*. My heart cracks in half when I see him look down at his bloodied hand—when I see how that hand trembles.

Though our lives were so different, I can't imagine that he ever envisioned having to murder someone in cold blood with a rusty knife.

Max and I help Alex into the bath. I keep his boxers on, and we slowly help lower him into the warm water smelling like lavender.

"You can go," I tell them. "Thank you for your help."

Otto hesitates near the side of the bathtub. His brows are knit together, and he begins to pace around the large bathroom.

"I'd like to stay, if that's okay," he says softly. He looks at Max, who nods once.

"Very well."

I wash Alex off, lathering shampoo into his hair and making sure to drain the bath once when it turns pink. When the water is clear and fresh, he turns to look at me, face wet and water clinging to his dark lashes. His expression is unsure—and it strikes me again just how handsome he is.

He sighs, eyes lowering slightly as he looks at me. "I realize I've been a massive baby, but I can't sleep alone tonight—"

"You don't have to," I say weakly. My hand shakes as I run it over the back of his neck. "Not anymore."

Max is leaning against the bathroom counter, watching him—watching *us*. I see him nod.

"You have all of us," Otto adds, kneeling on the other side of the bathtub.

Alex looks at him—truly *looks* at him—for the first time. My eyes flick between them, sensing something heated between the two Princes.

I shift my weight when I think of them together, squirming to get away from the throbbing weight that settles between my thighs. I shouldn't be thinking things like that after what Alex had to do.

After what we *all* had to endure tonight.

The area where Theo branded me throbs, as if it's reminding me of it all over again.

Alex reaches out for my hand, holding it behind his neck. "That feels nice," he says.

I shift higher and lean forward a bit, using both hands to slowly start massaging his upper back. He groans as his eyes flutter closed, and his skin is *so* warm—

Suddenly, his eyes snap open and he shuffles and leans his head back so that it's hanging over the back of the bathtub. The bump in his throat is pronounced and he closes his eyes as I continue massaging the front of his shoulders. The sounds he's making are... X-rated.

I squirm again, moving from knee to knee in order to dispel the tension, but as I knead his firm chest, I can't help but imagine joining him in the bath—

"You're looking a little dirty too, Astern," Otto says from behind me.

I look back at him and glare, and when I look back at Alex, he's watching me with darkened eyes.

"There's enough room for you," he says slowly.

His upside down face is open and interested, and as his tongue darts out to lick his lower lip, everything starts to pulse.

"If that's what you want," I answer.

He sits up and looks at me over his shoulder. "It's what I want."

I inhale sharply as Otto comes behind me. One of his hands hooks underneath the strap of my dress, and I'm suddenly *so* hot.

"Let me help you out of your dress, darling," he murmurs, helping me to a standing position.

When I turn to face him, I feel Max come behind me and hold my hair away from my shoulder as Otto works my dress down from the front. He's careful not to touch the sensitive area on my right side from the brand, and when my dress pools on the floor, I step out of it.

I take a step toward the bath, and Max's hand swipes at the back of my bra. In half a second, he has it unhooked.

"Whoops," he says, a hint of humor in his voice.

I look down at Alex, and he's watching me with a lopsided smile, so with a push of bravery, I remove my bra and let it fall to the ground. Alex's eyes flick over my chest hungrily as Otto helps me into the warm bath.

Spreading his legs, I go to sit down between them, and when I gently set myself down, he reaches out and pulls me closer—until I can feel his hard length against my back.

Lord have mercy.

I quickly close my eyes as Otto and Max drop to their knees, ready to bathe me—or to *watch*—I'm not entirely sure.

I gasp when Alex's warm hand comes to my back, and he grabs the bar of soap and begins to lather my shoulders. Like Otto, he's careful to avoid my right side. I let my head fall back against his chest when his large hands come around to the top of my chest.

"Such a filthy girl," Max says, eyes hooded. "Make sure you clean every inch of her up."

His words cause a spike of arousal to shoot through me, and I adjust myself against Alex.

"Mmm," Otto murmurs from somewhere behind Alex.

Alex adjusts himself behind me, and I realize with a start that he's leaning back, and—

The sound of kissing and low, male groans resonates through the bathroom as Alex's hands begin to explore my breasts while he kisses Otto. His cock twitches against my back when his fingers find my nipples, and I press my bottom against his shaft.

"Turn around," Max tells me, his warm arm coming to mine as he removes the plug for the water to drain.

I sit up and twist around so that I'm straddling Alex, and I'm not ready for what I see.

Otto bending down and kissing Alex with both of his hands on Alex's face. Otto pulls away and looks up at me.

"I'm starting to think death turns you on, little minx."

Alex groans when I stand up on my knees, move my underwear to the side, and slide one finger through my folds. His hands shoot to my hips, and he watches me with an enraptured gaze, flitting his eyes between my hand and my eyes.

"Starting to feel better?" I ask, smirking as I move my finger from between my legs to his mouth. He captures my finger, sucking hard and looking at me through his lashes. My mouth drops open as his tongue swirls around my finger, and then he releases it with a quiet *pop*.

"I'll kill someone every single fucking day for the rest of my life if this is how you'll take care of me after," he murmurs.

The water is mostly gone now, and he frees his cock from his boxers, fisting it with slow, tight strokes. I don't wait to ask—instead, I scoot up his body and line my core up with the purple head of his shaft. He's thick—nearly as thick as Lachlan, and veiny. My mouth waters as I lower myself over him, and his hands grip my waist firmly before he pulls me down roughly on his cock.

CHAPTER 23

LACHLAN

I walk back and forth in front of my bed and rub my mouth with my hand, considering.

Tonight was intense for all of us, and I'm torn between bottling everything up like I'm used to doing, or talking about my feelings. Astern and Alexander especially might need someone to check on them after everything that happened. I'd walked away like an arse, and they deserve better than that. We *all* deserve better than that. We're officially the Princes of Sin now, and that means we're one unit. I could've excused my behavior before tonight, but now? They deserve my best, and I expect the best from them in turn.

We'd only grow together if we were honest and open with each other.

Isn't that why I'm here? To find the family I've always craved? To get close to four other people who would one day become the most important people in my life?

I let out a heavy sigh and pull my bedroom door open. My heavy footsteps cause the old floorboards to creak, but I don't slow down as I get to Alex's room, instead knocking once and pacing in front of the door.

Feelings and *talking* about them make me uncomfortable—lord knows I'm not very good at it.

But I hope they can see that I'm trying.

That I'm *attempting* to go out of my comfort zone.

When he doesn't answer, I twist the handle and slowly push it open, wondering if he's asleep. There's no one in the bedroom, so I start to turn away, but then a low, throaty moan comes from the cracked ensuite door.

Astern.

I should turn around and walk away—I *should* give them privacy.

Instead, my feet carry me to the ensuite door, and what I see causes whitehot heat to flash through me. My cock instantly stiffens as I watch Astern riding Alexander in the bathtub. He's watching her with slightly parted lips—like he can't quite believe his luck. His fingers dig into her flesh as she expertly slides forward and up, and then back and down, rolling her hips every time she moves forward.

They can't see me, and I stay very still as I watch them.

Movement behind Alexander gets my attention, and I realize with a start that Otto and Max are here, too. Otto comes behind Alex and runs a hand down his jaw, and then he unsheathes his cock and presses it against Alex's parted mouth.

Astern moans, one hand coming to Otto's hand, wrapping her fingers around the hand that's around his cock and nudging Alexander's mouth open.

It's... *fucking* hot.

Especially seeing how our little minx seems to enjoy it, seems to beg for Alexander to suck Otto's cock.

"For old times' sake?" Otto asks, his voice husky.

"I've missed this cock," Alexander answers before leaning forward and swirling his tongue around the head of Otto's cock.

"Oh god," Astern whimpers, moving faster. The bathtub she's in is seemingly empty, and her body slaps against Alexander's with every downward motion.

Max moves behind Astern, but I still have a perfect view of the three of them. Astern turns her head toward Max, who slowly unzips his trousers.

"Yes," she whispers, opening her mouth and thrusting her flat tongue forward.

Max groans when she starts bobbing her head on his cock, and as my eyes rove over to Alex, I see him doing the same to Otto. Palming my hard erection, I stay hidden and watch the four of them enjoy each other—the soft groans and sounds of fucking and sucking permeating the air.

I could walk in and demand to be a part of it.

In a way, something akin to disappointment snakes through me knowing I'm the odd one out.

Knowing they're all perfectly content to be doing this without me.

A future without being this close to them causes my chest to ache, causes my hand to pause my ministrations.

"Fuck, I'm going to—" Astern pulls her mouth away from Max as her hips begin to jerk erratically. She throws her head back and her mouth drops open.

My balls feel heavy and desperate to empty themselves as I start tugging on my cock again. I can tell by the way it throbs in my hand that I'm close, and just imagining what it felt like to be inside of Astern when she came—

"Fuck," Max hisses. As Astern groans with her release, his cum begins to paint her perfect tits. He goes still a few seconds later, breathing heavily.

Alexander pulls away from Otto's cock.

"Turn around," Alexander commands, and Astern lifts herself up from his lap and moves onto her hands and knees. He mounts her from behind, grabbing a fistful of her hair and dragging her hips against him as he drives into her.

"Harder," Otto growls, working his shaft hard and fast nearby. "She's such a good, little slut. She can take it as hard as you'll give it."

The flush that spreads over Astern's chest and neck at his words causes my cock to jump in my hands. My balls tighten, ready for release, but I hold off. My hand lightly skims the sensitive head of my cock, and I edge myself twice—bring my pulsing cock close, yet not allowing my seed to spill.

I have to actively hold back a groan each time.

"Is that true?" Alexander asks, his cheeks pink from exertion. He pulls Astern's hair harder. "Are you just everyone's dirty little cum dumpster, then?"

She whimpers and nods. "Yes."

Alexander growls in response. "Except you're not everyone's, are you? You're *ours*."

Astern shatters on his cock then, her eyes squeezing shut as small, satisfied noises escape her mouth in tiny puffs of air.

"That's it," Otto says, moving around to face Astern. "Sit up and open your mouth, my little harlot."

She stands on her knees and Alexander moves closer to her so that her back is pressed against his chest. He continues to fuck her in the tub as Otto moves to the edge, and when Astern opens her mouth, he grunts.

"You love choking on my cock, don't you?"

She mutters something around his cock, and he places one hand on the back of her head.

"Swallow."

She groans at the same time he does, and I watch as her throat bobs repeatedly around his cock. I can't hold back any longer. As I close my eyes, I imagine it's Astern's warm little mouth pulling the cum out of me, and I explode all over the wall of Alexander's bedroom. My hips stutter and my cock pulses out the most intense orgasm of my life at the same time Astern comes again.

This time, Alexander comes with her.

"Oh fuck," he mutters, his mouth dragging over her shoulder as he comes inside of her.

Watching everything unfold extends my orgasm, and I recover slowly as I'm leaning against the wall.

Otto kisses Astern, and Alexander runs his hands over her tits, rubbing Max's cum into her skin.

I quickly remove my shirt and clean up my mess. The last thing I need is for them to discover I was here. As I walk out of the bedroom, I can't help but feel like perhaps I'd just crossed a line.

There would be no going back now, and I could either accept it—accept *them*— or be left behind in the shadows of this bedroom forever.

CHAPTER 24

Astern

"Your first kill," Alaric tells me, pressing the hilt of the knife into my hand.

My heart is pounding and my palms are sweating. I wipe them on my jeans and take the knife from him, settling my fingers around the ivory and gripping it firmly. As Alaric steps back, he removes the bag from the man's head and I stumble back as the blood drains from my face.

"What the fuck is this?" the man asks, his blue eyes flicking wildly across my face. "You," he seethes. "Listen, if I'm here because of what happened—"

"How did you find him?" I breathe out. My heart is pounding so hard that the hilt of the knife is pulsing, and I can't seem to get the words out of my mouth properly.

"Is that really your first question?" Alaric drawls, smirking.

I huff out a nervous laugh. "No. That was a foolish question. Of course you found him."

"Who is he?" Lachlan asks from behind me.

Alaric raises his brows, and I take a steadying breath before answering, looking at Lachlan over my shoulder.

I don't know what changed after last night, but he's been acting differently today. After waking up in Alex's bed–cuddled up with him on one side and Otto on the other–Lachlan sat down next to me at breakfast and asked questions about my life, like he was interested.

Like he *cared*.

"The hostel owner. The one who never made me pay him cash."

"I think you mean the one who molested a teenager," Lachlan growls, stepping forward as he glares at the man.

I can't even remember his name—it's been eight years since I've seen him.
But I remember the dread.
The heavy weight of guilt, thinking it was my fault.
The reluctance to be alone, because he would inevitably find me.
I didn't realize for *years* that what he did was wrong.
I was young, naive, and had lived a privileged life. It took me several years to figure out that everyone would take advantage of that, and when I went to University, I kept to myself. I hardly made any friends. I was too scared to tell them anything about my life, so I isolated myself from everyone and everything. I had no one to guide me, no one to *tell me* that it was wrong.

"I didn't know—she said she was eighteen," the man cries out, panicking. "I've gone to therapy for it now. My wife—it's an addiction, and I haven't *touched* anyone in years—"

Lachlan takes another step forward so that he's standing next to me.

"You think that qualifies you for redemption? You think that if you *apologize* and *go to therapy* that it erases everything you've done?"

"I didn't know she was underage. I didn't realize—"

"But you still touched her without her permission," Lachlan growls.

"I'd never do it today. I'm a different person—"

Lachlan lurches forward and clocks him in the nose—*hard*. The man screams as blood streams down both nostrils, yet he can't wipe it away because his hands are tied up.

"I knew a lot of men like you in prison. You say you've changed, but only a deranged and tainted soul would touch a child. You say you didn't know, but you must've suspected. You never confirmed it. So you may excuse your behavior, but I won't." He's breathing heavily as he looks back at me, and he shakes his hand out. "Make it hurt," he tells me with a furious growl.

Our eyes stay locked for several heartbeats, and when he finally steps back and looks down at the ground, something inside of my chest begins to ache.

He may act surly and distant, but he cares.

He's *trying*.

The thought gives me the courage to hold the knife tighter and take a step forward. The man is still whimpering, and when he sees me coming closer, he wobbles in his chair trying to get away.

"No, no, please, I'm sorry—"

I don't think. My mind goes blank with rage, and I channel every negative feeling into the force driving my hand into the man's chest. There's more resistance than I expect, and as he screams, I pull the knife out again and try again—and again, and again. His garbled screams start to sound wet, and I continue—mindless and thoughtless with rage. It *consumes* me—like a fire that rolls through every cell of my body.

I think of how he used to knock on my door, as if he was showing me courtesy by asking to come in.

I think of the times I pretended to be asleep, how I wouldn't be able to meet his eye the next day.

I think of how I'd scrub my body every morning in the shower—he never touched me below the pants, but I still felt like a whore.

I think of how his nightly visits would make me so anxious that I didn't have a period for over a year.

With each driving force of my hand, a half-cry, half-scream claws up my throat, and it isn't until Lachlan is pulling me away that I realize the man is dead already.

Slumped over and completely still with lifeless blue eyes.

There's blood—*everywhere*—

I look down at my arms. They're covered in blood, and the smell—

The smell—

I retch as I threaten to collapse, as the metallic smell hits my nostrils. I'm suddenly back in the hallway of my childhood home. The blood is already coagulating on my hands, and I let the knife clatter to the ground as the sticky feeling gets worse and worse—

Lachlan holds me close, his arms wrapped around me as his warm chest presses into my back. My face is wet, and I see the old Lords murmuring together in the corner. I flex my hands, squeezing my eyes shut as my heart thumps heavily in my throat.

"Astern," he murmurs, his mouth close to my ear.

"My hands," I whisper, my voice cracking. "I need—my hands—"

I see Max walk into my peripheral, and he holds a water bottle up. "Raise your hands, darling. Let me clean them up."

I do as he says, watching as the water slowly washes the blood off. Alex comes up behind Max and holds out a handkerchief.

Otto takes it and uses some of the water from Max's water bottle, and then he works the cloth up and down my bare arms. It's not perfect, but I don't feel the stickiness anymore.

"You did well," Sterling says from in front of me. Behind him, Alaric, Gideon, and Theo are untying the man from the chair. "I'd like for Alexander to stay—we'll show you how we dispose of the bodies." Sterling looks at me. "Tomorrow, we'll teach you, Astern. For now, go home and rest before training tomorrow."

I can't move my lips—can't nod or do anything as one of Lachlan's arms comes under my knees and picks me up. He carries me out the door bridal style, and I let my cheek rest against his chest.

In the back seat, I'm placed between Otto and Lachlan as Max drives us home.

Home...

Since when do I consider this home?

My body feels cold from the blood and the water, and even though I can still faintly smell blood, I press my face into Lachlan's chest so that I can only smell him. His arm snakes around my shoulders and he holds me close.

"You did so well, darling," Otto murmurs from next to me. I feel a finger drawing circles on my thigh, and it must be his.

"I never want to do that a-gain," I admit, stuttering. "I *killed* someone. I—I wasn't myself. Something overcame me, and all I could t-think about was...

snuffing the life out of him. Like someone spilled ink inside of my heart until it bled through e—every good part of me—"

"Hey," Lachlan murmurs, kissing the top of my head. "Let's not worry about the future right now. Let's get you cleaned up."

My chest aches as I attempt to hold back a sob. "I never actually w—wanted to do this. To be h—here. I thought it was the perfect opportunity to k—kill them, to avenge my parents. But they were horrible p—people—"

"No offense, darling," Otto says gently. "But did you really think you could take on the Lords of fucking Darkness? By yourself?"

"Y—yes," I hiccup.

"I believe in you and that you can do whatever your heart sets out to do," Otto adds. "But your plan was insanity. It's time to accept your fate—it's time for all of us to accept our fate."

My chest cracks open as I begin to cry in earnest, and it feels like an unleashing.

I haven't let myself think of what the Lords told me about my parents. About the people I loved so much, about who they *really* were underneath my rose-colored glasses. I can't let myself think about it, because over the years, I've held them on a pedestal. I've looked up to them and asked them questions at night when I was alone in the dark. I hoped that I've made them proud. But they weren't good people—not really.

Merging my image of them with who they *really* are... it hurts too much to even consider.

They're all I have left, and I need the perfect images of them in my mind for a little longer.

I'm afraid if I don't have that *one* tiny bit of happiness, I might get completely sucked into the inky darkness.

I continue crying as Otto rests his warm palm on my thigh, as Lachlan squeezes my shoulders like he *wants* to—

It hurts. Everything hurts, and I let it all out, soaking Lachlan's shirt in the process.

My mind dissociates and I hardly register pulling up to the manor, or Lachlan carrying me inside. I vaguely recall Max and Otto clapping Lachlan on the back and murmuring something about tea and biscuits before walking toward the kitchen.

I'm in a daze until Lachlan drags me to our joint bathroom and begins to undress me. I step out of my Converse, and then everything feels surreal. I snort as he tries to unbutton my jeans and fails.

"If you wanted to fuck me again, you could just ask instead of trying to get into my pants."

Lachlan glares up at me from his place on his knees in front of me.

"Astern," he warns.

"That's not my name," I say quietly.

"Is your other name better suited to you?" he asks, finally yanking the fly of my jeans open and helping me step out of them.

I open and close my mouth. "Maybe. I don't know. I have no idea who I am, because since that night, I've been planning on revenge. If I can't get that revenge, then who am I? I went to University for computer science. I wanted to be like Theodore Wolf. I wanted power, and I wanted to take them all fucking down," I growl, kicking my jeans off to the side. "But all I am now is a murderer, and that's all I'll ever be now."

"Charlotte," he murmurs, running his hands up my thighs.

Another sob escapes my throat as his soft touch, and goosebumps pebble my skin.

"Don't call me that," I whisper.

"You said Astern isn't your real name, and now you don't want me to call you Charlotte?" he asks, hooking a finger underneath my camisole. "That *is* your name, isn't it?"

I shake my head before pulling my camisole off and unclasping my bra so that I'm only in my knickers.

"I'm not that girl anymore."

"Tell me about her," he asks, hands flat on my thighs, blue eyes watching me through dark lashes. "Tell me about Charlotte Banks."

I swallow thickly as memories come flying back to the forefront of my mind. "She was happy. She was loved. She had a chocolate Labrador named Cocoa. She played piano and wanted to play music for a living. She loved Mozart and daffodils and lavender Earl Grey," I start, choking out a sob. "She never had to go hungry, and she never went to sleep cold. She got high marks in school and she was dating a guy who played football. She had grandparents who loved her. She watched rom coms and sang in the shower, and she never knew how strong she was until it was all taken away from her."

Lachlan's hands squeeze the tops of my thighs. "Will you play me something?"

My stomach flops. "On the piano?"

He stands up and nods. "After I clean you up. Will you come downstairs with me and play something?"

I hesitate, unsure if I'm hearing him correctly. "Okay."

CHAPTER 25

❦

Alex

The smell causes me to heave. Humans don't smell human—they smell like meat, and when I've thoroughly emptied my stomach of its contents, Alaric goes over multiple methods of disposing of a body. I'm familiar with most of them because I'd read through most of the binder Harlow gave everyone the other day, but seeing it all in action?

When the bones are denatured—a process that's incredibly long and boring—Alaric adds the ashes to the large waste bin with the name of the farm on the front.

Clever.

"In time, burning the bodies will feel like tending to a fire every night. You'll know which ones will hiss and scream as the fat burns. You'll know which ones will explode before the flesh is gone. You'll know the ones with hip replacements and pacemakers. Astern and Max will head up intelligence, while you and Lachlan will likely head up security and strategy. I'm still not sure where we'll put Otto," he adds, smirking. "Maybe espionage."

"He'd like that," I mutter, still feeling ill from the smell.

"Come on. Harlow will drive you home."

I don't say anything as Harlow discusses her latest scone recipe the entire drive back. I cover my mouth as I try not to laugh at the irony of it all, because I suppose it's completely normal to discuss baking strategies with *the* Lady of Darkness. When we get to the manor, she turns her Tesla off and faces me.

"I know this is a lot. Trust me. I didn't choose it like the others did."

"What happened?" I ask, leaning back in the leather seat.

"My father was the fifth Lord of Darkness, but he betrayed the order. The guys showed up in my bedroom the night of his funeral and that was that. There was no escaping it."

"And you're glad to be here now?"

Harlow considers my question for a minute before answering. "Yes and no. Yes, because I met the guys and we had Edith. Yes, because the world is a better place. Yes, because it's interesting and I get to work on my art—my passion—whenever I want to between jobs. But also... it's hard. It's grueling. I hate running, even to this day, and it feels like torture every morning. But I suppose there's a sense of duty attached to the role of a Lady. Because if I don't do it, who will?"

"A sense of duty," I murmur. "I understand that."

"I'm sure you do, being *Prince* Alexander. Did I ever tell you that whenever I played MASH with my friends, I always hoped I'd get you as my future husband?"

I laugh. "What's MASH?"

She stares at me. "You didn't play MASH? It's this game where you're supposed to predict who you'll marry, where you'll live, how many kids you'll have—" she stops talking and shakes her head with a smile. "Anyway, it's just odd that I'm now here with you. And I hope you know—I hope you all know—that you can talk to us. We're not going anywhere. Except for maybe a long-awaited vacation to Bali or Greece when training is over, but you can still call us for anything."

"Thank you, Harlow."

I say goodbye and exit the car, walking up to the manor in slow motion. When I open the front door, clean piano notes from a familiar melody sound through the whole house.

I walk into the lounge to see Astern sitting at the grand piano, her fingers flying over the keys. Her hair is wet, and she's in fresh pajamas. Her eyes are wild, and her body is straight and composed as she continues playing Beethoven's Sonata 14 perfectly. Otto and Max are on the sofa behind her, looking on in a daze, and Lachlan is sitting in a chair next to them. They're all watching her play, and a knot forms in my gut as the events of the last two days play out in my mind.

The song is sad, and I find myself drawn to her, and the piano.

I carefully sit down next to her on the bench, and I wait for her to finish the sonata while I tilt my head and look at her face. Her brows are furrowed, like she's concentrating hard. I have to wonder how long it's been since she's played. It can't have been that long if she's not reading music... surely she must still play if she's this skilled.

Or perhaps she's just *that* talented.

When the song ends, she closes her eyes and takes a deep breath. When she opens her eyes, they're clear and determined, as if the music is helping her combat whatever's eating away at her insides.

"Clair de lune," she whispers.

I nod once, and then I turn to face the piano fully. Her fingers hover over the keys, and mine hover over the other end of the piano, ready to play with her.

"Three, two, one," I whisper, and then I'm playing Debussy from memory. Exhilaration fills me as we play together—as the sound of the song fills the house.

It's as if we're resigning ourselves to this fate and to this life, but somehow finding the beauty in it.

Somehow finding our sense of duty, as Harlow said.

It's not fair—not in any sense. Especially not for me.

But if I can continue sitting next to Astern—or *Charlotte*—at the piano, then maybe things will be okay.

There are worse fates in the world.

PART II

CHAPTER 26

LOTTIE
Three Months Later

My alarm goes off at six sharp, and I hop out of Otto's bed to relieve my bursting bladder. When I'm finished, I brush my teeth and wash my face, and then I change into the leggings and long-sleeved shirt I brought over from my room last night. As I pull my hair into a ponytail, Max saunters into the bathroom shirtless.

"Morning, Lot," he says, rubbing his eyes and kissing my cheek.

He turns the shower on, and I admire his bare backside as he steps into the cool waterfall.

"Citadel is on the move," he tells me through the glass. "We should go over our plan one more time when you're done with your run."

"Sure. Have they made their move into Blackwell then?"

"Theo's system picked their car up in Oxford. Slow and steady."

"Bloody idiots," I murmur, looking at myself in the mirror. "They think they're so smart."

"But we're smarter," he replies.

"See you in a bit." I exit the bathroom and walk into the bedroom. As I pull my shoes on, Otto stirs in bed. "Come on, get dressed," I tell him.

"I don't want to go today," he whines. "I'm tired and sore from fucking my girlfriend all night."

I whip my head around. "Did you just call me your girlfriend?"

"Well, yes. What else would I call you?"

I smirk as I tie my laces. "Fuck buddy. Co-worker. Co-conspirator. Your little cumslut—"

"You can be all of those things at once, you know."

I stand and give him a kiss. "If you see Alex, tell him I'll make us a nice breakfast when I'm back. We'll need the energy."

As I leave Otto's bedroom, I nearly bump into Lachlan in the hallway.

"Hi," I chirp.

"Hello," he says, scowling at Otto's door. "May I join you on your run today?"

I nod. "Of course. Eight miles. Is that okay?"

"Already up to eight miles? Impressive."

"Don't patronize me. You know I'd rather be doing my usual ten or twelve."

He laughs. "You were stabbed in the abdomen four weeks ago, Charlotte."

"How many times do I have to tell you to call me Lottie?"

I'd decided to have everyone call me Lottie for the first time in ten years. It was my childhood nickname, and it felt more right than Astern or Charlotte once the dust settled.

It's also nice not having to hide that part of myself from the guys.

He smirks as we walk down the stairs together. "Not going to happen."

I wince as I take the last two steps as one, feeling my incision site pull tightly. It's a grim reminder that this job could be the literal death of me at any moment. I had a German terrorist group to thank for *this* particular incident. Lesson learned: Germans are ruthless. I barely got a word in before the guard stabbed me and ran. Fortunately, we were near a hospital, and Alaric paid the doctors off with a thick wad of cash so as not to be reported.

I grab a water bottle from the fridge and hand one to Lachlan, taking in his outfit. It's autumn now and the air is chilly, so he's dressed in joggers and a thin running jumper. I lead us to the door, and then we begin our warmup by power walking up the hill to the University.

Ten minutes later, we're jogging side by side.

Most mornings are like this. I don't always run outdoors, but on days we have big plans, it helps dispel the nervous energy. Otto has been attempting to come with me, but he finishes about four miles in. Max prefers to lift weights and swim—which isn't surprising, considering the size of his muscles. Alex joins me sometimes, but he's usually doing laps as well. Lachlan is the only consistent one.

He runs with me every time.

In fact, ever since the night of my first kill, he's been attached to my hip.

If it wasn't for him, I might've died that night in Germany. But he was there.

He's *always* there, and sometimes it feels like a blessing and a curse. A blessing because I like having him around, but a curse because I like having him around a little too much.

He hasn't broken his promise to stay away from me in that way, but I wish he would.

The way I catch him looking at me sometimes... the way I remember how it felt to be with him that very first night...

Most nights, I'm extra loud just to taunt him, but he seems unfazed by it.

There've been a couple of instances, though, where I swear he's about to kiss me—but then he doesn't, and it's the worst form of edging.

Luckily, I have three other men to tend to my wants and desires.

So while most mornings are spent with Lachlan, most nights are spent with Max, Otto, or Alex—or any combination of the three.

And my days are spent crammed with learning.

We take university-level anatomy tests, and the Lords show us where all of the important tendons and arteries are.

For death and immobilization, of course.

We learn about weapons, espionage, and reconnaissance from the Lords. We get private demonstrations from different military branches from all over the world. We learn to shoot guns, throw knives, and how to throw a deadly punch. We start on a regimen of highly effective immunotherapy, so we don't ever get sick, as well as very small doses of common poisons to build a tolerance.

Our fingerprints are burnt off with acid, and it *kills* me when I can't play the piano while my hands heal from the ordeal.

It's grueling and exhausting. At the end of each day, I hardly have time for anything fun after dinner commences, so my liaisons with the other Princes are often quick and desperate. We *all* need to dispel the nervous energy somehow, and the hunger to be with them hasn't left.

It's only gotten stronger as real feelings have developed for *all* of them.

Despite always being exhausted, I am stronger, healthier, and more clear-headed than I've ever been. Especially since, whenever I have free time, I play piano.

Sterling doesn't hate me anymore, and I've grown fond of Harlow. It feels like I have a sort of camaraderie with her now, especially since we're both the only females in the order.

I wonder—probably way too often—what life would be like if Quinn had lived.

I think of her whenever we talk about criminology, or if I see someone who looks like her in my lessons. I mourn the friendship that had only just started, and I wish she'd gotten a chance to be close with us. I wish she'd gotten to know the other Princes.

But, like all aspects of this job, I push it to the back of my mind.

Compartmentalize.

"Let's stop and get a coffee," Lachlan says when we jog into town.

"Splash of milk," I tell him.

He rolls his eyes and wipes his face with the front of his shirt. "Yes, I know how you take your coffee."

He walks inside the small cafe and I decide to do some stretches off to the side while I wait. I'm hardly paying attention when a large, chocolate Labrador jumps onto my legs.

"Down, girl," a male voice says, and when I look up, a younger man in a hat is smiling at me. I can't really see his face due to the shadow from his hat. "Sorry, she loves people."

I laugh as I crouch down and pet the dog, who licks my face and paws at my chest.

She looks *just* like my old dog, Cocoa.

"Helga, come on," the man begs, clearly embarrassed.

"Her name is Helga?" I ask, standing up. I haven't heard that name in over a decade, and I suddenly miss the older woman who was a constant companion as a child. My parents were usually busy, so the older couple—Helga and Bruno—took care of me. Their bloodied faces that night flash through my mind, and I shake my head to clear my thoughts.

"It is," the man answers. "And I'm Charlie."

I hold my hand out. "Hi. I'm Lottie."

He smirks, and as he shakes my hand, I study his face.

Realization hits me, and my skin pebbles as I drop his hand a little too quickly.

"Huh. Charlie and Lottie. That's short for Charlotte, right? How funny," he muses, his eyes taking on a dark glint. "Are you new in town? I haven't seen you before."

My eyes flick to the cafe, and I see Lachlan speaking to the barista.

Hurry up, I urge. When I look back at Charlie, he's waiting for my answer. He must know who I am, right? That's why he's introducing himself? Max said they'd been in Oxford... but they're not supposed to be in Blackwell yet.

Panic sets in, and I force my heartbeat to slow.

Everyone's okay.

I'm okay.

I let my eyes wander over the empty street as I try to implement everything I've been taught. Charlie seems to be alone, and from what I can see, he doesn't appear to be armed.

Fuck.

"Yes, I moved recently for work," I answer tightly.

Charlie nods like he knows. Because he *does*. His brown eyes study my face, and I utilize everything I've learned over the last three months to keep the emotions off my face.

"Well, Lottie. Maybe I'll see you around?" he asks, tugging Helga back with the leash.

Is the dog's name really Helga, or is he messing with me? It can't be a coincidence that she looks so much like Cocoa, or that she's named after my housekeeper.

"Yes, perhaps," I answer politely.

"Have a blessed day," he adds, tipping his hat and turning around to walk away.

I don't even realize that my hands are shaking until I reach for my phone to quickly text Max. I walk into the cafe and nearly collide with Lachlan carrying two takeaway cups.

"Char–"

"Citadel. They're here. In Blackwell."

CHAPTER 27

OTTO

I'm laying on the sofa in the lounge when my phone chimes with a text.
Max: Citadel in Blackwell. Charlie walked right up to Lottie a minute ago. Bold motherfuckers.
I sit up. "Fuck," I mutter.
Alex walks into the lounge, and he's holding his phone in his hand. "Fuck," he echoes.
The front door bursts open, and Max is breathing heavily. He must've been doing weights at the gym.
"Lottie's with Lachlan, but I don't trust those fuckers. Theo has no idea how they got past our security system. We've been monitoring every road into Blackwell–"
"They probably didn't come over a road. It would be very easy to suss out where our cameras are and bypass them completely," I tell him. "A year ago, these guys were amateurs. But ever since the ball, they've been studying us."
I sigh. "Alaric warned me this would happen."
"It's the first of many," Alex adds. "Unfortunately."
"So, what?" I ask, looking at Max. He and Lottie are the ones who've been planning the event tonight for weeks.
"They're trying to scare us," Alex says, running a hand over his mouth. "They want to intimidate us before tonight because they know we've planned something."
Max scoffs. "They can try."
"Is Lottie okay?" I ask Max.
He nods. "I think so. They should be back soon. I need to go do some recon-

naissance with Theo. See if I can figure out which side of town they came in from, and narrow it down from there. We've had all the roads from London covered, so I need to figure out what the fuck happened. Lottie said it was just Charlie, but I'd bet a million pounds there's more of them, and we need to make sure they don't come near the house."

"Keep us updated," I mumble as he leaves.

"Never a dull moment," Alex says, smirking as he sips his coffee.

"Not one," I agree.

"Are you ready?" he asks, his eyes traveling down my jumper and joggers.

"No. I need to shower. We can head to the office together?" I suggest.

His eyes darken. "Of course."

I smirk as I turn and walk up the stairs. My cock thickens when I hear him follow me, keeping his footsteps light as we make our way to my room. Once inside, I leave the door open and quickly shed my clothes. There's no hiding my hard on, and as I pull the shower door open, Alex's warm body presses against my back. His shaft slides against my arse, and his hands slither around my chest to tug me close.

"Figured you'd want company," he murmurs, his tongue flicking against my ear.

"You figured right."

As he kisses my neck from behind, my cock throbs heavily in front of me.

"Turn around," he growls.

I do, and he backs me up against the marble wall of the shower. His brown eyes pierce into mine as one of his hands comes down my cock, tugging it expertly.

"We should be quick," I hiss, the feel of his large, warm hand makes precum seep out of my slit.

"I can be quick," he says, voice low. Thrusting his hips forward, his cock presses against mine and he opens his palms. Adding a second hand, he wraps both hands around both of our shafts. "Fuck," he adds, mouth dropping open as he uses my precum, but it's not enough.

I reach over for the soap, drizzling some on top of us so that he can use it as lube. I roll my hips so that my cock gives him the friction he needs, and he tightens the grip of his hands around us.

"I don't think this will take long," he whispers, and pleasure sparks through me when he meets my tempo—sliding down when I slide up, and using his hands to hold us together.

"That's it, baby," Alex says, his eyes not leaving mine as we both fuck his hand. My hips stutter as my cock slips from the soap, and Alex's eyes flash. "Don't fucking stop."

A low, heady groan escapes my throat, and I drop my head back against the wall as my hips jut forward.

"I wish you were fucking me," I groan.

"Yeah?" he growls, squeezing us tighter together. My mouth drops open at the sensation of being in a tight hole with him, and I can't help but imagine being inside of Lottie at the same time. Of fucking her together, of feeling his cock swell and thicken with release... "You wish I was fucking your tight ass, Thorn?"

"I wish we were both fucking Lottie. I want to stretch her with you, feel her ripple around us–"

He groans and quickens his pace, spearing his cock against his hand and dragging it against mine in the process. "I want that, too."

Leaning down, his lips are on mine as we rut into his hands together, using the slippery soap to our advantage. He pulls away and moans, and the sound causes warmth to bloom everywhere. My balls tingle with release, and a white-hot sensation fires down my spine to the tip of my cock.

"I'm close," I tell him, whimpering. My hips begin to jerk erratically, and when I look down, I see two swollen cocks sliding against each other, and it sets me off. "F–fuck–"

"Yes," Alex hisses, holding his hands even tighter.

I pant and shake as thick, hot spurts shoot all over Alex's hand, and he immediately swirls it around our cocks for lube.

"Oh god," he says, voice hoarse. "I'm going to–"

I make a split second decision and add my hand on top of his, squeezing the heads of our cocks together. His eyes flutter and his mouth drops open, and a second later, I feel his cock curve and swell, and he pulses his seed all over my hand. I make sure to squeeze the head of his cock as he comes, elongating his orgasm. He groans and removes one hand, reaching out and digging his fingers into my thighs as his hips stutter.

"Jesus fuck," I hiss, collapsing fully against the shower wall.

"Jesus fuck," he repeats, smirking. "Guess I should clean us up then?"

I nod, still unable to fully form words yet.

He drags us both under the stream of the shower, and I start to lather my hair with shampoo. I close my eyes and let the suds wash me off, and when I open my eyes, Alex is watching me with an open expression.

"What?" I ask, smirking.

"Nothing. I'm just glad it's you."

My brows furrow as I run my hands through my hair to get the last of the shampoo out. "What do you mean?"

"The order. The Princes. I'm glad you're in this with me. I'm glad it's you."

I'm still smiling when he hands me a warm towel a few minutes later.

CHAPTER 28

Lottie

"You look nice," Max says, startling me.

I hold a hand over my chest and laugh. "Good god. My heart is racing." He smirks as he watches me from his place leaning against the frame of my bedroom door. He's wearing a three-piece navy suit and a silver tie that matches my dress perfectly. His wavy hair is slicked back, and his eyes search me through his glasses.

Now my heart is racing for an entirely different reason...

I clear my throat. "You look nice, too," I tell him as I insert the second diamond earring.

Watching him through the mirror, he pushes off the doorframe and saunters over to where I'm standing. My dress is made of silver sequins, and the material clings to my body perfectly. Stopping behind me, he runs a hand down my back as he watches me in the mirror, and when his hand skims my arse, I inhale sharply. He slides between my thighs, feeling for my gun holster. Then his other hand comes around the front of my dress and dips between my breasts, feeling for my knife.

"Good girl," he murmurs.

I scoff. "As if I'd go to an event like this unarmed."

"Are you worried?"

I shrug as I smooth my hair, which is pulled to one side with a diamond comb. "Yes and no. I feel loads more prepared this time versus our first event with Quinn," I start, my throat catching when I think of her. "But if I've learned anything, it's that we can never feel complacent, because that's when someone will strike."

His hands smooth over my abdomen, and I lean my head back against his chest.

The two of us will be attending the formal dinner in London together, and since Max is royalty, he'll be expected there.

Otto and Alex will also be in attendance, and Lachlan will be monitoring the mics in the van.

"Do you have it?" I ask.

He pulls out a silver container and shakes it, indicating the tasteless, scentless poison. I'm also carrying a syringe and needle in my holster in case it's easier to go that route.

We have our targets.

We have one goal.

Eliminate Citadel—all of whom will be in attendance tonight. It is, after all, a far-right dinner event. I just have to hope that no one asks questions about Maximillian Thorn's arm candy. As far as we had known, Citadel has no idea who the new Lords and Ladies are. No one knows our new name, as we've chosen to keep it secret until we take over the order in a couple of months. We've been careful to keep things under wraps. But Charlie's appearance earlier threw all of us for a loop.

He isn't supposed to know who I am.

"I don't think I should walk in with you tonight," I say quickly, turning around and placing my hands on his chest.

"Lot, we haven't confirmed that he knows yet, and we can't pass up an opportunity to take them all out in one swoop. You know as well as I do that the safe houses are nearly unplottable, despite multiple false leads—"

"No, listen. Charlie Hoeffler might know who I am now. It changes everything. Before, we might've been able to get away with it, but he could recognize me and we'd blow the whole thing. What if I stay in the van with Lachlan? Just for a few minutes while you scope the place out?"

Max's forehead pinches with worry. "You think that's for the best?"

I nod. "It can't hurt."

"Very well." He places a gentle kiss on my forehead. "I trust you."

Smiling, I rest my face against his chest. "Thank you for trusting me."

His phone buzzes, and he pulls it out of his jacket pocket. "Time to go."

I grab my handbag and shawl, and then I slip into my clear Louboutin's. They make me feel like Cinderella, and I smile as Max links arms with me.

The others are waiting by the front door, and I take in Alex's black suit, Otto's light grey suit, and Lachlan's dark grey trousers and white Oxford shirt. He's not as dressed up as us, because he won't be going in—but if need be, he'll blend in with the staff.

My heart races as we walk to the car.

Just the five of us—our first solo mission.

Once inside, I sit comfortably on Alex's lap and text Harlow that we're on our way.

Me: Driving now. Will keep you updated.

Harlow: Be careful. All of you. I know you're capable, but it doesn't stop me from worrying like a mother hen.
Me: Relax. You've all trained us well.
Harlow: I may have requested an audio feed from Lachlan's van.
Me: You are a mother hen.
Harlow: I'll feel better at least knowing what's happening in real time.
Me: *eye roll emoji*

The drive into London is quiet, and we hit traffic once we're in the city. I wipe my sweaty hands on my dress anxiously, and once we arrive in the nondescript parking garage a block away, Otto parks the silver Audi next to the white van Lachlan and Max drove here a few days ago.

Max explains the new plan, and before any of us are ready, Max, Otto, and Alex begin walking toward the door. Lachlan slides the van door open and then closes it once I'm in. It's eerily quiet, and his blue eyes flick over my face every few seconds as he boots the system up.

"Testing, three, two, one..."

"We're ready to party," Otto answers.

The plan was for Max to enter with me, and then Otto and Alex would enter shortly after. Since I'm in the van with Lachlan, they decided to go in one at a time.

Lachlan and I sit in nervous silence.

"It looks all clear," Max says a minute later. "I don't see Charlie anywhere."

My pulse spikes. "Okay. Let's give it another minute."

"Target Number Two," Alex murmurs. "Bar."

"Keep an eye on him," Lachlan tells him after pressing the mic button. He releases it a second later.

"Target Numbers Three and Four have just entered," Otto says. "I'm on it."

I press my mic button. "Stay on them."

Turning my mic off, I inhale through my nose and try to quell the nervousness. My leg bounces against the steel floor, and Lachlan gives me a dark look before checking the security feed they set up days ago. The grainy images show off a luxurious dinner event with formal place settings and fancy gowns everywhere. Considering it was over a hundred thousand pounds per ticket, I'm fully expecting every food item to contain gold flecks.

"You're probably fine to go in. It doesn't seem like Hoeffler is there."

I worry my lower lip. "He bought a VIP ticket. Why would he change his mind—"

A loud pop has me yelping, and it takes me a second to realize it was a gunshot.

"Fuck—" Lachlan grits out as his hand flies to his left arm. When he pulls his hand away a second later, there's blood.

My skin goes cold as my eyes fly around wildly, and then I jump forward and attempt to open the door.

"It's locked," I hiss, pulling on it.

"No shit. I locked it. The key—in my pocket—"

I'm not thinking of the key, though. And it doesn't matter if we never get the door open if Lachlan dies—*fuck*.

Compartmentalize, dammit!

I open my handbag with shaking hands, ready to call Kitt—our doctor on call—and Lachlan's face only grows whiter.

"Charlotte," he hisses. "Let the guys know and then get the key—"

"You need a doctor! I can't just—"

Another pop has me crouching down. "Start the car," Lachlan rasps out. "Spare key—in the console—"

My heart is racing at the sound of his ragged voice.

Please be okay... please be okay...

I climb over the seat, grabbing the keys we'd stored in the middle console. I'm just about to reach for my gun, but when I look up, my heart nearly stops.

Three men in suits are standing right in front of the van, holding guns aimed right at my head. One of them shoots the windshield, missing my head by a couple of inches but causing it to shatter.

My hands fly over my ears, and I glance back to make sure Lachlan is okay. He's clutching his left arm and glaring at the men.

Still alive.

Think, Lottie, think—

"Hello, *Charlotte*," one of them says.

It's him.

Charlie Hoeffler.

How did he know—

We were so careful to hide the van away days in advance... to ensure there were no cameras—

"I need you both out of the car now, or I'll blow the entire restaurant up, your friends included," he says cheerfully. "Oh, and Helga says hi. You might know her by another name... does Cocoa ring a bell?"

CHAPTER 29

Max

"Whiskey Tango Foxtrot," I murmur into my hidden mic. "No sign of Hoeffler. Alex is sitting next to Target Number Two at the bar. Or rather, he's being propositioned. Ot is still trailing Targets Three and Four, who seem to be making the rounds before dinner. I have no idea if you're even getting this because you haven't responded to any of our updates," I tell Lachlan.

More silence greets me, and I crack my neck to dispel the unease that works through me.

They're fine—they're probably just talking.

I casually walk up to the bar and lean on my elbows a few feet from Alex. "Gin and tonic with Hendrick's and lime, please," I tell the bartender.

Alex stiffens in my peripheral vision. *Gin and tonic* is our code word for something is amiss—code yellow.

He murmurs something to Target Number Two, and then he's walking past me to the other side of the bar. "Gin and tonic. House gin is fine," he tells the other bartender.

Code yellow for him, too—which means neither of us have heard from Lachlan or Lottie.

My eyes flick to Target Number Two, and he's typing something into his phone. I pull mine out and do the same, sending a message to the group.

Me: All good?
Otto: These idiots are so bloody boring. Save me, dear brother.
Me: Have you heard from Lottie or Lachlan?
Otto: Negative.
Alex: Maybe the mics stopped working?

Me: Even if they did, they should be getting these texts.
Otto: I say we abandon ship. Go back to the van and regroup.
Alex: Yeah, fair point.
Me: I'll walk out first.

Pocketing my phone, I don't touch my drink as I make my way to the exit. I curl my fists at my side, suddenly so damn nervous about why Lachlan and Lottie went silent. Best case scenario is that they got distracted and decided to do something about their sexual tension, or... worst case is, we botched this mission, too.

Pushing the door open, I stalk to where the van is, and my blood turns to ice when I see the shattered glass spread out all over the ground.

Flicking my eyes over every corner of the car park, I slowly pull my phone out and text the group.

Me: Code red.

Reaching into the back of my belt, I pull my handgun out and hold it up as I creep toward the van.

Please be okay.
Please fucking be okay.

My pulse is so goddamn high that I feel like my veins might burst from my skin at any moment, and there's a strange whooshing sound moving through my eardrums to the quick beat of my heart.

Walking around the van, I can see that the sliding door is open, and...

Blood.

"Fuck," I whisper, my voice shaky.

Lottie's handbag is sitting on the seat, and Lachlan's phone is still sitting on the console of the system he set up days ago. Most of the blood seems to be in that area, which means Lachlan was likely hurt. Backing up, I circle the van several times in case I missed any evidence, and that's when I see two bullet holes on the side of the van.

That would explain the blood.

The door slams open on the other side of the car park, I hear hurried footsteps coming toward me.

"What the hell happened?" Alex asks, eyes frantically looking around at the glass.

"I'm going to fucking *kill* Citadel," Otto growls, loosening his tie.

"Ot, call Alaric. Alex, look for *anything* that can be used for evidence—tire tracks, a button, whatever. I don't believe for a second that Lottie didn't leave us a clue. I'll call Theo to see what we can learn about Citadel's whereabouts."

I walk away and attempt to calm myself down.

Do I want to go on a murderous rage? Sure. But that'll help no one, and we need to figure out what Citadel wants from us. Still, I can't help the adrenaline that courses through me at the idea of either of them hurt.

Theo picks up on the first ring. "They have Lottie and Lachlan," I tell him, my voice cracking on the last syllable as I crouch down onto the ground several feet away.

"Fuck," Theo hisses. "What happened?"

"Someone shot out the front window. There's blood, but I don't think anything was fatal. There are two bullet holes on the side of the van. Can you track them?" I ask, thinking of the thin trackers we all had placed inside our forearms a couple of months ago.

"It's showing the car park. Citadel must've cut them out."

"Shit," I hiss, rubbing my mouth.

"And the security cameras were down because of Lachlan's system. We didn't want them to hack in and watch *us*."

"Yeah, we really shot ourselves in the foot with that," I grumble.

"I'm going to check CCTV around the parking garage. They didn't leave by foot. Someone had to have driven them away."

"Sure, okay."

"Max?"

"Yeah?"

"They're going to be okay."

My chest burns, and I rub at the back of my neck as I stare down at the ground. "Yeah. They better be."

We hang up, and my eye catches on something on the ground.

Reaching down, I pick up the syringe and needle–both of which are hiding in the crevice of the curb, like someone discarded them from the window of a car.

It's not just any syringe, either–it's the poison that Otto had created with Harlow.

Picking it up, I stand and walk over to where Otto is talking to Harlow.

"I found this," I tell him, holding up the small, plastic tube. "It's Lottie's. She left it."

"Or she dropped it accidentally," Alex says slowly, shrugging. I glare at him. "What? Unless she left us an actual scrawled word or something, it could've easily detached if they ripped her holster off."

I ignore him and look back at Otto. "Tell me everything about this poison."

Otto's brows furrow. "Like what? It's a mixture of thallium and a few other opioids–" He presses a button on the phone, and suddenly I'm talking to Harlow on video.

"Max? Can you show me the syringe?"

I hold it up with shaking hands, trying to keep it steady in the frame.

Harlow hums. "There's an air bubble in the liquid. See?"

I hold it up, and she's right. The syringe is pulled back a few milliliters. Two milliliters, to be exact.

"2mL," I murmur. "That's not a coincidence..."

"She would want us to know where Citadel is located. That would be her first objective," Harlow says. "The two of you were going over possible locations for their home base, right?"

My mind is racing as I mentally catalog every address and postcode we've combed over. There've been over a hundred, and most had been false leads. We'd ruled out a lot of them because we assumed Citadel was working out of London. The dots start to connect. If they're not based in London... that would explain how we missed them coming into Blackwell.

Fuck, this could be very bad.

"2mL..." I murmur.

"What about an anagram? She loves those," Otto offers. "LM2?"

I shake my head. "No." Pulling my phone out, I bring up the spreadsheet of possible locations, using '2' as the search term. Five come up—and one of them causes me to break out in a cold sweat. "ML2," I whisper.

"And where is that?" Alex asks, arms crossed.

I close my eyes. "Scotland."

CHAPTER 30

Lottie

My eyes feel heavy, and my wrists burn. There's a steady dripping sound from somewhere, and when I try to move my legs, metal scraping against concrete permeates the air.

"Charlotte?"

My eyes snap open, and I instantly begin to panic. Lachlan is across from me, and he's chained up to the wall behind him like a medieval prisoner. We're in some kind of dungeon, and I only know that because there are no windows. There's only the flickering light of the wall sconces. I pull against my chains, and the burning sensation returns. I'm wearing a silver sequin dress, no shoes, and my whole body feels heavy, like I've been drugged.

Suddenly, everything comes flying back.

The dinner.

The gunshots—

My eyes flick over Lachlan, and relief washes over me when I see a white bandage around his left arm.

I recall being corralled into a different car and having the foresight to quickly pull on the syringe out of my holster...

"We're in Scotland," I tell him. My voice is hoarse. "We were wrong. All this time we assumed Citadel worked out of London, but they don't. We're up near Glasgow."

"What? How is that possible?" Lachlan growls, tugging against his manacles.

"They disguise their voice. But tonight, when one of them was shoving me into the car, it slipped. Just one word—*aye*."

"Fuck," Lachlan hisses. "They think we're in London. They'll never find us up here."

I smirk. "They might. I left Max a clue."

"What kind of clue could you possibly have left?"

"One of the home base locations we'd been investigating was this one in Scotland—and the postcode starts with ML2. I had a syringe and pulled it back to exactly two milliliters. 2mL. Now it's just a matter of Max finding the syringe I dropped when we drove out of the car park and him figuring out what I was trying to say."

Lachlan's eyes go wide as they flick between my eyes. "You're a bloody genius."

I smile at his praise. "I know."

"What the hell are these?" he asks, holding up the metal manacles.

I look down at my own set, taking in the rusty chain links. "I think they came with the place."

"Very funny."

A loud bang makes us both jump, and a second later, a dog comes corralling into the cell.

My chest cracks in half when Cocoa—*it's her, it has to be*—starts to lick me wildly. A second later, Charlie saunters in.

"Someone's happy to see you."

"How—" My voice cracks as Cocoa begins nuzzling my arm as if to help me up. Even now, even ten years later, she still knows me.

I vow to protect her. Now that I have her back...

"Shall I start from the beginning?" he asks, his accent fully Glaswegian now —proving he was disguising his voice.

Disguising their appearance, disguising their accents... it all clicks into place.

When Lachlan and I don't respond, he crouches down to pet Cocoa, and I want to rip his fucking hand off for touching her. "Fourteen years ago, I started doing business with a man named Joseph Banks."

My heart catches in my chest, and the blood drains from my face. *My father.* I'm too stunned to speak, and Charlie continues.

"We were under investigation by the Lords for trafficking. Bloody fucking heroes. Your father wanted to stop all business immediately. He was worried about Alaric Cross coming for him—apparently, he'd heard the rumors."

My chest rises and falls rapidly.

"They're going to know," my father had said, his voice resigned.

"Darling, we don't know that," my mum had replied, sounding exasperated.

"Lord Alaric Cross has been watching me for years. Trust me. They know."

"The Lords of Darkness are a scourge on this earth. We have to trust that our people will take care of it before it becomes an issue."

"The night they were murdered, I'd gotten word of the plan, and I quickly transferred their assets to an offshore account so no one could touch them. Cocoa here paced in front of your house for days, and despite what you may think, I'm not a monster. I took her in. I presumed you were dead as well. So imagine my surprise when I showed up to a ball three months ago and saw someone who looks just like Charlotte Banks, except she's hanging out with the Lords? I quickly put two and two together."

"You're wrong about one thing," I growl, tugging at the manacles. "You *are* a monster."

He smirks as he stands up. "I never intended to eliminate the Lords of Darkness. We know the power you all hold. All we wanted was a free state—no more crown, no more monarchy. Our goals were simple—focus on eliminating the royal family. Restore Britain to what it once was—without the crown taking everyone's tax dollars. Being Scottish, I never wanted any part in the monarchy's *inclusiveness*," he spits. "It's all shite. England and Scotland need to return to their conservative glory days."

"Jesus fuck," Lachlan laughs. "Do you really believe in all of that?"

Charlie's face stays neutral, but his fists curl at his side when he turns to face Lachlan. "You should be thanking me. It's people like us—like Citadel—who work to release British nationals from prison."

"You're crazy," I scoff. "Do you realize what you've done? They'll come for you. Mark my words—by tomorrow, your skull will be smeared on the concrete you now stand on."

Charlie turns back to face me, and his eyes narrow as he crouches down in front of me again.

"Such filthy words for a pretty girl." Reaching a hand out, his fingers twist in my hair, and Cocoa whines uncomfortably. "There, there, girl," he purrs, tilting his head as he pets Cocoa. "You don't want anything to do with this trash anyway. Shall I see if you taste as filthy as you speak, Charlotte Banks?" Before I can push him away, he holds my hands down and lowers his face to mine.

"Fuck *you*," I hiss, turning my cheek. "Don't touch me—"

"Or what? Have your big, scary boyfriend throw a punch?"

Movement behind Charlie catches my eye, and I see Lachlan hold a finger up to his lips.

A finger attached to a hand most notably *without* cuffs.

I whimper, playing victim as Lachlan silently stands up. "He's not my boyfriend."

Charlie laughs, and it's low and filled with cruelty. "I know how the *Lords* operate. You expect me to believe you don't enjoy being used for their pleasure? It sickens me. Women like you are the problem," he snarls. "The minute we start giving you a voice, you spread your legs and spout that feminist bullshite. But not anymore."

Lachlan is right behind Charlie now, and I can't help but smile as I say, "Actually, *you* are the problem, Charlie. You fucked with my dog, so now I have to kill you."

Before he can respond, Lachlan swings one of his cuffs down onto the back of Charlie's head. I have to duck and move away as a sickening thud sounds through the dungeon, and when Charlie falls over on his side, Lachlan throws one heavy punch into the center of his face that collapses his skull completely.

I look away as Cocoa whines next to me, nuzzling into my neck.

"Impressive," I tell him as he crouches down in front of me. "How'd you get out?"

"Gideon taught me never to leave without certain tools. I had this clipped to the inside of my belt," he adds, holding up a paperclip. "These are Victoria-era manacles," he murmurs, taking my right hand in his and gently rotating it. "You can tell by the thickness of the cuff and the fact that they're iron." He presses the paperclip into a small hole and the cuff releases. "They also happen to be very easy to get out of if you have a paperclip."

I don't say anything as he releases my other hand, and before I can pull it away, he brings it to his lips and places a gentle kiss on the back of my palm.

"I'm glad you're okay, pet."

Pet.

He hasn't called me that since...

That first night.

Without thinking, I lurch forward and press my lips to his. A low, heady groan escapes his throat, sending vibrations through me. As his tongue dips into my mouth, I gasp and run my fingers through his hair.

"Fuck, Charlotte," he rasps, his breath hot against my lips. "I've been wanting to do that again for months—"

"I need you," I tell him, pushing him back into a sitting position. Charlie's corpse is only a few feet away, but I'm overwhelmed with arousal—with the desire to make sure he's okay. The gunshots—the blood—

I straddle his hips and bring his face to mine. His large hands run up my thighs, settling on my arse. Squeezing once, I feel him moan, though it's too low to be audible. I'm just hiking my dress up when footsteps sound just outside the cell.

"Fuck—"

The door crashes open, and several men take in the scene before us—Lachlan and me without cuffs, and Charlie dead on the ground next to us.

And then all seven of them raise their guns and point them right at our heads.

CHAPTER 31

Alex

The private jet lands in Glasgow just after midnight, and I work with Max the entire flight to ensure we take them all out at the same time.
    No more risks to our lives.
    No more second chances.
    We're going to eliminate the entire structure and kill them all for what they've done.
    The thought surprises me, because three months ago, I never would've considered murder. I never would've been thinking of ways to make their death slow and painful. But when Lottie and Lachlan disappeared... something inside of me snapped.
    It finally makes sense for me—what this order means, and how we all act in tandem. They're not just co-workers... as evidenced by all of the physical contact we take part in. And even though Lachlan hasn't taken part in *that* with us, I am developing feelings for him.
    We all are.
    No, we're something else now—something closer.
    I can tell when Max is about to argue, because his jaw tenses ever so slightly. I can tell when Otto is feeling insecure, because he'll make a self-deprecating joke. I know when Lachlan needs food or sleep down to the minute. And I can play Lottie's body like a fiddle—it's like they're all a *part* of me now, and I didn't realize it until someone threatened to sever that bond.
    Before my mother died, she used to read me a book before bed called *The Invisible String*. The main idea is that we're all connected by these invisible strings, so even in death, we're still connected. It never goes away. With the

other Princes, that string feels evident and obvious, and though I don't believe in fate, a small part of me wonders what would've happened to me had I not been in that back room three months ago.

And then I think... what if I was seeking something just like this? What if I *had* been meant to find the other Princes? I was lonely and sad, content to drink my days away in my own little shame bubble. My father–or the King who *thought* he was my father–hardly checks in with me. I have to seek him out. My sister is busy courting a Prince from Germany, and as she's set to be the Queen when my father passes, her duties are twenty-fold.

If I hadn't found the Princes...

I shiver to think about it.

Three months ago, it felt as if my life was ending. But being in this order somehow *saved* me. Taught me how to strengthen my body, my mind, my focus. I've learned more in these three months than I learned my entire childhood growing up to be the next King.

It just goes to show how much power we wield, and I'd be lying if I said I hated it.

It was *especially* gratifying to slit the throats of the four targets inside the dinner before we left.

Luring them to the car park had been too fucking easy, and I hardly felt a thing as I watched the life drain out of their eyes.

Such a contrast to my first kill.

It really does get easier over time...

"The thing is, we can't just barge into their home base and blow everyone up like we want to," Max explains to Otto, who sulks. "We have to be intentional. I don't know if they know we know where they're located–so we may have the element of surprise on our side."

"What if they've hurt them? Or worse?" Otto asks, his voice hoarse.

"Well, in that case, I give permission to exterminate them. Flatten the ground until not even a cockroach scurries out," Max growls. "Keeping Lottie and Lachlan alive makes the most sense. We have over fifty of our men in Scotland heading to Glasgow. Lachlan is head of strategy, and Lottie will do what Lottie does best: *survive*."

"And we're sure this plan will work?" I ask, nervously chewing on a nail.

"Of course not," Max barks. His face softens immediately. "Sorry, I didn't mean to snap. I'm just..."

"In agony? Barely holding it together? Fueled with rage and vengeance?" Otto suggests.

I huff a laugh. "You're so fucking dramatic and I love it."

Otto stands up and runs a hand through my hair. "I know you do."

After we land a few minutes later, the three of us get into a nondescript black sedan that will drive us as close to the compound as possible. The tension is thick, and I see both Max and Otto fidgeting nervously. My stomach is in knots when I think of what we're about to attempt.

Since we assume Citadel is armed and guarding their base, there's only one way in.

"The tunnels run underneath the city and extend out several miles. If I've plotted the home base correctly, we should be able to detonate the grenade just under the main room. If that happens, we need to be cautious about a collapse. If all goes well, we should be able to infiltrate the compound and perform our rescue with the help of our backup–"

"God, I've heard the plan a million times, brother. I know what to do. Let's just get there and blow this place to bits."

I smirk as Max rolls his eyes, but we're quiet for the rest of the drive.

Once we pull off near a bridge, I see several large SUVs parked nearby. "Backup is here," Max mutters.

There are men dressed in tactical gear holding machine guns, and when they see us, I give them the go ahead to scope out the tunnels. We have no idea if our plan is even possible. For all we know, the tunnel has collapsed and our plan will be futile. I pace along the side of the bridge until Max gets the go ahead in his earpiece.

"Tunnel is clear. Grenades?" He looks at Otto for this, who pats the waistcoat.

"Ladder?" he asks me.

I pull the small backpack out of the car and pull it over my back.

"Masks?"

I tap the pocket of my cargo trousers.

"I have torches," he says, standing straighter. "Ready?"

"Fuck yes," Otto growls.

I tighten the straps of my backpack and give Max a determined look. "Let's go get our Prince and Princess back."

CHAPTER 32

LOTTIE

Fuck.

 Fuck, fuck, fuck.

 That's the word that continues to circulate in my brain when I think of our predicament. Lachlan is tied to a chair on the other side of the room, and we're both gagged with rope. They moved us from the dungeon to another part of their home base. This room is more like a lounge—sofas and small tables make up the room, and there's a large window overlooking the countryside to my left. From what I can tell by the dark blue sky, it's very early morning—probably close to dawn.

 I'm on my knees being held down by one of the Citadel members, and his hand is fisting my hair.

 I hate to say it, but Charlie was the nicest of the lot. These guys? They're ruthless and cruel in a way that makes me wonder if we underestimated them completely.

 "I'm trying to decide if I should have fun with you before we kill you," the man holding my hair says.

 I let a low, threatening growl sound through the room. Cocoa whines in the corner while she paces.

 The man chuckles. "You're a little firecracker, aren't you? Small but deadly?"

 I glare at him, hoping he can feel just how much I hate him—how much I hate them all.

 "No one's going to save you. Not the man over there or your fucking dog," he adds, and Cocoa barks at that.

 My eyes well with tears. *Good girl.*

"We have no intention of taking down the Lords of Darkness. But that doesn't mean we can't weaken your order by ruining you before we snuff the life out of you. Just like your friend. What was her name again? Her pretty face was blown to bits."

A tear snakes down my cheek, and he laughs. He's a large man—black hair, icy blue eyes, long beard. His name is Andrew Campbell, and he's notorious for being a member of the East Glasgow gang. I study him, watching for any weaknesses so that I can fight my way out of this. Running through a list of facts, I let my eyes wander over the other members of Citadel. Like Andrew, they're disenfranchised by the monarchy and want change.

However, instead of going about it the proper way, they're set on terrorizing the very place they claim to want to protect.

I hear Lachlan grunt as he tugs against the rope wrapped around his body. He's yelling and his eyes are wild as he fights the restraints. His words aren't coherent, and I can tell from the vitriolic tone that he's threatening them all within an inch of their lives.

"One less whore in the world," the man muses, yanking my neck back.

I cry out because it fucking hurts—my scalp burns, and my neck aches. He could *so* easily overpower me and break my neck in this position, and that thought has me breathing heavily to calm myself down.

One of the things we've learned during training is how to keep calm. For example, I'm terrified of spiders—something I've tried to work on but can't seem to conquer. During one of these emotional regulation sessions, Sterling brought in a case with different kinds of spiders. The first exercise was easier—it was a smaller house spider I had to let crawl all over me while meditating. But as the days went on, the spiders got bigger. The worst of it was when a tarantula sat on my face while I had to breathe and relax like it wasn't about to sink its fangs into me.

I shudder every time I think about it—but it helped me learn how to be in control of my emotions.

One of the other guys laughs as he kicks Lachlan in the shin. Lachlan barely flinches, and my heart aches when I think of everything he's endured. He must sink down somewhere deep when he's in pain, because he was the same way when he got branded and even when he got shot. He acts like he *deserves* the pain.

"Should we make him watch?" Andrew asks.

Lachlan screams, and the rope around his body whispers against his determined fight to free himself. Cocoa barks loudly, the hackles on her back raised as Andrew tugs hard on my hair. I whimper in pain, and more tears leak from my eyes.

"Will someone shut that dog up?" Andrew growls.

My eyes go wide, my whole body begins to tremble, and dread fills me when one of the guys walks over to her with heavy footsteps.

"I never liked this fucking mutt anyway," the man says, reaching for the gun in his back pocket.

"Nffft!!" I scream, panic filling every crevice, every cell of my being.

Before the man can remove his gun, the room shakes underneath my knees, and dust from the ceiling floats down. One of the paintings on the wall comes crashing down.

"What the fuck was that?" Andrew asks, letting go of my hair. For the first time, his voice sounds unsure.

All seven men hold their guns up at the invisible threat, and my heart leaps at the prospect of the others finding Lachlan and me. *Please, please please—*

"All good out there?" Andrew asks, speaking into his phone with one hand, and holding his gun in the other. "Aye. Very good. Check it out and let me know." Hanging up, he smiles down at me. "Did you think your *Lords* were going to come rescue you? I have bad news for you. There's no sign of them anywhere—we have the entire perimeter to our property guarded."

My eyes flick over to Lachlan's, and he has the same hopeful expression on his face that I'm sure is mirrored on my own. I look over at Cocoa next, whose tail is wagging.

Interesting...

"Now, now, where were we?" Andrew asks.

The sound of cracking wood permeates the room as another blast—this one located where the wooden door stands—causes the men holding us hostage to yell and swing around with their handguns.

Otto strolls in holding a machine gun. His eyes are black with rage, and he cocks his head and grins as all seven guys cock their little weapons.

We all know they're no match for the machine in his hands, which is why none of them shoot. A few of them look between the others, and as my eyes drag over Otto's wild hair and clenched jaw, I realize they're in trouble because I've never seen him this fucking wrathful.

"Hello, boys," he drawls. "Fancy seeing you here." His eyes find mine, and something dark and possessive comes over his expression as he takes in my position. "Hello, darling."

And then he shoots—taking all of them out in less than five seconds. The sound of repetitive gunshots causes my ears to ring, but when I look back up at Otto, he's brushing a piece of white-blond hair from his forehead like he just swept up some crumbs instead of killing seven grown ass men.

Max and Alex walk in immediately after, each holding their own machine gun. When Max's eyes lock on me, he runs over and begins to untie the rope around my head.

"Fuck, are you okay, little minx?"

I nod as the rope comes away and I move my jaw around. Alex is untying Lachlan a few feet away, and Cocoa currently has her front paws on Otto, balancing on her hind legs as her tail wags.

"And who is this?" Otto purrs, reaching down to pet her.

"Her name is Cocoa. We got her from the shelter for my fourteenth birthday. She was one when everything happened..."

His eyes go wide. "She's yours?"

I nod as Cocoa trots over to me, licking my face wildly.

"Guess we're taking her with us," Max says, helping me stand.

My eyes find Lachlan's, and he walks over to me and pulls me into a tight hug. I feel Alex come behind me, and then Otto and Max group around us, and we're all holding each other as Cocoa yips and excitedly runs in circles around us.

"Let's go home," I whisper, my voice thick with emotion.

CHAPTER 33

Lachlan

I hiss as Kitt cleans my wound in the kitchen of the manor. It's midday, and after we confirmed that Citadel had been eliminated completely, we sent word to Buckingshire Palace to notify the King. He and Alex spoke for a few minutes, and the rest of the plane ride back to London was spent recounting everything to Harlow and the Lords. We were congratulated on a job well done, and when we landed, Kitt met us to look both Charlotte and me over.

"Sorry, mate," he mumbles, replacing the gauze and applying a fresh bandage. "Make sure to change this twice a day. If it gets red or starts to ooze—"

"Yes, yes, I know," I grumble. "Thank you."

"You're lucky the bullets embedded into your muscle and missed the brachial artery. You would have bled out in two minutes had that happened. It'll make healing easier too, though absolutely no lifting anything for a few weeks while the muscle heals, okay?"

"Sure, doc," I joke, smirking. "Thanks."

He walks over to his bag and begins to pack things away. I stand up from the chair I was sitting in, and just as I begin to walk out of the kitchen, Kitt speaks.

"I'm a bit jealous, you know. Of what you have."

I turn around. "What do you mean?"

Kitt finishes whatever he's doing, and leans against the counter with a sigh. "I just mean... the solidarity. Companionship. When my wife and I separated, loneliness ate at me for a long time. I'm used to it now, but it's... bloody fucking hard. You're lucky you have them," he adds, nodding to the door. "I've worked for the Lords of Darkness since my first day out of medical school. Charles Blackwell recruited me and we were both young and new at all of this, so I've watched the order both flounder and flourish. I've always been envious of how ruthlessly you defend each other. How much you *care* for each other."

I eye Kitt—an older man in his sixties now. "There's still time for you to find someone."

Kitt shrugs. "Maybe. All I know is if I had what you have... I'd never let it go."

I don't say anything as he walks out of the kitchen.

All I know is if I had what you have... I'd never let it go.

After walking out of the kitchen, I go upstairs and change. I've already taken a shower, and Charlotte is asleep, cuddled up in bed with Max and Otto. Alex's room is empty, so I go out to the back garden, where I see him doing laps in the detached indoor pool. I walk inside the large, warm room and sit against the back wall. My eyes track his smooth movements through the water. He does a flip and turns around, pushing off the opposite pool wall and heading back in my direction. When he stands, he sputters and coughs when he notices me.

"Christ," he mutters, removing his goggles and running a hand through his wet hair. "You scared me."

"Sorry. I'm not tired, but I— I also don't want to be alone."

Alex's expression shifts from surprise to sympathy, and even though I *loathe* the pitying look he's giving me, I let myself sit in the uncomfortable feeling.

It's okay that he's worried.

It's okay to be vulnerable.

Alex pushes up and lifts himself onto the side of the pool. I ignore the way his swimming costume clings to his muscular thighs, and I most definitely ignore the bulge evident between his legs.

"Do you ever think about your son?" I ask, and his eyes go wide at my question.

"Every day. Multiple times a day, in fact. Now that I'm no longer royalty, it makes things less complicated. I'm hoping to bring him and his mother out here for a visit once we take over."

My lips tug into a small smile. I'd never really considered having kids, but maybe one day. It might be fun—especially with... all of them.

"I'd like that."

"Is that why you came out here? To ask about my child?" His words are skeptical, and I don't blame him for being blunt. After all, the other Princes have done nothing but be honest and open with me.

I'm the one holding back—the one who's closed off.

It's now or never...

"Can I ask you something?" I mutter, brows furrowed as I look away.

Alex dries himself off and comes to sit down next to me. I can feel his warmth—and it's... nice.

"You can ask me anything, Lachlan."

I open and close my mouth a few times, pondering how to phrase my question without offending him.

"How did you know you..." I look down as my cheeks flame. "That you were attracted to men?"

Alex is quiet for long enough that I lift my eyes to his, and when I do, the look he's giving me makes me damn near breathless.

"Is there a reason you're asking?" he asks, his voice a low purr.

"No–I mean–yes," I stutter. "Maybe. I'm not sure. That's why I'm fucking asking you–"

He cuts me off by leaning over and pressing his lips gently to mine, and I'm so surprised that I don't move. I'm surrounded by the smell of his cologne and chlorine–it's an odd, masculine mixture that has my core swirling nervously. And his lips are soft–softer than I would've thought. My eyes flutter closed when he deepens the kiss, and we twist our bodies to face each other. His hands come to my neck, and when his tongue presses past my lips, a spark of arousal flashes through me. I groan when his fingers dig into the back of my scalp, and my cock twitches with need–

He pulls away, and we're both breathing heavily.

"I didn't know until a guy kissed me," he tells me, smirking ruefully. "So?"

I'm still panting, and my cock is pressing uncomfortably against the placket of my trousers.

"Uhh... yeah, it was good, I guess," I answer, running a hand along the back of my neck where his hand just was. "Was it Otto? The first guy who kissed you?"

Alex nods, but I can't stop looking at the way his lips are redder now–how he shifts slightly in his seated position to accommodate his stiffy.

"He kissed me for the first time when I was sixteen. So I took his virginity when we were eighteen," he adds, laughing.

I smile. "But you also like women?"

He tilts his head and looks at me curiously. "It *is* possible to like both, you know. I enjoy the masculine feel of a man. I like knowing they're strong like me. But I also get really fucking hard when I see a nice pair of tits. I like how women are soft. I like their curves. I like dominating–men or women, it doesn't matter to me."

I'm quiet as I contemplate his words.

Of course, I'd been around a lot of men who slept with other men in prison. In an all-male compound, it was only natural. I always fought against it–dedicating myself to learning instead. And then there was Abby... I just always assumed I was one-hundred percent straight.

Except, I knew something had changed that first night with Charlotte.

Every wank I'd had since that night included Otto and Max somehow–perhaps not directly, but I *did* enjoy sharing her. And in time, I might enjoy going further than that. Fighting against it for so long makes it feel... *wrong*. But I know, deep down, that Alex's kiss just now meant something.

What does that make me? Bi? Or heteroflexible like Max?

"You also don't have to put labels on anything, or make a decision today, Lachlan," Alex says gently. "Take the day to relax. You don't need to force anything, either–Max is straight, but he enjoys sharing Lottie. You can enjoy being with a woman at the same time as other men."

The instant he says it, I know it's not true.

Because I *do* want it—I *do* want to try being with another man.

I'm still bloody fucking hard thinking about Alex kissing me.

Alex stands up and holds his hand out. "Come on. Let's go back to the manor. You can hang out in my room—no pressure—and we can chat more if you'd like."

I stare at his hand for a few beats. *No pressure.* That sounds...

"Perfect," I tell him, letting him help me up with my good arm.

CHAPTER 34

Lottie

I sleep like the dead, only waking once to pee before climbing back between Max and Otto and passing out for six more hours. When I wake up, they're both gone—but Otto has my coffee sitting on a cup warmer with a note and a single purple rose.

Hope you slept well, darling. I'm so glad you're back.
Love,
Otto

My heart hammers in my chest.

Love?

It's just a casual sign off, right? I mean, I'd told Quinn I loved her the morning she brought me coffee—it's just a thing you do when you care about someone—

"Hello, beautiful," Max says as he comes out of the bathroom with a white towel around his hips.

"Hi," I say slowly, trying not to stare. It's difficult because the man has a body like a Greek God who ate all the protein bars on Mount Olympus.

"Ot left some coffee for you," he says, running a hand through his shoulder-length hair.

"I saw. He also signed it 'Love, Otto.'"

Max huffs a laugh. "And I presume that freaked you out?"

I shrug. "It just seems too soon for... that."

Sighing, he walks over and sits down next to me. The bed groans under his weight, and as my eyes skim over the corded muscles on every inch of his body, my mouth goes dry.

Stop ogling, Lottie.

"You know what our father did to us," he starts, leaning back slightly as his eyes skim over my face. "I'm older than Otto. Bigger. Stronger, though not by much these days. I tried to stop it—" He looks down and shakes his head. "Anyway, I did everything I could to protect Otto. Even though my father sexually abused all of us, Otto was barely touched. It only happened once, and I'll never forgive myself for it."

"I'm sorry that happened to you. To him. To your siblings. I don't blame you for letting your father die in front of you. I would've done the same thing."

"I know. And I don't feel remorse for it. I've said this before, but Otto loves with his heart on his sleeve. He doesn't play games. He's not mysterious like Lachlan. When he loves someone, he loves them with his whole heart. But don't take that to mean he loves everyone. He's selective with his love, so it's an honor."

I rub my chest as I digest Max's words. My eyes drag over the words again, and I see them in a new light.

"Thank you. Being with him is... uncomplicated. He's like a warm hug. He makes me want to be a better person. You all do," I add, brushing my shoulder against Max's. "I'm glad everything worked out the way it did."

"Me too, little minx." He kisses me on the forehead before standing up. "As much as I'd love to properly fuck you into this bed, we have the briefing with the Lords in ten minutes."

I jolt out of bed. "Shit."

After quickly brushing my teeth, washing my face, and changing into some leggings and a baggy jumper, I drink my still-hot coffee in four gulps before following Max out of the bedroom. He keeps a hand on me the entire walk down the stairs and into the lounge, and I like feeling taken care of by him. I *like* how he always seems to be touching me—like he's making sure I'm real. Like he's reassuring himself by constantly keeping us physically connected.

A small part of me wonders if he, too, has some internal scars from what his father did.

Everyone else is already seated around the large room, and the fire is roaring in the enormous fireplace. It's cold today—the first truly cold autumn day. Taking a seat next to Lachlan near the fire, my skin pebbles at the warmth licking my hands and bare feet.

I look around at Harlow and the guys, trying to gauge how they feel about everything that happened, but their expressions are indifferent and casual.

"Did you get some rest?" Harlow asks me from her place seated next to Theo, who has an arm around her shoulders.

"I did, thank you."

"Good. First things first, we wanted to congratulate you all on a job well done."

"Well, perhaps getting kidnapped wasn't ideal," I joke, my tone self-deprecating.

Harlow's brows furrow as she considers my words. "We wouldn't have done anything different. The guys and I have gone over the intelligence data, and there was no stopping what happened. They tricked you and they paid the price. You all handled it beautifully. Ultimately, we won in the end. It's a learning curve, and we won't always come out on top at the end of the day. But we *will* always come out on top at the end of the week."

Shivers claw down my spine, and I'm suddenly filled with a sense of pride.

We will always come out on top at the end of the week.

"Nice use of the tunnels," Theo adds, looking at Max.

"What they're both trying to say is that they're impressed, and we feel ready to complete the handover," Alaric says slowly, looking directly at Lachlan as the leader.

"We really just want to go to Greece next week," Harlow blurts, and I smirk at her honesty. "Relax on a beach, sip some wine, not have to worry about being targets or checking our emails twenty-four-seven..."

Harlow clears her throat. "If it's alright with you, we can do a soft handover this week while you recover. That means instead of feeding you the relevant information, we'll show you how to access it yourself. Lottie and Max will shadow Theo, Alex will shadow me, Otto will shadow Gideon, and Lachlan will shadow Alaric. Sterling will work with the technical handover, bouncing between everyone as the liaison."

"And next week will be a trial run. We'll have our jet at the ready should anything happen, but since there are no events scheduled, we're hopeful it'll be quiet for you all. Especially after the week you had. We'll be around if you have any questions, but other than that, we think you'll be able to handle the day-to-day."

"I thought training was six months?" Otto asks, leaning forward so that his elbows are resting on his knees.

"It is," Alaric tells him. "This isn't the end of training. We will have a lot to teach you over the course of the next three months. And even when we do the full handover, we'll be around to help with questions that arise. We'd always planned to do a soft handover a couple of months before the full handover, and after yesterday... we think you might be ready."

I look at Lachlan, and the corners of his lips twitch. I know what he's thinking, because I'm thinking the exact same thing.

Whose crazy idea is it to put us in charge?!

"Sounds good," Max says, ever the peacekeeper.

"Thank fuck," Harlow breathes, leaning back on the couch. "I really need a fucking vacation."

CHAPTER 35

Otto

At the end of our work day, I decide to take advantage of the evening sun while it's still around. Starting next month, it'll get dark at three-thirty, and I'll be depressed for five months until the sun comes back.

"I wonder if I can convince the Lords to move our headquarters to the south of France," I muse, sipping my cocktail as Lottie lounges next to me out in the back garden. We're both fully dressed because despite being sunny, it is still autumn in England, which translates to cold.

She laughs. "Doubt it. You remember the whole *five families* thing—five families protecting the five corners of Britain."

I scoff. "Well we're not *technically* one of the five families. We've started fresh with a new name, a new lineage... why can't we start over somewhere warmer?"

"I'd love to see you run that by Sterling."

"He likes me. And he seems to like you now, too. For a while there, I was afraid I'd see your fingers chopped off and placed on the mantel as a warning not to lie."

"Jesus, Otto."

I chuckle. "I wouldn't put it past him."

She's smiling when I look over at her, and with the afternoon sun reflecting off her silver hair and white-blond lashes...

She's the most beautiful person I've ever seen, and I can't stop imagining a future with her. With *all* of us.

"So... you and Lachlan?"

"No."

"What? Am I not allowed to ask? As someone with a cock that regularly penetrates you, I feel like it's something I should be privy to."

She glares at me. "You speak of me like I'm a sex toy."

"Don't pretend that doesn't turn you on," I purr. "Being my little fuckhole. Letting me use you, being the most gorgeous, little cum dumpster—"

"Otto," she warns.

"Am I making you wet, darling?"

The corners of her mouth twitch, and she looks over her mafia romance paperback at me. "You're ridiculous."

"But you love it." Her eyes flash with uncertainty, and her lips press together before I continue. "If not love, then something close to it?"

She nods. "Definitely something close to it," she whispers.

I give her a lopsided smile. "Come here."

She abandons her Bratva book to come straddle me in my lounge seat. The sun warms the grounds, but there's been a chill in the air all day. I don't like it, and I'm glad for her warmth when her thighs bracket my hips.

Pressing my fingers into her lower back, she moans. "Lachlan kissed me," she admits.

My fingers stop moving. "Did he?"

"Yes. And I liked it."

"I'm sure you did. Who wouldn't, knowing he's packing that absolute monster between his legs?"

She snorts. "I want him. And I want all of us... together. I never thought I'd say that. I never thought I'd end up with *one* person, let alone four."

I move my hand up her stomach and between her perfect tits, wrapping my hand gently around her throat exactly the way she likes.

"Me too, little minx." The slamming of a door startles us out of our daze, and I see Lachlan walking over to us from the manor. "Speak of the devil..."

Lottie looks over her shoulder as Lachlan approaches us. She shifts to move off me, but I hold her down.

"Hey," Lachlan says a minute later.

I watch the way Lottie eye fucks him, and if I wasn't already hard, that would do it. His massive cock may or may not make appearances when I'm having a wank.

"Can I help you, pretty boy?" I tease.

Lachlan's eyes go dark when they roam down to me—when they flick between Lottie and me, and where we're joined.

Sighing, he looks away for a second before muttering, "Fuck, I don't think I can do this." His voice has a nervous edge to it.

"Do what?" she asks, reaching out for him.

He just shakes his head, but I don't miss the way his neck turns pink, or the way he seems to need to adjust himself.

Hmmm...

"Lottie and I were just about to head upstairs for a little fun. Would you like to join us?"

Fuck it. Can't hurt to ask, even though he'll probably say no.

His eyes bore into mine before one of his hands comes to Lottie's face. He brushes a thumb against her lower lip, and I feel the groan echo through her body.

"I'd love to," he answers, giving me a defiant smirk.

CHAPTER 36

Lottie

My heart is pounding in my throat when my bedroom door snicks shut. I shouldn't be nervous—not when we've already done this before. But there's something heavy and significant in the way Lachlan is looking at both of us—the way his eyes flick between Otto and me, like he's ready to devour *both* of us.

"Some ground rules," he growls. "This is all new to me, but I'm open to exploring..." He gestures to Otto.

"Mmm, I can't wait to top you, pretty boy," Otto taunts. His eyes flash with mischief.

"I don't fucking think so. I'll be the one topping *you*."

"Whatever helps you sleep at night," Otto drawls, slowly making his way to Lachlan. "You should know that despite what you may think, I only bottom for Alex."

My eyes ping pong between them, and my core begins to pulse as I watch each of them fight for dominance.

"Until now," Lachlan growls, bringing a hand to Otto's neck. "Get on your knees and suck my cock—"

Otto shoves him backward onto the bed, and the look of pure, lustful wrath written all over Lachlan's face is enough for me to pull my jumper over my head.

"Ahem."

They both turn to look at me as I slip out of my leggings and stand before them in my black lace matching bra and knickers.

"Why don't you show Lachlan how it's done around here," Otto says, tilting his head.

He makes a sputtering noise. "I know how it's done. You forget I've fucked her before—"

"Ah ah," Otto says, holding a hand up. "That was three months ago."

"You know what? Fuck this," Lachlan murmurs, standing up.

Otto stops him with a solid hand against his chest. "Sit the fuck down."

Lachlan's blue eyes swirl with heat as he tries to maintain control. I saunter over to him and slide between him and Otto, letting my hands roam down his hard abdomen.

"Sit down."

He does—a vacant look coming over his expression. Once he's seated, I drop to my knees, and his pupils bloom with darkness. He stays quiet as my hands fumble for the zipper of his trousers, and when I tug them down his hips, his cock is so hard and so large that it pops out of the top of his boxer briefs.

"What changed?" I ask, palming his shaft and relishing in the hiss of pleasure that escapes his lips.

His darkened eyes track down my chest to where my hands are working his bulge, and I realize with a start that no one has touched him since that first night at Max and Otto's townhouse. Despite yearning to be with him, I've gotten my fix of physical contact from the guys almost every night since we moved into the manor. He must be so lonely, and I let my thumb gently swirl over the hole at the top of his thick cock. A drop of wetness pools against the slit, and his cock twitches away from the sensation, as if it's too much.

"Nothing. Everything. I don't know, Charlotte. Seeing you nearly murdered?"

I smirk. "Fair enough." I swirl my thumb over his slit again, and his whole body shudders. "You're so wound up, Lachlan."

"Then do something about it, pet."

There it is—that nickname.

Giving him a bold stare, I lower my mouth onto his cock. My lips stretch around his thick girth, and that's when I feel Otto come behind me and run a hand through my hair. He collects it at the nape of my neck, holding it back as I slowly work Lachlan's shaft deeper—until it hits the back of my throat and I gag.

"How does he taste? I imagine a big cock like that must leak sweet as sin cum."

"Fuck," Lachlan hisses, hips jumping at Otto's words.

He pops out of my mouth audibly, shuddering as my tongue flicks against the head.

That seems to be his sensitive spot.

I'm not quiet as I suck him back into my mouth, slurping and using my spit to lube up his cock.

"You like it when I talk dirty?" Otto asks him.

"Fuck—yes—" Lachlan's words are bracketed between moans as I cup his heavy balls with my left hand and wrap my right hand around his length, working them both in tandem with my mouth.

"You better watch out," Otto purrs, holding my hair back as my head bobs up and down Lachlan's cock. "She'll suck the life out of you and you'll be comatose for an hour after."

He groans in response, and when he starts to roll his hips, I know he's close. Pulling off his cock, I look up at him.

"Scoot back on the bed."

He does as I say, and I relish in the control he's relinquishing. I know, just because he's so aggravatingly dominant in all aspects of his life, that this is hard for him. I'm sure he'd love nothing more than to jackhammer me into the mattress, but I really want to ease him into this relationship dynamic. He needs to *see* and *feel* what we all do when we're together.

He scoots back to the middle of the bed, and when I press against his chest, he lies down.

"Still like it when we're fully dressed?" he asks, his voice a dark rasp.

"Yes," I tell him, lifting one leg over him as I straddle him. "I want to fuck you while Otto fucks my arse."

Otto is already reaching into my bedside drawer for the lube, and when I look down at Lachlan, his mouth pops open in surprise.

"There's no way—"

"Are you saying I can't handle it?" I ask, smirking as I work his taut shaft out of his boxers. I stroke him a couple of times with both hands, and he moans. Otto's hands come to my bra, and he unclasps it in an instant, pulling it off and baring my chest. This time, when the bra hits the floor with a heavy thud, he smirks as if he's remembering when I held that very knife to his throat.

"We'll break you."

I narrow my eyes as I lift up and take my knickers off. When I line the head of his cock up with my aching core, I watch his face as I say my next words. "Maybe I want to be broken."

I sink down on his cock a second later, and we both groan when I stop a few inches down. My heart hammers against my chest, because *fuck*—he's thick, and I can feel the stretch. It burns, yet along with the burn is a sense of fullness that makes my cunt flutter around his shaft.

"Fuck, pet," he murmurs, hands flying to my hips. "I felt that."

My mouth drops open when he presses up into me, and I can't look away when his eyes flutter closed briefly.

"She feels divine, doesn't she?" Otto murmurs. "Such a perfect little harlot." He uncaps the lube, and for a second, I think of telling him I can't possibly take them both. But when I look down at Lachlan, he's looking at me like I've given him the world. I *want* him to feel how tight it'll be with them both inside of me. I *want* him to feel the heavy press of Otto's cock. And most of all, there's nothing like taking two of them at a time—something I've only done a handful of times with Otto and Alex.

"Fucking divine," Lachlan murmurs, jerking his hips up.

I cry out as he fully sheathes himself inside of me, and it's too much and not enough all at once.

"Oh fuck," I whimper, feeling Otto's hand begin to caress the globe of my arse.

"That's it," Otto says slowly. "Get our whore nice and ready for me, pretty boy."

"Stop fucking calling me that," Lachlan grits out.

Otto chuckles. "You want to get me ready? Open your mouth."

I feel Lachlan shudder at Otto's words, his cock pulsing once. At least I know he's not faking it. He looks over my shoulder at Otto, and his hands stay on my hips as Otto crawls onto the bed. He unzips his trousers and pulls himself out, tugging on his hard length a couple of times. When I look back at Otto, he's eyeing Lachlan suspiciously.

"Go on, then. I don't bite," Lachlan growls, opening his mouth.

Otto lowers himself on my right so that his cock is hovering over Lachlan's lips, and as Lachlan's tongue flicks out and around Otto's slit, I brace myself as I ride Lachlan, whimpering at the thought of Lachlan *finally* giving into whatever this is. He groans as Otto presses deeper into his mouth, and his hips snap up into me immediately.

Otto pulls out and smirks. "You sure you've never done this before? Even in prison?"

"Fuck off," Lachlan rasps.

Otto chuckles as he moves behind me. I lean forward on my elbows to give him space to come behind me, and he straddles Lachlan's knees. I hear him dispense some of the lube, and a second later, he presses a calloused finger against my back end.

"Deep breaths, princess," he tells me.

My skin breaks out into a cold sweat. I take a deep breath to relax my muscles, and Lachlan pauses his movements to help me accommodate Otto.

"Slow," I pant.

"Don't worry," Lachlan murmurs, his fingers digging possessively into my flesh. "We'll take care of you."

"I know you will," I tell him, and he brings his hands to mine by his head. He threads our fingers together as Otto presses a finger into me.

"Fuck," Otto murmurs. "It's going to be a tight fit."

"She can handle it," Lachlan says, eyes locked on mine. It's intense looking down at him like this, and my stomach erupts with butterflies when Otto inserts a second finger. "Our little fuckhole likes that. Her cunt is gripping me with every move."

God, if they continue with the degradation... I'm not going to last long *at all*. It makes me feel all kinds of cherished knowing that Lachlan remembers something so specific about me from months ago.

"*She* can speak for herself," I bite, moaning when Otto inserts a third finger. It feels like too much, like I'll never adjust around both of them, but I know that's not true. Lachlan huffs a laugh, and then Otto adds more lube before he removes his fingers. "But yes, *she* likes this," I murmur, looking down at Lachlan specifically.

"I knew you'd ruin me from the moment I saw you in that club," he says gruffly. "And what a beautiful ruination it's been, pet."

My mouth drops open into a silent scream when Otto pushes inside of my arse without warning. It burns, and my nails dig into Lachlan's hands.

"Christ," Lachlan groans.

"A warning, please," I hiss. Despite glaring over my shoulder at Otto, the searing sensation is already giving way to a fullness I can't ever seem to get enough of.

"If you weren't hung like a horse, maybe we'd have a bit more room, pretty boy," Otto growls.

"Yeah? Just wait. You're next," Lachlan retorts, jerking his hips up into me.

"Fuck," I whimper.

Otto chuckles and his hands rove possessively over my arse. "You wish."

Lachlan breaks eye contact with me to look over my shoulder, and there's something vulnerable in his expression as he moves in and out of me.

Otto leans his body over mine so that I'm quite literally sandwiched between them, and Otto's hands wrap around ours. Lachlan's pupils blow out even further, and I feel him roll his hips up into me as Otto fucks my arse from behind.

"Can you feel my cock?" Otto asks. "I can feel yours, and I'm so fucking close to coming thinking about how you're filling our little cumslut so perfectly."

"F-fuck," Lachlan stutters, and his hips begin to jerk erratically.

They're watching each other with such reverence, and the thought of them both exploding inside of *me*—together—sends a lightning bolt of white-hot heat through me.

"Yes," I whisper, squeezing my eyes shut.

"I'm close," Lachlan tells me, gripping my hands harder. "Fuck, this feels incredible—"

"Just imagine Alex inside of your arse next time," Otto grits out.

I expect Lachlan to snap something snarky back, but instead his eyes roll back, and watching him lose control like this causes my own orgasm to rip through me. My toes curl and my legs shake as Lachlan fucks me through his own climax. I can feel the hot spikes of cum explode inside of me, and then I suddenly feel *so* much pressure—like a dam is groaning under the weight of a flood.

"Yes, fuck, yes—" I cry out.

"That's it," Otto murmurs, slapping me on the arse—*hard*.

I explode again, and this time, it feels like a true unleashing. Everything sounds wet, and Otto groans as he begins to come. They're both pulsing inside of me, and the feeling of that causes me to ride it out, circling my hips as I curse incoherently on top of Lachlan.

"Jesus," Otto murmurs, kissing my shoulder.

"That was..." Lachlan runs a hand over his face as his cock continues to twitch inside of me.

We're all panting as Otto slowly pulls out, and then Lachlan is lifting me off him and flipping me over.

"What are you—"

He opens my legs and grins, his cock still hard and glistening with my arousal. "I want to watch us both spill out of you."

I smile. It's not uncommon for Max to play with his cum—he has a bit of a breeding kink. But knowing Lachlan might, too? It's hot in a way I can't describe.

Otto drops to his stomach, and before I can push him away, he's lapping up Lachlan's cum with his long tongue.

"I was right. You do have cum that's sweet as sin."

The look Lachlan gives him—both heady and curious—sears itself into my mind. I'm honored to be a part of whatever happened tonight, but this whole thing was huge for Lachlan. Sure, he might've shared me with the others that first night, but he's never admitted to being turned on.

But the look he's giving Otto?

It feels like everything suddenly clicks into place.

The other Princes.

Lachlan.

Our soft takeover next week.

I laugh as Otto falls on the bed next to me, and Lachlan cleans me up before joining me on the other side.

And when Lachlan makes me use the restroom before pulling me against his chest, I can barely swallow past the knot forming in my throat.

Family.

They are my family now.

And despite how much I resisted this life—despite the revenge I was so set on—I am so fucking grateful the universe gave me these men.

CHAPTER 37

MAX
One Week Later

Me: Everything's fine. Go drink a mojito or something.
Harlow: I know, I know. And Edith? Is she okay?
Me: She's fine. Cecelia is here, and so is Archie. Still blows my mind that you had a little brother this whole time and you never said anything. He's a cool little dude.
Harlow: *laugh face emoji*
Harlow: Okay. I'll stop checking in. You know where we are if you need us.
Me: Go. Relax. Don't text me again. We have everything covered.
Harlow: Fine.
Harlow: That doesn't count. I just have to have the last word.

Smirking, I set my phone down at my desk and walk over to Lottie, who is bent over her screen with furrowed brows.

"Morning, darling. You're here early."

"I couldn't sleep."

"Mmm," I murmur, sliding a hand to the back of her neck. "I know how to tire you out."

She scoffs but doesn't look at me. "Have you seen this? I forwarded you the spreadsheet earlier. Their name is Obsidian. They're based in Hong Kong. Unlike Citadel, they never wreak havoc in person, but they have shut down the entire American government system. Twice."

"Yeah, I've heard of them. Fucking bastards stole a bunch of credit card information from retirees and pensioners."

"How did we not know about them? What are we going to do about it?"

"Calm down, Bruce Wayne. We'll get them in due course."

"Yeah, but—"

"Lot, this is our *job*. If there was no Citadel or Obsidian or whoever the fuck else is out there, we would be sitting around twiddling our thumbs. As long as they exist, *we* exist. There will always be someone to take down—someone to put in their place. We can whinge about it all we want, or we can actually fucking do something about it."

She considers my words for a bit, the corners of her lips twitching upward. "So what are we going to do?"

I laugh. "I have no doubt you'll come up with a way to take care of it. Right now, I'm just trying to fend off the worried, frantic texts from Harlow."

Lottie chuckles, her face relaxing a bit. "Otto calls her Momzilla. Fierce on the outside like a brutal assassin, but a warm mother hen on the inside."

"That sounds about right."

A minute later, I get settled at my desk across from her. We took Crowne Tower over this week, moving the Lords' stuff out and the Princes' stuff in. Alaric had clapped me on the back when the movers were finished, and he gave Lachlan a stern nod before exiting with the rest of them, leaving us newbies to our own devices. I don't even blame Harlow for worrying—it must be strange to have such an important job, and then one day you just hand everything over... it reminds me that one day, we'll be in their shoes.

"I just realized we'll never get vacations," Lottie laments.

I huff a laugh. "You *did* volunteer for this, little minx."

"Actually, I did not. My plan was to infiltrate the order and murder all of you."

I rub my mouth when I look over at her, and she's smiling innocently. "Alright, you might've been able to kill me, and possibly Alex and Lachlan, too. But Otto? I don't think you have it in you to kill Otto."

She twists her lips to the side. "Fuck, you're right. It would be like killing a puppy."

As if on cue, Cocoa whines and hops up from her luxurious bed that takes up a third of our office spice. Lottie even bought her a diamond collar, and she has little socks that she wears because apparently her paws might get cold when they go on walks. All joking aside, I'm truly glad Lottie has Cocoa now. Having that part of her childhood has changed her in so many ways. She's happier and she seems more content and comfortable with herself. Plus, Cocoa is an old lady, and I know Lottie is dreading the day she has to say goodbye for good.

It's both a blessing and a curse.

So yeah, none of us says anything about the collar or silly socks.

We're just glad our little darling has a companion.

Cocoa trots over to me and nuzzles my legs. She seems to like all of us, but she's taken a particular liking to Lachlan. I suspect it's because she knows he saved their lives, and she's appreciative of him. Personally, I do enjoy seeing him being followed by her constantly, and the way he's a total sucker for her. He even hides treats in his pockets.

"I'm glad you didn't kill us. And I'm glad this all worked out," I muse, running a hand over Cocoa's soft fur.

"We'll probably all be killed by Obsidian or some other entity. The Lords—the *Princes*—can't go on forever."

I turn my gaze on her again. "Why not? We appoint the next heirs. Who's to say we won't continue on?"

"Every empire falls," she replies, giving me a sad smile.

"Not us. Never us."

"Stubborn arse."

"Get back to work. We have people to kill, fingers to sever, and poison to administer."

"Obsidian is going to rue the day they entered my radar," she murmurs, going back to squinting at the computer and frowning.

"I'm sure they're shaking in their boots."

"They better."

I'm still smiling when Lachlan walks in, followed by Alex and then Otto. They each take seats at their desks, and it strikes me then just how damn lucky we are.

Sure, there will always be someone else ready to eliminate us. We are omnipotent, after all. But at the end of the day, at least I get to do it with my best friends.

A notification pings on my computer, and it's an email from Lottie.

You once said to come to you when I wanted to be fucked properly. I hate to admit it, but the last hour of plotting Obsidian's downfall has turned me on beyond belief—

I don't even finish her email before I'm jumping out of my chair. The other guys are busy, either typing or on the phone, so I quietly make my way to the soundproof conference room in the building next door. The Lords bought out the entire block once to hold an entire Swedish mafia organization hostage, and I still can't believe that the rest of the village has no idea what kinds of shit goes on here.

When I enter the conference room, I leave the door open. A minute later, I'm facing the window overlooking Blackwell Village and the door clicks shut. I don't even bother turning around—I can smell her from here. My cock is ready to burst from inside my boxers.

"Hands on the glass, Lottie."

EPILOGUE

Lottie
Three Months Later

The crescendo of the song lifts up into the air, the notes hanging beautifully suspended before crashing back down and pulling the audience into a stunned silence before the applause breaks out. I'm among them, clapping wildly as the members of the London Philharmonic stand up and take a bow. My eyes leak with tears as the emotions of the evening crash over me, and Lachlan must notice because he takes my hand as we walk out of our private box. The others are ahead of us, and as we hone in on our targets, Lachlan's hand squeezes me tight.

"Ready?" he asks.

"It's a shame we have to murder so many people just after such a beautiful concert."

He smirks. "Is it?"

My lips quirk to the side, but I don't answer.

Just as the words leave my lips, I see Max roll a smoke bomb into the cluster of people waiting to exit. A few people scream, and it's enough of a distraction for us to start running in the other direction—back toward the theater. Despite wearing heels, I've grown accustomed to running in them, and I haul my arse underneath the stage to where Obsidian is gathered.

"Nice hiding spot," I announce casually, and the men gathered all turn and point their guns at me. "I can see the appeal, but unfortunately, it's time for your eviction."

As the last word leaves my mouth, I duck—and the guys rush into the room behind me, guns blazing. Shots are fired, and I can only hope that the smoke upstairs is enough to distract people from the noise, because these idiots don't even have silencers.

I roll the grenade from out of my purse to where the eleven men are gathered. A few of them are dead already, but the grenade should take the rest of them out—and I want to weep for the beautiful instruments we're about to destroy forever.

"Go!" I shout, diving behind a wall furthest away from the blast. It radiates through the small room, and after a few seconds, the silence is deafening.

"Everyone okay?" Alex asks, coming to stand next to me.

"All good," Otto answers. "Max?"

"Yeah," he says, a few feet away from me. "Lachlan?"

"They're dead," he confirms, checking the area where they were standing. "All eleven of them."

"Eleven? Weren't there twelve at the concert tonight?" I ask.

"Maybe he's in the loo," Max jokes.

"That was too easy," Otto whines. "And we didn't even get to go to Hong Kong. My fans will be so disappointed."

"I think they'll manage," Lachlan growls, and we remember how one video of the five of us—taken without showing our faces and covering our brands—got him over a million new followers.

A door to the stage flies open, and a man looks around, completely startled. I recognize him as the twelfth member of Obsidian—a man so dishonorable he's stooped to creating a fake baby formula shortage so he can charge more for his black market variety.

"Goodbye," I snarl, lifting my gun.

When he collapses, I sigh a breath of relief. "Now that's really all of them."

We stand in silence for a few seconds before Otto clears his throat. "I'm famished. Let's get a chippy and go home."

༺༻

Two hours later, we're all gathered around the Christmas tree at Blackwell House, listening to Alex play Christmas music on the piano. Cardboard takeaway boxes are stacked on the coffee table containing the last of the chips, and the fire is blazing in the large fireplace to my right. Otto is stroking my hair while my head rests in his lap, and Max is rubbing my feet. Lachlan is on the other side of the couch, trying not to fall asleep.

We'd all moved into Blackwell House last week after taking over as the Princes of Sin—*officially*. Harlow and the guys had bought a country house down near the Cotswold's so that Edith could live near Archie and the six of them could start a new life without the weight of the order resting on them all the time in Blackwell. The other houses and manors will remain in our possession should we need them, but this house was the only one that felt right.

Cocoa trots in from another room and curls up against Lachlan's feet. I smile when I see him try to sneak a treat discreetly from his pocket and feed it to her.

No wonder he's her favorite.

The alarm goes off on my phone—a reminder to take my birth control. Alex pauses his piano playing, and I sit up and walk over to my handbag, rummaging around for the small packet of pills.

"That's weird," I muse, turning my handbag over and emptying the contents. "Has anyone seen my pills?"

The deathly silence that greets me puts me on high alert. Narrowing my eyes, I look back at the guys and see Max smirking at Lachlan.

"You're fucking joking," I grumble, throwing my handbag onto the table and marching over to where the four of them are sitting innocently—Alex included.

I pin my gaze on Lachlan—the most likely culprit. I thought Max had the biggest breeding kink, but Lachlan? He's always trying to convince me to skip a pill. When I suggested johnnies instead, he looked like I'd wounded him.

"Is this your grand plan? Hide my pills? I hate to break it to you, but I have more stashed in my bathroom."

"Yeah, he flushed those, too," Max says slowly. My mouth drops open but before I can yell and scream at them, he smiles. "I helped him."

"You bloody arseholes," I growl, stalking over to Lachlan, bending forward, and pushing him back against the couch. "I *need* those. You can't treat me like a fucking brood mare and make this decision for me—"

Lachlan grabs my wrists and tugs me forward so that I fall into his lap. In one quick motion, he flips me onto my back and hovers over me.

"You don't want us to breed you like the whore that you are? I beg to differ."

I open my mouth to argue, but my retort dies on my lips as a thrill works through me. "You... want to?" I ask.

"*We* want to," Max answers.

When I look over at Otto and Alex, they're watching me like they're waiting for my consent. Max murmurs something to Cocoa and she trots out of the room to give us privacy—something she's accustomed to.

"It doesn't happen overnight," I say quietly. "But you can try—"

Lachlan's lips are on mine in an instant, and his hands are zipping down my jumper. Once he works the zipper down, his hands move over my bare breasts, fingers playing with my taut nipples.

Someone starts to remove my socks, and when I lift my hips underneath Lachlan, they tug my joggers and knickers off, too.

I groan when Lachlan fumbles with his belt, and I arch my back against his chest.

"Sit up," Alex says from next to me.

Lachlan sits up with me in his lap, and I work my legs on either side of his hips so that I'm straddling him.

Alex removes my jumper completely, and now I'm naked. The thrill of being naked when they're all fully dressed will never get old.

Lachlan's lips graze my cheek, my neck, my collarbone... and then his hands grab my arse and lift me up.

"Breathe," he murmurs against my neck.

I gasp when he seats me on his cock, pulling me down as my mouth drops open. "Fuck—"

"That's it," he says slowly, his voice frayed. "Look behind you, pet. Look at your Princes lining up to fill you with their seed."

I'm panting when I look over my shoulder and see Alex and Otto stroking each other's cocks behind me, and Max pulling his cock free. He walks up behind me and runs his hands over my back. The sensation of his warm hands—the idea of what we're doing—sends prickles of arousal to tear through me. That they *want* this—with *me*—

"God," I whimper. "Yes."

"Such a beautiful harlot," he says. "Such a wanton whore for us to breed. Is this what you want? To be full of our cum?"

"Yes."

I can't believe how much his words affect me, and as Lachlan's thumb comes to my swollen nub, I explode unexpectedly. My eyes roll back into my head and Lachlan's breathing turns ragged as his fingers dig into the flesh on my arse.

"That's it, darling," Otto says. "Look at you losing control."

"Fuck, Charlotte—" Lachlan growls.

I look down at his heavy cock pumping inside of me.

When he's finished, he holds me down and kisses me reverently. I kiss him back, groaning when his cock twitches inside of me.

"Thank you," he murmurs.

He lays me down and pulls out. I feel sticky wetness trickle down my thigh, but Max walks up to me and uses his finger to push it back inside.

"Clench," he murmurs.

I bite my lower lip and do as he says, and when he's finished edging it back in, he knocks my knees apart and comes between them.

"Ready?" he asks.

"Breed me," I say, meaning it as a tease.

However, something dark passes over his eyes, and when he presses inside of me, he's not gentle.

"Fuck yes," he whispers, leaning back and hiking one of my legs over his left shoulder. "You're so fucking wet with Lachlan's cum."

"I want yours," I tell him, reveling in the way my words seem to affect *him*. All the guys are pretty dominant, and as much as I love submitting to them, it gives me a thrill when I can make *them* lose control. With that in mind, I clench my cunt tightly around his shaft, and he hisses in pleasure.

"Fuck, Lottie—"

"I want every last drop," I murmur. "Take what's yours, Max."

He groans, and I can tell by the way his hips stutter that he's close. "Christ, I'm going to—"

I squeeze him, panting as he pulses inside of me. When he's finished, he gently lowers my leg and pulls out. His finger plugs me up instantly, and I squirm when he curves it against my wall, teasing me.

"Halfway done," Max says, and then he pulls his finger out and stands.

"Sit up," Otto says. "Keep your legs closed."

It's difficult to do as he asks, but Lachlan helps me sit up without spilling any of the liquid inside of me. Crossing my legs, Otto lays down on the soft rug.

"Lay on top of me, back to chest, darling."

My brow furrows as I do what he asks, and even though he's much larger than me, I still feel like I'm crushing him.

"Open your legs," he murmurs, and when I do, he uses one hand to work his cock inside of me.

"There you go. Fuck, Lottie. You feel incredible tonight."

He drives his hips up and back, pistoning into me relentlessly. In my peripheral vision, Alex stands over me, fully clothed and stroking his shaft.

"Go ahead," Otto rasps.

I moan when Alex lowers himself so that he's holding himself up and hovering over me. When I look between us, my eyes go wide.

"You won't fit—"

"Trust me," he says, dark eyes glinting from the fire. "Deep breath."

I feel him scoop some of the cum that's leaked out and use it to coat his cock. This is *insane*—

He presses his cock against my entrance—the same place Otto is currently slowing his movements. Gasping for air, my toes curl when he slides against Otto's cock and slips inside of me.

"Fuuuck," Alex says, his voice hoarse.

"Slow," I beg. "Please."

I'm stretched to the brim, and even though it burns—like the wrong movement could tear me in half—it's also amazingly pleasurable. And when Otto slowly starts to move, I gasp again at the feel of both of them moving inside of me—both of them filling me so completely. Sparks of heat course through me as they work faster—as their cocks slide against each other inside of me.

I subtly roll my hips as the pain begins to dissipate, replaced only with the most fervent kind of need imaginable.

"Fuck yes," Otto hisses. His hands come to my breasts, and he pinches my nipples—*hard*.

My cunt contracts around them, and they both moan.

"Fuck, you're going to make us come—"

Alex groans on top of me, and then he pumps into me a few more times before his face goes slack and a low, heady moan rumbles through his chest as he comes. Otto finishes a second later, shuddering underneath me as my climax explodes through me. I see stars and my head lolls to the side as they both continue twitching inside of me.

We're all panting, and Alex gives me a quick kiss before pulling out. Otto moves his hips so that he slips out of me, and before I can react, Max is kneeling in front of me and swiping all the cum up onto his finger. He inserts it slowly—gently—and I hiss from the residual pain and soreness already setting in.

"Lift your hips," Lachlan says, placing a pillow underneath me.

I laugh. "You're ridiculous."

He glowers down at me but I do as he says. It's not like one night of a skipped pill is going to *actually* work, but the small chance that it will sends nervous butterflies through me.

Nervous and excited.

"Twenty minutes," Max says, starting a timer on his watch.

I roll my eyes. "I'm just supposed to lie here for twenty minutes?"

"Of course not," Otto says, zipping himself up and lying down next to me.

Alex lies next to him, and Max lies down on my left side with Lachlan next to him.

One of them pulls a blanket over us, and the five of us watch the fire crackle.

"What if it works?" I ask suddenly, my chest feeling tight with panic. "We haven't talked about anything. We haven't prepared, or discussed things like what will happen with our jobs. We just started. If I get pregnant, I can't do any of the fun stuff."

"We can talk to Harlow tomorrow. She would know and she'll answer any questions you have," Max offers.

I consider his words. "God, this is crazy. I can't believe I let you all convince me."

"You didn't like it?" Otto asks, rolling over onto his side to face me.

"I didn't say that. I would just like to have a choice next time."

"I'll drive to the pharmacy right now if you're truly worried," he offers, brushing a hand over my forehead and letting his fingers trail down the side of my face. "Is that what you want?"

I chew on my lip for a minute before answering. "I'll make you all a deal. I'll go back on the pill tomorrow, and if it doesn't work tonight, it's a sign to wait until we're truly ready. But, since there's a small chance that missing one pill means I can get pregnant, maybe it's a sign that we should—"

Otto kisses me, cutting me off. I'm still smiling as he pulls away. When he sits up and looks down at me with a devilish gleam in his eyes, I know I've awakened a monster.

"You have a deal. One night." He scoots over to where my hips are propped on a pillow, and he moves the blanket up with his hands, skimming my inner thighs in the process.

"What are you doing?"

He arches a brow and gives me his signature smirk before a hand comes to his belt. "If we only have one night, darling, I'm going to double my chances."

ಠ∴ಠ

Thank you so much for reading Princes of Sin. I wanted this to be the end of the Darkness series, but Otto stole my heart. I don't have a when or where, but little snippets of their story *will* continue somewhere. The best place to find out about any future plans for these characters is to sign up for my newsletter here:

www.authoramandarichardson.com/newsletter

Thank you again for reading!

ABOUT THE AUTHOR

Amanda Richardson writes from her chaotic dining room table in Yorkshire, England, often distracted by her husband and two adorable sons. When she's not writing contemporary and dark, twisted romance, she enjoys coffee (a little too much) and collecting house plants like they're going out of style.

For a complete and updated list of my currently published books, you can visit my website here:

www.authoramandarichardson.com/books

Printed in Great Britain
by Amazon

b403bfe0-5dff-4374-902b-6579a306a179R01